THE PEPSI SIGNS

A NOVEL BY

JAMES HANSEN

INKWATER
PRESS

PORTLAND • OREGON
INKWATERPRESS.COM

*Scan this QR Code
to learn more about
this title*

Publisher: Inkwater Press | www.inkwaterpress.com

Paperback ISBN-13 978-1-59299-904-0 | ISBN-10 1-59299-904-2
Hardback ISBN-13 978-1-59299-905-7 | ISBN-10 1-59299-905-0
Kindle ISBN-13 978-1-59299-906-4 | ISBN-10 1-59299-906-9
ePub ISBN-13 978-1-59299-931-6 | ISBN-10 1-59299-931-X

Printed in the U.S.A.
All paper is acid free and meets all ANSI standards for archival quality paper.

3 5 7 9 10 8 6 4 2

For Mrs. Bond, without whom, it would have never been possible.

God only knows. God makes his plan. The
information is unavailable to the mortal man.

- PAUL SIMON

DAY ONE

*I*t was a typical New York early February evening, freezing cold, windy, the remnants of a half dozen nasty little three-inch snowstorms that all came within eight days of each other still uncollected on some corners or halfheartedly scraped out of the way of an unwary pedestrian, everyone's strength and will to live sorely sapped minute to minute by the horrible weather and springtime, the greatest of seasons, impossibly far away. I work in the mortgage business for a large bank as I have for the past twenty years, and I am currently visiting a mortgage client in the famous Dakota building on Seventy-Second Street and Central Park West. While some people might think that was kind of cool, to me it was just another difficult coop loan. One has to approve the building as well as the borrower and it involves an additional layer of underwriting. The management company for the building has to get involved with questionnaires, budgets, and insurance policies and it always turns into an endless paper chase that very few borrowers want to try to understand. And that was before you arrived at dealing with the typical Dakota borrower...entitled and impatient were typical middle names.

I sat for close to an hour in a beautiful kitchen filled wall to wall with the latest Viking appliances that I bet were never used to cook a meal, listening to a pair of inane drones dissect bank attorney-approved, secondary market-approved, and government agency-approved documents that were the same for every borrower in the United States but these two...these two...they wanted the documents redrawn to their specifications or otherwise there would be no deal.

Now I know that even if they have tens of millions of dollars stashed away in some bank that they would not be able to have these types of documents *changed in any way, shape, or form. Somehow I have to get them to understand this painfully obvious point because if I leave this apartment without signed papers, the deal will be dead. They will ultimately sign with another bank after their similar requests for document altering are rejected in the same manner I am presently trying to describe to them without beating them both dead with the fireplace poker. And I will lose the chance to close on the deal. My commission… zero. Since the deals early in 2007 had been a little hard to find lately, I don't want this to happen.*

But that was exactly what happened. The shrew wife and the uptight prig husband decided to speak with their financial something or other and I had to leave empty-handed. Look strong and confident at the door, I told myself, keep smiling…maybe I can get them back somehow. How do you send a telekinetic message? You fucking drippy assholes…go fuck yourselves. "We'll be in touch soon, Mr. Pierce. Thank you for coming on such a dreadful evening," Mrs. Doesn't-give-a-damn-about-anyone-but-herself said to me, drawing out the dreadful in such a way that made me lose a bit of enamel on my molars. Yeah, great. "We'll be in touch, Michael," added Mr. Expensive-jacket-and-dockers-even-though-this-is-your-home shithead. Hope your Hermes tie gets caught in the toaster. I nodded, closed the door quietly and leaned toward the elevator.

As I was headed out of the huge courtyard, about to turn into the driveway leading to Seventy-Second Street, I put my head down to avoid catching the wind full in the face and lifted my collar around my neck, my Irish shoulders up around my temples, when a slighter, bespectacled man came briskly around the corner and we crashed right into each other like male bighorn rams, his glasses falling off his face in the process.

"What the fuck!" he snarled at me as he leaned down to retrieve his spectacles and I could think of nothing better to respond with than a good old-fashioned New York City, "Fuck you, too. What's your fucking problem?" To my surprise, the older man was on top of me right away. "My fucking problem is that suits like you are getting in my fucking way every day and I am sick and tired of it all!" The voice was the first tip-off, but now as he turned his head here and there, pulling the glasses back on his face, I could see clearly in the light that I had run into the most famous of the Dakota residents. At that moment I was thinking about his lost weekend with Harry Nilsson which I had read about some time ago, and I knew he was a fighter, not that I was scared. I mean, I was taller, bigger, and younger by twenty years, but still…this was…John. All of a sudden his wife was beside us and I could see that she was concerned with

the sudden violence. Since I grew up in Queens, I had a working knowledge of many languages, including Japanese. I bowed to her as correctly as possible for a Westener. "Honto ni gomen nasai. Sore wa watashi no, ano, fault desu. Sumimasen," which basically means, 'Sorry, it was my fault'...it would have sounded better if I knew the Japanese word for fault, but I figured I broke the ice anyway. I turned back to John and apologized sincerely. I bowed again to the lady, "Sumimasen, shitsurei shimasu," and started to leave. He called after me, "Hey, how do you know all that? I'm married to her for twenty years and all I know is that Ringo in Japanese means apple." I laughed and added, "To me Ringo means first drum teacher." It was meant only as a light, meaningless non sequitur, a string of words designed to allow the speaker to politely step off of into the night in the wake of any encounter, but I could instantly see the both of them had a sudden light in their eyes.

"Do you actually play drums?" he asked, taking a step toward me. I stopped my exodus from the courtyard and stepped back to him.

"Yes, I do. I mean, not professionally. I work for a bank. But when I saw Ringo on the Sullivan show, I knew what I wanted to do. I was five years old then and my mother got me a drum and a crappy little cymbal when I was ten and I beat the hell out of it until it made sense to me and I never stopped. So when I say Ringo was my teacher, all it really means is that I used to put the band's records on the Victrola, turn the volume all the way up, and hope my neighbors didn't break the door down to kill me." I had hoped to get a smile out of him, but instead I got a question.

"Do you still play? Are you in shape?"

"Uhh, yeah, sure. I haven't been in a band for a few years but my wrists and hands are still good. Why, do you want me to record some tracks with you?" I laughed when I said it but he didn't. Amazingly, he invited me upstairs. "Do you have a moment to show me how you play?" I followed, dumbfounded. Uhh, yeah, sure. Shit yeah. I would have been thrilled just to have a tour of his apartment. Maybe he needs a mortgage.

We took the elevator up to his apartment and, yes, you could imagine it was bigger and nicer than Mr. & Mrs. Snotty-as-Hell's place was. The entry parlor was as grand as any country mansion's and several hallways of black and white marble squares took off at irregular angles, each wide enough to accommodate a small car. The rooms beyond, well, I could only imagine what they were like. John beckoned me to the kitchen where two steaming cups of green tea already awaited us. There were two white director's chairs set on either side of a huge butcher block table. The floor was a type of red tile that exuded warmth and simple comfort and it helped me completely forget that I was on the street freezing and depressed just a few minutes before.

I took a quick look around and found that I could see a bit of Central Park out the large window in the center of the kitchen. I pictured having breakfast here, bacon and eggs and poppy bagels slathered with butter and tea and orange juice that would taste ten times better than anywhere else I had ever eaten. The window was partially blocked by crawling plants, the wall to the left featured a calendar with a photograph of an elaborately kimonoed Japanese woman and a water cooler of the type you would see in an office, with the big upside down bottle on top. There were shelves high on the walls on either side. One side held ceramic coffee cups, the other what appeared to be spices and vitamin bottles. John sat on the right and I stood there for a moment and watched him kick off his shoes and put his bare feet up on the table and look straight at me through the slightly-tinted, large-lensed glasses I had knocked off his face a few minutes before.

"Nice kitchen. Thanks for the tea," I said, making sure to hold the cup by the rim on the bottom and the lip, the scalding liquid inside quickly reaching through the porous ceramic to my skin. I could hear musicians tuning instruments elsewhere in the massive apartment. The phone on the wall rang and he pushed one of the extension buttons and picked it up. I could hear the guitars through the speaker as well as another English voice. He listened for about ten seconds and replied to whomever, "I think we have something here, I'll be right in. Yes, I think I've found the answer but of course it could all be a waste. Give me a moment." He hung up the phone without saying good-bye and then stared at me for a few disconcerting seconds. I was holding my ground but it was starting to get a little slippery. What the hell was this all about?

"If you don't know how to play and you're scamming me somehow, I'm going to be pissed and I'll have you carried out of here. Now is the last chance to come clean with me. Do you really play?" I put the tea down and returned his stare, Irish machismo to Irish machismo.

"Yes, I do play. I obviously didn't have the career you've had, but I do play and I love it. I'm not scamming anyone and I will walk out of this place under my own power unescorted later tonight whether you like me or not. As I remember it, you bumped into me first and then invited me here because it seemed as if I could help you with something. If you don't want me here, then I'll just go now." I took another swig of the tea and said nothing more, holding *the cup instead of returning it to the table. Maybe I could palm it in case I get the boot from the Dakota for the second time tonight.*

Instead he smiled broadly, laughed uproariously and jumped out of the director's chair with a teenager's bounce to his body, almost bumping into me… again…and he took me by the arm down an amazingly long hallway that might have traveled the entire length of the building, where I could hear someone bending a guitar note so…familiarly, along with a bass guitar that had a feel that was also…strangely familiar in its tone. He stopped at a large door that fit into the wall so perfectly I would have passed it right by and while pushing it open simply said, "In here."

I stepped after John into a large, totally white room and looked around the place as he closed the door noiselessly behind me. The room itself was larger than any other apartment I had ever seen, well over three thousand square feet. There were a few technicians running around checking connections and levels, a beautiful canary yellow Smith drum set on a slightly raised platform surrounded by a few highly polished Sabian cymbals, a Steinway piano off to the right and several large amplifiers set up on either side of the drums. Wires and cables snaked everywhere. As I stepped forward, I realized the entire room had a raised floor which I figured was to keep the music in here and not in the downstairs neighbor's living room. There were no windows and above me was a false ceiling still about fourteen feet high, made of a thick cloth material I guess to keep the peace with the neighbors upstairs. Paul and George were laughing together about something I couldn't discern and tuning their guitars; George, sucking on a cigarette; Paul, working the tuning pegs on his bass when they turned simultaneously to look at us.

"Hey," Paul said to John, "we were worried about you. Where did you go?" John moved straight into the room, to a guitar stand that held a 1960s Rickenbacker.

"Had to deal with some suit nonsense. Handed it off to the little woman. She'll take care of it." He slipped the guitar over his shoulder as easy as one would brush away a stray lock of hair and made no move to introduce me so I just stood there, unable to form any words. Where was Ringo? That's not his drum set. Ringo always played Ludwigs…black oyster pearl. George took a final deep drag off his cigarette and crushed it out in a silver ashtray on the floor. He turned to me still fingering his guitar fret board, the notes floating out of the amp. "Who are you?" he asked, not unfriendly.

"Uhh, I'm Michael Pierce, I'm from New York and I play drums and John

asked me to come up here. I'm a little surprised by all this, frankly. Do you need someone to sit in to get a level?"

Paul answered me. "No, we need someone to play with us. We have the band back together for some special shows and we need a drummer."

"The band?"

Lighting another cigarette, George jumped in rather impatiently, "The band, yes, the band everyone wanted to get back together since, well...a long time ago, I guess." Turning to John he asked, "How do you know he can play?" John answered without looking up from his electronic tuner.

"I don't. He said he could and I guess the karma was right because we've looked at the best session players in New York and London for two weeks and none of them had it. Maybe this guy does. We have nothing to lose and if he sucks, well, maybe he can carry the trash out on his way home. I forgot to take it out before." His guitar tuned, he rolled the strap around on his shoulder to get it comfortable and stared at me. "Well? Are you ready?" I nodded yes and he gestured with his head toward the Smith kit adding, "I guess that's yours. Get yourself settled and let's go." He then huddled with the other two and a couple of the techs.

I stripped off my coat and scarf and dropped them on a couch. I pulled off my suit jacket and loosened my tie and then, thinking better of it, took it off entirely, not wanting to hit it with a drumstick when I was leading on the hi-hat. I hit myself in the nose once during a live gig and it hurt like hell. I sat behind the kit and adjusted the heights and angles of the cymbals and drum stands for about two minutes, neither looking at anyone else in the room nor listening to their conversation which was not heated but I could tell there were mixed emotions banging back and forth. Impatience has a certain tinge to it. I broke into a quiet, gentle closed roll to test the snare, kicked the bass pedal a few times, touched the cymbals gently, hoped that I remembered to tighten the nuts sufficiently so that nothing fell over in the middle of a number and looked over at the three of them and waited for a signal to start. They broke their huddle and settled in front of me, all of them with their eyes on my hands. John asked me if I liked Buddy Holly and I answered that I did. "Well then count off 'It's So Easy' and don't speed it along. Give us something to stand on."

And so I did. And then some Carl Perkins and Chuck Berry. I was playing surprisingly well and I attributed that to the great room, the fantastic drum set, not having to worry about bothering anybody with the sound of the banging and playing along with these three guys, who were thorough professionals. I mean,

I have known how to play since my early teens, but it's much harder when your head is exploding with questions, your pulse is racing and your palms are sweating like a criminal who just listened to the words 'We, the jury.'

After we finished a rousing version of "Roll Over Beethoven," John looked over at me and smiled. He asked the others, "He's good, I think. What do you say?"

"He's a good slapper, not too technical, like Ringo. He fits well. I like him," said George. And he went back to re-tuning his guitar.

"He's good looking, too," said Paul. "Maybe he can help us round up some young birds." He smiled and I could feel his natural charm like a warm breeze. Not that George was unfriendly. On the contrary, he was just businesslike when it came to his playing and I could see him conferring with a tech about something or other. John took off his guitar, set it on the stand and stood in front of me with his arms crossed. I had no idea what to say or do so I asked him if he liked my playing. He ignored my question and got right to the point with one of his own in the manner of someone who knows what he wants and when he wants it.

"We are going to play several shows over the next few months. And we want you to play with us. What do you think? Can you clear your schedule?"

"Uhh, where's Ringo? Is he okay?" George answered without looking away from the tech, yet another cigarette dangling from his lips.

"He's on some sabbatical in the Himalayas. Decided to live like a monk for a few months to cleanse something from his soul and we couldn't locate him for weeks. Finally we did find him but he begged off the idea. We want to do this to raise some money and awareness about the wretched state of the world and have some old time fun at the same time."

"Is this a joke? I work for a bank."

"Not for the next few months you don't, unless you can't make it work in your own head," said Paul.

"It's a great opportunity, once in a lifetime, Michael," said John. "You shouldn't let it pass you by. But if you decide to take a pass, please see the lady in the kitchen and throw the garbage bag down the chute on your way out, okay?" Now he was impatient I could see. His arms were folded tighter across his chest and his hands gripped his elbows so that his knuckles were whitening. "Come on now. Do you want to play with the band or not?"

"Pays well," chimed in Paul.

"Could be fun," added George. "You play well. We've looked at a lot of players, but we want you."

I sat there for what seemed like a very long time before I placed the sticks back on the snare, thinking about my answer. What could I say other than, "Of course. I'm definitely in." John had his guitar back on his shoulder and he looked at George and Paul and said, "Let's test him." George then stepped away from the tech and hit the opening chord to "Hard Day's Night" and I reminded myself to keep my hi-hat open a little bit in order to create a sizzling kind of sound and I nailed it all the way through, following in similar fashion on "Twist and Shout," "She Loves You" and "Your Bird Can Sing." After a ten-minute jam on some Bo Diddley-type grooves, tea was brought in and we all sat around on couches and chairs, big white pieces of furniture with a raised pattern in the fabric that were amazingly comfortable. The three of them peppered me with questions and suggestions, all of them talking at once, but somehow never stepping on each other's comments.

"It's just like playing music in the garage," said John.

"Ringo had a good bass foot. You need to lean on it so we can feel it, stand strongly on the bottom you provide us," said Paul.

"Don't worry about mistakes. First of all, you already know all the material. You've listened to the songs since you were ten years old. And everyone will be screaming so they won't be able to hear a mistake. Nor will they really care if they do, in fact, notice." Another cigarette lit for George while he's telling me this.

"Just don't throw a stick and hit me in me bleedin' head," interjected John.

"No, I won't do that, I promise," I said. "If there's one thing I never do is throw a stick." Paul, the serious one, always so concerned with image and protocol and what might happen before it did, leaned forward and spoke directly to me.

"Michael, we like the way you play. We like you. You seem like a good bloke. But this is serious business. The world has wanted the band back together for years and now we're going to do it and we need to do it right. A lot of people are going to wonder where Ringo is and they are going to dig into your life once you're introduced as our drummer for this tour. Now is the time to tell us if you have, well, any problems."

"Problems?" Now John leaned forward.

"You haven't been diddling any little children, have you? Haven't taken the Lord's name in vain recently, have you? That got me in a bit of trouble some years ago. I'd like to avoid it this time around."

George added, "We don't care about what they say about you as a player. That decision is ours totally and screw 'em if they can't appreciate our musical opinion. But we can't have some bleedin' scandal leap out at us. So if you have tax problems, drug and alcohol problems, fifteen children by sixteen different women type of problems..."

"You always sucked at math, George," Paul jumped in. George continued, "You know what I mean, right?"

John then asked me quite seriously, "We don't need any surprises, Michael. So, are there any? You can tell us. We've seen it all." It was easy to answer them. I had no women problems, no tax problems, no bad hygiene problems. I might smoke a dubee once in a while and drink a beer now and then but otherwise I painted a pretty boring picture of myself. Which apparently was what they wanted. They were the stars; I was just a fill-in. But do you think I minded? Not a fucking chance.

"So you're in?" John asked me. My goodness, I thought, is he serious?

"Absolutely, I'm in. How and when and where do we rehearse?"

And so for the next month we all lived at the Dakota. It seemed as if the apartment was big enough for at least fifty people to live in. We would have breakfast in the morning, play music until the early afternoon, return about five for dinner and then play until midnight. Their stamina was limitless. I recalled reading somewhere that they would play in Hamburg for ten hours a day, morning shows, afternoon shows, and then two evening shows. We went through the band's entire catalog year after year, album after album. Some-times session players would come in and provide some horns, another guitar or keyboards. I was always worried that Steve Gadd or maybe the guy who plays for the great Beatles tribute band 'The Fab Faux' would walk in and take over on drums but it never happened.

"We have a number of our friends who are going to join us when we play live," John was telling me one rainy afternoon. We were sitting in the huge window staring out at the park. He was lightly strumming a nylon string clas-sical guitar, his right foot on the ledge, his left hanging down toward the floor, his comments coming at me while he stared dreamily at the park, nine floors below. The window casement alone was as big as my bathroom at home.

"Like who?" I inquired casually. I could only imagine.

"Eric Clapton will play some lead, Reggie will play most of the piano parts..."

"Who?" He put the guitar down and lit a cigarette, shaking out the match. The windows were always closed so the sound would stay inside...I always

wondered where the smoke went. I hadn't smoked a cigarette inside an apartment or a private home in years.

"Elton John. He'll play piano here and there. We have Phil Collins on some percussion parts." He leaned into me at this point. "He was pissed at not getting the gig. He's a brilliant player but we wanted an unknown. But there are tambourine and clave parts and so on, so he will be there for that. Don't expect to get too cozy with him. It's not his style." He slid down from the sill and walked over to the Rickenbacker. Paul and George returned to the room and their guitars as well. I made my way to the drums and sat down. John walked right up to me and told me, "You're in the band, Mikey. Don't worry about anything but holding onto the sticks. It's all going to be great." Then George started back toward me and I thought he wanted to say something as well but what I didn't see was that he had already plucked the strings on his guitar and was feeding it back into the speakers on either side of me and I knew without being told that we were going to jump into "I Feel Fine" which had a tricky drum pattern to it, some kind of pseudo-Latin thing, and I needed to work on it.

A month or so later, the news conference about the band's upcoming plans was held in Central Park. The four of us sat on a flat boulder that was nicely situated in front of another rock that acted as a headboard of sorts. There were media from every country in attendance, the live remote trucks lining the street just beyond a short wooden fence. There were print reporters in front of us and behind us, many of them squatting on their haunches lest they miss a note of what was being said, a hundred photographers snapping away.

I always remembered being told by some nun in school that God gave us two ears and one mouth for a reason so I mostly sat there with my mouth shut. But the members of the working press were having none of that.

"Michael, where are you from?" "Did you practice to Beatles albums when you were younger?" "Why you, Michael? With all the great session players in the world, and Ringo's own son being a great player himself, why you?" There seemed to be more than a few people who were less than pleased that I was sitting here and not Ringo. I was beginning to think that maybe it would have been better if this hadn't happened to me. Who needs all this scrutiny? "Michael, tell us about your family." "Michael what has it been like to play with what many consider to be the greatest band ever?" "Michael, what would Ringo say if he were here now?" That's when John stepped in, his shoulders starting to rise.

"Look gentlemen," he started, "have no doubt about it, Michael Pierce

is a Beatle for this tour. He is a good guy, plays well, and photographs well, okay? Ringo isn't here, and we didn't want to audition a bunch of guys. We just found each other on the street, started talking, and a half hour later were playing music. We clicked right from the start. If Ringo comes down from his mountaintop, and we do another tour, of course he gets his spot back because he is our oldest mate literally and figuratively. But today, tomorrow, and for the next few months, Mikey here is a Beatle." At that point we got up to leave. We were planning to just walk back to the Dakota from our rock throne which was about a half mile away. If the press and fans wanted to follow us, so be it. We didn't even have security. I felt like I needed to give these press guys something so I hesitated for a moment and then spoke up.

"If you really want to know, my true feelings are that it is an honor to sit in Ringo's chair." Paul clapped me on the back and John smiled thinly at my perfect sound bite.

We continued past a curved stretch of benches and I locked eyes with a gorgeous lady who was wearing a cute pair of black and white checked shorts and a black cashmere sweater while she stretched her shoulder muscles, her strong legs reaching for miles out from the edge of the bench she was sitting on. I remember wondering how such a beautiful woman could be alone on a Saturday evening but who knows? Maybe she was waiting for someone. She gave me a look and then a second look accompanied by a half smile and I was pleased to see she did so before she detected all the media following us. What would she think of a guy who was playing for the greatest band in the history of rock music? We started to cut across the great lawn when George sidled up to me, lighting yet another cigarette.

"Michael, you did very well with those guys," he told me seriously. "Just remember that even though they are just doing a job, they want something from you. So do virtually all the women you'll meet from here on in, and please be especially careful of anyone wearing a suit." He threw his arm around me. "Don't mind my moroseness with these people. It's just that we've seen it all and you haven't. We're just looking out for you. After all, you're a Beatle. Just always keep moving and be friendly until they become asses. Then just leave."

We continued across the lawn to Central Park West, never breaking stride, photographers running ahead of us, falling all over themselves for a money shot. Reporters were running alongside, peppering the four of us with questions, but we all agreed that no comments would be made during the walk back. We did stop for a couple of autographs. Two young hipster girls about twenty years younger than me asked for a picture and they got on either side of me and walked with us while a third who flew in from somewhere took the picture. They had to do that several times to make sure all of them got a shot with them in it and we pulled it off without an injury of any kind. The last one was about twenty-three, quite beautiful and sexy in a way I was not used to, so confident in her manner that she slipped her pinky below the waistband of my jeans when she embraced me for the camera and tickled my hip with it, but the tattoos, face-metal and cigarette she was smoking balanced it out, leaving it quite easy for me to say no to any future rendezvous. But I made sure to tell them thanks, and I smiled and told them to take care.

We rehearsed more and more and the night before the gig in Central Park, sat down for a big dinner and to go over the set list. At that point I was able to play any song from their catalog and the band was so tight we could predict each other's moves and thoughts several measures in advance. But how to start the evening? Several casinos in Las Vegas actually had a line on what song would be the first played. How do we lay out the set, what do we start with, end with, encore with? It was the subject of intense debate mainly between John, Paul and George, but then I had an idea which I presented within a minute or so. Like any good idea, it was easy to understand. The boys looked at each other and smiled and raised their glasses to me in appreciation.

So the next day we opened with "Don't Let Me Down," into "I've Got a Feeling," into "Get Back." My suggestion to open the set that way was to ease the fans jammed onto the lawn into the live music. These three songs were how most of the crowd remembered the last gig these guys had done, on the rooftop of the Apple offices in London. I said to them it would be like rewinding a tape that had been interrupted and now everyone would be listening to it again. After that opening trio of numbers, the band launched into an hour of the early hits: "Please, Please Me," "Help," "Twist and Shout," "Can't Buy Me Love," "I Saw Her Standing There," "I Feel Fine" and many others. We never stopped to banter much with the crowd. The audience was on their feet from the first moment the lights came up.

We then walked out to the middle of the lawn along a runway that rose about five feet off the grass that was ringed by fans, all of whom were calling our names and clapping. I caught the eyes of several of New York's loveliest citizens but didn't stop to acknowledge them as I knew in my heart that if I were in the crowd watching the band, they more than likely wouldn't give me the time of day. Plus, I had to keep up with the others as we neared the end of the runway which spread out into a small round stage that held a couple of armchairs, a few bar-stools, a harp and acoustic guitars on stands. From there we played another set of mostly acoustic music. Paul opened with "Yesterday" while the rest of us sat. My friend Fred Burke's girlfriend Lisa was there with Paul playing the violin parts perfectly, her blonde hair shimmering in the bright sun, every man in the place wanting her at that moment. Another woman appeared from... somewhere and took the harp for "She's Leaving Home." John, George and Paul standing together now, blending the vocals beautifully. I sat in one of the armchairs, popped open a beer, and kept my mouth shut.

George's sitar work was then highlighted on "Norwegian Wood" and I sat in the middle of the round stage with a set of tabla hand percussion, the sound of which I always loved and had to learn for this one song. John's version of "You've Got To Hide Your Love Away" was heartbreaking to anyone with even a smidgeon of emotion, the entire crowd chanting, "HEY," when the time came, and the rest who knew the lyrics accompanying very well. I had to keep my head down and concentrate extra hard on playing my maracas to keep from tearing up, it was so moving.

And so it went for another forty minutes or so, when Paul announced to the crowd that an intermission was upon us and that the music would return in a half hour. The sun started to dip below the roofs of the apartment buildings on Central Park West, the purplish pastels of the western sky impossible to resist, the colors and swirls impossible for any impressionist to recreate. We made our way back along the runway to the main stage. I again walked slightly behind the three of them and couldn't help noticing the way these guys not only owned their music (not literally, of course, but that's another conversation), their instruments, but the crowd as well. And I was with them. I turned to look over my shoulder at the Dakota and was hoping that Mr. and Mrs. Snotty-Asshole were watching me right now. Just before I got back to the main stage, a woman threw her bra to me and I caught it mid-arc. It was a fancy red lace number and I thought maybe I would hang it on a doorknob at my place as a memento.

We entered the backstage area, a huge white tent filled with hundreds of friends, celebrities and press. I continued to follow where the boys were headed. They told me there would be no interviews at the intermission. We entered a room that was strangely quiet and headed for a table filled with bowls of fruit, cheese cubes, chopped vegetable, grapes and dates. I picked out one of the dates and began stripping the delicious meat from the pit.

John asked me as I chewed, simultaneously reaching for a few seedless purplish grapes, "Michael, did you have a good time? Any problems?" I was halfway through the date, learning just recently how to strip the meat from the pit in one long piece, and I finished the task before answering. These guys taught me over the past few months to always think about what you are going to say before you say it. And if someone thinks you are slow-minded because of it, well then...fuck them.

"It is definitely the biggest gig I have ever played, that's for sure." That drew a laugh from the three of them. Months ago I had told them the story of my drumming career, up and down Bleecker Street in the Village, a hundred small bars and pubs on Long Island, loving every minute of it but never having the good fortune to meet the right group of players who had...something. The only thing I had to show for it was a lifelong-retained ability to play. You never lose that once you have it. I continued, a bit more seriously.

"The sound is great. That helps so much. You know how it is when you have terrible monitors and you can't hear yourself play."

"That was just about the situation at every one of our gigs in the sixties," deadpanned George. "I never heard anything I wanted to hear."

"Didn't you like hearing all the birds calling your name? C'mon, Georgie, you loved it. I know I did," Paul offered cheerily, scooping up a glob of onion dip on a stalk of broccoli.

"Yeah, sure, but my ears...Mikey, your ears would be ringing for days after one of those shows. Quite painful, actually. Maybe that's why I started to prefer a quieter life." John looked up quickly, but I could see his shoulders were down. I chewed another date and watched the exchange continue, John now speaking to the youngest Beatle.

"George, you loved the birds and they loved you. We all know that. Let's get back to this about now. We have to be back out there in ten minutes." He bit of a chunk of apple. "I think it's all going well. Michael is playing well." He gives a nod in my direction.

"Michael, definitely wonderful playing. Just continue to make believe it's a small room...same shit, just a lot more people," said Paul. To me.

"Thanks. I'm looking forward to the second set. Frankly, the sixties stuff was always a little harder to hold together for me." John waved a pita bread in the air, stuffed with...whatever and commented further, "You've been great with the material, Mikey, and you've handled the eye as well." The 'eye' was the glare of the spotlight, all of the people, organizations and causes that wanted your attention and time. George quickly agreed, adding, "You did just like I told you:

keep your head moving, try to keep your feet moving, and just smile as much as you can. You're a good student." John jumped up and proclaimed like an overfed lifelong politician, his pita pointed in the air like a scroll, "Michael Pierce was in the perfect place at the perfect time a few months ago and I made a perfectly natural discovery of this former real estate banker turning him back into the person he always wanted to be." We all laughed at that rehashing of when I met these men and I re-visited the moment for perhaps the millionth time since.

Back to the present. We finished our food and drink and stood to head back out for more music. This set would consist of all the White Album material, as well as Rubber Soul, Revolver, Sgt. Pepper's and Let It Be. The set would open with the reprise of "Sgt. Pepper's Lonely Hearts Club Band" right into the classic "A Day In The Life." On the stage with us would be the Harlem Boys' Choir, Elton John on various keyboards, Eric Clapton, Phil Collins on tambourines and other percussion, a string quartet that included Fred's girl Lisa, who played so well in the spotlight at Paul's side earlier in the show and an assortment of brass and woodwind players. But there was a problem, apparently, and John looked annoyed as he came up to me.

"Mikey, you have to work the clock, okay? Phil doesn't want to do it all of a sudden." I was instantly annoyed. The fucking guy is recognized as one of rock's greatest drummers. He's sold about a zillion records, toured the world as the drummer and then singer for Genesis, played drums for Eric Clapton and Robert Plant and the reincarnation of Led Zeppelin at Live Aid—although that wasn't one of his better performances. "Okay, no problem," I told him. What was I going to say...no? John handed me the Little Ben clock and he showed me the button that would set the clackers in motion.

"You know when, right?" I've listened to the song a million times and I knew exactly where the clock comes in, just before the 'Paul' part, the middle of the song. I nodded acknowledgment while staring at the clock, thinking that somehow this wasn't going to go right. "Just remember to keep it right on your snare mike so everyone can hear it. Toss it over your shoulder when you're done and get right into the groove." He slapped my shoulder as we entered the view of the crowd again, the swell of the cheers coming at us like a slow avalanche.

I was looking forward to getting the clock thing over with as soon as possible. I wanted to rock out on all the great songs we had lined up: "Taxman," "Revolution," "Day Tripper," and especially "All You Need Is Love," which would close the show and "Let It Be" which was to be the one and only encore.

The reprise went well and I loved the sound of the drum kit when I leaned into it. *This part of the set allowed me to play with a little more abandon. Some of Ringo's best drumming appeared on some of these songs, and I worked out some of my annoyance with Phil Collins by adding a little flourish here and there, being careful not to get carried away. The reprise melted into the beginning of "A Day In The Life," John's acoustic guitar and Elton John's piano bringing the crowd to life. I could also see the other musicians, the string players and others concentrating. They knew this was the tough one and they wanted to nail it.*

I had fun with Ringo's parts which I tried to match stroke for stroke. I looked over at Phil after my 'musically hesitant' fill right after John sang, "The English Army Had Just Won The War"...to stick it in his face, but he seemed far off somewhere, waiting for something. I chastised myself. How could I be thinking of anything else but playing well?

Now we were in the buildup, which the boys decided to double in length, the crescendo of notes and melodies crashing together between the strings, the brass, the woodwinds, Clapton's slide guitar, George and Paul and John strumming their instruments, the crowd being coaxed willingly to their feet, even those who didn't know the song realizing they were being pulled out of their sitting positions on the grass, unable to resist, and all of a sudden the lawn was filled with the familiar piano notes denoting the beginning of Paul's section of the song. The clock was in my hand, John was looking over his shoulder at me and I pushed the button with perfect timing, the snare mike picking up the chatter of the alarm perfectly.

But I can't put the clock down for some reason. All I have to do is toss it over my shoulder, let someone grab it as a souvenir, but I just...can't and I start to panic as I am supposed to come in semi-explosively with a quick five stroke on the snare right after the clock. Paul is now singing, "Woke up, got out of bed, dragged a comb across my head," and the clock was sticking to my hand like it was glued on. I tried shaking it off as if it were a nasty little rodent nipping on my fingers, but I couldn't dislodge it. John is glaring at me, George has his head down and I could see he's suffering for me but there's nothing he can do except keep it together without a drum track to hold everything up. Paul keeps singing and playing as if all were going well and then I look to Phil Collins, my fellow drummer, my favorite player...and he bursts out laughing which is louder than the music and I sit there dumbfounded. And now I can't see George anymore and John is gone as well. The crowd is sensing something wrong, the beautiful woman in the yellow dress whom I had noticed earlier watching from the wings of the stage has turned to leave, the lawn has quieted down and the sun now hits my face as if it were filtered by...slats, as if it were a window blind in a room, a bedroom specifically, and the slats are not completely turned to block the morning sun because I forgot to fix them the night before. And the sun is not warming a crowd of more than a half million in the park and I am not playing with the band. George and John are no longer with us on this planet and Paul has that great player the heavyset guy who plays drums with him now and Phil Collins really is a nice guy who would probably be thrilled for me if I ever got a gig like the...one...I...just...dreamed...about. My hand is on the alarm clock on the little table next to the bed. My six-year-old daughter, Sally, bangs into the room, an extremely unhappy child.

"Daddy, I'm hungry, the bus is gonna be here in fifteen minutes and Mommy says she can't make me breakfast *again*." She crosses her arms at the conclusion of this statement or demand, depending, of course, of your point of view, and awaits an answer. What else can I do? First things first...I have to look into these dreams. They've recently been frighteningly vivid, realistic, seemingly lasting for hours even though I know dreams commonly are very short in duration. Sally was screaming again. I silently point to the door and she thankfully gets the message and leaves. My feet are on the floor now. Be careful to stand up slowly and straightly as not to nudge any cervical or coccyx vertebrae out of joint. I stand to my full height, greeting yet another day that scares the hell out of me because, like everyone else too scared to admit, I'm just not sure how it will all go. So far it has sucked.

⸎

I know what it feels like to be in prison. I could have sat at the foot of Alexandre Dumas as he wrote <u>The Count of Monte Cristo</u> *and saved him a lot of time with his research into the feelings of a person who has lost the capacity to dream of escape, of freedom regained.*

No hope at all of escape to freedom, no escape from the toil of another dreamless day where your every move is analyzed, scrutinized, and your daily routine determined by others. Whether it is good or bad for you is never taken into consideration. I have never committed a crime, but I am in prison nonetheless. My cells change from day to day. Sometimes I am at the church, listening to endless streams of evangelism from a man who is sleeping with half the women in the town—including me—but thank goodness only in his dreams. I hated the way he would leer at me from the pulpit. I was sure everyone else knew what he was probably thinking when he looked in my direction. How many of them assumed I would give myself away so easily?

Sometimes my jail cell was my dreams of the family farm, where I was born and raised and for the first fifteen years of my life, treated to the best existence any young woman could possibly hope for. Our farm in Patagonia was made up of ten thousand acres of beautiful fertile land. We grew soybeans, maize, sunflowers and citrus fruits. We also had plenty of cows and goats for dairy and beef, and chickens as well. I loved my chickens...and my horses. The horses worked hard every day for my father and brothers, not only with heavy labor but also as transportation to nearby towns and pulling carts laden with the farm's produce. I was the only one the horses would allow to saddle and bridle them, though. They were always angry and stomping when the men were around. But they were loving and purring when I entered the paddock. I figured they must have known that they were heading out to work at some back-breaking task when I came to put the saddles on, but I guess they were just pleased that I spoke quietly to them and stroked their heads lovingly while I did so. At least they had a moment when I was near them where they could feel some genuine love.

But the farm has been gone now for several years, along with the aforementioned most beautiful life in the wake of our parent's death in a horrible accident that I truly can't recall. That's how I know the brain can block certain events from the past as effectively as removing pictures from a photo album. And I'm glad for that because there are just too many events that I don't want to remember, even if I can learn something from them. I was unconcerned that this kind of thinking would have made my father angry.

My parents were married at seventeen when they were seen kissing behind the church by our pastor. Their parents, my grandparents, got together to discuss this outrage as it was and decided they should marry to save their honor. My parents were secretly thrilled despite being forced to marry. They had been in love with each other from the moment they met, years earlier. And now they had everyone's blessing...as it were.

In the next four years, my mother gave birth to four sons and she and my father worked the fields and the livestock and became a regular Argentinean farming family, pillars of the community, the apples of my grandparents' eyes. My father stood with his fellow farmers against higher tariffs demanded by the government on soybeans and any other injustice the corporations of Argentina tried to lay on all the people who didn't happen to live in Buenos Aires and who didn't care to. Strange how all of that beauty came out of what so many initially believed to be a scandalous moment.

When my mother was forty-one, she surprised everyone by becoming pregnant for the first time in twenty years. My father prayed especially hard for a girl and to his and my mother's delight, I was born early in the second week of June. My brothers were all in their twenties by then and although I'm sure there was at first a smidgeon of joy in their hearts at having a new sibling, later on I started to discover how little they wanted to do with their little sister. My mother had to take care of me now and, as a result, my brothers had to wash their own clothes, mend them, cook their own meals, and I guess they harbored a bit of resentment for the person they blamed for the change in their lives. Hey, all I did was get born into the world.

It was my father who named me Laura, which was not a particularly common name in Argentina. Although a farmer and therefore at times looked down upon by the 'classier' citizens in Buenos Aires, my father was actually a very learned man. He never attended college, but through his love of books and reading became able to converse with anyone on a variety of subjects. He especially loved the life and works of Francesco Petrarca, the fourteenth-century Italian poet. He very much admired this man who is widely assumed to have coined the historical term, 'Dark Ages' and he did so in order to show disdain for those years which he believed to be full of ignorance on a social and ecclesiastical level. It was by reading Petrarca that he was also introduced to the writings of Saint Augustine, who apparently stopped both Petrarca and my father in their tracks with what was probably an almost random thought when he observed, "And men go about to wonder at the heights of the mountains, and the mighty waves of the sea, and the wide sweep of rivers, and the circuit of the ocean, and the revolution of the stars, but themselves they consider not." Petrarca was so moved by Saint Augustine's observation that he decided to devote the rest of his life to soul searching. My father, being a poor farmer, still needed to work to feed his family whereas Petrarca spent the rest of his life as a scholar and traveling intellectual. But both men knew also that the key to happiness and a fulfilled life was to have as strong and peaceful and just a soul as possible.

Petrarca wrote many poems about a woman named Laura, whose existence has mostly passed forgotten into the sands of time. My father easily sensed the true unabashed love the poet had for his Laura, unrequited as his love was, and he decided as soon as my mother was pregnant to name me Laura if I were a girl. He wanted me to have a pure soul and to be so lucky as to find a man who would write me poetry, professing his love for me through rhymes, clever phrasings, and sonnets.

But now I am seventeen, my brothers are in their late thirties and early forties with wives and children, all wanting to move to Buenos Aires to open a business or work for a corporation, the clean air and breathtaking beauty of Patagonia no longer interesting them. Our parents had been dead for a year and I had not attended school since the funeral, instead being enlisted by my brothers as a catch-all nanny, housekeeper, babysitter...whatever was needed, just give it to Laura. And I complied in order to gain favor with them. It wasn't my fault they were twenty years older. It also wasn't my fault that by seventeen years of age, my own physical beauty was blossoming while my sisters-in-law's butts and waists were expanding at the same rate of the national debt in Argentina. My life was ahead of me, theirs were almost finished except for the jealousy and thinly veiled hatred they felt for me.

My brothers sold the farm after the death of my parents to an American corporation that wanted to produce cattle feed with our soybeans. It was a good deal for both sides, I guess, but a terrible one for me as I now had to move to Buenos Aires with my brothers and their families. I shuttled from one apartment to the other, never being allowed to set up any kind of a permanent private place where I could listen to my records, practice a little dancing, read a book, dream a little or even display my orchids and my two little stuffed penguins which I won in a traveling bazaar by throwing a dart into a balloon. None of my brother's wives were able to break the balloon and they not only resented my easy athleticism, but also that I wanted to keep my prizes for myself. They couldn't have known those two penguins, whom I named Rosie and Charlie after the unlikely lovers in The African Queen, were my only friends in the world.

But that changed soon enough. One afternoon I was walking past a golf driving range where I heard whoops of laughter between the sharp pings of the clubs hitting the ball. I was immediately drawn to the laughter as I craved any type of smile at that point. I peeked through a hole in the fence and could see some well dressed men in their forties hitting golf balls in rapid succession. I didn't know how to play golf, but what they were doing didn't seem to me to be any type of practice. I shifted my gaze out to the large space covered by green artificial turf and I observed a young man about eighteen years old driving a golf cart in a haphazard series of circles, starts and stops. I realized the men were using him for target practice and wondered why he would be so stupid as to drive around picking up the wayward balls in an open golf cart like some kind of polo player.

I had to admit I enjoyed watching him dodge the shots and pluck the balls off the turf with the tips of his fingers without even slowing down. Any one of the drives would have cracked his skull had they connected. After about fifteen minutes of this, the golfers must have tired of the routine and left the stalls. Realizing the game with the golfers was over, he stopped his cart, wiped his brow and leaned forward on the steering wheel, resting his chin on his forearms. He must have sensed someone watching him because he then looked up and our eyes met and held.

I was about twenty meters away but could clearly see even from a distance that he was a handsome young man with a nice wiry physique and an amazing head of hair. He drove right over to the space in the fence where I had been watching and introduced himself. His smile was warm and his manner was easy going and I felt comfortable and drawn to him immediately. He said he was getting off work soon and would be right back after he parked the cart. A few minutes later he came bounding out of the front door of the complex where I had stood waiting for him and walked right up to me.

"Hello, I am Diego de Mendoza. I'm from Gaiman." I was astonished, as our hometown of Dolavon was not far from his. I told him so and he seemed equally taken aback. Only twenty kilometers or so separated us during our short lives and somehow we managed to find each other here among the throngs in Buenos Aires. I couldn't take my eyes off his two deep pools of blue that must have come from a Welsh ancestor gaining access to the bed of a local girl. Gaiman was known for its embrace of Welsh culture since the late 1800's. I was in love with him immediately and I told myself that this would be so even if we were both living in the clean, friendly environment of Patagonia.

We continued to see each other, allowing our relationship to grow as naturally as possible. We took a weekend trip without telling anyone. My brothers and their wives didn't seem to care about me at all, why would they display any concern if I disappeared for a few days? We went to Mar del Plata and strolled the beaches by day and slept in the dunes by night. We offered to help the local food vendors scour pots and bus tables for meal money and we swam in the beautiful water and told stories of our lives to each other without fear of judgment or misunderstanding. We made love every night under the stars. It was my first time and I was neither nervous nor guilty. I never asked him if he had this type of experience before but it was plain to me by his patient, loving caresses that he was not holding his first girl in his arms. But I didn't care. I felt alive for the first time since my parent's death and told him so. He told me that he couldn't believe a farm girl and a city boy—he had been in Buenos Aires for so long he considered himself a city boy now—could fall in love so completely.

My brothers and their wives took turns beating me when I returned after three days in paradise with Diego. They called me by every derivation of slut— obviously unaware of what their own daughters were doing in their free time— and said they would kill Diego if they ever found him. Luckily I never let them know where he lived or what he looked like. Later, I managed to sneak away here and there for a momentito with Diego who lived in a shack behind the artificial fairway of the driving range. We always laid in each other's arms afterward and discussed our hopes and dreams for being together forever in breathless coughs and spurts. None of it seemed impossible to either of us.

"Laura, when you are eighteen," he said to me once, "I want you to come with me to America. I have been saving my money for several years and I have some distant relatives that would put us up. We can get work and go to school and not have to deal with anyone who disagrees with our love for each other." It took me about three seconds to agree. I walked home to one of my brother's apartments—whichever one it was that week—after our conversation and I stepped into a nightmare. All of my brothers and their wives were there waiting for me, everyone had their arms crossed, and the atmosphere was severe. They started in on me as soon as the door was closed.

"Laura, we have a plan for you. It will be the best choice for you. Mom and Dad would approve you can be sure of that." My blood was turning to red ice by the second as I listened to them. I didn't dare sit down as it would have signaled my capitulation to their demands. They continued as their wives sat observing with their smug smiles and fat asses and overdone trashy makeup.

"Tomorrow we are taking you to live at the Seminary north of the city. They will educate you, house you, and feed you. We have responsibilities to our own families and we can't allow your emerging bad habits to cause us any problems." I stared them all down hoping against hope that they felt my hatred.

"I thought I was your family. I am of the same blood and body of your parents and if they were here listening to this nonsense they would disown all of you!" I screamed sequentially, each word rising in volume as the statement emerged from my throat, direct from my soul. "I am in love with Diego and I will go with him to America and make a real life for myself, away from you people masquerading as my family!" I started moving around the room, looking

for an escape but I was surrounded quickly. The wives grabbed me and pushed me into a small room with a gate on the window and locked the door. I pounded on the door until my hands bled, and screamed for help until all my strength was gone and then collapsed on the small bed and sobbed inconsolably until somehow I fell asleep.

I was startled by a noise at the window and I jumped off the bed, not quite sure of where or even who I was for a moment. The moon was full and I could see someone at the window. As soon as I adjusted to consciousness and I could see it was Diego at the window I rushed across the room and we pushed our faces as close together between the bars as we could and kissed as best we could as if our lives depended on it.

"Mi amor! How did you know I was here? Why, how, what?" I was blubbering uncomprehendingly and he puckered so he could kiss me again and bade me to be silent. "Somehow I thought it wise to follow you home tonight, to make sure you arrived safely. I'm sorry, my love. I wasn't following you for any other reason," he whispered through the window gate. "What was all the yelling about? I heard a little bit. And why are you locked in here?" I spent the next few minutes telling him what had transpired since my arrival home and my brother's plans for me. "They want to keep us apart forever, my love. They are going to send me away tomorrow." I gripped the bars and twisted them to test their strength. I knew I could never break out of there. "I can't live without you," I told him, stroking his hair and we kissed again through the gate. Then he told me about a plan he had been formulating for the past few weeks that we needed to enact right away, before I was sent away. He would wait outside the house all night and follow us to the bus that was to take us to the seminary.

"I know the bus route," he said. "It goes right by the airport. When we are near the terminals, we just need to jump off and lose ourselves in the commotion. We are younger than all of them and we will be able to outrun them easily."

"But what will we do once we escape? How can we get tickets and permission to enter the United States? Don't you need a passport and a visa?" I knew nothing of such things.

"We can hide out in the fields around the airport until we get what we need. I know someone who will get us a visa and who can fake a passport for each of us. I have the money for all of this and for tickets. I've been saving for three years. I have all the money we need to get out of here tomorrow." I was so scared I was shaking just thinking about it. It was a crazy plan, thoroughly haphazard and *practically designed to fail. But I saw it as my only way to freedom and a better life. And I loved Diego and trusted him and wanted to be with him.*

And that was how I came to be on this bus with my brothers surrounding me like I was some sort of dangerous political prisoner. Diego was sitting only ten feet away on one of the seats that ran parallel to the sides of the belching smoky vehicle and he was able to watch me surreptitiously from the corner of his eye. As the bus continued along its route, I sensed my brothers easing their moods and postures, probably anticipating dumping me off into the care of a bunch of nuns and priests and out of their lives. I looked at Diego but dared not acknowledge him in any way. I was so glad none of my brothers knew him. What they would have done if they found out who he was right then! My heart was pounding and I could feel his anticipation, his fearlessness growing as we neared the genesis of his grand plan.

But I could not move, my limbs were frozen with fear. The United States... my goodness, big and scary. I had no friends there, no family. All I knew about it was the name of the current president and some cities like New York and Los Angeles. I remembered reading in school about the big trees in Northern California. What were they called? Redwoods, right. I recalled the pictures of them thinking that if I climbed to the top I could probably speak with God, they were so enormous. I couldn't speak a word of English. How would I learn? Diego can't speak English either, but he is so sure of himself.

A jet passed low over the bus and I couldn't push off the moment of truth any longer as it was arriving shortly. I could see the signs guiding motorists toward the drop off areas for passengers. Diego was standing now and holding onto the bar above the seats, glancing in my direction. I was frozen with fear. Where would we stay? What would we do for money? Work? Would someone...take advantage of us...make me do...things for...men? The news sometimes talked about the danger for young South American immigrant women in America. The bus was stopping now and I looked right into Diego's eyes and I could see his disappointment and his understanding as well as he realized right then that I wasn't leaving the bus. I was only seventeen. My trepidation consumed me and rooted me to the seat. Diego smiled sadly and waved and got off the bus, the doors closed, and as we pulled away, I turned in my seat to see where he was going but I couldn't find him in the crowds. And I leaped off the seat, startling my brothers, and pressed the strip above the window that rang the bell that alerted the driver that someone wanted to get off, and the bell kept ringing and ringing and my brothers were just looking at me like I was crazy *and I could see the driver looking at me in the big rear view mirror and I was panicking because the bus wasn't stopping and Diego was slipping away and the bell, the bell, why couldn't it be louder because I love him and I want to be with him and, and...*and my hand is slipping out from underneath the covers and I'm fumbling for the clock which seems louder than ever, the ring of the alarm amazingly having the same pitch as the bus bell from so many years ago and I am finally in the United States, in the greatest city in the world but not with Diego, whom I never saw again except in my dreams. I find the clock, turn it off, and throw it against the wall. My feet hit the floor and I lean forward putting my head between my legs as if I am trying to avoid a fainting spell but all I want to do is rub the ache out of my scalp and try to make my hair look halfway decent because I am late to my job at Argent Bank where I toil in their Information Technology department and I do not have time to wash my hair. Diego, I wondered for perhaps the thousandth time in the past few years, where are you and do you still think of me once in a while? I am embarrassed to admit I have never been able to erase your face from my dreams which are getting more vivid as I get older.

Laura padded out of her bedroom and slammed the door to the bathroom, not caring about the noise and whether it bothered anyone.

—※—

The Long Island Expressway would never be voted one of the most beautiful roads in the country. The Taconic Parkway, winding its way from Albany to the city, would at least have been nicer to look at driving down to work. But as soon as he became aware of the average property tax bill in Westchester County, disinterest set in. He recalled the two weekends he and Georgia and their six-year-old daughter Sally spent looking at houses up there. Beautiful country, full of twisting roads, tall elm trees, stone walls, that sort of thing. But he put his foot down immediately, Georgia not happy at all and showing it, but he insisting it couldn't be done. He worked as a mortgage officer for Argent Bank, after all. He knew about these things. "I work at Argent Bank as a mortgage officer. I know about these things, Georgia," the comment coming out of his mouth with a slight touch of disdain for *her* disdain and aware that he didn't care as much about that as he once did. No way are we living up here, shocked at the cost of virtu-ally everything. Even gasoline was twenty cents a gallon more expen-sive than on the Island, and for what reason? Plus the tolls on the bridge...forget about it. *Fuhgeddaboudit.* Michael had to have access to a car all the time for his work with the bank. He did like the drive up and home...wide open all the way from Katonah to the Bronx, beautiful foliage that fall, but he also suspected a more brutal winter even though they were only thirty or so miles north of the city and he didn't want to shovel snow that much. Just thinking about it made his lower back hurt. He was also shocked at the speeds with which the locals drove on the parkway. What am I, going to roll the car down the highway at forty something years of age and go out of this life that way? What a waste. And all these fools tooling along in their benzes, beemers, and SUV's, did they have any idea they were a blown tire away from certain death? In spite of that frightening line of thought, this was the best part of the mortgage business he always thought... to be able to make your own schedule and hardly ever have to worry about being late to the office. Anyway, Michael and Georgia instead moved from Queens, where they both were raised, to Long Island, as close to the Gold Coast as they could get without going totally broke.

During these morning drives along the expressway, he allowed his mind to roam through what should be expected during the day, what he did yesterday, and what the morning at home was like. He usually found it is best to start with the most unpleasant issue and for several years now, that has been the morning routine at home.

Invariably there would have been an argument between Georgia, his wife of seventeen years, and their now formerly adorable eleven-year-old daughter Sally. The arguments usually start the same way. A Mon-day-morning-type bad mood by either to start, an ignored morning salu-tation, a utensil dropped in the sink from a slightly higher altitude than necessary, a snotty look, a comment made under one's breath. Not the usual type of argument you would expect in any of the thousands of suburban kitchens, those including 'Turn off Spongebob,' 'Brush your teeth,' 'Is your homework in your schoolbag?' and that sort of thing. No, in this house, for the last few years it is about Greek school.

Michael & Georgia met at one of his gigs when she walked up to him after he finished his drumming for yet another local rock band with the line, "You made me turn green with envy for your girlfriend when I saw you tonight."

"Well, I don't have a girlfriend," Michael answered, entranced mostly with the fact that she so brazenly announced her interest. "So you don't have to turn green." And, he thought turning green would have not gone well with her magnificent brown eyes that were tilted upward in such a way that would make any man melt away like a Mr. Softee cone on the hottest day of the summer. Her legs—she won a best legs contest at the age of thirteen—were flawless and she had a certain confidence that Michael felt instantly. They fell in love a few minutes later and were married a year or so after that.

So many years later he started joining in on the conversations with his married colleagues. What is it with marriage, he and all his friends wondered—men and women alike—that just killed the bedroom and any form of intimacy? Did we get used to each other too quickly? Take each other for granted too easily? Was it just easier to roll over on Sunday morning and face each other and do it that way than it was to lean your lover up against the wall and make love standing up on your way into the house after a nice evening out together? How much effort does intimacy really take?

A squeeze of the butt, a wet kiss goodnight, running fingers through your lover's hair in the car, a couple of hot lovemaking sessions per week...that was enough for Michael. But over the past eighteen years that turned into a long lost dream as Georgia became hyper-involved with her consulting business and new liberal European friends, new to the city from...wherever...and since she was doing business with many people in Greece and elsewhere in Europe, her day started at two in the morning. Michael was in bed by eleven-thirty, exhausted from the realtors, the lawyers and the borrowers he had to deal with on a daily basis in the mortgage business. Earlier in the evening, it was up to him most of the time to make sure the rest of Sally's homework was finished, and then invariably, he had to guide her through the Greek alphabet and some vocabulary, neither of which he understood. Michael always found that unusual because he had developed an aptitude in language from listening to his friends' parents speak in their own homes in Queens...Korean, Chinese, Urdu, Pakistani, some Spanish...what crazy verbs in Spanish. 'Estar'...a 'state of being' verb meaning 'to be' Ms. Grandes had tried to teach him...'Uh excuse me, but what the hell is that?'...and even a bit of Arabic came fairly easily to him. A few phrases in Greek stayed in his brain over the years, but it never truly took. However, he promised Georgia that he would help with the education of their daughter in this regard. But it seemed all up to him now and the resentment was growing. The battles between daughter & mother were becoming more and more severe as time went on and it wore on him like a heavy old coat.

"Why do I have to learn Greek? I am an American," it would usually start.

"It will help you get a better job. It will help your brain get stronger," was the typical refrain.

Sally was an unusually precocious child, with amazing verbal skills, which I was reminded of when she would respond, "Maybe I could accept that if you were teaching me Chinese, Spanish, or Japanese, but unless I am going to be a tour guide at the Parthenon, I don't see how this is going to help me. I hate being Greek." How did she know what the Parthenon or even what a tour guide was?

"You are Greek, half-Greek at least, and you can't change that, not ever. So get used to it."

"I hate being Greek and I hate you. Daddy is Irish so I'm half-Irish, too, and all-American!" Michael had to intercede at this point in order to maintain some sense of law and order as well as quell the pounding in his ears.

"Sally," he said to her in a voice that was gruffer than intended, "Don't ever speak to your mother like that. And you better get used to being Greek..."

"Half-Greek."

"...because you can't change it. And being Greek is a wonderful thing. Our entire civilization is built upon the ideas and philosophies of ancient Greek culture. You should find out a little bit about Plato, Aristotle, and Sophocles." Georgia was back in the kitchen now banging her way around the room, coffee cup slammed down here, spoon tossed there, bouncing around the porcelain sink like a roulette ball making a sound that was so high pitched and annoying Michael felt the reports in his teeth rather than in his ears.

And so it went on, beating Michael into the ground bit by bit.

Georgia ran out of the house to her appointment and Sally skipped down the driveway and caught the bus to school. Neither said good-bye and Michael continued with drinking his orange juice and reading the paper for a few more minutes.

It seemed like miles had gone by without his noticing any of the other drivers or scenery, Michael glancing in the rear view mirror just in time to see two street racers bearing down on him, a lime green Hyundai holding its own against a tricked-out Honda. Except that they were sharing the lane Michael was in…the middle lane…the cars in the left and the right lanes being forced to the shoulders. But there was no shoulder for Michael and these kids—probably racing from Montauk to Brooklyn for a five thousand dollar pot—were going to blast right through Michael's five-year-old sedan like twin Exocet missiles through aluminum siding. At the last possible moment, helped by his frozen in place method of dealing with these two assholes, they split from each other just enough that when they passed him going at least ninety miles per hour, they were so close that the side view mirrors clicked slightly…on each side of his car. In front of Michael there were several hundred feet ahead of clear sailing and the high-pitched whine of both foreign-born engines actually increased as they lurched forward even faster, the drivers seemingly oblivious of the destruction they almost caused behind them.

What a way to go, flipping the car on the expressway followed by a fireball. After getting hit by two kids. Not an exactly heroic death like performing CPR on a kid you just pulled out of the ocean. Just a lot of 'what a terrible tragedy' to be soon followed by general forgetfulness. Except, of course, for the family and friends, and Georgia and Sally. How utterly useless a death like that would be. But something like this happened at least several times per month. And a lot of other people didn't make it home after leaving for work.

Michael took the exit for the Brooklyn-Queens Expressway near the patch of triangular grass on Forty-Eighth Street where he had his first little league practice. The road ran under the raised portion of the LIE here, and then turned south, continuing to parallel Manhattan just a couple of miles away. With a deep sigh, Michael found himself at the point in his commute to his lower Manhattan office, doing what he did every morning for the past six years, looking downtown to make sure that it wasn't a bad dream, that maybe the towers were still there. The morning was still so clear in his mind. He was right here on 9/11, headed down the other side of the Kosciuszko Bridge on the way to whichever of the three lower East River bridges looked uncongested enough to use to enter into Manhattan. Hopefully the city would never put a toll on any of these river crossings.

Michael spent a few dazed moments that Tuesday morning trying to fathom what he was looking at and at first concluded that it must have been a bomb. What else could it be? The news had not yet gotten out since the first plane hit the building while he was under the LIE just a few minutes before. The smoke had just started its journey east. It didn't evolve into the hundred mile long plume it would become later in the day. His college roommate Steve called him just then. "Hey, what's up? Did another dentist lose his way to Teterboro? We're hearing that someone hit the Trade Center." He was practically laughing, seemingly figuring that a Cessna would just bounce off the building and land in the river. Teterboro was the site of a small airport in New Jersey that serviced mostly private, smaller aircraft. In the weeks prior to 9/11, there were several mishaps with private planes, and a dentist or two always seemed to be involved. The enormity of the hole Michael along with everyone around him on the BQE was staring at blew his mind and he was instantly convinced it was no little plane with two seats.

"Uhh, Stevie, I don't think it was a dentist, you should see the size of this fucking hole." The words slipped between his teeth and lips like vomit.

"Yeah, does it look bad?" How could he know? He wasn't looking at it like everyone creeping along on the raised highway. Michael's view was unobstructed, the skies as clear as they possibly could be. Severe clear. Everyone was moving slowly, the type of behavior that would usually result in a cacophony of horn honking, shouts, and raised fingers. A perfect early autumn day in New York City. And then the second plane came in, Michael watching it all, thoroughly convinced that the son-of-a-bitch who was driving the aircraft pushed the gas pedal to the floor in the plane's final approach to the seventy-seventh floor of the South Tower. He hung up the phone without saying good-bye as the fireball spread and opened and expanded like an ugly flower, the muted explosion reaching his ears a couple of seconds later, somehow not driving the car through the railing and falling to the street below in his shock and dismay, instantly knowing that at least several of his friends and clients just died alog with thousands of others. Whenever Michael was at this point in his journey, he had run this movie reel over in his mind without fail more than fifteen hundred times since that day. He sighed and brought his senses back to the present and continued onward to the downtown office.

About a half hour later, he parked the car near Fraunces Tavern and walked a few blocks north up to Wall. Upon entering the office, being unfailingly polite, Michael said good morning to the women in the front answering the phones and directing visitors for closings, meetings, whatever. He liked to joke that this was the only way he could get dates in college because he had very little money to spend and no car to drive them somewhere nice. But he knew that he could hold the door, pull out a chair, speak nicely and listen attentively, stand when a woman enters the room and help with homework, whatever the situation called for. Many times the rich kids would come by hours after Michael had composed a sonnet for a junior or senior in the wake of some intensive studying to pick up their girl in their Members Only jackets with their Dad's Eldorado idling outside, some of them openly wondering where the languid look on their girl's face had come from.

Passing by reception, he turned into the cubicle farm, stopping to say hello to Hank Fredericks, a salesman for a title company who was humping for more business. He was a good guy, who always seemed just a little overwhelmed and maybe too concerned about things he would never be able to control, but one of the good, solid guys nonetheless. Gaining a little weight now, Michael noticed. Hank was a few years past fifty and always looked like he was replaying his best moments from his youth in his mind whenever Michael saw him. He had a strange habit of writing things down whenever Michael spoke with him. He carried these small legal pads with him all the time. Strange…but harmless. He looked up and caught Michael's eye as he approached.

"Good morning, Mr. Pierce," he said with mock reverence, "how are things today?" Michael continued into his cubicle, pulling off his jacket and laying it on the back of the chair. He leaned back to answer him with a real answer. Michael always hated superficial small talk.

He believed that if someone asked you a question, you should give a truthful, thoughtful, complete answer.

"Good morning, Hank. We got a busy one today thank goodness." They both knew that their production numbers had started to fall off recently as interest rates rose. "A couple of very important closings are going on today," he continued, knowing full well that Hank did not have the title work for all of them. The first was a $2,500,000 loan on a nice townhouse in The Village on which Michael was earning a point and a half, a whale of a deal, and the client was going to love him because it was he, not the borrower's incompetent, lazy attorney, who arranged for the assignment of the mortgage tax at the last moment, saving the borrower more than $45,000 in extra closing costs. I am going to walk in there like a conquering hero, Michael was absolutely convinced of this. And the borrower's attorney would hopefully realize that Michael Pierce from Argent Bank had saved his ass, kept it quiet, and maybe he would remember that the next time a client asked for a mortgage referral.

The second was a smaller deal, but one that he worked on closely with Pia Enpiso, the hottest young realtor in the city. Ms. Enpiso had already closed a deal per week this year, and this was only her second year in the business. Last year she closed fifty million dollars in sales and had a reputation of being perfectly honest, and as firm and unyielding as a bridge cable. This particular purchase went so smoothly, it should have been nominated for the Deal of the Week. And with this closing, as with the first one this morning, in a building he knew she was trying to break into; he planned to parlay it all into an ongoing relationship with Ms. Enpiso that was going to bring a stream of referrals and income for several years until she got bored of him like she did with the last guy she worked with and would with the guy she chose after Michael. He told Hank about the deals and sincerely apologized for not being able to include him on all the business.

"The big guy, he's a property owner and therefore has his own title company connections and the second is a purchase. The buyer's attorney ordered title," Michael told him while lifting his palms skyward. "Hank, I promise to always keep you in mind." Hank sat there for a few more minutes while Michael answered e-mails, checked to see if the rest of his pipeline was moving forward, made sure that appraisals were ordered and that the next month's set of loans were getting further through the meat grinder of mortgage processing so he would be able to pay his bills. He tried to concentrate in spite of all the talk about sub-prime paper and the problems it was inevitably going to cause. He was hearing these rumblings in the distance, most of which was provided by his old friend Jeff Axel, who traded mortgage portfolios for a living. He couldn't worry about that now. Things were going pretty well for him. The bank was solid, he had some new referral sources percolating, he had a little money in the bank and a huge dream or two was within his grasp in the form of his friend Vinny's building project deal. He wouldn't allow himself to think about his home life until later. He gathered up his things for the trip uptown to the bank's office on Fifth Avenue, annoyed at Hank Fredericks, who didn't move out of the way quickly enough for him to have a free path, instead absentmindedly continuing to scribble on a little yellow note pad.

The 7 train travels back and forth from Times Square out to Flushing Queens all day and all night all year. Numerous times it has won some kind of Straphanger's Council award for cleanliness, on-time performance, and so forth. In recent years it has been referred to as the International Express, the reason for that moniker being that the route it took through Long Island City, Sunnyside, Woodside, Jackson Heights, Elmhurst, Corona and Flushing can be described much in the same way Henry David Thoreau described his view of traveling abroad and his disdain for the same: "I have traveled extensively in Brooklyn."

A passenger from Flushing to the city will start his or her run at Main Street in one of the largest Chinese & Korean communities in the United States, a place where the white people decided to sue the stores for signs in English. In Elmhurst and Corona you would encounter all types of Hispanic families, Dominicans, Puerto Ricans, Mexicans, Peruvians, the curses and arguments in Spanish and the bossa-nova grooves floating on the aromas of empanadas and cuchifritos from kitchens along Roosevelt Avenue all the way up to the train on the elevated tracks above. In Jackson Heights, Bengalis, Pakistanis, and Indians crowd onto the car, the women always dressed colorfully, smiling continually, the men looking much more somber, always appearing troubled and slightly uncomfortable with themselves. Rolling in closer to the city, the 7 arrives in Woodside and Sunnyside for its collection of Irish, although many more Koreans these days get on the train at Bliss or Lowery Street. African-Americans and Arabs are at the last stop in Queens, Vernon-Jackson Avenue, and this is also the station where Laura catches the train to work, just a few convenient blocks from her apartment.

Laura loved this crazy diversity, a patchwork of humanity if there ever was one, but had come to realize years before that the men in this country, including the different stripes of men from other countries who were on the 7 train every day with her, and probably in all others, would just not leave her alone.

She inherited her mother's great looks and figure, a body so lithe and elegant that she easily rivaled in this regard most women in their mid-twenties. If she were the type of woman to hit the clubs on a Saturday night, she could invite lovers to her attention fifteen years younger than she with but a crook of her finger. And she had in fact made the rounds of the city's fashionable hot spots over the years, a little bit here and there with her crazy but very nice friend Jordana.

But this was never her way, in spite of the efforts of the church and her brothers and then those teachers and her bosses at the seminary to make her fearful of her sexuality and desire for real passion. It was never their fiery speeches and dire warnings that set her feet on the love path she had traveled thus far. She wasn't going to ever just give herself to just anyone who had a pulse. She would remain forever picky, maybe to a fault, her friends would sometimes whisper.

Once she escaped the seminary, which she did six years after arriving there by simply standing up and telling them she was leaving...it took her weeks to get over the fact that fear had kept her there for all those years, fear of standing up for herself. But at least she got something out of it. Those people *could* teach and by the time she left, Laura was just short of several certifications in Computer Arts and Nursing of all things. Her brothers, who had not visited her once in the six years she was there, were all astounded at her level of education and how she blew them all off on her way to the airport, finally telling them the whole story of how close she came to doing the same thing that day six years before, running off with Diego to America.

She barely escaped the Chicano gangs in East Los Angeles during her first few terrifying months in the United States, although they promised her the world: "You'll be our South American princess, dulcita." The groping pimps along Hollywood Boulevard, the rich men who stalked her on the beach and at the mall, trying to lure her with promises of a meeting with this producer, that casting agent, a stalker boyfriend who seemed to know every cop on the Los Angeles Police force, all of them ignoring her pleas for assistance. Then on a whim she got in her car and drove straight through to Michigan, where it was so cold and so bleak she almost went back to Argentina. She still to this day traded Christmas cards and an occasional phone call with the wonderful family who took her in and let her stay in an apartment above the Mexican restaurant they owned. They had the cutest children, a boy and a girl, and although she was in her twenties by now, the husband and wife treated her like their own daughter.

Not a man up there, although her sponsors tried to fix her up with some of the auto company executives who would stop for lunch or dinner. One got into an accident on their first date and cried over the damage to his car while she waited for him to ask if she was okay. Another said he could never continue to date a woman who wasn't a 'real' American. And another spoke endlessly about his Porsche, Ferrari, and his Maserati, all of which he kept at his mother's house so his American car company executives would never see them. Not as bad a problem as the fact that he still lived with his mother in the same house. Big problem. The rest were just boys who wanted, demanded, felt they deserved her body after a few cheap dates. After her arrival in New York for the green card lottery there were some men here and there, even a husband for a few years, but none that made her feel the way her mother told her she would feel when she met the *one*.

"Laura, you will know you met the man you deserve, that you want, when you realize that you doing and saying things to and for him, that you never considered saying or doing before." She knew what her mother meant, about the deep well of secrets that every woman possessed, to be shared with no one...maybe not even the *one*.

There were some nice relationships in New York, but all failed ultimately because of the question she could never answer: why should she settle for this particular man? Many were funny, some were smart, a couple were drop dead handsome, most were adequate lovers, but all of them eventually snored like a freight train, were never curious of how her early life on the farm was, were unnecessarily jealous over her social dancing, or just acted as if they wanted to possess her very being and soul. None of them ever knew of the horribly lonely and confusing years she spent before the bus ride with Diego and her brothers, and the equally defeating months and years afterward. But if they did, they would have respected her need for a just a little distance. Just a few hours alone to think, read, watch a movie or anything at all.

Now she was forty-two with no children which didn't bother her so...much, no husband, and limited prospects. Well not limited, really. Maybe Adam, whom she met three months ago, would finally be different. Handsome and tall, working for one of the largest investment banks in the world, he seemed to meet all the prerequisites for Laura to even think about going further, but there was still an element of distrust, a wisp of insincerity emanating from him that she could not shake from her conscience. Outwardly, he was the type of man that ninety-nine percent of the eligible, good looking, horny forty-year old women in New York City would openly pant for. Nevertheless, she enjoyed the fancy parties, the way he spoke French to her, and she enjoyed his good manners. She had to admit she felt like a lottery winner when he told her that he was unattached, no old flames still hanging around in his mind, hoping they magically reappear in person once again.

"What the fuck is he single at forty-five years of age for?" spit her best friend Nadia, "He must be a fag or something." Nadia was the opposite of Laura in temperament and looks, short and twenty pounds overweight, fiery, not at all shy, but the two somehow got along famously.

"Maybe he never met the right girl," countered Laura, which was met with smacked, pursed lips, and an upturned chin which Laura knew meant, Are you fucking kidding me? The way Nadia cursed made her laugh and she wished she could have the courage to stand up to people the way her friend did.

"I am going to see him tonight and maybe I will find out a little more about him," said Laura, "especially since I will be staying over for the first time," wincing as she said it, waiting for the barrage of invective she figured was coming. But she was wrong.

"Amigalita," her friend implored not with harshness but with rare warmth in her voice that spelled real concern that touched Laura's heart, "please check this guy out a little bit more, call him at midnight to see if he answers, Google him, run a background check on him, just make sure he is what he says he is because I got to tell you, he makes my spider sense start to shake and rattle."

Laura laughed this off at the time, but admittedly could not shake her own little shred of doubt as her friend was full of street smarts. Once at a soccer game at a local college, shortly after they sat down, Nadia pointed to a group of young men and predicted, "They'll be beating the shit out of each other by the end of the first half." She was wrong only because they started beating the shit out of each other much earlier. She reminded herself to table these misgivings and look Adam over especially carefully tonight, because she believed that this was going to be the night for them to be together. And frankly, after five sexless years...how the hell did that happen?...she was ready to sleep with almost anyone.

In any event the 7 train offers all manner of perversion, pick-up lines and groping techniques imported from all over the world, the Chinese & Koreans brushing against your upper body if they could reach that high, the Irish preferring your lower body, the businessmen pushing past you with an open palm strategically placed on your thigh, the black kids sometimes brazenly grabbing a handful of butt. Her favorite place in the car was near the small seat by the door between the cars, so she could squeeze into the corner and observe anyone coming near her.

Not that she would have that much trouble handling any of these fools. Baling hay, breaking horses, and walking back and forth to school for so many years, followed by years of rollerblading and golf and ballroom dancing in New York gave Laura an incredibly strong and toned but nonetheless elegant body. Her legs were as hardy as any man's, and she had biceps that rivaled half of them. What she didn't have, would never have, never wanted to have, in fact, was the brazen manner of a woman like Nadia who once remarked to her, "I could have every man in this city at any time if I had your body and your looks. And if they didn't want me, I would beat the shit out of them until they did."

Laura rode the 7 through the tunnel into Grand Central station where she exited the car with a Chinese man hanging on her left breast, an Irish man rubbing up against her ass, and a businessman running his hand up her arm and somehow made it up the stairs without a major injury. She jumped on the uptown 4 train and rode to Fifty-Seventh Street, where she routinely exited the third car from the end of the train so she could be right in front of the subway stairs. The passengers here were not as aggressive as on the 7, but the stares on this line were harder, the leers more troubling. She always felt a bit menaced at times on the subway and she wondered if the other women riding next to her did as well. Some mornings the ride scared the hell out of her.

Three blocks walking west brought her to her office building on Fifth Avenue, across from Tiffany's, where she worked as an Information Technology Security Specialist for Argent Bank. The elevator took her to the fiftieth floor, which had beautiful views of Central Park, and she stepped through the double glass doors into what was another type of prison for her lately. Her long strides brought her past the public relations department for the bank, full of cackling young women from what she was told were the best schools, whatever that meant, and metro-sexual men who spent twice the time before the mirror in the morning than Laura did. The women's laughter and office socializing unnerved her not only because of the disturbing timbre of their cackling. In her work she had to concentrate totally on several jobs every hour, hundreds of lines of code, wires in and out of the bank, money flowing around the world in little electronic blips that were constantly in danger of interruption or theft from fake princes in Nigeria or fifteen-year-old nerds in the suburbs with the newest Apple computer. Many of these wires and files that accompanied them were voluminous, involved sums of money in the tens of millions of dollars and, although at times it seemed like a hi-tech version of an assembly line, she never ignored the importance of her work. It insulted her natural sense of pride in a job done well, no matter how small the task. She often considered that if these people from the so called best schools worked on the farm in such an indifferent manner, then nothing would grow and the cows, goats, pigs and chickens would eventually take over like in Orwell's novel *Animal Farm*. The men, well...several of them tried to lamely corner her in the kitchen over the years, armed with ridiculously inane come-on lines, some a little mean and others entirely too suggestive even for a salsa dance party let alone an office kitchen. She was ready for them all with her quick wit and sometimes more effectively her refusal to even acknowledge them or their actions or comments in even the most passing fashion. At times she felt like a fireman in a burning building, looking for hotspots in the form of a thirty-something metro-sexual man who thought he knew something about who she was or what she wanted.

No help was forthcoming from her own members of the gender team as Laura often found it impossible to have a decent friendship with most women. They acted as if they were worried about her taking their husbands or boyfriends. There seemed to be unspoken insane jealousy over the cheekbones, the legs, the figure, the hair, whatever. It probably would have served her better in the friendship department had she been less fortunate genetics-wise. Then maybe she would have more girlfriends. And the men, the asshole men who look at her and see nothing but her physical self, would stop bothering her, although she would have eventually liked to have had the opportunity to explain to a man with good ears and a patient heart what kind of difficulties shaped her life.

The phone is ringing on her co-worker's desk and as usual he was not around to answer it. Argent Bank was one of the few companies on the planet that did not use voice mail, a relic of customer service that many employees believed hurt the bank in these more modern days, one that forced Laura to interrupt her schedule several times per hour just to explain to some imbecile how to restart their computer.

Most days she enjoyed her work but was frustrated, as most women were at companies large and small, with the lack of support, education, and opportunity for advancement. One day she was going to do only her job, perform only her duties, and watch as her male colleagues were exposed for the lazy and ineffective employees they were. But mention any of this to management? No way, as they also seemed to have something against her, a triumvirate of bad luck in bosses that included a fleshy fifty-five-year-old, who resented her for being the type of girl who would never speak to him in high school; a guy from Paraguay who lost his girl in high school to a rich Argentinean playboy some thirty years earlier and therefore resented her for it; and the worst of the bunch, Andre, the West African, who seemed to regard her as less important than one of the goats she used to raise on the farm. This is what you get by helping them all these years, never asking for a raise beyond what they offered, never complaining about their constant lateness, about these same people getting the best classes, about their withholding information from her…it went on and on. And unless she won lotto sometime soon, there was little for her to do about it.

With a sigh she set out to clean up what was left over—again—from the night shift, millions of dollars that should have hit client accounts overnight that were still sitting in limbo. She started thinking about what she would do with Adam tonight as her fingers played over her keyboard. Nadia was dead set against him for some reason. Should she trust her friend's instincts? Maybe let him wait a little longer? No, I don't want to wait a little longer. I need something, anything, and I need it now. Decision made, over. The phone on Andre's desk continued to ring. It was up to seven rings before she decided to pick it up. As she brought the phone to her ear, she flashed on an image of Michael Pierce calling, announcing to her today that he was no longer married. For that, she would change her plans with Adam. Not hearing an answer of any kind on the line, she replaced the handset back in the carriage and went back to reading the codes sweeping across her screen.

⁓

Michael strolled into the building where some of Argent Bank's closing attorneys were located on lower Broadway, the picture of confidence, looking forward to this meeting. It was a convenient place for his Wall Street borrowers and borrowers from New Jersey to meet. He had no real work to do at the closing as the title representative and bank attorney were running the show now. Maybe he had to answer a few innocuous questions because these closings were designed to be just a big paper chase with mountains of documents to signed, dated, and notarized, the underwriting and science as it were of lending far behind them, every scrap of information about the borrower's finances already gathered and scrutinized. So essentially his role today was mostly to glad-hand the borrower and his attorney in an effort to convince them that they should never think of anyone else to call regarding home financing matters. A number of people waited in the lobby with him for the elevator and everyone piled in at once when it arrived except Michael, who had a certain disdain for tight quarters. Instead, he waited until the last minute and stepped in once he was able to discern the doors could close without packing him in like a sardine.

He was going to be a hero at this closing he thought, as he stepped aside to let an older woman leave the cab unobstructed. That earned him a smile…a smile from an old lady for a conquering mortgage Superman. A Superman who can take a snippy client like this one, this Matty Albano, who was denied for this loan by several other banks, a guy who inherited a fistful of apartment buildings in Greenwich Village and enjoyed passing himself off as some kind of wheeler-dealer, who thought his townhouse, his asset base, his tax returns—which he did not have to provide for this deal—were beyond reproach, and would get him closed with all the terms he promised from the beginning, amount of cash out of the deal, interest rate, points, everything.

In addition, Matty's New York State and New York City mortgage tax was going to be assigned—due to Michael's efforts alone—saving over $45,000 in closing costs. He would do his inept attorney a major league favor by not exposing his failure to arrange for the assignment himself in front of his client.

After being met by the receptionist, who upon his entering the attorney's office vestibule remarked to her equally young and pretty colleague, "Now that's one nice looking older man," Michael practically floated into the closing room, where he saw Matty Albano hunched over, signing one of the scores of forms, disclosures, and notes required of a residential mortgage closing these days. Before Michael could even say hello, however, he was greeted by a snarl from his borrower, the anger actually twisting his mouth and face in such a way that it would make a wolverine back off. He was astounded at the ferocity of the man's voice.

"I told you I don't pay application fees!" he yelled at the top of his lungs. Michael looked at the final Good Faith Estimate, the top of which was being twisted like a used tissue by his client's grip, his arm extended to its full length, the paper just an inch from Michael's nose where he indeed did see on line 808 of the form…Application Fee—$225.00. A simple thing to take care of. This is a $2,500,000 loan, the application fee can easily be absorbed into his commission. He silently grinded his molars, recalling asking the bank attorney to omit that item. Alright, forget about it, the attorneys really are good guys. They won't do it again. It's nothing to rant to them about. These were the main thoughts that flashed through his brain like lightning before calmly responding, "Okay Matt, this item went on the closing statement by accident. I will make it up to you by sending a check tomorrow."

"No, we will finish this now. I want a new Good Faith Estimate with no application fee appearing anywhere!" He was shrieking by the time he got to the last syllable. The borrower's attorney had his head down as did the title closer and the bank attorney. Michael put his left hand in his pocket and gripped his cell phone, much in the same way an electroshock therapy patient bites down on a piece of wood when the jolt hits the frontal lobe and extended his right palm toward his client in a gesture he hoped by itself would convey the fact that the new documents wouldn't be necessary.

"But Matt, that would mean a redrawing of almost all of the exhibits and forms, something that may take a couple of hours and then you would have to sign all of these docs again and it would throw off your day. Let me send a check. I promise you it will be in your mailbox before the end of business."

"No, Michael," Matty responded quite calmly as he turned his full attention back to the pile of papers on the table, something that simultaneously unnerved and angered Michael. "I want it done now or the deal is dead." And with that he put on his reading glasses, studied the papers before him and turned to stone.

Michael was dumbfounded. This was the guy from whom he was expecting a hero's welcome because of the assignment of the mortgage tax, but now he was being treated like shit, like a messenger boy. Bad enough it was happening in his own office in front of other professionals he has to work with going forward from this day. This guy owns real estate all over the Village. He knows what's going on. He knows what I've done for him. How could he not? There was nothing else for Michael to do now. The client probably wasn't going to refer any future business at this point anyway. This was what they all usually remembered, a tiny little bump in the road. Not the four denials from other banks that I overcame, not his incompetent lawyer whose job I did for no charge, and certainly not the enormous amount of money I saved him. Just an application fee that inadvertently appeared on a closing document. Michael somehow was able to sigh audibly while his shoulders were up near his ears.

"I'll do it for you, Matt, but please try to remember that I got the assignment done when no one else seemed able to do so. That's a lot more than $225." Michael peered slightly sideways at the lawyer who still had his head down, avoiding his gaze. You know what, screw his lawyer, thought Michael. If he thinks he's going to wriggle away from his responsibility to his client and try to make me look like the bad guy, well fuck that.

"So you are looking for credit for doing your job?"

"No Matt, I'm just trying to point out…"

"Just change the form and get that fucking application fee out of my face!"

Michael stood there for a moment like a statue, letting the ring of the angry words subside before he moved or responded. Slowly he took his cell phone out of his pocket, his grip on it so fierce it was in danger of shooting out of his hand the way he and his friends shot watermelon pits at the girls at CYO camp by squeezing them between their fingers. He called his closing department, told them of the change, parroting the suggestion of a check out loud so that everyone in the room could see he wasn't the only fool who thought that was the way to go, and he then apologized to his borrower, for Michael Pierce was a professional and a gentleman and a representative of Argent Bank. One hour and twenty minutes later, after the closing department had to interrupt their own routines, other borrowers' closings, wasting the time of about seven people, the new documents sans application fee were in the lawyer's office, Matt signing happily, the lawyer who couldn't get the assignment done now making himself look like a hero in front of the whole room, his head no longer bowed in fear. And it was at this moment that Michael was glad that he supported gun control because he truly wanted to shoot these two self-absorbed jerks in the knees. On Michael's way out of the closing room a little less than an hour later, without the business card of the lawyer representing Matty Albano, he once again passed the reception desk and the two young secretaries there who now were thinking that maybe they were wrong earlier because this guy really does look his age now.

—

"Laura!" bellowed Bobby Chitman, a Senior Vice-President of the bank. He was not Laura's direct boss. He didn't even work in IT, but he was someone to whom she absolutely had to answer. He should have had some sense of place, she thought, as he marched over to her desk, most of the rest of the people in the room now looking up. In the middle of this she realized that the only people not listening or watching were the young hires, mostly twenty-five-year-old tech geeks who listened to their IPods while at their desks. That was why they hadn't heard the bellow. And apparently, that was also why none of them heard the phone ringing when he was calling just a few min-utes before. Mostly, Laura and this man had spoken only briefly and politely over the years as he was not part of the IT department, and their hours were different, he coming into the office a little later each day in order to deal with some new clients in Japan and China. He arrived at her desk thoroughly flustered and out of breath, as if he had to climb a mountain to get there. Laura didn't even begin to try to understand what was happening so she just sat where she was and waited for him to speak.

"Laura," he began, the perspiration already staining his collar, "None of the wires hit the Asian accounts yet. They were supposed to be there hours ago. I was just cursed out in three languages that all sounded similarly hostile." He sat on her desk, one foot touching the ground, crossed his arms and leaned in, speaking softly, drawing the onlookers slightly closer. "Laura"—why was he saying her name so much as if she were a ten-year-old?—"I need to know what happened with this money which, by the way, totals about fifty million dollars, and I need to know in less than five minutes. That's all I can tell you. Just find that money for me, hmm?" With that, he unarched his eye-brows, slid off the desk and sort of half-stormed back to his office on the other side of the floor. He never asked where Andre was at that moment. That's what pissed her off the most. Andre, the Vice-president of the group, someone who was so blind to the concept of teamwork that Laura wondered if he could name half of the employees in this department, he was the one who should be handling this.

At the first moment, Laura had really no idea of how to proceed with Chitman's demand. Should I throw my letter opener at his back? Or should I try to figure this out for Andre? She decided to leave the letter opener for later and set aside the security jobs that were left unattended from the night shift and assembled her thoughts on how to approach this issue. First, get the list of these new Asian clients and their accounts. Review the history of traffic between our bank and theirs...how long and for what amounts. Check the specific wires for Mr. Shitface, uh Chitman, and e-mail him now before he gets to his desk asking for the exact wires to which he was referring. This she absolutely had to have and the ball was now in his court to get them to her. In five minutes she would call him and ask for them if he didn't respond. That's what she heard so much in her time in corporate America: cover your ass. It makes you look responsible and is good to have in the event of some inquiry later. Here, the e-mail is being answered from Mr. 'If-you-ever-sit-on-my-desk-again-like-that-again I'll-shove-you-right-off-so-you-land-on-your-ass' with the account numbers and names of the accounts, wire amounts and the following line: "Sorry if I was a little loud before." Nothing more. Nothing public. Fine. I won't let them bother me. I have a wonderful evening ahead of me with Adam Breezington. I've been seeing him for three months here and there and it's starting to get a little warm in the room when we are together, no matter what Nadia says. Maybe her friend is a little jealous. Tonight she would end one of her most embarrassing personal losing streaks...five years with no man, no sex... nothing but probably a hundred missed opportunities. Maybe she should be a bit more like Nadia. But let's face it, she always depressingly easily concluded, the men in New York are not what you would like to see in the men of New York. Not a Diego among them. But maybe Adam. He seems alright, at least decent enough to take for a little road trip through his bedroom tonight. She was turned on—a phrase she secretly hated— thinking about it but then was troubled once again not only by what Nadia told her recently regarding her instincts about him, but also by what her mother told her long ago. It was the first time while daydreaming about Adam that she realized she had ignored the advice of both regarding him. She shook her head to clear these thoughts away and concentrated again on this emergency. Her fingers flew over the keyboard of her computer in pursuit of the missing millions of dollars. I'll just take care of this, she reasoned yet once more, and maybe someone who cares about this company will actually notice. This was really Andre's job, his responsibility, she angrily thought again. He's the Vice-president. Where the hell is he?

———

Sometimes I think I should have made better use of my accounting degree, thought Jeff Parness, who was the owner and chief engineer of Parlalome Recording Studios in Manhattan, where he recorded music for commercial jingles, some B-list rock stars, and a whole host of wannabes. And he was here much earlier than usual, at the tail end of a marathon recording session, listening to another delusional singer who thought she had talent and her boyfriend, who was obviously desperately trying to hold onto her by financing this recording. The Beatles recorded some of the most musically enduring record albums in history in a day or two. But this one here has taken three hours just to lay down one vocal track for a listless, contrived pseudo country/reggae tune, whatever the hell that was. Such fools men were, he thought, especially when it came to women who would never love them back.

As hard as it was to listen to this woman's pitchy vocals, it was that easy to look at her. An Arab Denise Richards, he concluded when she entered his studio for the first time. A beautiful mane of auburn hair, dark eyes that flashed danger much in the same way a Magnum pistol would just sitting by itself on a shelf. The guy she was with, an African Muslim with black on black skin, a permanently furrowed brow and pitted skin, seemed to bark at everyone and anyone in his way, but was quite reserved in her presence to the point of almost bowing to her like a courtier. Jeff had to remind him a couple of times that he needed to respect the employees of the studio. They were not children and they did not take orders from anyone but him. The man would skulk away after each warning, muttering something about being a paying customer which Jeff responded to by accurately telling him that he didn't need this recording gig or the money and he would gladly refund the remainder of the man's deposit for the time not yet used. What a jerkoff, Jeff was thinking as he tinkered with knobs and dials and auto-tuning and filters and every gradation of treble, bass and mid-range he could think of in order to make this harpy sound like a vocalist. What a nightmare he must be to the others he works with in whatever hell-hole he works in, some fucking bank somewhere he remembered when he showed up with cash for these sessions. And you know what? Cash in any business speaks, and it speaks forcefully, even when it is offered by the likes of this guy.

No way is she fucking him, Jeff thought. Instead, it seemed like she was keeping him at arm's length, just enough to keep him wanting, but far enough so that he may as well be trying to stretch across the Hudson River. What a manipulative bitch, he was thinking as she scratched through take seventy-nine of the worst song he had ever heard. Some kind of weird effort to pull from every pop musical genre with inane lyrics and a bad pedal steel guitar solo. Once again, she ripped the headphones from her head in frustration at her God-given inability to remain in pitch, to reach the upper register that her weird arrange-ment required, which she had about as much chance of reaching as I do of supplanting Jeter at shortstop next year. Jeff stopped the tape yet again and rewound it. Jeff could see her manager/wannabe boyfriend in the window walk out of the studio control room and into the small vocal recording room just outside the door.

"Kismine," pleaded Andre Wyland, the same Andre who was sup-posed to be answering his phone at Argent Bank that very moment, "I told you it wasn't a good idea to try to start singing late in the evening into the morning. Your voice-box is tight from the chill spring air." He spoke to her as if she were a petulant child—which she was— but she was in fact a twenty-three-year-old young woman with the usual patience level of a rare beauty who had wrapped men around her finger since her middle teens. His voice was pleading, a little higher than usual. She could smell his fear like a shark at the blood bank.

That's the first thing he heard from this guy this morning that made sense, thought Jeff, but twenty thousand cash was twenty thousand cash so why should he talk this clown, this totally-smitten clown, out of spending the money? He knew this would go bad but was that his responsibility? She wanted to come in to record at one in the morning and cash was cash. What the hell did he care if she was unprepared? She should know the recording studio was not a place to rehearse.

"I told you we should have recorded in the Caribbean, where it is nice and warm, not in this filthy city, this freezing place," Kismine shrieked, Andre noticing she was off pitch even when she screamed. "And I also told you I want to be on TV! No one listens to the radio any more, I want to be seen! I need to be seen! Why am I making these recordings? No one buys compact discs anymore!" She threw Jeff's five-hundred-dollar headphones on the floor, but he didn't care because he also knew this session really should have cost only about ten thousand, not twenty. What an idiot this guy is, he confirmed once again as he remembered how Andre just offered him the twenty, when he would have done it for ten. What a fucking pigeon.

"Listen, Kismine, my flower, we need to get this recorded so we can send out samples of your work. We will send your photos with it as well so the television people will see how beautiful you are." He didn't come any closer than a couple of feet away from her although he painfully desired to stroke her face when he spoke to her.

"It is not TV," she replied as soon as the last word of his pathetically weak plea passed his lips. She continued, more subdued, brushing a lock of thick auburn hair out of her face, "I want everyone in the Middle East to know me. I can be the Shakira of the Middle East if you just get ME ON TV!" She was no longer subdued by the end of her sentence, her demands punctuated and accentuated by her stomping of her foot. She shifted moods as often and without a moment's warning the same way Steve McQueen downshifted his Mustang on the hills of San Francisco.

Jeff's business and life partner Sandy entered the studio just as Kismine continued to dress down Andre, whose head was hanging lower and lower with each complaint she hurled at him, shrill, shriller, shrillest, like a time lapse clip of a single rosebud left in a dry vase. Andre either didn't know the studio was wired for sound as well as video and all of his conversation could be heard and watched or he was beyond caring what others thought of him. Maybe he was just a king-sized lame-o. Sandy kissed Jeff good morning and pointed to the video screen. "Is this next month's rent?" she asked.

"Yeah. Beautiful girl, but painful to listen to," he answered, passing over the headphones and moving the last take back enough for a quick sample. Sandy's face screwed itself into a shape attainable only if she just ate a lemon sandwich as she listened to hours of expensive studio time completely wasted.

"God almighty, she is awful. You know, maybe we could do a reality show here, like American Idol, you know, people who think they can sing, pay big bucks for a recording, and it goes absolutely nowhere. Kind of like the show we saw the other night about the crazy young brides who drive the caterer, the band and their families bananas with their demands." Jeff loved these crazy ideas she would throw out here and there. At the very least she always made him laugh and every time she did so, he realized how glad he was that he kept asking her out even though she told him to get lost the first ten times.

"I could never be as vicious as you. Maybe if I would have been more ruthless, I wouldn't be here doing this sort of shit." Sandy threw her arms around his neck and pulled him close for a loud smack on his cheek. "I love you, whatever you do, as long as you only do it with me." She winked at him and spun around on the stool and headed out of the studio. "See you later," she said, spinning through the door and stopping momentarily to admire him.

He leaned back in his big leather chair making sure to suck in his stomach, and he playfully leered at her. "You know, you're as hot as ever," he said, and she smiled and spun through the door. The asshole was speaking to him once again, interrupting his thoughts about Sandy and what they would be doing later that day.

"Hey, Jeffrey," Andre called to the control room, stupidly craning his neck as he figured he had to in order to be heard, "Can we try it one more time?" Jeff saw him nervously looking at his watch, obviously distressed by something. He answered as interestedly as he could.

"Yeah, sure, palley. As many times as you want. It's your nickel," came the disembodied voice from the other room. Andre was pleased as he thought he had run out of time. "Kismine, darling, let's try it a few more times and we'll see what we can do in the mix later. I am sure it will be beautiful." He handed her the headphones and turned to leave the studio reminding himself to make a call to the office to make sure that bitch Laura was answering his phone for him.

Michael exited the subway at Central Park South and looked up at The Plaza hotel, never feeling uninspired by its beauty and perfect placement so close to the park, just off Fifth Avenue. For a moment he considered walking down into the park over to the pond which was tucked into the very southeast corner of the rectangular oasis in the middle of the city. He had fished there when he was a kid using the flip tops of soda cans as lures and a bent safety pin as a hook. The large goldfish would always swim tantalizingly close to the shiny metal and then dart away, probably laughing the whole time. He then recalled something that happened years later as a horny seventeen-year-old, spotting a pretty Latina with a huge head of teased curls frolicking on the big rock at the southeastern corner of the pond in a yellowy sun dress and he remembered that he wanted desperately to speak with her but never did other than saying, "Amarillo...muy bien." Yellow... very good. He could still see her face in his mind's eye. Did she smile at me because she liked it, or did she think I was a jerk?

He decided against visiting the spot of the pretty girl and went right over to the office on Fifth Avenue, about a block or so away from the park and entered the building that housed, among other things, Argent Bank's main office. It was here that he had his most special clients close their deals. The conference room overlooked the Plaza and the building that housed Bergdorf Goodman. And since they were on the fiftieth floor, they could see well past the pond and the Great Lawn.

This closing should go better than Matty's closing, he figured. This particular borrower was a young woman who was buying her third apartment, all financed by Michael, whom she once described as the coolest banker in New York. The other two closings went perfectly and the loan process for her this time also went well, the usual problems covered by Michael before they ever became an issue for her or her attorney. The only time there was a glitch in this deal was when she requested an interest-only payment option for her loan. Although that meant a lower payment every month, the rate was slightly higher than the traditional fixed rate. When he was explaining this to her, he couldn't shake the annoying feeling that he only had half her attention. He knew she was involved with a huge presentation at her job which had taken months to prepare, so he didn't press her on it. But he did fax her attorney the new commitment with the interest-only payment and higher rate, clearly calling attention to it with a big star in the column as well as circling the rate. An e-mail was sent to the both of them confirming this a few days ago, but it was never returned as read and understood. A loose end. Michael hated anything like that. Although he was a trusting kind of man, rare for a born and bred New Yorker, he had a copy of the commitment and the e-mail in his briefcase just in case. The elevator doors opened and he stepped into the reception area, the young woman buzzing him in without a request to do so. He was always forgetting his security card. It became their private joke.

He entered the conference room quietly, patting himself on the back for making sure that they booked the correct one, the one with the best view of the park. He was looking forward to meeting Pia Enpiso, who sold his borrower this latest apartment. Michael and Pia had spoken occasionally during the process, never in person, discovering that they had the same birthday and knew some of the same people in the industry. She was considered a rising star in the business, having sold as many apartments in each of the last two years as any twenty other agents in the city. Michael wanted her business and this deal worked perfectly for him to transition right into a discussion with her about that very subject.

But for the second time within two hours, he was unknowingly walking into a tempest, completely the opposite of what he was expecting.

"Hello, Christine," Michael said to his twenty-eight-year-old borrower, who was sitting ramrod straight, looking straight ahead. Something is wrong, the body language is screaming unhappiness: pouting, lower lip over the upper, arms crossed, back rigid. Shit, what's going on?

"Hello, Michael." Frosty the Snowman would have sneezed at her reception it was so cold. The room was silent as he scanned all the faces quickly and not finding any help, the bank closing attorney was his only friend there and he had that stupid kind of look on his face that said there was indeed a problem but you're going to have to figure it out yourself. Sorry, pal. Michael set his case down on the floor and put the bottle of champagne he bought for his client next to it. Something was going on here and he had to ascertain what it was...quickly. Just ask. It can't be your fault...everything went perfectly. He took a glance at Pia, sitting in the corner waiting on her commission check, furiously texting or e-mailing or maybe she was playing brick-breaker. Time to address the room and the problem that was hanging in the air.

"Everything going well?" he offered to the general population of the room. The lawyer for his borrower was not looking at him, the sellers and their lawyer were studiously avoiding his gaze. Christine, his young client, looked up at him, brushing a lock of hair away and set her face to furious, level ten.

"No, it's not well, Michael. Not well at all when I come to a closing and I see that you changed my interest rate at the last moment, when I have no room to maneuver, no time to go somewhere else. You trapped me and lied to me," she announced to everyone in the room. Michael was stunned to be accused of this highly deceptive and all too familiar practice of the bottom feeders in his industry, usually perpetrated on borrowers who trusted someone in the mortgage business of their own ethnicity, who used language skills—in New York it could be Korean, Chinese, Bengali, Spanish or Urdu—to gain the borrower's trust. This is quite probably the worst thing you can be accused of in the mort-gage business, but Michael knew how to deal with this, where to take this horrible accusation. He was unflappable. He was James Bond with a rate sheet. He spoke directly to her knowing that everyone else was hanging on his words the way they hang out the window to gaze at a car wreck or a fire.

"Well Christine, you requested the interest-only payment and as I explained to you several times, the rate *is* higher, yes, but the payment per month is three-hundred-fifty dollars less. That's what you wanted, the lower payment. The first commitment I secured for you had a self-liquidating fixed rate. You thought the payment was a bit much and you then requested the interest-only payment option which we did for your first loan. I even sent a new commitment with the new rate and interest-only terms," he finished, glancing ever so subtly at Christine's attorney, waiting for his assistance, waiting for him to point out to his young fiery client that he had indeed received the new commitment from Michael weeks ago and had indeed had a conversation with Michael about why he was receiving a brand new commitment, suspecting some kind of switcheroo, breathing out audibly when it was fully explained to him that his client specifically requested the new terms. Yes, sir, I have her request in writing, confirmed by e-mail, Michael answered to the attorney's staple query, designed to make sure he was in the clear, that his ass was covered at the end of the conversation.

"I don't care what you say, Michael. I never approved this rate. It's a quarter point higher than anything I see advertised. I never would have approved this. You lied to me!" The room was stunned into utter silence now, everyone openly watching him, the sound of Christine's voice reaching the corridor outside where through the glass windows he could see people peering in as they walked by. Michael was seething and saw no other way to deal with it other than with a bullet between the eyes. Fuck her...another client lost...Jesus, why is everyone so angry and unable to admit they were wrong? Well, he was not going to have his reputation skewered in this manner by anyone. Pia then decided to speak up and although he secretly hoped for it, he didn't believe for a moment that there was going to be any help coming from there. Not from a realtor with a closing being delayed.

"Michael," said Pia, addressing him directly without once looking away from the blackberry, I can't come to closings and hear my clients speak about interest rate changes without their knowledge. It's not good for business. Is this how you usually handle a mortgage application?" Now she was looking at him quizzically as if she would never expect any type of answer that didn't support her or Christine's position. What bullshit, Michael thought. Something is floated in the air and all of a sudden it crystallizes into truth.

Still going with being a rock, unmovable in the face of these assaults, Michael responded as calmly as possible as he reached into his briefcase for the paper he never thought he'd need but was sure glad he had with him. "Christine, here is the e-mail you sent to me authorizing me to lock *this* rate, the interest-only rate, the higher rate with the lower payment." He felt he had no other choice but to go for the death blow, bringing these people back into reality, rejecting this snotty girl's accusations, making them see her for what she is: someone who didn't listen to Michael when he was explaining the new terms weeks ago, someone who hired a lawyer who didn't explain anything to her, yet another youngster who had no experience with the word no. For his own survival, he had to stop looking like a punching bag, her personal whipping post. He handed the e-mail over to Christine, who promptly ripped it into a hundred pieces, tossing them into the air like caps flying in the air at a West Point graduation ceremony. She then launched into a tirade about general dishonesty in society, in the banking and real estate business. How could you do this to me? I trusted you. This is the worst thing you could have done, on and on and on, accentuated by a torrent of tears so unstoppable they were threatening to sweep them all out of the room on the crest of their wave. Michael was staring at her uncomprehendingly, wondering if the previous client had collaborated on some sort of hidden camera reality show and everyone was going to Alan Funt him, clapping his back, sharing a good laugh, Christine kissing him on the cheek and remarking to the room, "See, didn't I tell you he was the coolest banker in New York?" But no, this was not to be. Last night's dream of playing with the Beatles was going to occur sooner than an apology from this borrower. Her lawyer was speaking to him now and he swiveled his head slowly toward him, nervous that any quicker movement would fracture a cervical vertebrae, his neck and shoulders were so tight.

"I have a commitment from your bank for a fixed rate at 5.375 percent," he said to Michael. Nothing else was forthcoming from this bastard. This was the commitment that was produced before the change was requested to an interest-only loan and it was as obvious as the nose on his fucking fat face and it was obvious to Michael that his ship of truth was listing, that the band was tuning up. These people had made their decision to get on the borrower's side without even thinking that she might be wrong. He decided to plow forward.

"Christine, that now unreadable piece of paper proves to me and supersedes this unlocked commitment, that you were definitely consulted with about this change and that you yourself requested it. I changed nothing without your consent and when I did, I gave you exactly what you asked for," he told her, casting a sideways glance at the lawyer, ready to bury him and kiss off any future business from his office as he did this morning with Matty Albano's closing attorney. "I will re-send the e-mail later so you can see for yourself."

She was hissing through her teeth now like a cobra in a dentist's chair with too much Novocain, "I know what I sent to you, but obviously you didn't explain it well enough to me." A weak offering. Should he dial it down a bit, see if she would apologize? No, screw that. She needs to be hammered. Fucking people, I hate them all. He offered his upturned palms and continued as politely as he could.

"What's to explain Christine? Here is the rate. It is obviously a higher number, and the lower payment is spelled out on the first page. How much more information could I possibly have provided to make it clearer to you?" A mistake...he had embarrassed her, but he was beyond caring. All of the work he did for her on this deal, laying out the fees himself for the appraisal for *her* deal, hiring just the right appraiser who understood the building and the management company, the right bank attorney who knew how to get all of the official filings done promptly and who would never forget to remind the borrower's attorney not to forget to order the original stock certificate and proprietary lease from the current lender...all of this perfectly-executed concert of effort was going out the window now. His pride was all that was left and he was damned if he was going to be bested at this table by anyone. Christine was on her feet now, her lawyer gripping her elbow in an effort to control her.

"Are you calling me stupid? You? I am on my way to California next week by private Gulfstream jet to interview with an Oscar-winning director and producer to do set design for a one hundred million dollar film and you're a third rate mortgage broker who doesn't make sure his dynamic, young clients are fully informed about important financial decisions instead relying on the old tried and true formula of bullshitting anyone you can!" She plopped down in her seat again, more tears flowing now, her attorney hugging her around her shoulders, comforting her, while glaring at Michael as if this were all his fault alone. Michael made a mental note to stop at this lawyer's office later today to stand on his chest. He felt like Jack Lemmon in the *Out of Towners*, waving a piece of paper in the air at anyone who listened. "I have all your names and addresses!" But no one was listening.

Michael stood there speechless, totally unaware at this point of what to say other than to apologize for *somehow* not providing enough information, reminding her that he knew about the impending interview on the west coast which was why he made sure to include her lawyer in his correspondence about the new terms, how he understood exactly how much the impending interview was stressing her— as she told him about a million times when he was the coolest banker in NY—and remaining standing there like a squeegee guy, hearing nothing from anyone in return but feeling an almost physical sense of unease from everyone else in the room as if he had just had a load of shit run down his leg and fill up his shoe. He thanked her for her business, turned to Pia to say with as much dignity as he could muster that he looked forward to speaking with her again and headed out the door about three inches shorter than when he walked in. The champagne he left on the floor. He left the room, eyes straight ahead, shoulders tickling his earlobes, just wanting to get to the elevator before he did or said something that would never wash with Argent Bank client policy.

The receptionist was observing…nice looking man if just had better posture…as Michael strode past her desk and then Pia rushed into the lobby just as he pushed the elevator button to go down. He was surprised to see her. Was she coming out here to reassure him? He hoped so. He wanted to at least hope this young woman on the way up the business ladder would be able to discern the real score on what she had just witnessed in the closing room. She drew up to him at the elevator door and he looked down at her as she was only about five feet tall.

"Michael, I thought that was a bit unfair." He was momentarily impressed with the younger woman's thoughtful comment. He smiled lightly and was about to thank her but she started speaking again in a semi-robotic monotone that Michael and his friends recognized as the voice of the texting, e-mailing, cell phone generation, a soulless way of speaking that always jarred Michael a bit. The same tones, inflections and pitch were used to convey news of a tragedy or a triumph. "Be that as it may, Michael, when my client is unhappy, I don't care if they are right or wrong. And as a result, *I* or any of the other agents in my office cannot do business with anyone who creates an environment in which our clients become unhappy for any reason whatsoever." She crossed her arms across her chest as she concluded her statement. The elevator hadn't arrived yet

"Pia, you can clearly see that she is wrong and that I am being scapegoated. I can send you the e-mails that confirm everything I said in there."

"I don't want the e-mails, Michael. I want happy clients at closing. So now I will have to go to tell her I told you that you blew it here." She uncrossed her arms and leaned in to whisper to him as the bell for the elevator dinged softly, announcing its imminent arrival. "Between you and me, Michael, I thought you did quite well with the deal and in handling the little bitch in the next room. But simply put, I need happiness in my life and I excise anything or anyone who doesn't bring that to me. See you around." And with that she turned back to return to the closing room without saying good-bye or shaking hands and he knew that he would never hear from her again. The elevator door opened and he stepped inside, staying as close as he could to the walls, staring at the floor button panel until the doors closed, not moving at all until he felt the car start to descend.

⁂

SAUDI ARABIA, EVENING

It was a very warm, sticky evening in Jeddah, a cosmopolitan Saudi city of more than three million people located halfway down the west coast of the kingdom on the Red Sea. It was so hot earlier in the day that out here in an empty parking lot of the Red Sea Shopping Mall, the heat combined with the smoke from the spinning, burning tires of the young Saudi drifters to render it virtually impossible to take a deep breath. The cacophony from the high-pitched whine of the suped-up Hyundais, Kias, and Hondas racing back and forth, spinning sideways at speeds of up to one hundred miles per hour was not pleasing to any human eardrum, the squeal of the engines combining with the screeching of the tires to make the deserted parking lot sound like a barbecue gathering for banshees on steroids.

But this is where he wanted to be. Not in the construction offices of the company his father, an outrageously successful and wealthy member of Saudi society. He had no use for a job in an office although he did have what he considered to be some fairly visionary ideas of real estate development. However, as the third son of his father's third wife, he was about as far down the food chain in his own family as a rat was in a world of tigers. There was nowhere for him to go but sideways in that type of life.

Whathefu al-Aziz was twenty-five years old with a huge monthly stipend provided by his father and an even bigger chip on his shoulder.

He felt cheated in life from early on, being the third son of the third wife, in spite of the black Amex card with a fifty-thousand-dollar monthly limit that he used for everything from buying a stick of gum to a custom made Savile Row suit. But he was most angry at not having grown any since his fourteenth birthday, leaving him at five feet six and a wiry one hundred thirty pounds. No designer suit, high bouffant hairstyle, or elevator heels would ever make him appear manly—a staple of young Saudi desire—because of his slight build. He was able to grow a full mustache however, which he often compared to that of Tom Selleck, forgetting of course that he was not well over six feet tall and movie star handsome. Well at least he could buy the same car that was used in Selleck's television show that was based in Hawaii, a red Ferrari 308 GTSi that drew stares even on the very fashionable Tahlia Street, which was loaded with expatriates and native Saudis enjoying restaurants offering every type of cuisine on the planet, outdoor art exhibits, a remarkable display of numerous cultures existing side by side in a region of the world not entirely known for tolerance.

He could feel the stares of the mostly middle class group of men and it wasn't only because of the red Ferrari. The young woman in the car with him was an oddity because although Jeddah was a cosmopolitan city by Saudi standards, young women simply did not go out with, let alone ride in a car with a man who was not a direct family member or her husband. A few of the stares came from some young men who knew Whathefu on a more intimate level, the Saudi drifting community being full of homosexuality, with the winners of drifting contests often taking their pick of some of the younger, prettier boys. He had to admit he enjoyed the occasional carnal touch of his Arab brothers, purposely losing a few races in order to offer himself to a particularly virile and handsome driver of a tricked-out Kia or some other shitty Korean import. But he was troubled by it, at first considering these encounters nothing more than just some intensely exotic and adventurous form of masturbation rather than a natural calling for sexual relief, enjoyment and maybe even love. But now, especially with the very passionate experience with the young son of a German diplomat driving an embassy Mercedes-Benz he met here last week still burning in his mind, he started to wonder if he truly was gay. During his studies abroad, he participated in many orgies in Paris, Amsterdam, and Madrid with gorgeous interesting women—all of whom he amazingly considered immoral—but he increasingly found himself drawn to just watching men perform with these women and although he didn't concentrate entirely on another man's genitals, he found himself fascinated with the idea of replacing some of these women underneath their male lovers. But he only started down this sexual path a few months earlier, here at the drifting competitions and displays. Before his reputation was irreversibly damaged, he felt he needed to show these faggots that he loved and was in turn loved by women as well. And that was the reason for much of their stares of disbelief, not the car but the beautiful young woman in the passenger seat. Rare enough was the presence of a woman at a drifting competition, but this one was technically committing a crime by being out of the house and in the company of a man who was not her father, husband, or brother. And none of these young Saudis wanted any further reason for the police to show up at their little seaside party.

Leila was only seventeen years old, having been born and raised in Jeddah, her father the owner of a small but respected machine part manufacturer. Her father loved his only wife, his five older sons but most especially his youngest child, a jewel of a daughter that he named because she was his only child born at night, therefore dubbing her Leila...'night beauty.' She was a perfect child in the eyes of all who knew her. And all who knew her would never suspect her of attending a drifting competition on a Thursday night with the third son of a third wife who always seemed a day late and a dinar short. But none of her family and friends knew about her secret desire for adventure, to go somewhere, do something, get drunk, run away for a weekend, have sex with a stranger, something that would be shocking to all of them, even just once so she would never have to live with any regrets. Such was the thinking of so many teenaged girls around the world, completely unaware that painful regrets could be born in one's adult years as well as those of youth. So on this night, a night in which she had already lied to her parents about where she was going and with whom, she upped the ante by sitting in this car with Whathefu, who she didn't particularly like or dislike. He was, in her mind, as the girls in the American movies called it, 'something to do.' Maybe she would even play with his thing a little later if he was polite to her.

Whathefu could see some of the other drivers now openly sneering at him, their knowing smiles appearing from beneath their mustaches dripping with contempt. Rich kid, brings a woman here, he helps her put her whole reputation at risk. He read all of this in the looks he viewed through the windshield. He tried to look as cool as possible but this was a car event after all so he'd better get the Ferrari going a little bit. A sideways glance through the sunglasses he was wearing told him Leila was perhaps starting to become a bit apprehensive probably due to the attention she was garnering all by herself. Better make a move, give her a little thrill and drop her back at the mall. This was a stupid idea. If he wanted a woman, all he had to do was go to Europe and scatter some cash around and wait for them to flock to his side. He started the powerful engine and shifted into first gear, feathering the gas pedal like a jazz drummer plays the kick drum as he rolled forward slowly in neutral just to let the rest of them hear the throaty growl of a real engine in a real car.

"Where are we going?" Leila asked, glad to be moving away from the cluster of young men who were taking too much interest in her. What if one of them worked with one of my brothers or my father? she was wondering. What a mistake to come here, she concluded as she glanced at her watch. Six-thirty...I really should get back by seven. No way am I touching his thing. It's obvious I am nothing to him but a doll to play with. And he's nothing special either, I don't care how much money and power his father has. Whathefu didn't answer her right away because frankly, he wasn't sure himself. He moved the car out of the parking lot and over to a stretch of highway that ran parallel to the Red Sea. At this time of day traffic was very light, with only the occasional delivery truck passing by, sometimes a private sedan or taxi as well. The road was lined by a few palm trees and hundreds of people, the vast majority of them young men wearing either western style jeans, tee shirts and sneakers or more traditional flowing white robes. Some of them were drinking non-alcoholic beers and eating what appeared to be madhbi, chicken that was grilled on a stone. They were laughing among themselves, obviously having a good time, and Leila was a little sad that this was yet another social scene she was excluded from because she was a female.

"I'm not sure. Let's just stop here and see what happens." He knew what was going to happen, of course. He had been here many times. "Look at this guy," and her gaze followed his finger pointing toward some sort of imported car with florescent green paint and shiny wheels. Just then the green car accelerated down the road, Leila surprised at how fast it was. She covered her ears against the high pitched whine of the aluminum block engine which didn't roar with power. Instead it sounded like her old Aunt who was always ranting about this or that. The driver had started his journey about a half mile away from their position and he was passing them now, just a few seconds later. And without warning the car spun counter-clockwise wildly, the tires throwing off rapidly twisting plumes of white smoke, the sand kicked up off the nearby beach onto the asphalt, reducing friction, enabling the car to seemingly glide along the road sideways. The driver spun this way and then that, coming within mere feet of the spectators who didn't move at all, prompting Leila to wonder if it was really non-al-coholic beer they were drinking. The whole scene sickened her. The wasting of fuel, the wasting of time, the waste of such a large segment of Saudi youth who seemed drawn to anything that allowed them to even dream about breaking away from this oppressive society. She was about to insist she be taken home when Whathefu put the car in gear and took off down to the starting point of the car she had just watched spin down the road at terrifying speed. He looked over at her and asked her in what she took to be a very kind and concerned voice to fasten her seat belt. She liked that, she had to admit...maybe she was wrong about him. She fumbled with the latch, unsure of how to fasten it. It was her first time in a car in which she wasn't being chauffeured.

Whathefu raced down the strip of highway, but instead of turning west back to the heart of the city, he abruptly turned the car to face back up the road they just drove down. The crowd started to cheer and egg him on. She watched him run his fingers through his hair and adjust his glasses. "Why are we stopping here?" she asked innocently, naively.

"Make sure your belt is tight. We're going." She exhaled in relief at the statement.

"Oh good, thank you," she replied, still holding the belt in her hand, looking down for the slot she was supposed to slip the latch into. "Maybe we can go sit and talk at a coffee shop." He looked sideways at her as if she were an idiot, a lecherous no, an evil grin spread across his face.

"No, I mean we are GOING!" he yelled over the noise of the cheers, the radio spitting out American rock music, and the Ferrari's engine. And with that he slammed the gas pedal to the floor and popped the clutch, the vehicle leaping to life like a cat pouncing on a mouse that mistakenly wandered across its field of vision, spinning the extra wide Pirelli tires at an insane rate of speed, finally catching the asphalt, propelling the car forward. Leila was instantly pressed against the low bucket seat by the force of the car's forward movement and she dropped the seat belt in response to the sudden acceleration. She looked to her right and could see the palm trees and all the men on the side of the road whizzing by her as if they were part of an old-fashioned movie, the frames blurred into indistinguishable images of white robes, brown trunks, and green fronds. She looked over at Whathefu who was gripping the wheel with both hands, his concentration on the strip of road in front of them total. He doesn't even know I'm here, she thought and she forced herself to look through the windshield at the road ahead as if maybe that would cause the dizzying effect the array of images passing by her so quickly out the passenger window to dissipate. She could see the end of the road approaching. She knew he would have to stop soon and that momentarily filled her with relief. She turned back to Whathefu to placate him, remembering the words her mother had passed on to her...'You have to treat men with a bit of honey once in a while, my child, for they are all weak and in need of constant reassuring'...but before she could get any words out, Whathefu whipped the wheel to the left and stomped on the brake, sending the car into a terrifying spin that seemed to last forever. There was no way he could control where we wind up, she somehow instinctively knew, and she prepared herself for death as certainly the car would find a wall or tree and be pulverized by the impact. But all of a sudden the spinning car slowed significantly and then stopped and they were then enveloped in a cloud of white smoke and an acrid smell of burning rubber that apparently was chasing them during the spin. The sudden realization that she was not dead did not fill her with happiness. Instead she exploded at Whathefu, who was leaning back, lighting a cigarette and blowing smoke straight up in the air, smiling broadly at his accomplishment, absorbing the cheers of the crowd.

"You almost killed us!" she shouted at the top of her lungs, the lingering smoke causing her to cough out the last few syllables. He blew another set of smoke rings into the air and waved her comments off.

"We do this all the time. You were never in any danger." His casualness infuriated her. She hated him now, almost as much as she hated herself for allowing this to happen. It was her own fault, she concluded, for letting her guard down and agreeing to be part of this ridiculous evening.

"This is how you spend your time, Whathefu?" she asked contemptuously. She sat up in the bucket seat and waved at the spectacle around them, cars spinning and speeding down the road, the shouts of the men, always men only, almost as loud as the engines. "I don't think there is a greater waste of collective time in the entire kingdom." He drew on his cigarette again and flicked the butt out on the road.

"We're just bored, Leila. This gives us something to do. The kingdom's society barely acknowledges us, so we have to acknowledge each other and this is how we do so."

"You are all a bunch of pathetic half-men as far as I'm concerned. Why use these machines to test your skills? Why not, if you're bored, put together some sort of athletic contests, maybe a football league that at least teaches teamwork and a sense of accomplishment and brotherhood? Any fool with a foot and a hand could get in this car and play with it as if it were a toy. How many people have been killed or injured during these exhibitions?" she inquired like a prosecutor.

Whathefu didn't know the answer to that question, but he did know about the one driver, Faisal was his name, who had brought his three younger cousins to the track and spun out of control, killing the three younger boys instantly. He had been sentenced to three thousand lashes and twenty years in prison. Many others were just nameless, faceless, lesser members of Saudi society. Many of the non-apologetic homosexuals were total outcasts, with no other alternatives but to turn to the Wahhabists in order to become jihadists. Even his father approved more of these poor tortured souls than his own son. He now wished he had asked young Abdul to accompany him tonight, Abdul who was so pretty and well formed as to almost be as attractive to

Whathefu as Leila was. At least *he* had a sense of adventure. He had discussed with Abdul the possibility of leaving the kingdom forever, to set up a life in America, probably New York where he had read and heard that homosexuals were clamoring for the right to marry. He had discussed it with Whathefu just a week earlier, as they lay together on the beach in the darkness of the pre-dawn hours, their lovemaking—as Abdul called it—thankfully unseen from other eyes. What they had been doing just a half hour earlier could earn them both jail terms and whippings as well as the permanent estrangement and ostracism of their families. But neither could help themselves. For Abdul, it was the possibility of a life with a wealthy benefactor from his own country. For Whathefu, it was nothing more than the best blow job he had ever received. None of the European or Oriental women he had slept with could even come close. But he also knew it wasn't love because he was sure he would drop Abdul like a bad habit if something or someone nicer came along. He wished Abdul were here now instead of this snotty little harpy who was shrieking at him like a trapped rat. Time to dump her. He shifted the car into gear and turned it around, heading down the west side of the road at a much slower clip. He could see Leila out of the corner of his eye sitting ramrod straight in the seat, her eyes boring into him, awaiting an answer.

"I don't know, Leila. And the fact that you don't know either just goes to show how much all of us here are worth to you and your kind in the kingdom. If we're not connected to the royal family or the Wahhabists, then we are expendable." She sat back in the seat again and crossed her arms across her chest.

"This is nothing more than a monumental waste of time and energy, a pathetic grab at manhood." He swiveled his head at the insult to look her in the eye and couldn't help but stare at her breasts which were straining against her shirt which was bundled behind her, accentuating their swell. She noticed his stare and lifted her arms higher blocking his view. "Don't stare at me that way. You make me sick when you do that. I want to leave, NOW!"

"Fine. I'll drop you at the bus stop, you can walk home from the mall and that will give you plenty of time to come up with some sort of excuse for your whereabouts to tell your parents. My parents don't give a damn about me so you're the only one here with a problem."

The tears started streaming down her face as he passed by a group of drifters, many of whom continued to sneer contemptuously at the Ferrari and at the presence of a woman in their midst. He could see the bus stop about a hundred yards ahead and he decided to go out with a bang, show this snotty bitch some contempt, see how she likes it. He hit the gas again, aiming the car for the bus stop. He had seen something like this before in a commercial for...Audi maybe, just drift right into the spot, unlatch her seat belt, reach across her body and push the door open and tell her to get the hell out. How hard could it be?

Whathefu approached the bus stop at about thirty miles per hour and he heard her ask if she was going to be let off here. Those were the last words to ever leave her mouth. The breeze off the Red Sea was strong the past few days and more sand than usual built up on the sidewalks and roads away from the drifters. Whathefu hit the brakes and turned the wheel perfectly, the Ferrari performing beautifully, but the car wouldn't stop sliding, sliding toward the curb which looked a little higher than usual. Maybe it was that suckass brown nose in his father's company who built this sidewalk with the curb much too high. He could see it as he approached, Leila looking almost bored now with this little mini-drift because just a moment ago she was drifting at one hundred miles per hour and now she just wanted to get out and go home and get away from this...loser who was obviously trying to play her again with his little Ferrari that his father bought for him, all of these thoughts covering up what should have been a bit of fear that might have possibly reminded her to finally connect the seat belt which she never fastened earlier. And when the car hit the curb in front of the bus stop, it stopped on a dime and the centrifugal force lifted it on its side, the sudden deceleration snapping her fourth cervical vertebrae, paralyzing her from the chin down and sparing her the pain of her head slamming into the curb as the car stood on its side, this blow killing her instantly before the car settled back on four wheels.

Whathefu was shocked at the quickness, the suddenness of the accident and his first reaction was that he was angry to have dented the car. But then he noticed the strange angle at which his passenger held her head and when he lifted her head by her chin, blood flowed from her nostrils and her mouth, her unseeing eyes condemning him for her death. He let go of her chin and her body slumped forward, her forehead resting on the dashboard. The sound of the crunching metal and breaking glass was muted by the roars of the crowd for the other drifters, the cars' screeching tires and screaming engines apparently masking the accident. He would tell his father the car was stolen and he wasn't driving. He would blame it on someone...who? This was what he contemplated as he unhooked his seat belt, jumped out of the Ferrari, and ran as fast as his feet would take him back to Jeddah proper.

— ⚬ —

MID-MORNING

Vinny Malloy was utilizing, drawing upon every ounce of inner strength and resolve, resilience and intestinal fortitude...which he possessed in considerable abundance...to not absolutely blow his stack at the three people in the room with him, the founding members of the Sutton Place River and Environmental Preservation Society, who were assembled here talking about his dream, his life's work, as if it were nothing more than an ill-considered Christmas gift. He leaned back in the high-backed leather chair, which he figured cost more than the average person in Long Island City, Sunnyside or Woodside, Queens earned in some shitty job in a week and slowly, quietly drummed the black shiny conference room table top with his finger pads. One of his best teachers taught him years ago to channel the energy that would have, in his earlier life, resulted in a thrown punch into this type of limited physical activity. To anyone who didn't know him, it would have been seen as nothing more than a nervous, possibly unconscious tic. To his best friends and closest business associates, it was a signal that the steam was building.

He looked down the length of the polished black granite table at the two men and one woman in the room with him. He expected this meeting to take no more than twenty minutes, a simple meet and greet with people he had no interest in socializing with for what should be nothing more than satisfying the inquiries of wealthy-for-several-generations types, bored do-gooders trying to further themselves in the social register. Just one more hurdle in his attempt to construct two thousand rental units, complete with a riverside esplanade that would be the envy of the entire city, the abandoned factories around the site—which he had shrewdly bought up for pennies years earlier— to be filled with fitness clubs, shopping malls, big box stores, restaurants, maybe even a Wal-Mart if the city council would ever let the big retailer in, all of which would pay him rent. A lot of rent. His dream... now all of his friends' dream as well...a million plans, twists, and turns, a total gamble with differing levels of freakish, stomach-churning risk around every corner but what a payoff it would be. It had to work because it made complete sense and failure was never anything Vinny Malloy allowed into his life. All that effort had been played out for years just across the river from where they were all sitting. And instead of the rubber stamp he expected from these three, he was being dealt an iron ruler across his knuckles from a three-headed version of Sister Mary, or Angelica, or whatever. He concentrated only slightly on what the bald one on the left was saying, his razor sharp mind rushing ahead of this situation, trying to determine if these people were paper tigers or not.

"Mr. Malloy, we just cannot issue your permit to begin building on the site as you requested. The plans you submitted for approval just do not, well, fit the future vision of the riverfront any longer." Vinny stared at the man for a few extra seconds wondering if his stupidity was a ploy of some sort, very aware that the insanely dumb were uniquely capable of stumbling across something, anything more significant and thusly truly important at any time.

"I am not asking for a permit; I already have one," he answered evenly and quite truthfully. The permit process for a project of this magnitude was a massive undertaking, requiring thousands of documents, environmental tests, and approvals from almost every city agency and more than a handful of civic organizations. To Vinny's way of thinking, he had these two men and one woman—nice looking woman at that—right where he wanted them. They were behind, way behind. They couldn't stop him. He was just being courteous coming here to meet with them, hoping that maybe a kernel of a suggestion could emanate from them collectively that he could use. Vinny Malloy hated, among other things, those who thought they knew everything about anything. Another of his great teachers had taught him that knowledge is everywhere, comes from anyone, but not everyone knows how to recognize it for what it is, how it could be used. Part of his plan to change the angle of his building's footprints ever so slightly came was the result of an eight-year-old's suggestion that all the apartments should be able to catch even a little bit of the morning sun. The other one, the chubby one with the very unfortunate bow tie, was picking up the conversation.

"Yes, Mr. Malloy, but the removal of and subsequent decision to relocate the Pepsi sign makes your building permit subject to further scrutiny by a collection of interested parties. Once that process is concluded and all and any further concerns are addressed and dealt with to everyone's satisfaction, will you be permitted to continue."

Vinny looked them over from left to right...the balding one with the bony shoulders and the rep tie, the chubby one who looked as if he were raised like a veal, never allowed out of the house, and the woman. She was petite but she looked strong and athletic. Her face radiated intelligence and inquisitiveness, two characteristics he always found attractive in a woman and vitally important to whether or not he wanted to see her again. She hadn't said anything yet, but kept her focus on the documents and drawings on the table in front of her, studying them with much interest. Or was she ignoring the other two? Difficult to say at this point.

Vinny was somehow able to see something in her, as yet undefinable, but he thought there was something within her that he felt drawn to in some strange way in the absence of conversation. He shut his eyes tightly and rubbed the bridge of his nose in irritation at himself. Why was he thinking about a woman at a time like this? Why was he even giving these people the time of day? Now the woman was looking up at him and he hoped that she would distinguish herself from these other two.

"Why do you plan to move the Pepsi sign, Mr. Malloy?" asked Maxie Carter. Vinny was nothing if not polite to any woman and he turned toward her to answer, to make sure she felt his attention, that he wasn't blowing her off.

"The sign is in the middle of the building site and it serves no real purpose in being right...there. It's a beautiful sign, an iconic sign..."

"Befitting its protected status, Mr. Malloy," interrupted the tall, bony one. Interrupting Vinny Malloy was not usually an exercise in self-preservation but there was a woman present in the room and he kept his temper and disdain for the two men and these proceedings in check. He had his permit, he had the blessings of the community, the city was glad to look forward to the tax revenues and the local construction unions were salivating at the idea of more work for the members. He decided to press on and answer the woman's question without even a glance at her rude colleague.

"...but it serves much less purpose where it sits than a park would for the local children and families. The riverfront of Queens, actually of much of New York City, is wasted land and we intend to reverse that by providing a beautiful esplanade where people can walk, families can picnic, and children can play. The sign, in its new position, can still provide whatever importance it provides to whomever ascribes importance to such things." Vinny didn't disguise his contempt well with his last comment, but he made sure not to direct it toward Ms. Carter, whom he suspected was just trying to do the right thing by her conscience.

"The sign, Mr. Malloy, should not be moved at all because of its proximity to and apparent connection with the pier that extends out into the river," said the tall, bony one. That caught Vinny by surprise.

"The pier?" Vinny held out his hands palms up in the universal New York City gesture that meant 'What the fuck?' Or in other, nicer words...what are you talking about? The chubby bow-tie picked up where his bony friend left off.

"Yes, Mr. Malloy, the pier. In case you aren't aware, that pier plays a central role in one of the most iconic photographs ever taken in this city. A photograph that had raised the consciousness of the citizens of this city regarding the environmental issues our waterways were facing at the time, including the fate of the city's underprivileged youngsters." The bow-tie was leaning forward as he spoke, resting his body on his custom made French-cuffed encased forearms in a feeble attempt, Vinny guessed, to show his toughness and resolve. What this bow-tie didn't know could swallow him whole, Vinny thought. Vinny also leaned forward on the table, mimicking the bow-tie's body position, his powerful bricklayer type hands and forearms stretching past the cuffs of his Hugo Boss jacket which he had bought several years earlier at an upstate outlet center.

"First of all," Vinny started calmly, "I know all about the photograph in question, more than you could ever imagine. I attended the first exhibit of the photo at the International Center for Photography back in the early nineties. It was in private hands until then so don't tell me about any social concerns it raised to the public's consciousness because the photo was taken in the early 1970s, more than twenty years earlier, my point being the social and environmental concerns you are referring to had already been addressed by multitudes of bene-factors both private and official. I also find it interesting that you spoke first of the environmental concerns the photo allegedly raised and not of the concerns of the kids swimming in the river." The bow-tie started to object, but Vinny shushed him with an upraised hand. "Nobody on this side of the river gave a damn back then what was happening to the average citizen in the outer boroughs and frankly, I don't think in our *enlightened* times supposedly filled with *enlightened* people that anyone still gives a damn unless they're standing in front of a TV camera." Vinny managed to say this without a trace of anger in his voice but the continued posture of his body suggested danger and possible menace.

"You remind me of the type of person who would take sides with a snail darter over a project such as ours and your so-called concern for the health and welfare of anyone living outside Manhattan in anything other than a junior six on Park Avenue or some townhouse on West Eleventh Street who also might speak a different language in the home besides English and don't even get me started about if those same people live in a skin a different shade than yours." The men looked at each other quizzically in response while Maxie Carter allowed a corner of her mouth to turn upward ever so slightly in apparent appreciation of his metaphor. Vinny, a very observant guy, caught it like an owl grabbing a wayward squirrel trying to dart across a clearing. Maxie continued to flip through copies of his permits, comparing them to the blue ink mechanical drawings and colorful renderings with much interest and what Vinny hoped was admiration.

The snail darter, a fish about the size of a paper clip, was perhaps the most obscure marine organism in the world until its discovery by a university professor in the middle of a research project. The tiny fish and its apparent inability to live anywhere but a certain section of river, managed to halt the completion of the Tellerico Dam, an enormous public works project, for six years. The dam was ultimately completed, the snail darter ultimately re-introduced elsewhere where it thrived in its new surroundings, later being removed from the endangered species list. A gaggle of lawyers became rich, and innumerable workers looking forward to years of continuous employment went broke during the delay.

Vinny knew better than these fools how much great work the environmental lobby had done for America, cleaning up the air, highways, and waterways and reversing the criminal habits of many corporations regarding what they dumped into the ground and rivers, but this interest in the pier was ridiculous. He was starting to think that maybe there was some other agenda going on here that he couldn't quite put his finger on, but as he played it over in his mind again he felt, no...he knew that he had it all on his side. The truth was with him. The hell with this meeting and these people. He sat back to deliver what he figured would be his final words.

"The pier has no historical significance, no architectural importance. It was probably installed sometime early in the last century by some guy who just wanted a better chance at catching a striper on its way up the river. It is also, by the way, a possible invitation for some other kid who might not swim as well as the kids in the famous photo, to venture out on it, fall in, and drown. Did you ever think of that?" Not waiting for an answer, Vinny pressed down on the arms of the comfortable leather boardroom chair and rose to leave. The bow-tie jumped out of his seat with alarming agility.

"Mr. Malloy, we will continue to object to your project with all of our resources and might!" Vinny was going through his checklist before leaving a place...checking for keys, lighter, smokes, phone, and wallet. He looked at the bow-tie with contempt but was compelled to follow his inner sense of fair play.

"Look gentlemen, how about a sturdy reproduction of the pier, right down to the rivets, complete with a plaque describing its significance historically?" A perfectly acceptable solution, he thought, although he hated having to kowtow to these guys. Maxie Carter, he could see, appreciated his comment on some level and seemed to turn approvingly toward the bony man and the bow-tie.

"No thank you, Mr. Malloy. We have enough memorials around this city as it is," the bow-tie continued, as if he held the confidence of all eight million or so residents of the city in the palm of his hand. "Every street is being re-named for some obscure departed soldier and by the end of the next decade there will be a museum on every corner dedicated to something or someone that everyone wants to forget or never knew about."

"Should we replace the 9/11 memorials as well?" Vinny's fingers were starting to curl slightly, on their way to fists of stone. "Maybe take down all the little crosses that grieving families have put up on the highways where someone had died?"

"Your construction loan for this project is being provided by Shale Financial Corporation, is it not?" Vinny didn't answer as the loan was scheduled to close next week and it was not yet public record. How the hell did this guy know that? He apparently figured that Vinny was not going to confirm anything for him so he continued, "Sharon And Lee Skillman, the owners of the bank, are old family friends. I prepped with Lee and I had a hand in introducing them to each other. I will be calling them later today to ask them to put a halt to this financing. And believe me, they'll listen to our recommendations." The two men started for the door but the bow-tie was speaking again.

"And by the way, Mr. Malloy, don't even think of running over to Queens now and dismantling that pier yourself. Otherwise we will also be calling our friends in various government agencies, any one of whom could stop your project dead with the stroke of a pen." The bony one spoke up now leaning back into the room, his palm flat on the wall inside.

"If anything other than an act of God causes damage to that pier, Mr. Malloy, we will consider criminal charges against you and seek to permanently enjoin your efforts to raise your buildings. We have friends at the highest level of law enforcement as well as contacts at the largest and most powerful law firms in the city. I should think you don't want to take us on."

Vinny stared at the bony man, trying to keep his rage in check. The woman, he noticed, looked upset, embarrassed maybe, at the last exchange. Why would she feel that way? Vinny wondered, as he stared out the window of the boardroom across the river where he could see the plot of land on which his dreams lived. Isn't she on their team? He turned to Maxie Carter taking her in briefly, wordlessly, wishing her good afternoon before he strode out of the room, not quickly so as not to give away that he was very upset, but definitely with a power in his stride that would allow him to walk through a wall.

Vinny was steaming mad, positively enraged in the elevator cab. It was at times like this that he too was glad for gun control laws. Because these three, no...not the woman, Maxie, who was the only one he remembered by name. The other two he just left absolutely needed to be shot and dumped in the river right off their precious pier.

He exited the building and headed toward his Chevy Suburban which was idling at the curb with Charlie Mick, the son of one of his friends who was murdered on 9/11, and the Burke brothers, Ryan and Fred. He jumped in the front passenger seat and slammed the door shut startling the occupants.

"Hey, Vin, what's going on?" asked Ryan, startled from his concentration on the sports pages of the *Post*.

"You slammed that door like John Starks did on Horace Grant. What happened up there?" asked Fred Burke. Charlie Mick, brooding as ever, just sat at the wheel awaiting instructions. The Burkes were among his most trusted friends, also heavily invested in the project, but he couldn't handle their basketball analogies right now. He would lay down in traffic for them and they for him, but right now there was only one person he wanted to see.

"Let's go over to Steinway Street. I need to speak with J'lome." With that Vinny lit up a cigarette and stared out the window. End of statement, with nothing more expected from Vinny from anyone in the car, all of whom were smart enough and close enough to him not to even bother. Charlie Mick put the big car in gear and pulled away from the curb and headed up First Avenue to the Queensboro Bridge's backdoor Fifty-Ninth Street entrance that would take them along the outer roadway, the fastest way to their destination. None of them spoke for the entire ride.

⚯

The recording studio was only on the seventh floor but the elevator ride to the lobby for Andre was interminable. Kismine was wrapped around herself, arms crossed tightly across her chest, chin down like a bare knuckle boxer, even her legs were crossed at the ankles. Andre leaned up against the opposite wall of the elevator just hoping to contain the inevitable explosion.

"That recording session was terrible! They were laughing at me, I could hear them!" she bellowed in between floors four and three, punctuating her comments by stamping the floor with the utterance of each of the last three syllables. Okay, here is her scene for this day. Just calm her down, thought Andre. She's a woman after all and he knew it was up to him to keep her in check because she, of course, was unable to. Because she was a woman.

"They weren't laughing at you. They were just having a private joke among themselves." But Andre knew better. He wasn't that much of a fool. The engineers and the owner of the studio had recorded hundreds of singers, thousands of songs and jingles and they knew what they were doing. He was feeling stupid and used as it was. Those guys at the studio probably pegged him as some sort of whale, nothing more than a bottomless bank account to help them pay their bills, buy their cocaine, fill up their sports cars with gas to go to the Hamptons. As soon as they heard his accent and noticed the color of his skin, he instantly surmised that he would be treated like a second class citizen, because that's what this country is truly all about. That was what his friends and family in Algeria warned him of just prior to his departure for New York University, the recipient of a full scholarship granted to needy African students twenty years earlier.

He wanted part of that Hamptons life for himself and Kismine, who he had met a year ago in a nightclub in the East Village. She was singing backup for a pathetic sounding young girl in strange clothing... Stephanie something...and he had been besotted with her ever since. He sought her out after the set was finished and made it plain and clear that he was a wealthy banker and would be able to help her with her career. They had never truly dated in the American sense of the word, and they had certainly never even kissed, for Andre was Muslim—although he hadn't seen the inside of a mosque in years—and he wanted his future wife to be pure. Of course he kept these thoughts to himself.

The elevator reached the dingy lobby on Thirty-Eighth Street and she stepped out quickly, even before the rattly door slid entirely open.

Andre was following closely, feeling at that moment that the elevator ride was a metaphor for this phase of their relationship where it was becoming painfully obvious that that he would not be able to deliver what she desired.

As beautiful as she was, as much as *he* obsessed over her, it was becoming increasingly apparent there was no way she was ever going to record anything that would capture the public's imagination. Her voice was indeed pitchy, the absolute very worst quality any singer could have And she was an Arab—who refused to change her name—and he was convinced that she would always be suspect in this society with a name like that. Plus there were the men on the streets who followed her with their eyes, unable to shake from their minds the sinful thoughts that her thick auburn hair, lithe body, and fleshy lips had to produce in their fantasies, apparently unaware that her beauty passed into one eye and out the other for the vast majority of them, all too busy and concerned for their own lives and difficulties to devote more than a few seconds of the day toward the appreciation of a pretty girl. He did in fact know that hundreds of his African & Arab Muslim brothers were enjoying happy, productive lives here in New York and elsewhere in America, lives of religious freedoms and other pursuits that no other nation, certainly none of theirs, could provide for them. But he knew his limitations as all men whether they be stupid or smart do...or should...so he was aware of how weak he really was inside, always wondering if he could align himself with the rhetoric of Al Jazeera and the crazier jihadist websites he liked to frequent. And also with this type of girl, always a level above him, an Arab who must from time to time look down on his African skin and features, well she probably planned from the first moment of meeting him to use and twist him to her demands like a piece of Turkish taffy. Women, he was convinced, were the same all over the world.

"You can't take things like this personally. Otherwise you fail not only in show business, possibly the hardest business to break into, but in any business," he cautioned her like a parent once they exited onto the street. Hordes of New Yorkers passed them in all directions, some of the men stared at her as they always did but mostly this time because they were the only ones standing around with seemingly nowhere to go. Her arms were crossed over her chest again and she stared up toward Fifth Avenue, just a few steps away.

"Andre," she said thoughtfully, "I was told by every club promoter and producer in Beirut that I would be a singing star with the right backing, the right money, the right training. You know I have been cut out of my family's wealth entirely. You have done a magnificent job of funding me so far, the apartment, the clothes, the lessons, and this session…by the way, how much did it cost?"

"Twenty thousand dollars," gulped Andre, although he hid his alarm at the figure well. A man then stepped out of the building and brushed past the both of them, pausing briefly to offer a quick apology. Kismine nodded in appreciation at the stranger's gentlemanly gesture but Andre seethed that the man had come into contact with her body. He had not yet done so himself although a year had passed since their first meeting. She drew closer to him, allowing just the slightest touch between her jacket and his overcoat, and lowered her chin melting him with her large brown eyes when she raised them a moment later. But she cut him like a stiletto made out of glacial ice when she spoke.

"I need to be on television, Andre, so my friends in Lebanon can see me here in America performing for an American crowd, singing and dancing like Shakira. Can you do that for me, Andre? Can you?" The question was delivered with a voice of equal parts warmth and ice, like a cobra inviting a mouse into its lair for a beer. She wasn't asking for reassurance but instead using the question to challenge his capability as a man. He tried to be full of resolve with his answer. Women like that, he thought. She wants me to be in charge, to run her life for her, to provide all the answers and a path for her.

"Yes, I can," he stammered, losing control of his voice-box slightly, becoming as pitchy as she was. "Yes, I can. I believe, no, I am convinced I can get you on television. And if I do?" He moved an inch closer to her, trying to close the gap that always existed between them even when they were only inches apart, like now, raising his palms to hopefully hold her elbows in his big, ugly hammy hands. She leaned away slowly, like a leopard getting leverage on its victim's throat, and answered, "Then we will go away on a long vacation, just you and me, as lovers. But if you don't…I mean, if I am not on television being seen and heard in every café in Beirut within a month, I am gone from here, from you, and hopefully from your memory. Do you understand?" He nodded to her like a child apologizing for another oft-repeated transgression.

She turned without another word and strode off toward Fifth Avenue without looking back once and Andre checked his watch, becoming panic-stricken to discover that he was forty-five minutes late and still twenty minutes from his office. At least I no longer need to be watched so closely now, he thought, grateful of his promotion to a Vice Presidency in Argent Bank. He was confident he could cover his tracks adeptly, turning a forty-hour work week into one of thirty-two or less. As he hailed a cab heading west, he found himself turning from what could be a happy, comforting thought, that he as an immigrant to another country, had risen in stature in a large financial institution. Instead, as he slammed the cab door, drawing a look from the driver whose colorful scarf indicated that he possibly hailed from Tunisia, he told himself that he doesn't need any hassles from his stupid American supervisors, and especially not from the bitch woman whose password he had stolen, with which he had been stealing from the bank for the past several months. He had to plan quickly now, he had to keep Kismine in his life. He had to see his friend Fated in New Jersey, the one with the television dish store, the one who was making a small fortune illegally beaming the rants and hatred of the Lebanese terrorist Hezbollah into Arab-America homes. If anyone could help him, it would be Fated.

Twenty minutes later, Andre leaped out of the cab without tipping the cabby and five minutes later stepped into his office. It was now almost ten-thirty and Laura was furious, having spent the entire morning juggling her regular job duties, Andre's phone calls, and desperately trying to figure out the Asian clients' wire problem. She was just about finished when she saw Andre casually walk into the office and throw his jacket over the back of his chair. She strode over to his desk purposefully. She didn't give a damn at the moment that he was a Vice-President.

"Andre, where have you been?" she asked without a touch of annoyance although it was there in abundance. She recalled someone telling her once that one of the secrets to success in business in New York was to never let them see you sweat, never let the other guy know what you're thinking, but she couldn't help herself. Instead of answering her, he started up his computer and started to read his e-mails. She could see his eyes grow wide as he read and she knew then that he was not up to date on the problem. He was just finding about it now. She had hoped that he was hooked in via his home computer and had a head start on everything, but that didn't seem to be the case. What the hell was the matter with him? He had a Blackberry, a laptop, and a cell phone. He should have been able to read these e-mails wherever he was. She decided to continue, to at least force him to acknowledge her.

"Andre, the new clients, the big Asian clients the bank picked up in the last month have all complained that their wires are short. They claim that somehow they may have been tampered with."

"Don't bother me, Laura, you are not my supervisor," he barked at her. "Answer that damn phone over there. It's been ringing since I've sat down. Who knows who might be on the other line?" Okay, she thought, you're the Vice-President, you figure it out. With that she strode over to the desk with the ringing phone and answered just in time to hear the click of the other party hanging up. She replaced the receiver in the cradle and then decided to go to the bathroom to splash some water on her face to cool down, slowing her progress somewhat as she watched Andre leaving this area of the office ahead of her, probably, she figured, to visit the Chief of the department to kiss his ass a little more. Yeah, let him figure it out. Let him figure out that the situation has been contained. That she managed to get all three Asian companies on the phone to reassure them. That she had done so by calling several people elsewhere in the company with Korean and Chinese language skills and then summoning them to her desk to help her. That the account executives all called and profusely thanked her for her initiative, her brains, and essentially...for saving their asses. As she left the IT section to walk over to the other side of the office to the ladies room, she thought she saw Andre near her desk for a second, had he left something there on his way to the CIO's office?

The water from the tap felt invigorating to Laura, quenching the slight fever she knew was not caused by sickness, but by the stress of the morning. She looked in the mirror and thought how nice it would be to be at the beach right now...with Diego. Shaking her head to free herself from the unobtainable though satisfying image, she exited the bathroom, made a series of right turns to head to her cubicle, where she found Andre and the Chief Information Officer standing together, studying her monitor. Andre spoke to her without even looking up. How did he know I was there? Did he hear me or did he maybe see my reflection from the screen? How creepy this guy is.

"Laura," Andre started, "didn't you see my post-it note?"

"No, what note?" She wondered what he was up to. Did she really see him linger at her desk for a moment on his way to see the CIO?

"This one, right here," he said, pointing to the yellow sticker hanging from the lower corner of her computer. It was in a place that Stevie Wonder would notice, a place she would never miss. She marveled at the nerve of the man as he continued his outrageous lie. "Alerting you to a potential problem this morning and the solution for it?" Her voice was hardening as she answered him.

"I never saw that note and I have been here for the past two hours. Where was it?"

"Right here, stuck to your monitor," answered Andre with a slightly jovial bent to his voice. The CIO joined in at that moment. "Laura, you have to be in touch with the other members of the team in this office. Otherwise your next review will state that you can't work independently and that you can't work with others." His tone was grandfatherly. And why shouldn't it be? He was as old as dirt and he still believed a woman's place was in the kitchen and hadn't studied anything about computers since Fortran.

She wanted at that moment more than anything the strength and ability within herself to shout "And where in hell were you, Andre? What were you doing for the past ninety minutes?" Why didn't the CIO ask him? she thought. He's in charge of this unit, not me. The comings and goings of all the employees were monitored by cameras, the log-in times on the computers, and the security cards that opened the door to the office. But only silence and resignation emanated from her. It happened before. It would probably happen again. At times like these she wished she grew up on Flatbush Avenue instead of on the farm in Argentina. Then she would give these...men...a piece of her mind and maybe the back of her hand. Andre finished working at her terminal and walked off without a word, the CIO offering her a limp smile as he, too, exited. She stood there for a moment before she took the chair Andre had been sitting in and moved it into the storage room and retrieved herself a new one.

—الله ا سبح—

Just around the corner from where Laura had been dressed down by the CIO, Michael was struggling to maintain his composure against a torrent of bullshit coming at him like a mudslide. The third closing of the morning was turning into a disaster. At least he would be paid on the others. But this one was dissolving before his disbelieving eyes.

"Michael," said the client, "you have caused me to have to spend $77 more per month for the next thirty years and I am not happy." What had happened was that this particular client, who had taken out a one million dollar loan on his condominium, had asked Michael to lock the interest rate a few weeks earlier. The call was his and his alone, as Michael and any other loan officer in the business who had half a brain would never try to predict the movements of the interest rate market. If he could, as Michael often explained to clients, "I would be on my yacht in St. Tropez, not in the mortgage business." This particular client was a partner in some shit-hole of a hedge fund. He had his Harvard Business School MBA hanging over his desk in his office and took great pains to make sure everyone who sat here with him saw it. He made it very plain and clear that he had the pulse of the market. Michael secured his commitment with a minimum of trouble, cleared the file for closing and then closed it. That was two days ago. Today, the funding day, he was to appear at the office here for his cash out check. A million dollars...tax free...who could be unhappy, right? But this guy was. Because he didn't anticipate a couple of economic reports in the past week that spelled out a weakening economy which had the effect of lowering interest rates after he requested the rate lock which Michael made him confirm by e-mail. The borrower's rate for the mortgage he selected went down by exactly one-eighth of one percent.

"I'm here to let you know that I am exercising my right of rescission guaranteed to me by Federal law. I am not taking the loan from Argent Bank unless you change the rate to today's rate," the borrower said. Michael couldn't believe his ears. He struggled to keep his shoulders down as he answered the borrower, who had brought his lawyer along.

"Ivan, the rate has changed by only an eighth after *you* decided to lock in. It was a quarter higher earlier in the process. So you made out great, you made a great call as many others locked in two months ago, before the rate drop of a quarter. So instead of a grand slam in the bottom of the ninth inning, it's a hard smash off the wall that still wins the game. Why would you walk away from a million dollars?" With that statement, Michael unfolded the check he took from his breast pocket and put it on the table in front of the borrower and his lawyer. Dave Drucker, his old friend and mentor in the mortgage business, the greatest salesman he ever saw, would have loved it. But today was a black cloud day apparently as the borrower took the check and ripped it in half. A million fucking dollars, gone in an instant. Michael stared at the torn pieces of paper unable to comprehend the mindset of some people. It took the average American family twenty years or more to earn the amount of money this clown just threw away like a used hankie.

"Ivan, I can't believe you did that. What makes you think a better deal is to be had? Besides that, do you want to go through the whole process again? Do you want to fill out a new application? Pay for a new appraisal? Order a title report and make sure the whole thing goes through as smoothly as it did with us?" His lawyer spoke up then, raising today's desired body count of dead lawyers to three in Michael's opinion. Oh, why couldn't I have been brought up in the wild west? Or in Soviet Russia?

"Mr. Pierce I want your appraisal to be certified to whatever bank Ivan chooses. Furthermore, I want a complete package of the entire mortgage application copied and in my office by the end of the day. He paid for it and I want it." The lawyer was a small man, wiry, but not tough at all. Michael had had enough of this. He was going to eat this guy for lunch, but not before just one more try. He turned to his client and ignored the lawyer.

"Ivan, I can have another check drawn up in a minute or two. This is one million tax free dollars. You can't just walk away from it. Think about what you're doing. You asked for the rate lock, I have your e-mail confirming it." The lawyer started to comment, but Michael shot him a warning look. It did no good, though. Why, oh why couldn't he be with Saddam Hussein's Republican guard or maybe Savak?

"The Federal right of rescission law requires no reason to be given for this loan to be killed and for all fees to be returned," he said. "You are badgering my client and if it continues, I will report your behavior to the Chairman of this bank and the state banking department." Little suckass mealy mouthed prematurely balding...whatever. Time for lunch.

"Is that it, Ivan?" With the client's nod, Michael did what so many other loan officers, underwriters, and processors in the mortgage business wanted to do every day but had to avoid so they keep their jobs. Just let the client have it. "Well let me tell you, Ivan, I will indeed make you a copy of your appraisal, but I will not under any circumstance certify it to another bank. In the absence of egregious error, I don't do that. You want to go to another bank, then have them order an appraisal themselves and you can pay for it again." He turned to the lawyer, informed him that there was no law requiring he certify the appraisal to another bank and turned back to Ivan, who was getting red in the face. Good, Michael thought, I want you to lose your temper. Go right fucking ahead, you little shit.

"You just make sure you work with a bank that has a program that will take the average of your bonus for the last two years instead of leaning on the crappy bonus you had last year. You make sure the loan officer at the new bank takes about fifteen phone calls on the weekend from you the way I did. You also make sure they come to your apartment to write the application at eight o'clock on a weeknight instead of sending it to you with a bunch of arrows attached to show you where to sign. You make sure they will come to your office personally to pick up documents instead of suggesting that you overnight them. You ask them if they'll waive the underwriting fee. You see if they get you to a closing table in six weeks and then ask them if they even offer a fifteen-day rate lock in order to give you a better deal. Then make sure they don't turn around after five weeks and tell you your deal is declined because your building has more than twenty percent commercial space, that it also has thirty percent of its units held as investors, not owner-occupied. You make sure of all that. And if you get a better deal, well then enjoy it. I'm sure those pre-tax seventy seven dollars will change your life substantially. And if you don't, you make damn sure you don't come back here because we don't deal with losers at this bank, we deal with winners only." He stood and said to the both of them, "Now get the hell out of my sight. The both of you make me sick to even look at you." And with that he walked out of the conference room without looking back, feeling ten feet tall but unfortunately lighter in the wallet because the borrower's decision to rescind his deal also meant the loss of his commission on the deal.

Michael walked from the conference room past the doors of several executives, none of whom bothered to look up as he passed, but he knew they all heard everything that went on. They also recognized him from his occasional visits here to this office to meet with clients in midtown. They had nothing to say. They were just too relieved that they didn't have to be part of anything like what they just heard. Their jobs did not require any contact with the general public, none of the bank's customers spoke with them, and that was the way they liked it. And this, what they just saw and heard, was the reason why. Michael wasn't looking for any conversation with any of them at this moment anyway. The day was falling apart rapidly and he just wanted to be gone from this place…there had to be a rainbow around here somewhere, he thought, as he approached the corner on his way to splash some water in his face.

Laura felt uniquely capable of murder at that moment. The wire problem, handling Andre's calls, falling behind as a result in her own daily routine and duties. And to top it off, she knew Andre had planted that post-it note. She was very meticulous not only in her appearance but her surroundings as well. Not so much as a total neatnik, but she knew instantly when something was slightly out of place. And she knew that post-it note was not there from last night, but had been slapped on there before the CIO came by her desk with Andre. At that point she felt impossibly weary, more tired than when she would ride horses with her brothers and parents into town some fifty miles away to sell the farm's produce, sometimes galloping on the way back for a mile straight, her knees pounding in the stirrups, her body lifted off the saddle by legs that were already muscular and powerful, sometimes just loping around some low grasses, letting the beasts have a break and a little munch and then maybe stopping in the middle of a cool running stream to let them slake their thirst during which times she would wonder and dream. Her still-lively legs carried her back around the same corner away from her desk to the corridor and toward the bathroom where she just had to sit down for a few moments and collect her thoughts. And once again splash some water on her face as it felt as if it were on fire.

She seems immersed in thought, Michael concluded, moving as if she were on autopilot, her thoughts apparently a million miles away from this place, so maybe he should give her a wide berth this time, although he didn't want to. He had noticed Laura right away as she entered the hallway from the opposite end, just a second or two after he did. Halfway down the corridor was another hall that led to the bathrooms. They were perhaps forty feet apart and it only took Michael to get to thirty-nine feet apart when he felt the horror of his day instantly start to dissipate, as soon as he took her in.

It had always been that way between them. Michael and Laura worked for the same bank but in different departments, so they would only see each other at the holiday party and other bank functions. And two or three times per year, it was like this, usually right here as a matter of fact, that they would accidentally run into each other. He had never approached her desk and he realized a couple of years ago that he did not know exactly where it was. This was how it was for them for the past ten years, from the moment they first met.

"Hola, Laura," he said quietly, gently so as not to shake her from her thoughts too strongly.

She almost stumbled and fell forward at Michael's hello. She knew instantly it was him without even looking and she was momentarily angry that she had walked up on him without even knowing. She was so lost in her thoughts about the horses, about her hatred for Andre, that she must have been walking for several seconds in zombie mode. But it was his deep, sonorous voice that brought her instantly back in time ten years to when she first laid eyes on him. She was amazed once again that she felt so safe and warm when he was around and easily put Andre and the CIO and the Asian clients out of her mind.

"Oh," she started, a bit startled. "Hello, Michael. How have you been?"

It had been several months since the last time they ran into each other. Usually these brief meetings occurred in the hallway near the front lobby door by the elevator bank, once or twice only at his mortgage office, most of the time here in this hallway, on her turf, the exception being the last ten holiday parties where they usually found each other for a few minutes alongside the drunk executives and sec-retaries looking for a dance or to cop a feel. Each meeting was coincidental, they always included a decent amount of high level small talk that somehow managed some meaning, and every time without fail there was an electricity, something chemical that was in the air between them from the moment they had met, on the coat line at a hotel in Manhattan that served as that year's setting for the company Christmas party.

"I'm okay, thanks. You know, ups and downs, just like any other day, any other year, but doing okay overall. Always looking ahead, ya know? How are things up here?" One day, he always thought whenever he ran into her in this fashion and today was no exception, I would love to engage this woman in a real conversation…and anything else that might follow. But he never even made a pass at her, not even the most oblique reference to the smoldering, nuclear feelings between them. It was like one long first date…that spanned ten years. Each time they met, a little more information was exchanged between them, so they were getting to the point where the small talk was becoming unnecessary.

As it was with when they first met, he had the impression of some sort of slight amber, yellowish haze that seemed to settle around them, much like in the film version when Maria first met Tony in the gym in *West Side Story*. Those two kids from that great movie at that moment in the dance didn't know anything else about what was going on in the world around them, even anything that was happening just a few feet away. All sounds were muffled, all lights were dimmed as if the design was to lower any other sensory experience for the benefit of these two to concentrate on each other.

"Actually this morning is a bit problematic, but I can handle it," she answered, asking herself as she said it, 'Can I really?'

"I have no doubt you can. You look nice. Did you change your hair?"

"No, it's been the same for some time now." He looked perplexed as she said it.

"Well, it looked a little different from the last time but then again that was some months ago…but always nice," he added suavely, sure to be seen as a compliment as he said it while he started to lean towards the lobby doors, said in such a way to not be construed as a cheap come on. Like a dance partner sensing a change in rhythm or direction, she started to lean away as well. Their meeting today was over...two minutes of bliss. He smiled for her and her toes curled in her shoes in response.

"Always good to see you, Laura. Take care always, please."

He always has the most gentle, elegant good-byes she thought as she tilted her head back slightly, smiled broadly and said to him as she started down the hallway to the bathroom, "You too, Michael. See you again sometime, I guess."

With that he pushed through the glass doors and stepped to the elevator and she headed to the lavatory, neither of them daring to turn around, both of them experiencing the exact same thought at the same exact same moment which was, What was I thinking about before I saw him/her?

Michael exited the building onto Fifth Avenue a few minutes later, turned left and headed to the garage where he parked every time he had a closing here. Too bad I only see her once out of every fifteen times I come here, he thought. His mind drifted back ten years, to when he first saw her. At the holiday party. On the coat line. What an interesting accent. Could this be the woman with the amazing butt he saw a few weeks earlier?

At the time Michael was engaged in a heated debate with a credit officer when, out of the corner of his eye, he caught the slightest sug-gestion of a tall figure with an impossibly elegant way of walking. Michael always liked a woman who walked well...hips slightly for-ward, carriage and chin erect, exuding confidence, long athletic strides instead of clopping along like a Clydesdale. He was always cautious when he observed women on the street. He never wanted to openly stare at a beautiful woman as he felt maybe it was a little uncomfort-able for most of them. But this time, his eyes were drawn to perhaps the most perfect butt he had ever seen...muscular, each side totally in sync with not only each other but with the entire upper body of whoever this woman was, capable of being wrapped in a brown paper bag and still looking great. The debate with the credit officer ceased instantly and for the first time in his life, he actually turned fully one hundred eighty degrees and followed a woman, just to look at her again. She had already moved past him on her way to some destina-tion in his office so he couldn't see her face, just this truly magnificent ass that he could not take his eyes away from. After about fifteen feet of this ridiculousness, he broke off his stalking and returned to resume his conversation with the credit officer.

It was she, he realized, standing behind her on the coat line and he discovered as soon as she turned around that her ass was not essentially her best feature. On any given day it could have been her soft brown eyes which were a bit sleepy but somehow bright with intelligence and silliness. Soft as a chocolate cake in a sidewalk café in Paris. Or maybe her lips which were slightly crooked, giving her the appearance of someone who was always thinking about her next statement or movement. Not mere thin red lines or some pulpy mess, just a perfectly shaped mouth with straight white teeth that were so bright you could read by them. The rest of her bone structure was extraordinary, at least to his eyes. Maybe some other guy would see only a bologna sandwich when he took her in. But Michael was looking at a mixture of Cyd Charisse and Rita Hayworth. He wondered if Laura threw her hair over her head when she left the shower or after a dip in the ocean, as in that famous scene in the movie *Gilda*.

He was enthralled, openly staring at Laura's sharp features, cheekbones that seemed cut from a block of marble, a straight jaw line and strong shaped nose framed by a mane of black hair brushed back from her forehead, unstyled but cascading perfectly around her face down to her shoulders. She was able to look straight in his eyes, being almost six feet tall in her heels and he was instantly smitten, totally drawn to her the way a New York six-year-old is drawn to the Mr. Softee jingle. This was no ordinary beautiful woman. There were millions of those in and around the city. They were dime-a-dozen. Even though they were surrounded by several hundred raucous banking executives, the room, to them, was as silent as a forest after a winter storm.

What else was there to say to her but, "Hello. How do you do? I'm Michael Pierce from the mortgage department." Who are you was what he really wanted to know. If I could build the perfect girl, I would build her from your mold, he easily concluded as she stepped away just slightly as if to take him in. He could now see her entire body, not just her rear end. There was real strength there he thought, not some celery-eating anorexic. No, this lady had the figure of a beach volleyball player, long, lean, and strong. Oh my.

"I am fine, thank you. How are you?" she answered and asked with a voice that had a lovely, gentle South American accent, not the rapid fire chatter of the Puerto Riquenas and the Dominicas he was used to hearing in school, on the train, in the supermarkets and parks. It was a familiar sound for anyone growing up or living in any of the boroughs of New York City. To borrow from the novelist Charlie Carillo, if deer could speak, this is how they would sound. He felt like he was having a heart attack.

"Well I'm...okay, I guess. What is your name?" He usually wasn't so forward with women. In the past they complimented him for his gentlemanly manner, a tiny bit of James Bond in his mannerisms, but he was no player and didn't mind not being one. A movie track of the most beautiful women he had been privileged to meet over the course of his life played quickly in his mind and he easily concluded that they all slid down a notch in the last minute.

"I am Laura Rodriguez. I work in the Fifth Avenue office with the Information Technology department." She didn't extend her hand for a shake as many American women might have done. She was holding a drink in one hand, her coat casually held over her arm, and she was absentmindedly playing with the swizzle stick with the other. She was wearing a silvery, shimmering blouse, sleek black pants, and no jewelry of any kind that he could see other than a nice string of pearls. Easily the most beautiful living creature he had ever seen.

Laura lifted her head to look in the mirror of the bathroom in the office. The cool water dripped off the edges of her face which was losing the heat it picked up from her confrontation with Andre. But was it that? Or was it the heat that invaded her face and neck whenever she and Michael had one of their little hallway meetings. Sometimes at the holiday parties, when they had more time to speak with each other, the heat spread to other areas of her body, a sensation she had never known before. Sure, other men and boys were nice and handsome or cute and more than a few of them, starting with Diego many years earlier, piqued her interest. But not like anything she felt with Michael in her presence.

Again she thought back to Michael in the hallway just now. Not one bit, not one iota did her attraction for him wane over the years. Never did she feel threatened by him. He never made a pass at her, unlike most of the other pig men in New York in the past ten years.

Always a total gentleman, glib, charming, never repeated a story, all of which he told so well. Not once did he ever even ask if she had a boyfriend. Beautiful blue eyes, nice shoulders, trim hips, good strong voice. She laughed with embarrassment still when she recalled what she said to him after he introduced himself.

"I didn't know such a handsome man worked at Argent Bank." A perfect example of the mouth working before the brain has a chance to stop it. A blurt of truth the second before the gate of propriety slammed shut.

He was stunned to hear her say that as he was unaccustomed to such directness from women. He just didn't seem to ever inspire that sort of breathless comment. But in an instant, somehow he realized that she was the kind of girl that would never speak to a man like this. She seemed too poised, too reserved and demure. Of course she thought these things because he could feel the passion in her blood from a few feet away. But not to say it to a man, not ever. Well, at least not more than a couple of times. A nice change in these days of naked women on every television show, in every advertisement, and in every movie, women who didn't have a hint of sex appeal about them...just a lot of skin and pouty looks and not much else. Well, many of them anyway, not all. Michael was a little old-fashioned but never fancied himself a priest.

"Well, thanks, I uh..." and she also remembered the disappointment in that next moment as he said "I can't do romance. I'm married but I think I'd like to be your friend. Is that okay?"

Is it okay, she thought? Is it okay? No it's not okay because for the first time since Diego stepped off that bus so many years ago, she was aflame with desire, an uncontrollable urge to drop every warning and threat she had hammered into her over the years by parents, brothers, priests, and nuns, every device to keep her away from thoughts and feelings such as these. The holiday party was in a Times Square hotel and she wondered if she could actually go upstairs with him right now. A one night stand was an experience she never had, something her girlfriends kidded her about endlessly. She shook her head and smiled, still tickled like a little girl at what she said to him, one of the few times she could ever remember being so forward with someone she didn't know. I mean, I just met him, she told her girlfriends later. "You should have gotten a room," her new friend Nadia told her seriously. Many times, over many years, she had started to think the same thing. She should have gotten the room.

So they talked for the rest of the night, she disappearing for a few times to dance. He didn't dance except slow dancing in a circle, he explained, and no, she wasn't going to do that, allow him to put his arms around. Otherwise she would have just flapped her arms and floated up to the front desk to reserve a suite pulling him down on the bed by his nice burgundy tie.

Michael was turning onto Fifty-Eighth Street as she reached for the paper towel to dry her face, remembering how she and her new friend walked up Broadway that night after the party, the tourists parting for them as if they were royalty, actually standing aside as they walked uptown against the tide of Christmas time visitors to the city. Their strides matched perfectly and he felt as if he had known her forever, not just for a few hours.

They spoke every time they met accidentally in the hallways of the bank much in this same manner this morning, for the next ten years, with a little extra time allocated for them at the holiday party, but never a dance, a phone call, an e-mail, a stolen kiss, a lascivious look, not even a light touch on the underside of her elbow to dashingly bid a lady adieu. Nothing but an unspoken communication with their eyes and general mannerisms upon encountering each other that said, Yes, I want you more than anything.

But somehow, in an amazingly perfect storm of exclusion as they again only saw each other a few times in any one year, a friendship had been forged. He never asked after her social life, she never asked him about his marriage. Why should they? It didn't matter to them as neither was ever going to make a move on the other. Laura's moral core forbade her from even thinking about an affair with a married man and Michael's was the same regarding stepping out on his marriage. Michael had no idea if she, in the past ten years, had slept with twenty men...or none. Laura was equally oblivious to the state of Michael's marriage to Georgia. They could have been the types who still were very affectionate and silly with each other after years of routine and familiarity or they could be as cold as ice, just riding it out for the kids. Maybe he sleeps around.

But for the both of them, the real reason was the same. They secretly didn't want to imagine the other with someone else. They both knew that was ridiculous. She definitely had several boyfriends in the past ten years as well as a couple of unidentifiable...'things to do.' He was married and slept with someone every night. Their relationship truly was like a long first date that kept getting better with each passing meeting and though this remained unsaid between them, neither wanted it to stop. A candle had been lit, a barely perceptible source of light and heat and it was placed deep in their hearts from the moment they met. And even if they never saw each other again after this day's chance meeting, it would be another lifetime before either met anyone else who seemed to touch them so specially.

"Que caca di toro," Laura thought, with perhaps the appropriate amount of disgust and impatience with such daydreaming. She wiped her face dry, balled up the paper and tossed it into the garbage, pulled the heavy door open and headed back to her desk, unable to stop thinking that she would like to trade her date tonight with Adam, who was possibly a nice guy. He was good looking in a tousled brown hair and glasses kind of way, but he honestly seemed to possess about half of Michael's manners, a third of his story-telling ability, and shallow brown eyes that hadn't held a solitary sign of expression during any of their dates that inspired Laura to say, 'I'm enjoying just looking at you,' or just a delicious crinkle at the corners once in a while, some kind of silly young boy's intensity, as Michael's had every single time she spoke with him. Sadly, Laura had to admit that the only advantages Mr. Adam Breezington had were that he was single, not disgusting or gay, and also that he had not invoked the third-date-we-have-to-have-sex-now-or-forget-about-it rule. She was counting on that one fact as proof of his good character, that he wanted to build a relationship with her based on something other than the looks and body she was blessed or cursed with, depending on your point of view. With hers it was usually the latter, but Laura always hated the ridiculous notion that she would be required to give herself to any man, for what, to get a fourth date? Anyway, Adam had not pushed her at all, and it had been eight dates in a little more than six weeks and he was pretty good looking and he was single and Michael and all the others are not and she hadn't had an orgasm not brought on by herself for too long already. She knew however, that the undeniable truth was that if Michael Pierce were single, she would drop Adam like a bad habit.

She turned the corner with a new determination to figure out what had happened this morning with the defective wires. She wasn't going to allow this to just hang in the air of the office. Bastard Andre...they'll see what you've been doing all these months since your damn promotion which you didn't deserve.

Michael gave a two dollar tip to the parking guy, got in the car, and pointed it east toward the Queensboro Bridge to get him out of the city and back to Long Island. He was feeling a wave of guilt because he was thinking about Laura as much as Laura was thinking about him at the same moment. He had to admit she was the woman he wanted to see later, not his wife Georgia, whom he surely loved but who was leaving tomorrow for Tarpon Springs, a Greek enclave in Florida just north and west of Tampa. Georgia had many relatives who retired there and she wanted to show off Sally to them. It was to be a long weekend filled with family outings to the beach and the theater along with an inundation of Greek culture, too much to Michael's way of thinking, complete with reading, speaking and writing of the Greek language and alphabet.

He knew the layout of the approaching evening like a trained dancer knew his steps. This evening, like the hundred or so previous, would be filled with Georgia's work, Greek school for Sally, and packing and preparing for this trip which would be his daughter's first on a plane. He would miss them both in different degrees of course, especially Sally. He wanted to see her face bloom with joy and wonder at everything about the plane and the bustling airport, looking out the window from thirty thousand feet and pressing the bell for the flight attendant to order a soda. He figured with all that going on, the evening would be about as romantic as a visit to an STD clinic. He guided the car off the narrow outer roadway of the bridge after viewing Vinny's construction site as they passed over Roosevelt Island, into the streets around Queens Plaza which he knew how to traverse expertly on his way to the Long Island Expressway. Tonight he decided to take the local streets through the old neighborhoods of Sunnyside and Wood-side, just to see what was happening with the place. It also allowed him a little extra time to dawdle with the idea of dating Laura. He had no reason to get home earlier than usual. Georgia hadn't cooked a meal in years. Everything was takeout, pre-packaged or micro-waved. He started thinking again about it—funny how it could come out of nowhere—about a possible future conversation he may have with her...one that every married person in the world dreaded.

⁓

NOON

Vinny's Suburban pulled up in front of the People's Mosque on Steinway Street in Astoria, housed in a multi-level attached building near the Grand Central Parkway. He was on his way out of the car before Charlie Mick was able to bring it to a complete halt. He slammed the door shut and spoke to the son of his long dead and never found friend through the open passenger window. "Stay here and don't even think about moving."

"How long you gonna be?" Charlie Mick was learning to under-stand all of Vinny's mantras and employ them into his daily life, one of which was that time is the most important resource we have and all attempts to use it effectively will be appreciated and rewarded, which is why he asked when to expect Vinny's return. He was taken aback at the harshness of the reply from his father's friend.

"As long as it takes to finish what I gotta do and get back in the car, okay? Just fucking stay here, alright?" He turned quickly and stepped to the gold ornate doors of the mosque. Charlie Mick sank in his seat under the weight of Vinny's comments and stared out the windshield. The Burke brothers looked at each other and shrugged. Fred said to Ryan, "He's as surly today as Bill Russell at a Boston media outing." His brother nodded his agreement and added, "And he looks as pissed as Wes Unseld in the paint. Let's get out of here and get a cab back to the site. We gotta get the truck. Maybe Vinny forgot about that on his way over here. Hey kid," he said to Charlie Mick as his brother opened the door, "don't worry about him, we all have a little pressure on us these days. Just make sure you stay here, okay?" He laid a hand on the younger man's shoulder and gave it a friendly squeeze before he followed his brother out of the car.

Vinny approached the heavy doors of the mosque unobstructed by the three men standing outside. Nor did they watch him approach their spiritual oasis with a wary look as they had unfortunately been forced to do in the past six years, because they had seen him so many times before. He was the Imam's trusted friend, as close to him as anyone could be. They never knew how their relationship started or continued to jell to this point. He was a non-believer so close with a man as devout and dedicated as their imam, but they didn't care anymore as they had been attending this mosque for many years now and were always comforted by the lessons and sometimes the lectures they heard during prayer services. The door closed behind Vinny after he nodded hello and the men returned to their heated discussion, whether or not the Mets would ever make the World Series again in their lifetime.

Vinny looked for his friend as soon as he was inside the doors, his eyes adjusting to the softer light slower than he would have liked. He removed his shoes which he placed in a storage bin and then looked around some more. There were only a few worshipers milling about, the morning prayers having ended a few hours earlier and the *dhuhr*, or early afternoon prayers still to come shortly after noon time. This was the time to grab the Imam, J'lome, his best and most trusted friend in the world for a conversation. There was usually no furniture in a mosque, but J'lome allowed some chairs near the entrance. "Some of my congregants have pain in their legs, why would a house of God deny them a place to rest for a few minutes?" he had asked Vinny when the mosque was being designed in its early days. Vinny fell into a comfortable cushiony chair and tried to let the stiffness of his body to subside.

That was typical of J'lome's approach to Islam. Although his dedication to the teachings and ways of the Prophet Muhammad was total, he wanted most of all for Islam to gain respectability in the eyes of the average American. And he decided long ago that it had to start in his own house of worship not only with something simple as allowing furniture, but also inviting the local spiritual leaders here for discussions on topics of shared interest, such as the quality of the schools, crime, help for those residents of Astoria who couldn't or wouldn't help themselves. The Greek Orthodox church elders as well as the local rabbis and Catholic priests loved him and his programs and respected his efforts to bring everyone together.

Some of his congregants disagreed with this method of reaching out to various members of the community but he was adamant in his belief that the type of open discourse between the different strains of humans in New York City was sorely needed and had to come from the spiritual leaders of each and every community, to be allowed to trickle down to everyone including the agnostics and the atheists. His forceful personality won them all over, and in the ensuing years established the People's Mosque as a place of progressive ideas as well as a sacred spot on Steinway Street to pray and find comfort through the Muslim faith or advice about a business deal or how to deal with a less than attractive spouse. Even just for some relief from the oppressive summer heat or the biting winds of winter or the loneliness of being away from the family in the old country.

It was in the upstate prison Dannemora that J'lome, formerly of the Queensbridge Houses of Long Island City, was introduced to Islam. He had been selected by his mentor there out of the prison yard when he had noticed Elgin Barnes, now J'lome, standing up for some white inmates who were being set upon by a mixed Latino and black gang. He had stepped between the rivals, protecting the weaker ones with words and then with a blinding array of flying fists and feet and then with a staunch refusal to inform on the original instigators that left him by the end of the day with the respect of almost everyone in the prison. His mentor, an Iranian named Hassan Paria, believed in and promoted the very new religion of Bahaii which accepted all of the Prophet's teachings and promoted them as the true path, but also believed in the oneness of God and the unity of all people across a wide spectrum of race, economic status, and nationality. J'lome was interested in everything regarding his congregants' neighborhoods from their marriages and family life to environmental and ecological concerns, to the proliferation of handguns among the young men of the city and the prevalence of despair that hung around like a viscous stench. His mind was open, his intellect was unmatched by most and Vinny considered him entirely truthful.

They were friends since the age of five, collecting bottles on the street for the nickel deposit. They were inseparable, the Italian-Irish tough kid with the raw intelligence and fists at the ready and the cool quiet black kid from the Ravenswood Projects in Long Island City. They knew each other's moves on the basketball court, firing passes and effectively boxing out bigger and stronger players, never taking any shit from anyone. If any of the black players hassled Vinny, J'lome would step in and announce that no one was going to screw around with his blood brother. Conversely, if anyone tried a racist tactic with J'lome, well...Vinny would just beat the shit out of them.

It should have been an easy job way back in their seventeenth year. Vinny and J'lome had known of an abandoned blanket and pillow factory just off Van Dam Street and they wanted to break in to check it out for an inspiring game New York kids play called Joe Mannix, based on the 1960s television private investigator who not only always solved the crime by the end of the show but had been beaten, shot at, run down, and bludgeoned in a variety of ways in each installment prior to the crime being solved. J'lome liked the show not only because Joe Mannix would always come back from the dead and defeat the corporate/crime syndicate/drug gang bad guys, but also because it was one of the first television shows that featured a black actress. Playing 'Joe Mannix' meant swinging from ropes into each other, crashing into each other on huge dollys and diving onto each other from the different levels of leftover merchandise. It was always great fun and Vinny and J'lome figured a pillow and blanket factory would be perfect for a Joe Mannix recreation as they were all getting older and the prospect of broken bones and serious injuries was making its way into their fun.

However, after casing the seemingly abandoned factory, they quickly determined that there were hundreds of pillows and blankets left behind. The decision to steal them and distribute them around the elderly and poor population of the neighborhood was an easy one to make. Neither had ever stolen anything before, but they didn't care because they knew they were going to do something good with the proceeds of the heist and they also knew this would be the extent of their criminal enterprise, never to be repeated. After an afternoon game of Joe Mannix, Vinny and J'lome returned to the factory, leaving their friends the Burke brothers, Michael Pierce, Moose Miller, Ping the Router, Mikey Busy, and King Khan out of the plan. They had moved about twenty down comforters into a car that was 'borrowed' for the evening and then were stunned to see the cherry top of the police car through the translucent windows of the factory accompanied by a bullhorn announcing that they were surrounded and to come out. They decided to do just that with pillowcases over their heads, masking their identities while they ran for it. It should have worked as they could outrun any cop on the NYPD running backward, but J'lome slipped while executing a move between the two cops and went down before he even had a chance to slip away. The last thing he did before the cop's knee landed between his shoulder blades was to yell to Vinny to run away.

The cop with the knee on his back told him then, "Don't worry nigger, we're gonna grab your friend later," and he punctuated his statement by rolling his kneecap across J'lome's upper spine, blinding him with pain and shooting a panicky thought through his brain that he would be paralyzed if the bastard continued on his present sadistic bent. So he rolled out from underneath, kicked him in the gut, punched the other in the balls, and was about to make a break for it when the second responding radio car showed up and another man in blue jumped out with his service revolver at the ready, pointing right at J'lome's head.

The District Attorney piled on the charges: resisting arrest, assault on a police officer, grand larceny for the blankets and pillows. Combined with an apathetic legal aid lawyer and an all white jury that were collectively sick of the young gangs filled mostly with young black and Latino men running rampant through the city in the 1970s, the judge threw the book at J'lome and offered to lower the term to two years from four if he gave up the name of his accomplice. Vinny was sitting in the courtroom when his friend refused to turn him over for a reduced prison term and, at that moment, he knew there would never be anyone else in his world he would trust more with his life. So strange how a single moment can affect the rest of your days. J'lome knew the cop with the knee in his back sent him on a magical journey that ended with the knowledge of the Koran, the acceptance of Islam as his blueprint for righteousness, and the teachings of the Prophet as his guide for virtually every decision that would follow in his life.

Many of the old neighborhood rejected J'lome upon his release from prison, not because he had been there, because certainly on many of these streets a jail term was a rite of passage the way hitting your first jumper from the corner or the first time you felt a girl's tit was. No, it was the skullcap he wore on his scalp and the benign satisfied look he carried on his face that made most of them nervous and distrustful. Vinny was there at the prison gate when he was released and they embraced with pure love, adoration for each other's accomplishments in the past six years, as well as a fully cemented friendship. Vinny had visited as soon as he could and cried when he saw his friend behind bars all alone. He cried also at the selflessness of his friend, who warned him never to go to the court and confess his role to get his friend's time reduced.

"They would just throw you in here with me. They would never work a deal like that, you know that as well as I do. Listen, my friend, my brother...you have the most magnificent mind of anyone in the city in my opinion. If you want to make it up to me, then spend the next six years exercising that mind. I already know you love to read comics and newspapers. Read the classics. I'm talking about Hemingway, Fitzgerald, James Joyce. Read the great philosophers, Heidegger, Hobbes, St. Augustine. Read the Bible. Read the Koran. I've met someone in here who has changed my life, I never knew about any of this stuff before I got in here. Glean any and all truths from these texts and put them into daily practice. Read about how people make money. Learn about banking, math, and deal making. Learn the discipline of the mind, my friend, and show me what you have learned once I get out of here. That is how you repay this debt to me." Through tears he promised his friend that he would follow through on his request and therefore spent virtually every day for the next forty-eight months in the library with philosophy texts, newspapers—only the *Times* and the *Wall Street Journal* with an occasional glance at the *Post* for the sports section—business and banking manuals, biographies of every titan of business from J.P. Morgan to Earl Scheib, from Tom Carvel to Harry Helmsley. It was Helmsley's remarkably simple plan for gathering real estate like fallen leaves in autumn that set him on his course, the course that allowed him to accumulate twenty-five two- and three-family homes throughout western Queens through foreclosure auctions, twenty-four-hour, seven-day-a-week repair and upgrade sessions with the Burke Brothers, who he pushed through trade school to learn plumbing and electrical work.

Later Michael went into the mortgage business and he helped with the refinancing of all the smaller properties, taking cash out of them in order to buy six- and eight-family homes, then to take over the commercial spaces on the ground floors of these small apartment buildings and open a bagel store, a pizza place, a laundromat, the Pepperidge Farm bread route, the office cleaning service. Nothing glamorous, but definitely a money-making mini-conglomerate. When J'lome had a few months left on his sentence, he made an offer for the building where the People's Mosque now stood, bought it for cash, refurbished the bones of the building, installed all new utilities, and then handed J'lome the key as payment for the six years. He did much more for his non blood brother than most directly-related family remembers do for each other. Vinny ended up with the brother he never had. And so did J'lome.

He needed the kind of advice and counsel that he knew could only come from this one person, his best friend, his true unquestioned ally. And as if on cue, J'lome appeared from around the corner where he knew the gibah, the wall that faced east toward Mecca was. Vinny preferred to meet J'lome away from the most spiritual places in the mosque mostly out of respect for the congregants. J'lome was walking with a young man who was dressed in jeans and a leather jacket, his prayer rug over his shoulder. Vinny sized the young man up immediately as a bit of a rogue, trying to figure out how to be a tough guy, but he could also see that he was listening intently to J'lome. His friend had that kind of rapport with others. One felt compelled to listen to him the same way you felt compelled to stare at a beautiful movie star when she appeared on the screen. J'lome raised his eyebrow at Vinny when he saw him which told Vinny just to wait a moment while I straighten this kid out. He walked the young man to the doors of the mosque, stood for a final moment with his hand on his shoulder and then sent him on his way earning an earnest smile and handshake from his young charge. He turned immediately to greet Vinny, who was out of the chair already and reaching out to embrace him.

"How are you, my friend? It's been a while since I've seen you," he said to Vinny once they broke away from each other.

"I'm sorry," Vinny answered, his head hanging a little low for J'lome's liking. "I've been trying to deal with this building situation and..."

"And you are running into forces you can't scare away, or think away, or drop with a left hook, right?" J'lome smiled as he said this, knowing he was probably the only person in the world who could speak with Vinny this way. He turned toward his office which was just inside the front door and bid Vinny inside.

"If only it were that easy," Vinny said as he turned with him, his shoulders sagging as well, giving away to J'lome exactly how troubled he was. He craved some counsel now, some spirituality, some reminder of what he had turned his life into in the past twenty-five years. J'lome could see he was in a hurry to unload. This must be heavy, he was figuring, as Vinny plopped down in a chair in front of his desk. The Imam of The People's Mosque dropped into the high-backed leather chair he loved so much and leaned back, steepling his fingers under his chin. He couldn't stop a scary thought regarding his friend from entering his head because he was, after all, only a man, but he shooed it away and opened a new page in his brain. First thing was to put him at ease. Why not a joke?

"You want a beer? Got some good Taliban brew here. Strained through the eye mesh of an Afghan burqua." J'lome smiled, he thought it was funny. Apparently Vinny was going to let it fly over his head like the red-eye over an Iowa cornfield.

"No, nothing, thanks," Vinny said as he wiped his face from his hairline down the sides, to the hinge of his jaw, trying to quell the headache that had existed since he left the meeting earlier in the day with the two assholes and...the nice lady. Maybe if he wiped hard enough, the memory of the meeting would go away as well and he would somehow find the answer in between his worry lines.

"What's happening, my friend? You look like a reluctant groom on his wedding day."

"J'lome," he started, looking out the window, while picking at his fingernails, a nervous habit that he hated, "How long have we known each other? Thirty-five years?"

"No, a little more than that. We were seven when we went on our first bottle collecting mission. So it's more like, oy vey, thirty-nine years. I'll bet you a dollar that I am the only Muslim on this earth who uses that phrase. Can't break an old habit." He regarded Vinny closely and leaned forward, his forearms on his desk. "Talk to me, please. What is it?"

Vinny looked out the office window to Steinway Street and he could see Charlie Mick flipping through the pages of the newspaper. He could see the Burkes had left. Have to remind the kid later to read the articles instead of just checking out the pictures and the captions. He sat up and turned back to his friend.

"You know, I thought it would be easier when we got older. Do you remember when we used to say that to each other? Can't wait to be an adult. Everything would be easier once we weren't kids anymore. Remember?" There was bitterness in the question. J'lome could feel it like an electrical shock on wet skin. He said nothing at first, trying to allow the silence to pull it out of him.

"Yes, I do," J'lome replied after a few seconds, "we always thought we would be able to do whatever we wanted as long as we were eighteen years old. No one to stop us from doing whatever we wanted, no parents, no teachers, no priests getting in our way."

"Right...how fucking wrong were we?" J'lome let the language slide as he knew how respectful Vinny was of his mosque and the choices he made. If it were anyone else, J'lome would have thrown him out the window for using coarse language.

"Very wrong," said J'lome. "We knew nothing about the fleeting nature of a youth's existence at that time. What is happening with you today? I haven't see you like this since I can remember." Vinny blew a breath out and rubbed his face again with quick up and down strokes. And then he blew it all out in a rush.

"These fucking people, these two guys and some woman on this preservation committee, none of them have probably had a job since they were born, none of them produce anything, employ anyone, or perform any function I can see except for busting my fucking chops over the building and this stupid sign they are in love with." J'lome let the obscenities pass once again without comment because he knew Vinny would not make the mistake again in his mosque. These are only words his teacher had taught him, not thoughts or beliefs. Ignore them until they disturb your own sense of peace and harmony or until you discover unequivocally that they are more than words but a true representation of one's philosophy of life at a bitter moment. Then either turn the speaker around to a truer path or throw them out. Vinny's face scrunched up in apparent embarrassment and frustration. "I'm sorry J'lome, I don't mean to speak this way in your place."

"It's okay, my friend. Without you this place wouldn't even exist, so I'll grant you a little latitude. But I'm getting a little bored with this." Vinny sat up straight like a bolt, highly annoyed.

"What do you mean by that? I've been your brother for years ever since..."

"Since the first time you put a beating on Butchy from Thirty-ninth Place right there in the park in front of everyone in defense of me." J'lome was fairly adept at answering people's questions not only with the correct answers but at the right time. It was quite the disarming technique. "Yes, ever since we protected each other from anyone else who tried to take our bottles, our bicycles...our pride and self-respect. Now J'lome looked out the window dreamily. "I will never forget how you took on every tough guy in Sunnyside, Woodside and beat all of them."

"So now why are you telling me that you are bored? I have a real problem here."

"You don't understand what I meant by what I said. I am bored because I have heard this before. I heard it when you were trying to get the bread truck routes and the other drivers tried to stop you. I heard it before when you offered all the merchants up and down Roosevelt Avenue a legitimate cleaning service so they wouldn't be assaulted by constant summonses for a candy wrapper twenty feet from their door and so many dismissed you. You said these very things when you were trying to buy all the buildings in Long Island City...the bankers, the mob, the shop owners associations, the unions. All of them didn't understand you or what you wanted to do. But in the end, they did in fact understand and they did work with you through the sheer force of your will and your own very particular way of getting things done."

"What do you mean by that? My own particular way?"

"People are scared of you, Vinny, you know that," J'lome answered quickly. "You look tough, speak tough, and you are tough. You don't need a backwards baseball hat, rap music, tattoos up and down your arms, or gold teeth the way these other fools do. So that in itself is going to give the average person some pause from the get-go. But what really scares them is your spectacularly elastic mind that can turn anything into a deal that somehow benefits both sides. That makes you irresistible to anyone who bothers to listen to you. It's an incredible talent to possess, one that no college course could ever teach."

"So what are you saying I should do with these shi, sorry...these people?"

"First of all, these people are nothing to your problem. I don't even need to meet them to know that. You haven't even told me what the real problem is and you don't have to because it doesn't matter. I am saying you should do whatever it is you have always done to achieve your success. And that is, find a crack in the system, the one flaw that will allow you to enter their world and clean the offending substances out while at the same time allowing you a quick and clean getaway, and then seal up what you have to in order to succeed." J'lome thought for a moment. "Did you mention there was a woman on this board?"

"Yes, a blue-blood from Sutton Place named Maxie Carter. Why?" He cocked his head quizzically at J'lome, unsure of what he was getting at.

"What about her, is she good looking? Attractive to you in any way?"

Vinny regarded his friend closely. "I'm not looking for a date here, my friend. I got a real problem to contend with. My bones are telling me these people have some sort of reach in this situation and because of that they can't be ignored. Besides, I haven't been interested in women since Stacie left me. You know that."

"My friend, not only do I think you need a good woman in your life, but I think maybe this woman could be the path to successes for you in this situation. I notice that she was the only one on this board you mentioned by name. That means something, maybe just a little bit, but still something. There was some...cosmic connection maybe between you two, a greater level of understanding that neither of you probably realize yet. I'm not suggesting you try to impress her with nonsense. The average woman is much smarter than the above-average man and quite capable of detecting a whiff of nonsense from a mile away. But try to see if there is anything there. Is she happy where she is, with what she's doing? There may be something there. You never know."

"And if there isn't anything there?"

"Then at least maybe you can get a date for Saturday night."

"And what about the buildings? I need this, J'lome, I need this badly. All of my other properties are folded into this. It's my shot at something really big and, well...you know. Everyone is involved with the deal. You are, too, I needn't remind you."

"It's just money...anyway for what? For what do you *need* this, hmmm? Some sort of validation of your life?"

"Yes. To show everyone from the old neighborhood that I turned out the exact opposite of what they thought. And also, these buildings will last longer than I will on this earth, like my own personal pyramid. And frankly, the money would be great for you, Mikey, the Burkes and Moose. Everyone's in it, J'lome, I've lost on other deals before, that's just part of the business, but always with my own money. This is the first time I've had everyone else in on a deal."

"Then do what you have to within the reach of the law. Use your brain, your guile, your charm to bring this dream to fruition. And remember, there's no crying in real estate." J'lome's hugely bright smile split his face and Vinny felt uplifted just by the sight of it.

"Will you be my brother for all time?" Vinny asked the question like a child who needed assurance from a parent who was leaving him at the end of a visitation hour.

"That you will always have. That is solid, concrete, a foundation that can never be moved by anyone or anything. You knew that yesterday, you know it now, and I hope you don't have to ask me to remind you tomorrow."

Vinny returned to the present. "How are things here?"

"You mean in Astoria?"

"Yes, but well, no, more specifically in the mosque business. Are you still getting hassled?" Now Vinny could see his friend's eyes dim a bit. He already knew the answer and it pissed him off to no end.

"Sometimes, but not as much as before, you know, shortly after 9/11. My members unfortunately will carry one slight with them the rest of their life. If someone curses them or accuses them of being a bomb maker, all of the other hundreds of positive experiences they will go through every week will be lost. It's kind of cultural with a lot of them, honor of the family and all of that nonsense."

Vinny liked the congregants of J'lome's mosque. He had the opportunity to speak with many of them, funny, hard working men from Bangladesh, Pakistan, Indonesia, and Lebanon among other countries who had all the same problems and complaints he or any other American man did. Bad weather, bad wives, bad Mets teams, wayward sons and daughters. More than a few times he stared down some of the local toughs who hassled these people—staring them down was all he had to do—and if there was one thing all the congregants appreciated, it was a man who would stand up to an enemy for nothing more than the honor of his friend's friends.

J'lome said, "I have been lucky that none of my people here have that strange, unfocused rage in them that can immolate the brain, turn it into an instrument of destruction."

Vinny answered as if he were a cop or the local Hell's Angels enforcer, "You always make sure to let me know if you have any hassle with people like that."

"I will, my brother," he replied warmly just as Vinny's phone rang. He checked the screen to see who it was and J'lome could see his eyes roll a little.

"Another voice from the old neighborhood, Moose Miller. Let's see what he has going other than that he wants to try to impress his wife enough to keep her from walking on him…Hey, babe, what's happening?" Vinny said as he got up from J'lome's comfortable chair, feeling much better than when he had walked in, but of course that was what he expected, what he always got from these visits. He walked to the window to check on the car and Charlie Mick and to continue his conversation with Moose Miller.

"Vin," interrupted J'lome. Vinny looked over his shoulder and shrugged his shoulders, 'What?' "Tell Moose to come see me some time." He was rewarded with a thumbs-up and a wink from Vinny as he told the caller to hold on for a moment. He stepped around J'lome's desk as the Imam of The People's Mosque also rose and went to his friend. They embraced warmly and held each other at arm's length. "Always be well, my friend. These doors are always open for you, don't ever forget that. And never forget that no problem is truly devastating...unless of course it's cancer. If you don't hear that word, then there is always a solution, somewhere." That earned him another thumbs up as he stepped out of J'lome's office. The Imam stepped back around his desk, once more fully appreciating the turn his life had taken so many years before. What better thing could I ever be doing in this life than helping another child of God to find the way? he asked himself. He took out his pen and paper for the sermon he intended to accompany the evening prayers and started to write about the previous ten minutes he spent with Vinny. Not once did he worry about all the money he invested in Vinny's project by the river.

—•—

Whathefu stared in the mirror in the aft bathroom of the American Airlines 747 at the damage to his face and contemplated the damage to his life. Less than twenty hours earlier, he was the somewhat handsome and somewhat desired son of one of the wealthiest families in Saudi Arabia. A third son of a third wife, yes, but still a young man from a family of means. He couldn't marry into the better families in the Kingdom, but the lesser daughters would step up quickly, especially after they passed their twenty-first birthday. Shortly after that day passed for them, they started to decompose in the eyes of the average Saudi man like Christmas cake on December twenty-seventh.

Whathefu owned a Ferrari. Well, at least he used to, and he owned one of the nicer apartments in one of the best buildings in a nice part of Riyadh. A flat in London was available to him at any time, as was a one-bedroom in Greenwich Village in Manhattan. Vacations in the Cote d'Azure...European and American women and the best restaurants available at a snap of his fingers. There was almost no limit to what he could acquire, not with the mostly unlimited funds provided by his father. That state of perpetual pamperedness morphed into an insatiable desire to push whatever limits his family, society, and religion placed on him. Debauchery seemed to propel him forward, instead of repelling him the way most young men in the society he grew up in managed to do. Nothing he tried in order to abandon his destructive thoughts and actions had worked. He just finally admitted to himself that he liked screwing around, fucking foreign women and getting drunk. His father was largely absent from his life other than the occasional visit to his mother for an afternoon tryst but he was indeed smart enough and honest enough with himself to know it would be too easy to blame his life's aimless trajectory on that.

A vicious hangover, social ostracism, abandonment by his family… those unfortunate states of being for so many young men and women in the Kingdom…he was always able somehow to give them the slip, he not being smart enough to admit to himself that pushing the envelope this way would certainly lead to something that would disappoint everyone, to say the least. But now…with the death of the girl, that had all changed. And he was surprised by it, the reaction and finality of it all as the girl's father wasn't nearly as powerful, as well-connected as his.

He abandoned the wrecked Ferrari immediately after the accident, running from the scene without calling for an ambulance, without standing by the young girl who lay broken in the passenger seat, ignoring the shouts to stop from the other racers, all of whom were then running to the accident scene to assist. It was such a stupid, illogical course of action on his part as about a hundred spectators were able to identify him by face and name and, if they could not, certainly a red Ferrari's owner would be tracked down with relative ease. If he had stayed and made a show of trying to rescue her, what would have happened? Maybe none of the others had seen the risky maneuver so close to the curb. It was just an accident he would state to any police inquiry so sincerely. The girl would be buried quietly and within twenty-four hours as Islam prescribed, the family not wanting any more publicity than a quiet story in the press lest they be shamed by her apparent indecent actions. But no, he panicked, ran, and as a result incurred the wrath of her father, who was one of the legions across the Middle East who were slowly building up the resentful kind of human steam on which insurgencies, revolutions, and general types of uprisings first got their legs.

Her father was a small business owner, nothing like Whathefu's father in terms of financial and social stature, but one nonetheless much respected by the average man on the street as an honest and decent man, a regular guy who deserved all the best things life had to offer. One of the drifting spectators that night knew him and upon recognizing his daughter, called to notify him immediately, telling him the whole story. Wailing with grief upon arrival in seeing his daughter's lifeless body pulled from the wreck, he ran to the marina where he knew Whathefu's father kept a one hundred-foot Ginerva motor yacht. Whathefu was surprised to receive a call later from his father summoning him to the vessel. He must have found out, but how? He didn't think much of it as his father sounded calm and friendly on the phone, lulling the young man into a very false sense of security. The abuse started as soon as he stepped into the yacht's main salon which until that moment had always been Whathefu's favorite room on the vessel. He loved the room's dark wood flooring, the black leather sofa that ran fifteen feet down the wall with the beautiful orange and yellow pillows that broke up the dark colors. He also loved to watch the yacht's crew at the far end of the salon in the wheelhouse maneuver the magnificent craft in the Mediterranean, able to see the hills of Cyprus and Crete as they headed north to the bluest waters of the Aegean Sea, perfectly dotted with the Greek Isles and colorful fishing boats. He loved the uniforms of the crew...the white pants so tight...that newest one, might he? Hmmm.

He boarded quietly and as he reached the top of the spiral staircase that separated the main salon from the wheelhouse he saw his father standing before him, waiting for him, towering over him, glaring at him with more contempt than any mere man could summon from the deepest, darkest part of his soul. The first blow, a vicious half-fist backhand made contact under his cheekbone before whatever remaining natural instinct for danger left in his modern brain could begin to react. Whathefu staggered back against the polished frame of the staircase, unable to block the follow up punch to his gut that doubled him over like a wet cardboard box. His father grabbed a handful of hair and yanked hard, straightening out his body, pulling him into the salon and threw him into one of the orange armchairs that Whathefu once thought were a perfect addition to the room. Helped break up the dark colors. This time one of them helped him break his fall.

"What position have you put me in you stupid bastard, you loser?" his father bellowed, each syllable accompanied by another open-handed slap...forehand, backhand, every third blow a closed fist to whatever part of his face was pointed toward his father.

"It was an accident, Father, just a car accident," he weakly blurted out. He received a kick in his chest that toppled him and the chair. His father stepped around the upturned furniture and pulled him to his feet again by his hair. He was much taller than his son and he was able to look down at him as he maintained a death grip on his son's thick locks. He shook his son's head a few times to get his attention. Whathefu's eye's were full of water, his mouth was filling with blood, his lungs were still trying to fill up with air, and he was amazed that he didn't feel one of his teeth lolling about in his mouth.

"Shut up, you disgraceful insect. You have not a clue as to what this does to me. Everywhere the whispers are in the air for the common people to bring down the ruling classes of our neighbors, the gap between them and us never to be breached by any of them, hordes of them just waiting for a reason to go out into the streets and now you have given them one!" The backhand slap came again, the shame of the reality he now faced, of his cowardly actions hurting Whathefu more than the blow. "All you care about is your liquor, the European girls who offer themselves to you just because you have some money for pretty things. People of no honor, no morals, and they are drawn to you like flies to a dead body and you think this validates your existence and your worth." He released his grip on his son's hair with a flourish and motioned to him to pick up the chair. He waited until his son sat down once again before continuing to speak. Now his voice was gentle, almost comforting to the shivering young man.

"But your body isn't dead, your soul is. You have no consideration for anyone else but yourself and I am not even sure you have even that as you abuse your body and waste your mind with trivial, pointless, hedonistic pursuits." Whathefu turned slightly at the sound of one of the stateroom doors closing not so quietly. He wondered which of his father's mistresses was aboard. All of a sudden he was angry and for the first time he could remember, he spoke back.

"I watched my father and my brothers, and everyone else in the corrupt government and business community of this country enjoy the same pursuits you describe. That is how I learned what I have learned, my father." As the last sound of the last word left his mouth, his father drove his fist into the middle of his son's forehead, once again knocking him and the chair to the floor.

His father stood there looking at his son crumpled on the floor, then at his own hands, ashamed at not being ashamed quite enough for beating his son. In his heart he truly loved this boy and his dear mother, but he was equally troubled and repelled by him. The lack of concern for his life, honor for his family and culture, and total lack of responsibility sickened him. Now he would have to show his son what Saudi responsibility was all about for someone in his position. He was not a man who liked being backed into a corner. The girl's father demanded justice and in another time, his boy's head would already be in the sand. And maybe the girl's father's as well. But he couldn't bring himself to order it done and in the end, came up with a solution that satisfied both.

"Whathefu, you have shamed the family and yourself and you can redeem yourself in only one way at this point. I just had to sit through a tirade by Leila's father. The man was wailing in such a way I thought I was at one of the big zoos in America at feeding time. And why not? She was his princess, his only female child, and you corrupted her and then killed her and left her to die, abandoned and shamed. He couldn't help himself and then also quietly declared, "but she also acted like a whore, going out with you unescorted, wearing cheap-looking, suggestive clothing designed for prostitutes and thus she sealed her own fate." His voice rising again, "But you allowed yourself to be trapped by her and the western thoughts and values or rather the lack thereof that you seem to value so dearly, and it shames me that my son could demonstrate such an astonishing amount of stupidity along with an appalling lack of basic caution. No seat belts while you and your queer friends hurl yourselves around on a sandy roadway at insanely high speeds. Holy shit, boy!"

He was shrinking like a flower in a heat wave, slowly but surely, and his father could see it. And for a moment Whathefu thought he detected pity and a semblance of filial love in his father's brow. He watched him sit wearily on an orange ottoman and look at his son with great effort, lifting just his head, his shoulders too heavy to follow.

"What do I do now, Father?" Whathefu asked through free-flowing tears, like a fountain turned on after a month of maintenance, the water's flow hesitant, gurgling through the pipes and then rushing through in a torrent, the weight of the rest of his life pressing in all around him. The new reality, the changes that are coming, what would it be, he wondered.

"You must go to America immediately," said his father, his son looking up in a flash at the impossible statement, stunned at his father's pronouncement. Go to America? Instantly, in spite of the horrible state of his life at that moment, he thought of the beautiful women in that glorious island city, the beautiful men as well, walking on the newly-developed Christopher Street pier, all of them so willing. His father was going to take care of him, wipe it all away by sending him away for what, a year? Maybe two or three? His thoughts were then interrupted.

"Don't expect to be going there with an idea of partying the night away like some European half-prince, although if that is how you decide to spend your last days on this earth, that is your choice." Whathefu blinked uncomprehendingly and waited a moment before speaking, wiping his hair away from his brow, swallowing the blood that was filling up in his mouth again, feeling sick to his stomach and deathly afraid he was going to vomit on the polished floor of the yacht's main salon.

"Last days? What do you mean by that?" Whathefu gulped noticeably.

"I mean that I had to agree to compensation to Leila's family for his daughter's death and the shame to his family. I mean that the amount to be paid in order to restore our family's honor is seventeen million dollars. One million for each year of her life. And it has to be delivered in one week." Whathefu was not stunned at the enormity of the figure as his father could write a check of that size from any number of accounts in banks from Riyadh to Geneva to the Cayman Islands.

"But, the family could afford that. What is the problem with paying them off? Why do I have to go to America? What am I supposed to do there?"

The father resisted bashing his son's skull in at the absolute thoughtlessness and stupidity he was sometimes capable of, instead choosing to inform Whathefu that HE, not the family, would have to raise the seventeen million." This revelation had the young man jumping from his chair like an overanxious salesman trying to close a deal that was rapidly slipping through his fingers. He walked around the chair completely and then sat down again.

"How am I going to do that? I don't have any accounts in America. I have nothing to sell there. This is an impossible task, Father. It is unfair."

"Maybe so, but you have to come back here with seventeen million dollars in one week. Otherwise you will go to your grave in whatever manner the father of the girl deems appropriate. He may decide to shoot you, drown you, maybe he will run you down with his truck, burn you alive, maybe he will decapitate you with his scimitar. It's his choice and I cannot interfere. I won't interfere."

Whathefu was still completely stunned as he asked his father, "You would sanction the death of your own son?" A great weariness dripped off the man's face as he seemed to age seventeen million years in that one instant...yes, he replied with total conviction, yes I would. He went on with an explanation that to Whathefu felt like a speech to an employee that had to be let go from his job. "Because there are many other things to consider. The family's survival is of paramount importance. You will disappear from this earth, my son, unless you pass this test. And although it will be reported that you died in a tragic accident, so that I can salvage what little bit of my honor I have left, believe me, my son, your death will not be pleasant at the hands of this common man."

Whathefu shook with fear at the thought. He knew what his father and Leila's father had decided. That he would die by the sword, in some basement somewhere, where other men had been dispatched, the dregs of society, rapists, thieves, murderers. His life would end there and drip down the same drain those others bled into after his head thumped on the floor and rolled away from the rest of his body. His father interrupted his thoughts by standing and giving final orders to his son.

"Get your things together. The late night American Airlines flight will be delayed one hour just for you at gate 42. Take only what you need to last one week in New York. You have the use of a hotel room for one week. You can have a car if you like...but this is all the assistance I will give you."

Whathefu was already contemplating hiding in the vastness of the United States the way Bin Laden has been hiding out in the mountains in Afghanistan. Maybe Wyoming, or Alaska, or why not in New York City? Plenty of people there, filled with different neighborhoods he had grown to know well and love. They would never find him in Brooklyn or Queens. A plan was formulating in his head when his father once again interrupted his thoughts in such a way to suggest to Whathefu that his father was capable of reading his mind. "And, my son, do not think of any plan to escape into the west. We have had a man in America working for our religious friends in certain ways that is all too eager to keep an eye on you. He has already been contacted and is on his way to Kennedy airport as we speak. He will meet you at the airport as soon as you clear immigration. If you try to escape, he will kill you with my pre-granted permission on the spot with all of Allah's rage motivating him. He will be with you at all times and, at any time, his is the final determination to terminate your worthless life. Do you understand?" After a few seconds' silence between father and son, Whathefu nodded and descended the spiral staircase and left his father's yacht, exiting the ramp directly into a waiting car.

Now he was an hour outside New York City, wanting to just wrench open the large emergency exit door, decompressing the plane and taking himself out of this impossible situation. He didn't care about taking all of the other passengers with him. An honorable death, he told himself. So many others take their own lives and for what? The twisted teaching of the Koran's rules for a righteous life? Idiots and depressed, worthless souls dispatched to police stations, shopping malls, with twenty pounds of dynamite, aluminum shards, ball bearings and a plunger hidden in a jacket pocket. At least in a plane crash he would be sparing his family further shame. And he would also be sparing Leila and her family further shame as well. He was angry at her in the car, that she had caused his bad mood which caused him to lose concentration with the maneuvering of the car but he realized that he missed her. He wanted her still, not believing that she was gone, disappointed that he would never have the opportunity to sleep with her. And who was this person he was meeting? He was given no description, no name, just an assurance from his father that he would be met at Kennedy Airport. He threw some water into his face, studied his reflection one last time, hoping some semblance of an answer would appear and when nothing did, he yanked a few pieces of coarse paper towels out of the receptacle, dried himself off, buffed some foundation he always carried with him onto his face to cover the bruises and headed back to his seat.

—◦|◦—

Vinny stepped out of J'lome's mosque, passing the two men he had seen engaging in a heated debate on his way in. They may have been discussing the end of the world what with all the angry gesticulating, but Vinny was still in the car when he first noticed them. I should have been a CIA officer or a homicide detective, he thought, considering how he tried to notice as much as possible around him, before most others became aware, if they did at all. He couldn't hear them once he arrived earlier, but now as he exited, one of them, a thirtyish young man with a bushy beard, skullcap, and otherwise regular New York regular guy attire, reached for his arm as he was saying, "Hey, brother, help us out with this, will you?"

Charlie Mick was out of the car the instant the young Muslim touched Vinny's arm, but a stern look told him not to come any closer. He got back in the driver's seat and Vinny turned to the two men, seeing that the second man was considerably older, about fifty-five, dressed in a flowing white robe, keffiyeh and matching taquiyah, with an immaculately trimmed white beard. The younger man spoke first.

"Tell us, brother, we see you coming here to our mosque to visit our teacher, so we will take your word on this. Do you think Derek Jeter's passing Lou Gehrig's Yankees hit record is anything to be truly impressed with? This guy doesn't think so," he finished, gesturing with an open palm to the older man who answered with a little exasperation for the younger man.

"Of course it's not. Jeter makes twenty million a year, doesn't have to travel on trains, has a full medical training staff at his beck and call, and doesn't have to face the pitchers today Gehrig and the other great players had to face. The major leagues are totally watered down with what, thirty teams or so? You have a bunch of Triple A players in the majors now. And plus the ballparks are smaller. My sister could hit a home run in some of these tiny places."

"Are you saying Jeter is a minor leaguer?"

"No, I am just saying that the records, when they are broken today, just shouldn't count as much because of the differences between base-ball then and now. Frankly, the same thing should go for most basket-ball and football records as well." He turned to Vinny, "What do you think, Mr. Vinny?"

Vinny grabbed his chin in thought for a moment, as he discovered during his many hours spent with J'lome and his followers, that these people respect someone who contemplates before answering. "I under-stand your comments, my friend, about the differences in the way the game was played then and now."

"No night games back then so the ball could be seen easier by Gehrig," said the younger man.

"Yeah, and like I said, ball parks today are about the size of a one bedroom apartment. Half of Jeter's home runs and Bond's and Rodri-guez' home runs, for that matter, would have been either doubles or long outs in the old stadiums."

"Gentlemen," Vinny interrupted, looking each in the eye and in that very special way he developed of lassoing people into his thoughts, not allowing the attention of either to stray, "you are arguing about things that at the end of the day do not matter, because they do not help you earn money, gain knowledge, feed your children, or bring comfort to those in need. That being said, we have argued baseball in New York for generations."

"As new Americans, we do not have that advantage," said the younger man.

"Right, said Vinny feeling compelled to add, "You know, true Amer-icans would love to hear this conversation between you two. But that aside, I am sorry, my friend," turning to the younger man, "Gehrig was a much better player than Jeter. Just look at the stats and ask yourself, Who do you want at the plate in a tough spot? And who knows what statistics he would have finished up with had he not passed away at such a young age, right?"

Before the younger man was able to respond, Vinny continued, turning to the older man, "You have to admit, my friend, that Jeter is going to slide on the ice right into the Hall of Fame and has conducted himself like a true Yankee. You gotta admit that, right?" The older man's head was already nodding in agreement when Vinny added how Gehrig never faced the top black or Latino players of his day due to the racist policy of the Major Leagues prior to 1947. He closed with something to bring the combatants together. "Face it, you could have been Met fans, forever resigned to bad trades, free agents that other teams sign, and five tool prospects that don't do anything but swing at ball four and suffer career-ending injuries at age twenty-three." He smirked and lifted his head in a jovial manner to the younger man to drive his point home.

"I would rather be dead than be a Mets fan," he plaintively stated.

"So would I," agreed the older man and with that, Vinny clapped both on the shoulder and told them proudly, "Welcome to America, my friends, where we are free to engage in ridiculous arguments like this one just so we can escape the drudgery of the daily grind if but for a moment or two. And tell me, gentlemen," he looked at the both, "how great is it that usually these arguments end up with the combatants understanding each other a little bit more than when they started?" Not waiting for an answer, he waved and turned to the car, jumping in the open door and asked Charlie Mick to head to the building project on the river. The car was barely moving before the son of one of Vinny's old friends started to speak.

"I thought I was going to have to help you out there a little with those two sand niggers," he said casually, staring into the side view mirror waiting for the cars clogging Steinway Street to pass safely. Charlie Mick, a lumbering, perpetually angry kid, the son of his now dead friend Mikey Busy, killed on 9/11 when the kid was only twelve, with enough brains to do okay but a lack of common sense that could negate all of it. Vinny, in the next millionth of a second, reached over with his left foot and slammed it down on the brake causing the large vehicle to shudder to a stop. He ordered Charlie Mick to park the car again, and when they were settled in once more at the curb, ordered him out of the driver's seat. Vinny jumped across the console, got behind the wheel and slammed the door closed, leaving the uncomprehending younger man standing in the street looking in the driver's side window.

"Let me tell you what you're gonna do," Vinny said with ill-concealed malice, "You are going to stand there, on that spot, for as long as it takes for me to conclude whatever I have to in the rest of this day. I may be back in twenty minutes or maybe twenty hours, but you are going to be standing right there, on that fucking spot in front of the mosque when I return. And if you do not produce for me a satisfactory answer as to why I am doing this, you will not only lose your association with me, my continuing support for you, but I will personally beat your ass to within an inch of your life to get my point across."

Once again, as with the Muslim men arguing about the Yankees, he turned away, not waiting for an answer, this time not inwardly happy as with the first exchange just two minutes ago, but seething with rage at the kid, the son of his dead friend. The phone rang and Vinny could see it was Moose Miller again, another of his old friends from the neighborhood, now a twenty-year veteran of the NYPD harbor patrol, a diver who pulled bodies from the river like you pulled on an overcoat. He must have hung up, figuring that his call was lost. Vinny was embarrassed to realize that he forgot Moose was hanging on the phone when he was talking baseball. Vinny knew his friend was troubled at home and that he was troubled at work, but for his friends…J'lome, Mikey, the Burke brothers, AJ, well…he would lay down in traffic for them as they would for him, and this call, although he knew he was about to have a Oprah-type moment with Moose, was a welcome change from the young asshole he just deposited on the curb. "What's up?" he asked as he pulled the car away from the curb and headed down Steinway Street.

⊷ ⊱

Whathefu tightened, as he always did when the wheels of the plane touched the tarmac, knowing that this was when most crashes occurred. His fear once the plane was down did not recede this time, however, as it always had before on his trips to New York, Paris, London, where he knew he could shed his religious restraints and be the hard-partying jet setter he aspired to be. No, he was still on his father's yacht, watching him retreat to his stateroom, where the aspiring model from California waited for him, shocked at the last words he had said. "You will be accompanied my son during your time in New York by one or our operatives, an American we recruited a few years ago into our fold to maybe conduct future jihad against the west for our Wahhabist brothers." Whathefu always figured his father, as with many others in

Saudi Arabia's elite ruling class, had some contacts there, in that strange world beyond Islam, that world that hated everything performed and thought of that was not in line with what happened in the daily life of the average Muslim from five hundred years ago. He knew that these people were secretly reviled by the ruling and business elite of the Kingdom but had to be dealt with occasionally and appeased most of the time. Leila's father was in contact with the Wahhabists with much greater frequency than Whathefu's father, and he insisted that his son be accompanied at all times in America by a carefully chosen 'warrior,' an American-born convert to Islam, who was absolutely trustworthy and faithful. In no way, shape, or form was Leila's father going to let Whathefu slip away. As he passed through customs, and walked down the hall to the common area where families, friends, and lovers anxiously awaited the return of the special people in their lives, Whathefu wondered about who he was going to meet. Certainly, it wasn't going to be anyone with whom he wanted to spend casual time.

─ ※ ─

"Vinny, how's everything, waddya say, waddya know?" Moose asked ebulliently, repeating Cagney's standard greeting line from his favorite movie, *Angels with Dirty Faces*. Even the Bowery Boys are in it, for crissake, and they even mention Sunnyside in the first few minutes of the movie." He would always say this to anyone who either looked confused at his greeting or dared challenge his movie critic's opinion.

"Always good for you, Archie," Vinny replied, the only person who could call Moose Miller, a six-foot, three-inch mass of muscle and bone by his given name and live to see the next day. It's good to hear the spring in your voice again." Vinny turned the car onto Thirtieth Avenue and headed west toward the East River, where his construction project was.

"I'm sorry about the other day, Vin, but everything was just boiling over for me at that point. My fucking head was exploding and I was feeling sorry later for bothering you with this domestic bullshit. I know you have a lot going on." Earlier that week, Moose had opened up to Vinny about his dissatisfaction with the job: "Vinny, I got twenty fucking years in and I can't get a break because the Irish run the fucking department since the days of the draft riots and I'm like the token Jew. I should have stayed in the office, doing research or forensic work. I got no chance for any advancement as I see it." Once again Vinny tried to control the path of the conversation. After all, there were only so many minutes in the day. He crossed over Twenty-First Street, passed the Queensbridge Houses and continued to Vernon Boulevard where he turned left.

"But Arch, you decided against going that way a long time ago and you requested harbor duty because you used to love the river, swimming and being in the water. You were always like a fish, teaching us how to handle the currents when we went there to cool off in the summer, remember? *You* chose your path, Archie, and you can't allow yourself to get upset with how it has turned out because you can't unwind the spool of time and go backwards to fix it. None of us can. Once you signed on for duty on the boat, you knew you were going to be doing something you loved or at least liked a lot, you would be performing a brave, necessary duty and service, you would be getting a ton of overtime and retirement with full bennies in twenty years. But you also knew that you weren't going to get any detective work on the boat."

"It made sense at the time, to go this way." Vinny jumped at the weakness of his friend's answer.

"It made sense because Joanne told you at the time it made sense, Archie," said Vinny, purposefully cutting him short. "When are you going to suggest to her that you are plenty capable of running your own life and as a result becoming a better person for her to spend her life with? I mean, holy shit, Archie, I hate to say it. I know she's your wife, but how do you deal with her pressure all the time?" Moose Miller's wife Joanne, an Italian princess from Long Island, was only five feet tall, cute as hell, and totally absorbed in running everyone's life except her own. No one argued with her much anymore because as far as she knew, she hadn't been wrong about anything, ever. She could convince you that two plus two equaled five just by wearing you down.

"I love her. Well, I guess I know I loved her once, but she is my wife, the mother of my three girls, and the priest and the rabbi said it was all for better or worse."

"Right, Arch, I know where you're coming from with that, so please just accept responsibility for your own career choice and woman choice. Either that or just quit, take early retirement, then divorce her and go on Chick.com for a new woman."

"Yeah, sure. Look, I'm sorry about all this. I know you hate hearing this nonsense." Vinny responded with affection for one of his oldest friends.

"Don't worry about it, Archie Miller, all was forgiven at the moment you called. You and Mikey, J'lome, and the Burkes are all my brothers for life and we will always stand with each other. You just may not hear what you want to hear all the time. That's a good thing, you know," he added.

"Thanks Vin, I appreciate it. Somehow it always works out, doesn't it?" Vinny knew the answer to that stupendously overused and ridiculous statement was no, but he was turning west onto Forty-Seventh Avenue now, the project site only a couple of blocks away and he had no interest in bringing his friend any further down than he was already with some sort of existentialist conversation.

"Where are you now? Are you in Jamaica Bay today? I hear planes."

"No, I'm actually in a car doing some surveillance work at Kennedy Airport, following some schmuck up from North Carolina. The Feds think he's some kind of link to the Middle East, but the fucking guy looks anything like one of those guys. Actually looks like he stepped out of one of those Abercrombie & Fitch commercials, but meaner looking. And bigger, he's a tall bastard." Vinny was at the chain link fence that separated the construction site from the street. He had been out of the car for just a moment, unlocking the padlock and pulling the heavy chain through the openings in the fence when he let it fall to the sidewalk on its own, clinking faster and faster until it ran out. This situation, Vinny decided, would not go uncommented on.

"Arch, so what you're telling me is that you're doing surveillance work for the FBI, following a guy they think might be dangerous. Do I have it right?"

"Yeah, so? It's a major fucking bore." Vinny squeezed the bridge of his nose to stave off the growing pain, to keep his frontal lobe from dripping through his nostrils.

"I'm sure it is a major fucking bore, as you say, but you never know what may turn up here. Even if this guy is nothing what the feds say or think, you're helping them out. They'll remember that, *if* you don't let them forget it. Who are you talking to? A field agent or someone in the N.Y.P.D.?"

"Ya know, it's strange. I don't know who it is. Either they decided not to tell me from the get-go or he's got some secret agent name for this operation. I don't know who I'm talking to and I never met him. Wouldn't know him if he walked in the freakin' door." Moose was silent for a second and a half and then switched gears. "This is what you always mean by looking for opportunities, right? When you say they pop up anywhere, anytime, and only those with prepared minds can be aware of it and take advantage?"

"I didn't say it, Arch; Louis Pasteur said it. Or something like that. I was paraphrasing."

"Who was he? Some fag Frenchman?"

"No, Arch, just one of the greatest scientific minds that ever lived. Your kids drink milk with their breakfast?"

"Uhh, yeah, sure."

"Well, then think about it. In any event, keep a close eye on this guy at the airport. You never know what it could be. Something big possibly but more than likely, nothing at all. You should definitely remember to call the feds during and after this gig they gave you. They love constant communication. Make them remember you, my friend, and something good will eventually come of it and maybe just this once, Joanne will realize what a great guy she has."

"Yeah, and maybe I'll play in the NBA this year. Okay, look, I gotta go. My friend from Tarheel country is on the move. Best to Mikey and the rest of the boys."

"Right, I was supposed to call him, Archie. Thanks for reminding me and remember something."

"What's that?"

"Woody Allen once said that success is ninety percent just showing up…so keep your eyes open for anything even slightly unusual and make a note of it and pass it along to the Feds and your boss on the job, okay?"

"Thanks buddy," he said, adding, "Sorry again for last week."

"Never a problem, *ever*," he answered coming down a little harder than he had to on the last word, to instill just a little bit of confidence he knew his friend needed and probably wouldn't receive anywhere else. He started to dial Michael's number, wondering why he hadn't heard back about his construction loan extension, which may not mean a thing anyway if he didn't find a way to get through this lame preservation society. What was it J'lome said...just at the end of their meeting? Right...solutions. Something he needed quickly if those clowns were truly able to reach out to his construction lender before he closed the loan.

⁓اﷲ⁓

MID-AFTERNOON

Michael was leaning back in his office chair trying to crack some of his thoracic vertebrae which would always ache when the stress of a problem deal got to him. For about an hour upon his return – not wanting to get home early after all – he discussed the day's disasters with Hank Fredericks, the title company representative who seemed to have a calm, well-thought-out answer to almost everything. He thought it a bit odd that he was still hanging around the office, but he was glad to see him again. For a fleeting moment, he thought he was going to escape from this terrible day, make it home and have some sort of peaceful existence if only for a moment. Then he heard his desk phone ring behind him and even before he excused himself and swiveled his chair around to pick up the call, he just knew somehow this was going to add another dose of heartburn to the day. He didn't bother to check the caller id. He decided to test his resolve and his ability to deal with a situation as soon as it smacked him in the face so he picked up right away.

"Good afternoon, Michael Pierce." He could hear splashing and the sounds of a party from the other side. It sounded immediately like a place he wanted to go to. Michael recognized the voice of Lee Skillman, who with his wife Sharon owned Shale Financial, a private bank he used occasionally for commercial mortgage deals. They were in the middle of ordering drinks, and Michael could hear them giving the formula for what they wanted to a waitress. Sharon and Lee were a pair of financial and business wizards who also loved to party like college students. They would run down to their villa in Montego Bay every weekend and drink Red Stripe beer, smoke the local marijuana, and regale anyone who would listen with tales of how they rose from poverty to near billionaire status. Easy for them to do, as they kept a private Gulfstream fully fueled and ready to go at a moment's notice out at Republic Airport. They appeared at first glance to many to be nothing more than a couple of crass garmentos, but all you needed was five minutes with them to see what great people they were, a fun and loving couple who lived to make money and then have fun with each other—as well as incredibly bright, visionary, and frankly, ruthless as a pair of hawks. A few weeks earlier they had finally approved and then quickly cleared for closing the largest loan of Michael's career, a one hundred million dollar construction loan for Vinny's project. Even asking for an extension for a few weeks was easily done...not yet obtained but it wasn't going to be a problem.

Why are they calling? The beads of sweat started above Michael's hairline and he quickly wiped them away. Please, oh please don't tell me you are withdrawing from the deal. The drink order was apparently finished and now Michael was being spoken to directly.

"Mikey! How the hell are you?" Lee had a booming voice that could cut through concrete. He could hear Sharon then calling over the phone, "Hello, Michael. How are you?" She laughed uproariously and it sounded like she was slurping a liquid something. Lee then came back on the phone.

"Mikey, you know, they have these drinks here. It's a beer topped off by a martini, how they get them to stay together without mixing is the ninth wonder of the world but what the martini does is keep the beer cold by floating on top somehow and when you finish the beer, the martini kind of moves to the side when you tip the glass to drink it, so when you finish the beer, there's a martini waiting for you. A truly awesome drink. You gotta try one."

"It sounds great, Lee. Maybe after we close our deal you can invite me down for your next party." Why is he calling me now? Sharon then came on the line. He could hear her dial down her party voice and settle into business as if she had anti-lock brakes on her drunkenness.

"Michael, you know we love you, but we just got a call from one of Lee's dweeby friends from prep school. Some rich kid who always played on the third team, you know? Couldn't even make junior varsity and I guess he spends his days now spending his family's money and dreaming up ways to get back at those who didn't choose him in back in high school." Michael could hear her slurp another dollop of the beer-martini concoction, if that was in fact what she was drinking. His heart was racing and he just wanted to scream at her to get on with the reason for the call. Lee came back on the line, shushing some close by revelers. Apparently they called together from their hot tub, conferencing themselves on the line so they could speak together. Not a good sign.

"So anyway, Mikey this guy, who we blew off by the way—I mean why the hell should I interrupt my long weekend to speak with him, right?— he leaves a message that he wants to speak with us, wants us to pull the loan on the development in Long Island City. Says that there's a problem with some landmarks or environmental commission." Michael had not yet spoken to Vinny and was unaware of his meeting that morning with the bow-tie, the bony man and Maxie Carter. Had to answer quickly and firmly with Lee and Sharon to keep them from talking themselves out of the deal. Even though it was approved and practically scheduled for closing, they could kill it at any time before then, for whatever reason they wanted to come up with.

"I never heard of anything like that. The only landmarked...anything near there is the Pepsi sign and part of the permit process was that it would be moved to a specific spot and all of that was going to be done as soon as ground is broken. I don't know what this guy is talking about." Sharon came back on the line, but she asked Michael to wait while she ordered another of the beer and martini thingys— that's what she called it—before speaking.

"Michael," she began—another bad sign...what happened to Mikey?—"We don't lend to anyone who may have a landmarks problem. We hate these people for what they did to us a few years ago with the townhouse on Tenth Street." Michael remembered the story. Lee and Sharon wanted to add a penthouse on top of their beautiful home just off Fifth Avenue, a block away from Washington Square, but some local preservationists blocked the project basing their argument on how the added height would be out of proportion to the rest of the block which they then tried to landmark. "They tried to landmark the entire block," Sharon reminded him. Michael was dumbfounded.

Could any deal close today without a major problem coming up at the last moment?

"Well, we don't have any problem with that here, that's for sure." Lee came back on then.

"Mikey, you know we love you, and sooner or later we'll have you down here, but if we get a whiff of some sort of preservationist bullshit around this deal, we're going to pull it. I'm sorry, but we have a policy between us that we will never break regarding this sort of thing after the Tenth Street debacle."

"There's no problem like that, Lee, I promise you."

"Well alrighty then," Lee answered. "Listen, I'm not going to call this clown back until after the weekend. So don't worry about it, probably total bullshit. But we will get back to you on Monday regarding this, okay? We'll finish it off then."

"Yeah, sure, Lee. Have a good time and you as well, Sharon."

"We always do, Mikey. Why worry about things? That never gets you anywhere. And if this deal doesn't work out, then we'll do another. Ciao." The line clicked off just as Michael's stomach shrunk to about the size of a walnut.

Oh my God. Michael's chest tightened and he instinctively rubbed his left pectoral. Was that a pain he felt? Right over his heart? He wouldn't have been surprised. Vinny's commercial deal...the biggest and most important real estate project going in all of Queens, arguably in the city. The deal of both their careers. Vinny told him a few years ago that he had a vision since childhood for the large plot of land on the Queens side of the river south of the bridge, where the Pepsi sign had stood forlornly for so many years when they were jumping off the old pier into the river during the summers of the early seventies. It was a project that even in his wildest dreams he couldn't have envisioned. Only Vinny's fertile and disciplined mind and courageous nature could have shaped such a massive venture of two thousand apartments with a third set aside for lower income families, the rest at market rents. Just a few blocks away from the subway, one quick stop to Grand Central Station. The buildings would load up within weeks. The park would be filled with kids and weekend warriors, the riverside esplanade would have been the site of numerous first kisses, wedding photos, marriage proposals. Film producers would have made the western shot over the river a new identifiable iconic portrait, like the Brooklyn Bridge, the Empire State Building or, well...where the towers used to be. The empty commercial buildings surrounding the site that Vinny snapped would be filled to overflowing with commercial tenants.

Michael daydreamed about the Sunday night seven months ago as he sat in the car alongside Vinny on Thirtieth Avenue a block away from the el, who earlier that day had sold off the last of his properties, twenty two-families, ten three-families, and a handful of small mixed-use buildings. He even sold the pizza store, the bagel shop, and the fruit and vegetable store he had in Astoria, cash cows all. It was capital he needed now and in one year, he sold everything for a net profit of a little more than four million dollars. Enough for an option buy on the land, to hire architects, and acquire the massive amount of permits. Everything fell perfectly into place like well-placed dominoes as he used the still-strong market to his advantage. He made sure every buyer offered a new two year lease to his tenants and then he bade them farewell. The sale of the little stores touched him a bit emotionally, however, and he could see it on his friend's face as they exited the café after chowing down on some burgers. "Do you remember that pair of black-haired beauties we saw at the vegetable store that night?" he asked. Michael nodded yes, easily remembering the sisters...Noelle and Amy...gorgeous creatures they were.

"What the hell was a pair of nice girls like them doing there at nine-thirty on a Sunday night looking for potatoes and broccoli?" They were sitting in Vinny's car at the light on Thirty-Third Street losing themselves, reminiscing about a singular moment that stayed with the both of them all these years. Michael had asked the sisters if he could help them pick out a perfect pair of peppers and they giggled delightfully and hooked arms and left quickly, but not before the taller one gave him a glance over her shoulder.

"I guess they knew somehow we would be there and they were waiting for us."

The light then turned green and some cabbie who should thank his creator he's still alive blared his horn mere milliseconds after it changed, and Vinny started to move, which he did at ten miles per hour down Thirtieth Avenue just to annoy the prick. He loved the stores and his buildings as if they were his favorite nieces and nephews.

But he had a vision, a life's dream to realize. And nothing was going to stop him. The stores would be replaced or reborn in the commercial warehouses he snapped up at bargain prices. The warehouses would be little cities unto themselves, indoor malls for big box stores, fast food franchises, another movie theater, and many small local businesses that he purposely set aside room for. It couldn't miss.

Or then again, maybe it could all be slapped down in a minute by some complaint by a little known group of preservationists with a possible ax to grind.

It wouldn't just be the loss of a half percent commission on a one hundred million dollar construction loan, or the income generated by his own personal investment in the project, his 401k, an IRA, all his stocks sold, bonds cashed in or, in other words, every penny he had, would be gone like a fart in the breeze. It would be the final nail in the coffin that held his marriage together as he, the Burke brothers, Charlie Mick with his 9/11 settlement from the government and all of J'lome's money from the People's Mosque were all in on the deal along with Vinny. They would all be like Rocky Balboa returning in triumph from administering a beating on Drago, just in time to learn his business manager lost all his money.

His thoughts drifted off as he bent backwards over the chair to relieve the familiar pain in his back as his phone started to ring, causing him to groan audibly, as he could see it was Vinny calling. Well, his father did used to say, "Call all your clients back right away, sooner if you have bad news. That's the only way you will ever succeed and impress anyone." He leaned forward quickly and reached for the phone, ignoring Hank Fredericks, wishing he would just leave. He was becoming a little annoying, taking notes and drawing pictures like he was writing a screenplay. He reminded Michael of Jim Bouton writing *Ball Four* on the bench between innings, his teammates watching and wondering what he was writing.

—◦|◦—

Laura arrived back at her desk, momentarily brightened by the splash of water. Or was it the quick little meeting with Michael in the hallway earlier today? She allowed herself to think about him in an absent-minded way, allowing her thoughts to wander as if they were a two-month-old puppy on an adjustable leash. The last couple of years, she found that he lingered in her thoughts for longer periods after they parted. Did she secretly wish that her date with Adam tonight was with Michael instead?

No, she told herself, admonished herself…maybe probably well… most definitely if he wasn't married, she allowed. Why lie about it? But that was it. He was married, an eight hundred-pound gorilla always in the room with them, a mountain range standing in their way. She would not sleep with a married man and attempt to learn how to endure the no-shows of her lover at holiday time, birthdays, the bittersweetness of the two of them parting after an afternoon lovemaking session. Whatever, she thought as she once again brushed Michael out of her brain for the thousandth time since they met so many years ago. Adam is available and Michael is not and neither is Brad Pitt, for that matter, so onward with Adam, whom I will go out with tonight and sleep with tonight for the first time after several months of dating. He is handsome, sophisticated, and rich, although that last part really didn't matter much to her. Chiefly he was available, and although she could turn half the heads on any New York sidewalk, the fact was that she was forty-two…ancient in the eyes of all of them, including the forty-two-year-old men in Manhattan. She was discovering in the past few years that that was not an advantageous age for dating in New York. Easy if a woman wanted a man for a plaything, a 'Hey, I'm in town next weekend, let's go for a couple of cheap dinners and have a few boinks together.' That was fine for others, but not for her. At least not permanently. She tried that once, it lasted or a year before she decided to just stop answering his calls. He didn't even bother leaving a nasty message on her answering machine or a letter filled with curses and prognostications of her impending lonely life. That was all the proof she needed to know the relationship, as it were, was ultimately a waste of time. But maybe she hit the jackpot with Adam, who knows? She sighed in slight frustration again, still not able to completely erase the latest meeting with Michael from her mind. He was indeed comforting to be near, she realized. That's a nice quality to have, but she decided Michael Pierce and his nice blue eyes, gentlemanly manner, broad shoulders, and sense of humor was not going to be part of her thoughts anymore as she turned back to her computer. The wire problem was fixed, it seemed, as she read several e-mails from account executives at the bank thanking her for saving their asses. She wondered again why it happened. Just then her concentration was interrupted by the phone. She didn't glance at the caller id as she reached for the phone and answered "Laura Rodriguez, Argent Bank, can I help you?"

"Why so businesslike?" It was Adam's voice on the other end which she strangely still hadn't learned to recognize right away although they had spoken by phone numerous times. "What happened to hello?" She didn't feel embarrassed at all by his query. She wondered quickly why she wasn't moved to any great reaction or emotion by this man.

"Sorry, I had a problem just now. How are you?"

"I'm okay. Just wanted to make sure you knew where to meet me later." Uhhh, he's not picking me up, she thought, a little annoyed. She asked him the obvious question after she told him she was aware of the restaurant's location.

"No, meet me at my apartment building, in the lobby, okay? Be on time and look good. See you later." And he hung up quickly, without saying anything else. Laura stared at the phone and asked herself, wishing he could hear, 'Don't I always'? A sudden chill went through her, a sixth sense of some kind that as a modern human being she ignored or let pass over her head, but she waved that away. No, tonight is going to be good, she semi convinced herself, I will look especially hot at the restaurant and frankly I don't even care if Adam knows what he is doing in bed, I need something…five sexless years was just too long and unhealthy.

⁓⁂⁓

Michael placed the phone back in its cradle once he concluded his call with Vinny. He did indeed break the news about the call he received earlier from Lee and Sharon and their concern about any preservationist activity. Vinny reacted as if he wasn't surprised and suggested they talk later. His friend sounded almost defeated, something Michael had never seen or heard in all their years together. The headache then started in his ankles and surged through his body like a missile, coming to rest in his temples leaving him with a feeling as if an incompetent surgeon accidentally left a sharp instrument behind after a little brain surgery. A comment from Hank Fredericks, whom he was surprised to see was still sitting there, still scribbling as if he were writing a novel in his spare time, grabbed his attention. "That sounded like it really sucked." Michael leaned back in the chair, not even bothering to suck his stomach in the way he had become accustomed to do in the past couple of years.

"You have no idea," Michael responded in the middle of reaching into his top drawer for the ever-present bottle of extra strength Excedrin. He gulped two of the tablets before he unscrewed the top off the bottle of water Hank was offering him.

"I never do title work or get involved with loans for friends. If something goes wrong, it's very damaging to the friendship," Hank informed him. Michael was in no mood for a lecture, especially from a title guy.

"Yeah, me too," he answered tersely. Michael had learned that lesson the hard way years earlier. But this deal was different. This wasn't some refinance of a single family home or a purchase of a condo for a first-time buyer. This was a commercial deal, a business deal, not a consumer mortgage, with a borrower who knew exactly what he was doing. He recalled the night when Vinny approached him and the others to join in the project as angel investors. They all remembered when he was eleven years old, standing on the bulkhead on a sweltering July afternoon and pirouetting slowly like a ballet dancer, his arms held out wide as he proclaimed, "One day, all of this will be mine. And I'm gonna share it with all my friends." We all thought he was crazy then, but as we grew up we could see with each passing year, with each new business and piece of real estate he acquired, that if anyone could do it, it was him. "I don't want anyone else in here except a bank with a mortgage that I can pay off early and then kick out," he had said. This deal, this project was for all of them, all of the boys who looked after each other like blood brothers from the time they used to swim in the East River all the way into adulthood. It was a story he had told many people over the past six months from the genesis of Vinny's announcement that he had the option on the land. And now, for perhaps the third time, he had retold the story to Hank partly because he thought with the retelling, the reality of the phone call he took earlier would just go away. He looked Hank in the eyes, unaware of how tired he looked to the older man.

"You know, my friends and I are all invested in this project. Some of us, including me, have everything we have riding on it." Hank shook his head and squeezed his lips together in the way that some of the president's men responded to Sam Ervin during the Watergate hearings.

"I'm stunned that this happened. It seemed like you were all on your way a few weeks ago when you got the commitment from Shale Financial. What the hell happened?" Hank's attitude was not unlike that of a passerby coming upon a car accident. Can't keep their eyes off the carnage. Hoping to see some blood or maybe a severed limb. Michael liked Hank but had no interest in pursuing the matter much further with him. Not if he was interested in feeding off his misery. Lots of people in the mortgage business liked to do that. Compare how poorly everything was going with you so they would feel better about their own problems. Michael knew that many people were more interested in your screw-ups rather than your successes. He had never felt that was the case with any of the boys from the old neighborhood, however.

"You can never count your freaking chickens, you just can't count on anything anymore," he said matter of factly. "The most mundane of tasks is a crap-shoot these days. You know, I can't get excited about many deals anymore what with everything that has tightened up in the past year. You take a couple of million dollar loans, a year ago you could look forward to a streamlined process of sorts on the way to a relatively pain-free closing and a nice commission. Today, I see these types of loans as problematic from the get-go and I think long and hard about even taking them on. This was...is...a major deal for all of us, not just financially, not just for the mortgage fee for me, the rental income we all would earn through the fractional ownership agreements. A couple of my friends are plumbers and electricians and this would have been work for life for them. Vinny was also looking to hire men and women from the neighborhood for the other businesses that would come into the commercial buildings. If they wouldn't make a commitment to hiring people within the 11101 to 11105 zip code, he would double their rent. It was Vinny's dream to be able to deliver for his friends and all of the other unconnected people from the old neighborhoods and surrounding environs as he was clearly the smartest of all of us and the one with the most balls."

Hank also leaned back and set himself to listen to Michael tell the story once more about his friends from the old neighborhood, how they grew up together and where they all wound up. He actually had grown tired of these stories about growing up in Queens some time before but he recognized his colleague needed an ear most of all right now, so the indulgence was on.

"Vinny has always been a dedicated student of the great philosophers, completely grounded but equal parts dreamer as well. Not afraid of anything or any man. He was the guy I told you about…"

"The one who won the Attica boxing tournament?"

"No, that was a guy I used to play basketball with." Michael was a little embarrassed. "Sorry to bore you with this stuff."

"No, it's okay. I will probably call on you some day to perform a service for me in payment for the indulgence I have done for you." Michael continued on, ignoring the sarcasm.

"He is a living testament to home schooling. He spent every day in the library as a kid, and every day after all of us graduated. He taught himself math, history, he read all the great philosophers and incorporated much of their thinking into his everyday life situation by situation, shifting from discipline to discipline as was needed. Martin Heidegger for this, Thomas Hobbes for that, Ben Franklin for just about everything. And he never came off like some phony Ivy Leaguer about it. He knew the disciplines back and forth and how to apply them to modern situations which, if you think about it, were really no different from what Plato and Socrates had to deal with. He could quote Shakespeare by rote as well as sing any Grateful Dead song from beginning to end. A truly amazing mind." Michael heard his phone ring, leaned forward to check the caller id and shook his head no, allowing the call to go to voice mail. "I'll get right back to them." He leaned back and looked over at Hank, who was once again scribbling in a little yellow legal pad. One day he planned to grab it out of his hand to see what he was writing about.

"The real estate business was a natural for him. He knows as much about it as any lawyer, can figure all sorts of complicated financing and tax consequences better than the best bean counter, can assemble a package of property with the best of them and was just, well...never scared. That's what happens when you're homeless at fourteen years of age and fending for yourself. Him and J'lome, what a pair. They were on their way to a life of crime together, two homeless kids thrown out of the house by their parents. They were so lucky to find each other."

"J'lome is the Muslim guy?"

"Yes. He took the rap for a burglary he and Vinny committed together, never ratted him out, did some years upstate for him—that's why Vinny will never allow anyone to screw around with him—and it was in the clink that he discovered Islam and he finally found a family and peace and a way for the rest of his life. Threw himself into it with all he had, studied the Koran day and night, made his pilgrimage to Mecca already, the whole nine yards. And now he has The People's Mosque in Astoria. Everyone is welcome there, Jews, Christians, Hindus, everyone can and does go to J'lome's mosque. He has built a model facility, a model for the world, really, welcoming everyone at any time. As long as he is there, the door is open. A bit of social paradise in Queens."

"Is he invested in the project, too?"

"Yes, along with a few of his followers, but just for a few bucks. I mean it's a sizable sum, but the other guys, Moose Miller, myself, the kid Charlie Mick, the Burke Brothers..."

"The basketball guys?" The Burke brothers peppered their everyday speech with basketball colloquialisms. They loved the game and the Knicks and St. John's basketball, and if they were running the team instead of the Dolan family, with their collective knowledge of the game and every player up to and including Bubbles Walker, they would have created a dynasty.

"Yeah, those guys. They also kept the bread route that Vinny bought years ago, the Pepperidge Farm route. It was his first business and he purposely kept it out of the sales he made to buy the option on the land." Michael laughed as he said, "He bought the route not only to make some money but because we all loved to skitch on the back of their trucks when we were kids. They had these huge bumpers that you could grab onto with ease and when you got tired, you could pull yourself up on them and take a seat. They were very comfortable. They were like our own kind of ski lift chairs." Hank watched Michael closely and was a little uncomfortable with Michael's dreamy faraway look. He was about to ask if he was okay when he started up again like a drunk coming off a bender.

"Also Moose Miller the harbor patrol cop and Charlie Mick, who is the only son of our friend, one of them, who passed away on 9/11. We have adopted him and Vinny is trying to mold him correctly, you know, with knowledge and fearlessness. The kid is big and tough, a good kid, but so angry still over his father's murder. Who could blame him? My other friends, you know, I told you about them probably too many times by now, Ping the Router, Roger Khan—a Muslim by the way, killed by those assholes, and Mikey Busy...all great guys, and all gone along with so many others. But their kids are all okay now or so they seem, their wives have either remarried or moved back to the old country to try to assuage their grief." Michael's cell phone rang again and he picked it up without checking the caller id and just dropped it in his drawer. He ran his hands through his thick salt and pepper hair, unconsciously making Hank a little jealous as his own hairline was receding like a glacier in Greenland.

"Shit...and now I feel like I have let them all down. God, my wife is going to go fucking bananas when she hears this. She was counting on the commission and the future profits from our investment." Normally Michael hated the indiscriminate use of curse words. He firmly believed they were a sign of lesser intelligence, but he couldn't help himself in some situations of stress. Sometimes the city kid in him would want to just let loose and verbally assault a cab driver who was blocking a side street, a kid on a rice rocket recklessly speeding and weaving on the highway, or a kamikaze bicycle rider in the East Village with a barrage of language that would make a soldier blush. He felt a hand on his shoulder and he flinched. Hank kept his hand there as he spoke like an old friend.

"Michael, you don't know how it will all pan out. Don't write the ending before it happens." He then wrote something on a yellow post-it note which he stuck to his briefcase which Michael took to be a reminder to stop somewhere else in the building. But he didn't seem to be leaving any time soon...guys like him, they need a reason to hang around the office as hovering unnecessarily is frowned upon. But as long as he is engaged in conversation, then he could stay all day. Hank's phone buzzed and he asked Michael if he would mind if he answered it quickly, leaning forward at the same time to slap the post-it note on his computer, and he received a casual wave, 'of course' in return.

⚓

Whathefu's British Airways flight touched down smoothly at Kennedy Airport just as Michael was deciding whether or not to throw out Hank's 'Smile' post-it note or to leave it on his computer as a reminder of how to approach each day. The taxi time to the jetway was just a few minutes but it seemed to take hours because this was not another ordinary fun visit to New York City for the young Saudi jet-setter. Not this time. This time it was all about the business of saving his own skin. His anxiety was on the rise again, coming to his consciousness in waves measured from barely tolerable to coming within an inch of fainting. He felt as if the upswings of these blasts of nervousness would cause his blood pressure to pop at the slightest provocation.

The pilot brought the massive airliner to a halt with barely a lurch and the flight attendant made the announcement welcoming everyone to New York City and some jabber about the weather and times of other connections and have a pleasant visit to New York City, seemingly oblivious to the fact that everyone just wants to get off the fucking plane. Disembarkation had already commenced by the time she stood from her jump seat and turned around to speak back into the cabin.

Even though he was poised to spring out of his seat which was at the front of the first class cabin, he was blocked by an older, heavyset man who was struggling with a piece of carry-on luggage. Whathefu was steaming as precious minutes ticked by. He wanted to deck the guy...I don't fly first class to be delayed by some New York Jew, he thought. When the passenger gained control of the over-sized piece of luggage he had somehow stuffed into the overhead bin, he angled his corpulence slightly to settle the bag on the seat, and Whathefu took this opportunity to slip his skinny body past him, swearing under his breath in Arabic as he did so.

Ignoring the flight attendant's suggestion that he have a nice day, he hurried down the jetway to immigration and visa control. The lines were mercifully short as he was one of the first off the plane and he knew where he was going, but the length of time it was taking the immigration officer to study his Saudi passport was not. Another racist bastard, Whathefu figured, as he maintained a detached smile, answering all of the officer's inane questions. Whathefu snatched the passport back, drawing a hard stare from the Port Authority cop who was watching everyone: what they wore, how they spoke, and their mannerisms. He scooped up his small carry-on and headed to the exit doors. He paused for a moment wondering whether he should attempt to seek out an Arab cab driver, one that he could speak with in his native tongue, maybe such a man could help him disappear in the city and possibly begin a new life away from his father, away from the grip of Islam, and away from everything about Saudi Arabia. But whomever was waiting for him outside those doors was there because of his father's vast wealth and international connections. He would be able to secure the type of body guard quite easily. Hopefully I can dodge him somehow between the time I leave this terminal and I find a cab to take me to Manhattan. Hopefully he was a few minutes late, figuring I wouldn't have gotten out so quickly.

Aubrey Epstein moved towards the reception area, keeping a highly trained eye for his assignment. He had a recent head and shoulders photograph of Whathefu but he did not know his exact height and weight, "average and skinny," his controller had told him. Or if he has changed his appearance in any way since he received this assignment. Aubrey is having difficulty remaining anonymous in this crowd as he is a six foot four, blond, movie star good looking man, with a body that appeared sculpted from marble by the pharaoh's top stone cutter. The very last thing he wants is to be noticed and risk possibly being recalled, but half of the women and a few of the men in the terminal cannot help but openly leer at him from head to toe.

They all disgust me, he thought to himself, especially the men, but he will not allow his concentration to waiver. Aubrey was a converted Muslim for several years now which was a secret back home on the base and in his private home. His benefactor, his controller in Saudi Arabia, has charged him with an incredibly important and personal mission. He knows he is going to hate Whathefu before he even meets him, just as he hated the rich Kuwaiti sons who partied in Berlin and Prague while his boots were filling with blood during Desert Storm. As he hated into his adult years the memory of the rich kids who tortured him on the school playground because of the horrible name his mother insisted on and his remarkably unblemished face. But this time is different because now he has permission to kill this rich kid if he screws up and since he has spent the last twelve years as an Army Ranger, he has more than enough skills and knowledge to kill any man within a minute of meeting him.

Andre rode the elevator down from his office with a young girl with pink hair, her head bobbing to some unfathomable musical beat that was fed directly into her head through tiny headphones, her face a mask of euphoria. Also in the cab was a young black man checking a delivery schedule with some sort of electronic device that scanned the packages and envelopes in his arms and a tight-faced lawyer type who was studiously ignoring them all by seeming to study the numbers on the control panel as if they were hieroglyphics. As the elevator reached the lobby, the lawyer and the young black man stepped aside to let the pink-haired girl out first, but Andre brusquely rushed past them. He turned left upon exiting the building, heading uptown on Fifth Avenue, past Harry Winston Jewelers and Bergdorf Goodman. The weather was turning out just fine, the weatherman's prediction of morning showers wrong again. The tourists were out in force on the street, dreaming about buying something in Tiffany's across the street, going in and out of the Apple store on the next block or taking pictures of themselves in front of the looming hulk of the Plaza. Andre was searching for a place of quiet and relative solitude in order to make a phone call. He decided to head west on Fifty-Eighth Street and hide himself in an alcove of a commercial building, his face buried in the corner. It never occurred to him to cross the street to Central Park and sit down by the pond as he had never taken a walk in the park during the entire time he lived in New York. He dialed the number of his friend Fated who lived in New Jersey.

To Andre, Fated was one of those people with the golden touch. Anything he did or became involved with seemed to work in his favor without effort and subsequently pay well for himself with a minimum of hassle. Always perfect timing. Andre figured it was a sort of divine intervention or the belief that some people were preordained for success, never coming to grips with the fact that most successful people actually made their dreams and efforts bear fruit through trial and error, repeated failure, and guts. Andre estimated this phone call was similar to one of the connections to be used that most of these rich people had in abundance at their fingertips to get low rate mortgages, tax breaks, and any velvet rope lifted.

Among many other businesses and concerns and silent partnerships, Fated was the owner of a satellite dish store in Jersey City. One of the many scams and illegal activities he had been involved with is the broadcasting of the Hezbollah propaganda channel Al-Manar to whomever wanted to watch it in North America. Al-Manar was the broadcasting arm of the terrorist group Hezbollah and had been declared illegal throughout the western world. Even the New York Civil Liberties Union didn't object to the blocking of its signal completely although they were publicly concerned that some 'ideas' other than the obvious anti-Semitism and commitment to the destruction of Israel and all western culture which usually permeated its broadcasts would be silenced. They tried to hold publicly that all speech in a free society is protected regardless of the viewpoint despite the fact that the network was obviously nothing more than the stump Sheik Nasrallah stood upon during the Hezbollah-Israeli clash. The other side quite rightly pointed out that sales of the terror network went toward funding future terrorist actions. Of course nothing would ever be investigated until someone got lucky or unlucky. Flush with the confidence of an unmarried entrepreneur with no children to worry about, Fated quite reasonably figured that at least a few thousand in the *uuma* were not finding the hundreds of cable channels beyond basic service available across the United States entertaining or interesting enough, so it was easy to extract a couple hundred dollars a month from each to send them the signal. And he thought the MTV-like channel that pushed violent jihad videos would keep them interested month after month.

Andre appreciated on some strange level how Fated was able to make so much money illegally. Once he stole ten license plates off government cars that were parked in a lot separated from a public street only by a six foot high chain link fence and sold them for five thousand dollars each to some crazy bastards in Yemen. He pulled off countless Craigslist apartment rental scams, straw buyer mortgage rip-offs, and now the Hezbollah channel. It was Fated's idea, a suggestion made a year ago to Andre when he started dating Kismine, that he steal money from the bank but only pennies at a time through the use of his 'salami scam', in order to pay for the recording studio time, jewelry, clothing, and other gifts for his beloved. A 'salami scam' allowed only the cents two digits to the right of the decimal point of a cashed check to be deducted and sent directly into an account of the scammer's choosing. The person running the scam banked on the presumption that the amounts were so small they would be easily missed. And it worked well until the bitch woman Laura got involved this morning. It wasn't entirely her fault, he knew, as he should have been in the office to intercept the calls from the new Asian clients. Damn those people and their love of details. But he just had to be in the studio to help Kismine record her songs. Also, he didn't trust her to be around any of the musicians who laid down the basic tracks. Their leering stares unnerved him, it never occurring to Andre that she was the recipient of leering stares of the same type wherever she walked. And also that most of those stares were those of pity at her complete lack of talent. Now Andre wanted Fated's help in getting the object of his affection on television, even if it was just one of the Iranian soap operas or as a newscaster for one of the many anti-Zionist programs the Hezbollah channel featured. She told him she had some family and friends in Lebanon. If he succeeded in getting her on television there, she would certainly then declare her love for him. He frankly didn't care if her career went anywhere. He just wanted her in his house every day when he returned from work. He wanted his eyes only to look her over. He wanted to be the sole recipient of her attention. He dialed the number of Fated's store and hid his face from the passersby on the sidewalk.

Fated listened to his friend patiently which was the only way he had been able to speak to him recently, and told him he will meet him later at the People's Mosque in Astoria. But not before he had a little fun with him. "Have you fucked your little princess yet? Ha Ha Ha, just kidding, I'm sure she is as pure as the driven snow. Let's just meet in Astoria later, okay? I'll pick you up by the Thirty-ninth Avenue train station and we'll go there together."

"I don't like that place anymore," Andre said after regaining his composure, "the imam there invites Jews and Christians inside. It's a sacrilege." Fated hated his soon-to-be-former-friend's aggressive racism. Fated had no love for Jews, tolerated Christians as long as they weren't evangelical, but he himself worshiped at the temple of the almighty dollar, Euro, or yen. He was a Muslim, would always be, but just couldn't completely fathom the idea of an invisible man in the sky who was watching and judging everything he did. He figured all of the thousands of men from back home he watched on the news—where were the women by the way?—were lazy fools, somehow unaware of how often their middle Eastern leaders broke every rule and precept laid out in the Koran, only pulling the great book out when it satisfied their own ambitions. One day, Fated thought, there will be an uprising over there. I wonder how I can take advantage of that? First things first...he had to take care of his friend once and for all. These calls were becoming more frequent, their annoyance factor increasing geometri-cally with each one. Fated had to live half his life in shadows. Andre was the type you had to distance yourself from.

"It's an okay place," Fated responded, "just be there in time for eve-ning prayer and I will meet you in our office afterward to discuss." Andre agreed and hung up the phone. This will be a good use of my time, Fated thought. While I am there, I can check on the empty storefront on Thir-tieth Avenue. Maybe some sort of hookah café can be stuffed in there, pull in some young liberals and hipsters who want to hang out with the oppressed Arabs and other middle easterners, and use it as a place to move the cash from his other operations around. First though, he had to put this dummy Andre in his place once and for all.

━

EARLY EVENING

Maxie Carter stared through the sliding glass door at the Pepsi sign from her penthouse high over Sutton place. She enjoyed studying and admiring the architecture, the history of old New York and she supposed the work with the landmark board would be interesting when she started, but she could see now it was just full of bullshit. She disliked the two other members on the board about five minutes after meeting them as they were apparently involved not for the love of architecture and a commitment to the preservation of deserving landmarks in the city but just so that they can get a little bit of power in their hands. The meeting with Vinny earlier had been only her second meeting with the bow-tie and the bony one, friends of her husband, 'we prepped together', it was obviously nothing more than a means to an end of some kind for the both of them, nothing more. She stepped out on the balcony, the breeze heading downriver sweeping her hair out of place, and continued to stare at the Pepsi sign as she brushed it away from her eyes recalling an afternoon here with her father some thirty-five years earlier. Standing here with him, a tall, proud, self-made man, pointing to the kids on the Long Island City side of the river, swimming in the filthy, dangerous currents. "That's all they have, Maxie. Remember always how much more you have and the responsibility that goes with it," he had told her with gravity. She knew as a young girl that this was something her father wanted her to remember forever.

Remembering her father's words from that day, she quickly surveyed her life. A thoroughly empty marriage, devoid of any passion or silliness. Why did she marry this trust fund guy anyway? You know why, she admonished herself. He was tall and good looking and a good dancer, full of what she thought was confidence then, but what she now knew was supreme smugness. He never got his hands dirty like my father and my grandfather, men who built and expanded their fortunes literally from the ground up, developing small buildings in the outer boroughs of the city, doing business with concern for their employees and the neighborhoods they worked in and near. Now all he does is live in my apartment—she inherited the apartment after the death of her mother some months before—ignoring me while he probably arranged dates with old high school hookups. She didn't know the password to his computer. She was brought up to be a trusting sort. She could only imagine the pornography he viewed and the dating sites he frequented. Maxie wouldn't presume to ask him for the password. That would only serve to show him how concerned she was and she would never allow that. She briefly considered hiring a private detective to hunt him down and finally get some dirt on him, getting hold of a real reason for divorcing him.

She sighed deeply, realizing once again how bored she was with her life, how underutilized and unappreciated she was by her husband and all of his friends. I have a law degree as well as a nursing degree. I have worked in a courtroom and a hospital. What the hell am I doing with my life except wasting it away? How could she have agreed to resign from the hospital? She loved the work she was doing there although she was often frustrated with the doctors, overwhelmed by the misery, and pissed off at the bureaucracy. She quit to live a life of leisure, flitting around the world with her husband and his colleagues, friends, associates, none of whom impressed her in the least. For a year she lived this way and when she announced she was going back to work at the hospital they quarreled fiercely. Why? Any man with half a brain would welcome a wife who worked and made a good living. He was embarrassed somehow. He wanted her to be a princess, his little bauble to show off, nothing more. No, she didn't have to work. She had plenty of money left to her by her parents. But what would they think about that? That was the final nailing down of her decision, how she could see them in her dreams, angry with her, disappointed. She reluctantly agreed to help out on the preservation committee for a few months to appease his sense of face.

She stepped away from the door and went out further onto the balcony, drawing in a deep breath of fresh spring air. Her thoughts wandered back to the meeting with Vinny earlier in the morning. That man earlier today pleading his case before us, that man had a real passion, a true vision. He was in the middle of creating so much from nothing. Just like her father and his father. Hundreds of jobs, beautiful open space on the riverfront which would certainly be a better view from her apartment, nice moderately-priced rentals for working families to live in, a greater tax base for the city. Why would the others be so opposed to it? They hadn't let her in on it. Her questions to them after Vinny had left went unanswered. The meeting was hastily arranged, but it seemed obvious to her halfway through that her colleagues had put some thought into this...without her. She had spent much of the meeting studying the plans for the development and she was impressed, hard-pressed to find a flaw anywhere.

What was wrong with all of this? Why are we letting a sign for a soda company stand in the way of all this well-thought-out progress, a model of entrepreneurial spirit? It was apparent to Maxie that the others were jealous somehow of a man like Vinny Malloy. She surprised herself by her quick and easily-arrived-at realization of just how attractive, interesting and exciting she found him. She decided that a walk through the city streets would clear her mind and grabbing her coat upon reentering the apartment from the balcony, she didn't stop to say good-bye to her husband and headed down to the street for a breath of fresh air.

⁓⁂⁓

Vinny had been at the development site on the East River at the foot of Forty-Seventh Avenue for the remainder of the afternoon. His visit to J'lome had been, as always, fruitful in a spiritual way. If there were a religion that Vinny one day would decide to adopt it would be Islam only for the fact that J'lome would be his Imam. Other than that, he had very little use for ecclesiastical dogma other than the writings and teachings of the great Christian thinkers such as Leo the Mathematician, Roger Bacon, and Blaise Pascal. All of these men were deeply involved in their faith—in their cases the Christian faith—and they studied and wrote about math and science without a regard for any criticism they might have received from the church. Michael Stifel, an Augustinian monk and mathematician who was an early supporter of Martin Luther, Bacon with his emphasis on empiricism and the scientific method, and Pascal's wager about the existence of God...which led to groundbreaking new territory in pragmatism, existentialism, and voluntarism and decision-making as a whole. In Vinny's point of view, these men had real balls, they were meant to be emulated for questioning the conventional wisdom and doing so in the face of the church which would stop at nothing to silence dissenters and heretics. Vinny spent his years after J'lome's trial devouring these brave and innovative men's philosophies and studies, coming away with not only admiration for them, but with a method of living the rest of his life.

Vinny liked people with real stones, anyone who was ready to take a chance on something that everyone else told them couldn't be done.

J'lome also introduced him to the great Muslim thinkers and scientists like Avicenna, a Persian regarded as not only the foremost physician of his time, but also an Islamic philosopher of the same stature. Essentially the man wrote a medical journal that was so complete that it was still used well into the nineteenth century. As for Islam and science, the Prophet Muhammad said it simply: "Seek knowledge from the cradle to the grave." That was all Vinny had to know.

The Burkes had spent the afternoon at the site with Vinny as well. Fred and Ryan Burke, a couple of hotshots on the courts at Astoria Park and Lost Battalion Hall on Queens Boulevard, then four great years at Rice High School, if they were born with some height, they would have at least gone to play at Fordham or possibly St. John's. But they stopped growing at fifteen and sixteen, both of them topping out at about five feet ten. Not bad for high school, but terrible for anything beyond that. As good as they were in the game, with great instincts and a nose for the ball, you couldn't teach, buy, or exercise your way to six foot five or six. By the time they graduated from Rice, it was Vinny who persuaded them to get the plumbing and electrical licenses. He convinced them that the work would always be there, not only with his own properties but others as well. And they agreed easily. They wouldn't allow themselves to be caught dead in a suit. And what they heard about college was that other than the hot young girls away from home for the first time and the easy availability of beer and pot, it was probably a waste of time. There were plenty of unemployed suits around these days. Why would it be any different in four years? So they went to work on the Pepperidge bread route in the early morning and spent their afternoons in trade school, obtaining their licenses a year later. It wasn't glamorous, but it was good honest work and they hadn't had a day of unemployment since they were teenagers. They owed all of this to Vinny and they were as loyal to him as one could be.

Tomorrow morning they would start the day in the Pepperidge Farm truck delivering bread around the city and then performing the electrical and plumbing work for a few of Vinny's properties that they retained as accounts after they were sold. They never seemed to require much sleep and this was great for Vinny as these brothers, his friends for the past thirty-some-odd years, were the perfect complement to his entrepreneurial mind. The only other thing they ever did beside plumbing and electrical work was talk about basketball constantly. They were able to tell you anything and everything about virtually every player who ever played in the NBA. They had an unusual and sometimes annoying habit of peppering their speech with basketball related non sequiturs. Vinny thought there were many much worse habits a human being could have so he always just let them ramble on about the Knicks and the Lakers, and the Cincinnati Royals for goodness sake. In any event, they ran the bread routes for Vinny for thirty years now, and helped to manage his properties from the very beginning up to now, this potentially sorry state of affairs.

Vinny all of a sudden had an extreme case of happy feet and an idea for action struck him like an jolt of electricity in his marrow. He jumped back in the car and turned up Vernon Boulevard, then east on Thirty-Ninth Avenue, and then ran down Crescent Street, heading over the Fifty-Ninth Street Bridge and then over to the little park on the FDR Drive by Sutton Place. He wanted to take a look at his project, his life, from the view across the river. Maybe it would provide him with some new perspective. Like looking down at your body when you are floating away to heaven. Maybe it would be a complete waste of time. But what else would he do now? Moose is working, chasing some ghost for the Feds. Mikey was probably on the expressway headed home. The Burkes were going to watch replays of NBA games from...1973 probably. No wife or girlfriend to go home to, he had no kids, plenty of friends at least, but most of whom are unfortunately currently busy with their own lives and problems at this moment, and ah, what the hell, let's just go take a look just to get the hell out of here. He grabbed a copy of John Cowper Powys' *Philosophy of Solitude*, which he had read some twenty years before. Vinny didn't have a photographic memory, but he did recall Powys' assertion about nobler instincts being born into solitude and that the soul that has re-created itself in isolation has gained something of the humility of the grass and that the escape from one's difficulties was to simplify, simplify, simplify. He figured it would do him some good to be alone to work this situation through. It wasn't horribly bad yet. Normally he could destroy a pair of twits like the bony guy and the bow-tie in seconds, but this situation was unnerving him. It wasn't just his money he had on the line, it was all his friends' as well he reminded himself. He couldn't see himself living any normal kind of life if he failed them now. He parked the car in a garage and told the attendant that he'd be back in an hour or so.

—●●—

Whathefu stepped through the customs control amidst hundreds of people consisting of New Yorkers returning home, tourists coming to the city, businessmen arriving and departing. He started thinking about dinner and where should he go. It was just after five in the afternoon, close to the time for the evening prayers, which he fully intended on skipping. Will the man, bodyguard, jailer, whatever and whoever he is supposed to meet insist on going to the mosque? He hoped not. On some of his prior trips to New York, he met many Muslims who prayed only sporadically. They were proud of their faith, claiming their religion as a national heritage, not the country they were born in or emigrated from. But they balanced the requirements of the Koran with cars, family, sports, love, along with all the difficulties of being a Muslim in America.

Whathefu knew, as most Muslims did, that America and most ironically, Israel, were the best countries in the world for practicing their faith and establishing a life beyond that faith. His father had the construction company, the yacht, several wives, numerous girlfriends, luxury cars and real social as well as business power. Why couldn't the average Arab man live the same way if they put forth an effort that bore fruit? Where was the freedom of the individual in the kingdom for men and women as well? Did the Wahhabists control the Royal family that much?

He knew his father paid millions in tributes to them and Leila's father also paid tributes lest they ever think he was an unworthy Muslim. Political capital was the reason why, his father explained to him years before, they keep the world unbalanced enough to keep the Saudi royal family powerful enough to keep the West somewhat at bay by feigning friendship and diplomacy. God help them all, Whathefu considered, if the Western governments and businesses ever truly decided to pursue the possibility of solar energy grids handling the power needs of large cities. They would wipe out the Saudi economy as well as the economies of the other OPEC nations in about five minutes. Whathefu might secretly enjoy that after all. Would his father ever think of buying a couple of buildings in New York his son could manage, maybe finance the opening of a restaurant or two, just a bit of money to help him out a little? Not a chance. He knew as he knew his own image in a mirror, his father was sure to drop a million on some new girl from eastern Europe without a thought long before he would help out Whathefu. Seventeen million dollars! How was he going to ever do this? He peered out the scratched window door of the terminal scanning the line of taxi and limousine drivers, desperately searching for a Middle Eastern face. So many Indians and Africans. Where are all the Arab drivers? Maybe that one there, he supposed, as he spied a young man with the same coloring and build, about the same age as well. His car was only twenty feet away, so he quickly pushed open the door and ambled over to the driver, hoping to turn invisible. All he needed was to get into the cab and disappear into the city for a while.

Aubrey spied Whathefu instantly even without the photo. The Middle Eastern features were there. That wasn't unusual as he heard and understood a bit of the Arab and Pashtu dialects slinging back and forth at the taxi stand a few feet to his right. He thought it a good idea to situate himself here at the head of the taxi line in order to watch all the cars at once as this kid would probably try to make a dash for it into the city where it would take months to find him, if he could at all. But the finely-tailored clothes, the stylish haircut and the gaudy jewelry all made him as the sort of Muslim Aubrey hated. He remembered the type during Desert Storm in Kuwait, fighting and dying to save whom? These rich playboys who were busy fucking any western women they could get their hands on in the discos of Europe while Aubrey and his friends were riding in tanks that were choked with dust and sand, eating shitty MRE's—Meals Ready To Eat—and wearing the same underwear for a week at a time. He witnessed soldiers on both sides die horrible, agonizing deaths, and he also saw the brutality of the war visited on the peasants and non members of the royal family, and he was disgusted by how the rich boys treated them. Just a farmer or a goat herder, that was how they would refer to their less fortunate countrymen, and then the next crappy disco song would blast through the speakers and they would run back onto the dance floor, arms above their heads, sweating through their silk shirts, the American girls and the Europeans fawning all over them.

He began his second life on those sandy battle grounds finally finding some religious nourishment, something he didn't even know he craved until he was able to observe the quiet dignity of the peasants answering the several daily calls to prayers. He obtained an English version of the Koran and read it voraciously, taking in every word and lesson, rejecting any and all notions of the teachings of Jesus Christ which his parents tried to instill in him in between all the other sick, crazy moments of his upbringing.

He was thrilled to be in the region of the world where all the great prophets honed their beliefs and traveled by foot and on camels to spread their word. Moses, yes...Jesus too and his disciples. And of course the Prophet Muhammad, all dedicated to pulling the people ignored or oppressed by the upper strata of their society together with a simple set of rules to live life by. The godless princes of Kuwait, like their equally disgusting Arab brethren the Iraqis, laughed at him while they were shooting at him, killing his friends, his commanders exhorting him and the others to kill as many of the ragheads as they could, whether they carried arms or not. He found an everlasting peace in the Koran and his sponsor, this little shit's father, assured him a place in the holy land of Saudi Arabia when the time came, when he would be able to perform a favor for his new overseer like a true jihadist. Aubrey had met Whathe-fu's father during some very light security duty while attending a state dinner in the kingdom. He was quite the impressive figure in his dress uniform and at first he thought the older Arab man was going to come onto him. But he was wrong, so wrong. Somehow Whathefu's father had seen the copy of the Koran he kept in his pocket...maybe it was peeking out in an unguarded moment. He asked if he were Muslim. Aubrey answered yes, and the man, who was obviously one of great import in this land, recoiled slightly in apparent shock and then asked him to dinner the next day at which he outlined his desire for Aubrey to be his eyes in the American military.

"You must have been chosen by the Prophet himself to reveal yourself to me. There is so much we can do together when the time is right to bring Islam to all those who thirst for true knowledge," said Whathe-fu's father to what he considered to be his new son. He gave Aubrey a pre-paid cell phone that he was not allowed to use other than answering a call. He was never to dial out, just wait for a call which could come at any time. The phone never left Aubrey's side for many years and never rang until the other day. The time to prove himself was apparently now and none too soon as he once again scanned his immediate surround-ings for any sign of police, military or not. He felt so close to his goal of becoming the new American An-war al- Aliki, spreading the word of the Koran around the world on YouTube...but he was going to be the new face of it. At least his parents gave him these good looks and the tall fit body that so many women and men desired. And that none of them would have again. His contempt for these types, like this little shit just entering his line of sight in his purple shirt and white pants, nurtured slowly but surely on the battlefield, was rising like bile in his throat as if he just consumed a plateful of spicy empanadas when he reached out and placed his hand on Whathefu's shoulder, not knowing completely if he would follow his assignment to the letter or if he would snap his little neck right here on the sidewalk.

"You are with me, I believe," Aubrey said quietly to Whathefu as his grip slipped down to the frightened young Saudi's elbow, the iron grip suggesting to Whathefu's ulnar nerve that resistance was ridic-ulous to contemplate. The notion of escaping was draining from his mind rapidly, soon to be replaced by abject terror, as well as something else he was struggling to understand, to come to terms with. The tall handsome American steered him away from the line of yellow cabs.

"My car is over there," said Aubrey, gesturing to the short term lot. "It's almost time for *asr* and I have no intention of disrupting my per-sonal *salaat* schedule for you. I saw what appeared to be a mosque just off the highway on the way here, we're going there now." They were in the large parking lot now and after scanning around for unwanted visitors, Aubrey's hand shot up quickly and he now stabbed his thumb into Whathefu's armpit, his hand being large enough to grip the top of his shoulder with a lot of strength simultaneously. He spoke again, but now it was quite different than just a minute ago, a menacing growl that seemed out of place emanating from the handsome man.

"Let me make something clear to you, my little friend. I am here at the behest of your father, for whom I have the greatest respect. He is my controller and he has charged me with the task of watching you. I know all about the girl you killed in Saudi Arabia...what a waste of life as well as a waste of anyone's time. Sliding cars on the sandy streets, what the hell is wrong with all of you?" He continued to pull/push his prisoner along, reaching his Saab station wagon in another minute. Aubrey clicked the remote, the car chirped like a bird and, after yanking open the passenger door, he shoved Whathefu inside like a full laundry bag. He slammed the door and walked around the front of the car to get in, staring down his passenger through the windshield, never taking his eyes off the cringing young man in the front seat. He got in, slammed his door, put his eyes on Whathefu once again causing him to shrink even further into the seat, in order to pound the message home that he would not hesitate to kill him if given the chance. He had already been given permission by the little shit's father to do so at his discretion. He did not reveal this to Whathefu because he wasn't instructed to. His passenger was now trembling like a cold wet cat, which was exactly the result he wanted.

Aubrey backed out of the space and maneuvered to the toll lane pulling on his seat belt and instructing Whathefu to do the same. They pull you over for anything in a big city these days. He smiled at the attendant, slipped the ticket in the slot, arrows up, something which even he, a big man, had to lean far out of the car to accomplish. He waited for a moment while the thoroughly bored attendant, who looked as if he wouldn't help you place the ticket in the slot if you offered him a hundred bucks, relieved him of four dollars for about a half hour of parking before lifting the gate so they could exit. He guided the car along the confusingly labeled streets of Kennedy Airport until he reached the exit for the Van Wyck Expressway heading north out of the airport, driving up a few miles to the merge with the Grand Central Parkway, staying in the right lane as he knew he would be exiting soon after. He couldn't go over the Tri-Boro Bridge, he knew. The mosque he had seen was somewhere near the foot of that bridge. He considered his silent passenger. Maybe this prince of wealth could possibly be some kind of ticket for him. A ticket out of the States and out of the reach of the Military Police not to mention the local cops down south who were surely looking for him. Could they know where he was headed? He couldn't believe his good fortune that after so many years his controller had contacted him with such perfect timing. It had to be Allah's will that guided the events of his past twenty-four hours. He dismissed the thought as all that wasn't important to the rest of his life and hit the gas, cutting across three lanes, exiting the highway onto the service road and then re-entering the highway a few blocks later, putting quick distance between him and anyone who might have been following him.

Moose Miller had clicked his radio to signal his FBI agent partner of sorts a few minutes earlier, who was supervising the shadow of this guy. He liked this particular Fed, probably the only one he ever dealt with who didn't treat him like an errand boy. He was a big bastard, this subject, thought Moose, wondering why the Feds were watching him. He didn't look like a Russian mobster and he was definitely not Middle Eastern, not with that blond hair. "This is car one, we have a moving target and he has a friend over."

The Federal agent Moose was communicating with but had not yet met in person—he wondered what he was all paranoid about—was named Tony Craig, which Moose also did not know, clicked his radio to respond, "Tell me about the friend, please. Over." Moose was now following a few car lengths behind and in the right lane of the Van Wyck as he did not know which way the subject was going to turn at the merge, either north over the Whitestone Bridge or west along the parkway. He was lucky he had maintained his surveillance in the right lane as he would have been made had he followed Aubrey in the left lane and tried to copy his maneuver up to the service road and back onto the Van Wyck. Whatever it was this guy is suspected of, Moose was now convinced he was guilty.

"Twenty-five years old or so, well dressed, Mediterranean features, thin build, about one hundred forty pounds, black hair. He looks nervous and unsure of himself. The big guy grabbed him under his arm and muscled him to their car, a Saab station wagon, by the way." Mediterranean features, thought Moose. He is a fucking Arab. Why can't I just say that? Well maybe because he might be Jewish, Vinny would admonish him. Ha...this guy is as Jewish as George Bush. His FBI contacts in the past counseled him against racially insensitive comments—as well as the lame-ass new boss of the harbor unit—and apparently someone who looks like an Arab, walks like an Arab, smells like an Arab can't be referred to as a fucking Arab. "He doesn't impress me as a friend of your subject," Moose finished.

"Why"?

"For one thing, they look like they're from totally different worlds. Your guy looks like a movie star, tall, fit, and handsome and the new guy on the scene looks like a weasel. A slick-backed little euro-trash weasel." Or he just looks like a rich Arab kid looking for some foreign tail, he wanted to say, but this FBI guy was ultra-polite and deferential. Or maybe that was just in front of his boss, whom Moose met over the phone earlier as well. No love lost between those two, he thought at the time. Even over the phone he could detect the strain between the two Feds, but what did he care? Maybe Vinny was right, that this gig, other than the overtime, could turn into something nice for him. Maybe then his wife would stop nagging him. Had to remember to be careful with his language over the FBI airwaves.

"Okay, make sure to stay with them, don't lose them. Keep me informed." The guy clicked off without a 'Roger and out' or a 'See you later' or anything that suggested to Moose that he had even a half of a heart. Fucking Feds, Moose thought, they have to lay details, details, details on me all the time like I gotta be reminded of this basic shit between every breath I take. He settled the Crown Victoria a few lengths behind the Saab as they passed by La Guardia and then returned to his all-day attempts, which were quickly becoming a daily grind, to try and put his wife's disappointment in him and his career choice out of his mind.

―‌⊕‌―

Bob Berg Al-Amin was equal parts miserable, happy, and satisfied. Strange combination but nevertheless true. What else could it ever be for a man born a Jew, then forced by his parents to follow them in a conversion to German Lutheranism in his teens—who does that, all his relatives used to ask—and then in his mid-twenties changing his religious affiliation once again but on his own this time to Islam, the Wahhabist brand, a fiery, take-no-prisoners kind of religious intolerance. He only had one purpose in life now and that was to spread the word of the Prophet Muhammad anywhere and everywhere he could. Unfortunately for many, he usually did this at the wrong time and place, in front of synagogues, at Ground Zero during the annual reading of the names of those killed on 9/11, or at the funerals of soldiers returning from overseas in a coffin. He had his ass kicked too many times to remember, been arrested several times, but his wealthy parents bailed out their only child every time, providing a law professor from Columbia University at his side every time, half-heartedly promising to cut him off from his family stipend if this sort of transgression ever happened again. They were intensely ashamed of him, but the memories of watching him in his Little League uniform, his first bicycle ride without his Dad holding him upright, holidays and vacations with the rest of the family overrode the wishes of their friends and family to dump him from their lives. "Maybe he will come back to us," his mother often said. But he continued to delight in pontificating even in front of any one of the hundreds of mosques that dotted the city, exhorting Muslim men to always wear a skullcap and a kaffiyeh, regardless of their profession, nationality, or professional career from which most of them were leaving when they stopped at the mosque for afternoon or evening prayers. He extolled the virtue of incessant prayer and devotion to jihad to men who were running businesses, attending school, raising families, all the while trying to fit into the fabric of American society within a twenty-four hour day. He pushed for the adoption of Sharia law, if not on the streets, then in their own homes. Put the belt to your wife, or wives if you can afford more than one, and your daughters if they engage in any type of immodest behavior. Have them at least be veiled whenever they are out of the house and indeed you should put the burqua on them. Have your sons adopt the way of the Wahhabists in Saudi Arabia as they and they only practiced the religion purely and properly. They were his heroes, the imams and financiers of the countless madrassas slamming the reading of the Koran into the thousands of young lost minds across the Middle East and somehow some way he was going to create an army of followers that would establish a brand of Islam in the United

States that was absolute and unyielding, unlike the moderate imams who preached tolerance and understanding, respect for the community and for the beliefs of others. They were just as much an enemy to him as the Jews were as all of western society was. He rejoiced on 9/11 the way scads of Arab teenagers on Atlantic Avenue in Brooklyn did, running in groups to the esplanade in Brooklyn Heights for the better view as the buildings, firemen, police officers, secretaries, and bond brokers fell to the ground just across the river. He delighted in the scene of ululating women in the West Bank and Gaza basking in their joy at the destruction of the towers, the Pentagon, and the lives lost in the field in Pennsylvania. He dreamed to be a player in an operation of that sort, not as a mere participant, but with his name on it, his followers carrying it out, his website, not yet built, claiming responsibility. The reporters from Al-Jazeera would be placing him on their speed dials soon enough.

He wouldn't hide in a cave in Tora Bora like bin Laden, that coward. He wanted to take the word of his convictions to the street, all streets in all towns in all states across America. He believed this as fully as any man could believe in anything without ever pausing to check the level of the gas tank of his life, of his conscience, of any responsibility toward others. His own wife ran off with his daughters several years before in fear and disgust of him. Even his parents would not tell him where they were. Well, one day I will find out where they have been, and I swear I will have them under my influence soon enough, and the music, the makeup, the earrings, the sex...all of that would be replaced by obedience and chastity. He looked out the window of the N train which had emerged from the tunnel that ran under the East River a few minutes earlier, and could now see that he and scores of other straphangers were barreling along Thirty-First Street in Astoria toward the last stop at Ditmars Boulevard. He checked the address of the People's Mosque once again. It must be near the parkway, he thought, as the doors opened, the air brakes emptied their lines with a whoosh and he exited with his head down, stalking toward the stairs, bumping into several people along the way without turning to apologize.

───

Laura was still sorting out why the wire protocol went haywire this morning. By now, she had almost completely brushed Michael out of her hair, but not entirely. It had admittedly been getting harder to do just that the past couple of years. He was aging well, his thick brown hair gaining some streaks of well placed gray that to her relief he didn't try to color. But she needed to eliminate him from her thoughts in order to concentrate on her computer screen and the problem at hand, even though this was outside of what her superiors at the bank wanted her to do.

But once again she wavered...why does he distract me so easily, just by standing there, or by saying hello? She wondered. She never in her life looked at any man in a purely sexual way. Several of her past relationships were mostly sexually satisfying, but ultimately boring as her self-aided orgasms were helped along by visions of what she believed real lovemaking should be. And none of her boyfriends even came close to her private visions and she wasn't about to try to suggest certain techniques to them. Let them figure it out, she thought time and time again as they sprawled heavily on top of her, the patterns of their huffing and puffing almost as interesting as the patterns the light made through the drawn shades in whatever room they were in. Deep down she knew this was unfair as well as unproductive, but a girl from her background expected a man to know what to do, with talent and fearlessness, without having to be told.

She continued to stare at the endless rows of commands and data streaming across the computer screen like army ants in pursuit of a meal. Now she was regaining her focus, searching for the one fatal flaw, a fat finger resulting in a missed keystroke or misplaced command that caused the crash of the system earlier this morning. But she was also looking for something else and that was evidence of tampering. For several months she suspected that her computer was being doctored somehow, that it was compromised and that someone had possibly gotten hold of her password. Several more minutes of studying the rows of information produced no evidence, however, and she moved on to the other assignments she had that morning. But her suspicions were still nagging at her, some sort of sixth sense, a self-awareness she generated more fully after moving from the farm to Buenos Aires. She always felt thankful for the beautiful countryside, the majestic mountains, the freshest of fresh air and water, her brothers and sisters working in the fields, always barefoot, baling hay, breaking horses, fixing, building, always in motion building muscles and strength that no gym membership with their ridiculous machines and trainers ever could do for her, as well as developing a strength of character that no school, self help book, psychiatrist session or advice from a priest could either. In the city she used all of those acquired strengths and attributes to hone her bullshit detector, spotting a bad business deal, a man who just wanted to screw her, a friend who just wanted her around because she looked good.

All of that effort to build a human foundation of strength, just to dissolve in a few years after her parents' death in a plane crash, their first time on a trip out of the village and their first time on a plane as well. It had taken so many years to build it back up and here she was in her early forties, wondering if it all had been a waste of time. Maybe I just should have married this one or that one and spit out a couple of kids and wait to divorce him when the children were done with school and out of the house. Ahhh, she thought, pushing the heels of her hands at her eyes, why do these silent scenarios plague me this way?

She pushed away from her desk, and shook her head to further clear these introspections away, along with any lingering thoughts of Michael Pierce. She leaned forward, placing her head between her knees as if to stave off a fainting spell, and allowed her hair to fall forward. She scratched at her scalp, massaging with her fingertips to smooth out the tension headache she felt developing. Was it this job that was causing the increasingly frequent bouts of worry? Or was it the comment by Adam earlier? No, I didn't like what he said or how he said it, for that matter, but should I just let it go or skewer him with questions like so many of the brassy New York women she knew? Forget it, she told herself, he's quite possibly as nervous about tonight as she is. Tonight was to be their big night. Three months of dating was enough, she concluded. He seemed to be a complete, honest guy. Too many married men had lied to her in the past looking for a quick lay only to be read by her like a comic book. Didn't they know the wedding band they removed just before they met her still left an impression on their finger? Or a tan line for some of them. Or that they wouldn't be living in some Westchester or New Jersey suburb if they weren't married? Did they think that she and the other women in New York were idiots? But they still tried all the time which is why she told

Adam on their third date, the traditional sex or no more dating for us date in New York, at least it seemed, that he would have to wait much longer to hold her in his arms.

And she told him, as lasciviously as she could muster, "It will be worth the wait." And it would be, she guaranteed herself as she felt her sexual prime revealing itself to her in so many different ways. She was the rare woman who became more beautiful as she entered her forties. Her body was magnificent, flat stomach, taut legs, muscular butt and pert breasts that still scoffed at gravitational forces. Hopefully he would be the man who would be able to kiss her, hold her, and make love to her in the way she always wanted...not some medieval pounding, as she had had enough of that. "Sorry Laura, but if I don't go really fast and never stop, I'll lose my erection." She actually had two lovers who said that to her and at the time she momentarily wondered if they were both comparing notes regarding their sexual sessions with her. She, like all women, craved a patient, confident man, who could hold her gently with one hand while the other grabbed her with real strength, who looked at her with eyes filled with molten passion, but who spoke to her respectfully and quietly. Someone who was in some sort of shape but not a slave to his body, shoulders out to here and hips well, in here, not outrageously good looking, but not ugly either. Someone who...well, knew what he was doing in the sack. She was aware she had eighteen different types of passion inside her body and her brain, all of them searching for an exit. No man had ever been able to do that for her. Although she enjoyed sex, she was just as bored by much of it and as a result never really desired a session more than once in a while. No penis ever delivered an orgasm for her. At the very least, she hoped that the slightly over-the-top self-assuredness which was necessary to a degree for survival in New York City that she noticed in Adam wasn't his true self. Some humility would be nice as she continued to massage away the tension from her scalp. But then again, in the laser-like directness of some of her New York girlfriends, she reminded herself that at least she was going to get laid tonight. More than sixteen hundred days had gone by since her last relationship. Sixteen hundred days! How was that possible!?

Michael entered her mind again as she finished her scalp massage, remembering several years earlier when he caught her performing the massage scalp outside the ballroom for the latest bank holiday party. He was actually interrupting her at the moment by saying hello in that thick New York accent, "Hey, howyadune?" She recalled the memory with ease, a pissed-off Latina type explosion on the tip of her tongue, when she flipped her hair back and before she could stand and walk away in a huff, he asked her, "Did you ever see the movie *Gilda* with Rita Hayworth?" Here she was, mortified and pissed off and this man was asking some ridiculous question. "No," she answered, standing taller, throwing her shoulders back and straightening out her dress. He continued, "You should rent it some time, a classic American film and at one point in the film, Rita Hayworth flips her hair in exactly the same way. You remind me of her." He smiled and walked away at that, turning to look one more time before he pulled open the doors to the ballroom to reenter the party. She rented the movie later that night and thought he was crazy to compare her to this amazingly beautiful and glamorous actress. Even before she left the party that evening, she felt more relaxed and sure of herself, more in control of her anger, which that night was the result of yet another insult by Andre, even allowing herself a dance with a notorious womanizer from the Mergers team just to let him know what he would never have.

Her scalp massage was over, the headache momentarily abated, and she admonished herself silently for once more thinking too much about Michael—goodness, was I going to call out his name later tonight when Adam was making love to me?—allowing herself a smile at the silly thought, and when she brought her shoulders up, just like Rita, she was staring into the face of Andre, who had apparently silently sidled up to her desk like a panther.

"Are you still looking for the answer to the wire problems from this morning?" He was practically barking at her like a junkyard dog, drawing attention from all over the office. He wasn't asking so much, as the question was framed like an accusation.

"Yes," she answered turning toward the computer screen, her composure rescued, "I think I found an anomaly here."

"Forget that," he barked again at her, reaching across her body, much too closely in her opinion, taking control of her mouse and wiping her screen clean with a series of point and clicks that she would never be able to follow. "Just stick to what you are told to do and stop trying to be a detective. Stop trying to run the department, know who you are!" His voice boomed over the office again and Laura knew without looking that many eyes were on them. He's very skillfully trying to show I was to blame for this morning's disaster, she realized. His cell phone then chirped and he stalked away without another word, leaving her seething, desiring to put him away for good. "I want to kill him," she said under her breath. She had never held violent thoughts like these about any other human being at any point in her life, but she felt it completely now. "Do you think you could get me the documentation on that procedure you just performed?" she called to him as he turned the corner, phone glued to his head, not expecting an answer or the documentation or an explanation of what she had seen on her screen in the instant before Andre wiped it away. But he wouldn't have heard her if she screamed directly into his ear as Kismine's number appeared in his screen. He answered immediately, "Hello, my dear, how are you?"

"I am not fine at all" she screeched at him in a voice so shrill half the dogs within twenty miles yelped in pain, "That's how I am!" His stomach dropped to his weakening knees, "Wha...What is it? What's wrong?"

"It's apparent to me that what we have been doing isn't working. I hated that guy in the recording studio this morning. I was embarrassed and I felt like a fool!" Her voice rose with each syllable like a Mariah Carey vocal exercise.

"Hold on, baby, we'll get the recording straightened out." He sounded desperate and he knew it. She jumped on his desperation like a lioness on a tired wildebeest. "I want to be on television, I want to be seen in the cafés in Beirut, my homeland. I want to be a star at least there if not in the rest of the Middle East and maybe Europe. I don't care about America. It sucks here and it's cold! I know I can be the Shakira of the Arab world if I had the right manager, someone who knew what he was doing!"

"I can do this for you. Just believe in me and work with me a little bit more." He remembered that he was meeting Fated later and he believed it would be a good idea to introduce to her now before she went over the edge. "Listen, my love, I have someone lined up who can definitely help us. He's..."

"You mean help *me*, don't you?" she interrupted.

"Yes, my dearest flower. I am helping you, that is right...help *you* get on television. Which would help us, too, don't you think?" The desperation dripped from the phone into her ear like a disease and she instinctively held the phone a little further away from her head. She was already far away spiritually from Andre, his weak voice annoying her all night. Instead she was thinking of the young man she met on the Great Lawn in Central Park after the recording session ended who was now washing up, post coital in her bathroom, "Okay, fine, Andre. Call me when you have something figured out," was all he heard along with the sound of running water which confused him...why was she taking a shower in the middle of the day?

Nearby, in the same office, Michael had resumed speaking with Hank Fredericks, wondering if he was keeping the poor bastard trapped there. Well, he does want title business from our company so he can sit around for a few minutes while I ramble on a bit. The fact of the matter was that Michael just didn't want to go home right then and he wasn't interested in walking around the city streets like a zombie. Besides, speaking about the old neighborhood, regaling the guys who were raised in the suburbs or younger yuppie types with tales about how different it was just, oh...about five minutes ago it seemed, but it was really thirty-five years ago, retelling war stories of him and the boys in their youth and their therefore youthful exploits always relaxed him. He found that they were not a little fascinated with some of his *Eastside Comedy*-type upbringing with colorful characters who all sounded like Leo Gorcey.

"We used to dive off the pier by the Pepsi sign in Long Island City during the summer. You had to be able to read the currents and the tides so we would be carried into the next pier, or rock, or anything instead of out into the middle of the river. Just to be sure, we always tied a rope to something heavy on land that we would hold onto so we could pull ourselves back in. Those currents would have swept us up to Hell Gate in a matter of minutes. Mark Spitz times ten couldn't escape that current unless you were incredibly lucky and caught the change of the tide from inbound to outbound. For a few minutes the river would be relatively placid. We always had a rope tied to the bulk-head and we would dive in holding onto the rope with a death grip, but still it was amazing that none of us drowned. We watched these clowns once, bunch of teenagers from the Island probably, they were water skiing in the river and one of them jumps off the front of their eighteen footer and before he comes up for air, the current takes him down river the length of the boat plus another fifteen feet or so before he even comes up for air. At the rate the guy was being pulled by the current, he would have been under the Brooklyn Bridge in about five minutes. His friends didn't know where he went, couldn't find him, and we yelled to them and pointed downstream. They went nuts trying to get the anchor up and get turned around but they finally picked up the guy in the water about a half mile away. We all laughed not aware of how dangerous it all was for the teenagers in the boat. That freaking current is unlike anything in the world."

"The people on the General Slocum found that out the hard way," Hank contributed. The General Slocum was a day steamer taking tourists up the East River to a church picnic in 1904 when fire broke out and hundreds of passengers clothed in the heavy woolen clothes of the time armed with their outrageously substandard life preservers jumped into those currents and were drowned. The burning ship was ultimately beached nearby where the Triboro Bridge would be built over thirty years later, taking over one thousand lives, still to this day it was America's worst maritime disaster. Michael remembered hearing the story from his grandmother about so many lives destroyed that day, several of her friends among the passengers, all the promise gone, the best days for them just ahead, taken away in an instant. Michael always found it difficult to even imagine an early death for himself, an accident on the highway or in the home, death by terrorist assholes like his friends and several mortgage clients, the devastation it would cause his mother, his brother and sister, the utter waste of potential, potential, potential.

"Anyway we always looked out for each other." Me, Elgin Barnes—now J'lome, he's a Muslim Imam now—the Burke brothers, Moose Miller, and of course, Vinny, our de facto leader. He was always the strongest in our group intellectually and physically. Toughest guy I ever met."

"How did he turn out to be your leader?"

"Two reasons. He has the most disciplined mind I have ever seen. He thinks geometrically, studying any and every angle in any situation and always coming up with a solution it would take others weeks to figure out if they did at all. I once joked that he was born in the wrong century, that he should have been arguing philosophy and drawing math equations in the sand with the ancient Greeks. Answers to challenging situations come to him the way women come to a handsome rock star. And so it just happened naturally, as if there was no need for discussion, he just led us without being asked and without taking advantage of any of us. It would have been stupid to disagree because we all knew we were in the presence of great talent. We have been like brothers to one another all these years."

"Where did he go to school again? You told me this part, but I can't remember."

"He never even graduated high school, although I think he eventually got himself a G.E.D. He had a hard life growing up because his old man split, his mom's new man kicked him out of the house with her permission so he wound up sleeping here and there, doing odd jobs to survive, fighting anyone who got in his way or who screwed with us. He studied everything, devouring books on philosophy, logic, business and management schemes and, of course, real estate which he loves. He loves all types of philosophy disciplines and he applied what he read to just about everything he did, everything he dreamed of."

"What was his dream?"

"To create an oasis in Long Island City, by our dock. A place for kids to play, families to live, even a floating rotating beach that he would have anchored off the bulkhead so no one would have to dive into the river the way we did. The rotating part would help everyone to get an even tan."

"What was the second reason?"

"He is quite possibly the most fearsome man you have ever seen. A white Mike Tyson, if you will, and I'm talking about the Tyson who scared his opponents out of the ring before the first round." He and J'lome used to screw around with the low level gangsters who were roughing up the local business owners, shaking them down for small cash...sometimes they would deal weed in front of their stores and apartment buildings and hassle some of the older residents."

"He was a criminal?"

"No, he was an anti-criminal. He did have a year or two where he and J'lome walked the razor's edge, but when J'lome got busted and went away for a few years, he dropped all of that from his life. But he still made sure to let everyone in the neighborhood know that they'd better be careful who they screwed around with." He always hated drugs, there was so much heroin around in those days in Sunnyside, and he especially hated the dealers who worked the neighborhood. Never saw him steal from anyone else or bother anyone else other than the dealers or any junkie who tried to turn one of the younger kids on. When J'lome got busted, Vinny was with him, but he was a faster runner and J'lome never gave him up. The judge tacked on an extra year to his sentence when he found out he beat a guy senseless with a baseball bat the year before but the judge didn't know the guy was a heroin dealer hanging around the park on Forty-Seventh Avenue, trying to get all of the twelve-year-olds to try a sniff in between hand-ball games. Eddie Brown was his name but he was forever known afterward as Eddie Black 'n Blue when J'lome was finished with him.

"He sounds on the surface like a possible menace to society. I guess it depends on your point of view."

"No, quite the opposite. He is intensely loyal to all of us and to anyone who lives in or even comes from the neighborhood, as long as they are doing the right thing. His fearlessness could have been used to incite and inflict violence, but instead he used it ninety-nine percent of the time to educate the mooks that would hang around with a simple message: Leave me and my friends alone, leave the neighborhood alone, and I won't beat you to within an inch of your life. And believe me, people listened to him. He won the lightweight boxing championship put on by some local boxing promoters strictly for guys who lived or grew up in a project. Vinny lived in the boiler room of one of the buildings in the Queensbridge houses for a few months after J'lome went away and I guess that qualified him. Only white guy in the entire tournament and he whipped everyone. He has a trophy in his office with a caption that reads "Toughest White Man" New York

City Projects Boxing Championship. He actually hates the caption but never altered it out of respect for those who gave it to him."

"Why?"

"Because Vinny believes, as we all do, that racism and reacting to anyone because of their race or religion is the true root of all evil in this world."

"And what does J'lome do now?"

"J'lome found God through the Koran in jail and he has the mosque now. He's quite the community leader. He knows how to gather people together. I feel bad because I'm still finding myself occasionally pissed at some of the Muslim community because of 9/11 and other things since, but in my opinion if there's one person who can bring peace to the Middle East, it would be J'lome. As different as our lives are now, I still enjoy seeing him and still consider him my brother."

"It sounds a bit like the Jets and the Sharks from *West Side Story*." Michael scrunched up his face at that one.

"You know, we all hated that movie when we first saw it. We considered it totally lame with all the dancing and singing. We wanted to see some real fighting, hear some rock and roll, but also because the story was based upon racism. Vinny hated that more than anything. We had a diverse group of friends and if he ever heard anyone uttering racist remarks, he would get the glare and a verbal warning to knock it off. There was never a second time allowed to anyone for that lesson. Anyway, J'lome discovered Islam, in jail and opened the People's Mosque with Vinny's help in Astoria. He welcomes any faith, any person, any time. Vinny gave him the building after he refinanced it, and then used those proceeds to buy other buildings in and around Astoria, Long Island City and Sunnyside. The neighborhoods were mostly ignored back then by New York magazine and developers, but they are hot now...his timing couldn't have been better. He made millions on all the sales. He convinced the Burkes to go to trade school to learn plumbing and electrical work. He bought the bread routes at first and put the Burkes in charge of the deliveries so they could earn some dough—no pun intended—while they were in trade school and they kept the routes to this day. The Pepperidge Farm trucks were absolutely the best for skitching."

He had a cafe in Astoria, a pizza place, a couple of bagel shops.

The buildings surrounding J'lome's Mosque on Steinway St. were all at one time owned by Vinny and he sold them to people who wanted to open Muslim-related businesses there, coffee shops, food stores, clothing stores, that sort of thing. He got some shit about this from others in the neighborhood, but he told them all to go fuck themselves. I don't know how he kept it all together in his head but he did, and as a result he helped transform several blocks in several neighborhoods. He collected two- and three-family homes and then small apartment buildings like he was playing Monopoly. But he always had the goal of consolidating it all to build his dream, like Larry Silverstein did when he bought the Trade Center in the summer of 2001. And now I've got to go tell him and the others that this dream may start looking as dead as Elvis, terrific." Michael sighed audibly, running his fingers through his hair, wondering where all of those years he was just describing went. He could remember them like it was yesterday, smell it, almost touch it. He looked at Hank Fredericks and knew he was thinking the same thing, where did all of this time go for all of us and what have we become? We used to be strong, fearless, and we would fight anyone because we firmly believed we would never lose. Now he was scared to death to go face Georgia about not only the lost commission, but about so many other things. His wife and mother to his daughter, how could he be scared of her? Just for speaking his mind? Wasn't he allowed to do that? He pushed his hands onto his thighs in order to help him out of the chair."

"See ya, Hank. I gotta get going...thanks for listening."

"Take care, Michael." Hank Fredericks said as he packed himself up and shook Michael's hand. He then stuck the post-it note he scribbled on earlier on the computer on Michael's desk. "Smile" was all it said.

⁂

The subway ride back to her apartment in Long Island City was at least free of any random touching, men or women accidentally on purpose rubbing up against her on the way in or out of the car, or overtly lecherous stares from any homeless men or Wall Street types. All in all she figured that the disaster portion of her day was over and she was to leave it back in the office. She hadn't spoken again to Andre, who disappeared as he usually did for a good part of the afternoon. Good, she thought at the time...get the hell out of here. Without him skulking around, she was able to finish the remainder of her assignments for the day on time. The usual assortment of rats, delays and filth of the subway was at a minimum for today's return commute. So as a result she was hanging her hopes for a fantastic evening on the basis of this better-than-usual train ride which she had to admit was a little flimsy. Admittedly as well, she was a little put off that Adam wasn't coming to pick her up and she was annoyed with herself for still thinking about...him.

She started to get ready for her evening out almost as soon as she returned to her place. The first thing was a hot shower and shampoo. After she was done washing and in the middle of toweling off, Laura once again appraised herself in the full length mirror on the back of the bathroom door. The hot jets of water had been nice and relaxing to her stiff shoulders and upper back, the pulsating action of the water loosening up the knots caused by what was becoming, unfortunately for her, a normal day. A pat on her butt on the subway in the morning, a problem at work just before noon and a possible hitch in her love life in the early afternoon. She was still harboring a little bit of annoyance at Adam's brusqueness with her today on the phone. But maybe it was nothing. It was possible he was having his own issues at that moment. Everyone has them, she told herself, all different varieties and degrees of problems and issues, big and small, mildly annoying and life threatening. So it was probably nothing, she shouldn't allow it to bother her.

She looked again in the mirror and, setting aside her disdain for vanity, admired for a moment the image that looked back at her. The flat stomach, the muscular curve of her quadriceps, her taut biceps. She had little use for physical beauty; many times she thought that she would have been better off had she been five inches shorter and thirty pounds heavier, but she wouldn't deny that she enjoyed the fact that into her early forties, she had a figure and looks that could attract a man half her age. "A lot of good it did me, however," she said aloud. She only had a handful of boyfriends in all that time. She was aware of her inner passions, her fantasies, the way she needed to be touched and held, but had mostly never played them out, never even spoke about them during the fun, rousing discussions she had with the other Latina women she met in her early days in the United States. She had to be honest with herself about the fact that no man had ever managed to touch her in quite the correct way, although some did come close and would have lit her up if they were a little more patient, so that a perfectly natural connection could be made. There were certainly plenty of fun moments to look back on in the early autumn of her life, several of them a whole lot of fun, good vacations, fun parties, but never had she felt a real primal urge for any one man. Her orgasms were mostly manufactured by her own manipulation of her clitoris during lovemaking, never having had a penis deliver that feeling for her while she laid back like Cleopatra, hands behind her head... Do it that way please, she figured the Queen of Egypt would have commanded. Most of the men she had known intimately were strangely repelled when she reached for herself during lovemaking. They seemed almost insulted that she wasn't relying totally on their own equipment and prowess. She didn't bother to explain to them that not only did they not know what they were doing—at least with her—with their dicks, but maybe if they told some jokes or a nice story beforehand, just say something, anything that would pull her toward them. Not looks, not money or power, not some perfect physique, but a certain... something that would reach into her soul. Diego was the only one who was ever able to do that.

"No necessitamos parables," he said one day while they laid on a blanket under a beautiful summer sky, looking for shapes in the clouds. "We don't need words." And it was true. They enjoyed each other's company so much that they could go for hours without any words between them. She always remembered her response, "No one can do what we can." She truly believed, and so did he, that there was no other couple in the world like them. She rubbed her hair vigorously with the towel and told herself to be through with that nonsense. I am forty-two years old, and I am twenty-five years removed from that day, I haven't been held properly but maybe once in so long and tonight that is going to end with Adam. I hope he knows what he is doing, she thought, and the fears starting to gather again. She was annoyed once again, these sort of emotions coming to her a little more frequently these days, that Adam wasn't picking her up, that she had to take the subway into the city in a dress and high heels. That would mean much unwanted attention from her fellow subway riders. Maybe one day she and some other women would band together and beat the hell out of some of these men who lose all sense of propriety once they step into a subway car. Her annoyance level shot up again when some synapse in her brain she would love to strangle so it would stop repeatedly pinging her with unwanted information once again suggested that Michael Pierce would have picked her up at her house and would have probably stood outside the car holding the door for her. She concluded this latest silent scenario by toweling the remaining water from her thick black hair, hanging the towel carefully on the rack and slipping into a lacy pair of black panties and bra. She decided on a pair of sleek black pants instead of a dress, high heels and necklace of colorful stones she found in a Tibetan knickknack store in the East Village and a violet sweater. She would wear her black top coat which was light enough to move around easily enough in but would help her ward off any chill in the weather that may come up later. He doesn't get the black dress and pearls she knew she looked fantastic in. Not yet, he hasn't earned it.

ـﷲﷻ

Whathefu looked around with ill-concealed disdain at the somewhat dingy neighborhood on Steinway Street. He could see the towers of Manhattan down the east/west avenues just a mile or so away. He felt their pull like an iron filing to a magnet as Aubrey turned into the larger two way street replacing his view with cheap-looking but busy stores. He could see some Middle Eastern dress shops and cafés with Arabic lettering on the windows. He marveled at how these people could start such a business in America or any other foreign country and felt a twinge of envy that they could somehow make it work. They pulled into a metered parking spot across from the building that housed the People's Mosque, whatever that meant. Mosques were typically given a broad scope for what name they were to be called, mostly dealing with the person who built the mosque, the city it was located in or after an Islamic scholar. Whathefu found it interesting, "The People's Mosque." Maybe there was a solution of some sort here, in the form of a back window he could slip out of and into an alleyway through which he could escape. This guy watching him probably didn't know

New York as well as he did. As beautiful as this man is, Whathefu had to admit to himself, and as much as the personal confusion he felt was making him think sexually about Aubrey, wondering what it was like to maybe blow him in the car on the highway earlier, he knew he had to get away from him. He couldn't think of overpowering him; escape was the only answer.

"Let's go," Aubrey brusquely announced once he pulled the car close to the curb and shut the engine off. They crossed Steinway Street after depositing a dollar's worth of quarters for an hour's worth of parking in the meter, heading for the golden double doors when they came upon an argument between a couple of Pakistanis, one in a dark colored shalwar kameez, the other in a leather jacket and jeans topped off by a black Jinnah Cap, and a strange-looking guy in a bin Laden t-shirt and skullcap, who Aubrey thought looked Jewish. They paused and listened to the argument just as the Pakistani men were telling the other guy to get lost.

Rob Berg al-Amin was incensed with these two, arguing about baseball in front of the mosque, so close to prayer time. He didn't mind the imbroglios he stirred every day in front of mosques around the city as he had suffered through some of the worst family clashes in New York. Imagine a Jew from Bayside Queens denouncing his faith and culture... many of his relatives having spent time in the camps in Poland...the arguments were profound and loud and they tore the family apart. He compounded his problem of having not a single person in the city on his side by openly proselytizing on the streets in front of the mosques, enraging the patrons and the Imams as well the local cops who had to save him from what he considered to be his, well, own people. But he kept at it like so many other strange beings in every city in every country, oblivious to everything except their own manic drive to be the next Moses, Jesus, Gandhi, or Jim Bakker.

"Please explain to me and every Muslim man how you two could be talking in earnest about some pampered athlete just before evening prayers," he shrieked at the two men.

"Because it is indeed *before*, you asshole, not during prayers, that is why we are talking now," answered the younger, tough looking one in the leather jacket.

"And also because we like to discuss these sports, my friend," the older man chimed in. "Maybe the Prophet was an athlete in his early life. Did you ever think of that? What is wrong with sports? Active participation in them keeps a body healthy and the mind refreshed, does it not?"

Whathefu's chaperone had taken all of this exchange in as they approached the door to the mosque and his ire was being slowly raised by the idea of the Prophet Muhammad entering these talks. It was important for him to be invisible for the next few days but for one, he was on an anonymous street in New York where he didn't know anyone and vice versa and two, he didn't care where he was or who was around if the Prophet's name was being taken in vain. As far as he was concerned, this conversation had now gone over the line. He stepped right up to the two men pulling his prisoner with him and ignoring Berg al-Amin.

"Is it wise to speculate on the life of the Prophet in this way? To try to compare him to a shortstop?" He stood there with Whathefu at his side. The question was delivered with cool detachment and with a voice that seemed to come from the bottom of a tomb. It said that any attempt at an answer might result in something that involved more than just words. It wasn't a question he wanted answered but instead was merely used as a threat. Whathefu watched him carefully during this exchange, very impressed with his self confidence and becoming more and more appreciative of his height and his obviously very athletic and strong body. His crazy fantasies started to take him away again, entering his mind as they usually did without warning or reason or any real stimulation, picturing Aubrey on his father's boat in a tiny thong, tanned and magnificent, but he squashed them immediately reminding himself that he had to develop a hegira of sorts some time soon.

The two Pakistanis and Rob Berg al Amin looked quizzically at the tall, blue-eyed stranger with the southern accent as he interrupted their argument. "Hey country," the younger one said, "Mind your own business, okay?" He turned back to his friend and jerked his thumb at the two interlopers. "Just another clown from out of town who thinks they know the way of this city five minutes after their arrival." He turned back to Aubrey, whom he almost matched in height, and snarled, "Fuck off country. Please go fuck yourself with a dry splintery pole as quickly as possible and don't ever talk to me about what you think you know about my faith."

The movement by Aubrey was lightning quick. He was like one of those actors in movies out of Hollywood lately that are shot mostly with a hand-held camera, Whathefu thought, those that keep the viewer somewhat off stride, a dim of colors and shapes. Just then, a certain car with a harbor patrol cop driving was attempting a U-turn to continue to watch the two from the airport from across the street, but he was blocked by a huge SUV with Jersey plates.

The younger Pakistani found himself up against the wall of the mosque, suspended under the armpits, unable to move, the terror working its way from his toes northward, astounded at losing the sensation of the ground through his soles as he was pinned securely to the wall. The shame he was feeling at that moment because of his impotence at being subdued so easily and publicly was then trumped by the pain in his head after Aubrey banged him against the wall as if he were beating a rug free of dust. Aubrey was now shouting at him, not caring who heard, "Don't ever speak to me again with those filthy words and don't ever, ever link the teachings of the Prophet to this decadent, undeserving society in any way, ever!" He was positively roaring, attracting stares from a few passersby on Steinway Street. The tall Pakistani and his friend were astonished at the quickness and the level of the violence, Rob Berg al Amin was thinking of prostrating himself in genuflection, wanting to worship at the knee of this obviously dedicated, odd-looking Muslim brother and Whathefu was thinking again about being on the boat with Aubrey, coming to the conclusion that maybe it wouldn't be bad if he was killed on his mission for the seventeen million dollars by this man because he didn't have the slightest idea what defined him anymore. Charlie Mick, standing about fifteen feet away, took it all in as well but remained where he was because that was what Vinny told him to do.

J'lome was alarmed at the loud thumps and angry voices outside the door of the mosque. He knew there were problems here and there around the city with its Muslim civilians subjected to random shouting matches and slurs from mostly young drunk men stretching their patriotism and their balls as far as they could go. He quickly ended his call with the local CYO official with whom he was discussing starting a new basketball league for middle school kids as well as some other charity work they might be able to get involved together with. The Catholics, he realized, as he moved swiftly from behind his desk, knew how to do charity. He pulled open the front door to his mosque and was shocked and angered at what he saw. "What is this? Put him down and stop this desecration of this house of God." He was calm and controlled but on the edge of the abyss of really losing his temper. He knew, his street smarts told him instantly, that there was no discussion here and now with this big guy, that whatever it is that started this fracas had to be put down instantly. There were many lessons he learned long before the first time he cracked a Koran and they came from places like the Queensbridge Houses, Bushwick and Dannemora. Plus, the surge of confidence he felt every time he read his Koran and wore the vestments and lead the prayers would lift him past any man. It also didn't hurt that he noticed Charlie Mick, all six-foot-five of him watching from about fifteen feet away. What was he doing there? Didn't he leave with Vinny earlier? he wondered. He addressed Aubrey directly as the Pakistani was being lowered slowly to the sidewalk, "You are not a member of this mosque and you will never be one if you conduct yourself in this manner against anyone in this mosque and the surrounding community. The surrounding community being, in my view, everywhere in this beautiful world Allah has created for us. This is not the way to settle conflicts."

Aubrey stared at J'lome in an appraising way. He saw strength of purpose in this man and some physical toughness he picked up somewhere along the line. Could he be ex-military? Or maybe just a jailhouse Muslim thug. If he wanted to, Aubrey believed, he could crush him in an instant but he didn't need the further attention. He had already blundered twice, first by letting this Pakistani fool get to him so easily, next by drawing attention to himself unnecessarily. He released the man from his grip once he settled him back on the ground and straightened out his jacket, the glare of absolute menace and hatred never completely leaving his face. Aubrey spoke to J'lome as the young man cupped the back of his head with his hand feeling the warmth of the blood dripping on his collar. "I'm sorry, Imam. Please accept my apology," Aubrey said as he moved toward the door, now being held open by Andre and Fated, who arrived in the last seconds of the fracas. He smiled thinly at Andre, "Thank you, brother," and he strolled into the People's Mosque with Whathefu at his side.

J'lome's eyes followed them into his mosque, surprised to see Andre and Fated, casual attendees at the mosque, J'lome knowing that thought was generous. Strange that they were there right as this was going down. A coincidence…or…probably nothing. Is the big guy Muslim? He focused his mind on not acknowledging his appearance, instead deciding to watch him once he was back inside the mosque. "Good to see you both again," he said to the two men, "Hurry along, the drama is over." He paused at the door addressing the two Pakistanis sternly, "The language you were using is unacceptable in the world of educated men. Once you introduce it into a conversation, you lose. Please remember that."

"The man lowered his head as a show of reverence and acceptance and said, "Yes, Imam. We are sorry." J'lome waved them inside and then addressed Bob Berg al Amin. "If you are here to join us for prayers, come in now and conduct yourself accordingly. If you don't, I will have you removed and arrested. Try to learn something by listening. That is why Allah in his wisdom gave you two ears and only one mouth." J'lome cocked his head a bit to the side. "Wouldn't you agree, my friend?"

Bob Berg al Amin responded instead in disgust, "This place is for infidels and whatever you practice behind those doors is not Islam!" he roared, waving his arm across the expanse of the building's facade. "People's Mosque, what is that?" And then he added, "I can stand here as long as I want and speak about anything I wish because those are my constitutional rights." J'lome started to turn away halfway through the tirade when he surreptitiously signaled Charlie Mick and made a V sign and then brought his thumb and forefinger to his ear. The SUV finally moved out of the way, allowing the U-turner to complete his maneuver, angry that he lost his subjects for a moment before he thankfully picked them up again entering the mosque. Charlie Mick nodded ever so imperceptibly, knowing that J'lome was asking him to call Vinny and to get him here right away. This fucking clown in the army jacket, Charlie Mick was thinking…J'lome could probably swat him like a fly but he wasn't worth his time what with everything he has to do in a typical day, and he certainly would not allow the armor of his dignity to be even scratched by some like al-Amin. He recalled his Dad talking about J'lome from years before, when he was still alive. "You can always trust him, my son, he has a pure heart. And because you are my son, he automatically loves you as if you were his. Always remember that." No, it was the tall blond guy that was the real problem, he and his little buddy. They didn't belong, he knew somehow. Everything about them was wrong, why they were together, why they were here, all of it. He pulled his phone out of his pocket and dialed Vinny who was at that moment staring out over the East River at his dream project, wondering if it was possibly stalled forever.

⟶⟵

Vinny could feel the phone vibrating in the inside pocket of his jacket but he ignored it. How the hell was the Empire State Building put up so quickly without the benefit of cell phones, computers, and e-mail? He recalled the first time he received a vibrating page on a beeper he had clipped to his belt. He thought it was an amazing piece of technology. He continued to stare at the lot and the Pepsi sign with equal feelings of frustration and desire much like an older man in love with a young girl who would never return his affections. His mind was working furiously to solve his problem, although anyone who looked at him now while passing by would conclude that he was in a fog, thinking of nothing in particular. That damn Preservation Society, what was their problem? Their obvious indignation at his mere presence in their fancy conference room and their snottiness was overwhelming. What assholes, living off interest accumulated on top of interest from trust funds established by their grandfathers, men who actually did something. If those same men were here right now, they would side with me, Vinny knew. At least they accomplished something, created something of worth.

He thought of the lady at the meeting, Maxie Carter. There was something in her posture earlier today at the meeting that suggested she understood where he was coming from, that this was not just a pile of unattainable dreams, he was sure of it. The way she was studying the plans, the simple questions she asked, the apparent marginalization of her by the other two. Did she truly understand that five hundred jobs were on the line as well as the personal fortunes of many people including all of his friends? Or was she just another society girl, pampered to the extreme and looking for something to do during the day to control her boredom? Maybe she wasn't so far removed from a life in the tenements, in some crappy neighborhood that was filled with despair, from understanding the human condition of always wanting to strive for something more, something better. That's what motivated Columbus, Magellan and Armstrong to reach way beyond the borders of their countries, their planet, and especially their minds.

And the banks, the damn banks bushwacking Mikey, my friend, ambushing him with this cowardly threat to cave in to the Preservation Society. Unbelievable. Fucking banks, there was not an adventurous, entrepreneurial spirit anywhere within their walls. It reminded him of some grass roots organization turning companies, dreams and progress on its collective head just because they have fancy stationary and someone on staff who can construct and knit together a few coherent sentences like those clowns who tried to get the FCC to ban someone's radio show. Meanwhile they had maybe a few hundred members, most of whom were professional gadflies, mostly just consumed by jealousy of the success others had attained. The drone of the cars on the FDR Drive below was lulling him to sleep and his head started to droop a bit. He started at a voice that floated out of nowhere...how did someone get so close to him without his knowledge? "Mr. Malloy, are you trying to will the pier into the water?" He turned and found himself staring at Maxie Carter. She was more casually dressed than this morning, in a pair of black jeans, a burgundy sweater, and a patterned jacket with some kind of fur on the sleeves which Vinny deduced was real. She looked quite cute in her casual clothes and Vinny suspected that with her pageboy bob, trim figure, complete with an intelligent sparkle in her eyes, she would look great in anything. She pulled the coat around her in response to a stiff breeze off the river.

"You look like you are trying to talk the Pepsi sign into dismantling itself," she said to him. She was smiling still but Vinny was not. She was surprised to find herself thrilled to meet him by chance like this, and he in fact, unbeknownst to her was working overtime to contain his composure. She found him attractive mostly because of his roughness around the edges, the way she remembered her grandfather. His blue eyes, fit physique, obvious intelligence and drive combined with an undefinable feeling of personal safety when he was near also didn't hurt. Her father also had a keen innate intelligence and the ability to marshal others to his way of thinking. He was able to turn dust into gold as a result, and she could never remember a time when he raised his voice to do so.

"No, just thinking about a million things," he answered evenly and politely. He reminded himself that she couldn't read his mind and therefore shouldn't be held accountable for smiling in the middle of his semi-malevolent brooding. "I don't have much formal education, but I have always been able to see a problem or situation more clearly if I just sit with it quietly for a spell. And sometimes that just means staring at it for a while."

"That's how I dealt with a calculus problem in college. I felt if I eagle-eyed it for long enough, it would finally make sense to me," she answered somehow expecting this statement to solidify her bonafides with him.

"Exactly" Vinny quickly agreed, if you don't have some sort of inner discipline, all the Harvard degrees won't do you a bit of good."

"Just how did you acquire so much discipline? I read your curriculum vitae and your business accomplishments are quite impressive. Do you mind if I sit down?" She had settled on the other end of the bench about a second after the last word left her mouth, clearly not interested in his answer. Her interest in this man was growing geometrically. It wasn't only the powerful set of his shoulders and his sleepy look, little crinkles permanently affixed around his eyes indicating wisdom and experience, not tiredness. It was something else she couldn't quite articulate clearly. But she knew there was something compelling about him for her. He turned away when he answered in a profoundly succinct and slightly admonishing tone, "Hunger." He turned toward her now, amplifying his remarks, "Not only the type of hunger as when your mother feeds you a bowl of apple sauce and Fruit Loops for dinner because that is the best she can do and the check doesn't come until next week. Not only a physical hunger, Ms. Carter..."

"Maxie."

"...Maxie, but a metaphysical one as well. It propels many men and women to strive for something better. That is a realization that not many people on this side of the East River understand, remember, or ever knew." He turned away from the river and his building project and leaned back against the top rail of the bench, trying to use it as a fulcrum to crack a few bones in his back which might deaden the ache there. "There are not many men, and I mean adults, who were able to best me in a fight from when I was sixteen, but I learned soon after that real power was to be found in words. Used skillfully, with good timing, the correct words and phrases delivered with supreme confidence could set any college boy down faster than a straight right hand to the jaw." He smiled at her, not yet aware that he was melting her like a skinny candle on a birthday cake. "It also hurts a lot less."

She laughed and was then mortified when her stomach turned over quite audibly. He joined her laugh, inquiring, "Did something escape from the zoo?" For that humorous comment he was treated to a pair of pursed lips and a playful smack on the shoulder. "Why don't you join me for dinner?" he asked and she answered with no hesitation at all. "Yes, where should we go?"

"I know a place downtown we could go to, do you like Vietnamese food?"

"I never really tried it, but I will now. Is it a fancy place?" She detested the overpriced restaurants her husband and his friends favored.

"It's definitely a nice place, but the people there are great, not too many tourists and we can probably get a corner seat even without a reservation. Come on, I guarantee you'll like this place. My car is over here." They stood together and moved over toward his Suburban when he felt his phone vibrating again. Glancing at the screen, he saw it was Charlie Mick, whom he had almost forgotten about. He'd better have something to say if he was going to interrupt him at this moment. He opened the passenger door and held it until Maxie got settled in and clicked the phone on when he closed the door after her. "Hello, what's up?" Or in other words, get to the fucking point, kid.

"Vinny, sorry to bother you, but I think J'lome needs you."

"Now?" he asked, glancing at his watch. It can't be now, he concluded, because it's prayer time. "What's going on? Come on, get it out," he said with a little more urgency in his voice. He stood outside the driver's door, his hand on the handle but he hadn't opened it yet.

Maxie was watching him now from inside. He wanted to know every-thing Charlie Mick had to say before his ass hit the driver's seat.

"Right, well...prayer time seemed as if it were about to start and J'lome had to get between some guys outside the mosque." Even Maxie, who had known Vinny for all of fifteen minutes was able to see the change in his face, in his voice. Playful to serious in an instant, like her father. "Tell me quickly, without breathing, exactly what happened." He opened the door and glanced at Maxie, who smiled in return. "Sorry, this will be done before we get downtown." She waved him off with the universal sign of 'Don't be ridiculous, do what you have to do.' Charlie Mick then recounted everything about the Pakistani duo arguing about something he couldn't overhear, the appearance of Bob Berg al-Amin and his rantings, and then the scrawny Arab guy and the big blond bastard who looked like a movie star, who he thought was going to kill one of the guys arguing outside the mosque, and the two sleazy looking guys who came upon the scene afterward, but they may have just been innocent bystanders, who entered the mosque at the same time J'lome quelled everything and brought some order.

"Vin, I wouldn't have called if he didn't signal me."

"Where were you standing when all this was happening?"

"Exactly where you left me." He added," I was ringside for the whole thing. Happened in a flash and I gotta tell you, Vin, these people didn't look like they belonged, it's just my feeling. Not a racial thing, I'm sorry about that this morning...this is the real thing, my spider-sense is telling me these people, the big bastard and his little buddy, are no good. And they're all in J'lome's place right now."

After about 1.5 seconds of thought, Vinny told him, "Stay there, do not speak with anyone, including J'lome. Listen to everything that is said and follow the blond guy and his friend if he comes out. I want to know everything they do, what they are wearing, driving, eating, everything, understand?"

"Yes."

"Hail a cab now and tell the cabbie to wait with the meter on. Tell him he has a fifty dollar tip coming when he drops you off. Do not move from there until you see them come out."

"Okay, I got it."

"CM"?

"Yeah?"

"Do this right and this morning is forgotten." He was about to sign off when he thought to ask, "This guy was blond and big you say?" He was remembering what Moose told him earlier about his surveillance.

"Yes, blue-eyed, blond and very fit and strong. He lifted this guy and pinned him against the wall like he was a rag doll."

"Okay, thanks...don't forget what I told you." He clicked the phone off and turned to Maxie, "Sorry, but I believe it's best to deal with things right as they come up."

"I agree," she answered, "Otherwise they just accumulate and start to stink." She smiled and he smiled in return. He turned the engine over and headed west on Fifty-Third Street and he fiddled with the radio to find something nice to listen to, finally settling on a station that was in the middle of a Motown marathon. He just caught the end of Smokey Robinson's "Tears of a Clown" and now the deejay was segueing into the Four Tops, thankfully not talking up the musical intro of the song. Vinny started to sing softly, "Sugar pie, honey bunch," and looked over at Maxie again out of the corner of his eye, who was bopping her head slightly to the great sounds. He had to admit to himself as he crossed First Avenue that he liked how he felt when she smiled. Amazingly, the street was clear of slow drivers from Jersey, trucks, stopped cabbies jutting out in the next lane as they dropped off or picked up passengers and he was able to catch the light before it turned red. He made a left down Second Avenue, settling into the middle of the road to avoid any gridlock overspill or bicyclists who were becoming more manic as time went on. He stared down Second Avenue as far as he could see and all the lights were green. That has to be a good sign, he considered, but of what? Is he going to be lucky in love or is he going to get a call from Michael any minute informing him that everything is going to be fine with his financing? Something just still might come together naturally, he was hoping against hope as he continued downtown. So there, his decision was made. He was just going to enjoy dinner with this lady. Evening prayers and J'lome's lesson and discussions with the congregation typically ran ninety minutes or so and he planned on being there at the mosque when the first of the faithful were leaving. His stomach growled and she quipped,

"Maybe the zoo lost a couple of lions tonight." They both laughed and he sped up a bit down the avenue.

—※—

Michael turned off the Long Island Expressway about an hour outside of the city into the town of Cuchino which he always thought was a name better suited for somewhere in California rather than Long Island. He would have preferred one of the old Native American names that dot the Nassau and Suffolk county map like Montauk, Sagaponack or Massapequa to this place. He would have preferred someplace about forty minutes closer to the city and where they both grew up. The taxes were much lower and Sally could have attended the Catholic schools if the local Gangster Vocational High School was too much to deal with. But no, after very little discussion, it had to be Cuchino for some reason when he and Georgia set out to buy a house six years earlier. He started to navigate the twisting turns of their neighborhood, longing for the grid format of laying out streets.

Forty miles east of the city and ten miles north of the Long Island Expressway, hardly out in the boondocks and yet he felt totally isolated. For most of the ride home he had the cruise control set at sixty-two miles per hour and still most of the other cars on the expressway were passing him like he was standing still. Once again he recalled the events of the morning and afternoon and he said aloud as if someone were in the car listening, which he and probably everyone else liked to do but would never admit, "I have no interest in dying in a car accident. If I am going to depart this world at this age, I need it to be for something noble and grand. At the very least halfway worthwhile."

He needed this humor injection because he knew what he was going to face when he arrived at the house. He and his wife were barely tolerating each other these days. Last week, at yet another fancy dinner party he had zero interest in attending, he finally just let it all hang out in the face of some pseudo-intellectuals that were trying to measure him, to pigeonhole him. He probably shouldn't have done it, definitely should have done so more gently, but he had decided that if he had to give up his time for something Georgia absolutely knew he was going to hate, well he might as well just be his Irish self and enjoy a good lively discussion. The Greek school that Sally was attending was getting on his nerves, and their very independent-minded daughter was starting to flex her vocal and intellectual muscle, constantly complaining about the extra studies, but Georgia wasn't hearing any of it. None of what they are teaching her could help her in business some day," he told her time and time again, but he was not reaching her, not even chinking her armor.

"It is good exercise for her brain and it will make my family happy," she usually retorted.

"But does it have to be Greek? A language with a different alphabet? I mean, even if we lived in Astoria, it wouldn't help you as much as it would have fifty years earlier. And how about her, Georgia? Have you considered her feelings at all? She clearly hates the new school and it will start affecting other areas of her life as well if it keeps up like this." Yeah he thought, as in how much our own kid hates us. He could see his beautiful daughter at eighteen, with piercings, tattoos, orange hair and attitude all over her, living in the East Village with some loser boyfriend ten years her senior. He didn't know how to deal with his daughter hating her mother; that wasn't in any manual for child rearing that he had heard of. Sure, he was ready for the trials and tribulations of parenting, but not for the knock downs and drag outs that were becoming an all too frequent part of their evenings. "And please try starting to consider what might make me happy. I don't like having to get in between the two of you as much as I have had to lately." As in most of the past two years.

But it was her loopy new NPR-listening friends who embraced all things progressively liberal no matter how bizarre that drove him especially nuts. Michael was a registered Democrat and would always be, but he was a Robert Kennedy Democrat, not a Michael Moore Democrat. These people were in the habit of jumping on any bandwagon they could if it were anti-capitalism, anti-Republican, anti-American, or anti-regular-white-guy regardless of any pertinent facts or someone else's learned and/or earnest opinion on the subject. Rational political and social discourse was an alien concept to them.

And so, as he privately predicted, a few recent dinner parties sent Michael over the edge where good relationship sense nosedived into the abyss of on the couch sleeping, no sex, perpetually wearing of pained 'but what did I do?' expressions, in other words, matrimonial hell. But he didn't care anymore, he just had to speak his mind. These people were not his friends nor would they ever be and frankly they were not Georgia's either in his opinion and he had long given up on trying to understand why she didn't see that as clearly as he did. She was also born and raised in western Queens, and should have been able to mark these types as soon as she came within twenty feet of them. Ideally, Michael and Georgia would have gotten a few laughs out of their ultra snottiness, the intolerance of their beliefs. But that wasn't the case as she seemed to be joining them the way a wayward son joins the Hare Krishnas.

Anyway these pseudo-intellectuals, these sycophants were just asking for it too much and Michael believed they knew and enjoyed what they were doing. He felt like that little white rat Ernest Borgnine skewered with the sharp stick in Willard. They wanted to argue exclusively, with someone, anyone, as civilized discourse seemed to be permanently off their list of things to do along with the aforementioned rational kind. They had picked on him from the first get together and now he decided to take out his inner Philistine and finally oblige all of them who dared venture further with him.

"What did you really think of Clinton and the Lewinsky girl?" This question was asked by some guy with a whisk-broom mustache in a cheap suit while lighting a pipe, an intellectual poser if Michael had ever seen one. They had been going back and forth for a half hour, back and forth over this issue that was dead one and a half presidents ago. Why were they discussing it now? Maybe to justify their own affairs? Michael wondered. They were all down on Monica and totally up on Bill. As if the guy was some fucking saint for banging a young girl, playing Svengali in his own wife's house. Michael was no priest, but there was a line somewhere with any issue. The guy with the pipe probably would have given the ex-President a blowjob if he happened into the room. Why was he asking him this question? What could he possibly offer that was new and relevant considering these events happened over ten years ago? Michael took it upon himself to conclude that the guy was screwing with him. So he answered accordingly. But before he did, Michael looked around the room and saw that virtually everyone was looking at him. It was a set-up question, to make him look foolish. He knew it then and there. Fine, I'll give them my uncensored opinion if that's what they want.

"Well, if I were the President of the United States" he began, "I would have been able to get a better looking girl." He loved the line... perfect deadpan delivery, the smirking cheap suit nearly swallowing his pipe expecting to hear Michael go off on some type of evangelical morality tale, but hearing this response instead. The other guests either frowned or turned away rolling their eyes at the Neanderthal in their presence, Georgia positively glaring at him.

The next one was worse, just two nights later. The same kind of crowd, some of the same population from the Lewinsky/Clinton debate overlapping with this one. At least the subject of this party was more timely. They were all going on about global warming, carbon footprints, how humans are destroying the planet, America's refusal to sign the Kyoto Protocol, and so on. Michael was a man who clearly remembered the air around the city clogged with chemicals, fire burning incinerators in every apartment building adding up to a daily thick miasma that hung over the city. He remembered the headaches he would get inhaling the exhaust of the cars, trucks, and buses using leaded gasoline. He remembered the garbage in the Hudson River, the disappearance of the snappers from Reynolds Channel out near Long Beach where he and his beach friends used to fish off the pier at Bay Lot. He remembered the clams on the beach, hundreds of them just waiting to be scooped out of the mud at the shoreline, all also disappeared now. He recalled the stench from the Wrigley factory in Long Island City reaching into the deepest recesses of his olfactory system.

The environmental movement of the late sixties and early seventies remedied all of these injustices to the planet and he would be ever thankful for their efforts. But the global warming campaign was never one he could get behind. He clearly recalled discussions about global *cooling* during the seventies. How could it change so quickly? This was a five-billion-year-old celestial body we are talking about. How could we know anything about the climate patterns when we only had a little more than one hundred years of data? It just didn't make sense to him, although he did think the warming trends and shrinking glaciers needed to be studied further and he also believed that living green was a good idea. And furthermore, he couldn't understand why solar power still wasn't a part of every American household as he seemed to remember that NASA had a couple of their astronauts tool around on the surface of the freaking moon in a car that ran on solar power.

Anyway, many of the guests at this gathering were almost hysterical with fear, spouting cataclysmic scenarios about the future of the Earth, polar bears, and probably their oceanfront property, although that wasn't mentioned. Michael just couldn't quite stifle a groan at yet another slew of doomsday predictions. And in a room filled with people all having conversations at once, somehow his barely audible displeasure reached everyone's ears like a loud wet fart brought on by a broccoli and mayonnaise sandwich. It was an amazing moment, Michael recalled, because the entire room seemed to focus on him right at that moment. It reminded him of those old commercials where everyone in a room buzzing with conversation all of a sudden leaned in to hear some secret stock tip. They were indubitably astounded that a single note of doubt about their passion had crept into their world. Michael was feeling set up again and then it happened. A short woman, who was wearing a pair of army boots and a spiky pink hairdo, walked right up to his face holding a large photograph of a polar bear standing on an ice floe about twenty feet by twenty feet. In the photo the polar bear looked to be peering thoughtfully into the water. The woman held the photo at the corners between her index finger and thumb, her other fingers held straight out, reminding Michael of one of those lizards with the cowl that would fan out when annoyed.

"Tell me what you think of this," she shrieked, the photo inches from Michael's nose. It was all he could do not to punch the host of this affair—a ridiculously tall and handsome asshole—in the face because he was the real problem here. He had always felt looked down upon by Georgia's friends and this guy in particular—he didn't know his name because he never offered it or a handshake to Michael—and Georgia, to his annoyance, kept up numerous fifteen-minute conversations with this guy, often leaving Michael standing there like a chauffeur, and this particular clown seemed guilty of planning these types of traps for him. He struggled to keep his composure and answered the army boots, "Well maybe this bear is trying out a new way to hunt seals. Did you ever think of that?" The question was not meant to be rhetorical and it was delivered a touch louder than the hunting comment. He wanted to provoke her now, just take the bait. Please, please, he begged the gods of social behavior.

"This bear is obviously floating away on a piece of the polar ice cap that has broken away! And that is due to your Republican friends rejecting every piece of environmental legislation brought before them. The combustion engine was never necessary to our culture and it is clearly the worst invention of all time." This she said in a 'pronunciamento' sort of tone. Not to be questioned. But that wasn't going to happen here as Michael just threw the last of his social decorum out the window.

He started by asking, "How do you know what is beyond the borders of this photo, hmmm?" No stopping him now. The woman started to back away a bit, looking left and right for support. He continued, following her slow retreat, "Maybe this ice floe is only a few yards away from the edge of a glacier that consists of thousands of square miles. Unless of course you believe every photo you see only within the context of what you believe. And why do you care so much about the polar bear? I agree it's a magnificent animal, but if you also believe in Darwinism and basic evolutionary theory, if the bear can't find something to eat then it will just die off like any other species that can't hack it. There have been thousands of species that have died away in our lifetimes and probably close to the same amount that have also been discovered. But all you want to talk about is this stupid bear on an ice floe because it is a beautiful animal. What about the echidna and the effect on global warming on its natural habitat? Do you care as much about an ugly animal" He figured that was enough at least on the Georgia scale. He knew he was dead with her again as he watched her disengage from her knot of friends, now heading in his direction with her furrowed brow leading the way. Friends. What the fuck do these people know about real friends? he thought, as he remembered the boys and all they shared for so many years. Oh well, he was finished with this pink hairdo anyway. He was about to turn away when it spoke again.

"Global warming will kill us all within the next century, I can guarantee you that," the woman said with much finality. Michael was ready for her again, a little embarrassed at himself for purposely prolonging this argument but he was like a drunk heading directly into nonsenseville after a few shots topped off by a few beers before dinner.

"All that can be guaranteed by the likes of you is a lot of fear. Try to remember what Roosevelt, he was or maybe still is a darling of the Democratic Party, isn't he? Try to remember what he said during World War Two before he sent over one hundred thousand Japanese American citizens into containment camps for a purely racial reason, something about fear...it's a good way to live. You people don't seem to want to embrace that, however, because you are indeed fear mongers, nothing more. I consider most of you to be intellectual morons. Your theories about the Himalayan Glaciers disappearing within the next thirty-five years, that it would never snow in England again, that the farmlands of California would dry up and blow away. Meanwhile the glacier report was totally debunked, there's ten inches of snow in Piccadilly, and California is in the middle of a flood. And by the way, the population of polar bears has been increasing at the rate of five times their population in the 1960s. You have global warming alarmists screeching about how we are going to be able to surf the ocean swells in Iowa, but these same people were talking about a coming ice age just thirty years before. It's always conspiracy time with you people. Do you think Bush brought down the towers as well?" His adversary stepped up to him at that comment and he could feel the growing presence of a crowd as if they were in a Jersey Shore bar, waiting for the first punch to be thrown. He had to admit, upon reflection later, that he loved it.

"I have no doubt that not only did the government place explosives strategically throughout the World Trade Center..."

"You're nuts," Michael interrupted her. Georgia was now at the side of the pink-haired woman, facing him down—not her husband's side—his hands waving in the air in frustration. He wanted at that precise moment to be very alone, with a Met game on the TV and a Mozart string and oboe arrangement on the stereo, a tumbler of Jameson in his hand.

"...but also that every Jew that worked there received a call the night before warning them to stay away from their offices." Her anti-Semitic comment caught him by surprise and he was filled to the brim with loathing by the seemingly lack of horror on the faces of the other guests, all of whom by now were circling him and the pink-haired woman like a pack of hyenas. He waited for someone to say something, anything to help him bury this bitch and actually pleadingly searched their eyes for any one of them to object to her horrible comment with him. He was naively astonished to realize that he was never going to hear what he had hoped to. He recalled what Vinny always told him, "Never let that sort of shit go unchallenged; it's the root of all evil." His eyes bore in on the army boots woman, unafraid of the whipping Georgia was planning for him later.

"You are a mental midget to think anything other than crazy Islamists brought down the towers. They burned right in front of all of us here and on television for the rest of the world to see." He stepped right up to her now, towering over her, wishing she were a man. "I saw the second plane come in with my own eyes. That murdering rat bastard slammed the gas pedal down and tilted the plane's wings for maximum destructive effect."

"There are plenty of scientists and engineers who believe otherwise," was her weak retort.

"Such as who? Who are these scientists, engineers, metallurgists, physics professors you are referring to? All I've ever seen and heard is a bunch of conspiracy nuts with dubious videos narrated by anti-American nut-jobs with too much time on their hands."

"Well, Mr. Republican, why don't you tell us what you think?" She stepped back and folded her arms across her chest, a smirk growing on her face. Was that her best insult, calling him a Republican? Wasn't Lincoln a Republican?

How many times would I slam a car door on her head? he was wondering. He instead replied evenly, "I will give you a completely plausible reason why the towers came down. An indisputable fact is that the towers were built with a new architectural design of curtain rods hanging off a central core, radically different from the steel and mortar buildings we are used to here in the city. Unfortunately the construction method used was uniquely susceptible to this type of attack. But that aside, think about this if you want a conspiracy. When those buildings were being built in the late '60s and early '70s, the entire construction business in New York was completely run by the mob. Truck drivers, cement companies, all the union workers, all of it was under the thumb of whatever mafia family was in charge of what. This one had the carpenters union, that one had the Teamsters, that other one had the rebar concession. And one faction must have had the fireproofing contract. And I can just see these two guys walking around the interior of the building, miles of unprotected steel beams and curtain rods in front of them and one of them says to his buddy, "Hey, isn't the drywall going up here tomorrow?" "Yeah it is, why?" "Well, let's just give it a little spritz and get the hell out of here. They're never gonna notice. What are we worried about, a fucking plane hitting this thing?" Michael stuck his finger in her face to drive his point down her throat. "That, my dear, is a completely plausible reason for the buildings coming down, after, of course, they were stuck by fully loaded jet planes that weigh about a half million pounds, traveling at about five hundred miles per hour, filled with fifty thousand gallons of gasoline which ignited and set everything on fire including rugs, draperies, furniture, drywall, bond dealers, stock traders, insurance men and women, cops, firemen and secretaries by these homicidal maniacs." He brought his finger out of her face and started to step away but decided, What the hell, let's kick her when she's down. He turned back to her, now with his hands on his hips.

"And I'll tell you another thing, you racist anti-Semitic pig. The idea you just casually floated about Jewish people receiving warnings the night before the attacks is so disgusting it makes me want to puke all over your stupid pink hair and those lame boots. I speak for all decent people in this city when I say to you to go fuck yourself. And for your information, I am a registered Democrat, a Robert Kennedy Democrat, and I would rather be you, an ugly, pathetic, imbecilic piece of shit before I sign up to be a member of the Republican party." Georgia was now at *his* side, fuming so much that Michael thought he could feel her body heat from two feet away. He turned to his wife and told her, "I'll be downstairs. I'll wait for you there when you're done with this crew." With that he turned away from the rest of the party goers and was out the door in a minute and down on the stoop of the building a minute or two after that, where he consumed ten cigarettes in ninety minutes before she came down and joined him for a wordless ride back to Cuchino.

"I'm still not interested in talking to you ever again. I'll probably never be invited back to their house, thanks to you." She never looked in his direction and stared out the passenger window the entire ride home.

"I never asked to go to these things, you know. There's no reason for us to be joined at the hip, especially when it means leaving Sally with yet another baby sitter. I tried to get along with these people and frankly, they never showed any interest in being friendly with me, in case you didn't notice."

"Well you certainly won't be asked again."

"Is that a promise? I'm sorry Georgia but I wouldn't mind as much if these people would allow even a mildly dissenting opinion. But they just go crazy if you disagree with them and they look at me like I'm some sort of neoconservative buffoon. They know nothing about me except that my wife won't come to my defense in public which I always asked you to do, Georgia. We're married and you couldn't even do that for me."

"They are my friends and you have to accept them."

"I have to accept your family, not your friends. And these people, by the way, would probably abandon you in a heartbeat if you really needed them. And another thing, I am your husband. You're supposed to show a smidgeon of loyalty to me, at least in public. You can pull me apart at the joints later if you wish, but do me a favor, okay? I'd appreciate it if you don't make me look or feel like a fool in public again, especially in front of those people."

"You did just fine making yourself look foolish all by yourself. Even your group from Queens would have thought you were out of line."

"My group of friends, whom I have known since the age of eight, would do anything for me and I for them. They have never judged me nor have they ever held any of my quirks, weirdnesses, or whatever else you can find against me. They know who I am...do you? And the last time I checked, you came from the same neighborhood, so maybe you should remember who you are and where you come from...or were, for that matter."

"Yeah, I know who you are. You're an asshole." And with that the argument was over, but unfortunately not the ride home, which took about an hour. He was wondering for the rest of the ride and later when she was lying on her side next to him in bed, facing the wall if she was thinking about splitting up, which would have been fine with him as the same subject was occupying his mind as well and for the first time, he had started to wonder if it would be manageable.

After a few minutes of navigating his car through the neighborhood, he arrived in the driveway of his home. He waited a moment as he heard Bob Dylan's "Knocking on Heaven's Door" come on the radio. He tried to sing along to the amazing first verse of the song—"It's getting dark, too dark to see"—but he couldn't follow the Guns 'n Roses version they were playing on the radio all the time now. In disgust he turned if off. "Nothing, absolutely not a fucking thing remains the same, even when it's perfect," he said to the moon and stars as he strode toward the front door of his home, his daughter's screams of protest penetrating the walls, amazingly reaching his ears out here, and he instantly felt as if he were carrying a sack of bowling balls over his shoulder. Thank goodness they were going away for the next few days, although Michael didn't like the idea of Georgia and Sally being around her parents at this point in time, whispering into each set of ears. Her parents were pure xenophobes, hating Michael for not being Greek, her father chasing him down Queens Boulevard with a baseball bat when he first discovered they were dating. He also didn't like the immersion techniques Georgia was recently insisting upon, it was as if his opinions didn't exist. He was looking forward to a quiet house this weekend because he sure wasn't going to have it now. He knew that as soon as he heard Sally's shriek, "I hate this extra homework and I hate being Greek!" He slammed the door to the car and trudged up to the porch.

⁂

Laura was trying to shrug off her growing concern regarding Adam and their soon-to-be-unfolding evening, and a multitude of other items large and small, the usual nonsense clogging the average human's psyche. She exited the Lexington Avenue subway at Seventy-Second Street, walked north for a block and turned east on Seventy-Third. Adam's apartment building was halfway down the block. As she walked along the sidewalk, the instinctive gnawing feeling that was instilled in all human beings since the beginning of their time on this planet to warn of any type of impending danger from an imminent velociraptor attack to rushing water crawling inch by inch up your body toward your nostrils was flaring in her brain. I truly looked forward to this night, she told herself as she admired a beautifully gnarled cherry blossom tree in the courtyard of a townhouse...for weeks, if not months or even years...a nice dinner coupled with some nice conversation, and for a grand finale some wonderful first-time lovemaking with a handsome decent man she had vetted for several months, looking and searching with all her female instincts for any indication of a problem.

Maybe a drinker or drug user. Maybe a gambler, maybe...anything. There was a sense of humor in him, she was pretty sure of that, some intelligence and certainly good looks with his wavy hair, bookish charm, and she loved the way his glasses fit his face. No, he was a good one. Maybe not a winner, she wouldn't know that for a long time. That was a big reason but not the only one why so much time had passed with only one lover, if you could even call it that. And in the two years before that, two. In between were a mountain of catcalls, a boatload of ass grabs on the subway, every fifth or so involving some serious physical contact, clumsy propositions, and a few dates with a few men that she never allowed to progress past a halfway decent kiss good night. Most of those men were genuinely surprised when the next three or four phone calls went unanswered. That was how it was for her lately, a typical single girl's existence in New York City, until she met Adam on the great lawn in Central Park. It was a late February afternoon, an unusual sixty-degree day and the lawn was filled with tourists and New Yorkers soaking up the rare winter sun warmth.

She noticed first off his athleticism as he played football with whom she presumed were his friends. Just as she was hoping he would return her gaze, an overthrown pass landed near her bench and their eyes met when she flipped it back to him. Right out of a beer commercial. Not in a million years would she have asked him for a date, but she tried with all her might to somehow convey her interest in him starting with flipping the ball accurately and with a tight spiral back to him, then opening her eyes wider and wider as he strode toward her, finishing off the wordless flirt with pursed lips and a smile.

"Thanks," he said, and continued back to his game but after what seemed like some sort of consultation with his football buddies, he did return to ask her for a cup of coffee sometime later that afternoon. Adam was definitely handsome up close, she remembered thinking as she continued past the townhomes, although she did have a preference for blue eyes, and his voice was not as deep as she would have liked.

Her father had a deep voice. Coffee and cake turned into a lunch here and there, a dinner and movie once in a while, an art show this weekend, a play that weekend. A perfect gentleman throughout, never pushy about anything. The last week, however, had been a bit strange, she was thinking. It was going to happen as she knew she wanted him maybe, probably, no definitely. She didn't completely desire him with everything she had in her heart, but she wanted him that was for sure. She would have preferred that it all came along in a bit more natural way instead of two boxers trying to get through a late round, waiting for the bell.

A weekend in The Hamptons sounded nice, something like that. Maybe a weekend trip to San Francisco, ride some cable cars, go to Muir Woods, a nice dinner in Carmel after a run on the beach, maybe meet some locals and make love three times per day and carve our initials on a tree. I don't give a damn how silly or stupid that sounds to anyone else, that's exactly how I would like it to be. But all of a sudden it had to be tonight, a weird sense of urgency poured out of him for their first lovemaking session. Alright, she told him, over the phone yet. Why couldn't it have been under the moonlight somewhere as they strolled lazily along? But at least they would get some dinner beforehand and then they would do it, she figured. She was afraid to admit to herself that her inner instinct, the same instinct that had guided her all along throughout her life, was telling her that something might be a little wrong. Maybe it was his horoscope, she laughed to herself. Maybe tonight with the full moon hovering overhead would give him strong and unimpeded circulation. She was tired and terribly bored with masturbation, all alone afterward, her body wanting to be held, stroked, looked at. No, that was not going to happen tonight, it was to be a penis that would deliver her an orgasm tonight, as long as he was patient and knew what he was doing and she was able to relax.

She arrived at his building and there he was already in the lobby, unaware that she had arrived. The doorman eyed her in an appraising way and tilted his head back in an effort to take her all in. The black pants she had chosen for this evening definitely worked their magic on the doorman. She stepped to the side and noticed Adam texting furiously, then answering a call that came through in the middle of it and, after he was done speaking, went right back to finishing his text. She wondered what it was about and was not a little annoyed that she had been standing there unnoticed. The doorman looked perplexed as he opened the heavy glass and latticed door for an older couple on their way out somewhere. She kept an eye on her date as he put the phone away in his jacket pocket and only then did he look up. She had been waiting for this moment, to mark his reaction to her outfit, remembering that Diego was almost moved to tears the first time he glimpsed her in a dress. But Adam merely strode a little too purposefully toward her, took her by the arm kissing her perfunctorily as he did so, and curtly ordered the nice doorman to flag him a cab. Her disquiet at these tiny bits of what she considered bad social behavior was growing bit by bit as the cab headed over to the west side for their dinner.

Nothing happened at the restaurant, a fancy overblown affair with high prices, small portions and snotty waiters, that was able to quiet her disquiet. He was not nearly as loving as he should have been on a night like this. He didn't gaze into her eyes the way a man who loved her should have. He took a couple of phone calls at the table and a text as well, something that Laura as well as most civilized people hated. He asked for the check without checking with her to see if she wanted anything else. In the cab on the way to dinner she took a picture of him with her cell phone as he was focused on whatever was outside the window on his side, and at that moment, a stray beam of light played off his earlobe in such a way that it looked in the photo like he had an earring. Earrings and tattoos were something on her list that would eliminate any man from her favor, along with a number of other negative traits, the usual things. It depressed her seeing so many men in New York with earrings and tattoos and now this strange photograph of Adam with the apparition of an earring...it was just too weird. And then he stiffed the waitress on the tip. Laura was horrified at a five dollar tip on a one hundred twenty-five dollar dinner. Did he just make a mistake? Did he forget to leave a twenty along with the fiver? And as they were leaving he openly stared in appreciation at a beautiful woman on the street outside the restaurant, enough so that Laura felt compelled to tighten her grip on his arm which did bring his attention back, but she knew that there were thousands of attractive women in the city, most of them single, it seemed, and he seemed so... interested in that one. On this evening. Would Diego have done that?

she wondered. Sure, he would look at a pretty girl for an instant, but never when she was on his arm. No, never. Not a chance. And once again she thought of Michael. Would he have done that? Probably, she figured, as men couldn't seem to help themselves. But I bet he wouldn't have stiffed the waitress. And I also believe his gaze wouldn't have lingered on the woman's legs as long as Adam's had. All of these thoughts were crowding her brain like passengers on a Tokyo subway train as the cab was taking them back to his apartment. Couldn't we have walked together arm in arm or at least held hands on our way back here? Wouldn't that have been nicer? Just at that moment, when she was about to tumble head over heels into an abyss of self-doubt and endless analysis, when she was seriously considering feigning a headache and going home, she heard Adam announce to the driver, "Here we are."

ـﻟﺍﻊ

Dinner at Michael's house was predictably, a disaster. The tension was greater than that of a cable on a suspension bridge swaying in a high wind. The argument was moving along like a whisper jet, the presence of their daughter the only reason they weren't throwing plates, knives, and forks at each other across the table. The rift over Sally's continuing education was widening by the day. Exacerbating the general situation was that Georgia's work was involving more and more travel out of the country, leaving him alone for a week at a time at least once per month, her willingness to answer to any travel request baffling and sometimes infuriating him. The nights were filled with Sally attempting to e-mail her friends and doing homework and him watching *Law & Order* re-runs.

The battle for the television at dinner was a lost cause for Michael as monotonous re-runs of *Seinfeld* and *Friends* were insisted on by Georgia. For the first time in his marriage, he wondered what it would be like to be unmarried again. What would it do to Sally? That was his primary concern. It came across to him that Georgia was getting ready to move on, as it was painfully apparent that they had lost each other somewhere along the way. The dinner finished and the plates and glasses piling up in the sink, Sally was leaving to finish her homework and Georgia was back in the bedroom, silently returning to packing and replying to her e-mails from work. So Michael turned his attention to the television, clicking through endless two-star movie possibilities on HBO before settling on a documentary about a native tribe living a Stone Age existence somewhere in the jungles of Peru. He started to wash the dishes, watching a man in a loincloth fire an arrow at the camera which was apparently filming from the safety of a helicopter. At that moment, Michael understood the primitive man's helplessness and fury at things he could not understand or control. Georgia then came out of the bedroom putatively just to issue an order to him, "Please clean out the turtle's water, its green." The N in green was barely out of her mouth before she was turning back to her packing and e-mailing. "That's all I'm good for here," he muttered to himself as he continued cleaning the dishes, psyching himself up for the evening's only entertainment, chasing Sally's turtle Francis around the tank so he could clean it.

—◦|◦—

Maxie wiped away a bit of sauce from the corner of her mouth, a finishing touch to a surprisingly excellent meal. They both had the same thing, spring rolls with peanut sauce and spicy chicken over rice. Vinny asked if he could order for both of them once they arrived, assuring her she would love it, turning to the elegant, young, out-of-work model and telling her, "Number fifteen and twenty-nine, please, two orders." He handed back the menu which he never looked at and turned to Maxie, who was sitting just beside him in the corner of the restaurant. "I hope you don't mind that I ordered for both of us. I don't usually do things like that. I'm in a bit of a hurry as something may come up later and I didn't expect to come here tonight."

What a nice way to spend an evening, so unexpected, far removed from her usual dull routine, she was thinking. Was this a date? It had come about so innocently and simply. A walk around the block turned into a meeting with this gentleman and now a meal and conversation she found surprisingly refreshing and stimulating. She admitted to herself that she was enjoying the company of this man from Queens, with his understated swagger, obvious intelligence and guts, his will to succeed, and frankly, his manliness. She asked him about the construction site and found it amazing not only that he didn't speak endlessly about his work as most men do, but that she actually had to ask him about it in spite of their difficult meeting earlier in the day. She remembered how impressed a friend of hers was who had broken up with her boyfriend and then run into him many weeks later and they enjoyed a lively conversation, never, not once mentioning their failed relationship. Her friend married the boyfriend a year later and they never looked back. "I knew he was the one after that, the thoroughly mature way he handled himself," she had said to Maxie, as if it were a lesson she should always revisit whenever necessary.

"What settled you on the site?" she asked him between scooping the spicy chicken into her mouth with a heaping of sticky rice balanced on elegant chopsticks. "There seems to be some emotional attachment to it, beyond making a good buck." She put her chin on her hands once she finished chewing and swallowing and awaited her answer trying to look as good as she could.

Vinny liked her, that was for sure. Not too tall, thin but not bony, he appreciated her patrician manners and speech. He detected a desire on her part to be free of Sutton Place but wondered if she had the nerve to effect a plan to escape it. He realized all at once that he was very comfortable with her and did not mind telling her anything she asked about. The meal was excellent and they were both shoveling it into their mouths in spite of their not knowing each other.

"My friends and I used to go swimming there when we were kids. We used to dive in at the south end of the pier and fight the uptown currents to get back to the very dock we were all fixated on today." Her head started to spin at this revelation as she wondered if Vinny and his friends could possibly be the boys in the photograph her father showed her as a little girl. How very cosmic, but it couldn't be him, could it?

They finished the meal and a tall bottle of Vietnamese beer in about a half hour. She watched him closely as he signaled the waitress, paid the bill and left a nice tip in cash on the table. He started to rise and extended his hand to her in order to help her out of the corner once he was standing straight up.

"I have to get back to Astoria to help J'lome. He seems to have a little problem." He had told her so much about his friends and the tightness of their relationships during the course of the dinner. How she would have loved that same sort of loyalty in her own friends as well as her husband.

"My friends are the type of friends you can count on as long as you maintain your social standing and in some way you remain useful to them," she said a little sadly as he gallantly helped her on with her jacket. She noticed a few of the women in the restaurant eyeballing the old-fashioned scene appreciatively.

"The guys in our group would lay down in traffic for each other," he responded while retrieving her pocketbook from the back of her chair for her. "You sure you don't want dessert?"

"Yes, thank you, Vinny," she replied as she turned like a ballerina to step between the tightly arranged tables, pulling her coat around her with not a little bit of grace. "I have to get back now, but next time you're definitely on for dessert." Her smile blazed its way into his heart and he held out his hand just past her, palm up to guide her to the door of the restaurant.

—⚓—

Andre steered his companion into the bathroom of the mosque immediately after the prayers were concluded. He was sweating profusely and Fated noticed his friend seemed overly anxious to talk, as if he wanted to confess to a crime. He started jabbering as soon as the door was shut.

"I need to do something for this lady, something big, my friend. Otherwise she will leave me," Andre blubbered, pushing the door closed before its pneumatic mechanism had a chance to.

Fated turned to the urinal and unzipped. "How about you do the following for her, my friend? Send her back to where she came from because she has poisoned your mind, corrupted your morals, and turned you into a dog, a sniveling, begging little dog." He shook himself free of any loose droplets and pulled on the handle and his zipper in succession as he finished at the urinal. Stepping to the basin and splashing water on his face, he looked up at Andre while still leaning over the sink. "She is poison to you, why do you not see that? Anyone else can, but you don't. Or you choose not to." He buried his face back in the basin close to the faucet's rush of water and cupped his hands to run the cool liquid over his face. Andre resumed his pleading, leaning on the other end of the vanity for support or maybe to get as close to his friend as possible, to try to show him how important this was to him.

"Just please help me get her on the Hezbollah network you are importing to some of your satellite dish clients. Maybe someone will see her and recognize her talent and beauty. At least she will see that I was able to accomplish that for her." He was pleading now and Fated snapped at him, "Keep your mouth shut about my businesses and affairs. They are not for everyone's ears." And Fated realized at that moment they were no longer for Andre's ears either. He no longer cared about their friendship of the past ten years as just now, he felt the beginning of the possibility of blackmail entering Andre's mind and he wanted to stop it immediately before it gained any further momentum. He lifted his face out of the water, shut off the flow, and ripped a couple of paper towels from the dispenser on the wall. He dried his hands vigorously, threw the soggy papers in the garbage, and faced Andre, throwing his shoulders back as he spoke.

"I hear American Idol starts shooting a new season soon. Maybe you can bring her to the audition," Fated said, starting for the door. He would pay good money to hear Simon Cowell blister her on the show in a way this besotted fool never could, and then ask her out to some villa on a beach far, far away from his friend where he would have her legs over his shoulders in about five minutes.

"Can you still get the images broadcast here? Please just do this once for me, that's all I ask."

Fated sighed as a new fool was born in front of him. My God, they are not in short supply in this country and now that he no longer considered Andre his friend, he decided to pick his pocket. He kept his hand on the door handle as he replied in an even tone. "Yes I can, but it's expensive."

"How much?"

"Two hundred thousand per appearance." Fated turned fully toward Andre as he said it, pulling another towel from the dispenser and blowing his nose loudly not only to clear his sinus passages but also to show his soon to be former friend how disgusted he was with him. Andre was literally staggering under the weight of even thinking about such a sum. It was almost twice his annual salary at Argent

Bank. "I can't raise that much, you know that," he said glumly. Fated jumped into Andre's face like a hungry cat, now that his opportunity presented itself.

"I am tired of this *can't* answer from you all the time," he hissed in reply to Andre's sniveling. "I have run fifty or more scams over the past twenty years as well as my own legitimate business to cover my expenses and more while you toil for this fucking Argent Bank, playing with pennies." Fated leaned in and looked at him closely then sideways, the way a father would question a seventeen-year-old son or daughter he suspects of lying. "You have stolen what, twenty, thirty thousand dollars in the past year with your stupid salami scam, and for what? For this despicable woman and her utterly ridiculous unattainable dream of being a singing star." He turned away again from Andre to grab the door handle and leave forever but came back blazing. "You are taking all the chances for her, paying her rent, paying for her recording studio charges, musicians, her clothing, and she isn't even screwing you!" He leaned in even more closely again to Andre's fat face, "You could, if you had some real balls, you could set up your life for all eternity by instead of diverting just the cents out of a bunch of checks, you just grab ten or twenty million out of the bank at once, send it to the Cayman Islands with the push of a button of one of those fucking computers you love so much, and then send yourself to Brazil. You could then take that bitch there with you and pimp her out, that's all she is good for."

"Watch what you say about her, my friend."

"Or you'll do what?" Fated stood back a step now and put his hands on his hips. "I used to be your friend but I haven't seen or heard from you in the past year because this woman has taken over your life. I will not watch you destroy yourself any longer. If you want her on television, it's two hundred thousand per show. And don't tell me you can't do it because I know you can. You told me about how you compromised some woman's computer at the bank and with it you can run everything through there without detection. So why sit around in this cold, dirty city, feeding your heart to this witch a spoonful at a time? Get some money, my friend, and let's go to Rio. You will get the same jail time for ten million as you would for ten thousand, so you might as well make it worth your while. Otherwise, don't call me anymore.

I'm sure I'm going to be busy." And with that he stepped past Andre, pulled on the door of the bathroom, and was then out of the mosque onto Steinway Street a minute later, heading to his car, convinced that he would never see Andre again.

The wire problem of earlier today almost exposed him, Andre recalled, with not a little bit of horror. Somehow, somewhere, something went wrong with his program, or maybe the computer itself was compromised. Maybe that woman Laura, whom he hated for reasons he couldn't remember, maybe she was fooling around where she had no business and tripped over something. But at the last minute he was able to cover his tracks and also make her look like a fool in front of the entire office at the same time which was about the only satisfying thing to happen to him today.

Much of what Fated just said was true, except of course about his girl, who he knew loved him. He had twenty years in at the bank and he was never going to rise any further than where he was. He was only able to spend what he earned, and like most workers in America, he was living month to month and he hated it. He knew he could get the money as Fated suggested he do, as he completely understood the wire system of the bank and the Fed, and his only problem would be moving it around the world fast enough. How long would it take? he asked himself, and he started running it through his mind. Setting up foreign accounts, transferring the funds the instant they hit. He could get a functionary to do that for him for a few hundred dollars. He would have to get out of the country and possibly buy a new identity. Where would he go? Is the beach in Rio truly a possibility? He had heard the government there is totally corrupt so maybe he could just buy whatever he wanted. And why stop at ten million? Why not twenty? Or fifty for that matter? He bent over the washbasin and splashed water on his face hoping the cool water would soothe the fever starting to erupt in his brain. And it was then that his blood ran ice cold in his veins as the toilet in the last stall flushed, the occupant strolling out and right up to him at the basin, and Andre realized with a rush of dread that his entire conversation with Fated had been heard by this young, Arabic looking man. Did he even understand English? He knew that many members of the mosque had poor skills in this area but was disheartened when the stranger said to him in flawless

English, "Good evening brother, I am Whathefu from Saudi Arabia and I think you and I need to talk about some things."

—·•·—

Maxie was thinking about the ice cream and mango dessert she turned down. Not only did it sound delicious, but it would have meant a little more time spent with Vinny on their 'date.' She said to him as they turned onto Sutton Place, "I'm glad we had this time together. It was very enlightening." He had miraculously found the same parking spot they left a little more than an hour before and jumped into it. It was about a hundred yards to her front door, about twenty to the spot where they met tonight. Would he walk me to the door?

Vinny turned toward her without breaking stride and smiled his agreement in such a way that had Maxie thinking they could possibly go an entire evening without words and manage to communicate better than in a full-blown conversation with her husband. "It was for me as well. I don't get many chances to hang out with truly elegant people." His eyebrows raised as he complimented her and his finishing smile engulfed her heart. He jumped from his seat and came around the car to open her door for her. She took his offered hand although she didn't need the assistance. They started walking together slowly toward her building. There were a few people out on the street, joggers, residents and some tradespeople packing up for the day. Maxie noticed not only that a few were taking notice of them—do any of them know me, she thought with a sudden touch of concern—but also that she and Vinny were walking almost perfectly in stride. She always disliked when she dated a man who couldn't keep up with her gait. I wonder if he can dance. They arrived back at the same spot they found each other and stared out past the FDR Drive, across the river toward the Pepsi sign. She noticed Vinny seemed to slip into a state of being that was difficult to define but she knew to interrupt it would be unwelcome. His strong profile and his hair pulled this way and that by the breeze off the river was enough for her to concentrate on for the next few minutes. He didn't look at her when he started to speak.

"When I was growing up, it seemed like a completely different world over here, even though it was so close, geographically speaking.

Thoroughly unattainable and frankly, I didn't even know if I wanted to be part of it if I were ever able to afford it." He was silent for a few more seconds before continuing. "It was a sad time for me and most of my friends, the guys I told you about earlier. But we always watched out for each other when our parents refused to, when the schools didn't care, and the cops would just grab us off the street, or try to, just to meet some quota. And we all wound up okay, some better than others, of course, but we're all okay...those of us that are still here. We still have our dreams because we all believe that without dreams and dreaming, life isn't worth anything." He turned to her and asked, "Don't you agree?"

She was falling for this man, a little bit at first in today's meeting, more at dinner, and now it was tumbling forward like froth over Niagara, doubling over itself, creating layer after layer of interest. She didn't care about the husband who was sitting in his library with his stinking cigar and brandy snifter...in the apartment I was raised in, no less! She was ashamed of herself for thinking this way. She was married, even though her husband had become a disgustingly snotty sloth. But she was also excited for the first time in years about what tomorrow might bring and it all came about with a chance meeting with this man whom she barely knew. He was a dreamer, that was true. Her mother always warned her against a dreamer, "That's all most of them ever do, dear," she would say. But Vinny was also a doer, a delicious combination in a man, especially when it came with twinkling eyes, a certain mental and physical toughness, a helping of straightforwardness spiced with an ability to make me laugh. She knew right then that if she were single, they'd be in her living room sharing a coffee in about five minutes.

"Yes, Vinny, I do agree. And I know that surely because I stopped dreaming a long time ago." She looked out at the Pepsi sign and then up at her building and said to him, "But I recently started to think about dreaming once again." She took his arm and looked into his face, "Vinny, that pier, somehow, some way I believe it will come down. Maybe a river bore will somehow shoot up the East River and knock it over, maybe it will get hit by a bolt of lightning. Just don't go there and do something that is man-made. That will cause you more problems than you want or need. Keep your eyes peeled for the faintest sliver of opportunity and make good on it. Let me know if you find out or figure out anything and I will get your project off the agenda of these people. I think it's a worthy and beautiful project as well as a profitable one." He looked back over the FDR Drive, out at his dream across the river and simply said, "Thanks, I will." He turned back to her and announced rather abruptly, "Look, I gotta go, Maxie. I loved the dinner and this time and I don't want it to end, but I gotta go help J'lome. Something's happening over by his place and I have to be there." He lightly guided her away from the bench and toward her front door. She was momentarily nervous that he would kiss her, but he just squeezed her elbow a bit, smiled and told her he might reach out to her some time. "Good night, Maxie, I'll leave you off here," he said, and turned back to his car. She continued to the doorway of her fabulous building on Sutton Place, staying there for a moment to see if he would look back when he got to the corner. To her immense satisfaction and some relief, he did but he didn't wave as she could see he had his phone glued to his ear.

—•—

"So what is the plan?" Michael inquired of Georgia, more in an attempt to thaw out the room rather than gain some information. He knew she would ultimately write it down for him and stick it up somewhere. It was perfectly arctic in their bedroom as she packed two large suitcases, answering without looking up.

"The plan is to go to Florida, see my family, share some old stories and maybe some laughs and continue Sally's cultural saturation, and playing a string instrument, preferably the viola. I have a cousin who made all of her children learn a musical instrument." Or in other words, to get away from here and you as quickly as I can. There was no forthcoming question from Georgia about what his plans for the next few days might be and he wondered if she cared. He wouldn't allow her to even consider that she had annoyed him with the way she answered him.

"Why are you packing so much for just a few days? Are you planning to stay longer?"

"I want to be prepared for anything," she replied. They were like a single hungry lioness and a herd of zebra on the Serengeti, each eying the other, little pokes and jibes of movement to discern any hint of weakness. Michael wondered who was the hunter in their case. Sally appeared in the door just then, her freshness and innocence a body blow to the reality of the marriage relationship right in front of her.

"Daddy, can I bring my Barbie?" Georgia answered for him.

"Yes, sweetie, bring her here and I'll pack her nice and comfy in my suitcase. But also bring along your new doll so your grandparents can see you playing with her. After all, they bought her for you." Sally's grandparents had sent a beautiful doll made out of polished alabaster that had articulated limbs. The ancient Greeks made dolls such as this one for their children for thousands of years. Yeah, sure, Michael thought, at your suggestion or their prodding, or a combination of both. But he wouldn't allow himself to take the bait. She was angling for an escalation, just hovering above the fault line, but he wasn't going to rise to it. No, just pack and go and I will sleep late, order in pizza for a couple of days, and go back to the old neighborhood, maybe for a card game with the boys, his friends, real friends. Then again, why not? You can't be a pussy and look at yourself in the mirror in the morning.

"Sally," Michael said to his daughter, "bring your Barbie onto the plane in your backpack instead and introduce her to the flight attendants. Maybe they played with Barbies when they were little and it will make them smile at the memory." He cursed himself for breaking one of his most cherished rules, using his child for leverage in an argument.

"That's a good idea, Daddy. What do you think?" she asked Barbie, skipping away. Georgia slammed the massive suitcase shut and pulled the zipper around from back to the front in one grand sweeping motion that had the contents of the suitcase sweating for their lives, but luckily nothing got caught in the track. "Thanks a lot, Michael. Just thanks so much for all your help."

"What is it now, Georgia?" he asked her, but not as a wounded male might ask. He was tired of it all now, the dancing and maneuvering and the manipulation of their daughter. If she wanted to fight then now was a good time. She'll be gone for a few days in the morning anyhow. He'll deal with it then.

"I wanted to take some time on the plane for her to brush up on a little Greek before she sees my family, not play with a fucking Barbie," she spit at him. She threw the other suitcase onto the bed in preparation for the death zipper pull like she was wrestling a sheep to the ground in preparation to be sheared. No time to back down, as Michael's shoulders were creeping northward.

"Why not let her brush up on being a little kid? You are trying to dump a million things into her lap all at once. It's nothing more than a race between you and your friends over whose kid is the cutest, the smartest, the most talented, and it's going to continue right up until she becomes a parent of her own children with everything between now and then judged over and over as if she were in a beauty pageant with eighty-seven categories that never ends. It's obvious she wants a little down time, obvious to anyone who looks at her. Or any of your friends' children as well," he added. All of the kids around the city and its affluent suburbs were so naturally perfect, full of wonder and joy. But he noticed they all started to change a bit around age seven, when the teachers at these ridiculous schools started talking about the 'academic careers' of these second graders.

"What is obvious is that you don't give a damn about anything or anyone that is important to me."

"Georgia," he said, using the more conciliatory tone because he still had to get through the rest of the night. If they were at the terminal at LaGuardia Airport, he might just suggest to her to take a much longer flight...by herself. "Please separate this issue with Sally from the arguments I had with your acquaintances."

"Friends. They are my friends."

"Sorry, but for me they will never be more than just acquaintances and not because we hold opposing viewpoints on a few issues but because they refuse to consider anything other than their own point of view. Half of the problem is what I just told you but the other half is that you never back me up in front of them."

More silence from her as the contents of the second suitcase practically huddled like Emperor penguins trying to stay warm during an Antarctic blizzard, holding themselves together to stay away from the ferocity of her zippering. Michael knew silence was never a good thing with Georgia. In a second he would know if this particular silence

would bring forth fury or a tabling of the conversation. He was prepared for both, but greatly preferred the latter.

"You don't even make an attempt to care about their point of
view which happens to be increasingly my point of view, if you didn't
notice." She ripped this suitcase off the bed and flung/placed it next to
the other by the bedroom door.

"From what I have been able to observe, they are not your friends.
They seem to be collecting people for their cause, whatever it might be
at the moment, so they can be fawned over. They remind me of Paris
Hilton. Do they really know anything about you? Where you grew up,
how we met, maybe your birthday or favorite singer?"

She stared right at him as she asked, "Do you?" Short sentences...
another warning sign.

"Do I what?"

"Know me?"

He sighed out an answer, "We've known each other for twenty-five years, from the old neighborhood. We grew up together, went
to school together, had our first kiss behind the junkyard wall on Thirty-Ninth Place, snuck on the 7 train together, your birthday is June
12th, your favorite singer is Joe Cocker and everything else in between
then and this moment we have shared together in one way or another.
Yes, Georgia, I think I know you except of course for the well of information that every woman keeps hidden from a man."

Wearily now, "I used to think the same way, Michael, but I'm not
so sure now. The weariness was strangely disappearing at the end of
her sentence, like a second wind was coming to her spurred on by a
shift in her acceptance of something in her existence. "Maybe I should
have listened to my father when he chased you down the avenue with
the baseball bat." Normally an exchange like this precedes a fuzzy
moment between people in love. Not here and not now.

"Oh, really. So what did he tell you?"

"That I should stay with my own kind. He said you would never
truly understand me."

Michael was finished with the conversation right then. Time
to wrap it up with a tight bow. "Well then maybe you are having
an epiphany of some sort. You figure it out over the next few days,
Georgia, and so will I and we'll see what happens when you get back

from Florida. He left the bedroom to watch the Met game on the basement television.

It was indeed true, as Vinny reminded Moose Miller earlier, Woody
Allen's observation that ninety percent of success is just showing up,
and Whathefu was feeling just that way at the moment. This amazing
gift apparently had fallen into his lap in, of all places, the bathroom
stall of some mosque in Queens. A few minutes earlier, he had excused
himself from Aubrey citing a call of nature, his 'chaperone' waiting just
outside, watching the door from across the corridor after first making
sure there was no window or door from which an escape could be made.

Whathefu didn't have to relieve his bladder. Instead he wanted
to have a few moments to himself and get lost in a dream about him
and Aubrey, his jailer, who to Whathefu's eyes looked liked a perfect
masturbatory, if not actual sexual, subject. Whathefu was once more
giving in to his gay sex fantasies, in spite of the danger he was in and
that barely a day earlier he needlessly caused the death of a young girl.
Exactly what he wanted in his dream was a week-long boat outing on
his father's yacht, just the two of them visiting the hundreds of beautiful islands along the coast of Greece and Spain. In his fantasy, each
island would hold a collection of people who had bullied and taunted
Whathefu over the years: teachers, relatives, neighbors, all the horrible
bastards who had marginalized him and his mother from his earliest
days. Aubrey would then beat the hell out of all of them—in a Speedo,
of course—and then he would scoop Whathefu up in his powerful
arms and they would have a marathon sex session on each and every
beach that dotted the Aegean and Mediterranean Seas.

And it wouldn't be some hit and run in the bushes in Central Park
or some glory hole action in some Chelsea dump. No, it would be real
lovemaking, better than with any of the European women he had over
the years. After each sandy encounter, it would be back to the boat for
a hot soapy shower, oil massage, and some wine and food to loosen the
both of them up for the next island.

Amazing what he would allow himself to think about with this
impossible task handed to him, his life probably over in a week or so.

Even with the threat of imminent death, his inner turmoil regarding his confused sexuality was in his frontal lobe once again. Women or men? Which did he enjoy more? Could he have one without the other? Could he stand the social pressure in the world that although was increasingly liberal, regarded homosexuality as an aberration? He knew there were reams of literature and art in the Arab world devoted to men sleeping with each other. Maybe they regarded it as nothing more than an extremely exotic form of masturbation, but after his few encounters with the drifters, he was discovering to his chagrin that he liked it. But he liked Leila as well, her beautiful eyes and strong body also fascinated him. If only the world would allow him both, then he could truly feel free, he thought. In the meantime, he would have to relegate most of his activity to masturbation with a gay theme in his mind. And so it was as the hot surge he was feeling in his balls was reaching a friction point, the door opened, the new occupants of the bathroom not noticing that he was holding the broken door of the stall closed with the soles of his shoes, balancing himself on the toilet while he jerked off.

He was able to hear two men speaking privately and it was apparent that they did not know he was there. What to do? He didn't move a muscle or even breathe lest he give himself away. He wanted to continue his fantasy about Aubrey in a Speedo on top of him as soon as these two clowns did their business and exited. So he sat and listened to the conversation, fascinated to be a fly on the wall, observing another human's distress about love and attraction when it all came together for him at the suggestion by one of them to steal the money he needed. Apparently one of these fellows was a computer expert at a bank and he was already stealing money electronically. He listened to his friend suggesting he make one huge score and disappear. At that instant he was transformed from a self-loathing, lecherous, somewhat homosexual Arab rich kid into a ruthless, murderous opportunist. His salvation was delivered to him, in the middle of a jerk-off session in a mosque's bathroom, and he found the intersecting ironies delicious. This guy was a gift from Allah, he thought, as the second man left the room leaving only himself and the now key to his future, who was apparently washing up. I will make good use of this man, Whathefu decided. He released his penis, pulled up his pants, and stepped out of the stall. He walked right up to the startled man and spoke directly to him.

"You work for a bank? In the computer department? Is that what I understand about you, my friend?" asked Whathefu with the confidence of a CEO questioning a junior sales executive. Andre was furious that he had made such a critical mistake in allowing this...person to hear about his ongoing thefts from the bank.

"Yes I do," Andre replied, shaking the water from his hands and reaching for a paper towel. He pulled two sheets from the dispenser, wiped his hands and his face, hoping his concern wasn't too obvious. "Were you listening to my private conversation? Do you normally hang out in bathrooms this way?" he asked Whathefu. Andre was struggling to maintain his composure, hoping that his imposing size would intimidate Whathefu into leaving him alone.

"I could not help but hear you and your friend speaking. This area after all," Whathefu said sweeping his hand in an arc around the bathroom, "is a public place. You should take extra care when speaking about such sensitive subjects." He stepped up to Andre, who was six inches taller and about forty pounds heavier, and tried to summon every bit of malice that he knew lived in every man, no matter how short and scrawny, "My associate and I would like to speak to you about a business opportunity that will be mutually beneficial to us all." He took Andre under the arm and guided him to the door. Andre easily pulled away saying, "Call me some other time, not now." Whathefu once again gripped Andre's arm, this time more tightly and further up near his armpit the way his had been gripped only a few hours before by Aubrey, "No, my friend, I will not call you later. Now is the time for us to speak about our futures." He pulled the door open taking Andre with him, Aubrey on guard immediately, crossing the corridor quickly to meet them, thinking Andre might be Whathefu's ally. "Hey, this is somebody we should definitely talk to," said Whathefu, slapping Andre on the shoulder as if he were an old friend. Aubrey fixed Andre with an reptilian stare, chilling the marrow in his bones and making him wonder if he would ever be able to make up for his mistake in the bathroom.

—

Vinny's phone went off as he was heading over the bridge on his way back to Astoria. He loved cell phones, not just for their convenience communication-wise, but for the fact that he could see the incoming caller on the screen and, before two rings were out, he was able to decide if he would take the call and if he did, what he would probably hear and have a half dozen possible responses ready as the question was still forming on the caller's lips. He would never, ever answer a call from a number that came up private. He himself was an intensely private man except with the boys from the neighborhood, with each of whom he was quite the opposite. He shared everything with them simply because he wanted to and also as time went on, they became his angel investors in a few smaller projects. He wanted them involved as he wanted, no...craved financial success for all his close friends and if he was able to secure deals that he could bring them in on, he would do so without hesitation. He could see the caller was Moose Miller, whom he had forgotten about a bit since the meeting with Maxie and the call from Charlie Mick in front of the mosque. He figured he had about ten minutes before he would arrive at the mosque on Steinway Street. And he also figured he was going to hear about either the shit he was taking on the job, from his wife and kids, the surveillance he was on with the Fed—didn't he realize that this could be a great opportunity for him?—and from life in general. But he was an eternal bud and therefore the phone was flipped open halfway through the second ring. "Moose, what's up? Where are you?"

"I'm on Steinway Street, by J'lome's mosque" he replied, taking Vinny by surprise.

"Why are you there?" he asked as a sudden feeling to go faster came alive in his right leg. He pressed the accelerator to the floor, passing a sanitation truck on the right and rocketed through Queens Plaza, the roar of the overhead subway lines failing to cut into his concentration.

"I followed that guy the Fed has me on from the airport over here. Seems like he is a Muslim as well as the guy he picked up. He looked like an Arab, the guy he picked up at the airport, but not this guy. Anyway, he started some trouble outside with a couple of guys who seemed to be with J'lome's congregation."

"Did you recognize these guys?"

"No, they were typical Islamics, I guess. They looked like foreigners from another fucking planet to me what with the long shirts and the stupid hats. Although one of them had jeans and a leather jacket on."

"Moose, you know what I'm about to say right?"

"Sorry, brother, you know what I mean."

"They sound like they're dressed like Pakistanis, like our depart ted friend's Dad, you remember? Don't forget that, Archie." He said it like an angry parent trying to instill a life lesson.

"I'm sorry, Vin. I loved him, too."

"You gotta keep that bullshit out of your life. No one will ever be able to accuse you of weakness because of that and I'm tellin' ya, it just might set your mind free a little bit, ya know? Maybe one less thing to get pissed off about? Waddya think?"

"I think you're right but I'd rather take the lecture later." He quickly related the argument and the violence that ensued, at least what he was able to see once he cleared the SUV with the Jersey plates. The fucking mayor should really charge these bastards triple on the toll to come into the city. "Anyway, J'lome broke it up and I guess by now they're all finishing up facing Mecca."

Something was happening, Vinny thought to himself. Nothing truly tangible, he knew, but his inner voice was telling him to be quiet and observe. He remembered what the cops he came to know over the years, professionally and thankfully on more friendly terms, would say, "we always look for something, anything out of the ordinary, unusual in any form, and more often than not this is what points us toward the action. Coincidences, coincidences, coincidences. There's no fucking such thing as a concidence."

"Moose, how long are you supposed to keep following this guy?" he asked. He reasoned that the Feds would have a rotation on this person at the very least so that the first team doing the surveillance would have time for a bite to eat and, more importantly, to lessen the chance of being made by the suspect.

"As long as the Fed guy, I can't remember his name..."

"That's something else you're gonna have to fix, you know," Vinny interjected. "How the hell do you plan on getting any recognition from something like this if you don't even have the guy's name?"

"Yeah, right. That's for tomorrow. Anyway, the Fed, he's a good guy, the only decent Fed frankly I've ever met, most of them think who they are. I mean this is our fucking city, right? As a matter of fact, he sounds like he's originally from somewhere in the city. So as I was saying, when he orders me off, which will probably be within the half hour, I'll be off. Maybe it's a budget thing. I heard him arguing with his office about costs versus opportunity, that sort of thing. In the meantime, it's good overtime for me. I don't have a clue where this is supposed to go, what it's supposed to mean and frankly, I'm not sure I need something else on my plate so I'm not asking what it's all about."

"Are you on the boat tonight?" Moose spent most of his professional time with the harbor patrol for the New York Police Department, fishing out bodies mostly, some genuine heroics here and there, but for the past few years, just sitting in the East River across from Vinny's project watching the U.N. Building. Not a place for any career advancement, but he loved the water and hoped for some involvement in an important undercover type of operation. Maybe that would show someone what he was capable of. Then again, maybe he would be out of the department in a week if that goddamn Lieutenant continued his assault on him and his career. Stupid bastard gets drunk, plows a cruiser into the side of the precinct, and he's coming after me because I won't lie for him?

"No, not for a couple of more days. Saturday night, why?"

Vinny thought for a millisecond before deciding against giving Moose too much information. Not that he didn't trust him. On the contrary, although he moved to the neighborhood and fell in with the boys when they were fifteen or so, some years removed from the swims in the East River, he was accepted immediately what with his quick wit and jolly demeanor...how couldn't they? But he wanted this situation, whatever it was, to play out naturally. Because he just couldn't ignore some sort of sixth sense tickling his brain cortex that was telling him that something was happening here. Something very...unusual. Coincidences, coincidences abounding everywhere.

"Do me a favor, I know I'm not a cop and you can't take orders from me, but just sit on this guy even if the Fed tells you to take the rest of the night off, at least until I talk to you. But don't interfere unless you see a gun, okay?"

"Yeah okay. Where are you now?"

"Five minutes away, listen, don't acknowledge me in any way when you see me, okay? Listen, do you see Charlie Mick anywhere?"

"I do. I saw him when I was watching the tail end of the fight. I was about to jump in when J'lome came out and calmed it all down."

"Did the kid get involved?"

"No, he was just standing by, watching. What's he doing there?"

"Learning about life. Listen, just be invisible, okay? Just make sure that if the guy leaves the mosque between now and when I arrive, follow him and let me know where he goes. Remember, invisible. Okay?"

"Invisible like Elvis."

"Right." Vinny folded the phone and put it back in his inside jacket pocket while starting to work his neurons and dendrites into providing him with the most plausible of options his disciplined mind could form. It seemed quite possible that this would just be an exercise in scaring the crap out of these guys, whomever they were, into never coming back to J'lome's mosque under the threat of a certain beating. J'lome was his closest friend. He had given up years of his life so that Vinny could stay out of jail. He never gave up Vinny's name when he could have, when most others would have. Vinny figured J'lome had some hard-line Irish in him even though he was black, like those guys he read about at Long Kesh prison who would stay silent for months, years at a time, rather than tell their jailers anything at all, even their name. And basically, someone was fucking with his best friend, his brother, and Vinny was pissed off enough about that alone to put aside his troubles with the project, his interesting dinner with Maxie and his physical well being to teach whomever this prick was a lesson. He reminded himself not get carried away, but rather to let it all play out with great patience and practiced intellectual reflexes. He was confident that not only could he beat any man hand-to-hand, he could out think any man as well. He believed that he could react to a situation better than anyone he ever met, like a pro athlete seeing a virtually invisible seam in a defense, a tiny mistake by a defender, a little bit of daylight. That combined with his legendary patience would lead him to some sort of promised land of answers. But then again, maybe this was just all bullshit analysis, leading to mental paralysis. Maybe the guy was shaking hands with J'lome right now, asking for forgiveness. And he was wasting all of this mental exercise on a situation that was probably a whole lot of nothing. Sitting now at the light at Northern Boulevard behind a diplomat's limousine, a couple of yellow cabs and a tanker rig looking to back into the gas station on the corner, he started to again feel like an idiot for letting his thoughts get away from him, for not concentrating on the important matter at hand, that being what the hell he was going to do with the clowns he met this morning. He knew they indeed called the husband and wife who ran Shale Financial. Ninety-nine times out of a hundred, a decent banker worth their salt would have blown them off. But somehow they struck a raw nerve with those two...unbelievable. If the Burkes were here they would probably compare it to Tate George's last tenth of a second shot against Clemson in a long ago college basketball game. But unlike the players on the losing team that night who had to trudge off the court in resigned acceptance once the ball fell through the net, Vinny was not finished by their call to the bank. Hurt, stunned maybe, but certainly not dead in the water. The tanker then somehow fit itself into the gas station, the cabbie stopped leaning on his horn and everyone moved forward. First things first, he thought. I'm going to go stand up for my brother and then I'm going to somehow find the answer I need to begin breaking serious ground on this project next fucking week.

⁕

It certainly was a nice apartment, Laura thought upon entering Adam's place, but oddly cold. He should have put the heat up before he left, made it a little cozier. A one-tenth deduction from the Czech judge. There were no pictures of family members, nothing interesting hanging on the walls, not a plant anywhere. She couldn't put her finger on it, but Adam didn't seem quite settled here and she wasn't referring to the lack of 'lived-in-ness'. Maybe he just moved in. She never asked him how long he'd been here. Should she ask now? Or might he think that was prying? A recent move-in date would explain the relative lack of furniture. There was only a sofa with a small coffee table in front and a halogen lamp in the corner. The view from the high floor west-facing windows over the avenues and the Hudson River made her think the summer sunsets must be magnificent to see.

Adam invited her to sit on the sofa and he looked around for a place to deposit the keys. It was becoming apparent to Laura that maybe this wasn't his place at all. Men usually drop their keys and wallet in the same place every time they come home. If they had landed here earlier in the relationship, when he would have known that there was no chance of sex, just conversation, she would have asked then. But she was on a bit of a mission now and she truly wanted him to work out nicely. Why shouldn't he be a little nervous as well? She answered herself simply, Because a real man wouldn't be nervous about any-thing other than making me feel beautiful, loved, and desired. We're in our forties, for goodness sake, we should know how to do this. She stood and went to the window for a look but instead of the horizon, she found herself instead looking down at the pedestrians and cars in the street below. Adam returned then from the kitchen, she figured, because she heard the keys hit a stone type of surface she figured was a counter-top. She had to guess because he hadn't offered a tour of the place. He also didn't ask her if she wanted anything to drink. She wanted to give him a "No thank you, Adam," with a coquettish look, which should have at least prompted another request just to make sure, but nothing. He moved to the sofa to sit and Laura noticed that he didn't seem to know his way around so well. He didn't move well around the low coffee table and he didn't instinctively go to one part of the sofa that should have been his favorite. He brought out a bottle of wine that Laura guessed had been sitting on the side of the sofa, perhaps on the floor—very strange—but then couldn't find a cork-screw. It was too obvious. She had to start asking some questions, at least start a conversation, maybe to uncover something, some reason why maybe she should consider leaving.

"How long have you lived here? It seems like you are stumbling a bit." Laura sat at the far end and crossed her legs. That he noticed she, well...noticed.

"Uh, not for long," he replied, taking care not to spill the wine. "That's why it's kind of bare." Laura was a bit miffed because he was expecting her to drink some wine and he didn't have the slightest bit of decency just to ask if she even wanted some. Alright, just relax, she told herself. She looked around toward the other end of the apartment where she figured the bedroom was.

"It's a nice place, though. Do you like the neighborhood?" She didn't get an answer so maybe he was still looking for the corkscrew... or condoms. She stood again and walked over to a stereo, which was perched on a multi-level silvery metal kind of 1980's piece of furniture. She pressed the button on the tuner and found a college station that she knew played soft music, the kind with nylon strings and romantic lyrics sung by people who could actually sing. She was startled to hear the young deejay play a Camilo Sesto tune, "El Amor de mi Vida," a beautiful song she used to sing together with Diego back in the late 1970s, which she took for a major sign that this was, in spite of everything negative that happened so far, going to end up being a wonderful night. She had some of his CD's back at her apartment. She closed her eyes and listened to the elegant Spaniard croon, whispering the lyrics to herself, astonished that they came back to her so easily.

She had been absolutely concerned in the past hour, several times, that she was making a mistake with Adam, but she started to brush off those thoughts one by one, dismissing them as silly schoolgirl stuff. Instead the glow of anticipation was emanating from her again and she started to feel like a vital, desirable woman. The boorish behavior in the restaurant was behind her as she turned to see him come toward her with two glasses of wine. He was indeed handsome, a debonair, kind of academic look she liked. She started to wonder just what his body looked like, felt like.

"I hope you didn't mind that I turned on some music," she said, looking up into his eyes when he arrived. He leaned in perfectly and kissed her softly and Laura opened her lips, allowing him to explore her mouth, but he pulled away. He was looking past her shoulder at the stereo system with what she thought was some kind of concerned look.

"Please ask me next time you want to turn on any of the electronics, okay?" He then leaned in for another kiss and she answered once more with slightly parted lips, but again that chill was in the air. He leaned past her and turned the channel to a rock station that was currently playing AC/DC's "Highway to Hell." As much as the Camilo Sesto music was starting to raise her carnal desire, this music was now starting to raise her blood pressure instead. Just relax, Laura, she said to herself. It's his first time with me so he's bound to be somewhat nervous as well, even if he is a forty-two-year-old man. He finished adjusting the stereo, locking in the station and turning up the bottom on the equalizer which made the drums and bass leap out of the speakers. The singer was positively screaming the lyrics.

"Here, sit down again," he said invitingly, patting the sofa close to him. Oh boy, Laura thought, that's exactly what an old boyfriend used to do, pat the couch or the bed to summon her. It made her feel like a dog. She ambled over and sat down, taking his offered glass of wine. Please do something to make me feel like a woman, she wanted to cry out.

"Do you want to change that?" he asked, pointing to the stereo with the wineglass.

She started to stand immediately, "You sure you don't mind?" He waved her off and drank from his glass. No toast from him, she thought. Stop judging everything, she admonished herself. In front of the stereo again, she found the college station and listened to the last third of Camilo Sesto's song. The notes of the guitar floated out of the speakers and into her heart, once again transporting her to a simpler time, a simpler place. The drummer at this part of the song played powerfully but was in perfect balance with the rest of the band, the lyrics enunciated so clearly anyone could discern their meaning even if the listener didn't speak a word of Spanish. She closed her eyes and started to sway slightly to the easy rhythm. She could hear Adam get up from the couch and come up behind her. She leaned back against him and raised her chin still with her eyes closed and waited for him to kiss her neck, maybe even cup her breast tenderly. But instead he reached past her and turned the radio off and then put a compact disc in the player...a singer she didn't know, and frankly didn't want to. The music was not as monotonously pounding as the earlier song, but this one was sung by a young girl with a screeching voice that reminded her of the wild parrots that used to raid her father's crops.

"This is better," he said. "I need something to keep me invigorated." Laura wondered what he thought she needed to keep her invigorated as he never bothered to ask. He downed his wine, pointed to her glass and asked, "Will you finish that?" She barely had a moment to acknowledge his question as she was still working on how and why he changed the music but it didn't seem to matter to him what she would have answered as he downed her glass as well, smiled...and then came in for another kiss and a gentle push toward the bedroom.

"Adam," she spoke to him in a voice slightly above a whisper as he was kissing her neck now, still angling her toward the bed.

"Hmmm?"

She put her hands on his shoulders and stepped away, smiling sweetly, "Hold on, let me get ready."

She pirouetted into the room, walked around the other side of the bed and kicked off her shoes and after looking around for a moment said, "Don't you have to brush your teeth or something?" She was reaching for the top button of her pants, fingering the material—seductively, she hoped—as she asked the question, at the same time breaking her knee and sweeping her foot slowly in a small circle, the big toe pointed like a ballerina's.

He smiled and came to her for another kiss. Laura liked to be kissed deeply with her head titled to the left, which was unusual according to nine out of ten men she had kissed already. She also bowled as a righty but strangely ended up on her right foot, the incorrect foot, when she threw the ball down the alley. She always thought these little quirks were strange but hopefully endearing to any man that tried to get to really know her. Anyway, she couldn't change either habit or any of the others that Adam would never know about. Most of her boy-friends just learned to deal with the lefty kiss, but Adam took her head in his hands while planting a noisy, sloppy smack where something much more sensual would have melted her on the spot, and a little too strongly titled her head to the right, which sent a minor stinger down her neck. He sucked noisily on her lips, causing a vibration that felt like she was sucking on a piece of dry ice. He pulled away looking deeply into her eyes and disappeared into the bathroom.

"I'll be right back," was all he said as he closed the door and it wasn't even said over his shoulder. It was as if he were speaking to someone in the bathroom, which he entered without turning around, shutting the door behind him, the click of the lock echoing around the room.

Laura's shoulders slumped as she heard the faucet opening with a squeak and the water running around in the sink. She sat on the bed, pulled off her pants and casually dropped them on the floor along with her sweater. She slipped beneath the covers and put her head on the pillow and admitted to herself fully what she didn't want to, that Adam had failed his test miserably. She was so horny that even the slightest, most indiscernible piece of charm, with a tiny dash of mischievousness—how else would a man think and act if he knew he was going to have a new woman for the first time in a few hours, she wondered—anyway, it would have made her jump on him. The texting in the lobby, the stiffing of the waitress, that she arrived for the date on the subway not having been picked up by him for this special night, his clumsiness from the moment they walked into the apartment, the music, the sloppy kiss, taking my wine, not talking, no patience, just a teenager looking for his first lay. All he had were his looks and what he had in his drawers and by the way this night was going, she wasn't expecting much there. Even if he were blessed with size and girth, he probably would prematurely ejaculate, or be soggy in her vagina as the big ones usually were, or maybe he would have the strength and duration of Priapus and not have the good sense after twenty minutes of rhythm-less pumping with no orgasm in sight to roll off the woman sparing her some cracked ribs, flattened breasts and serious facial burn and complete his mission by himself. Laura had one boyfriend who did just that when he was lasting too long, and she found it to be a wonderfully intimate and thoughtful deed.

Anyway, she was seriously considering gathering up her clothes and just leaving the apartment as when it came down to it, she didn't have to explain herself to anyone. If she wanted to on any given day she could get laid within the hour...a couple of drinks at some fancy hotel bar, a traveling businessman, a few silly jokes, maybe somewhere nice like the Four Seasons or The Plaza, and she could be banged, showered and then home in bed for the evening news. But maybe she would give Adam one more chance as the last thing she wanted to do right now was to go home by herself...five years without getting decently laid, again she wondered, how did that happen? But okay, she put in the time with Adam, three months of dating and she could sleep with him at least just this once and put a stop to it shortly after. If he turned out to be an Olympic champion in the sack, she'd keep him around for a few months, her 'last minute' guy, dumping him at the end of the summer or until someone better came along. At least she would gain a little more experience—what a funny thought for a mature woman to have—and she thought again that maybe, just maybe, Adam would emerge from that bathroom with a towel around his waist, a beautiful smile on his face, and a boyishly shy comment like, "Sorry, I'm not as smooth as I'd like to be tonight. I've just never known such a beautiful woman before."

And then of course he would walk toward the bed, lose the towel and make love to her as no one else ever has or even thought of. They would laugh often in the ensuing years of their relationship about his ineptness their first time. She would tell her girlfriends the story also, but she would include for their envy and enjoyment how he had her number as soon he touched her. That was another page from the sonnet to be written about her perfect world that she thought of often, how things should be, at least once in a while in order to keep us hoping for something better the next time.

Well whatever it was, sex was going to happen soon, so she started to stroke the inside of her thighs, reaching up to her right nipple in an effort to get her juices going a little bit as she realized Adam was taking an uncommonly long time in the bathroom. A minute later the water stopped along with her breathing and she noticed the light from underneath the door turning off and Adam opening the door and emerging...well a nice body he definitely has, but he's also wearing an atrocious pair of underwear, a half jock strap contraption with its own pocket for his junk that she realized from her days in the fashion industry were specifically designed to push everything forward. She could read the brand name, which was printed on the band in bold black letters, 'Cockthrusters.' She remembered from her time in the garment district that gay men loved them. Jesus, is he gay? she wondered. He walked across the room and her head swiveled from left to right, following him. Yes, he definitely was gorgeous, she thought, strong legs and powerful shoulders and everything else you need to be a model for a Michelangelo creation. He was a bit shiny and she guessed that he had applied some expensive body lotion, and maybe too much as she could smell it from a few feet away. He stood at the end of the bed, kind of showing himself off for her. He was slipping badly in his approach now and the thoughts of a great night in the hay with this guy were fading fast.

What she wanted to do was kneed his muscles, take in his natural scent, and not have her hands slip around on his slick body as if she were massaging an ice cube. The normally delicious fragrance of lavender really started to hit her nose as he leaned down and started to crawl toward her up the bed, this action pushing the unnatural lavender smell of the oil he took so much time applying toward her the way an offshore storm pushes the tide toward a barrier beach. It was a misplaced scent, not belonging on a man's body, like delicious smelling hazelnut coffee brewing in a disgusting greasy spoon diner. He rolled left around the foot of the bed and she could see now that he was carrying a phone. Was he texting his friends with it while he was in the bathroom?

"Someone you need to call?" She had turned slightly on her side, facing him, resting her head on her fist. He had rolled to that side of the bed, not taking the direct approach straight up her legs as she had hoped.

He looked at her and shook his head no and put the phone on the nightstand. It was a flip phone and it was still opened, standing on its side, the blank screen facing her. He lifted the covers and slid to her and she turned fully toward him. His hand went around her waist and he pulled her toward her a little roughly, that was okay, she thought, she liked a little of that...very little. And he started kissing her neck again, but this time his kisses were so wet they were leaving a liquidy feeling on her neck which she despised. His saliva was mixing with the lavender oil and that was producing a viscous slop that felt like she had been spit upon. Plus, his eyebrows still contained some water droplets from his recent ablutions and as a result she was wet in another, wrong place. He was failing her fast and furious and at this rate she was inches away from jumping out of the bed and leaving. Just then his hand slid down to her crotch and he ran his fingers over the lacy underwear she picked out especially for this evening that he didn't comment on, causing her to buck her hips slightly.

"You like that, huh?" he asked in diction lifted from a male porn star's first acting lesson, complete with raised eyebrow. God, what a loser, she thought as he pushed her hips flat on the bed and climbed on top of her, reaching behind himself to pull off his jock strap under-wear. She was reminded of several selfish lovers—had she had any other kind? she quickly wondered—all of whom climaxed quickly after no attempt at foreplay. Maybe Adam will at least be quick, she rumi-nated as she took her own panties off and dropped them off the side of the bed, where she knew she could find them quickly once this was all over. He slid his hand to her breast and pinched her nipple, of course too hard, and started to kiss her mouth again, she allowing him to let his tongue inside because at least that would keep him from talking.

Oh, just put it in me already, she thought. I will dream of Diego and a few of the other decent men she had been with and soon it would be over. Maybe she would even make believe it was Michael Pierce inside her. She had done that a few times before, Michael making love to her expertly, not a wrong move in her mind's eye when he was with her, her only words being 'otra vez, otra vez,' again, again.

Those were the only words she would need because in her mind, the most perfect lover and man for her would understand the concept she and Diego perfected, 'no necessitamos parables'...we don't need words. Her thoughts were interrupted by Adam, now guiding his knee clumsily between her legs, opening them with his patella on the inside of her left leg, at the south end of where her quadricep narrowed, where there were about a billion nerve bundles that needed to be dealt with gently, not like this, and she could feel his cock now, a good size she had to admit and at least it was kind of hard and ready to go.

He was kissing her again on the neck and actually he was much better than he had been earlier, his lips drier, his breathing even and he was keeping all of his weight off her. She felt herself returning to the moment, thinking, This can be saved...this is going to be okay... maybe extraordinary. His cock was inches from her vagina now and she wanted to reach down and guide him but frankly, the kissing on her neck was now really turning her on and she turned her head toward the right so he could have a better target and she raked her fingers into his hair to hold his head in the perfect place at a perfect angle. Wait, was he pulling away a little? He indeed was and she was angered to see him smooth his hair back into place. He buried his face in her neck again and just before she grabbed a handful of ass to pull him inside her—oral pleasures for her apparently not being on his list of party favors tonight—she found herself startled by a buzzing and a flash of light as if a large lightning bug was hovering over the bed. She turned her head a little further right, toward the vibration and the light on the edge of her vision, her attention drawn to the phone still lying on its side on the night table and it seemed to be moving slightly as it rested on the edge of a small piece of fabric stretched across the table the lamp stood upon. The fabric was muffling the sound. She saw the phone ringing, in effect, instead of hearing the vibration against the hard material of the nightstand. And the screen was lighting up with each pulsing of the incoming call, displaying the phone number and name of who was calling. Adam brought himself up on his straightened arms, ready to insert himself when she placed her hands firmly upon his shoulders and stared in disbelief at the screen. It was a one-word caption identifying the caller, the word flashing in a pulsing manner with each subsequent ring...WIFE.

—⚓—

The dishes at Michael's house were done, stacked neatly in the dishwasher. He filled the soap compartment with powder, slammed the door, and turned the machine to maximum clean. The newspapers and magazines were tied with cord and put out along with the garbage cans by the sidewalk in front of the house ready for pickup in the morning. Michael sat down at the now empty and clean kitchen table to watch yet another episode of *Law & Order*. Damn, Mariska Hargitay looks good, he was thinking. He always wanted to accidentally run into the production of the popular television series on the streets of Manhattan so maybe they would cast him somehow. It was embarrassing to him to realize that he knew so many of the lines from the episodes he watched in syndication. Had he been watching these shows that long? That many years with nothing more productive to do? Anyway, maybe he would be lucky enough to share the screen with that blonde actress with the glasses who plays a District Attorney. Have to Google her tomorrow, he thought, find out her name and other films and TV work she may have done. He heard Georgia's footsteps striding with purpose out of the bedroom toward him.

"Where's Sally?" The question was launched at him as if she were a crossbow.

"Finishing her homework," he answered as he continued to stare at Mariska's beautiful features while she was wrestling a 200 pound suspect to the ground with the greatest of ease.

"Clean the turtle's water. I don't want it to stink while we are away." This statement came at him like a dum-dum bullet shot out of a 44 Magnum. He turned his body halfway toward her.

"Georgia, can you try to ask me something without it sounding like an order? I feel like an employee here sometimes." He did not immediately twist back to the television. He waited for her response, his spine starting to protest. Screw it, why not amp it up, she's leaving tomorrow anyway. He watched her tearing up a pile of paper on the counter as if she were looking for a winning lottery ticket. She didn't even look up when she spoke.

"Michael, I am busy and upset. Please don't try my patience with your mid-life crisis ruminations." She found what she was looking for and turned to walk away when he jumped up to head upstairs to clean the turtle's water.

"What makes you think that I would have reacted to how you speak to me any differently if I were twenty-eight instead of forty-five or so?" He didn't try to hide his anger, like an employee who was tempted to belt out a Johnny Paycheck song to the boss. Not waiting for her answer, she was gone from view now anyway, he ascended the stairs to Sally's room. Could she hear us arguing he wondered. He then heard the familiar stomping coming back. He turned back to listen to an answer from Georgia he really didn't care about anymore.

"Michael" she started like an impatient third grade teacher ready to scold an petulant child, "I warned you not to start with me. This trip has me nervous enough as it is." Hmmm, maybe she's reaching out to me, actually sharing an inner fear with him? He stopped his ascent and looked down at her with soft eyes.

"Why? It's only to see your relatives and they all love Sally," he said comfortingly. She was not comforted, however. Exasperation was spilling out of her along with a familiar complaint and lamentation.

"They want her to be one hundred percent Greek.. My sister's kids are Greek on both sides and I feel like I am failing them and her."

"Georgia, your sister's husband is named Constantinos and mine is Michael. I am of Irish extraction on both sides of my family, I can't change what I am and you can't change what Sally is no matter how much you try. She is an American kid and even if we were both Greek, just off the boat from the Mediterranean, she'd still be an American.

"And it's not important for Sally to discover her heritage? For me?"

His answer stayed in his head because voicing it again, now, would just escalate everything unnecessarily and he was getting tired. It was a lost cause displaying his opinion here and now. It should have come out, "I know it's important for you, Georgia, but I don't think as much for Sally." He struggled for the strength to sweep his hand toward the large living room window, and explain that it was America out there and that speaking and reading and writing Greek was nothing more than a skill, much like playing a saxophone. It might have been somewhat more justifiable if it were Japanese, Spanish, or Chinese, even Russian, language skills that were becoming more and more important in the business community. But Greek was more and more part of the ancient world, its importance left behind by the global economy and its stronger European partners. The speaking part he felt Sally could absorb through daily conversation and he was cool with that, but the fights over the reading and writing were driving him and the child over the edge.

Michael had in his early years acquired more than a pedestrian knowledge of Korean, Chinese, and even some Urdu and Pashtu from the constant comings and goings between his friends' homes and apartments in the old neighborhood, sitting down to dinner and lunch several times per week with his other friends, Ping the Router, Roger Khan and his gorgeous cousin Jasmine, 'Mikey Busy,' who got that name by always being just too serious even when he was having the time of his life, and Pak-man all dead now along with some others, crushed by a falling building on 9/11. But he could never fathom learning the written discipline of these languages. Why was it important if you could just point to something and ask "Please translate this for me?" All of a sudden he missed these friends who were buried under tons of concrete, steel, desks, computers and airplane parts, buried like whatever dreams he once held so dear. He shook his head, angry at his uncharacteristic self-loathing and terrible habit of comparing his small problems to something so tragic and unbearable...he brought himself back to the present, realizing that if he just changed the turtle's water, he could then go to bed and start to look forward to three days alone and maybe a card game with Vinny and the rest of the boys. There's an idea. He said nothing more to her and headed upstairs to finish his latest household task.

"Tell me about your job with this bank. What was its name again?" Whathefu knew the bigger man wasn't intimidated by his small stature when they were still in the bathroom, but now Andre was backed up against a wall just outside the prayer room which was now spilling the faithful out to the lobby of The People's Mosque and then to the streets of Astoria. He warned him to keep his voice low and to not draw any attention to them.

"I work for Argent Bank," replied Andre, who was being closely watched by Aubrey. He was terrified of this evil-looking, blue-eyed 'Ice Person' looming over him. His own bulk was clearly insignificant to this man, who seemed as if he were incapable of any type of compassion or understanding of any other point of view. He had already recognized him as the same guy who was pinning the Pakistani congregant against the outside wall of the mosque as he was entering with Fated. Andre was able to look into his eyes then and found them to strangely be equal parts fury and calm resolve. Scary bastard, he thought as he entered the mosque, dismissing him earlier with ease as he was at the mosque only to speak with his friend about Hezbollah TV, but now he could feel the man's menace and killing ability as if it were an old heavy blanket draped over his shoulders. "I am a Senior Network Administrator for the bank's computer systems," he answered timidly.

"Did I hear you and your friend discussing your ability to transfer money electronically?" asked Whathefu, feeling stronger by the minute. He could see the pieces of his life falling back into place before his eyes.

Andre laughed and waved his hand in mock exasperation, "He was just kidding. I can't do anything like that." Whathefu pursed his lips and shook his head slowly from side to side.

"No, my friend, he sounded to me like he knew what he was talking about. As if this was either something you had discussed previously or at least, he did his own research and was just trying to convince you to act upon it." Whathefu turned to Aubrey, "This other guy also made reference to some woman our friend here seems to be involved with, one that he apparently was already stealing money for, though on a small scale." He turned back to Andre. "I think you're lying to me, my friend. I think you can walk out of the bank with whatever you want, whenever you want, and quite easily at that."

Aubrey grabbed Andre's elbow discreetly but with tremendous power, gaining his attention as he softly growled, "Tell us now how we can get this money out of your bank or I will smash every bone in your body starting with this arm." Andre's eyes were practically bulging with fright now, his body twisting in fear as well as pain. He licked his lips and said, "Yes of course it's possible. With computers today, you can steal virtually anything. But there's a trail of messages and codes that would ensure your eventual capture."

"You haven't been captured yet," said Whathefu.

"Yes, alright, yes," answered Andre, fully aware that for the first time he was admitting his guilt to someone other than Fated about his embezzling monies from Argent Bank to pay for Kismine's studio time. Damn that bastard Fated for not being my supportive friend, damn myself for being so weak! He continued, "But an enormous amount of money would attract instant attention. And it would lead everyone right back to me. And ultimately to you as well."

"We have no intention of sticking around this disgusting city any longer than we have to," said Aubrey, still gripping Andre's elbow. "As soon as we have…fifty million dollars in a certain bank account in Switzerland or the Caymans, we will be far away and quite unreachable."

"Fifty million?" asked Whathefu in surprise, turning to Aubrey with a raised eyebrow.

Aubrey released his grip but kept his stare on Andre's round sweating face. "I have my own plans that include no one else but me. You can do whatever you like, but I suggest you pay your debt to the family of the girl you killed otherwise death will stalk you the rest of your days. But I want twenty-five million for myself."

Whathefu thought, as did Andre, that now was the time to finally do something big, something that will change someone's life. "Make it sixty million," said Whathefu. "I need something to live on after I pay off my debt." Aubrey liked this idea as he had already decided to kill this Saudi rich boy and make off with his share. It would be easy to do, easy for him to justify because he could see this kid was infatuated with him sexually as so many men in his past were. Damn queers…I'll just make him think he has a chance with me and I'll let him set up the accounts and a short while later, deposit his body in the river, along with this fat bastard. His controller would understand. All he would have to do is tell him that Whathefu had tried to escape. That would be readily and quickly accepted as truth.

"I can't do this," came Andre's pitiful, pleading whisper. The pain reentered his elbow and Aubrey spoke to him from an inch away, his voice becoming even more menacing as it lowered in volume.

"Let me be crystal clear with you, my friend. Unless you do this by the end of this weekend, you and your whole fucking family as well as anyone else you hold dear will be dead. Don't even think about what we will do to you because the reality of it is beyond your comprehension. Starting tonight, you are going to explain to my friend here exactly what your set-up has been at the bank and how you can get hold of this money we want and transfer it where we want it to go. Until that task is finished, your life is in constant danger and under my control." Aubrey released Andre's elbow and reached inside his jacket, ripping his inside pocket away so that his wallet just fell out. "I'll keep this," he said, sticking the wallet in his back pants pocket and then demanded as he was extending his hand again, "Give me your phone, too." He put Andre's phone in his other pants pocket after shutting it off. He asked, "Do these computers at your bank run all night?"

"Probably," Whathefu answered for him. "I'm sure they have someone on duty even at 2:00 in the morning."

"I asked him," said Aubrey in a most unfriendly way that Andre didn't fail to notice. Who were these guys? he wondered. Were they really friends? What is their connection to each other? What dead girl? "So fat man, tell me where the computers are and who is there monitoring them now?"

"Well, like your friend said, the system is always in operation as we receive hundreds of files containing wires and transfers of millions of dollars from all over the world all day and night. Right now after regular business hours, there is only one person on call because of budget cuts and automation. Many of the programs just run themselves now," he explained.

"Can you get in there now?"

"Yes, as a Senior Administrator, I can come and go almost as I please." He felt the pain in his elbow again. "Let's go there now; I want to see this place," Aubrey ordered as he edged Andre toward the door.

—⚬—

"Stay here, watch the car," said Vinny to Charlie Mick, who had stayed put in front of the People's Mosque since earlier that day. He continued purposefully to the door despite being on edge for several reasons. The project was uppermost in his mind, its possible death just days away, all of his friend's savings as well as most of his own wealth poured into it. Even J'lome was uncharacteristically nervous. He hadn't seen his friend so unnerved since he brought Islam into his life. And the woman, Maxie, she was swirling around his brain as well. He had to admit, she was something else, a perfect combination of elegance and fun girl, the kind you could have a farting contest with on the lawn of a fancy Westchester wedding and still look like a million dollars to anyone who saw her. But she was married, and he wasn't going to take that on, no way. Maybe he should get to know her a bit, but wouldn't that just be a very slow bullet to each of their hearts? The bitter sensation overtaking what would probably be the obvious sweetness of a relationship with such a vital, attractive woman.

She said she was unhappy...screw that, he thought, I'll just wait around until she does something, if anything. This evening was full of such strange dynamics, he continued to muse, wondering how it would all come together or if it were just a wisp of happenstance, to be blown away into nothingness like the spores of a dandelion settling on a city block. A card game with the boys would probably be a good idea, he started to think. We always came together during the games which were becoming as rare as a Knick winning streak. He looked at the full moon overhead, a wolf's moon it was, the time of year when it passed closest to Earth. He basked in its simple beauty, remembering the exercises J'lome taught him when he needed to relax: Breathe deeply and surely and focus on one of God's creations, be it a flower, a tree, a laughing child, a cool breeze, or the moon and the stars, and within a moment or so whatever you were so concerned about should melt away. It had actually worked many times before, but he would really need to concentrate on something truly beautiful to settle him this time, especially when he was suddenly getting a face full of door. His anger started to rise like a missile as the pain of the blow from the mosque door being pushed open too quickly shot through his hand which had not yet completely gripped the handle all the way to his elbow and back. He glared at Andre, Aubrey, and Whathefu as they moved through the door with no obvious concern for anyone else who might be in their way. He summoned his best Cagney, "Howyudune?" The question was not a greeting, but a retort to their selfish behavior, a way of expressing annoyance in a diplomatic, New York kind of way. It was supposed to be followed by an "Alright, sorry about that," kind of response. Out of the corner of his eye he could see Charlie Mick lean imperceptibly toward them but not so much so as to draw attention to himself, not identifying himself as an ally. Good, thought Vinny, he's learning. Vinny also knew that Moose was nearby watching as well. Not that he was afraid. Vinny feared no man either intellectually or physically, but he was full of comfort knowing he had his back covered.

"Yeah, okay, sorry, excuse us," the big blond bastard said as he pushed past Vinny. The rudeness of the answer, the obvious racial disconnect, I mean, there were not many blond, blue-eyed Muslims in the world and there were none in Queens, he was sure of that. And he could see that although the big bastard was concealing it well, he was directing the fat guy as if it were a quiet kidnapping. Then it hit him, these are the guys J'lome called about. Could they also be the same guys Moose was following for the Feds? What are the chances of that? Vinny stood in the door like a Japanese businessman saying good-bye to a client, watching the trio head south on Steinway Street. They passed by Charlie Mick, who showed no acknowledgment of them, turning toward the same direction the three were heading after they passed so he could observe them without drawing any attention to his actions. Vinny looked past Charlie Mick and he noticed Moose Miller's brown Ford Crown Victoria idling across the street about fifty feet further than where the trio were at that point. When were the New York cops going to get cars that didn't stick out so much? he wondered. Couldn't they have SUV's on Monday, Chevy's on Tuesday, Buicks on Wednesday, and so on? He could tell it was Moose behind the wheel, his telltale bulk filling the windshield. The driver's side window went down and Moose's hand came out, not waving, just stuck up in the air for a moment before being withdrawn. Vinny put up his index finger and quickly pointed at the trio, 'Is that the one you're following?' Moose's head bobbed up and down just once and Vinny then saw him bare his forearm, tapping his watch as he did so. Vinny knew Moose was going off duty soon. He must have heard from the Fed who was running him and if he didn't get home on time, his wife would eat him for dinner. Also, it was very much frowned upon by the powers that be in the police department. If you weren't on duty, then go home and don't get involved with anything unless you absolutely had to.

So Vinny turned to Charlie Mick and pointed to his eyes with index and middle finger, cupped his ear with his other hand, and then twirled his finger in the air, pointing it at the young man. 'Follow them, watch them, listen to them, take your time.' He finished by holding his pinky to the corner of his mouth and his thumb to his ear...'call me'. All of this took about three seconds and Vinny was again comforted by the close relationships he had with these people. He observed the trio once more and he could definitely see the big bastard gripping the fat bastard's elbow and the little bastard was looking up at the big bastard in a strange kind of way and Vinny could see that he was smiling and actually rubbing his hands together in glee as if he had won the lottery.

—⊕—

Laura was staring incomprehensibly at the phone as Adam was saying, "Guide me, guide me in." Doesn't he know the way: Which was the last thought she had prior to her exasperation with her almost-lover metamorphosing into turning to barely controlled fury. She grabbed his penis in her left hand and squeezed and twisted as she reached for the phone. She maneuvered deftly from underneath him, pushing him on his side and getting her feet underneath her and she now had one knee on the bed, one foot on the floor and the still vibrating phone in her right hand as well as Adam's semi-limp penis in her left which had naturally twisted along with her body's movement from underneath him. He looked at her in a state of shock and pleaded desperately, "Don't answer that," which only got him a not-so-subtle twist from

Laura's hand, not the one holding the phone. He grimaced in pain as she pressed the talk button.

"Hello?" A sigh from the other end.

"Is Adam there?"

"Yes, who is calling, please?"

"His wife." A tremendous, pregnant silence followed before the caller added, "Do me a favor, honey, just make sure he showers before he comes home. I don't want any of your disgusting whore scent on my husband when he returns. Just make sure you understand, whatever your name is, you're not the first and you're not the last. I'll never divorce him, ever. You're just the latest bimbo to fall for his charming, lying ways." The line clicked off and Laura, in a rage she had never known could exist in a human being let alone herself, threw the phone against the far wall in such a way that would have made Dwight Gooden proud and further twisted Adam's still engorged penis with such strength he thought it was going to separate from his body.

"You're married?!"

"Please," he begged, moving his hand to his groin to try to relieve her grip which he amazingly realized got even tighter.

"Just answer me, now!!"

"Yes, yes, dammit! Now let go of me!"

Laura released her grip with a flourish and Adam fell back among the fancy three thousand count linens cupping his groin and letting out a breath of relief. "What's your problem, Adam?" she demanded. Why would you do this to me or to any other woman?" She was pulling her clothing on as she spoke. Her exit from this den of horrors was imminent, but she had to try to understand what motivated this man, and so many others like him in the city. "What was the point of lying to me all this time?" Why not just be charming and honest, why don't you get divorced, why not just go with a hooker or one of the sluts on Screwme dot com?"

"It was a bet I had with my friends, the ones you saw me with on the lawn in Central Park." She was finishing pulling up her pants as he said it.

"A bet? For what? I demand an explanation from you."

He pulled himself up to a sitting position, still breathing hard from the pain in his groin. "My friends and I saw you in the park a few months ago, you remember that beautiful day in February?" He was smiling at the memory of that day and it disgusted and enraged her.

"All of us wanted you, but we're all married. A few of the boys knew that I played around when I wanted to—my wife and I haven't had sex in almost eight years—and they said to me that a classy woman like you would never fall for me. So I bet them all a thousand bucks each that I could get you into the sack within three months." He was smiling now. "Several of them are lawyers and I can see them tomorrow arguing the point of getting you into the sack and not consummating the act and maybe that would turn the bet on its head. In other words, who won the bet, because I did get you into the sack didn't I?"

He stood and came toward her, still naked except for his shit-eating grin and deflated unit, "You definitely wanted me, didn't you? This doesn't change that simple fact." His hands were reaching for her and the horror of his Olympic-sized selfishness and clueless actions were quickly overwhelmed by another prehistoric impulse, one that lived in all of us, that was strangely taught to her by Michael Pierce: "Always punch from where your hands are laying at the moment of attack. If you pull back to land a haymaker, your opponent will see it coming from a mile away and duck or worse, grab hold of your arm. Just start the motion from down here near your hip and remember to put your shoulder into it and you will have the same or more power as if you reached back and swung with all your might."

He had been speaking to several women at the bank holiday party when she overheard him. In the weeks previous, there had been a series of attacks against women around the building's neighborhood, and he was giving an impromptu self-defense lesson. She took in what he was saying that night along with his nice gray suit and burgundy tie combination and she even recalled quickly her twinge of jealousy that he was talking to these other women.

Her left hand launched upward like the Saturn 5, curling into a fist on its way, finding Adam's nose on the right side, that strong Roman nose she had admired only hours before, and she remembered to twist her core as Michael had instructed so many years ago, putting her shoulder into it and she felt the cartilage snap and, like a perfect golf shot, not rattling the shaft of the driver after really laying into the ball, she couldn't feel the violence of her blow through her arm. But she instantly knew she hit him solidly. Adam tumbled back onto the bed, the blood streaming from his nose on both sides of his face like Bash Bish falls. She moved to the edge of the bed and leaned over it as she pulled the sweater over her head and shoulders. "You're right, Adam, I did want you. And I would have made love to you with more vigor and passion than any other woman you have ever known. I would have given my all to you, in the kitchen as well as in the bedroom. I would have explored every limit of my sexuality with you and not have felt a single bit of guilt or shame. All of your friends and colleagues would have wanted to fuck me because of my muscular ass, my long legs, my flat stomach and pretty face. But you would have had enjoyed that privilege alone and you could have scoffed at and been amused by all of the men who paid me attention on the street. And now," she continued while bending to the floor for her panties and bra which she stuffed into her pocketbook, "Now I wouldn't screw you for a million of anything. Not even everlasting world peace."

At the door she turned once more to the pitiful man on the bed, not knowing what hurt him more, his penis, his nose, or his pride and not caring either. All she knew was that by now she should have been climbing the staircase toward a gushing orgasm, a connection with what an hour ago she considered was an eligible man, maybe someone she could finally trust and actually look forward to seeing at the end of the day. She summoned all of her disdain and tried to wear it like a mask as she stared at him, still not believing the events of the previous fifteen minutes.

"Please, please don't go."

"Go fuck yourself Adam," was all that she could think of saying... it was her first time ever to use the F word out loud. She turned and left stomping out the apartment's door, slamming it behind her, not at all concerned about the neighbors. She quickly pressed the elevator button, nervous all of a sudden that Adam might make it out into the hallway before the elevator arrived. The elevator doors finally opened, she jumped inside and pushed the lobby button right away, followed by repeatedly pressing the 'close doors' button. She was there less than a minute later and she hustled out the building's front door, the cooler air awakening and refreshing her, remembering with amazement that it was only an hour ago she passed through this very door with Adam on a different type of journey. Although she had no idea of where to go, her feet went to auto pilot and carried her along the street away from the jungle.

—※—

"J'lome, brother, what's happening, what's going on?" Vinny said to his friend who was already coming out from behind his desk for a hug. A small sea of followers were still streaming out into the night, back to families, homes, work and their own set of problems and most of them recognized through the open office door the man the Imam described as his true life-long brother. They all appreciated the depth of the friendship and bond between these two very different men.

J'lome released his embrace and extended his arm to the chair in front of his desk, inviting Vinny to sit, who was already halfway there. They could communicate wordlessly these two friends, usually one of them starting on a course of action milliseconds before the other suggested it.

"We had this guy causing problems on the sidewalk. Somehow he decided he had to get violent with a couple of my followers outside the front door because he objected to their discussion about Derek Jeter and some hitting record." J'lome shrugged his shoulders.

"Does any real Yankee fan give a crap about that record?" Vinny asked. Vinny was a Met fan for all his life. That was all that they ever disagreed on, which baseball team to follow.

"Only the Sportscenter addicts. All they care about is stats and championships as a measure of excellence. If I remember correctly, Ted Williams never won a World Series ring. Neither did Ernie Banks, Don Mattingly and a host of others. Anyway, it was pretty crazy for a minute or two."

"I'm glad they felt they had a good reason to kill each other," Vinny said sarcastically. Vinny was always fascinated with how easily most people put their lives at risk and/or made painfully stupid decisions based on well...stupid things like arguing about baseball that have the ability to turn into something tragic that would then haunt them in the days and years to follow. He considered his friend, "You afraid of these guys?" he asked. J'lome steepled his fingers under his chin. It wasn't easy for him to admit the following.

"Just the one, big bastard. He scared and confused me as he was not what anyone would call a typical follower. Allah forgive me for profiling another human being, but he looked like a California surfer boy. Not a wisp of beard or anything about him that would identify him as a practicing Muslim." He considered Vinny right back, "Just in case you need to know, I am still not afraid of any man in any way. I am least afraid of the unfortunately large number of my fellow Muslim believers who are against what we are trying to accomplish here at this mosque." For J'lome, it was as easy as acknowledging the simple fact that Isaac and Ishmael, essentially the fathers of Judaism and Islam, were brothers of the same father and therefore all Muslims and Jews were intertwined through the millennia and anyone who had as much brains as God gives a goose would have to understand that very simple concept, if J'lome were to ever have his way. Two thousand years ago, before the arrival of Islam, virtually everyone in that region of the world were Jews. This was the basic tenet of The People's Mosque. He continued, "However, I am definitely afraid for all men, as I have so painfully found out time and time again, that our weaknesses plague us although the answers to most of our problems are right here." He cupped his right hand under his heart as if to catch tumbling bits and crumbs of a crunchy snack.

"So why did you call me? You sounded concerned, I didn't know what I was going to find here. What's bugging you about this clown? He probably won't be back, right? He's gone and forgotten." J'lome laid his muscular forearms on the desk and leaned forward and lowered his voice.

"The blond guy, I watched him praying out of the corner of my eye. His mannerisms were not that of someone who develops a rhythm with their prayer, thus finding some peace and contentment. This guy was rigid and judgmental of everyone around him. Just like he was with the two guys outside. His incantations were perfectly enunciated, louder than the others, like he was on some personal quest to take over my congregation. I could see that he was watching the others, checking the depth of their prostrations, the duration of them." J'lome leaned back, took his chin in his hand and thought about his next statement and he hoped he wasn't getting paranoid. "I wonder if he is part of the Salafi."

"What's that?" Vinny asked. "Some kind of ultra-orthodox sect, some radical Islamists?"

"The Salafi is indeed a sect of Islam. The American media typically refer to them as Wahhabists but they themselves reject that term. When anyone in America or Europe who ever bothers to lift a newspaper sees that word they think, extremist, terrorist. The principal tenet of Salafism is that the Islam that was preached by Muhammad and practiced by his Companions, as well as the second and third generations succeeding them, was pure, unadulterated, and therefore, the ultimate authority for the interpretation of the two sources of revelation given to Muhammad, namely the Qur'an and the Sunnah. They are like strict constitutional constructionists in that way. They are only interested in the fundamental beliefs of Islam. That is their aquidah, their fundamental belief system." He finished his appraisal and looked at his friend once again. "I don't want these people here," he stated flatly, and then asked, "Who did I say I was afraid of?"

"No one."

"I was lying, my friend. These people scare me. With their radicalism, their outmoded ideas of the world and Islam's place in it, their intolerance and their penchant for senseless violence." His voice was trailing off, as this subject depressed J'lome most of all. Vinny got out of the chair and came around the desk to embrace his friend once more. "Forget these guys, J'lome. Between me, Mikey, Moose, the Burkes, and maybe Charlie Mick if he ever grows up, we will break them all if they step out of line with you again."

"I wish we were all here now. I know their spirits are with us, but I miss them sometimes, now especially." He was talking about their friends who were killed on 9/11, Ping the Router, Mikey, Pak the man, and Roger, who was Persian not Iranian, as he always pointed out to anyone who would listen, whether they asked or not.

"I know. I wish they were here, too, but the rest of us are here, and we will continue to look out for each other, right? No way these guys, these slimies, salamis, whatever, fuck with this neighborhood, this mosque, you or anyone in this congregation or anyone else in our group, ever. Forget these clowns. Moose and Charlie Mick will continue to watch them, by the way. J'lome nodded, totally confident of this one fact along with the will of Allah, death, and taxes. "By the way" Vinny continued, "who were the two guys who left with Blondie, the little guy and the doughy bald guy?"

"I never saw the little guy before, looked like a Saudi based on his dress and haircut. The other guy I know a little, his name is Andre I have seen him here and there for a few years. A classic ne'er do well, always fat and jowly. My friend once told me Andre was where leftovers go to die." J'lome lifted his chin and looked past Vinny who was smiling at the joke, "You know, he works for the same bank as Mikey...interesting."

"Doing what, mortgage business?"

"No, he handles the computer network security, money trans-fers, wires, that sort of thing." This answer caused Vinny to now gaze blankly at the wall beyond J'lome's shoulder. He knew this look; it meant that something was tickling his friend's brain.

"What is it, what are you thinking?"

Vinny stayed with his thoughts for another moment or two, unable to let them go, kind of like pulling your leg out of quicksand, and then coming back to J'lome, "I'm not sure, but something is there and I'll find it some time. You know what? We need a meeting, I've just decided. I feel something coming together somehow, but I think I need a meeting with everyone to pull it all together." At least he hoped so. "Plus" he continued as he came back from his mini reverie, "I think everyone needs to share with each other, we need to remind each other that each of us is involved in the shit storm of life and none of us are getting any younger. Mikey's got troubles at home, he's freaking out about the loan, Moose Miller is also getting double doses at home."

"Yes," J'lome cut in, "She's a difficult one, his wife."

"And he's getting shafted on the job as well, he can't get put off the crap duty guarding the United Nations building, he just sits out there doing nothing and his career is going nowhere. The Burke's, well, you know nothing bothers them but they haven't had a Knicks playoff appearance in years and are probably still pissed over Mikey and you taking the tournament pool earlier this year."

"I told them Allah provided me with the wisdom to go with Florida last year. I mean how could we not pick a player named Noah? And I liked George Mason. They were a tough little team that we lucked out with. This year, I had to push Michael on it but I believed all the way that Florida was going to repeat. They're lucky. I just helped Michael pick the teams...if I were allowed to gamble, I would own that truck they love so much by now. I promised them that next year I would purposely pick two Butler players and that we would ride that to the Final Four as well."

"Right. For your information, the truck is ready to finally give it up and they are like, emotionally affected by it. I wish they would find someone to date, fall in love with."

"That would be nice, but what woman would ever put up with them?" He was smiling when he said it. Vinny started to smile again as well, the spell of despair was starting to lift thanks to the magical nature of his best friend who could somehow find a rainbow anywhere, at any time. He nodded at Vinny, "Maybe you need a woman as well my friend."

"Yeah right, who would put up with me?"

"J'lome leaned forward and placed his hand on Vinny's knee, and he spoke softly, "Any woman with as much brains as Allah gives a goose would find you to be the most attractive man and candidate for a full life they have ever met." He leaned back. "I have even seen a few of the young faithful women noticing you. They struggle to contain themselves and they ultimately manage to do so, but I have seen them a few times looking over their Korans at you. But seriously, my friend, it's been years since that lawyer woman broke your heart. Have you in response to her selfishness closed it altogether?"

Vinny was angry at his friend for just the quickest of moments. Be it priest, rabbi, or Imam, all of these people of the cloth could probe you ever so gently just skirting the edges, and then they plunge right into your heart to rip out a cancerous growth of negativism, of fear, of regret, of a refusal to move ahead in life...sneaky bastards.

Beth. It had been a long time since he thought of her. Vinny had loved her with all he had and she dumped him unceremoniously, dumped him for some Wall Street clown and he could still see the smile on the guy's face when he unfortunately ran into them walking hand in hand through Grand Central Station, saying to her not completely under his breath, "You going out with that?" Mr. Goldman Sachs turned but she took his arm and quickly led him away knowing how easily

Vinny could and would have taken him apart. That was all the credit he was willing to give her, even after all this time, that's all there was. At least, he believed, she knew how much of a mistake she made. The last he had heard, she was living in a mansion in Darien with two bratty kids and her husband was screwing anything that walked in front of him. Fuck them all, he thought then and he declared a moratorium on dating and love, instead re-devoting himself entirely to the business of providing for himself and his friends better than that loser MBA piece of dog shit stock market analyst could ever do for her.

"No, I haven't," he answered, and almost told him about his increasing interest in Maxie Carter, who had definitely touched him in a most special way. He was fighting it, though. "I'll keep you informed. Anyway, I'm also struggling with Charlie Mick. The kid is still completely at odds with himself over his father's death on 9/11, and I don't want him to stray too far away from the right path. That's why I had him out here today, because he messed up again and I told him to stand here until he knew what my philosophy of life might be all about. I had no time for his nonsense this morning, what with the bad Preservation Board meeting and Michael's news about the bank's commitment. I guess it was good that I did that because he called in the fight with the blond guy to me and I guess in a way he helped avert a potential major problem for you and the rest of your flock."

J'lome smiled, "Interesting how that happens, isn't it?"

"Don't get all religious with me." J'lome threw up his hands in a conciliatory gesture.

"Please, you people loved it when Pope John Paul stepped outside that time when he was in the city years ago, and the sun shined for the first time that day. It was a rainy day, remember? And he pointed to the sky as if to take credit for the sun coming out just as he hit the sidewalk. See what faith can do, was what he was saying and I have to tell you, that man knew how to use the stage." J'lome started to rise from his seat which was the start of the end of the conversation. Neither man enjoyed small talk and they were both busy.

"Vinny, my lifelong friend, all I am reminding you is that practiced patience rewards people with tremendous profits. It is a time-honed truth. Keep your eyes open, your ears as well because I can see it in your eyes that somehow, a solution to this thing is somewhere floating in our little universe, and I wouldn't want any other man searching for that solution than you." The two moved to the door together and embraced before Vinny stepped outside of the office. Vinny asked, "What are you doing tomorrow? Come to lunch at AJ's place. I'm going to call the others and set up a general meeting. Everyone needs to be settled down a bit and I think it's a good idea to get together, face to faces."

"I do, too. I'll see you there at noon if I can."

"Later brother," and with that Vinny turned and left J'lome's office and a moment later was back on Steinway Street. Moose Miller's Crown Vic was no longer on the street as apparently there were no more funds available to watch these guys. Charlie Mick was not in sight either, and Vinny cursed himself for not flipping him the car keys to make sure he could follow the three assholes. I hope that the kid was thinking and he found some way to keep a tail on them. He would call him shortly. Better yet...let's see when the kid calls me.

He was thinking heavily again, the drone of cars entering the parkway a block away and the horns of drivers trying to get past double parkers was all around him but it wasn't touching him, as he was falling into one of his well known 'brain locks' when he was capable of intense thought and creativity. J'lome was right as always, our solutions are right in front of us ninety-nine percent of the time, he was quickly reminding himself. Well anyway, he continued in his thoughts, a solution had better come along within two days otherwise I'm dead meat, and all of my friends, my brothers, my business partners and investors, are dead meat as well. He jumped in the driver's seat of the Suburban and headed home, reminding himself to check in with Charlie Mick within a few hours regarding the three clowns and what he was able to observe if he didn't hear from him first.

—◦—

As the evening wore on, Laura was quickly composing herself, surprising herself with her resilience. Maybe she was feeling better and stronger than she thought she would have because in the day or two before, more so in the hours prior to her date with Adam, the doubts about him began to crowd her thinking, taking over her enthusiasm like an over-watered house plant.

Therefore, she concluded, maybe I was already mentally prepared for disappointment so that when the phone buzzed and she saw who the caller was, it was more of a release from stress rather than a flagrant violation of the most basic rules of decency on the part of Adam. Unbelievable, what a prick he is, she thought. In the months and years since her last lover, she started to develop a resolve that was becoming more frequently employed by women of her generation, that being the desire and will to just be alone forever. A vacation here and there, some fun here and there, a lover on call or the occasional one nighter—even the thought of that made her gulp—here and there.

But no more love, no more exchanges of plans and dreams with a man. They were all shit. This was the only logical conclusion she could reach after this evening's adventure. And furthermore, now at this point in her life, she would start to use men strictly for her own pleasure, she would start to become a little more selfish herself. "Oh, you want to take me to dinner, the theater, a ball game, the beach? Sure. Why not? Just please be aware that I won't limit myself to you, that is, if someone else wants me to accompany them to a museum, social dance, party or an afternoon on the Great Lawn playing frisbee, and I find them physically attractive, then I will do that. And maybe I will sleep with each of you once or twice a week so that *I'll* be satisfied. And if either of you ever tell me you love me or complain about the situation as it stands, I will toss you to the curb without a shred of regret and replace you within a couple of weeks time.

Once more she ran down the movements after she left the apartment. The elevator arrived mercifully quickly at her floor, she was able to find the button for the lobby immediately, a relief as so many buildings in New York had so many different types of elevators, all of which seemed to have different panels. Sometimes it was as if she were searching for the Holy Grail rather than the lobby button and at times, the 'close doors' button. But this one time, she was smiled upon by someone, something, as she found both immediately. She had to steady herself against the wall on the way down, not daring to look up lest a camera catch her image in her present state. She exited the cab before the doors were fully opened, turning her body sideways in an attempt to slip out as quickly as possible. This apartment building was like a skin she was trying to shed. If there had been a public shower in the lobby, she would have jumped in for a head-to-toe scrubbing. The doorman started for her as she was nearing the door. Did Adam call him to try to stop her? Was this doorman in on the bet? She wasn't about to engage him or any other man for that matter in any type of conversation because they were all pigs and not worthy of her time. She dealt with the doorman with a stiff arm to the upper chest, the strength of which surprised him enough to not even think about another try at stopping her. Hell, he thought, get the door on your own.

The chill was in full force this early spring night, the temperature dropping into the upper thirties. It was quite pleasant earlier today, certainly no foreboding of the night's coming events, no pun intended. She walked west at a brisk pace, lest Adam was able to make it to the lobby quicker than she thought. She never would allow him to look at her again. He wasn't anywhere near her level, certainly not anywhere near the level of man she wanted in her life. Unfortunately, he seemed to be a part of a vast male conspiracy, that is, to be as uncaring, dishonest, and slimy as a human being could possibly be.

She reached Park Avenue and turned south. Here on Park, she passed couples smiling at each other, laughing with each other, arm in arm. Men with men, women with women, men and women together, all shapes and sizes, ages, some looked wealthy, others looked as poor as church mice. But Laura hated them all at that moment because she, a good lady with a pretty face and a great body, a sparkling personality was totally, thoroughly alone. A drink, she thought, that's what I want...a shot of Jameson and a Guinness...she remembered Michael talking about that combination one night. "The liquid of the gods" he called it, the reason why the Irish could and would never take over the world. "No, Laura, I'm not a drinker, but if I'm on a Caribbean Island with a special lady, and we spent the whole day playing golf, swimming with the colorful fish in amazingly blue, clear waters, hitting the numbers in roulette, dancing salsa for an hour or two, I might be moved to put a buzz on as long as I don't have to drive anywhere, keeping sure of course that I don't lose my balance as well as my dignity as a result."

She was a little nervous about Michael at first when he started talking about beer and shots of whiskey because of her previous association with a so called 'social drinker' whom she had to drag into the bed by his shoulders and then undress him more times than she cared to remember. But as his story progressed, his method of telling it calmed and comforted her, as if he instinctively knew what would turn her off and he introduced that portion of his personality in such a way to make her understand what he was all about so that in case they ever did date, they might have a chance at being in love from the moment he picked her up to go out.

After about a half hour of zombie-like strolling past the tourists, fancy looking 'how do you do' types, and shrieking kids from uptown on skateboards, she came upon Grand Central Station. She skirted the building through the tunnel to Forty-Fifth Street where she found an Irish pub, a true New York kind of establishment she decided looked tame enough to sit down in. She walked right to the bar upon entering, ignoring the stares that always came her way, and ordered her drinks. Two shots of Jameson and a ginger ale...the Guinness would have to wait. She wanted numbness, not oblivion. The bartender, an old world gentleman from the Emerald Isle complete with red hair and a twinkle in his eye, brought them over, asked if she was okay, and when she shook her head no, told her to let him know if she needed any help before giving her the room and solitude she craved. Wow, a gentleman here in New York City, she thought, what a concept. She threw back the shot of Jameson, and sucked air in through her teeth to cool the heat of the liquid as it descended through her throat. The very smooth whiskey hit her stomach with a thud and then settled pleasantly in the mash of her earlier dinner meal with Adam. She stared at the small glass in her hand, twirling it on the tips of her fingers, concluding that Michael was right, this is quite good stuff. She motioned the bartender over again, "Can I have another please?" she asked. The Irish gentleman had seen this before and he wanted to do the right thing for this lady. He reached under the bar and brought out an old-looking bottle and uncapped it.

"Listen, I'll let you have a shot of this Crown Royal whiskey I found in my grandmother's house after she passed last month. It has a stamp of 1955 so it is as smooth as silk. But that's the only one I want you to have. These two shooters and a bad mood will hit you hard and I can't have a nice lady like yourself feeling worse than you already do.

Is it a deal, lassie?" He had a wonderful singsong brogue that helped to settle her mood unlike that other bastard, the Brit con man she met a year earlier. She wondered what this older man was like about twenty years ago. He's part of a dying breed, she concluded: a classy gentleman who somehow knew how to act and behave like a man.

"Okay, deal," she agreed with a smile, raising her glass to him. She threw this one back as well, not feeling it at all as it traveled the length of her esophageal tube. She smiled at him as warmly as she could, "Thanks."

"No charge, lil' lady," and he moved off to the other end of the bar to tend to some refills after depositing a ginger ale in front of her. She leaned forward, elbows on the bar and watched the bubbles in the glass start to fade. She felt the fire subsiding as the soda mixed with the alcohol, and she started to once again assess the events she experienced just a couple of hours earlier. She looked around the establishment through the use of the enormous mirror over the bar, studying each of the faces briefly, convinced all of the patrons of the tavern could look right through her and that they would soon start breaking out in unstoppable guffaws at her plight. She turned back to the bar and stared into the ginger ale which still had a few bubbles rising, her concentration on the upward flight of the carbonation not deterring her from thoughts about Adam, that bastard.

How unbelievably clumsy he was, the fact that he had lied to her in a most horrific way becoming almost secondary. His boorish behavior at the restaurant, his complete lack of understanding of what probably any woman needs or desires from a man. Maybe she would have forgiven his behavior, written it off to nervousness if he had taken her in his arms correctly, kissing lightly but passionately, stimulating her with touch as well as words. Instead he showed himself to be just like virtually every other man she had known intimately, that is completely unaware, strictly into it for themselves, only interested in their ejaculatory payoff. "Yeah, I fucked her so hard," they would say to their friends the next day, not even beginning to understand that they had been with another human being, a woman who trusted them enough to allow their vulnerability to show, to allow them into their body and heart. Certainly, she realized, as she drew on the ginger ale, the fire in her belly not as hot, the bubbles tickling her a bit on her upper lip, there were plenty of women around the world who were having sex at that moment just because they wanted a good hard bang, nothing more. But she liked to believe that most women were not like that. She knew for a fact that she wasn't.

She learned to be patient with men who pulled and squeezed her nipples too hard, sometimes nibbling on them like peanuts at the ballgame in some bizarre belief that this was actually pleasurable. Maybe it was so for some women, but not for her. It would take weeks before she finally complained or made a suggestion to her lover which usually resulted in a hurt look that disgusted her.

"Well, hell, buddy, let me bite your nipple and see how you like it," she would think but did not dare say out loud. There were too many chunky, unclean fingers with untrimmed nails, she recalled, probing her clumsily, searching for her clitoris as if it were a needle in a haystack when it was right...there, you schmuck, the same place it is on every woman. Why don't you even ask me how I like it so you don't have to continue like Australopithecus Man? And the oral sex, if she ever got any after the first few times with a new lover, was just as clumsy, full of sucking and slurping sounds that made her feel like a popsicle, the razor stubble on many of these clowns—did they think that style still looked good—burning her skin like the summer sun. Wasn't Miami Vice on the air about twenty years ago? Didn't that go out of fashion? Maybe I ought to rub their balls with sandpaper, see how they like it. And the intercourse, well, half of her lovers just inserted their penis, and went back and forth as fast as they could, no change of direction, no holding themselves inside her as they strained their bladder control to give themselves a little pulse through their penis which a woman most definitely could feel while they kissed her softly but deeply, no love tap on her butt as they started again, no ability to read her own hip gyrations, looking for the combination of strength, thrust and rhythm that was so necessary and so different for all women to achieve orgasm, several of them telling her that they had to keep going as fast as they could so they could maintain their erection and she believed them until she realized a few more lovers later that they were just selfish, talentless losers. And the others who just wanted to masturbate next to her...she learned to love intercourse in spite of the rookies she had unfortunately bedded in her past, and mutual masturbation lying next to a great man might be fun once in a while. "Hey, let's have a race!" But like any other woman, she wanted a man inside her for a decent duration before lying together, but these guys just shut their eyes tightly and flailed away at themselves, not even bothering to hold her closely with their free arm.

She had pretty much given up by now on the prospect for real romance. She would only dream about a weekend in Paris, touring the Louvre and the West Bank, renting a slick sports car for a two- day drive to the French Riviera, stopping along the way at a beautiful bed and breakfast for an evening of dinner, and wine in front of the fireplace, and warm, soon-to-be-very-sizzling lovemaking in a large comfy bed, sleeping on his shoulder afterward, naked and satisfied. Running off the beach at Cannes for a quickie before hitting the casino, she in her favorite black Michael Kors dress she saw in the window of the store on Madison Avenue and he in a white dinner jacket and nicely pressed black pants, all the women looking at him and all the men looking at her, tables of men staring at her as she stood to excuse herself to the ladies room, her man appreciating their inability to keep from staring at her and feeling like Superman for having such a woman in his life, almost being reduced to tears when he first sees her entering the lobby in her ensemble, complete with a beautiful set of pearls he had given to her on the plane over the Atlantic, hitting the number at the casino before returning to a gorgeous room overlooking the Mediterranean where they would make love all night, his hands, lips, and penis all perfectly synchronized with her needs, her desires and a couple of her fantasies. She laughed out loud at her little schoolgirl fantasy and drew on the ginger ale again, the magic Michael told her about starting to work. All of her friends told her it wouldn't be that way after a few years with any man, and she believed that to be true because all of them were saying it, but hell, why was that? It seemed easy to be able to please men, let them watch some sports on the tube, have a card game with their friends, keep the sex interesting and fairly frequent, a couple of times a week with a quickie massage in the middle here and there, what was so ridiculous about the idea of a man who was so turned on by her that he would still be chasing her around the room well into his eighties? She remembered a conversation with Michael several years ago at yet another drab holiday party.

"It's easy to care for someone you truly love," he had started, prompted by a comment from her crazy friend Lulu in accounting that she would never understand men and what they believed love was. "All you have to do is pay attention to the little things. For example, when you go to pick her up in the winter, turn on the heat on the passenger seat so when she sits down, it's not cold leather awaiting her. Make up some private pet names for each other and use them fairly often, but not all the time so you don't burn them out. Maybe a little private language, something ridiculous to anyone else who hears it but very special to each of you. And do silly stuff. We're all wrapped as tight as an eight-day clock. Try carving your initials in a tree or in newly poured concrete. If you do stuff like that consistently, if you hold your girl's hand, maybe kiss it at a red light, or you take your man's arm not just to hang on, but to draw the two of you close on a cold wintry day in the city, maybe tap your girlfriends knee affectionately when you're driving, I don't know, there's a million things. With real love and trust and honesty mixed in along with some physical attractiveness, then the love flame will never go out."

He didn't wait for a response to his soliloquy, she remembered, but looked off into the distance a bit, past her and her crazy friend from accounting and she recalled thinking at that moment, What was his own marriage like? They had known each other for ten years by then, as well as you can get to know another person passing them in the halls of the company or speaking at the holiday party, but they had never shared anything about their personal lives. He had never asked her once if she dated, if she had a boyfriend, nothing. That was how she knew she could trust him, because he had proven himself over time to be a gentleman and not a pig like that awful Adam, who was quickly receding into the dusty drawer of her mind labeled 'Men I've had or came close to, anyway.' But what was it like for Michael at home...good or bad, interesting or indifferent, hot or cold, supportive or selfish? She brushed the daydream away before it carried her all the way back, ten years before, to when she first met him.

Standing on a coat line at her first holiday party for Argent Bank, she was surveying the room nervously, not knowing anyone except a few of her immediate managers and them only for a few months. Her new career was starting and she was alternately excited and frightened at the prospect. But she was pushing ahead into uncharted waters because that was what she had always done or was forced to do. She turned to her left when the door to the ballroom opened, filling the anteroom with sound, and she saw him in his well-tailored suit, tall, confidence dripping off him, and ridiculously good looking. Their eyes met and the chemicals in her brain tried to grow fingers out of her hips to help her wriggle out of her new black dress. She had never felt such an instantaneous attraction before, it was like when Cyrano first noticed Roxanne. It actually became a little hazy around him as he smiled and walked toward her, jacket buttoned, hair a little out of place, but oh boy, look at him brush it back with a careless sweep of his fingers, how...mmmmm. "Hello," a sonorous baritone voice greeted her and she felt her knees go weak. Please, please God, please let this man be single, she was thinking as she blurted out the first thought in her mind, "I can't believe such a handsome man works at Argent Bank."

She immediately felt like a fool when she said it, it was the sort of thing she never had said before, but he smiled warmly, not a bit off stride, and thanked her although with a bit of boyish embarrassment to show that he was not above understanding at least a little bit of how a woman's mind really works. Of course, not more than a minute later he did inform her that he was in fact married with a little girl at home, showing her the picture of his attractive wife. "So I can't do romance, but let's be friends." And that's what they did all these years, never sharing a dance, a phone call, the only time they were alone was when he drove her home from the holiday party about seven years after they met and, of course, their walk up Broadway together the first night. She remembered how the holiday tourist traffic on the famous street parted for them like the Red Sea did for Moses, letting them by as if they were on some red carpet at a movie premiere.

Her hand completed its upward arc bringing her hair behind her ear and she reached for the ginger ale again, the sweeping of the stray strands keeping her from looking like a raging drunk out for a quickie and also closing the door, again, on her thoughts about Michael Pierce. Now she was back in reality and she was pissed off. He lied, that bastard Adam, he lied to me in the worst way possible. And that wife, what was her problem, seemingly allowing this type of behavior to continue unabated? What woman or man would put up with that? He degraded the love of two women, one of them obviously a lost cause by now. Fine, she concluded, if that's the way he wants to live his life, so be it. At least I am not on his list of women he's screwed, although she was sure he was texting all his friends that he had finished the deed and therefore won the bet. She took another sip of the ginger ale, this time downing about half of the glass. "You didn't damage my spirit," she thought as the effects of the alcohol were really starting to get to her. It provided a sudden motivation instead of its usual desired effect, a clouding of judgment and slumping of the shoulders and head. I have to start over, she knew, clear out the garbage in my life, the friends who only call when they have a problem, the men who just want to lie to me and fuck me, and the stream of bad news in the papers and on television. Back to square one it was going to be for her as she drained the last of her soda. Thing one: I want my career back from those assholes at the bank who have sabotaged it, with my permission, as she wasn't going to get anywhere if she couldn't make some admission of her own mistakes and complicity which caused this toxic mess she was now in at the office. I want my respect, my respect that I have earned, slaved for in that bank, and I am starting right now as she placed her nearly empty glass on the bar. The delightful and cheery brogue was back, "Would you like another?"

"No thanks, I'm fine." She giggled a bit more noisily than she would have preferred, now imbued with self-purpose and quite pleased with the ease that she blew Adam out of her brain. She started to push away from the bar, getting ready to stand, drawing down the last bit of the bubbly soda, not getting a chance to swallow when a different, unpleasant voice intruded. "What's so funny darling?"

She was only slightly startled by the interruption of her private thoughts and was then severely disappointed to look into a pasty face on top of a body that was thirty pounds overweight, topped off by a bad haircut. The voice came at her again as she cocked her head to one side and raised her eyebrows in a mixture of puzzlement and annoyance, "I bet I could tickle you in a way that would make you really laugh." Her two-second assessment took in the details in milliseconds: bad breath, bad suit, a little shorter than I first thought and, on top of it all, probably the worst line ever offered to a woman. The ginger ale, which she had planned to savor for a moment or two before swallowing, was still swishing around her mouth. Without a moment's extra thought, she blew it out of her mouth like Linda Blair did with pea soup and was pleased to see it all landing squarely on his twenty-nine dollar shirt, silencing and astonishing not only him, but herself. Not for a second did she feel bad or embarrassed. She pushed past her interrogator, who had a nameplate on his jacket that she just now noticed, identifying him as Tom. "Hey Tommy, just don't ask your wife to clean that okay? She has enough to do already."

Tom's friends burst out laughing, the Irish gentleman behind the bar smiled a tiny little smile and she hit the door, the crisp New York City spring nighttime air on Madison Avenue acting like a stimulant that started pushing her uptown to her office.

—◦‖◦—

NIGHT

Georgia entered her and Michael's bedroom at about the same time Laura was exiting the tavern on Forty-Fifth Street. Michael was reading a novel, the covers pulled up to his neck without a crease in them like Felix Unger. She knelt beside the bed right next to him and opened one of the drawers built into the frame searching for something else to pack. It would have taken him five minutes to pack for this trip. It's taken Georgia about three days so far. Michael put the book down carelessly, losing his place which was okay since he had read this particular novel about eight times already. He took off his glasses and with a soft voice asked, "Looking for something?" Without even looking up she answered perfunctorily, "Just wanted to see if I had forgotten anything." With as much sincerity and suaveness as he could muster, he countered with, "Maybe you have to make love to me before you leave tomorrow." Her answer came quickly without looking up, "Stop being stupid, Michael," she answered, still rummaging through the drawer, "I'm busy." With that she pushed the drawer shut and strode out of the room. Stung by her rebuke, he picked up his book without a word, put his reading glasses back on and was angry only that he lost his page.

—◦‖◦—

Whathefu and Aubrey finished their meal of hummus spread on turkey sandwiches they bought at a deli near the safe house owned by a paper corporation which was owned by a subsidiary of his handler's construction company. It had not been inhabited for some time, the only furniture being a pair of chairs surrounding an ancient formica-topped table, a sofa that was hard as cinder blocks, and two queen-sized box springs and mattresses that mercifully were clean. There was no television, but the bathroom had a radio on a rope hanging from the spigot. What a dreary shithole, thought Whathefu, who was more accustomed to the grand hotels of Paris and London as well as the Waldorf Astoria, just across the river, less than two miles away. He looked out the window of the three-family home in Astoria and was able to see the glow of the city against the cloudy night sky, but not the actual buildings giving off the light. His view was blocked by an equally dreary apartment building across the street, its windows letting him look in on the less fortunate of New York City's citizens. At any time, he could see that there were several grizzled men and overly tattooed women gathering on the stoop for a cigarette break, apparently their only chance at something remotely pleasurable.

He let the flimsy curtain fall back into place and he looked back into the room. Aubrey was clearing off the table and cleaning the dishes in the ancient sink. He was clean at least, the young Saudi observed, still hoping against hope for a sexual encounter of some kind with this gorgeous specimen of man. But that was not his greatest desire at the moment. I am going to get over there, he thought, past the ugly building across the street, over to Manhattan where I can find luxurious surroundings, with a proper bath, a change of clothes and myriad opportunities for hook-ups of all sorts. He turned his head when he heard Andre call out from the next room. Aubrey had secured him to the bed with a pair of handcuffs when they arrived, and now that he was finished in the kitchen, was returning to the room, he figured, to secure their guest for the night.

We can't lose this guy because he was specially provided by Allah. That guy in there is going to deliver me to the promised land...what a stroke of luck! He felt more sure of himself now. What was her name again, the young girl in the Ferrari? Who the hell was she to die in his car that way, the selfish bitch? All he could see now was the future.

The present held no meaning other than its use for his end gain and the past is well, just that. He would pay off the blood debt, fund a lavish lifestyle with the remaining ten million or so, and then maybe even return to his homeland, a prodigal son in his father's eye? Was that possible? He could be, might be, welcome to the private yacht kind of world again and this time if he were so blessed with that good fortune, he would embrace it and forget about these foreign women and men he had been wasting his time with. He quickly undressed and got into the queen-sized mattress and box-spring, where he hoped against hope he would be joined by the magnificent creature in the other room. This would be the last time, the very last time he would have sex with a man if it were to happen here tonight, he promised to someone or something.

Aubrey returned from the next room and Whathefu asked, "Is he giving us any problems?" His question was answered with a harsh look, a flash of white seeming to cross his face the way an old-fashioned computer indicated the programs are changing. He stood over the bed and impatiently addressed the young Saudi.

"Let me explain something to you. I work for your father, I answer only to him in this world and the merciful Allah overall. You are in my control for the next few days and you will do everything I say. That guy in there is our prisoner, so I have to trust you a little bit to help me understand the computers at his bank as well as keep an eye out for him. But don't ever think there is an 'us' or a 'we' in this equation. You are what you are, and you know what it is. If you try to escape, I will kill you without hesitation. Your father has completely sanctioned this. But I want that money as well because I have bigger, better, and more important plans for it than you do. Do you understand?" Whathefu nodded, his hopes as full of holes as a New York Met bat with runners in scoring position.

"Good. Now get the fuck out of the bed," he commanded, and Whathefu hopped to it, nervous for his well-being, even more so for the pathetic skinny body he had to show to this man. Never had he felt so weak and helpless. Aubrey positioned the mattress and box-spring in front of the door, effectively blocking any attempt at opening it.

"Now you can get back in." Whathefu crawled back under the

covers and positioned himself close to the front door, making sure that Aubrey had enough room to consider sharing the mattress with him.

"Where are you going to sleep?" he asked.

Aubrey was already starting to lay down on the floor as Whathefu was finishing the question. "Give me the other pillow," he barked. He turned on his side facing toward the door to Andre's room, making sure the pillow supported his head without impairing his hearing. "Go to sleep. We have a long day tomorrow. Don't wake me unless the room is on fire or if you hear something outside the door or from the other room. If you can do that, we'll get along better tomorrow. It'll be an early day. We go to the bank just after morning prayers, long before the rest of the staff gets there. Our friend inside then does his magic and we just might have all the money before twelve noon. Until then, just always remember what I told you before, no one leaves this room or goes anywhere or does anything unless I approve it, understand?"

"Yes," answered Whathefu, but his thoughts were running away with him now. The hell with you, he thought. In spite of your sculpted body, beautiful face and obvious military talent, you are nothing but an unbeliever. I don't buy into your conversion, not for a minute. You are an American dog, a modern day Philistine. Yes, I love your women and your boys and I have loved your liquor and drugs from time to time, but this society is doomed because you have absolutely no restraint. These days you allow events that would shame the lowest families of Saudi society to wash over yourselves and then you broadcast it on a reality show. You are selling all your technology and expertise for pennies, your national debt is racing away from itself and the Chinese are soon going to be in a position to crush your nation financially. Tomorrow I will have millions in my pocket and my father will appreciate how I put it all together. It was I, you bumpkin fool, not you, who heard the conversation in the bathroom, who immediately put it all together as a course of action. I will pay my debt to that stupid girl's pathetic family and it will all be forgotten in my father's eyes. He is my father not yours, and he will always choose his blood over anything or anyone else. With that he turned toward the door and tried to stop the shaking feeling in his bones that would keep him awake for hours, hoping that he was correct with everything he just thought about.

Andre couldn't hear anything from the other room although the door was open. He looked to his left and could see the fire escape outside the window, just a few feet away from the brass bed to which he was handcuffed. His view of Manhattan and the fire escape was blocked somewhat, however, by the collapsible guards on the window. That big white bastard made sure to check the mechanisms and the locks before he left. Andre wanted to go to the bathroom before he fell asleep, but no, said his new warden. He wasn't going to uncuff him before morning, before going to morning prayers, damn...so early in the morning. Why was he worrying about these things? he thought, as he looked away from the window and at his manacled wrist. Certainly he was in much more trouble than having to worry about the early morning call to prayer which he routinely avoided. His inability to keep himself focused annoyed him before, ten times as much now. But he was seeing some kind of light at the end of the tunnel. Fated was right...this society didn't care a whit about real security. He could have walked out of the bank years ago with ten times what these fools were asking for. He did have to admit to himself he was not a little impressed with the general basic honesty he found in the vast majority of New Yorkers. It was the opposite in his own country, where everyone was involved in some sort of scam or another. The politicians grabbing foreign aid to buy planes and real estate, the mid-level managers of foreign corporations grabbing any kind of item or advantage from the local businesses, the poor grabbing whatever they could, usually whatever was left over or unwanted or owned or inhabited by someone weaker, more pathetic than them. Even during the recessionary times, the terrible economies, he had been able to make a living, have some laughs with these people. Never truly comfortable, but however he did it, he managed to forge ahead and become a success by the measure of just about anyone in the old country. No wife, but these American women, such horrible morals. The ones with morals were busy hiding from their own shadows, nothing to love or live for him there. But sweet Kismine, she was the love of his life and for once, he found a true inspiration in his heart to help another human being. He wanted to do everything for her and had in fact put his career and freedom on the line for her this past year, although the bank would probably just fire him and avoid prosecution to save their own reputation if they ever found out about his salami scam. No, they wouldn't want any publicity like that floating around. Besides, he set it up for Laura to take the fall, so what was there to worry about?

But satisfaction was not his, not by a long shot because he always felt smarter, more capable than any of the faces he saw staring back at him from the television, the business pages, and magazines, their fancy cars and limousines and tall beautiful women in apparently endless supply. They seemed as if their lives were perfect in design, right down to the smallest detail that was nothing but a consistent mocking of him personally. His own body was just too round, a little too short, his brain just the wrong side of capable. His looks were as average as they come and his hair was starting to recede. He was a man on the verge of full panic mode, and that was long before these two assholes came into his life, kidnapping and chaining him like an animal.

He was besotted with Kismine. Fated was right about that, no matter how much he hated to hear it from someone else. His own admissions of that fact tortured him enough for several men to feel the pain. Her beauty thoroughly beguiled him and he strove to possess her from the day he met her. He knew how to treat her, what she really wanted. He, in his heart and in his mind, had seen her wearing the veil at some point in the future, when she was his wife, after he had made a success out of her, an Arab woman deemed one of the most beautiful in the world, just like the ancient queens of the Nile. Yes, he knew exactly what she wanted. The corruption of values in this city and in this country for a woman was overwhelming to her. That's why she had not yet slept in his bed, always resisting his advances. She wanted to be pure for him in her body as well as her heart. She wanted to be first class all the way. Well, why not? Why shouldn't my love feel that way? And I will give it to her because with the money we can steal tomorrow, I can set her up anywhere she wants to be. He would get her on the channels Fated was illegally importing and she would become a star because she had to. How could anyone resist her? After that, they would settle into a more traditional setting, she would retire, and he would enjoy her all to himself. By then, her debt to him would take fifty years to repay, and he wanted to savor every moment with her, as her guide to a righteous life. Oh yes, he thought, actually smiling about it while a chained captive in a strange room. I will have her soon, she will be all mine. It was a thought that traveled through his brain like laughing gas. In spite of his surroundings, and with the handcuff digging into his wrists, he fell asleep quite easily dreaming about a veiled lady in a thong on a beach in Rio.

Vinny switched off the light on his desk, plunging his apartment into darkness, the way he liked it when he was ready to end his day. He enjoyed a few moments to himself without any other sensory intrusions. No light, no sounds, no touching, although he had to admit, he missed the presence of a nice lady. It had been so long, but he had to take care of other matters for now. His love life could wait, would have to wait, had been waiting for years anyway, so what was the hurry? The building project, it had to be done, nothing could be allowed to stop it. The jobs, the park, the development of the surrounding factories into vast indoor shopping and cultural centers, the rotating beach, all of it was to become a centerpiece for the revitalization of the neighborhood. It would also be the culmination of years of haggling, cajoling, risk taking upon risk taking, begging bankers for extensions, the local population for concessions so that he could get it done under a certain budget, on and on it went in his head. And then he would get to the expenses and what he would lose personally if this project went down in flames and his options were exhausted.

He kept his long-ago promise to J'lome and studied every book and article he could about real estate and lending, in addition to the philosophy and history. The effort had brought him millions in profits over the years, all stashed away, ready for his dream project on the river. A massive project, incorporating everything he ever wanted in a real estate venture, to say nothing of the amazing rent rolls he would receive, the permanent jobs for his friends, and the mountainous profits for each of his investors, the Burkes, Charlie Mick's family, Mikey, AJ, J'lome, and a few others. They all threw in on the deal because they knew it was really their only way to make a real score, something big to lift them to the next level of economic certainty, whatever that meant to each of them. For some of his older partners, working class people from Sunnyside and Maspeth, it meant a chance for a condo in Florida with enough left over to start a bond account with his friend Tommy Lundon. "Didn't you ever hear rich people say, never touch the principal?" he would instruct them. And in they came, with their nickels and dimes because he was the one they could trust.

It was Vinny who kept the drug dealers out of the local parks, who collared a wayward son or daughter for a lesson to be delivered on the consequences of hanging out with knuckleheads. It was he who took out the crazy Eberlin twins and Nuck Horan and the Willis boys, all local hoodlums who never stood a chance against his bravery, his raw intellect, or a garbage can being banged against the side of their heads. He was the sheriff, the mayor, and the general of the neighborhood all rolled into one and for years he relished the idea of this respect, never once allowing his growing power to corrupt him, always remembering his origins and all the people who helped him along the way, even if it were just a smile or handshake offered on a crappy January day with nothing in return expected. He cataloged all of these moments throughout his life and vowed never to forget them.

He was no Carlo Ponzi or Jay Gould, corrupt men who reveled in the idea of any type of scam. He could have ripped people off left and right, the local rackets lining up for his services, be it beating the sense out of someone or calibrating their various criminal enterprises to the point where they might have considered an IPO. But no, he had a strong moral core that would not allow theft, racism, or any other type of stupidity that passed for comedy or television programming today. He couldn't look his friends and partners in the face like Ponzi or Gould must have, smiling the moments away while their savings were being ground up by boundless greed. Vinny promised to deliver and he always had. He was the tacit leader of his group of friends from the neighborhood, although he would never accept any such title from them. Then he wondered again about Maxie Carter, whom earlier today he considered an enemy, only to turn into the biggest enigma for him in many years. The dinner on Lafayette Street was fantastic if only for the fact that they didn't speak about the project at all. Kind of like running into an old lover completely by chance, going out to dinner on a whim, and never mentioning how much you missed the other, just enjoying the unexpected and very welcome moment with them. The Vietnamese beer washed it all down quite perfectly. He was finally admitting to himself that he was very attracted to this very married woman, her personal style, her look, the way she adapted to a situation as it unfolded. Nice lady, he mused once again as he rolled over on his side and punched the pillow.

—※—

The Burke brothers settled in front of their Mitsubishi fifty-five inch flat screen HD television with a couple of beers to watch a Madison Square Garden network re-run of a Knicks-Bullets playoff game from 1970. Willis Reed versus Wes Unseld in the paint...all out war. The bigger centers of today, Garnett, Shaq, and Yao Ming never had wars like theirs. Walt Frazier versus Earl 'The Pearl' Monroe, two of the classiest guards in the league going head to head, ace against ace. And the mini-wars between Gus Johnson and Dave DeBusschere, who never got over the fifteen points Johnson scored in the third quarter alone, finishing with thirty-one in all in the sixth game. They knew all the stats of these old games, the colleges the players attended, who was drafted in what round or traded for whomever. They carried this knowledge forward to today's Knicks as well as the rest of the NBA. It was often said the Burke brothers could take over as General Manager of the Knicks and do a better job than Isaiah Thomas and Scott Layden combined.

"Let's only watch the first half," said Fred, popping open his beer. "We have to be at AJ's at noon tomorrow so we have to run and gun with the bread deliveries and then meet the suppliers who have the new fixtures we're installing in the new condo uptown."

"Maybe it won't even be worth it to show up," his brother replied. "Kind of like the Knicks versus San Antonio in the finals. What's the point?" He popped open his beer as well and drew noisily on it.

Fred was quietly sipping on his own beer thinking about their position. They owed Vinny so much, but they also had given much to Vinny's efforts as well. They became electrical and plumbing geniuses at his original suggestion, but they also did a lot of work for Vinny. They were always on time and under budget, the sort of thing you could say about maybe ten percent of the contractors in the city. It was a nice trade-off. It was therefore pretty easy for Fred to come to a conclusion.

"What's the point? Are you nuts? The point is we gave our word to the guys uptown so we have to follow through." He downed the beer in one shot, crushed the can and banked it off the wall into the basket. "Two." He stared down his brother from across the room and then pointed to him.

"You're thinking selfishly," he said to Ryan. "We have to stand behind the project, hang in there with Vinny and everyone else. Without him and the rest of our friends, where would we be?" He leaned into his brother, "I know it's hard to admit this about your friends, but let's face it, Vinny is definitely our fearless leader, always has been and I am confident he will run this problem through the way Kareem decked Kent Benson in their first game together."

Fred didn't bother to maintain the stare when he continued, "Besides, we gave all of our money to this project, you know. If it goes under, we'll be the L.A. Clippers in their worst years. I don't know if we could ever recover." He looked back again at his brother pushing the old school videotape into the machine. Some gravitas had to pass between them now, no use denying the obvious anymore. Ryan returned his brother's gaze as the tape started to turn in the machine and the grainy images they had watched so many times before started to appear.

"This will all work out somehow, I feel it in my bones," he said. "We just have to stand aside and let the situation work itself. Nothing else we can do now." He pointed at the television, "Look at Willis back Unseld down in the paint. How strong and confident do you have to be to do that?" They watched the rest of the half in silence, enjoying every minute of a game that had been played some forty years before, a game to which they knew the ending, the final stats of the players and exactly when Clyde would pick the ball from The Pearl as deftly as a hawk takes a pigeon out of the sky, laying it in, never having to slam dunk the ball, the both of them secretly, silently hoping that it would indeed all work out for them and the rest of their friends the way this game would work out...April 26, 1970, Knicks 127 Bullets 114, and then onward to the Bucks and then the Lakers in the finals. Maybe, just to help them feel a little better, they would also pop in and watch Larry Johnson's trey in the final seconds against the Pacers in 1999. They always loved the way the Garden exploded when the ball fell through, the ref's hand in the air signaling a possible four point play, good if it goes, good if it goes.

⁓∘⁓

Charlie Mick sat back in the driver's seat of the car he borrowed from the nice girl he had been seeing from Ridgewood, sweet Diane, and watched the lights go off in the apartment where he knew the three guys Vinny wanted watched were holed up. Earlier he promised fifty dollars to a homeless guy if he woke him in time to see any of the three leave the building. He was so tired from standing in front of the mosque all day, he just didn't see how he would stay awake much longer. He was gulping coffee and chocolates, hoping the caffeine would keep him going. But just sitting here like this? Not a chance he would make it all the way through. So he took a page from Vinny's business mantra of the week, of the year, of the decade: CYA. Cover your ass. "Listen, Charlie," he would say, "you must always think of every angle in a deal because it is stupid to assume that the other guy isn't going to. If you cover yourself at every possible angle without exposing your position, even if it goes wrong, you know you did the right thing." Therefore the fifty was well spent because these guys up in the apartment on the third floor seemed to be true assholes if they got J'lome and Vinny this riled up. And calling Diane worked well also. She was glad to hear from him and he loved her smile and her little dog Zippy, and the fact that she was so generous with him. Vinny would think that was a good idea as well.

He had an epiphany of sorts earlier in the day when Vinny left him on the sidewalk and he decided at that time that he would never let any of the men in this group down again. They were his Dad's friends, and Charlie Mick believed enough in the church's teachings so that Heaven was real enough to him and therefore his Dad was watching him right now and would be pleased that he was with this group of guys, all of whom he had trusted and loved. He let the driver's seat fall back so he could relax a bit, the lower angle allowing him to still see the window up on the third floor without being so obvious to anyone walking by. He hoped the homeless guy stuck around long enough to help him out and he also strangely hoped that the third guy in the apartment wasn't suffering too much. He wished Diane were here right now, to massage his aching muscles.

—¤—

Maxie Carter feigned sleep once again as her husband got in their bed. She had not had any acknowledgment from him in over a year and in the three years prior to that, she could count their 'encounters'...as he referred to their lovemaking...on her fingers. Therefore her thoughts were ensconced with her 'encounter' with Vinny earlier that evening. She had to struggle to keep from giggling about the whole thing. She felt like a teenager now, hundreds of contrivances racing through her brain about their next meeting, if it did in fact happen, and what they would talk about and possibly, well...do together. She sighed and not imperceptibly at all. Only she knew that it was for a good thing, not as a statement of remorse to her husband, who was already snoring.

—¤—

Kismine lifted her face out of the crotch of the drummer of the local band whose music she heard through the open doors of The Bitter End nightclub on Bleecker Street in the Village. She loved it down here, much more so than midtown Manhattan. So many different people, most of them young like her, certainly full of the same fears she felt. But also full of the same impulses, most of them harmless to anyone but the impulsee, and each adventure possibly affording a window to a magical discovery. The music drew her to the huge doorman to whom she paid a five dollar cover charge, and then informed that she was interested in the band on the stage at that moment. She looked at the chalkboard and read the name aloud, "Internal Affair." She sat down right in front of the stage and felt herself go limp watching the drummer flail away at his small drum kit, keeping perfect time, alternating between a rock solid groove and tasteful but powerful fills that fit between the twin guitars and the vocalist like a glove on a cold hand. She seduced him wordlessly before he even stepped off the stage, knowing he wouldn't be able to resist her. Why would he want to unless he had a girlfriend? "Do you have a girlfriend?" she asked within thirty seconds of their meeting. "No, but I think I might have one now," he retorted, fairly smoothly for a young man who couldn't have been more than twenty-one years old. "You're right, you do," she countered. "Where is your car?"

"Van...I have a van," he answered. And with that she was in his arms much in the same way Goldie Hawn fell for that French guy as soon as he told her he was Jewish in *Private Benjamin,* which was to say quite instantly. And now, as she looked past the tip of his penis into his angelic face, pausing for a second to admire his perfect set of abs and sinewy arms. She knew exactly what to do and that was to move like a panther up his body without a word because SHE was in control of the situation, reaching his face now and kissing him deeply, sucking his tongue noisily and then settling back on him, her sopping vagina enveloping his hard penis like a plaster of paris mold causing her to let out a howl of delight that was full of the kind of passion and truth that a clown like Andre would never experience, at least never with her.

DAY TWO

MORNING

*M*ick Jagger is asking me if I really do play drums and he is serious as hell. He is a short but tough- looking, absolutely no-nonsense guy. His chin is high in the air and he appraises me somehow, wondering if I can really play, at the same time probably trying to decide if he can kick my ass. Keith Richards and Ron Wood are tuning their guitars and couldn't be bothered with our conversation. But I think I saw Ron Wood looking over a few times and then whispering to Keith, who looked like he responded with some kind of mumbled gibberish I was sure was along the lines of, "Who the fuck cares?"

"So listen, I'm not here to help you get laid or to get one of Ronnie's paintings for any less than what it's worth and neither am I here to help some middle-aged Yank find his lost inner rock star, am I being clear?"

He's very serious but I'm not intimidated, not yet. That's probably due to the fact that this whole thing is a total lark. I'm at an art gallery owned by my friend Tony LaSala on West Broadway in Soho, just south of Houston Street. Somehow he landed the contract to show and market Ron Wood's paintings and drawings which surprised me with their originality and flair. Georgia is with me and I couldn't help but notice she seemed kind of displaced here, even though we were in Soho and it was a pretty cool gallery opening, filled with beautiful people types and plenty of hyper-progressive liberals that she could commiserate with over the issue of the day. There was quite a buzz not only in the room but out on the street as many fans of the Rolling Stones were trying to get a look-see inside the gallery in case the rest of the band showed up to play a few numbers.

I never thought of Ronnie Wood as anything else but the great guitar player for the Rolling Stones and Faces with Rod Stewart before that. At the gallery, which was by invite only, some four hundred people milled around admiring the many pieces, which were mostly of the other members of the Stones, though some were of Eric Clapton, Bob Dylan, and other musicians. I originally had no interest in buying art but then decided on a drawing of Stones drummer Charlie Watts titled 'Blue Charlie.' I asked the sales clerk if I could have the frame autographed by the artist just as the artist himself appeared from what seemed out of nowhere. I guess these people, these celebrity types, the real ones who have actually accomplished something, somehow learned to move around unseen, silently, so as not to be swamped by their fans. But I haven't stalked him; he was just all of a sudden there, paper thin skin, a mop of jet black hair all askew, black leather jacket and pants, and a cigarette that could not have been anything but permanently affixed in the corner of his mouth. "Hello, love," he greeted the gallery worker in a surprisingly polite and gentle voice, "How we doing?"

"Great," came the enthusiastic response from the saleswoman, who was about twenty-five years old and gorgeous. I could see her nameplate now that I was done looking at her legs and everything else, Marilyn Coop. I don't remember anything other than that she regarded my request for the frame to be signed to be bordering on blasphemous. But Ronnie saved me by just showing up at the right moment, just like his guitar riffs on countless musical jewels. "I think we are well on our way to a successful opening," Marilyn continued.

"Thanks, love," and he turned to go back to the rear of the gallery which was cordoned off by billowing sheets hung from the ceiling. Timing is everything, I reminded myself.

"Hey, Ron, I loved this blue Charlie. Is he around tonight? I would like an autograph on the frame and I would also like to say thanks to Charlie for all the drum lessons." He turned at that comment as I knew, well...hoped he would, and stepped back in my direction. His hair looked as if he brushed it with a boot blacker's polishing shammy. The cigarette bounced up and down in the corner of his mouth as he spoke.

"You know Charlie?" The question was asked without the ash ever moving from the glowing end of his smoke. Explain quickly, the little voice in my brain shrieked at me as I realized as he was already leaning toward the billowy closed-off area, which resembled a Bedouin's tent, a mix of hastily hung thick material. I sensed other people behind it along with some kind of mildly frenzied

activity on the periphery of our conversation, equipment moving around, people talking hurriedly.

"No, I never met him. I learned how to play a drum set by beating the hell out of a crappy kit in an apartment in Queens to every Stones record I could. The first song I ever played all the way through without a mistake was 'Wild Horses.'" This was a true story. I can still remember using my bicycle seat for a hi-hat because we could barely afford the drum set which was a super cheap kit with a couple of tin cymbals and no floor tom. I also played plenty of Beatles, Motown and Buddy Holly, but I figured I'd tell him that later.

"Do you still play?" he asked me and I saw the ash finally fall from his cigarette. He dropped the still glowing butt on the floor, causing Marilyn to wince slightly, and he exhaled out the side of his mouth, directing it down but not enough as he squinted against the burning smoke as he held my eye. Somehow, for some reason, I have his interest. Gotta move with it, although it's been several years since I was politically moved out of the last band I played with, the last band I would probably ever play with. A band that went through three drummers after my dismissal in a space of eleven months and then imploded. Idiots. Anyway, I didn't tell him about that as I was in a 'moment,' something that most people wouldn't recognize if it slapped them in the face. I just didn't quite know what the 'moment' was all about just yet.

"I do, but not professionally. I work for a bank. I played all around the city and Long Island, had a lot of fun, but never hooked up with the right group of players," I said with a shrug, but also a smile as how many people ever learned how to play any musical instrument at all?

He lit another cigarette and asked me, "Can you play right now?"

"Uhh yeah, sure...what do you have in mind?"

"Hold on a moment, stick around," and he disappeared behind the fabric and I heard him speaking to someone, all the other voices around them hushing in unison. In a moment he reappeared at the entrance, which was nothing more than a fold in the wall of drapes, and asked me to come in. I glanced quickly at Marilyn, who seemed to have a higher opinion of me all of a sudden and feigning any ignorance of her heightened appreciation, quickly followed Ron Wood into the closed-off area. He welcomed me inside as if all of a sudden I had some sort of answer for him. Inside the drapes was an area much larger than I imagined, about eight hundred square feet. I could see a basic PA system with three mikes set up, one in front and two off to the side, a few amps, an upright piano and a drum set. I recognized it as Charlie Watt's instrument, a small

Gretsch wood kit, painted a nice mustard yellow. Basic in its configuration, two tom-toms, a piccolo snare, ride cymbal, two crashes, and some kind of inverted splash cymbal that I remember that Charlie used quite often. On the records, it had a really nice flat sound that worked so well with his understated grooves. I was feeling quite thrilled being around other musicians, especially these guys. It was apparent to me that the Rolling Stones were about to answer the prayers of the fans out on the street with a few numbers. I turned to Ron Wood and desperately tried to be casual about what I was hoping would happen next.

"Oh, so the guys are playing tonight...nice," I said.

"Yes, but we have a problem." He looked up into my face before continuing. "Can you really play or were you bullshitting me before? And I mean really play so that you don't make a fool out of yourself and us, for that matter."

"Well yeah, I can play...really. I've been playing since I'm eleven years old. I know most of the Stones' material, my chops are okay and my timing is solid." It was a sales job I was in the middle of and I was daring to think what it was all about. I didn't want to imagine it, but I couldn't help it. Ron Wood lit another cigarette and blew the smoke toward the open flap in the drapes. He turned back to me with an appraising eye, and finished half the cigarette with one puff.

"Charlie is held up at Heathrow Airport, couldn't get out in time for some bloody reason or another." He lit yet another cigarette after dropping the one he just sucked down in about two drags, his third in the last fifteen minutes. "Do you want to sit in for a few numbers?" He raised his chin at me, seeking a quick decision.

"Huh?" Annoyed now, he quickly dropped and crushed this new butt on the floor, again drawing a wince from Marilyn who had been spying through an open flap.

"Do you want to play, mate? We haven't much time to discuss it. Can you play 'Rip This Joint?'"

"Yeah. Up tempo blues progression, right?"

"'Jumpin' Jack Flash?'"

"Yeah, since I'm thirteen years old." Easy now, they aren't technically difficult songs, but they have their nuances and these guys never wanted to be Frank Zappa, never had to be with about a zillion albums sold over the past forty years or so.

"'Heartbreaker?' 'Shattered?'" Another cigarette was lit as he now seemed to feel a little more at ease with my answers.

"Yes, I can play all of those. I'll just hook into the bass player and I'll be right there." I scratched the back of my head, "You really want me to play?"

"Yes, we need someone. I asked all of these guys for a favor to come play here tonight and Mick won't play without a drummer."

"Mick?" My eyes were glazing over with disbelief, "The band is here, the whole band?"

"We're all here except for Charlie and ready to go in ten minutes, so get your wits about yourself and get ready for the big interview. I have to tune." And with that he left to join...was that Keith Richards? Yes it was. He was sitting on a Fender Twin amplifier, one skinny leg crossed over the other, also smoking furiously, the same wild jet black hair bursting out from a face that looked about a hundred years old. The small area was starting to feel like a typical misty London evening but with cigarette smoke instead of light rain. I was just noticing that Bernard Fowler, the Stones' back-up singer was now in the room and I was thrilled to see him once more. We were never the buddy-buddy type friends, but I remembered him well from junior high school in Woodside, great basketball player I played with often and very stylish, way ahead of his time. I had heard years later he was singing with a fairly well-known R&B group but never saw or heard him until an HBO telecast of a Stones concert in Madison Square Garden in which at the instant I turned it on, caught Mick Jagger announcing Bernard as the back-up singer. I nearly fell off the couch and I was instantly jealous of and thrilled for his success. And now Mick Jagger, arguably the greatest front man for arguably the greatest rock and roll band ever was beside me, sizing me up. He was smaller, shorter than I imagined, but like I said earlier wiry and tough-looking, someone you'd size up in an instant as the sort of man who never took any shit from anyone.

"I do play. I wouldn't lie about that and risk making a fool out of myself," I told him. I started thinking about a long ago visit to the dentist, the rich fancy one on Fifth Avenue my mother used to take me to. I was only nine or so and after getting drilled like an oil field for what seemed like an eternity, we took a walk down Fifth to go to the park at Washington Square. And then all of a sudden a cacophony of squeals of delight rose up and rolled toward us. Apparently there was a band playing on the back of a flatbed truck and as they passed by us at only about five miles per hour. I recognized the song and the band instantly...the Rolling Stones, playing Brown Sugar. I learned later it was a publicity stunt to kick off their 1973 or 4 or 5 World Tour, done in this fashion because they didn't have a record out at that exact time. I remembered *that I thought Charlie Watts looked very cool playing his drums and it was then I decided I would learn how to play as well.*

"It's not you looking like a fool I'm concerned about," he countered.

"Well, what do you have to worry about? You have a great legacy, great material and if anyone here doesn't like how it turns out, you've earned the right probably since 1965 to tell them to go fuck themselves. If you want a player, I can play. If you need Charlie to play, then you're not going to get him for about seven more hours. I'm not looking to join the band beyond whatever you've got going on here tonight, but you seem to have a problem and I might be the solution, so if you want to cancel whatever you set up here for tonight, it's no skin off my nose." Screw it, I'm not going to kiss anyone's ass, not for any price or privilege. Keith Richards then moseyed over with his guitar on his shoulder, butt in mouth and whispered in Mick's ear at that point, shrugging his shoulders, his lips forming an upward sneer that I couldn't tell was excitement at the prospect of allowing me to play or if he just said that it might be fun to see this guy screw up or maybe he was just trying to keep the ash on his own cigarette from falling on the floor.

"Okay, let's go," Mick said and turned away, Keith Richards giving me a friendly wink before he too turned back to his tuning.

"Where's the bass player?" I asked anyone within earshot.

"That's me pal." I turned and shook the hand of Darryl Jones, who had been playing bass for the band since the early 1990's. "Just keep your eyes on my fingers and we'll be okay." He was tuning his bass as he spoke, not looking at me directly, but I didn't feel he was being rude. He nodded to Charlie's kit, "You better get yourself situated, gonna start in about two minutes." And he walked away to join Ron and Keith, presumably to get in tune with everyone else. Mick was walking in small circles apart from the others, his fingers pressed together, their tips touching his lips. He seemed as if he were trying to remember the lyrics he was about to sing, but how could he have forgotten something he had written himself? I sat behind the kit, thanking the gods for the fact that a pair of sticks were there. I didn't dare adjust anything...this was someone else's instrument, of course...I just wanted to eye the placement and angle of the cymbals, the snare drum, and test the tension of the pedals. I needed to center my body so I could reach each element of the kit with ease and strike them just right. I needed my feet to feel comfortable on the pedals and I also hoped the knot in my back that had been acting up recently wouldn't start hurting until I was done.

What was the set list again, what did Ronnie Wood say before? Right, "Rip This Joint," "Jumpin' Jack Flash," "Heartbreaker" and "Shattered." But what order? I was about to ask, but everyone was settling in at their stations, Ron and Keith to my right, Mick in front, Bernard behind everyone and off to my left along with Darryl Jones and now I could see Chuck Leavell behind the upright piano. How did I miss all these people stuffed into the small space? I was being ignored by everyone and now I could see a stagehand off to the side ready to pull some sort of cord that looked as if it would lift the curtain. Seconds away and I am awash with fear that I am going to look like a fool...more than likely they are going to start with something the whole band comes in on the 'one' with, but what? But then I remembered Vinny telling me once "God loves details, Mikey, we can never ignore them," just as I noticed Mick picking up a cowbell. An unseen emcee was announcing to the crowd that something special was about to happen, could everyone stop what they were doing and face him. I could hear the crowd's decibel drop as I realized I wasn't the only one here who had hoped to hear music tonight. The cowbell; the emcee announcing quite calmly, "The artist of the evening and a band he plays with want to perform a few numbers for you, we hope you enjoy it," the curtain going up instantly as he finished, the crowd gasping and then coming to life as they were realizing how lucky they were to be seeing this, only about four hundred in the crowd, and I heard it...the cowbell starting...one two, one two, one, one two, one two... "Honky Tonk Woman" it had to be, and it was and I made it in on the and of one and the and of two with the snare and then the floor tom by the skin of my teeth and continued the groove against Mick's more Latin type rhythm on the cowbell and then Ronnie's bluesy guitar entered the fray to be joined by Keith's layover, bringing everything into the first verse, "I met a gin-soaked bar room queen in Memphis."

The crowd went nuts, dancing and singing along. Darryl, like a good bassist always should, checked in with me at the end of the second measure and we locked in so tight you could have hung your coat up on the groove we created. We never had to look directly at each other again. All the band members checked in with each other at certain sections. Part of my groove was on hi-hat and snare and bass drum, the rest was riding on the floor tom during the verses. Had to be careful coming into the chorus, had to keep perfect time. My confidence is soaring and now I check out the crowd. About two hundred men there all wishing they were me at that moment. About two hundred women all looking at Mick with occasional glances toward me. My smile is so firmly in place my cheeks hurt and I am playing on muscle memory alone, like a bullet train zipping along on a magnetic track. No way will I fall off this groove.

I catch a few glances from some of the women, most of them twenty years younger than me, all of them gorgeous, but I am especially distracted and then drawn to a pair of shapely legs in a yellow dress, dancing and swaying in perfect time but I can't see her face. Did I see her when I played with the Beatles in Central Park? Black hair waving back and forth, but I can't see who it is and I realize she is taking my concentration away. The song is ending and I have to one, two, three, crash…and then roll out gently on the floor tom. But they are starting again immediately into "Shattered" just a beat after I finish "Honky Tonk Woman." Good…a nice straight path of a groove all the way through. I recall Ringo saying he used to watch Paul's butt twitching so he could keep time and so I locked onto Mick's ass, which was shaking back and forth like a metronome on cocaine. Gotta remember the off-time little thing Charlie gets into during Keith's solo. I get there on cue and in the groove and I am all over the odd timing and Mick is now looking back at me and smiling, announcing to the crowd while pointing to me, "He's a good one, ain't he?" The crowd responded with applause, Keith looking up briefly before spitting out his butt, Ronnie Wood smiling as he looks my way, the cigarette with a half inch of ash holding on for dear life. I see the yellow dress again for just a moment. I see also that whoever this is is quite shapely through the hips and very tall, but I still can't see her face at all. We take a break after "Shattered," Mick thanking the crowd for coming out to see Ronnie's paintings, "Buy some art please, he needs the money." Everyone in the band laughed as did I because for that moment, I was a Rolling Stone.

"Here's another just for you people here in the greatest city in the world," and then Chuck Leavell started the intro to "Heartbreaker," my groove settling in nicely for a couple of measures, Keith and Ronnie strumming their axes, wah-wah pedals providing a beautiful sixties Motown feel to the tune, reminding myself about the very brief rest before the verse then Mick coming in shortly after, "The police in New York City," which brought a roar from the small crowd, "chased a boy right through the park." A much tougher groove I just had to match, dropping the snare on the and of three and the four as well. Powerful, short solos at the right times. But there was no problem. The kit sounded great, I was comfortable with the material and the guys in the band were all cooking along. I can't see Georgia anywhere, but I had to figure she could see me from some vantage point. I wish I had the chance to alert her before the curtain came

up, but it all happened so quickly. Hopefully. she has a camera going right now. The band brought "Heartbreaker" to an end, an improvised ending at that, which was nailed perfectly. I was feeding off these fantastic musicians the way Pippen and Kerr fed off Jordan's genius on the court.

Mick Jagger announced to the crowd, extending his hand backwards toward me, "Thanks for being here, buy some of Ronnie's art, and please also say thanks to a great drummer from New York City, Michael Pierce." How did he know my name? I wondered. I listened to the crowd clap its approval at my drumming. "One more and we gotta go," he announced and looked at me and counted quickly, about a 125 meter marking, and I joined in with a couple of staccato shots on the snare and then right into "Rip This Joint," a two-minute quick up-tempo shuffle that brought the house down. I stood up at the end of the song, Mick slapping me five quickly as he left the area, a toady appearing instantly with a comfortable looking white robe he draped over the singer's shoulders, the other guys in the band giving me the thumbs up, and then Ronnie Wood pausing briefly in front of the drum set, "Didn't you want an autograph for the painting?"

"Yes, here it is. Right around the edge of the frame, if you don't mind," and he whipped out a white ink marker and drew some squiggly lines around the border of the painting capped by a couple of open mouth and flapping tongue Rolling Stones logos. He shook my hand and disappeared with the rest of the band somewhere behind me. I stepped back out into the main area of the gallery to handshakes, shoulder claps, and attaboys from all these people I didn't knew, a little wary of it all, frankly. How did Ringo deal with all of this? I thought. No wonder he went to live on a mountain for a year. I see Georgia now as I make my way through the crowd, some of the women actually touching my shirt as I approached her. Uh oh, she looks pissed, but why? At this incredible moment for me? I only left her for fifteen minutes and she was perfectly capable of handling herself in a crowd. She was certainly attractive and intelligent, maybe she could brush up on some flirting skills. But no, it was frown time, arms crossed against the chest time in classic pissed-off woman pose made famous by Julia Roberts in virtually every movie in which she appeared. I approached her with a big silly smile on my face, not giving a damn about her mood, "Did you see me playing with the band? Please tell me you got a picture."

"What are you doing in bed?" she was half shrieking in my face, in my ear, the chill of her question seeping into my marrow. "I told you a week ago you had to take us to the airport this morning."

And with that, the room faded from view, the instruments were gone as were all the people who were watching me play drums with the Rolling Stones a moment ago, a dream come true for any drummer or any other musician, for that matter. The last thing I remember was the woman with the yellow dress departing into the mist, and I was still unable to see her face. I could see, however, on her way out that she had a great figure and particularly alluring way of walking, one that the rest of the faux beauties in the city with their tight jeans and wrap frocks could never touch.

"Yes, dear, I remember," he said, pushing the covers off the bed and placing his feet sturdily on the floor. "We can leave in ten minutes," Michael added as he padded off to the bathroom not unaware at all of the sudden drop in temperature in the room.

⁂

Aubrey was leading the morning prayers in the other room and Andre couldn't help but admit that the American thug was quite good with his pronunciations and dedication. But he still felt contempt for him— and not because he was his prisoner—but because this newcomer to Islam dared to hold over his head, a born Muslim, the idea that he was more pure and dedicated to Allah than he was. Bullshit, he thought. What were you before you read the Koran the first time? Christian, maybe a Jew perhaps, but more likely one of those detestable Southern Baptists, the evangelical ones on television in silk suits and diamonds, always with their hand out looking for nothing but more money from their mostly welfare state congregants. And now you think you are better than me? Why, because my own dedication to prayer and my pronunciations to Allah are lacking in beautiful, sonorous qualities? Aubrey reminded Andre of someone who started listening to a band or going to a restaurant because they just recently discovered the music or the great menu, although both had been available for years before. And now they considered themselves experts, self-proclaimed historians of... whatever, as soon as they came on the scene and Andre hated that along with so many other characteristics of other people in the city.

He would see it all the time with the new young guys coming out of college with their degrees and certifications in the Computer and

Information Technology business and on their first day they would be quizzing him about this or that, and not with the type of normal enthusiastic behavior you'd find in a young new pup of an employee, but rather like, "Hey, old dude, I know more than you do in half the time for a third of the salary." In any event, Andre spent the first few minutes of this day as he usually did, angry at those whom he felt owed him something, actually mouthing the words to this one and that one, the words he wanted to scream, at all of them, "Go screw yourselves, all of you. I'm better than you, smarter, purer in mind and soul." But the ending of the prayers in the next room snapped him back to the present.

He had to admit there was something exciting about confronting the demon that stalked him for the past fifteen years at Argent Bank. For that he was secretly grateful to the American thug and the Saudi prince. The endless rows of numbers on his printouts and reports representing dollars, yen, and euros being wired into and out of the bank mesmerized him. Out of and into other people's accounts, not his. Hundreds of wires per day, millions, no tens of millions each day to here and there, but never to him. He wanted that money for his own use and often felt like an alcoholic living in a college town with seventy or so bars on the main street catering to thousands of underage students. He knew how to get the money; he had been stealing for a year already and was confident that he could continue this way for years to come. But he had to make a big move at some point in his life and here it was, forced onto him of course, but he had already figured that if he got caught stealing the seventy million—yeah, why not raise the amount?—he could blame it on these guys, and even the salami scam was secure as he set it up to look as if it were Laura who was doing the stealing. No, he wasn't going to jail. Instead, it was looking more and more like he was going to Rio very soon with Kismine. All he needed was for Laura to stay away from the bank for the next few hours or so. The Asian wire madness from the previous morning had made him nervous at first, but not anymore. His plan was still intact, not only to steal from the bank but to make it look like someone else was doing it. And in Andre's mind, Laura was the perfect pigeon for his plan. It was a beautiful set-up, the others at the bank helping him without their knowledge. The only other South American, placed in her area because of some deluded Human Resources executive who just figured they would get along because they grew up on the same continent, not even thinking of the possibility of him constantly riding her because of resentment left over from some centuries old land grab; the other a skinny, nerdy know-nothing who proudly wore bow ties, who hated her because she came in as the department head's protégé years before, displaying a tendency toward showing up on time and being remarkably adept at finding solutions on her own, which of course pissed off her managers even more.

So as a result they had it in for her without his prodding and without any apparent voice from her—he was thankful she wasn't from Brooklyn, for if she were, she would have punched both of these guys out years ago—but she didn't seem to want to even try out her voice lest she shake her good reputation. Therefore, he could keep on doing what he was doing as long as he liked.

Hell, if discovered, she would probably fall on her own sword, he always figured. It had been so easy for these other managers to shut her out of meetings, classes, any way to demean her in the eyes of the executive management of the bank. As a result he was convinced that he had found the perfect patsy for his operation. She seemed weak to him, like a sapling bent easily by a small breeze, seemingly content to at least have a job even though it allowed her spirit to be pulverized a bit more each day. But he had always reminded himself to be just a little on guard with her because of what Fated had told him some time before, "You have to be careful with the South Americans, no matter what country they come from, they have this desire to kill left over from ancient times and at any time, they can slice you up either physically or intellectually and you never see it coming. And their women? Oh my God, even the nuns have three times the passion of a European or American woman. The quietest of them are boiling just below the surface."

But as always, these concerns were again swept away by what he saw as her apparent acceptance of her lot in life, another victim of the economy in that there was no way she would complain or quit, and his now geometrically increasing obsession with the money in the bank that he believed really should have been his all along as well as a woman that also should have been his all along, she was his now, wasn't she? Well, in just a little while it will be official. When Aubrey entered the room a few seconds later, he was just starting to wonder where she might have been last night, but was jolted back to his current reality by Aubrey's painful twisting of his arm to get at the handcuff keyhole. "Let's get going, you two, and remember, if either of you screws around, I will kill you on the spot." Aubrey lead the way down the stairs lest either of these two tried to bolt once they hit the sidewalk, surveying up and down the block before heading to the battered Saab station wagon. All he was able to see was some homeless guy fifty yards away who seemed to be trying to break into a car. Worthless, disgusting city, he thought as he crossed the sidewalk and grunted to his prisoners to follow him.

⁓

Laura woke from a fitful sleep mostly caused by sleeping at her desk, her head resting on her arms crossed on her desk. Her computer was still on but in sleep mode, the blue of the on/off button illuminating the empty cubicle at three second intervals. She pushed her chair away from her desk and put her head between her knees and ran her fingers through her hair, shaking off the past twelve hours which included not only the fiasco with Adam, not only that she made major inroads into what happened to her computer and was pretty sure who did what and how, but also one of the best dreams she ever had. Strange how that happens, she thought. Is that the way the brain works? Does it automatically bring you to a better place when you are troubled? Probably not, she concluded quickly. How else would you explain nightmares if that were true? Or the lack of beautiful, inspiring, entertaining dreams on so many lonely, desperate nights. All of the pigeonholing she had put up with from the men in her life...her brothers, who had her pegged as a future spinster, "Laura will take care of our kids. Who would want to marry her? And if one shows up who does, we'll just scare him off." I would have had plenty of suitors, she knew, starting with Diego and even if she never saw him again, there were plenty of stares on the street, double looks, and even one young banker who followed her down a hallway staring at her butt twitching beneath her suit. Laura knew she was a desirable woman; she could see what the mirror reflected. So many of the other women in the bank secretly envied her lithe, taut body, her high cheekbones and lustrous hair. But she secretly wished to be plainer, more average, able to blend in instead of lighting up a room when entering. Then, maybe then, a man would love her for herself, her sense of humor, strong moral core and infectious laugh instead of her physical beauty which was nothing more than an accident of birth. Again maybe then, she would be taken a little more seriously. Maybe then the other men in New York City wouldn't expect her to be just some lovely Latina from South America that they could manipulate into whatever they wanted, be it an exotic doll on their arm at fancy parties, a housekeeper, or someone they could expect to screw every night regardless of her mood. Probably they would be surprised to find out that she carried a fire inside her, a desire for respect and success as well as for happiness on her own terms, not theirs. So many of them could have done so much better with her if they had just listened a little bit.

She brought her head up quickly, flipping her hair up in the way Michael said reminded him of Rita Hayworth. She recalled something he said once to a group of people who surrounded them at the Christmas party, "A big part of success is not taking any crap from anyone and speaking up for yourself, no matter what the consequences." She realized now that he was completely right, that she was the only one in control of her life, that she had to put aside everything that wasn't working. That began with her walking out on Adam, although she would have preferred a night of intense lovemaking or at least some sweaty sex and a hearty breakfast the next morning. It continued with her rebuke later of that clown at the bar. What was his name?...Tom, right...what a loser. But it really picked up when she came back to the office and began work on the professional portion of her life. Michael was right. You have to push back, no matter who it is. She glanced at the clock on the wall...4:29, ugh. She would close her eyes for a few more minutes and then run to catch the 5:45 at Penn Station out to the Long Island office. She felt ultra-confident that her final piece of proof rested there and that she would find it. And if it were as she suspected, it would take only five minutes from when she entered the office to disable Andre's scam and leave. She could conceivably be back at the office by nine o'clock in time for her shift. And then she would bring her evidence and shove it up Andre's ass, staples and all. But for now, as soon as she readjusted the alarm clock on her cell phone, she would return to the dream she had last night. It was sometimes unfortunate to have such an active mind, she was reminded from time to time. Her night-time dreams were vivid and easy for her to remember. Unfortunately, they weren't always soothing, which was the rough side of the cloth. She was thankful, therefore, in the wake of such an awful day, that she dreamed vividly once again, in spite of sleeping mostly at her desk.

The geography class had always been her favorite. After reading about so many varied peoples, customs and languages throughout the world, she wanted to travel and see with her own eyes the great cities she studied about: Paris, London, Amsterdam, Jerusalem, Tokyo, New York. An endless list of places filled with people to talk to, laugh with, secure an understanding with. And the natural wonders of the world thrilled her as well. She would pore over photos of the beaches of Bermuda and Thailand, the Pyramids, Mt. Fuji, the canals of Venice, a sunset in Hawaii. But it was San Francisco and Muir Woods that always remained the first place she wanted to visit.

The city itself she was sure would be as beautiful and welcoming as the stories and textbooks and articles she would manage to get hold of always said. She rented any movie that was filmed there, and faithfully watched reruns of *Streets of San Francisco* with Michael Douglas just to look at the scenery, although that particular show revealed the gritty side all cities had. She had an itinerary all laid out should she ever make it there. A ride on the cable car, a sightseeing boat trip in the bay followed by dinner on the Wharf, maybe a drive down to Carmel for a delicious al fresco dinner where she could drink wine with people she didn't know at the adjoining tables and laugh all night with them. But the trees were what she wanted to see.

The gigantic Northern California Redwood trees at Muir Woods were a historical landmark just north of San Francisco. These largest living things on the planet captivated her from the very first time she saw the photos. The largest trees around the farm in Argentina were barely fifty feet tall. In some of her favorite dreams, a visit to Muir Woods was always present. But last night was different in that she was able to truly enjoy the behemoths found only in that section of California as easily as she walked along the shore, dodging the incoming tide of cold water like a ballerina.

Now deep in REM sleep, she saw herself standing at the base of an enormous tree, looking up, awed by the size and the majesty of this three-hundred-foot-tall plant, watching the clouds pushed along by the offshore breeze possibly touching the uppermost reaches of its branches. She was surrounded by tourists from all over the world with clicking cameras, screaming children, even some fool who was lighting up a smoke, the stink intruding on her space. Deciding at that moment to get far away from these people, she drew gasps as she started to climb hand over hand, making quick upward progress like the squirrels playing on the maples in a big city park. The rough, grooved bark of the Redwoods provided plenty of places to grab hold and she found herself climbing along as if she were on a ladder built specifically for her. She climbed to about the halfway point of the behemoth within a few minutes and relaxed for a moment on a perch created by a huge burl, probably the result of a lightning strike that could have occurred centuries before. The smaller branches closer to the zenith were not bending under her weight as she continued upward.

"Toque las nubes," her father used to say, reach for the clouds. The clouds she saw from the ground were so close and she discovered, now that she was at the top, she was able to brush them with her fingertips, causing specks of cottony material to fall away as if she were in the middle of the gentlest snowstorm ever. An eagle soared past, looking her over, seemingly beckoning her to try and follow and well, why not? The swaying of the massive tree and the others surrounding it brought their crowns into greater proximity than what was apparent at the base. She searched out the next step and then took it, utterly unafraid, completely confident in her balance, the support of the next Redwood branch and where she wanted to go. She timed the swaying and bending and leaped for a new foothold and found it, but this time she didn't stay put. This tree seemed to bind itself with others near it, the falling burls from previous lightning strikes or high winds or age falling, crashing into their neighbors on their descent to the ground, but instead forging—as Redwoods many times do—a network of boughs she meant to traverse, this path unseen by the humans nearly three hundred feet below.

It was as irresistible to her as anything she ever experienced and she lit out on the nearest branch, the moss that covered it easing the way for her feet which sank comfortably below its surface, as if each step was with a different, perfectly-worn-in house slipper. When did she take her shoes off? She started to run at a brisk clip, each of her toes individually finding the ridges of the boughs, sending signals to her brain in incalculably small units of time, helping her to maintain her balance and speed. Her fear dissipated, there was nothing to stop her from testing the metes and bounds of carelessness and lack of respect for her health and welfare and her surroundings, leaving caution far behind, somehow aware this was the path to discoveries of all kinds.

She was reveling in her physical strength and the suppleness of her body. The eagle dove past her, alerted to some prey on the ground possibly, her wings folded back, her body rippling through the air currents. She watched the eagle until it disappeared from her sight and returned to a level gaze that allowed her to see for many miles, the San Francisco Bay and the distant peaks of the Sierras. All of it just perfect, the cool breeze on a blazing summer day, the air so sweet and refreshing, the fog lingering up here at the top of the world, providing the perfect climate for this old-growth forest to thrive. The only part missing were the stars and the moon, but since it was daytime, this was not about to happen anytime soon. But that was alright with her because she truly felt as if she were the queen of her domain. The wind, considerably stronger at these great heights than on the ground, started to pick up and Laura alighted on another treetop that swayed close enough. The currents of air whistling through the needles of the tree seemed to speak to her, so loneliness wasn't any concern for once, though there was a strange consciousness to her dream that seemed to remind her she was very alone on the crowns of these trees. This was fine with her as she knew herself like no other person ever could and she long ago became accustomed to her solitude. None of her past mistakes intruded up here, none of the people who plotted against her with their selfishness were here either. I do want to see the stars from here, she thought, and she continued along a series of criss-crossing branches and burls, then arriving at a section with a pile of small pliable branches and needles collected in the middle of several fused branches that was so inviting, the perfect bed. The zephyr whistled a lullaby that hurried her to sleep, awaking peacefully later to the magnificence of the clear and cool night sky, the stars more magnificent than any long-time city slicker would ever know. The moon in perfect opposition to the sun stood over it all like a doting parent, and to Laura the cratered and pockmarked heavenly body appeared as if it were only a few feet away. The serenity of it all brought tears to her eyes. It was a moment that so few people could ever experience, a moment of pure contentment with themselves and their surroundings.

It was the best dream I ever had, at least in the last, well, I don't know how many years. And so in spite of sleeping on a short vinyl covered couch in the same clothing she wore to impress Adam just twelve hours before, she immediately upon wakening felt as strong as she ever had in her life. She had Andre cold, his testicles in her hand and she was going to squeeze and twist them until he begged for mercy. Her dogged pursuit of the truth proved it beyond a shadow of a doubt. So many injustices dumped on her by Andre the shit over the past few years were about to be reversed and deposited into his lap. There was no doubt about it all, it was going to happen. She would bring him crashing down like a Canada Goose on its third Bloody Caesar. But the intoxication of revenge was not touching her as it would so many others. She just wanted to have her good name back, her reputation restored, and the company to which she dedicated the past twelve years of her life protected against what could be one day manipulated into a massive theft of their client's identities and monies, causing horrible embarrassment for the bank.

It was during her research into the wire problem from this morning that she uncovered Andre's little salami scam complete with a phantom computer probably set up in a broom closet or somewhere else out of sight that he presumably used to both steal the money as well as cover his tracks. Bastard. Laura abhorred theft of all kinds, from government corruption to the petty robberies on the streets of virtually every city in the world. But Andre tried to pin it all on her. It was certain in her mind that this computer set-up was also designed to point an investigator right to her desk. What a turd you are, Andre. Not only do you steal other people's money, but you try to blame it on someone else. Well, I'm not going to take this crap anymore. I am a new person, with a renewed sense of purpose toward attaining justice for at least myself. God help anyone who gets in my way from now on.

She knew she had to share this information with someone, but had initial difficulty in deciding whom to trust. She couldn't know at that moment if Andre had an accomplice in his crime and was suddenly nervous of some sort of retaliation. The police? The FBI? Her old friends, the twins Linnea and Lorielle? What about HR? The answer came to her a second later and it was now crystal clear what she had to do. For the first time in the many years since they first met, she would reach out to Michael Pierce, ask him his opinion, pick his mind and frankly, get a chance to sit next to him somewhere not surrounded by other Argent Bank employees. She tingled at this idea, but quickly reminded herself that it would have to be all business. This was not to be fooled with, how to deal with the theft of funds, the corruption in her department. No way could she let it go any further. She laughed inwardly at the impossible idea that somehow she forged a friendship with this man borne out over many years, without the benefit of a date, a shared dance, a personal e-mail or any kind of personal moment between them other than a half hour or so of shared table conversation at a company party and a few captured moments in the hallway per *year.* She was actually glad, relieved he didn't work in her building.

The very last gentleman in New York City, one who has proven his integrity, his decency, his sense of fair play...that's what he is, she concluded easily as she had many years to think about him in so many ways as she gathered up her things to head back to the office in Manhattan. She found herself almost tingling with excitement at the prospect of calling him. She wondered what he sounded like on the phone and hoped against hope that he would indeed agree to meet with her because, the high school girl type excitement aside, this was her whole career on the line as well as the reputation of the entire company.

—⁂—

Whathefu pulled Aubrey's Saab into the parking lot of Argent Bank's offices in Mineola, Long Island. He recalled driving through Nassau County many times on his way to or from the Hamptons, not ever stopping in any of the seemingly miserable little towns on either side of the Long Island Expressway. The lot was practically deserted owing primarily to the early time of day. It was just past seven in the morning and most of the employees of whatever company had offices here were undoubtedly just rolling out of bed, getting the kids up and out to school and then hurrying to make it into the office on time.

"Not right in front," ordered Aubrey, who was sitting in the passenger seat. He turned to Andre, who was handcuffed in the back. "They have cameras mounted in the lobby, right?"

"Yes, they do."

"Do they also record out here in the lot?"

"I'm not sure. I don't think so because the bank doesn't own the building. But I'm sure the management company that does own it has some cameras out here." Andre was hoping just that, so he could more easily quell the knot of fear in his stomach that was overtaking the excitement of seeing Kismine on the beach in Rio.

Aubrey thought for a moment and instructed Whathefu to park further away than he ever would have intended. Whathefu was not the type to usually park any further away than he had to, his formerly privileged life allowing him clear access to any open door with just a few steps from his car. He used to laugh at those unfortunates in the kingdom and in America who would spend twenty minutes trolling for a closer parking spot to a restaurant or a mall. But here and now he could suddenly see the sense of it all, so he swung the car away from the building, bringing it to a stop at the far end of the lot.

Andre was thinking about all the times he had come out here. He relished the hour long train ride which he could use to pad his overtime and the ease of working here with no managers in sight. "Oh yeah, that will take a few hours to set up at least, not including the ride back and forth," he would always say to whatever Vice-President was in charge of overseeing assignments and therefore overtime that week, knowing full well that the entire job he was assigned to do would take a halfway competent and somewhat diligent worker about thirty minutes. He loved that overtime, something the Argent Bank shareholders would go bananas over if they were ever able to determine just how much money was siphoned away in this manner every single day. But this office was much more special to him than all the accrued overtime he had basically stolen from the bank. This was the location of the genesis of his salami scam. He conceived it here, set up a computer terminal here in an unused locked office here, set aside his moral code, and then proceeded to steal close to twenty-five thousand dollars a tiny little bit at a time for the past two years. And even if they found the computer, it would all point back to that bitch Laura thanks to his ingenious and, frankly, simple manipulation of her passwords. As a result, in case anyone came sniffing around and discovered the set-up, she would be the one to get canned and Andre would come out smelling like a rose, something of which he convinced himself of at the exact moment he stole the first few cents.

He recalled when she came out here for the initial set-up of the department, walking around with boxes of cables in her arms, carrying monitors and PC's around like a man. She would even get down on her hands and knees to make connections, a woman doing a man's job and obviously enjoying it, getting her hands dirty and putting another man out of a job when she should be home with babies and a husband. She was always oblivious of the doom that was coming to her one way or another as he had planned to destroy her as soon as she joined the department ten years earlier.

Well, now was the time to end all of this guesswork, albeit he had to admit to himself that he never would have gathered up the courage to do what he was now doing if he hadn't been threatened by that big bastard in the front seat. Reminding himself that he was a prisoner still, he tempered his dreams of being on the beach in Brazil with Kismine. Andre listened to the big bastard directing the little shit away from the building, wondering if he should have said there were no cameras watching the lot instead.

"It's quiet here at this hour," said Andre. "We may not even see a security guard."

"It's good to be cautious," replied Whathefu, trying his damnedest to be useful. Aubrey turned in his seat and was able to watch the both of them as he spoke. "Here is what we are going to do. We are going to go in there and move the money as quickly as possible. I'm not that all interested in what you have to do, but this guy here," he pointed at Whathefu, "will be able to tell me if you're screwing with the machine to send a signal to the cops or anyone else. If there is a problem doing so," he angled his large body to fully face Andre, "I expect a solution in under a minute. I want your explanation to be succinct and worded in such a way that anyone could understand it. In other words, if you try any tech babble in an attempt to bullshit me, I will kill you on the spot, understood?"

"Yes," replied Andre, not knowing what else this bastard would expect him to say at such a moment. Aubrey kept his gaze mostly at Andre, but he turned slightly to Whathefu, who was searching the steering column for the ignition, unaware that Saab engineers located them between the seats for whatever reason. He continued in a voice not unlike any business executive issuing an order that was expected to be followed without question.

"I want to be sitting in this car within fifteen minutes tops, a very rich man," Aubrey stated matter of factly. He stared hard at his two accomplices/prisoners for a moment or two to drive his message home. Neither said anything.

"Okay then, let's go do it." They all got out at the same time, the three doors making one sound as they were slammed simultaneously. They moved toward the building, Andre leading, Whathefu slightly behind him, Aubrey closely bringing up the rear, careful to make it appear to any watchful eyes that they were indeed friends or colleagues, but keeping the both of them in front and in his sights, his hand on the Glock pistol in his jacket. After about twenty feet however, Andre stopped and shook his head in frustration.

"Sorry, I forgot the security card for the door; we will need it at this hour." Whathefu, annoyed that he was walking through a parking lot and not parking right at the door, the velvet rope already being lifted for him, tossed him the keys to the Saab adding with a tough guy's demeanor, "Here you are, dummy." Whathefu then heard Aubrey's whispered admonishment close to his ear. How did he get there so fast and so silently?

"If you speak to him again, or make any decision regarding him which includes what you may assume is an innocuous gesture or action on your part such as giving him the car keys without my permission, I will snap your neck right here. Don't think for a second that I won't do it. Your father would probably thank me for it." Andre skipped back to the car in just a few seconds, unlocked the door and retrieved the pass from his jacket pocket, his fat ass hanging out of the door, managing to look even more ridiculous and pathetic when he balanced on one foot and reached into the cabin for the jacket, sticking his leg straight out for balance. Whathefu and Aubrey turned away in tandem with equal pity and disgust, Aubrey also taking this moment once again to survey the surroundings.

Laura was full of life with the spring to her step returning after a couple of years' absence. This in spite of the fact that she, in the past twenty-four hours had ended a potential long term relationship by twisting a man's jewels in her hand, gotten slightly drunk afterward, hopped an hour long train ride out here, had worked for several hours hunting down the problems with the printers and wire system and several other programming glitches that had bothered her over the past few months. Staring at the computer screen for hours on end always made her weary, but not this time. This time it was like a movie, or a revelation coming to life on her screen. For there it was, everything she had suspected. Her password had definitely been compromised, her account was used for what appeared to be a scam to steal money from the bank, and the dummy computer she stumbled upon in the locked closet was used to facilitate it all. It was all Andre, she knew now with complete certainty, that self-righteous bastard, misogynist pig. Do all of the men who come from his part of the world act this way? she wondered.

She quickly corrected herself, admitting that she had not met any other Muslim African men. Who was she to paint millions of people with a tar brush? No negative waves for me today. Today is only for my personal glory and vindication. Maybe the Chairman of the bank will want to hire me as his special assistant. She left through the office's front doors, crossed the lobby and pulled the train schedule from her jacket pocket as she pushed open the door that led to the parking lot, suddenly thankful Argent Bank took a suite on the first floor of the low-rise office park on Long Island rendering the usual waiting for a crowded elevator in the city office to an inessential event. She had a funny feeling that she might be cutting the time a little close and she absolutely did not want to miss this next train back to the city. She turned immediately right upon exiting the building as her eyes concentrated on the small print of the schedule she found tacked up on a message board in the kitchen, not noticing anyone else near the building or in the parking lot.

⁂

Andre helped to pull himself out of the car by walking backwards on his hands across the back seat. Boy, do I have to get in shape, he thought, as he stood huffing and puffing from this small exertion, again picturing himself on the beach in Rio in a few days with Kismine. He slammed the door shut and started back toward Aubrey and Whathefu, both of whom were concentrating on something by the building. Did they see someone? Did I just catch a momentary flash of a person rounding the corner? He wasn't sure as he approached the other two but was not overly concerned either. "I found it. Now we can get in," he told them unnecessarily.

Whathefu and Aubrey were both watching the woman leave the office building. She was reading something, totally engrossed in what she was doing. Aubrey especially noticed her increased speed of gait once she put her reading material away in her pocketbook. He filed away her approximate age, her height, weight, her hair color and style as if he were in a battle in the streets of some city and he couldn't yet tell the combatants apart. It was unusual for anyone to be here at this time, he knew, and anything unusual was worth filing away.

"She has a great ass," was all that Whathefu could add.

"What? Who has what?" as Andre attempted to enjoin his...comrades...as he drew even with them.

"Who would be here now, in this building at this early hour?" demanded Aubrey.

"Well, none of the banking executives would be here, not the receptionists and assistants either. The overnight technical employees are at the branch in the city for twenty-four hours straight; they never leave the system alone."

"There are other companies in this building?"

"Probably, I guess so. Law firms and CPA's, other professional offices, a couple of small restaurants, sure. Why? Did you see someone?"

Aubrey ignored his question and implored them to follow at a quicker pace. These two are so beneath me I can't even muster much contempt for them. That's good...I will be able to kill them both later without hesitation or tears and as for this Saudi rich kid, well, he's going to feel it more than the fat guy. As they stepped up the curb leading to the small plaza in front of the building's front door, Aubrey spoke again. "Fifteen minutes, I'm serious about that." He turned his attention to Whathefu, "You follow what he's doing. I want a running explanation of what's happening, like a pathologist describing a dissection. Other than that, keep your mouth shut."

I'm sorry, but she did have one of the greatest asses I have ever seen. Lighten up...Allah has provided us with this wonderful solution. That was what he wanted to say. All he did say was, well...nothing. He just nodded quickly in agreement. They were at the door now and Aubrey turned to each of them again, "You know what to do and what not to do. Let's go."

⁓ I ⁓

Although it had been some time since she last visited this office, she remembered the short cuts to the station and she was able to breathe a little easier now that she realized she wouldn't miss the train. It had been years since she last rode the Long Island Railroad, spending most of her time in the city or in Queens. She had no use for suburbs, the sameness, the lack of friendliness, neighbors hardly ever speaking to one another. The last time she rode the railroad was to attend a party in the Hamptons where she discovered to her dismay that nearly all the men wore pink or too-bright yellow shirts.

Laura reached the south end of the station and skipped up the stairs to the platform, putting her recall of that particular one of hundreds of dull Saturday nights aside for a moment. She bought a one-way ticket to Penn Station and walked slowly to the center of the platform, gathering her breath. There were only a few additional people on the platform and she was glad that a seat would probably be easy to find. Falling back into her memory of the party out in the Hamptons several years earlier, she recalled there were about forty human males at this party, without a single man among them. The food and wine were both good and plentiful, however, and she suddenly felt an impending urge to laugh right there on the platform recalling an unfortunate scene of unintentionally burping a mouthful of wine and cracked crab onto some suburban man's bright aqua shirt—red wine, of course—which she felt bad about even to this day, but she couldn't help almost laughing out loud at the memory whenever it entered her mind much in the same way the average American man usually can't suppress a smile if not outright laughter recalling his favorite *Three*

Stooges episode. A businessman in a trench coat reading a newspaper edged away from her, wondering what anyone could be so happy about at such an ungodly hour.

—◈—

Andre strode immediately through the cubicle farm to the large computer room where virtually all the bank's servers were located, becoming quite alarmed as soon as he got to the door. A month previous, the staff in this office put up a written attendance sheet. Apparently some staff members were passing their security cards around to anyone who wanted access to the computer room and, as a result, they couldn't control who was where and when. And they didn't want anyone just walking around. So they decided to go old school and made everyone sign in. If your security card showed you gained access at a particular time, then you better have left a corresponding signature that also showed who else was in the room, what they were doing there, and when they left. It was a pain, and it offended many of the younger set, who seemed to not have used a writing implement in years, but ultimately was quite effective for controlling traffic in and out. Salespeople, electricians, air conditioning technicians were in and out fairly frequently, but that had to be more tightly controlled now. Andre was stupefied as he now read the sheet...*Laura...1:30 AM—6:20 AM*. What the hell? Was she here earlier this morning? And why? The sweat at his receded hairline started immediately, beading up with alarming speed near his temples and dripping down within seconds as if he were in the middle of a rainstorm. Did he underestimate her? Did she figure this out just today or last night? How can this be happening now, this display of the most awful timing? And as if he were telegraphing his every move and thought, Aubrey asked him after reading the sheet himself, "Do you know her, this Laura?"

"Uh, who, do I know who?" Andre's brain was on overload, ready to explode at any moment.

Resisting the urge to chop his larynx, Aubrey stepped closer to Andre, reading him the name and the time right off the sheet. "Who is Laura and does she usually work here at this time?"

"Maybe she's the one with the great ass we just saw," Whathefu guessed aloud.

"I do know her, but I can't imagine why she or anyone else would be here at this time of day. She works in my office in Manhattan. She would only come out here if she was assigned here for a particular job." Andre spit the words out rapid fire, like a kid sputtering to the principal.

"Or if she unfortunately figured out that you set her up and she came here to test her theory," Aubrey countered. "What does she look like, this Laura?"

"I don't know, tall, long black hair..."

"Is she fat or thin?"

"Does she have a great ass?" asked Whathefu. The question almost earned him a chop from Aubrey, who stopped as soon as he recalled the woman leaving the bank. She appeared to be in good shape, he remembered. He was able to tell even though they had been over one hundred yards away.

"I don't know about her rear end, but she is very trim, almost like an athlete in fact. Why?" And then he remembered their gaze when he pulled himself out of the car after he recovered the security card. He also did see something, just a flash of movement and color. Was it her? "Do you think you saw her just before we came in? I thought I saw someone."

"Quickly," Aubrey told him, "Try to sign in and see if you and your little scam was discovered. Just tell me if it is still up and running."

Andre went immediately to the broom closet where he kept the dummy computer, unlocked the door and went inside and sat at the terminal. He pushed the on button and waited, but nothing happened. What's wrong now? He looked under the desk and to his horror could see that all the cables had been removed. The internet connection, the power cables, the network cables were all removed. The computer was effectively dead. It had to be her. My God, is there a worse piece of timing recorded in recent human history? Why couldn't she have come here later this morning? He had to tell them now. "It's not working. Someone sabotaged the system. I guess she did." He sat there speechless, aghast at realizing that he would probably be arrested within the next forty-eight hours. Aubrey grabbed him by the lapels, jerking him out of the chair.

"Where is the nearest train station?" Aubrey barked as he hustled the two of them toward the lobby door.

"A block and a half away. We can cut through the parking lot of the diner, over through here," Andre replied, terror in his mind at the thought of going to jail, for how long?

"Let's move now! We need this woman right now!" Aubrey commanded as they burst out into the parking lot, following the same path Laura had used just a few minutes before. The three of them broke into a dash, spurred on by a realization that their dreams and schemes were possibly permanently fading away as the not too distant whistle of the train just about to pull into the station reached them.

——

"For once on time," the man reading the newspaper commented to Laura as the train pulled into the Mineola station and opened the doors. He had moved a little closer to her once he discreetly took a better look at her. No passengers were getting off here, so Laura was able to step right into the car, vaguely aware of a group of people running to catch the train, hearing hurried steps like the old Dashing Dan commuter logo of the railroad back in the 1960s. She turned left upon entering, choosing to sit in one of the seats just inside the door that had a matching pair of seats facing it, perfect for the commuting pinochle and gin rummy games in the morning and also perfect for her to put her feet up for a few minutes before the conductor came around to punch her ticket. The doors closed and the train hesitated for a moment before slowly pulling away. She turned to look out the window and did indeed see that a tall, handsome young man did in fact miss the train by a second or two. She felt bad for him and was also annoyed that the conductor didn't wait for him. What was wrong with waiting for an extra second? Now that guy's day was possibly ruined. As the businessman said a moment ago, this train was hardly ever on time. Oh well, not my problem. Other people's problems are not mine anymore. The only problems that matter to me going forward are mine and I am going to take care of a big one today. With that, she closed her eyes and fell asleep, ignoring the agitated group on the platform.

—⫶—

Michael turned into the exit for La Guardia airport off the Grand Central Parkway, dodging the yellow cabs who were fighting with the black Ford radio cars for a sucker tourist or two they could charge a hundred bucks for a ride to Manhattan. He continued along the byway on the outside ring of the airport, coming around to the Delta departures area. They had an hour drive from Long Island, the only sounds in the car coming from the radio and Sally's singing and nonstop questions about the plane, what was its color, could I talk to the pilot, can I fly the plane just a little, where they were going, why weren't you coming, Daddy, and on and on. He wasn't the least bit annoyed. In fact, it was much more peaceful than trying to have a conversation with Georgia. He pulled up to an empty space and squeezed into it in one shot. As soon as he turned the ignition off, he heard Sally opening the door.

"Dad, please open the trunk so I can get the bags out," she asked impatiently. Lately she had been interested in showing off her physical strength and independence.

"Okay sweetie, but be careful behind the car," he replied, very aware of the cabs looking to drop off their passengers and get back to the city for another fare. He reached for the button under the dash that worked the trunk lock and held it until he heard the metallic click of the latch releasing. She slammed the door shut and ran to the back. He could see her in the rear view mirror between the bottom of the raised trunk lid and the top of the rear console. He turned back, briefly catching Georgia's profile as he did so. She was staring straight ahead, fumbling in her pocketbook for something, probably keys or a wallet. Whatever it was, she didn't seem to be about to let him in on it. Ten or fifteen seconds passed before either spoke. It felt like ten or fifteen minutes, so he decided to break the ice.

"Have a nice time, say hello," he said without much energy.

The resulting silence was as loud as an avalanche of boulders. It spoke volumes, the most obvious of which was that for many years you have known this woman, lived with her, married her, produced a child with her, and the stark realization that maybe, just maybe, you didn't know a thing about each other was a serious jolt to his existence.

"Before I leave for the next few days, do you even want to try to explain to me who the hell you have been lately?"

"Is it that important to you that I act as if I were your beard at these events?" He unfastened his seat belt and turned in his seat toward her. Sally continued to struggle with the big suitcase. He figured he had about one, maybe two minutes to continue this conversation. "Do you expect me to stand by dumbly, if that is even a word, while I listen to nonsense being pounded into your head? And if they are in fact not reaching too deeply into your brain, at the very least most of these people freak me out with the aggressiveness of their progressiveness. They don't object to anything and they love lame conspiracies involving the U.S. government. I never hear them talking about all these Arab governments treating their people like shit, or about Kim in North Korea who has a political prison in his country the size of Washington D.C. filled with people who didn't cry hard enough at his father's funeral, or about..."

"They are important to me! Why can't you understand that?"

"Fine Georgia, they are important to you. Then you go see them alone. I have no interest in ever seeing any of them ever again in any forum. There is no reason for me to go. We don't have to be glued to each other. Do you want to go to my next card game?"

Again silence, the kind of silence that precedes pigeons in a city park taking flight milliseconds prior to a temblor's initial shakes and rolls. He heard only the satisfied grunt of his daughter dragging the last suitcase out of the trunk, the one hundred pound bag landing on the ground with a thud. She came around to the passenger window and spoke to her parents.

"What are you guys doing? The plane is leaving!"

"Sally, pull the bags up on the sidewalk and bring them over to the man in the uniform with the red hat, okay, honey? Mommy and I need to talk a little more."

"Try kissing each other good-bye, that might help," she replied before setting out to move the bags over to the skycap stand. Out of the mouths of babes...who came up with that piece of wisdom? He would have to ask Vinny about that. The rage he felt was receding as was always the case when his daughter was near. How long would that last? he thought. She'll be a young woman soon. Running out on dates, studying in college for a career, planning the rest of her life, partying, working, getting—gulp —laid. He stared out the windshield, struggling to find the warmth and sincerity in his voice.

"You used to say I was important to you, Georgia." He sounded stupid when he said it, like a pathetic man begging a woman to come back while she was thinking about the great guy she has been screwing the past few weeks. He felt no warmth in his words, there was no conveyance of love. It was merely a statement of fact for him. He felt ashamed that he couldn't summon anything more. She picked up on it and reached for the door handle.

"Have a good time, Michael, hanging out with your friends from the old neighborhood. I have better things to do, better people to speak with and listen to and better places to go." The door was open now, her right foot on the pavement as she was about to lift herself out of the car. He angrily grabbed her elbow, the pigeons lifting off somewhere, "You'd do well to have friends like mine instead of the self-important pseudo-intellectual morons you think are your friends." Not waiting for a response, he released her, got out of the car and slammed the door, as he was physically exhausted in a mere few seconds from this conversation and just craved to be alone. Not even Sally's smile could cure him of that. He did his best to fake it for her, though, as he came around the back of the car. Georgia was all the way out of the car, her door slamming as well, doing nothing but startling their daughter and drawing the attention of the Port Authority cop about twenty feet away.

"Sally, be a good girl and take care of Mommy," he said leaning down for a kiss and a hug.

"Not here, Dad. There's too many people. Shake my hand instead." He stood up straight and took her tiny hand in his and shook it straight up and down rather comically. "Okay, big girl, have a nice time and I'll see you in a few days." Sally turned toward the skycap who came over to help her without another word for Michael. Goodness, in about two years she won't even say good morning to me. He turned back to Georgia, "Call me if you need anything," he said, quite aware she would never call. It was just another weakly-delivered statement. Frankly he didn't want to hear from her at all. She affixed her pocketbook on her shoulder and called after Sally, passing him by without even a look. He watched them pass through the door into the terminal and Georgia looked over her shoulder rather coldly, certainly not the way every man likes to see their girl look back over their shoulder at them. This look was a smidgeon above obligatory, wordless, but effectively delivering a wave of contempt and resignation which he recognized as his cue to get in the car immediately and get the hell out of there. At the last minute he heard his daughter's voice, the words fluttering toward him like a butterfly over the din of the cabdrivers yelling, their horns blaring, tires screeching, "Bye, Daddy!"

"Bye, sweetie," he called back, but Georgia pulled her along quickly and so it was likely she hadn't heard him. He hoped she had. He felt the presence of the Port Authority cop the next moment. "Yeah, yeah, I'm outta here, I'm going," Michael told him as he got back in the car. He clicked his seat belt and was about to turn into traffic when his phone chirped. He checked the screen before answering, and he saw that the call was coming from his largest mortgage client ever, a commercial loan that would carry a commission equal to more than a year's earnings in one deal. He remembered his father's advice regarding bad news for a client from years before, "Deliver it immediately, never hold onto it for a moment longer than you have to," and he clicked the talk button.

"Vinny, good morning."

"How's everything? Gonna see you later?"

"I heard, yes. Twelve noon at AJ's place?"

"That's when everyone else will be there, but I'd like to meet you earlier, at about 11:30. We have things to go over before the rest of the boys arrive. We have to talk."

"I know. I'll see you then." They clicked off their phones without saying good-bye. They had known each other so long it seemed unnecessary. We have to talk...the four most dreaded words in relationship land, the precursor to a breakup or really bad news, sometimes both, such as, "I'm breaking up with you and it burns when I pee."

He wondered if he would be saying those words to Georgia sometime soon or maybe he would be hearing them from her. He shook the thought from his head, put the signal on, looked in his side mirror for a possible yellow cab missile coming from out of nowhere, threw one more nasty look at the Port Authority cop and pulled away from the curb and headed toward work at the mortgage office of Argent Bank.

⁓ﷲ⁓

Andre was in deep shit. He knew it and his jailers knew it as well. Strangely, even though he knew this crazy big bastard could break him in half at any time, and also that he may be exposed as a thief at the bank by the end of the day, subject to arrest and prosecution, his primary concern was that the prospect of continuing to finance Kismine's singing career was now in doubt. It had to be the Laura woman, she must have been the one the others had seen. They just missed her at the train station, if she was on the train at all. The big bastard and the little weasel both were sure they had seen her entering the train, the weasel adding that she seemed quite happy, a spring to her walk. But they weren't one hundred percent sure and if there was one apparent quality to this big bastard, it was that he wanted to be sure about everything with no loose strings left to chance.

Aubrey asked him, "How long does this train take to get back to Manhattan?" Andre delayed his answer for a second as he mentally calculated for an accurate answer and that earned him a crack under his cheekbone, a short but vicious blow that made his entire face feel like it was on fire. The man in him wanted to inquire in a certain way why it was necessary to hit him, but he just palmed his cheek to make sure it was still there and in one piece. "How long?" Aubrey snarled.

"I don't know exactly, but about an hour I guess, maybe a little more. It depends on whether she has to change at Jamaica Station and when the connection gets there."

"Where does the train terminate in Manhattan?"

"At Penn Station." He thought to add the location of the stop and was rewarded with a smile from Aubrey when he said, "That's at Thirty-Fourth Street and Seventh Avenue."

"And where is your office? She works there as well?" Aubrey asked.

"Fifty-Sixth Street and Fifth Avenue, about a thirty-minute walk from Penn Station and probably close to the same amount of time if she took the subway, and yes she works there." Aubrey was in motion immediately, grabbing both of them by the collars and dragging them off the raised platform, "We have to get to her office right away. We need to intercept her before she gets inside. We need to assume that she's told no one of her discovery yet. It's still early so probably the main executives and managers are still driving to the train station in their hometowns." He checked his watch as they hustled along the sidewalk back to the parking lot. "We need to get there as quickly as possible."

"Or what?" This from Whathefu.

"Or I seriously consider immediately killing you both." They reached the car and Aubrey instructed Andre to drive. This would tie him up as effectively as handcuffing him again would and he must know the roads here better than either I or the little Saudi prince would, Aubrey reasoned. Andre was fitting the seat belt when he said, "There's going to be a lot of traffic on the way. I hope I can get us there in time." Aubrey was on him like a Great White Shark on a hapless body surfer, grabbing the seat belt and wrapping it around his neck with his left hand, his right hand taking Andre's right hand and bending it up and back in such a way that Andre could soon scratch his scapula with his elbow. He cried out in pain, but Aubrey showed no interest in letting up. Whathefu watched with a detached fascination mixed with a healthy dose of fear at the sudden violent burst from the back seat as Aubrey told him, "You have been delivered to me..."

"Us," chimed in Whathefu earning a look from Aubrey that could chill a volcano.

"Right, us...yeah, sure. Listen, you fat turd, Allah the most merciful has delivered you to us and I will see that His vision for this gift is fulfilled. So the next time I detect a gloomy feeling from you, I will break a bone of my choosing. I have spent the last ten years of my life as an Army Ranger and I can smell your bullshit from a mile away. I can read you like a comic book, my friend, don't doubt that for even a moment." He released Andre and let him continue to get the car going. They pulled out of the lot and Aubrey continued.

"You're still a foreigner in this country, although you probably at least have a green card. I bet you're one generation removed from a straw hut that served as the family compound, am I right? Some place in Africa, Sudan, the Ivory Coast, or maybe Somalia? Is it Algeria? Is that where you get that faggot French name?" Aubrey snarled condescendingly, apparently forgetting his own name which brought him so much grief in the schoolyards of his youth. "Let me continue...you're over-educated and you will never land a top job that will pay you what you want because you are a Muslim AND a nigger. You toil and dream for years, envisaging all that money passing through your fingers like shit through a duck. So you got a little frustrated, pissed that you may never get your shot and then started a little scam on your own, earning a couple of bucks along the way. Well good for you, my friend. I don't know why you wanted the money so badly that you would commit a Federal crime. Maybe you gamble too much on slow horses, maybe you hold a fondness for some white powder, maybe you just want to buy some land in your home country, maybe some woman has convinced you of something that will never happen because I can tell you, my friend, that's what they all do because they are all completely full of shit and completely unaware of what they want out of life." This last comment drew a curious look from both Andre and Whathefu, but he continued on.

"You never had the balls to go all the way, however. Well, my friend, now I am your balls. And they are telling you that you are going to succeed today in not forcing me to kill you. Now drive the car and get me to your office in one piece and on time, okay?" Andre nodded yes and Aubrey patted him reassuringly on the thigh, "Just remember the mission, my friend. We have to beat this woman to Manhattan and it is your responsibility to help us do exactly that. I have confidence in you. Now go."

Andre settled himself best he could, found he was sweating again in spite of the cool morning, checked his mirrors and headed up the street to the entrance ramp for the Long Island Expressway, racking his brain for alternative routes in case he hit traffic, which was a virtual certainty.

—⚓—

The Long Island Railroad train was filling up quickly with each stop and Laura was now crowded into her seat by a foursome of businessmen playing cards on a folded piece of cardboard. At least she was able to sit down, she thought, unlike the N train where giving up a seat to a woman was as rare as an elephant trudging down Park Avenue. She wound up not calling Michael as of yet as she forgot how early it was and she figured it would be better to get him once his day got underway a little bit. She stared out the window as Nassau County flew by, soon to be replaced by the danker neighborhoods of Queens.

This train would probably be nicer to commute on if not for the same heavy eyes on her. Well, men were men, she knew, as her mother always told her. It would be much less disconcerting if there were any warmth behind the stares aimed at her body. "I don't mind if you look at me, I know I'm lucky to look like this," she wanted to say. "It was all my mom's doing, she passed her beauty to me and her brains as well, by the way. But can any of you just say hello or good morning or allow a slight upturning of the corner of your mouth in a semi-secret conveyance of appreciation? I know virtually all of you want to bed me—you don't even need to know my name probably—but can any of you possibly exhibit even a shred of gentlemanly behavior?"

This frustration with the male human animal almost always brought her back to Michael Pierce. Here was a man who never hid his interest in her as a woman, but it was so well concealed, so dart-like in its accuracy that in a roomful of people, his desire could not have been detected with the Hubble telescope. He didn't wear it on his sleeve as so many others did with their ridiculous questions, stupid posturing, and banal, innocuous statements. He never, not once ever asked her whom she might be dating, never touched her in any way at all, not even a casual acknowledgment on the inside of her elbow, not even coming close to sharing a dance. She saw him watching her once when she was dancing a silly salsa at one of the Christmas parties and he looked almost jealous. She thought at that time he would finally ask her to dance, but it never happened. In fact, in all the time she knew him he never stood any closer than three feet away when they were talking, only bending from the waist to hear her soft voice over the din of the deejay's music and the conversations carrying on all around them. Well, he was always just nothing more than one more man that she found an attraction to that she had to avoid. But he was well, so freaking perfect, why did he have to be married? She checked her watch, figuring that it was still a little early to be calling. She would wait until she arrived in the city. At least then and there she could call from the street and have a bit of privacy as the train was filling up even more as it neared its final destination.

Forty minutes later Michael was officially in a daze sitting in stopped-dead traffic on the parkway. The ability to make the transition from the drop-off of Georgia and Sally at the airport to the phone call from Vinny and the deal of their lifetime coming apart at the seams, to the mortgage business in general made him feel like he was in a washing machine. One disaster to the next, boiling water into a frying pan then directly into the fire. Part of him was looking forward to the gathering at AJ's later as it was always comforting to be with the boys. But this was not going to be an ordinary meeting. They were all tied up in one amount or another into the waterfront project in Long Island City and it would be laid out on the table for them to collectively gag over. It was inconceivable and truly unbelievable that all the carefully laid plans that had taken years to put together were going to be trashed by a group of people from Sutton Place or Park Avenue or whomever these losers were who mostly treated places like Long Island City as nothing more than somewhere they pass through on their way to the airport.

Michael knew in his bones that this group ultimately would be squashed by the Board of Estimate, local politicians, even the mayor would line up to hang them all by the balls. But they had the one little piece of juice that mattered and they played it perfectly. What were the chances these clowns would know the owners of Shale Financial as well as know a tidbit about them that would drive them bananas, possibly resulting in their pulling their financial commitment to the project?

Everyone he knew, the Burkes, Moose Miller, Charlie Mick, they all poured multiple tens of thousands into the project for start-up costs, architects, materials, permits, an endless cycle of preparation for what appeared to be turning into the Hindenburg of deals. Those dollars were already spent, gone, into the wind, never to be retrieved except in the form of future equity in a huge development project and a nice piece of the rents for the rest of their lives. The Burkes put many hours of work into the project and were as interested in making it work as they were in any Knicks game. All they all had now was a huge dream that was quickly turning into a nightmare, complete with financial ruin for virtually all of them, public embarrassment in front of all those who doubted their collective ability to bring the project to fruition, even though none of those types ever came close to even jotting down a plan for their dream on a piece of paper. Scores of people waiting for it all to come together, construction workers desperate for wages, electricians, plumbers, suppliers of masonry, rebar, concrete, heavy equipment operators, truck drivers, all of whom just wanted to make a buck in the middle of a miserable economy. And all the people in the neighborhood who were sick of the stinking, reeking waterfront that always had so much promise along with apparently no one throughout the decades who wanted to take the chance on creating something worthwhile. Except Vinny and us, he thought. Damn, what a mess. The selfishness that all people possess but don't like to admit then started to take over his thoughts. His commission from this deal would have come close to five hundred thousand dollars. With that payment in the bank it would mean no more debt, mortgage paid significantly down, new car, and a college fund that he would give over to his friend Tommy with the strict instruction that it would never be touched until Sally was ready to go to school. Poof, all up in smoke.

"Shit, damn, fuck!" he screamed at the windshield. The classic rock station on the car radio just started yet another Doors tune—don't they have anything else to play?—and he punched the radio button to silence it. It was creeping into him again, a general feeling of malaise when nothing at all seemed like it was going to work out. No more mortgage clients were going to call, his general assortment of aches and pains would never go away, etc. He was seeing in a more and more vivid fashion the possibility of divorce, more debt, and the loss of stability and at least mild routine. Michael always considered himself to be pretty light on his feet, but frankly he craved his routines, his schedules. One of the advantages of growing older, he realized, was that he finally understood that every man and woman and many of the children fought the same fight every day. So he knew he had company in his misery. There was divorce, bankruptcy, loss of relationships and love going on all around him, most of it much worse than what he was feeling at these moments. As a result he was able to finally come around and count his blessings and move on to more fruitful thinking, but he could never shut the door entirely, the silent scenarios would come on like a thunderstorm in Kansas, quick and powerful. These had been a bitch to deal with, he was realizing, and he was keenly aware that these moments were more frequent in the past eighteen months.

He sighed and opened his driver's window for a breath of fresh air and was met by a flatbed truck driven by the toughest looking Hasidic man he had ever seen pulling up next to him, its brakes squealing with effort. The truck was piled with steel wire cages filled with live chickens piled five high. He locked eyes with one of the birds just as a dollop of poop landed on its head from the upstairs neighbor. The chicken didn't move a feather, he couldn't stand up as it was, and Michael figured there wasn't a more pathetic existence in New York City at that very moment than that of this poor bird. He was probably looking forward to the rabbi's razor across his neck prior to being part of a chicken salad sandwich. It was certainly preferable to this cage. The traffic then opened up a bit and the driver of the flatbed grinded into first gear and pulled away. The chicken seemed to keep his beady eyes on Michael as if to say, "Don't even think about complaining about your lot in life to me."

—

Laura was exiting the subway at Lexington Ave. and Fifty-Third Street, just a few blocks from her own office at Argent Bank. She headed west on Fifty-Fifth Street, turning about eighteen heads in the process with the barest minimum of effort. But she didn't notice them this time, no definitely not this time as she was interested in something much more important than receiving a wolf whistle or a casual fling with any of the men and boys who would be talking about her later: "You should have seen this broad's/ chick's/ babe's ass this morning, Mama Mia, Holy Shit, Hay Chihuahua, she was a piece of ass, a slice of Heaven, my greatest dream girl."

Her steps were full of power and the requisite natural grace she possessed since she was a teenager. Maybe I should call from here on the street instead of in the office, she thought. Yes, that's a good idea. Keep it close, don't want anyone else to hear. She checked her pocketbook for the bent and tattered business card Michael had given her many years earlier. "Call me if you need a mortgage or if a friend needs a mortgage, or if you, I don't know…need a piece of advice about something." And he smiled at her and said good-night before he left and she thought her knees would buckle, but thankfully that didn't happen. What had happened instead was the creation of a barometer of sorts for her to draw upon for the next ten years whenever she was out on a date, and that was simply, Does this guy make me feel the way Michael did the first time we met and all inside of about fifteen seconds? If no, and they were all ultimately a no in the last ten years, some much faster than others, then maybe she would consider a fling with the person, but nothing more. Maybe it would have been nice once in a while if she actually ever got around to doing it. She still hadn't at that point in her life.

She finally found the card at the bottom of the bag, fished it out and started to dial Michael, momentarily concerned that maybe his number had changed. She dialed the 10 digits and then paused, realizing that this would be the first time, since they met ten years before, that she had ever spoken with this man outside the walls and eyes of the bank. Would his voice be as strong and resonant over the phone as it had always been in person? But then she stopped dead in her tracks, stabbed by a thought that she had never considered, and she was surprised to be slightly horrified by it seeping into her little stream of thought about a man she had so many nice conversations with, each one ever so slightly stoking a fire that had burned for years within her... would he be glad to hear from her? Exactly what would his reaction be?

She knew now that total disappointment would come over her if she were rejected by him, but that was silly, wasn't it? She had never had any kind of romantic relationship with Michael, never danced with him, met him anywhere socially, was never alone with him and certainly never kissed him or even touched his arm to accentuate a point in conversation. What they had, in essence, was one very long first date, stretched out over ten years. And what woman ever knew if she would hear again from a first date after they were dropped off? Several first and blind dates had gone well in the past, she recalled, and then...nothing. Not a phone call and, in today's more modern world, not even a text or e-mail...or even a fax. "Sorry, it was nice, but not nice enough. Have a good life." Even something like that would have been preferable to nothing at all. At this point in her life she was having difficulty recalling certain moments of intimacy with old boyfriends so how could she recall all the first and only dates she went on in the past twenty years? Oh enough of this nonsensical pop psychologist bullshit, Laura, her inner voice cried out, Just dial the freaking number. With that, she placed her thumb once more over the talk button, but paused yet again.

She tried to relax but she knew her alert level would be on ultra high, as it had been since she came to the United States, never fully trusting anyone, the women less than the men even. Always on guard for the slightest of slights, she estimated that she probably misjudged many situations and people in her life because they made in her mind some sort of critical mistake early on. A wrong word, gesture, or anything else that so many in New York would deem inconsequential meant so much to her. And it was rare that any offender would get a second chance. Laura knew this was terribly unfair, but she didn't care as she very much ascribed to the rule that first impressions are usually true and everlasting. In other words, a man who burps, curses, or touches her inappropriately in the first half hour of a first date is probably nothing more than a selfish slob.

So what would his first words be like? Enthusiastic? Surprise certainly, but that would be a great way to determine how he deals with the unknown or unexpected, a quality she found very attractive in a man, much more so than a washboard set of abs or a full head of wavy sandy hair. Maybe he would be impatient with her intrusion into his daily routine, as she was aware the mortgage business was very difficult the past year what with all the doom and gloom predictions she heard in the halls and read in the Wall Street Journal regarding the sub-prime business and accounting shenanigans with Fannie Mae and Freddie Mac. Maybe he wouldn't display any noticeable enthusiasm, but he could then refuse to meet with her. He does work for the same company and might feel exposed to accusations of being a whistle blower. And he had a family to support and he wouldn't entertain anything that could put his job in jeopardy, no matter how he felt inside about her. And what was that exactly? she continued thinking as the phone once again dropped to her side. I wonder what he thinks about me...really. Well, it would all come out shortly but she promised herself to be patient with him because, after all, she was the one intruding on his day. The phone was facing up once again, and this time she dialed, remembering her new self, her new mission. If Michael didn't want to help her, she would still push forward on her quest to expose Andre and his crimes. Her new self reminded her that she needed no other person in her life, including Michael Pierce. But she had to admit, deep in her heart, that she hoped this call went well. Why not? she asked herself as she punched talk with her thumb, Why the hell not?

Michael turned away from the chicken truck to see if he was going to be moving anytime soon and shortly he was able to see the problem. A cesspool collection truck was being ticketed for whatever reason and the jerk was taking up the whole right lane instead of pulling off on the shoulder. The banner on the side of the truck read, "We flush your problems away," and all Michael could think was that this massive toilet on wheels couldn't handle all of the shit coming his way today. Just then, the phone which was laying on the driver's seat started to ring. He couldn't recognize the number right away but he could see it was local, with a 917 exchange. Someone's cell phone. Good, at least it would probably be a short call. Maybe a piece of new business. He picked it up and pressed the talk button.

"Hello, this is Michael Pierce," he said, twisting the screen so that he could read the whole incoming number again, which he still didn't recognize.

"Hello, Michael. This is Laura from Argent Bank. I hope I'm not bothering you." Several seconds of silence, the stunned kind, ensued while he contemplated an answer.

"Uh, no, of course not. How are you? Que Pasa?"

"It's a little early and I thought maybe you wouldn't have been on your way to work yet. Sorry again if I've intruded." Her voice settled into his ears like warm hands touching an athlete's cramping muscles. A delicious ecstasy was spreading all through his body. He could no longer see the chicken's rolling tomb and he had just passed the shit sucker truck and now the highway opened up. He stepped on the gas and sped off on his way to the office. He was immediately aware that this was the first time he had ever spoken on the phone to her...the first time in what, ten years?

"No, no, it's okay, just fine. I was up early this morning for an, uh, appointment. It's nice to speak with you." He couldn't help it and hoped against hope for some reason that he didn't sound lame. "I think this is the first time we ever spoke on the phone." He felt like a twelve-year-old having his first conversation with the cute girl in the front row in science class.

Is he happy to hear from me? she wondered. He sounds as if he is, but he also sounds a bit wary. Well that makes sense because of what he just said, she concluded. It was their first time on the phone and as a result figured that he should be a little startled. She was surprised to catch herself trying to read his inflections and choice of words, looking for a meaning other than what he was plainly stating. Mellow out, she cautioned herself, just talk to him. You're calling him above all others because he has already proven himself to you. You need his help and advice, nothing more. She brushed all this away and continued.

"Yes it is. Isn't that amazing?" Ugh, she felt like a child back on the farm. What do I say now?

"How have you been?" Michael asked her.

"Fine, thank you. And you?" Lovely, lovely voice.

"Ups and downs, Laura, you know, the usual ups and downs," he replied quickly adding, "But somehow we all get through it with some effort, no use complaining about it, right?" Why is she calling me? His heart was racing as he recalled the last holiday party, several months before. She had chosen a dark blue vintage dress to wear, with just a little bit of frill and some perfectly placed white beads. Dark blue stockings covered her legs accentuating her calf musculature. She wore a nice set of pearls and her high heels, in which she was always able to walk so well, completed a perfect package of taste, style and elegance. Many of the other women at the party were wearing horribly shaped rags, most of them resembling stuffed sausage casings. Not one of them could approach her terrific display even if they had the space shuttle at their disposal. Michael was sure they all wanted to kill her. He just wanted to talk to her, as he had done for the previous nine years. And they did, extending their strange first date for another year. No kissing, dancing, no exchange of truly emotional issues but, as always, a very easy, honest exchange between adults. He drove her home that night for only the second time, unfortunately along with her crazy friend from accounting and one of the managers from the IT Department. He made sure to drop her off last and they exchanged more stories about their lives for an hour in front of her house.

"I never liked people who complain constantly. There is beauty everywhere if you just look around," she replied. Dripping class and style over the phone, he wondered what she was wearing at that moment and was dying to ask her.

"Too many people out there who are full of negative waves, ya know? It's a struggle to avoid them, but avoid them we must." He had to know now. The time for small talk was over and he wanted to push aside the bromides and get down to brass tacks. "I'm surprised, but admittedly pleased to hear from you." He continued, "What's happening, what's up?" He almost asked ,"Que Pasa, amiga?", but he decided against it. He could hear the rushing of the blood in his head as his heart pumped furiously.

"I've suspected a problem, well, that is, I've had a problem in the office for a couple of years and just recently I discovered something related to that problem that well...is a real problem." She almost spat the words out because she just wanted to paint a picture as quickly and easily as possible for him. Somehow she figured he would get it despite her stammering.

"I understand, I think. Do you mean that you believe some person who has been hassling you for a long time now is doing something, I don't know...sinister? Are they evil or something? Or is it a personal thing, maybe a relationship issue?" Please tell me you don't have a boyfriend. But why should I care? I've never asked her that before.

He never asked me anything like that before, Laura thought at the same time. I guess it's a natural question under this circumstance and then she replied, "No, I don't have a boyfriend to have a problem with." One question asked, two answers given. "It's in the office, a political problem that I am having difficulty with."

"At Argent Bank?"

"Yes."

"Do you want to tell me now what's been happening? Are you there in the office now?"

"No, I'm in the city, a few blocks away from the office. I didn't want to use the phone there," she replied, starting to feel less and less anxious about whether Michael was the right person to call about this situation. She continued, "I can't really explain everything over the phone, but I can give you some background," she replied, then filling him in on the basics of the political marginalization, her difficulties with some of the other executives at the bank, this and that, that and this, that had gone on so long and that was totally out of line and undeserved. He listened without comment and Laura had to stop a couple of times to ask if he were still there.

"Yes, I'm here," he reassured her. What a nice voice. And he felt bad then that he had been engaging in, probably for her, meaningless chit-chat in the bank hallway and at the Christmas parties, no doubt boring the hell out of her, completely clueless to this maybe years-long issue that was apparently starting to consume her a little. "It sounds like something we should meet for. Is that okay?" Please say yes. I would just like to speak to you for a little while and I don't care about what, we could talk about the weather for three hours and I wouldn't mind. Suggest a very public place, quickly. "We can meet at your favorite coffee shop if you like." His head was spinning. Maybe the chicken had a special connection with the creator of everything and for his last wish, he worked this out. This was happening barely fifteen minutes after dropping his family at the airport and then a grim call with his biggest client—and best friend—and now this lady drops a call to him in the middle of all that and he essentially is about an inch away from meeting her somewhere for coffee. He was totally jazzed by this turn of events, more so than if he won a lottery, had Georgia run back to his arms with everything back in their lives as it always should have been, all the bad karma removed, Lee and Sharon no longer threatening to pull out of the deal, or if Angelina just called and said she was going to drop Brad, put him in her movies, and marry him without a pre-nup or if a Mets batter ever got a base hit with a runner on third with two outs. What would she say? If she truly had a problem about which she needed some advice, then he wanted to help her. Absolutely with no strings attached as she had always been, frankly, the nicest person he had ever met. And the most beautiful. And now he calmed down a bit, quickly coming to the conclusion that it would be better if she actually had a man in her life she was in love with, in order for them to talk without really any sort of...tension between them, right? He added...

"You know Laura, I'm not really all that great with the technical computer stuff, I can barely cut and paste and copy or whatever, but I can listen to your story and give you, perhaps a new perspective as long as we were away from the bank. Waddaya think?" He was always of the opinion she found some of his New York stories and accent funny to listen to.

"Yes," she said a little quickly, her answer blurted out somewhat inadvertently, a little loudly, drawing the attention of some people on the street. Michael wondered if she actually thought he would refuse to meet with her. Not for a million dollars. And especially not now, what with all the shit flying around him. A little bit of serene conversation with the most beautiful woman he had ever seen, why not?

"Alrighty then...when and where?"

"Is later on today too soon?"

"No, actually it's perfect to do now. I'm free most of this weekend and I have just one big meeting early this afternoon. How about later this afternoon?" He continued, "Do you have a favorite coffee shop where we can sit?" Thank you for being a gentleman, she was thinking, suggesting a public place that I know and am comfortable in.

"How about a Starbucks? Is that okay?"

"Sure, which one? Somewhere in the city?" Michael didn't drink much coffee, preferring tea, and if he did, he wouldn't pay ten bucks for one. But to sit down with Laura for a cup of coffee, he would swim to Jamaica and harvest some of their Blue Mountain special blend himself. She was thinking strategically, can't be near the bank, or near anywhere any of my friends work or live. But you know what, chuck the strategic thinking and go wherever. You're allowed to talk with this man. It's not as if you're going to run off to Paris for the weekend. Goodness, I'm forty-two years old and I'm still worried about...the most inconsequential stuff found anywhere. She knew where they would meet and said so. "How about the Starbucks on Fifty-Seventh Street down the block from Carnegie Hall? Do you know how to get there?"

"Sure...practice, practice, practice."

"Huh?"

"Forget it, just a stupid old joke. How about three o'clock?"

"Yes that will be good, that'll work." Fantastic, wonderful, she was so glad to be able to share this weight with someone who had earned her trust over the years so naturally. She was weary again, the excitement of the phone call on top of the job stress added on top of sleeping on the couch in the Long Island office. All of a sudden she decided to take the day off. She had accumulated several personal days. She wouldn't have missed a day unless she was truly incapacitated, unlike most of the rest of the staff down there, all of whom would be first-class programmers if they actually dedicated themselves to the job instead of figuring ways to pad overtime, or to turn a half hour task into a three-hour project. She decided to go home and rest until the afternoon and then she would meet Michael later on at Fifty-Seventh Street.

"I'll see you then, okay? Three o'clock?"

"See you then. Hey, will you remember what I look like?" he asked teasingly. Close with something funny, he decided. She tittered at his question, "Yes, Michael, I think I'll be able to find you. See you later."

"Okay, hasta la vista."

"Bye, have a good day. Oh, and by the way, do you remember what *I* look like?" She realized she was fingering the ends of her hair, like a schoolgirl. She had no desire to stop either. She was within an inch of twisting her legs into a figure eight.

Yes, Michael thought, I will always remember you as the tall, lovely, elegant woman that captured my attention from the moment I first saw you walking down the hallway at the mortgage offices. He had pulled himself away from a conversation with a credit officer to follow her and study the mechanics of her gait for a few seconds.

"I think I'll be able to pick you out, yes." Time to get off. Don't drag it out; save something for later. "I'll see you later, bye"

"Good-bye."

They both clicked off their phones simultaneously, both looked off into the distance simultaneously and both smiled. She could see the vines starting to come to life on some of the fancy town homes she was passing by, and was that the first hint of pink on a cherry tree in front of one of them? It was her favorite time of year, the spring. Another beginning of life.

He was looking at a beautiful willow tree sitting by its lonesome on the expansive shoulder of the eastern side of the parkway, the long wistful branches starting to show some buds. He loved willows, massively strong at the trunk and in the branches, but so supple in a summer breeze, changing with just a little effort, but always remaining grounded with powerful roots. Well, he thought, I'm going to learn something later today. Something about himself. He would never know it, but Laura was thinking the same thing. Her thoughts were interrupted by a construction worker's catcall which she accepted with a smile. She made one more call to her office to report her absence for the day. Michael and Laura were both feeling quite dreamy about their impending rendezvous but they were also wondering at the same time, What am I doing?

—※—

Whathefu, Aubrey, and Andre made it into Manhattan at about the same time Laura entered the subway on Lexington Avenue. Aubrey, aware that he was wanted by several authorities and that he possibly compromised himself by receiving his overseas call in front of his soon-to-be-ex-wife before leaving South Carolina, had to remain as invisible as possible. This wasn't easy to do being six foot four, ridiculously handsome, flanked by a diminutive Saudi national and a rotund chocolate dark African. The were the 'odd triple'.

They entered the city by taking the Twenty-First Street ramp onto the upper level of the Queensboro Bridge. No tolls or EZ-Pass sensors here, Andre was explaining, as Aubrey noticed just a single traffic coordinator casually waving the cars onto the bridge's roadway in a listless fashion. What a joke security here is, he was thinking as they turned onto the ramp that circled around and then pointed due west, affording them a glorious view of the skyline of the greatest city in the world. I could come up with a hundred operations that would bring this city to its knees and they would never see it coming, he continued musing silently. He looked south down the length of the East River at the mid-span of the bridge and could easily see the United Nations Building, the Empire State Building, the Chrysler Building...all possible targets with thousands of potential casualties on the streets below in the form of the average New Yorker. But at this moment, until he had the money securely in his hands and his two accomplices were dead, he craved invisibility above all. He didn't doubt the effectiveness of the Military Police or the police here in New York or anywhere else in the United States for that matter. Anything unusual, anything just slightly out of place would draw their attention like a journalist drawn to a politician's gaffe. His plan was formulating in his head like a rose that was unraveling itself on the first warm day of spring, a tightly wrapped bud to folded-out splendor. A straight route north into Canada. I could drive there in about seven hours. One phone call is all it would take, no visa problems to worry about, not for a man like his benefactor. The ticket paid for directly out of the new account—why did I care at that point if there was a paper trail? I am out of here, gone from these United States permanently and quite willingly—an eleven-hour flight to where I want to be for the rest of my life. And I will never be touched. None of these Arab states will ever be toppled by a popular uprising. Egypt, Libya, Jordan, Syria, they were all run by men and their families with two goals: suppress the people and suck up every dollar of foreign aid meant for roads, schools and hospitals, and line my pockets with it. Or can they?

Hmmm, a new thought...maybe I can carve a new Islamic republic somewhere. With fifty million dollars, I'd have a pretty good start. He could fund thousands of followers and warriors for his own brand of Islam. As with all zealots, his was the only interpretation of whatever good book they followed that they believed in. He would be able to present an amazing image—former Army Ranger, tall, blond, handsome, Aubrey knew what he was and decided to use it for something useful. He wouldn't be like that pathetic John Lindh, some fucking counter-culture type's disaffected kid from California. Nor would he be the tool of Al Jazeera, like that fool Al-Awaki in Yemen. One day the Sixth Fleet is going to show up about a hundred miles off the coast of that shit-hole of a country and put a missile through his eye. No, he would be a rock star, nothing less. A regular Billy Graham of the Muslim world. How many wives should he have? He was allowed four if he could afford them. And if one of them became troublesome in any way, she could and would be dispatched either to some cold distant place. Look at all those Soviet ministers who disappeared and then died, all from a 'cold.' He would ultimately wield real power against a succession of Presidents, Prime Misters, all manner of western despots. But first things first. Must get the money. Aubrey watched the streets closely as Andre steered the car through a poorly designed off ramp that squeezed north for a couple of blocks, all of the lanes forced to turn west at a traffic light. They were at the corner on Second Avenue and Andre started downtown.

"Come back down here, by the apartment buildings over there." He pointed southeast, off to the left as they passed the entrance to the outbound, lower level lanes of the bridge. "There are no stores around there, it looks like a bunch of rich people living on the river. Cops won't be looking for crime around here; they'll be cruising in other parts of the city. Look for a spot to park over there and we will walk the rest of the way."

After a series of turns, they found themselves on Fifty-Third Street, on what appeared to be a private block. It wound one way in a horse-shoe fashion and was rather charming, and also totally hidden from view of the trucks, cabs, tourists, deliverymen and anyone else who might be looking for them. They waited for a few minutes and mirac-ulously, a spot opened up. The other driver startled all three of them for a moment when he waved and pointed to his own car which he was trying to tell them would be available in a moment, in a prime, non-parking-meter-encumbered spot. Andre waited behind the other driver's Mercedes with his signal on, and parallel parked perfectly.

"Allah delivered us right here, my friends, so we could continue to remain undetected," Aubrey said to Andre as he turned off the engine. Andre quickly agreed but Whathefu was momentarily chilled by the dissimilarity of Andre's parking maneuver and his own attempt to draw the Ferrari up to the curb as he had seen in that commercial...was it for an Audi? He just wanted to scare her a bit, that was all, wanted to show her that despite being the third son of a third wife son, he had his own life and he intended to live it the way he wanted. He did not start to rethink once again of the tragedy visited upon a teenage girl, nor of the weakness of a man who would leave a dying girl's side. Instead he thought how stupid the American sounded with his proc-lamation for Allah, and how thin the line was between success and failure, triumph and tragedy, sheer stupidity and conservative sensi-bility, between good and evil, and that neither Allah, Jesus, or Buddha could guide a man one way or the other with a either a timely and well delivcered parable or a push in the back. Aubrey continued, "Here is the drill. We are going directly to your office. Where is it again?"

"750 Fifth Avenue, across the street from the park. That's Fif-ty-Eighth Street." Aubrey remained silent for a half a minute, sketching out his next moves in his mind before speaking. "We are heading due west with no stops, no conversations with anyone. If anyone stops you to ask the time, keep walking. We're in New York so everyone here understands rudeness," despite the evidence to the contrary just offered up by the man and his parking spot. He continued with his mission plan, now fixing Andre with his eyes. "All three of us are to enter the building. No one's waiting in the lobby. We go to your office and I want you to make a straight line to wherever it is to find whatever it is in order for you to determine that your scam is still alive. If it is, we move the money right then and there and we leave to await final confirmation the money has been transferred. You do not answer any e-mails or phone calls while we are there. Your only job is this one." Andre pondered the practicality of this plan for a moment, his hand rubbing his chin, concerned especially with the part about the transfer. It was simple enough, he didn't even have to sit down. Create a file— in her name of course—enter in all the necessary information...where it was going to be sent and how much. He'd have to make sure he got his cut after all and maybe he should run this off into an account he could create right there in front of these two unwitting boobs and ultimately he could hold them ransom with the information they would require to cash in...he would call them with it from Rio. He was seeing her again in a thong on the beach. You should have done this years before, he told himself for the hundredth time since he left the Long Island office. How great would it be to buy her whatever she wanted? He knew she would learn to love him, as long as he was able to buy anything for her. Aubrey was giving him a little latitude time-wise before deciding to bend his elbow once again because he wanted this buffoon to be comfortable with the plan. He wanted him to think he would actually live to see another day.

"I guess we could do that." But what if, and it was sure to happen, what if someone in the office started to speak to him? "Oh Andre, I was looking for you. We have to talk." He looked at the both of them, "Once we are in the office, just act like you are my friends from out of town and I am going to show you around the city a little bit. Drop you off quickly at the Plaza or something like that, okay? He looked only at Aubrey now, "You have to figure that someone will want to say something to me, at least good morning."

"We also have to find that woman."

"What for? We are not friends. We're barely colleagues. I don't even say good morning to her or to wish her a nice weekend," replied Andre.

"It's very apparent to me that she knows something. I need to impress on her that if she ever says anything about anything she might have found out, then I'm going to kill her and her whole fucking family. Then again, maybe I've already made that decision to end her. I'm not sure yet."

Andre and Whathefu were astonished at the matter-of-factness of this statement, as if it were something he didn't mind at all, the death of this woman. Whathefu almost concluded that he no longer wanted Aubrey around at all, in spite of...no. No, now he just wanted the money and then to disappear somewhere in America. Maybe, probably would have to be Los Angeles at this point, he figured, what with his second murder to be involved with within a few days. He was lost in his own little daydream of beautiful boys and a few women around in barely anything, all of them falling over themselves to be invited to one of his parties. At one of his new restaurants. Or nightclubs, maybe several of each. He loved the Western life, or what he thought he knew of it, all of the culture, the food, and the freedoms and protections it afforded, even to its criminals. A life that everyone in America dreamed of, or did they? What did it matter? It was his dream and he could practically taste it. What was the death of another woman to be concerned about?

Andre was wondering why he had ever mistreated Laura in the first place. Didn't the Koran have a saying that such deeds would come back to hurt you? He was sure it did, but he just couldn't get that thong out of his head. What could he say? He looked at his watch and saw it was a little after eight.

"We should go now, before the office building really starts filling up with people. From here it's about a twenty-minute walk." The three exited the car wordlessly, walked to the corner, and turned right to head uptown on First Avenue. They would use the smaller side streets for the journey over to Fifth Avenue. They pulled their coats closer as an unexpectedly cool and strong breeze hit them in the face. As they crossed First Avenue, Aubrey asked Andre, "What exactly do you have to do up there? I want you to explain the mechanics of it to him," he said, jerking his thumb in Whathefu's direction. They hustled across the final third of avenue in order to avoid being flattened by the uptown traffic which was capturing the sequenced traffic lights perfectly. They fell back into step on the next curb and Aubrey turned to Andre for his answer after instructing Whathefu to pay attention.

Andre proceeded to lay out the step-by-step process of moving the money. He explained the configuration of the building, the office and the personalities and titles of people they might encounter, everyone from bank tellers to the President of the company. He explained the potential problems, all that he could think of, and he came away from his explanation satisfied that it was sound.

"What about the woman? Where would she be in all of this? Does she sit near you?"

"No, she is on the other side of the office. Chances are we won't even see her." He could see Aubrey absorbing this, thinking about something.

"How will you know that she hasn't figured all this out already? Is there a way for you to determine instantly that you have or have not been figured out?" Once again Andre pondered his response before answering.

"If she has changed her password, that's an indication that something is wrong. For her to change her password this morning—which is not as easy as you think—would be more than just coincidence." They were approaching Second Avenue now and pedestrian traffic was getting heavier. Aubrey kept his voice lower and drew his collar higher around his face.

"Can you divert her somehow? Get her out of the office to somewhere we can intercept her?" Andre looked at him, perplexed. Aubrey bore in on him, "Can you? Order her somewhere?" Andre now realized he was treading close to a kidnapping. Whathefu, already comfortable with another murder on his resume, seemed not to care. He was also waiting on an answer. Andre realized that he had no choice anymore. This guy would kill him if he didn't comply and he knew he couldn't go to jail. He opened his phone and dialed his office, not sure who was in at this hour.

"Good Morning, Argent Bank, how can I help you?"

Andre asked the unfamiliar voice, "Who is this?"

"This is Tom Randazzo. You are speaking to the Help Desk."

"This is Andre. Are you new there?"

"Yes, it's my first day actually. Can I help you with something?"

Great, Andre thought, how will he know what to do? "I need for you to get a message to Laura. Do you know her?"

"No, I'm sorry. I don't know anyone here yet except for the HR people I met. I mean, I know who the CEO is and the Chairman of the bank and the head of the department, but not anyone named Laura, sorry." Andre had to come up with something quickly. And an idea struck him. "Do you know where the assignment sheet is?"

"You mean the daily assignments for IT department employees to move around the branches of the bank?"

"Yes, do you know where it is?"

"I do," he replied looking up at the list just over his head, "I actually have it right here."

"Good, this is what I want you to do. Put Laura's name on there up at the top for an assignment at our Fortieth Street branch at nine o'clock, okay? She'll see it later when she comes in. Make the order as if it came from the branch manager up there, Jim something or other. I believe the cables need to be changed on some of the computers, some sort of impedance problem. His full name and number will be on..."

"Oh, wait a minute, Laura...right...I think I just took a call from her. She called in sick so she won't be in today." Andre snapped his eyes shut. The headache was coming. It felt like a rope tightening itself around his forehead. "Okay, I'll be up there soon and I'll take care of it, thanks." And he clicked off the phone. He said to Aubrey, "She's not there. Apparently she called in sick."

"Does that happen often?" Andre made sure to conceal the fact that Laura hadn't taken a sick day ever, not once. Damn, what had she done and where was she? Not waiting for an answer, Aubrey grabbed both of them by the collars at the corner of Fifty-Third Street and Third Avenue and snarled, "We have to move. I want to be in that bank office in five minutes. I've had it with coincidences with this woman. I want her and I want that money." And he pulled them along as if they were reluctant children, ignoring the stares of the increasing number of passersby. They continued across Third Avenue, Aubrey convinced that they wouldn't be able to pull this off in one visit to the bank's office. He knew that any unusual activity merited a second, more appraising look at any situation and even though he was unaware of her perfect attendance record, he couldn't shake the coincidence of her presence at the Long Island office followed by her missing work today. His legs started to work at a more furious pace, his hands gripping the elbows of Andre and Whathefu, pulling them along even faster.

⁓

At eleven-thirty later that morning, Michael pulled up to the coffee shop on Queens Boulevard and Thirty-Ninth Place, which was housed in the ground floor of a building owned by his old friend, AJ. She was the only woman who was able to penetrate the world of Michael, Vinny, the Burkes, and the others. She was their Darla Hood, the cute girl who hung around with Spanky and Alfalfa on the old *Little Rascals* television show. He got out of the car, grateful for a parking space with a meter that was broken. He looked up at the imposing limestone structure of the elevated 7 train, not immediately appreciating its fairly recent renovation, instead recalling running in between stations with his friends when they were younger, cheating death probably more than a hundred times. He shook his head in wonderment at the absurdity of so many past situations, how they were all so dangerous and stupid but he only saw that in retrospect as an adult. As a thirteen-year-old, it was quite a thrill. He was a half hour early for his appointment with Vinny and the others, but he didn't care. He wanted to have some personal time with AJ, who was perhaps his greatest and most trusted friend in the world. She was also a brutal assessor of a situation, perfectly willing and able to tell you straight to your face what she believed. And if she needed to tell you to go fuck yourself, well she would. That's what he needed right now, a brutal assessment although he wasn't sure he wanted to hear what she would say. Like most people, he always tried to find some rationalization for an action or inaction, but she would be able to cut right through that sort of nonsense like a knife through butter. He stepped up to her door and went in. The bell over the door tinkled his arrival and he found her staring right at him as he stood in the door.

"Hey you," she called to him, coming out from behind the counter as she said it, her arms open for an embrace which he received and returned warmly. Michael loved this woman as much as he loved anyone else. She stood on her toes and gave him a wet kiss on the cheek and pulled him over to the counter. She leaned over to the old-fashioned fountain and drew Michael a Coke in a tall, bulbous glass and placed it in front of him.

"You're still drinking this crap, right?" she asked.

"Yeah, it always served me better than the quarts of Colt 45 everyone else around here used to drown themselves in. It kills my teeth but not my liver." She patted his side.

"Yeah, but at your age, you gotta be careful of too much sugar. Getting a little hefty here and there, Mr. Pierce." Michael downed half of the coke and answered her with his own warm and thoroughly sincere smile. He could tell her anything and feel comfortable about it. He was glad he was able to see her before the meeting with everyone else, he hoped it would settle him.

"I'm in the same shape I was in when we found each other in Amsterdam," he replied to her dig which drew an eyes-to-the-ceiling look from her.

Michael and AJ met when they were seventeen years old on a trip to the Dutch capitol, a trip that Michael saved for a year in order to make happen. He had always wanted to travel and through research he determined Amsterdam was the least expensive of the big European cities and also the friendliest to visitors. There were plenty of hostels for him to stay in, some for as little as ten bucks a day.

He waited on standby at Kennedy Airport for almost two days in order to get a seat and finally paid a hundred bucks to a guy who was on his way to Amsterdam to propose to his girl but when he called to let her know he was about to get on the plane, some other clown answered her phone and told the guy his girl was in the shower. The man had a conniption right on the spot and Michael, sensing an opportunity, told the guy he would buy his ticket and even hand deliver a hate letter to his almost-betrothed. Amazingly, the guy accepted and Michael even followed through on his promise and delivered the letter to the woman, who promptly invited him in for lunch. She lived on a houseboat on one of the myriad canals in the wonderful city and upon leaving after being served a delicious piece of apple strudel, ran into a group of American high school students on some sort of foreign exchange program. He immediately settled his eyes on one of them, AJ Scott. He fell right into step with the group and she was very glad he had as the group was getting a little dull. They were both amazed and delighted to discover they both lived in Queens, he in Sunnyside, she in Forest Hills. She laughed when he explained she might have well lived in China. They bonded immediately and she promptly dumped her exchange program for the next few days. Together they explored the city, walking all the time, wanting to feel the pulse of the life there. He was almost killed by some manic bicyclists, but he knew this was their town and in Amsterdam you better not stand in the bike lane. The Van Gogh, the Rijks Museum of the Dutch Masters, these buildings held some of the most exquisite works of art he had ever seen. They cried together in Anne Frank's house and had a beautiful dinner at a Malaysian Restaurant which for years after Michael referred to as the Night of The Green Blouse, because she picked a simple green top to wear that although not particularly fancy, reached some sort of perfection on her when the candles on the table played on the angles of her face, her thick lovely brown hair falling around her face perfectly, long before the 'Jennifer' made its appearance.

Some years later, she told him that the people at the bar behind them were looking at the two young kids sitting together as if they were movie stars. They spent the rest of the evening strolling through very charming streets and the not-so-charming streets, smoking a little pot and drinking some Grolsch beer in a cafe in the Red Light district, listening to a young couple from England with Cockney accents so strong they made the lead singer of AC/DC sound like George Plimpton prompting both of them to say to each other at the same time on their way out the door, "What the hell were they talking about?" They laughed so hard at their shared amusement they both had to bend over, almost falling into the canal, and Michael farted inadvertently and she almost lost a lung she was laughing so hard and then she farted and Michael thought she was the coolest girl he had ever met. They argued with other young and old Europeans in a MacDonald's about everything that was the United States of America. They slept that night in the cheap hostel he had found in a travel guide, her head on his chest, the thought of making love certainly all around them, but not that night. It was a perfect day, why screw it up? As Humphrey Bogart proclaimed in Casablanca, this was the beginning of a beautiful friendship. It was the next night, upon their return from yet another day of boat rides, some roulette in the casino, and a dinner at an Italian restaurant, AJ excusing herself to the bathroom, Michael taking in all the men in the room stopping to watch her walk between the tables. She was full of grace and confidence at only seventeen years of age, but silly too, a perfect combination for any young man with half a brain. That night they made love furiously back at the hostel, ignoring the fetid conditions, the filthy mattress and blankets, the rolling of the bed on the wood floor, and the squeaky springs. To this day, Michael still counted it as his most pleasurable sexual experience. Yes, men do remember these things, he told her many times over the ensuing years. She hooked up with her exchange group once again and he accompanied her to Schipol where they said good-bye to their love affair, a sad moment for most, but not for them as the memories of their excitement and the purity of their days together would in the future help them overcome any negative wave that came their way.

As she waited for her flight behind a glass wall, he quickly composed a sonnet for her and held it to the glass for her to read. He gave the paper the poem was written on to a security guard to give to her and many years later during a visit to her home, she pulled it out of her desk explaining she would never part with one of the most beautiful things anyone had ever written for her. Upon his return to New York later that same week, they got together and quickly agreed again that their brief but intense affair would stay in Amsterdam, but they should remain friends and with that a beautiful, trusting relationship endured to this day. Michael introduced her to the rest of the boys and they all quickly accepted her as an equal. Michael told all of them that they were forbidden to date her unless she made the first move, but she never did. He would lay down in traffic for Vinny, the Burkes, J'lome, and Charlie Mick, but this woman and he shared so much more that he obviously couldn't share with any of the guys. He was closer to her than anyone else. He trusted her completely. She looked right at him and smiled at their shared memory, a private smile which was unnecessary as they were the only people at the counter, the few other customers sitting at the tables, reading I-Pads or working on laptops.

"Ahhh, Amsterdam. It was so great there, wasn't it?"

"I'll never forget it."

"And you're *not* in the same shape you were in there, Mister," again poking him in the ribs. "But you are getting better as you age."

"Like a fine wine."

"More like a great blue cheese." She lightly tapped his shoulder, "What's going on? Anything getting better from the last time we spoke?" Michael had unburdened himself in the months before to AJ about his marital difficulties. She knew the answer before he spoke it because she was able to recognize his 'intense face' and correctly surmised his home life was the cause of it all.

"No," he replied. "I just dropped her and Sally off at the airport. They're going out of town for a few days, they'll be back on Sunday."

"Was this planned in advance, or was it a result of a fight?" She was stirring a bit of cinnamon into her cappuccino, the aroma settling him for a moment.

"It was planned and as it turns out it couldn't have come at a better time. The heat was rising between us and I'm not sure where it would lead to if she was at home tonight."

"And you're not there on vacation with them because....?"

"Because I have a ton of work to do with the mortgage business, and frankly." He didn't want to admit it.

"Frankly what?" No way she would let that unsaid item dangle any longer than it had to.

"Frankly, AJ, I needed a break. I wanted to be alone for a few days. There, I said it." He continued, "Her family hates me anyway, figures she would have done better with a Greek doctor or something like that, and I didn't want to hang around all these people faking like I either belonged or wanted to belong." He spent the next ten minutes recounting the argument they had last night, the insanely poisonous, loud silence this morning in the car, the final little darts before they disappeared into the terminal.

"Why do you have to go with her to all of these functions anyway? Is your presence there mandatory for some reason?" She asked him like a district attorney. She shifted her weight on the round counter stool, turning it to face him. It was her serious pose. "Let me ask you a question, Mikey, I've wanted to ask for a long time now, way before Georgia, way before marriage, really since I've known you. Why have you settled for so many things so many times in your life for something or someone that was less than what you really wanted? I remember that lunatic you dated from Long Island for two years. I distinctly remember you telling me you were disappointed to find out she had an ass the size of a bus when she opened the door on your first date. You were so excited because the picture your work colleague showed you of her was only from the chest up and you were so excited because she looked just like Vivian Lee. 'Fat ass,' was what you told me your very first impression of her was. But you stayed with her for two years through bad sex, fights with your friends over her, and having to drive her all the way to the end of the expressway every time you would get together." She noticed his embarrassment about his past crass remark regarding another woman's anatomy. She always liked Michael's gentlemanly manner and she felt a little guilty bringing the comment up.

"I was too nice then. In my next life I'm going to be a ruthless bastard." He laughed quietly, but she wasn't feeling humorous at all about anything at the moment. She was getting angry now, he could see that. She could simmer slowly like a pot of water on a low flame, finally bursting forth like Mount Saint Helens. "What exactly are you saying... or asking?" he asked her. She looked at him as if she were his parent.

"The question you never answered to yourself," she replied with a half sigh. "The question the vast majority of people never ask themselves. The same question I just asked you." He hung his head before answering. He always knew the answer despite what she believed. He knew it the way he knew his own name.

"Because I am scared shitless every day, AJ."

"Of what?" She took his hand, the warmth and gentleness back in her voice. He laughed at her query, laughed at the ceiling and then looked directly at her.

"Of everything, of being broke, which is why I am in the mortgage business instead of a number of other businesses I would have enjoyed more. Certainly I'm frightened and concerned for Sally's health and welfare. I could never stand to see her ill or injured or even unhappy. I am scared still of dying alone even though I have plenty of good friends."

"I'd come to your funeral."

"Thanks."

"No problem. I'll wear my favorite red dress."

"Thanks, I always liked that dress, that wrap thing. Do you still have it?" She nodded her head very slowly, a lascivious grin forming. "I'd like to see it again at least once before I die," he added.

"We'll see." They were quiet again. He said, "I'm also lonely in my own bed, AJ. I wish I don't have to leave this earth without ever knowing true love." He looked right at her, "What we had for a few days and nights a long time ago. That experience, to me at least, was perfect."

"That was indeed a few days of utter bliss and excitement, I'll admit. Do you remember when we tried on the jeans together in the Levi's store? I bet those Dutch store clerks are still talking about us."

"Of course I remember. How could I forget that?" He didn't want to move the conversation to a lighter place. He needed to talk to her, only her, not any of the guys, not about this. She then continued, "What is true love for you, Michael? What is your interpretation of it?" She touched his arm lightly, "Do you think you ever experienced it with Georgia?"

"I'll answer your first question first. True love to me is simply looking forward to seeing the other person at the end of the day and in the morning. That doesn't mean I'm looking to be married to Donna Reed's perfect suburban wife from her television show although that would be nice."

"She did wear an apron better than any other woman anywhere."

"But seriously, I know that some mornings either of us can be grouchy, or the daily grind can be crushing and you wear it like an old coat when you walk in the door. I don't live in the world of Donna Reed's TV show. True love to me is an armor both participants in a relationship wear to protect each other against anyone and everything else. Each one is the air mattress to the other's potential fall from success. Each one is a warm blanket on a freezing February night. I want to be able to look at my lady as she is offered a dance at a ballroom convention with the most handsome, debonair man in the room, and then hear her say with utter conviction, "Thanks, I'm flattered really, but my man Mikey is all I could ever want and need." I want to see her smiling in her sleep. And I would feel the same way about her. I have no interest in collecting women like some asshole politician or sports star. I would feel great just to be with a woman who looks and acts as if she wants to see only me in her field of view. I want to be able to think she is the most beautiful woman in the world, no matter what she is wearing. I want to do things together with her, go places we both enjoy equally. And I want intimacy, as well as sex. And frankly, I want the intimacy every day, even just a tiny little bit of grab ass in the kitchen in the morning. Maybe a whisper in the ear, a little sweet nothing. I want it to be playful as well as passionate. I don't want to hear a list of her fantasies, I want to be able to discover them on my own, through trial and error. I don't want to hear about her past love life, I just want to be her best. How does that sound so far?"

"That wasn't an answer to my first question, but that's okay. All of that sounds nice, Mikey. Do you think any of that is possible?" He was confused, what was her first question?

"Yes I do," he answered. "I'll never stop believing in the possibility of its existence."

"Hell of a statement for a married man to make."

"I know, let me answer your second question."

"It was my third, I think, but that's okay. I'll bring you back in a moment because I'm sure you forgot by now." Boy, she really did know him, he was thinking. Can she read his mind?

"Anyway, Georgia...yes I love her. I would take a bullet for her, I would give her my kidney if she needed it, I would never let anyone fuck with her, ever. I had a lot of fun with her in the beginning. I was at peace."

"Big deal, you were at peace. Sounds pretty one-sided to me."

"Hey, don't be harsh. Being at peace is part of the true love thing I was trying to explain earlier."

"Yeah, you're so peaceful sleeping in the same bed at night, reading your books together, facing away from each other. When was the last time you really squeezed her tight before punching the pillow?"

"About the same time the last time she did that for me. I don't know...years, I guess." It sounded defiant and he didn't want it to be.

"I guess there was a lot of comfort for her in you as well, but no true love as you describe it. Even though you knew each other for years, as it turned out you were both in your thirties when you married, time possibly running out—especially for her—and all of a sudden, there you were with the diamond ring."

"Having a child had also complicated things as well," he offered.

She screwed up her face, leaned back and threw her hands up in the air when he said it.

"Oh bullshit, Mikey. You know, I don't know what's wrong with you marrieds. I know how hard it must be to have children. I don't have a child so I really don't know, but how hard is it to grab her butt a little in the morning or for her to slip her hand behind your neck and pull you in for a wet one? How difficult is it really to find fifteen minutes to ravish each other sexually? Sally must have two or three play dates every week, right? So there you go. And just go to sleep a little later, after she's down for the night. How hard can it be? True, some of the romance tends to go away for a while, for practical purposes, but that won't be missed after a few minutes of steaminess between you two." He now leaned back before he spoke, growing weary of the topic by the moment.

"It's a corporate marriage, that's what it has become. And I did love her, I thought she was fabulously beautiful when I first started dating her as well."

"Well maybe you should have an affair. This way you could find out something about love and sex and intimacy and how all three operate without any input from the other for so many sad, sad people."

"Maybe I have someone lined up for that possibility already." He shocked himself with his straightforwardness, but this was AJ after all. She would understand. Or then, maybe not. He figured as such when she jumped off the stool, walked away for a second or two and then returned with a fire in her eye.

"Who do you have in mind?" The question floated toward Michael as if supported by a thunderhead, ready to explode in a shower of lightning bolts. He didn't care; he hadn't done anything except admire Laura from afar, something half the men who pass her on the street do.

"Someone from work, you don't know her."

"How long has this been going on, whatever it is?" She seemed very far away when she asked the question, like a woman he didn't know that he was confessing something lurid to, expecting anonymity to cushion the response.

"We met ten years ago at the office Christmas party, on a coat line. We literally bumped into each other and when I apologized, she turned around and it was like Boom! for both of us." He couldn't help but smile at the memory, even though he knew it would not be received well by AJ.

"How often did you bump into each other after that?" came the arctic reply, an accusation, a question posed in such a way that the hurler of it was absolutely convinced of the answer. Michael had been lifting his glass of soda when it hit him and he stopped in mid air.

"Hold on, we only saw each other a few times a year, and always by accident. We would cross paths in the office and stop and talk about the weather. The only time I ever saw her outside of the office was at the Christmas parties. We would sit and speak in public, in full view of the entire bank staff, her kooky friend was always there anyway, and it was there, at those times...well, after a few years went by, that we would talk about dreams, some talents we had, places we've been, the mortgage business, stuff like that. We never socialized outside of what I just told you." He completed the arc of the glasses trip to his mouth and downed the rest of the soda and continued.

"I'll freely admit I enjoyed seeing her and speaking with her. She's a beautiful, charming woman. She seems very sweet and I detect a fire of some kind in her stomach. I'm willing to bet she had a hard time coming to New York as an immigrant but I really don't know. We never shared such intimate information with each other. I told her thirty seconds after meeting her that I was married and therefore unavailable for romance, but I suggested we could be friends. And that's what we did. In almost ten years I never held her hand, danced with her, spoke to her on the phone or e-mailed her. I never asked her if she had a boyfriend or was otherwise involved. For all I know she could have been alone all this time or she could have had thirty different men. I never asked because it didn't matter because we weren't going to get involved." He could tell AJ was finding this hard to believe. She was looking past him now, her arms folded tightly across her chest.

"Look," he continued, "We never met accidentally at a neighborhood fruit stand on a Sunday night like they do on some ridiculous sitcom. I did e-mail her a few times..."

"So you lied to me a minute ago," AJ interjected bringing her gaze level again with his eyes, boring into him now.

"I didn't lie. Listen to me. I e-mailed her and a bunch of other people at the bank as part of an e-mail blast a few years ago to invite them to some open mikes at a club in the East Village, just to see me play drums. I always suggested that they bring friends, I never sent her a personal invitation."

"Did she ever show?"

"Never, not once." She leaned in closer, and conspiratorially asked, "Did you want her to?"

"Of course. I already admitted I liked her, but I had known her by then for seven years or so and nothing ever happened between us. I never even came close to making a pass at her. Perfect gentleman, always." He now leaned back, trying to relax. "But I'll admit I did look out past the lights on the stage for her, but she never showed." He remained slumped in the chair, his upper back starting to strain but he didn't feel like sitting straight up again. He continued speaking in that position and he could see she was not looking past his shoulder anymore.

"When I met her the first time, it was like Michael Corleone meeting Apollonia on the hillside in Sicily. The attraction was instant, chemical or nuclear." He left out what Laura said in that first minute, what she blurted out to him because he felt that was an ultra-private moment between the two of them and didn't want to share it with anyone, even AJ.

"And strangely, I always remember this when I think of that moment: somehow I just knew she was a very nice lady with a good moral core. Not a nun, but a good lady. And that was before I knew her for even one minute. She already was the most beautiful woman I had ever seen, impossibly classy and elegant, and I thought, If I could build a girl, this is what I would have built." He sat up now and stretched his aching shoulders. He drew his breath in deeply and let it out. "It was love at first sight for the both of us." AJ shifted in her stool again, now facing more toward the counter.

"How the hell do you know that?"

"Because of something she said to me, she blurted it out and I won't repeat it here, but believe me, not only was I very touched by what she said, but somehow I knew that this was not something she would ordinarily say. Especially to someone she just met. I'd bet a dollar I'm the only man she ever said this to." He added by way of explanation, "It was very complimentary."

"So there hasn't been any sex, no emotional affair, no dating, or in other words are you two the only attractive man and woman in the world who apparently were completely turned on by each other from the moment you met that actually did the right thing and kept your distance from each other? Is that what you're telling me?"

"That's what I'm saying. If I were single then, I would have begged her to go out with me, but I didn't even consider it an option, so I told her right away I was married."

"What did she say to that? What was her reaction?"

"She was grateful that I told her the truth. She said thank you, most men would have lied to me."

"So no dating between you two? Please, Mikey, tell me the truth, between you and me, I swear."

"Nothing, I swear."

"Keep it that way, Mikey. You have to stay away from this woman the way you've been doing." She leaned right into him again, "You, like most men, know nothing about women."

"I'll give you that."

"Thanks for confirming for me something I already know. Anyway, you just painted me a picture of some kind of angel, almost a deity. Jesus, Mikey, you were practically gushing." He blushed, embarrassed now, looking away from the counter was all that he could think to do.

"I'm not trying to embarrass you, Mikey, you know I love you. But you gotta understand something. Are you listening to me?" She poked him in the shoulder.

"I want you to understand what I'm about to say has nothing to do with her. I wouldn't know her if she walked in the door. But the fact of the matter is that you don't know anything about her in spite of the fact that you think you do. I'm gonna let you in on a little secret, my male friend. It is entirely possible that this nice girl with the solid moral code you mentioned is a slut, a wack job, a woman who would fuck anyone who buys her a cheap dinner. Someone who would stalk you, don't look at me like that," she almost shouted, admonishing him when he rolled his eyes. "You don't think that happens? Look, I'll admit you may know more about her than some guy who has taken her out on a few dates, but in the end, at this exact moment, you don't know shit about her." She said this with finality, an implied threat hovered between them that more strong words would follow if he didn't agree completely.

"My instincts usually are not that far off, AJ. I think by now I would have been able to identify her as a nutcase," he replied. He felt a little weak when he said it. Like a wounded Thompson's Gazelle on the Serengetti plain, limping along, wondering if he was close to where the lions were dozing. She leaped at him verbally, and her claws were out.

"Don't be surprised if she's screwing some guy right now, some poor slob she keeps in her back pocket for a quick monthly bang after a cheap dinner while waiting for something better to come along, this little angel of yours. She probably has more problems than a math test. It's entirely possible you could get involved with her and then fall in love with her, and you're going to spot her coming out of a hotel with her blouse buttoned wrong, freshly washed and shampooed hair, hanging on some guy's arm and you're going to rush up to her and a second after you ask her what she's doing with another man, she's going to rightfully tell you to go fuck yourself."

"Look, I admit I don't truly know anything about her personally, but looking at it as if I were thinking about a date with her, I would say yes quickly...I would go out with her. Maybe later I would find out she's kooky, but I would go out with her." He swung his legs out away from the counter. "I'll find out later today, actually." He didn't look at her when he said it but he knew her eyebrows were now on top of her head.

"Why?"

"She's having a political problem of some kind at work and she called and was asking my opinion."

"And you are the only one she can talk to? She has no girlfriends, no family, no one else she can confide in? Seek counsel from? Maybe someone she doesn't find very attractive?"

"Maybe. Remember, I've never made any type of pass at her, nothing at all. I have always been the perfect gentleman with her for ten years, during which time she must have been hit on seriously at least a thousand times, probably jumped on her fair share of them, I have no idea. Maybe she was bored and lonely the entire time, I don't know. But that was never part of our relationship. Sure, the desire seemed to be there, but it was never acted upon, I'm tellin' ya." He turned to face her.

"In some weird way I've built up a foundation of trust with her. I was honest and straight with her from the very start as I told you. She once told me she was very impressed that I was honest with her when I told her I was married. And I figured out why much later."

"Why?" she asked, practically yawning now, completely bored with someone else's story of their own romance.

"Because it seems to me that maybe people in her life have been bullshitting her since she was a kid. Her parents, family, the boys in the town where she grew up, her girlfriends here in the states, and probably ninety percent of the lovers she had. That's why she made a point of being impressed with basic honesty, because she didn't have any or much experience with it. Hearing the truth so consistently, that is. Look, I'm not trying to make myself out to be a beacon of virtue or virtuosity for that matter. She's just a nice lady who happens to be very nice to look at. And I have nothing to do for the next few days."

"Is that some kind of joke?" He was confused for a moment before realizing that she was accusing him of celebrating the absolutely perfect timing of it all.

"No, it wasn't. It's all purely coincidental and if Georgia was home and not in Florida visiting her family I'd still meet her in public, and if I as much as shook her hand at the end of the meeting, that would be all there would be to report. She trusts me apparently, and after all these years, I can't violate that trust by simply abandoning her. She obviously needs some help and she asked me and so I'm going, end of story." They were silent for a minute before he capped the conversation with, "She seems kind of lonely." Just then the bell over the door tinkled and Michael knew it was Vinny without looking, punctual as an atomic clock. She didn't turn around to make sure it wasn't a customer, instead looking Michael right into his eyes when she answered, "Those are the most dangerous kind, those lonely ones." She slid off the stool. "See me on the way out, I'm not finished with you." And she pirouetted like a ballerina into a perfect little hug and a peck on the cheek for Vinny.

"Hello, lady," Vinny said, simultaneously reaching for Michael's hand.

"Hello, you. Coffee? Sit over here." She guided them to the last table along the wall, a semicircular booth she knew would be best for their conversation. Michael and Vinny entered on either end and slid in a couple of feet. "Coffee's great," they both said at the same time and they then both watched her slide effortlessly between the other tables and chairs in a most approving way, looking like she was dancing salsa with each piece of furniture. One final moment of happiness before the darkness settled in. Although they were friends for life since the age of eight, right now Vinny was the client and Michael decided he had to speak first.

"How is it going with the historical preservationists?" Michael asked. Might as well start with something they both knew the answer to. Settle in a little bit, try to make up for the unpleasantness soon to follow.

"Yeah, lots of bullshit from people who have nothing else to do," he replied, picking a few peanuts out of his pocket and cracking the shells on the table. He still carried them in his jacket pocket even though they mostly helped cure him of his smoking habit years before. He had read about a New York detective in a novel about a hydrogen bomb hidden in the city many years before who had quit by keeping peanuts in his pocket and thought it was a great idea to help him stop. The shelling of the nuts kept his hands active and the chewing replaced the need to inhale. He popped a few into his mouth and turned to Michael, "You know, when Lord Acton said absolute power corrupts absolutely, he was absolutely correct." AJ returned with two steaming cups of her excellent coffee, a commercial blend she sprinkled a little cinnamon powder in to create a marvelous taste with which she could charge double for to all the new professional and student types who had moved to Sunnyside in the past fifteen years. Wordlessly she slipped away again, but this time the two friends kept their concentration on the problem at hand.

"What do you really mean? What's the bottom line?" Vinny continued as if the question was not even posed. Michael knew he was not pleased and although Vinny wouldn't admonish his friend for wasting some time with small talk and puff questions such as the one Michael just asked, he was letting him know that it was time to get down to business. "Because these people are getting a little taste of power and it is intoxicating to them," he finished. "I scare them because I am a guy who is making it step by step like their grandfathers did years before. They've forgotten that whatever fortune they have, the trust funds set up in their names, were established by men who did what I"...he turned to Michael and continued, "What we are doing." He crushed a few more shells, a little pile accumulating in front of him and started talking again, not giving Michael a moment to answer his question of a minute earlier.

"These people on that board are rich, well-connected, and soft. If their ancestors could see them now, they would be disgusted at what they've become and *I* would have their favor, that I'm sure of." He sat straight back against the wall and continued, "They seem drunk with power over me right now. The poor little orphan boy from Sunnyside with dirty fingernails. For some reason I make them nervous, I can tell you that with total certainty. Because there is no reason why this should be a problem. We dealt with the Pepsi sign before we did anything else. We had to; it wasn't like we could just knock it down without answering to anyone. But we had the plans approved, the sign was down anyway for renovation, and we were picking up the cost of putting it back up, only twenty feet from where it originally was." He was slumping in his seat now, embarrassed slightly, realizing he was doing the same thing Michael had a few minutes before, talking about things to which they already knew the answers. A little lightness from him now. "You know, even though you look like them in that suit, they wouldn't let you into one of their buildings even if you paid cash. They'd kick your Irish ass right out onto the street and probably wouldn't have allowed you to even apply for a board meeting, let alone pass one."

Michael stared at the pile of peanut shells and started to move them around with his index finger. "Vin, the bank, I've called everyone I know there. I spoke to Sharon and Lee, the owners of the bank. I turned this over in my mind a thousand times since yesterday and I can't get them past this historical issue. It has always been a quirk in their underwriting guidelines that you had better never, ever run a deal past them that even had a whiff of historical significance. It would be instantly declined. Apparently it dates to when they got burned on some townhouses that were deemed historical or whatever a week after his closing and he couldn't develop the property or change the existing buildings in any way, not even the color of the paint on the hand railings. I mean, ultimately they made a mistake or two. It was one of their first deals, they got bad advice, whatever. Now they own the bank and they're good people, but if you mention landmarking to them, they go freakin' bananas. They took it to heart and although they are still aggressively lending in other areas, this is something you can't even talk to them about. It's a privately held bank, it's their baby, so all the top executives together couldn't move them on their decision."

"Is there anywhere else we can go?" Vinny asked, although he knew the answer. Everyone knew what was happening in the market. Michael shook his head as he answered.

"Even the most beautiful deals...good credit, fifty percent equity, excellent properties, plenty of assets in reserve, builders with solid credentials, they're not even giving anything a look-see. Vin, without a solution to this historical preservation society thing, we're dead in the water. We bought some time because the co-founders of the bank are on vacation, but they're coming back on Monday. And they know about it, Vin. These little shits you met with may have had only one card to play, but they played it well."

There. It was said, and the shock of it felt like a taser in his gut. Professionally, personally, they would all be cooked by this situation. This project was...is huge for a multitude of reasons. The jobs, the transformation of the neighborhood, the steady stream of income for all of them forever, Vinny's dream for all of us as well as himself, the Burke Brothers' electrical and plumbing business that would be supported by the building, apartments for life for Ping the Router's wife, Yung, and his parents, and places to stay rent-free for a while in the city for the relatives of other friends who didn't come home on the second Tuesday in that September. Vinny was grooming Charlie Mick to take over his property management business, creating permanent employment for this orphan of 9/11, if Vinny could mold him properly and turn his anger into something positive. The commission for Michael was to be huge, close to five hundred thousand which would ensure a college education for Sally as well as allow a bit of the steam in the marriage to be released. But that wasn't even the worst of it.

"Do the guys know how much trouble we're in with this thing?" Michael asked.

"No, not yet. We'll be telling them as soon as they get here." With that, both friends fell into a silence that was as deafening as the one between Georgia and Michael during the car ride to the airport. They knew without saying that both of their entire fortunes, as they were, were sunk into the project. They both also knew that everyone else in their tight group of friends, all of their money was in it as well, everyone in the group, the IRA's set up by Vinny for the Burke brothers, AJ's refinancing of the building enabling her to take a $500,000 position in the project, Charlie Mick's money from the government pay-out from his Dad's murder on 9/11, pensions, 401k's...these were all drained to satisfy the asset requirements of the bank that was to lend on the project.

Income taxes were paid on the retirement money and everyone subsequently lost out on a run up in the Dow. All of Vinny's properties were sold, save for a couple of six-families in Brooklyn that were now financed to the eyeballs. Everyone was looking forward to a fractional ownership of the project, everyone was looking forward to their own rent-free apartment for life in addition to a piece of all the rents... forever...for everyone. It was emblematic of the group in that they were always looking out for the other's welfare and if that meant that someone had to be told they were acting like a jerk, so be it. These opinions were always taken at face value and were always respected. None of the friends in this group were ever able to comprehend when they heard about other people using an attorney, a plumber, a mortgage broker or an electrician from outside their own group of friends. They mutually hated the types that would quiz you for hours about what they should do, whether it was how to install a dishwasher or something with electrical work, or a point of law...and then go to someone else and pay *them*, not the friend who gave them hours of free consultation. That never happened with these guys. They were a self-contained, closely-held collection of tough kids from Queens who ignored the call of drugs and malt liquor that created a morass of despair in Sunnyside, Woodside, Long Island City, Maspeth and other neighborhoods in the '60s and '70s. They took care of each other with fists, words, advice, and tough love long before it was coined on some afternoon talk show. They would lay down on subway tracks for each other just as any one of them would have jumped in the river so many years ago in case one of them misjudged a current and were threatened to be carried away. Vinny was the one everyone knew from early on would be the vanguard of their interests. With his ability to think of eighty-five details at once, to see solutions to problems in ways they never could, to never accept defeat, whether it was a game of three-on-three against the rich kids in Bayside—and some of those rich kids could play—or a bargaining session with a team of Harvard lawyers and bankers, he would never accept a loss. He was the most natural leader Michael and the others had ever met. In addition, it was also a nice feature that he was absolutely fearless when it came to a physical confrontation. In his wake were a number of biker toughs, a few connected guys, some suits in the city counting on a bit of liquid courage and anyone else who threatened any of his friends.

"I'm gonna have to lay it all on the line for everyone. No sense in sugar-coating it," Vinny said into his coffee.

"Do you see any cracks in these people?" Michael asked. "Anything at all?" Vinny leaned back and lifted his coffee. He could see AJ looking over at them now. Was her hearing that good? Or maybe it was a women's natural intuition he had always heard about. He wished he had some of that now. Maybe Michael with that deep voice of his spoke a little louder than he wanted to. But what did it matter if he did? AJ was in this with them financially as well. She had a right to know everything.

"I don't know if it means anything, but I ran into the lady on the board last night, actually." Michael was stunned at this news and it made him sit straight up.

"Are you kidding me? Where, when, how? What happened?"

"On the street, just by coincidence. I was at Fifty-Third and Sutton Place in the city, looking out over the river at the construction site, trying to sort it all through and she just happened by." Michael was dumbfounded by this news and Vinny's holding onto it for so long. If it were him, he would have blurted it out as soon as Vinny walked into the café.

"So?" Michael's shoulders were up around his earlobes, his palms were upturned, and every gesture he could think of was screaming at his friend of thirty-plus years, "Why didn't you tell me this?"

"We went to dinner, we talked about all of us, my upbringing, my education in the library, all the properties, the bread routes, how we all got to where we are now. We talked about the differences in our upbringings, that sort of thing." His obtuseness was infuriating to Michael and he couldn't hold back.

"Vin, holy shit, did you talk at all about the project, about this ridiculous position she and her friends have put us all in?"

"No, I didn't." This brought forth an explosion from Michael that had been building for several days, inquiring loudly why the hell he hadn't. AJ stopped wiping the counter and now looked over at them, concern riding her features. Vinny faced his long-time friend and Michael could see he was as calm as a lion with a full belly.

"Going at her that way would have been the absolute wrong thing to do. Why would I ever let her know how nervous I was? Instead, I took her to dinner, we had spicy chicken and spring rolls, a couple of beers, and a few laughs. Do you think that was wrong?" Michael looked past Vinny at AJ, who was coming over with a slice of marble cheesecake for them to share. She sat with them now, glancing at her other customers from time to time.

"I guess we won't know if it was wrong until we analyze what happens later. Right now it's part of a plan I guess to get what we want, right?"

"I'm not that devious. I didn't know she would be there. A big part of it was that I was quite attracted to her." Michael could see AJ smile at this. She always wondered why Vinny was unattached for so long. "I liked her. She had some substance to her that I didn't see in the meeting earlier in the day. In front of those other stuffy guys, she came off as more than another cold blue blood...sort of."

"What do you mean sort of?" This from AJ.

Vinny responded without hesitation, "The lady came from some money, but I could see intelligence and dedication that many of her type usually don't pursue. Most of them just live off of compounding interest. I thought there was something there behind her eyes that was telling me that she disapproved of the others, that somehow, she was on my side. I can't offer up anything concrete, it's just a hunch, but that's what I felt. And then when I ran into her later on, I decided to talk to her about anything else, but the project. I wanted to peel her back and see what she might have really been all about."

"And did you?" This from Michael who was ready to explode again.

"She mentioned something at the end of the evening which, by the way, was perfectly perfect other than the fact that she is married."

"What did she say?" This now from Michael and AJ. Vinny sipped his coffee and cracked a few nuts.

"All she said was, Just get rid of the pier Vinny. Figure out what's wrong with it and then get rid of it. And then she said good-night and went into her building. That was the end of the evening. I don't think she knows about anything substantially wrong with the other two guys, their motives or whatever, but I definitely do believe she suspects something. And I have to find out what."

"All we need is a tsunami to come up the East River and take it out," Michael said tiredly.

"Right, because we can't just go there and rip it down. Somehow they are connecting the pier directly to the sign, which is why they want the sign to go back up in the middle of the lot instead of off to the side so we can build what we planned."

The three of them fell into a silence, interrupted only by AJ excusing herself to welcome some new customers into the café. She greeted the new arrivals warmly, and directed them to a table far away from Michael and Vinny. Michael knew Vinny well enough to know that he was working the problem. The best thing for him to do was to let him go to work on it, like a slow computer.

Sooner or later, a sliver of hope would emerge and they would act upon it then. He didn't dare introduce a new subject, the weather, his marriage, the Knicks. Lord knows the Burkes are going to be talking about the Knicks nonstop as soon as they sat down, and everything else, well...you can't do anything about the weather can you and Vinny didn't want to hear about anyone's marriage troubles. So he started daydreaming about the meeting with Laura later this afternoon, which was just about a couple of hours away. What would she wear, what was she going to talk to him about, how would he be able to keep his act together sitting so close to her? These questions were all running through his head when the bell over the door tinkled again and he smiled at the familiar voices and vibes entering the café.

⁂

"So, Andre, who are your friends?" asked Sheila, the chirpy office manager. She was speaking to Andre, but her eyes were locked on Aubrey as if he were the last piece of food on Earth and she was looking to break fast. Andre did not want to speak to Sheila. She had a high-pitched, annoying voice. She was the type of employee everyone couldn't stand to be around. She was constantly stopping by everyone's cubicles to chat and pry into every area of anyone's life. She constantly played the lottery, announcing her numbers to anyone within earshot. She was the last person Andre wanted to see at this moment. He had to get away from her lest the maniac lost his cool and killed everyone in the office or if the FBI all of a sudden showed up to haul him away. That damn woman Laura, what did she do? It was apparent to him now after three minutes working at his computer that she found out somehow. Why else would she have been out at the Long Island office at night? Sheila was waiting for an answer and he had to give her one.

"Just some friends I went to school with," Andre replied, hoping that would satisfy her.

"Strange, they look much younger than you to have attended college at the same time." Andre turned to leave, gesturing to Whathefu and Aubrey to follow him, "Not college, Sheila, just some certification courses." He reached for the door handle. She was speaking again.

"Andre," the voice was firmer now. "They can't be hanging around here, you know the rules. Please end their visit now, okay?" With that she turned and left but Andre knew she would not leave the hallway until she knew they all had exited the office.

Aubrey asked Andre, "What was that all about?" His eyes were searching Andre's face, looking for the faintest glimmer of a lie.

"We have to leave here. There are proprietary programs running on these computers, there are tons of privacy issues and security regulations to deal with. Even the Chairman of the bank would be stopped in these hallways if he is not recognized by someone. We have to go before we are exposed." He could see that indeed, Sheila had not turned the corner; she was lingering to make sure his 'guests' had left. He then felt Aubrey's iron grip again.

"Can you get into the Human Resources files? I want to know where this Laura lives."

"Yes, I guess so," he replied, very aware of Sheila now turning toward them again, looking annoyed. He couldn't risk her coming back again.

"Then do it. I want to find her today, right now. She's obviously the key to our success." Aubrey didn't add that she would be extinguished as easily and quickly as these two as soon as he had the money. He continued, "Let's go, your workday is done. Where will we find the HR File on her? We can come back at night if we have to and make the transfer when no one else is here." he asked as he pressed the exit button that unlocked the lobby door which finally made Sheila reverse course and turn the corner.

⚊ ▎ ▟

EARLY AFTERNOON

Laura was at that moment running her fingers through her hair in the shower, trying to get the last remnants of the conditioner out of her scalp. She didn't want her hair laying flat on her head today. Normally fairly meticulous in her appearance—not overly so like her friends she used to go to the clubs with who would labor over every stroke of lip gloss—she decided that she would look nice for this meeting. Maybe even wear high heels. Why not? She hardly ever dressed more than what was necessary at the office. She never wanted to give those people even a glance at her very fit and toned figure. Her fingers started to squeak now that the conditioner was rinsed out completely and finished with the shower, stepped out while she twisted her hair into a knot and squeezed the last bit of excess water from it. She was amused with herself, feeling like a teenager getting ready for the prom. But she tempered these thoughts of fancy with two others, one that Michael the married guy was unavailable to her and also that she was about to enter into dangerous territory. She did not relish the idea of being a whistle blower. Hollywood may like the movies they create from these types of stories, but the fact of the matter was that whistle blowers usually became pariahs in their organization, even though they helped clean up internal corruption and sometimes criminal activity. Many of these people became unemployable afterward. But she no longer cared about all that.

Recalling what Michael had told her years before, when she had asked him about a friend of hers who was experiencing some trouble at her office, "You can never allow yourself to be fed a shit sandwich every day, not from anyone. To do so, will cause a lifetime of bitterness and lingering regrets that will eat at you the rest of your days. Even if you have to go down with the ship, doing so with zero regrets is preferable to carrying them over your shoulder like a sack of bowling balls." He was right, she remembered thinking at the time. And her friend took his advice and earned the praise of her bosses and co-workers as a result of it. Again she reminded herself that he was married. Her moral compass was strong, always had been, so why was she fretting about what to wear?

Maybe she was approaching the point where she was going to do whatever it takes in order to feel good again. Laura was aware of who she was, she knew her inner strength could carry her gracefully past any situation, lord knows enough boulders had been placed in her path already. Family members who expected her to take care of them and their children for the rest of their lives, a spinster- on-call, a permanent solution to someone else's last-minute Saturday night plan difficulties.

"Don't worry about it, Laura will be available, she'll take care of it." The church damning her for daring to dream a little bit, whether it was for higher education, a more rewarding career than being a nun or staying on permanently at the seminary, labeling her with ugly, hateful words just because she wanted to dance with a handsome gentleman, one who knew how to ask her properly as well as how to move on the floor. And the total condemnation from church and family members if she expressed a desire just to kiss a boy on the beach, under a beautiful moon, all the stars twinkling their approval. She almost toppled out of the shower, so dizzy with trepidation and anticipation, steadying herself on the edge of the vanity. Looking up she could now see herself in the nice half length mirror the landlord installed last month. She studied her taut abdomen, muscular arms and shoulders, her strong rear and long athletic legs. She half-laughed and then fully scoffed, "Adam, you jerk, I'll bet you never had a woman who looks as good as I do now." She smiled at her reflection, allowing her bit of vanity to pass, and then deciding to wear her violet sweater, black jeans—her 'old faithful' pants—along with a pair of flats. She was close to deciding on wearing heels, but she had remembered Michael commenting to someone at the holiday party that high heels with jeans was not a good look in his opinion. She remembered and then asked herself why she should care. She thought it was a good look, as did several of her old boyfriends. But she went with the flats and complimented everything with her favorite necklace, a dainty chain of small purplish stones that faded from bright to dark as they traveled its length. Checking the time, she saw that she still had a little more than an hour to kill before her meeting. She reminded herself again that she was going to see him for his counsel and for that only...or was she?

⁓·‖·⁓

Andre, Whathefu, and Aubrey stepped out onto Fifth Avenue looking like the three most mismatched people in New York City, one of if not the most ethnically and economically diverse city in the world. Aubrey, tall as a small forward, powerfully built with movie star looks. Whathefu, skinny, short and oily-looking although wearing expensive designer clothing. Andre, squat and ugly, sweating on a cool but beautiful May morning in a suit that would never have shouted successful man even five minutes removed from the rack. Whathefu was the first to speak up, "Are we going to go to her house?"

After leaving his office, Andre went to the HR office on the third floor thinking he had to log onto another computer—administrators like him could log onto any one of Argent Bank's computers whether he had the password or not—in order to find Laura's home address. But all he had to do was ask the young receptionist to see her paper file and she readily complied. What a joke the security here was, all three of them thought as Andre thumbed through the file, explaining to Ms. Ditzy as he did so that he had to drop off something to her. After just a few minutes, he had her last few addresses and personal phone number. He looked to Aubrey for the answer as he was not in control of his life since yesterday afternoon.

Aubrey asked him, "Do you know where this address is?"

"I do. It's in Long Island City, not too far from the river. Not too far from the mosque where we first met."

"How do we get there?"

"We have to walk cross-town to the Lexington Avenue line, take the 6 train down to Grand Central Station, and then the 7 train under the river over to Queens. We can get off at the first stop and then walk to this address. All in all less than an hour's traveling time."

"What's it like there now?" asked Whathefu. "I remember the last time I was here that there was a lot of talk to build apartments on the river, make it into another artists' colony, take over the warehouses, like Williamsburg." Aubrey grabbed his skinny bicep, his fingers nearly able to close around Whathefu's arm.

"Why are you interested in that? Are you looking to become a real estate broker? Rent some apartments?" His voice was truly menacing and he was barely speaking above a whisper. Aubrey turned to Andre, "What is it like there? Is it an industrial neighborhood?"

"Well," Andre responded indicating Whathefu, "It's like he was starting to say. It's a neighborhood dominated by long-closed factories that are being considered for development. Some two- and three-families scattered about, but mostly commercial. During the day or night, it can be pretty quiet."

Aubrey hated Whathefu more than any of the pretty secretaries or successful businessmen passing them on the street. All of them non-believers, once my countrymen, but no longer. His plans for killing Whathefu and the fat one were overtaking his plans for the fifty million or so he felt would soon be in his hands. He'd have to exert his discipline to remember that obtaining these funds were first and foremost. Killing Whathefu would be easy to justify. "Sorry," he would say to Whathefu's father, "but he tried to escape and you did order me to prevent that at all costs. Yes, he drowned in the East River trying to run away."

He said to Andre, "Take us there. I want to see where she lives. We don't want to make contact with her now, even if we see her. I want to wait until later to try to take her so we can have the weekend to work with her in addition to tonight as the offices will be quiet. She is the key to this whole thing now so it has to be played correctly." He grabbed their lapels, pulling them both toward him, violently and quickly enough to attract the attention of several of the passersby on Fifth Avenue.

He snarled at them, "Again, you two remember who is in charge here. The both of you follow my instructions to the letter, are we all clear?" The two weakest and most pathetic people on the street acknowledged yet another threat by shaking their heads yes, like an old slave on the plantation with not a hint or chance of disagreement. "We're not taking the subway, too many cameras and cops. Instead we are going back to the car and we are then going to sit on her apartment and watch everything she does until it is time to take her." He released their lapels as he ordered them back east toward Sutton Place.

The Burke brothers were aghast. "That's a stupid pick, double Butler, they're going to be a number five at best, what's the matter with you, Mikey?" Michael was leaning back, sipping another of AJ's excellent coffee, the only kind he ever liked, listening to the Burke brothers go apeshit on his future NCAA tournament pick of Butler University. It didn't matter that the next pool was ten months away, they were already waiting on it. He had passed on two Big East teams, Georgetown and Notre Dame to pick a mid major a couple of months ago and it worked out perfectly. The friends were involved in a tournament pool for many years whereby they chose players in a draft and earned points as their players' teams advanced in the tournament. Michael and J'lome picked Winthrop to beat Notre Dame and Nevada to win over Georgia Tech and Wisconsin. Heck, UNLV came within a whisper of knocking off Oregon.

"J'lome told me that the double Butler move will be a good one for next year and he has a line to God so I'm going with it. Look, it looks like there's no great team next year. I'm willing to bet that no more than two number one seeds make it to the Final Four. These kids at the mid-major schools, they tend to stay in school instead of the draft so they're more mature than the kids at Kentucky or Duke, the big schools."

Both Fred and Ryan Burke, basketball geniuses who could tell you not just the college attended and stats of every NBA player but the trades that brought them to their present teams, stared at Michael, mouths agape. The Burkes knew who scored how many points, the number of assists they had and how many rebounds each and every player grabbed. They knew each and every liability as well...injuries, bad attitudes, deficient defensive skills. Their knowledge was encyclopedic. And they thought Michael was crazy to even consider doubling on a mid-major team like Butler.

"You're gonna lose next year, Mikey, plain and simple," said Fred.

"As simple and elegant as Earl the Pearl driving to the hoop," added Ryan. Even Vinny had to chime in.

"Hopefully you're better at the mortgage business than you are at picking teams for this thing," he said. "Then again, what the hell do I know? I've never finished in the money." Vinny drained his coffee and asked AJ for another. He was tired and his head hurt but the tournament was a serious business for the group as were their occasional poker games. These were very spirited affairs, with opinions and jokes never in short supply. Michael had to quiet the Burkes before they went off for an hour on their analysis of the field of sixty-four teams.

"Look, you two, Kansas was the number one seed you were going for in the tournament, right? I virtually guaranteed you at the time the only easy game they will have is their first round match-up against Niagara. They couldn't play defense, they couldn't shoot free throws and they were just another Big Twelve team that was never going to live up to the hype. And as it turned out, they were lucky to make it to the Sweet Sixteen before they got whacked by UCLA. We'll see at the end of next year's tournament who's still in it come Final Four time. You guys are gonna be out of it by the Sweet Sixteen and me and J'lome are going to ride our double mid-majors to glory."

This drew whoops and hollers from the Burkes and Vinny as well. Michael felt more alive than he had in months. This back and forth banter, totally good-natured although an outsider might not think so had they witnessed it, served to invigorate the friends, all of whom were experiencing the various pains and aches and worries common to forty-five-year-old men. Even Moose was smiling, Vinny noticed. Thank goodness because he couldn't take any more of his whining about his marriage and career malaise. Charlie Mick had joined the group a few minutes before and was quietly sitting on the periphery, waiting for an opportunity to jump in. Good, Vinny noted to himself, the kid is finally starting to learn. He turned to him and asked, "Did you stay on those guys like I told you?"

"I did," Charlie Mick answered swiftly and simply, the best kind of answer delivered the best way. He waited for Vinny's next question which anyone could have anticipated, but he was determined to show his worth, that he was growing up finally. The whooping and hollering between the Burkes and Michael was continuing with Moose Miller now joining in with all his effort. Vinny continued his conversation with Charlie Mick under the roar.

"Where are they now?"

"The three of them are in a car, a Saab station wagon, parked on Vernon Boulevard, down the block from the construction site." This caused Vinny some concern and it showed momentarily as he twisted more to face the young man. Was there a connection to these guys being so close to his project and the little confrontation he had with the big bastard at J'lome's mosque? Couldn't be deduced. There was nothing in their brief meeting that would have led them there. Still, it is unusual. He rubbed his chin and asked another question.

"Where were they before they made it to Vernon Boulevard?"

"I followed them to the city, on the east side. From there they walked together to an office building on Fifth and Fifty-Eighth Street. I had to circle around a few times because the ticket cops were hassling me. But I caught them exiting about fifteen minutes after they entered. They headed back to their car and I followed them over the bridge."

"Who's watching them now?" Vinny's eyes narrowed, ready to give the young man another lesson.

"I gave little Jackie Stevens, you know, the kid who works in the hardware store near the 108th precinct? I gave him twenty bucks to keep an eye on the car. I gave him my number with instructions to call with anything that looks unusual." He decided to follow up, "And as soon as I'm done here, I'm gonna race back there." Vinny was especially pleased and he told him so. "You're learning, I'm glad." Charlie Mick's resulting smile could have lit up a small city.

Don't look so fucking happy yet kid, because I'm going to have to bring everyone down right now, he thought. He raised his hands and everyone quieted down quickly like Catholic school students in the schoolyard when the principal rang the bell to gather everyone. Once up and then down was all that was usually needed to get the kids in line. AJ glided back to the table without a sound. Vinny continued, trying to sound confident, unsure of how it was all going to come out. The best way was to just go right at it.

"We have to talk about the project, guys. We have a major problem." Just shock the shit out of them and this way he could keep the conversation flowing from his side with Michael to help. He looked into the faces of his best friends and could see without a doubt, that they were indeed shocked into silence. Vinny turned to Michael and asked him to explain the attitude of the bank regarding any preservation committee findings or hassles. With that Michael laid out all the terms of the commitment it took a year to obtain. He explained the bank's rock-like stance about any preservation board nonsense. He left the poison pill about the sign and the expiration date of the commitment for last.

"Usually you can get a month's extension from any bank on virtually any deal, no questions asked, but these days the banks are looking for any reason to bail on a project or even an individual mortgage loan for a small house or apartment. I'm not kidding you, gentlemen, it's fucked up out there right now, in plain language." Vinny put his hand on Michael's knee, signaling him that he was going to take over the rest of the conversation. He spent the next few minutes recounting his meeting with the bony man, the bow-tie and Maxie Carter yesterday morning, leaving out the dinner meeting with Maxie. It was Moose Miller that reacted first.

"What the fuck, Vin, are you saying they're going to put the fucking sign back up in the same place? What the fuck for? Why can't it go where you planned for it to go, who gives a shit about a fucking sign anyway? I mean honestly." He leaned back in his chair with so much force it almost tipped over, his meaty hands going to his face to wipe away the sweat that would soon be pouring down. The Burkes were silent. AJ spoke up quietly and calmly.

"Vinny, is this something we can work with somehow? Certainly the bank can't be that concerned about this sort of thing. It has no bearing on the whole project, none at all." She started wringing her hands, unable to fend off the freight train of disappointment hurtling toward them all. The Burkes were next.

"So what are you telling us?" asked Fred. That this commitment is as useful as a Scott Layden game plan for a winning team?" Ryan's turn came a millisecond later, "It seems like we're going down like

John Starks' shooting percentage in game six versus Houston. Holy shit, Vin. Mikey, you're the mortgage guy. Any way we can slam dunk this bank? What's their problem?"

"Their problem is that these people at this grass roots preservation committee have hit on the only thing, the one item that drives the bank nuts. Apparently they have some sort of line to the owners of the bank and also apparently they knew this was their hot button. The bank will allow no wiggle room on this subject." Vinny continued, "Can you believe it's all about the pier we used to dive off of? They believe it is somehow connected to the sign because of its proximity, or some other piece of bullshit. And therefore the sign can't be moved and the pier can't come down which stops us from building the esplanade and the buildings the way we need to, the way we want. I mean I'm sure I can fight them and destroy them, but the problem is that when the owners of the bank come back from their vacation this Sunday, they will pull this commitment out from underneath us if they even get a whiff of preservationist controversy." Both Burkes jumped in at that, "They moved the Lakers out of Minneapolis and now we can't move that stupid pier which is about as useful as Tim Curry in the paint? These people are destroying this plan the way Mike Jarvis destroyed the St. John's program. Totally and thoroughly."

Everyone was spent despite the shortness of the arguments. Charlie Mick was silent but the enormity of Vinny's words were hitting him between the eyes just as they were with everyone else. These guys and AJ had managed to find many hundreds of thousands of dollars in a down economy and they all took their shot at greatness collectively. To have it brought down by a group of faceless people for what seemed to be the most absurd of reasons was giving them all a massive headache, the kind that a boulder made of Excedrin couldn't touch. All of their focus returned to Vinny.

He was their leader in a situation like this. He had always brought it home for them. The bread routes, the never-ending string of two and three purchases and refinances to buy more and then the apartment buildings he renovated in Astoria, Williamsburg, and other neighborhoods, long before New York magazine decided that the hip crowd should live in these places. The pizza joints opening wherever they could and the bagel shops as well with their huge profit margins.

The simplest of ideas had moved these along...making sandwiches on bagels and maybe a pizza slice made with spinach, bringing internet access to these places long before anyone else did. These simple ideas brought in so many people that they wouldn't have otherwise, and the dollars rolled in as a result.

Vinny was the brains and the strength of the group, that had been undisputed since they were all twelve years old. He came up with the ideas and presented them in such a way that made it easy for everyone to understand. He was their antidote to any neighborhood bully. When he showed up on the scene, the fight was over before it began, whether it be intellectual or physical. Without him, they would just be another collection of guys from Queens with city jobs if they were lucky, their dreams of really making a difference either long behind them or totally out of reach. The pressure he was feeling at this moment was all consuming. He knew he could not lose his cool.

He started, "Listen, guys," and they all turned toward him, like little kids in a burning building looking for a way out. "You gotta let me handle this with Mikey. He'll deal with the bank and I'll deal with these historical preservation knuckleheads. I may have an idea germinating in a seed one of them gave me. Let me work on it, okay?" Quizzical looks all around. These guys and AJ could all smell a secret of some kind or bullshit a mile away, but they didn't dare interrupt.

"In the meantime, we have something else happening to one of us that may require some attention." He leaned into the table, forearms resting in front of him. The rest of them huddled like the Giants around Phil Simms in the Super Bowl. "J'lome is possibly having some problems with three guys that showed up at the mosque yesterday. I've had Charlie Mick on them since and he's been tailing them all over town. Nothing has surfaced, and it may all be a waste of time, but we have to draw tight and keep an eye on things, make sure these assholes don't get any ideas that they can fuck with any of us, correct?" Vinny's comments had several desired effects. One, to galvanize the group again and keep them together mentally and physically in the face of the news they just heard regarding the project. Two, it was the most basic rule they always had, we watch out for each other, always. That would hopefully keep everyone thinking that all was going to be well.

And three, well...it was something for everyone to keep their mind on and away from the consideration of financial ruin.

"Who are these three guys you're talking about?" Moose wouldn't say here in a matter of fact fashion he was following Aubrey and Whathefu; his surveillance had to be secret at all costs. He was annoyed with himself that he had let on to Vinny where he was, what he was doing. The question was posed by the Burkes, and Moose Miller asked Vinny without exposing his assignment to anyone else at the table at the same time, "Do you want me to check them out when I'm off duty?" AJ slipped back to the table just in time to hear all of this and she cast a nervous glance at Michael. He shrugged his shoulders as he knew nothing of these people or their involvement with J'lome. He had too much else on his mind to worry about this which he figured was probably much ado about nothing.

"No, Moose. Remember you shouldn't have any extracurricular activity when you're off duty. I'm sure your captain wouldn't like it and your wife would bust your balls for not getting overtime for it. You stick with that assignment strictly as the Fed you were telling me about earlier wants. I mean, if these guys were truly bad guys, they wouldn't be taking you off them because of a budget cut. The kid will watch them without interference. We'll let you know if it gets hairy and maybe you can get the collar, okay?" He looked at the rest of them, "We don't know who they are, just a few guys who were screwing around at the mosque. J'lome's radar went off and he called." He waved it away, "More than likely, it's nothing. But until we know it's nothing, I want everyone to stay close, until the end of the weekend. Stick to the neighborhoods, Long Island City, Astoria, and Sunnyside if you can. Keep your phones on at all times and be ready to converge wherever something might happen. Remember what John Lennon said, 'There are no problems, only solutions,' okay?" He looked all of them in the eye. "Let's keep our eyes open for solutions. You never know where one may come from or when." He then had a brilliant idea. "You know what? Let's have a card game tomorrow night."

The Burkes jumped on that idea as they were always up for a game, especially Fred. They voiced their approval the only way they knew how, "Hey Vin, that's a slam dunk of an idea if I ever saw one, I'm in."

Ryan countered, "Vin, that's as clutch an idea as Keith Smart hitting that baseline in the tournament to bury Syracuse." As soon as he said it, he winced because he knew what was coming.

"And that's what you have to look forward with any Syracuse pick in the pool, you fool," said Michael. Groans erupted from the Burkes and the others. The Burkes were dying to counter this point, and the others were dying not to hear them counter. Michael did them all a favor by turning quickly to Vinny. "I have to go, Vin, I have to take care of this thing I got." He started to get up, a signal that the statement was made without any allowance for discussion. He looked into Vinny's eyes to give his friend and business partner, at least he hoped he still became his business partner, a little something to work with. "I promise to be available. I just have to help out a friend in need." Vinny studied Michael the way a father studies his sixteen-year-old daughter when she asks permission to go to a party. He extended his left hand and Michael grasped it firmly, "Alright, Mikey...you can make it to the card game, right?"

"Absolutely, I have to get a head start on taking these guys' money." He slapped the Burkes five, grabbed Moose Miller's shoulder for a squeeze and said good-bye to Charlie Mick. "Everyone, make sure to bring all your money, I need a little extra padding in my pockets. Vin, when are we getting together?" Looks were exchanged around the table. Ten-thirty was agreed upon. Michael left the table trying to turn his mind toward his meeting with Laura which was in a half hour, but he knew he couldn't get out of the café without talking with AJ again. He had noticed she slipped away again once the Burkes started in with more basketball talk. He figured it was equal parts not being interested in the sports nonsense and wanting to finish ripping his head off. He would never leave without saying good-bye, so he started for her without being called over. She called him over anyway, "Come here, you. I'm not finished with you." He obeyed, as any sane man would, and sat down in the same counter stool he sat in earlier. This time she was on the other side of the counter and she leaned over to make sure their conversation was only between them. She touched his arm affectionately.

"Mikey, I'm sorry about the way I came down on you before," she told him. Continuing like a guidance counselor, "but I had to check your enthusiasm because you certainly weren't going to. You sounded like a besotted fool." He started to get up, his lips drawn tightly across his face with a classic, I'm-not-interested-in-yet-another-lecture face. She gripped his arm, softly, "Mikey." He sat down again, and in respect of their friendship and her intellect, he leaned in again.

"I wanted to also remind you that it is entirely possible that you and this lady, if ten percent of what you've told me is true, that you and her somehow found each other and in spite of the bad behavior exhibited by just about everyone else in the world, you two managed to form some kind of nice relationship that can only be defined as pure love and respect. I'm sure you'd like to bed her, Mikey, probably ninety nine out of one hundred men would want to, but you have her trust, Mikey, which, as a woman, I can tell you is a lot more important than any sex session she may have had since you've known her." She continued unabated, not even allowing Michael a moment to interject, she admiring him for not doing so.

"You may discover that the two of you can, without effort, share a level of love and respect that the rest of us can only dream about. Ten years you know this lady and you have had no contact on a social level, no romance at all?" She stood up, shaking her head in apparent amazement and disbelief, but still touching his arm continued, "Life is not only short, Mikey, it's very, very strange. You get the test first and the lesson later. Try to treat yourself well from now on, okay? That's what I'd like to see you do for once. I do have to say I am very impressed with you both, but remember that if you do decide to be with this woman and she decides to be with you, we will all support you as long as you respect Georgia and love Sally." She came down hard on the names of his wife and child and Michael knew why. All members of the group had at least one parent that was largely absent, and yes...it did hurt and it did result in a hole of some sort that could never be repaired. Jesus, she has him divorced already. Time for some cold water.

"Thanks AJ...but I'm not going to do anything. Maybe I'll be able to help her a little bit and maybe, just maybe a coffee with a different woman might get me to remember why I married Georgia in the first place." He smiled the perfect warm smile she remembered seeing for the first time in Amsterdam so long ago. She was equally elated and fearful for him. He looked great, she thought, as he stood and leaning over the counter, kissed her on the cheek, telling her that he would let her know what the meeting with Laura was like and turning back to the table of friends, waved and told them he would see them all tomorrow night for cards. He hit the door, the bell tinkling, the harsh glare of a late spring afternoon sun not bothering him at all.

MID-AFTERNOON

Goodness gracious, thought Michael, she's absolutely beautiful, as beautiful as the first day I saw her. He was sitting in the Starbucks on Fifty-Seventh Street in Manhattan, down the block from Carnegie Hall. He arrived straight from the meeting with Vinny and the others and was glad that he planned to be a little early. This particular Starbucks was arranged as a square, no cozy nooks for privacy, save for one. To the right of the door as you entered, there was a table for two set up against the window looking out on the street. It afforded some privacy for them and it also meant that they would have to sit next to each other. Aside from the obvious advantage of sitting next to her— who knows, maybe my leg would rub up against hers—he would be able to hear her better. He loved her soft voice but he sometimes had to struggle to hear her over the cacophony of voices and bad deejay music at the office Christmas party.

But this wasn't the Christmas party. This was a Friday afternoon and he was now watching her crossing the middle of the street, from north to south against the light, like a real New Yorker. The traffic literally stopped for her and she covered the eastbound lanes with a few jaunty steps, waving thank you to the cabbie, who never thought of honking his horn at her, instead following her progress with a sleepy, desirous look. She was moving like a gazelle on an African plain, carelessly and effortlessly, as if she had utter conviction in her movements and also somehow knew the lions and hyenas were taking the day off. He could see her powerful and shapely quadriceps rippling beneath her jeans. The jeans were topped by a sweater that went with her black hair perfectly and a checked jacket that seemed tailor made, it fit so perfectly. She slowed as she approached the door and then she saw him through the window and their smiles of acknowledgment were so bright they could have powered a small city. He stood as she entered and he took her in unashamedly from head to toe as if he were in a dream, not believing the two of them were actually here. She did the same, thinking that Michael looked so good in a suit, the wide shoulders, trim hips, love that burgundy tie, at least he knew how to dress unlike three out of four men in New York with their clunky shoes, floral patterned ties and rumpled shirts. She extended her hand feeling oddly awkward as they had known each other for many years and shouldn't feel so strange in each other's company. He took it lightly and was the first to speak.

"It's good to see you in a place where we don't have to shout over bad 1970s music." A winner, he thought, as she smiled genuinely in response.

"Yes it is. I like loud music actually, but not when I am trying to speak with someone." A Brooklyn hipster, a half of an anarchist in his army jacket, ratty looking dreads—does any white man look good in dreads—and old-style, low black Converse started inching toward the table. Michael quickly deduced that this guy had as much chance of taking this seat as he did of cracking the Yankee's starting rotation. He took the back of the chair in his left hand and beckoned Laura to sit on his right, giving Mr. Bad Hair his very best Irish diplomatic look, which was equal parts peaceful and threatening. Laura maneuvered herself into position to sit and he got a sidelong glimpse of her rear which transported him back to the hallway sighting so many years before. Wow, she's as trim and in shape now as she was ten years ago. "Thank you, Michael," she said, thinking that he is definitely a throwback to a nicer era as she settled into the offered seat. The dread-head slinked away. He would have to plot his next action against corporate America and environmental missteps somewhere else. Michael sat to Laura's left, and then stood up quickly.

"Would you like something? What do you get when you come in here?" he asked her. She answered quickly, "I'll have a cappuccino, thanks. She watched him walk away. He moves like an athlete, she thought to herself, struggling not to say the words out loud. He stood in line for a few minutes, looking back to their table where he could see she was unloading a few sheets of paper. He picked up the cappuccino and as regular a cup of coffee as he could get in this place—it was his first time in a Starbucks—and brought them back to the table. He placed her cappuccino in front of her along with a small pile of napkins and sat next to her after she thanked him for the coffee. They both regarded each other for a moment. Her perfume was heavenly. He recalled the old Pepé Le Pew cartoons where the French skunk would float along, buoyed under his nose only by the beautiful scent of a woman's perfume. Neither had any idea of where to start so Michael went basic.

"So, the weather has been very beautiful."

"Yes it has. Spring is my favorite time of year. I love to see the flowers come out in Central Park." Please, Laura thought, let it be easy. She thought she could feel some beads of sweat forming under her sweater. But there isn't any reason I should feel nervous now. He has more than proven to me his sincerity over the years. And I asked him here, not the other way around. "I hope you don't mind that I asked you here."

"No, not at all." I would have paid a million dollars for this. "It's one of the great things about the mortgage business, that I can move around as I like. And these days, well, the business has been kind of dead so I can move things around a little easier. I have a little more time on my hands than I usually do." He sipped his coffee to take away the dryness in his mouth. "So what's going on, what's happening?"

I have only been here for a few minutes and I already feel more comfortable with him than I ever did with any of the boyfriends or lovers I've had, she concluded quite easily a few seconds later. The beads of sweat she felt forming were gone. Is he that great of a guy or was I just used to dating and sleeping with fools and losers? She decided for once to open herself up a little, let this man see what is going on...don't be shy with him. He obviously is enjoying this as well. Laura couldn't help but notice the intensity of his gaze when he saw her, not only here but whenever they encountered each other in the hallway or at the company party. She may not have had as much experience as many other American women, but she knew what was needed to be known when it came to men. She said to him, "You have no idea how bad it is in my office. It has been a disaster there for years, everything from padding overtime in the six figures annually to political groups all fighting for control. Nobody there works together to resolve or solve issues."

"I had no idea it was so bad for you. You never gave me any indication that anything was going on over the years. What is the central issue, Laura? What was it that pushed you to call me?" He leaned in towards her slightly. "I think that was the first time I ever heard you over the phone."

"No, you're wrong, it wasn't the first," she replied.

"Really?" He was taken slightly aback. Then it came to him...right, that time.

"I called you at your office, remember when..."

He interrupted, making sure that she would see this episode embarrassed him a bit, "When I was having a particularly frustrating day and I announced that I wanted to go to Paris and you happened to be sitting there and I asked that you go with me for the weekend and you called me later in the day asking me to never say that sort of thing again in the office." He added by way of explaining, "I never meant to embarrass you that day."

"I almost died right there at my desk, you know." From embarrassment or hunger for just that type of weekend...she didn't know which. Because by then, she knew that she wanted to say to him, 'Yes, Michael, I would love to go to Paris with you and walk along the River Seine at dusk, and eat chocolate cake and drink coffee in a café of our choosing on St. Germaine Avenue. We could spend hours there watching Paris walk by and frankly, they would watch us as well. I want to tour The Louvre and eat baguette fromages for lunch and then rent a car and drive down to the Mediterranean and go to the casino with you in a beautiful black dress and a shiny set of pearls. She awoke from her momentary daydream to see that he looked slightly distressed.

"I'm truly sorry about that. I never really apologized to you properly. I never should have said anything like that." But I meant it, Laura, he thought. I could very easily see us strolling through the Bois du Bologne, listening to jazz in one of the many music joints they have there, and doing silly tourist stuff like the Eiffel Tower and a trip to Versailles. But mostly, I want to make love to you in a non-air-conditioned room, the French doors open wide to the streets below. What the hell, we don't know anyone here, right?

She replied quickly, "It's alright, I may have overreacted a bit. I just don't want any of those people there to think that maybe you and I...you know." Goodness, what was she saying?

"I understand, but you can never control what people think. You can only control what you do."

"I have to try to control them as much as possible. Michael, I appreciate that you came here today, but I have to insist that you tell no one about it, promise? I don't ever to want them to know anything about my private life."

"Of course, no problem. Just between us." She was deadly serious with that demand. Mikey...make sure to honor it and also to really listen to her. She looked sad when she said this and Michael was guessing that she was sorely disappointed in these people as human beings. Probably nine out of ten men she has known listened to barely thirty percent of what she had to say, he surmised easily, but wondering how accurate that really was, maybe he was wrong. In any event, you better make sure you're different than those fools.

"Laura, tell me what's going on. What's the bottom line? Tell me in one sentence if you can so we can concentrate our efforts." She detected no impatience in his request, no reluctance to move on to other matters as so many others had done to her in the past and that made him more handsome, more attractive, more...desirable than she had ever realized. Be careful, Laura, she warned herself again as she brushed her hair away from her eyes. Boy, do I love the way she does that, thought Michael. She began, "Basically, I am politically marginalized in this office but that's not the worst of it. I can handle that by myself. In the last day I have uncovered a scam at the bank that has been ongoing for some time and it seems to me that I was set up to take a fall for someone and I need to know how to deal with that issue." Michael could see in her eyes how serious and concerned she was. And this was definitely serious business. Since 9/11, the banks across the United States had implemented myriad security checks and balances to prevent any monies from being laundered to fund terrorism. But given mankind's need to continuously fool around and find newer and better ways to steal, cheat, manipulate and basically screw around with the system instead of turning their obvious talents toward industrious efforts that would produce legally gained fruit and legitimate profits, there still remained plenty of con artists, scammers, identity thieves and assorted assholes who just refused to live inside the boundaries of lawful society. This was serious shit and he made sure to think before he spoke. He sipped at his coffee again, and looked out the window at Fifty-Seventh Street, the sidewalks jammed with tourists, native New Yorkers pushing their way around them, hundreds of semis, yellow cabs, Porsches, and twenty-year-old Toyotas heading east and west, from one side of the city to the other, and harbored his thoughts.

"You have to come forward with this, Laura. There's no doubt in my mind that you need to get in front of this as quickly as possible at least in order to protect yourself against any suspicions that you were involved," he told her. "What do you have in the way of proof? For something like this you need to show the paper, as they say in the lending business. No one is going to believe you unless you can produce something that is unassailable, not just a suggestion of a crime, but a clear path of evidence to a clear conclusion, you know what I'm saying?"

"Yes, I do," she responded, not at all annoyed that he expressed some doubt in her because she also detected genuine concern on his part. It was then she knew she had made the right decision in seeking his opinion. Smart, honest, and willing to say what was on his mind. What a concept, she thought as she continued rummaging through her bag. She pulled about fifty pages out of the bag and placed it back on the floor, under the table. "Here, look at these."

He could see that the pages contained thousands of lines of code and endless columns of numbers and he felt useless, as computers and math, well, they would never be his strong suits and he told her so. But maybe it would be better this way. "You're gonna have to show me so it's perfectly clear even to someone like me, a guy who looks at technology and rows upon rows of numbers on a sheet of paper like that, and usually runs away." Laura picked up the papers instantly and straightened them and put them back down in between them on the table. He moved closer to her—he had to in order to read what she was pointing at—she now had a pencil in her hand, and it was pointing to the first line of code.

I better not touch her leg with mine under this table, he thought, so he leaned over for the last few inches, balancing most of his body weight on his right butt cheek which caused half the muscles in his back to clench in protest but he didn't care. In this position, she was only half a foot away from him and he was enjoying it immensely. Plus it was practical as well as he had to strain somewhat to hear her voice which was as soft as a feather. "Here, follow me on this and listen. I'll take you through it line by line," she told him, very aware that he was all hers at the moment.

She began by sketching out her entire career at Argent Bank, how she was recruited by the then-Chief of Technology, who left the post after a heart attack three years later, an apparently generous man who recognized her zeal for technology combined with an immigrant's dedication to work. He had told her that technology would change virtually all businesses forever and that he had projects and interesting work available for a mind such as hers for the next ten years. She told this mentor a few months in how she sensed some confusion at first and then a dash of resentment among the others in the department, which consisted of nineteen males and only three females, including her. She remembered him waving it off as just jealousy so she put her nose to the grindstone, performing any job, answering any call, saying good-bye to any sort of social life, not that it had been so great anyway. She left that part out, continuing her story with the abrupt departure from the bank of her mentor. She soldiered on for several years, performing many unwanted tasks and, without her mentor to protect her, started noticing there were meetings she wasn't invited to, classes she wasn't included in, whispering around her desk that made her feel paranoid. It was starting to make her think that maybe she had to look for a new job as the office atmosphere was decidedly chilly. She described some of her colleagues with blunt honesty: "Backstabbing, political maneuvering, lazy, slimy snakes."

The worst part was when in a reshuffling of staff, she was assigned to Andre's group and as a result, he effectively became her boss. He dumped all the ordinary tasks of the group on her. He never picked up a phone or explained a procedure. His absences became more and more frequent. He was fiercely protective of his territory, not sharing anything with anyone on the team, and even going so far as to write up phony warnings for everything from improper dress to a missed appointment when there was no appointment. He fired the two older men, nice guys, who had been with Argent Bank for close to forty years and took over the monitoring of the entire check encoding and bank wire system for himself. He was constantly making and receiving calls on a cell phone that had the most awful song with some wailing banshee of a female singer as a ringer and he would either be in ecstasy at the conclusion of a call or in agony. If the call ended badly, of course he would take it out on whomever crossed his path at that particular moment.

"It's peace I crave, Michael," she said with much earnestness and yearning in her voice, "I don't want any part of a political office war. I like a quiet life with no extremes in thought or deed."

Michael listened, somewhat astonished at what she was saying. Ninety-nine percent of his conversations with her in the previous ten years only lasted a few minutes. But it was immediately apparent to him right from the start of their friendship, not ever receiving any indication through maybe fifty encounters with her in the hallway or at the Christmas party that she was anything other than possibly the most pleasant individual he had ever met. How could these people see her any other way? He was embarrassed then, realizing how much she must have been suffering while he was talking to her about...whatever.

"I'm sorry, Laura...you must have thought I was an amazing bore whenever I approached you at the parties. I never had any idea you were being treated like this," he said to her. I wanted to tell you Michael, I really did because I knew I could trust you, but we had to maintain a certain amount of distance for our own survival, she was thinking right then. She shook her head and smiled at him, "No, I always enjoyed speaking with you but I have to admit I was kind of nervous, worrying about whether or not anyone else was watching us."

"Well, in the end all we ever did was talk, we're allowed to do that. Imagine what it would have started had we danced together," he answered, chuckling quietly, almost privately, loosening things a little between them. Back to business, listen to her. He asked her to continue.

"On Thursday we had a major wire problem with some new business clients located all over Asia. Without warning, the system failed, none of the clients' money hit their accounts on time. We were alerted to what was happening because apparently these new clients have some kind of proprietary software that tracks their wire amount to the penny. They called and started to freak out, saying how could this happen, we are your new clients, all this sort of thing. They were going crazy and I don't blame them." She explained how she gathered up a Chinese programmer and a Korean administrative assistant, then traced down the executives overseas through numerous time zones and spoke to several companies in an effort to cool them down.

He asked her, "Were you working with them or in their vicinity at that time? Even just walking by?"

"No, why?"

"I was just wondering. Sorry for interrupting, please go on," he insisted, lightly touching her elbow from underneath, withdrawing his fingers right away, impressed with her ability to effectively deal with a problem by searching out others who can immediately help. She gathered up her papers and started in with them again.

"These snapshots," she lifted them all by the bottom and held them up near her face. Michael could see them clearly now, and he knew he wouldn't be able to make heads or tails of them even if he had a gun at his head. She continued, "These are snapshots of computer runs that point out very clearly what I suspect." She put them down on the table again and continued, beckoning him closer to follow her pencil.

"What I see here is I think, no, I am sure that someone infiltrated my computer, set up some kind of passcode so they could hide themselves and their crime by setting up a dummy computer outside of the network. Through my analysis of these snapshots I was able to tell how long it's been going on, what they've done, and most important, who it is. Last night I went out to the Long Island office and discovered the dummy computer and I disabled it."

Michael was leafing through the snapshots, looking for any semblance of something that would make any sense to him. Not finding one, he looked up sheepishly. "I'm not much help deciphering these. What kind of crime are you talking about, identity theft? Or are they looking at porn?" He was realizing that part of him wanted to get to the heart of the matter quickly. Maybe they would have some time for a walk through Central Park, which was just a few blocks away. It had been a beautiful day but the sun was now going down and it would get chilly quickly. He was already sure of his advice to her and didn't want to seem bored by all of this technology talk, although it was making his eyes glass over a bit.

"That may be going on, but what I am sure of is that money had been siphoned off a little bit at a time. They call it a salami scam, where someone can slice off a little bit at a time and not get noticed. Say a customer of the bank writes a check for $25.87...the scammer would make sure the check was encoded properly, but the eighty-seven or just the seven cents would disappear somewhere along the line into his account." She put the papers back in her case as she was noticing his eyes drifting a little bit. He came back to life with a question, "Where did you get those papers? It must have taken hours to search for and print these." He looked her in the eye. "Did you do this during business hours?"

"No, I uhh did it last night...I had a last minute change of plans and I decided to use my newly found time to research this."

"Bad Thursday night date?" He was glad she was putting the papers away. They looked like Greek to him, which he actually tried to learn once. He didn't hear an answer from her about last night so he looked up to see that she was staring out of the window and he could tell she was miles away, the vehicles and pedestrians on the street just a blur to her. It was then he noticed a slight welling in her eye. That was a stupid question. This is no time for flippancy, he thought. He reached out with his right hand and as lightly as he could, brushed the tear away. "Laura? I'm sorry about that crack. That was stupid of me. I know how serious this is, but I've always tried to keep things light because I've discovered that when you grow up in a city like this, with a ton of different people and cultures, you just have to not take even the most serious things too seriously. I don't know if that makes sense to you, and it was most probably ill-timed, but please don't think I was making fun of you or this situation. And I'm not suggesting in any way that one should just ignore obviously important and weighty issues." She turned back to him, the subtle curl at the end of her mouth not betraying the sadness she felt.

"Michael, I have always appreciated how much of a gentleman you always were these past ten years," she told him, looking deeply into his eyes for the first time ever. "You never even made a half of a pass at me. I always admired your honesty with me from the start. When you told me you were married, when it was obvious we had some, well... electricity between us, it made me respect you even more. Most men would have, actually did lie to me about their status."

"I'm no priest, Laura, but I would never lie like that, just to get a woman into bed," he answered with all sincerity. He was recalling that night so long ago, when they were both rendered speechless for an instant when they first took each other in. He wished he could take her in his arms right now and provide a well of comfort for her to draw upon if she wished. It suddenly seemed stupid and illogical to him that they weren't together. She maintained eye contact with him and he resisted leaning in any more and he started, "I learned early on in life that intimate contact is much better when you have a real attraction of the heart and the mind. One-nighters and friends with benefits relationships don't appeal to me on any level." And he meant it when he said it, at least at this point in his life. They did have some appeal on a couple of vacations to Jamaica many years earlier. Now, however, he would rather be at a card game with the boys than hunting eligible women around the clubs and parties of the city. She responded quickly.

"Not for me either," she said, and for some reason she couldn't fathom opened up to him easily. "I have only had a few boyfriends as I always preferred relationships over anonymous, loveless sex. I have experienced both, very little of the latter by the way, and your way, I agree, is much better." She felt her left quadricep suddenly tighten and without thinking, lifted her foot and leg to relieve the pressure and she inadvertently let it rest on his knee for a second or two, the left tendons at the back of her knee hooking a bit on the edge of his right patella. He didn't move as he savored that tiny bit of connection with her. An earthquake couldn't have moved him. She placed her foot back on the floor and blushed noticeably while turning away from him, looking out the window again.

"Sorry about that, I'm actually very athletic and I don't like sitting for too long. It tightens everything up." She pressed her shoulder blades together and lifted her chin and Michael didn't even try to not stare at her flat stomach. She then pulled her arm across her chest to lessen the tension in her rotator cuff, instantly reminding her of the injury she suffered while skiing many years ago. Her boyfriend at the time left her laying in the snow for a few minutes, not believing that she was in that much pain and protesting that because he was a member of the ski patrol, he couldn't show her any favoritism. And later that night he had the nerve to ask her to have sex in the snow outside. She dumped him at La Guardia airport upon their return. Wait a minute, what am I doing? Michael could see that she was suddenly embarrassed again and she said, "Sorry again, it's tough to get old. I really shouldn't have..." and her voice trailed off. Michael leaped at the opportunity to tell her one more of the maybe ten million things he always wanted to say to her.

"I don't mind, don't worry. I'm kind of glad that you feel comfortable sitting here with me. It's very...natural." He looked out the window again, "I knew that if I had been aggressive with you at some point in the last ten years, it would have ruined our friendship. Being aggressive with you, even floating a double entendre would not have been natural at all."

"Yes, it would have. I doubt that I would have been able to trust you anymore had that happened." And she knew that was the truth. She might have never would have spoken to him the same way again even if he had ultimately shown her a divorce decree. He was sitting back now, still looking out onto street, when he came to a decision. He didn't care if she slapped his face, he had a sudden uncontrollable urge to just tell her...something. He didn't know if he would ever see her again, life was so...unpredictable and he needed to just tell her. And so he did.

"Laura, I would like to tell you, in case you ever wondered..."

"What, Michael?" She was leaning a little forward now. She had turned toward him again, his voice a magnet to her entire body. It was as if she were made of iron filings instead of flesh and blood. His deep sonorous voice was wrapping itself around her like a warm cloak. All hesitation disappeared from him now.

"Just that..."

She loved this boyish charm of his, she realized as he tripped over his words, not knowing that he was still fearful of not only getting his face slapped, but of the territory he was broaching with her. He touched the underside of her elbow ever so slightly, "When we first met, it felt like I was in a movie. I felt an instant, almost chemical connection to and with you that I never felt with any other woman. Seriously, I couldn't hear a thing, even though the deejay was already playing music, I couldn't hear anything but your voice and I couldn't see anything on either side of you or behind you in spite of the fact that we were surrounded by hundreds of people. It was a very strange feeling, and I sensed that you were experiencing the same thing." He looked at her for a reaction but couldn't read her face at all. Her focus on his words was obvious but he didn't know if the slap or a smile was coming in the next few seconds. So he continued, "But being who I am as a person, I couldn't make a pass at you, ask you out on a date. But I really wanted to."

She interjected, "I would have said no because I knew already you were married." He leaned back and slightly raised his hands defensively.

"I know that, and frankly I felt that I knew that in the first minute of our friendship. What I'm trying to say is that it was a conscious comfortable decision on my part to act the way I have. It was very... natural." He put his palms flat on his legs and gripped them slightly. "If I couldn't date you, then I decided that I wanted to have a beautiful, decent, elegant lady like yourself in my personal ledger of people I can call my friends. If I were single when we first met, I would have asked you out immediately."

And I would have agreed to go, she thought but did not dare say. Maybe she would never tell him. Even if they had dated for ten years. Some things a woman has to hold close to her heart. He was continuing, "If you had a boyfriend then, I just would have waited him out. Not that I wanted you to be lonely or in the middle of a painful breakup, but I would have probably called you every few months to see if you were still unavailable." She watched him sit back and look out on the Starbucks crowd. It was a busy place, the tourists from Carnegie Hall and the Russian Tea Room clogging the air with a hundred different accents and languages. She was just realizing that she hadn't heard a sound other than Michael's voice for the past few hours when she heard him say, "I just wanted you to know that. I thought it was important to tell you this, so I did. I hope you don't mind." The longest two seconds in his recent history went by and then he heard her say, "I don't mind, I've thought about it as well. For about five years now." This revelation hung in the air between them like a beautiful lilac scent. Time to get this back to business, they thought simultaneously, but it was Michael, to her relief, who spoke first. After another gentle elbow touch and warm smile. "Let's get back to this; it's more important now. Tell me, what do you want from this? You must answer that before you choose a course."

Wow is he smooth, she thought. Another minute of spill your guts out conversation and I would have probably just sat in his lap. A warmth she never experienced either in its suddenness or brazenness, was spreading throughout her body with its epicenter about three inches below her navel. Business...right. Better get back to that. Because frankly, when she was describing earlier what she discovered in the past twenty-four hours about Andre's set-up, she realized that unless she cleared herself immediately, the FBI could come knocking on her door. It was an excellent question that Michael just put forth, it would help her focus on a clearly-defined goal and with that she could set herself on a straight path and not be bumped off it.

"I want my good name cleared first and foremost," she said with utter conviction. "I've never stolen anything in my life, never been accused of even thinking about stealing. It seems to me that there is something illegal going on here and I need to disassociate myself from it immediately so I don't get caught up in it somehow. I think I can prove with these snapshots what has been going on and how I was being set up like a scapegoat."

"Is that all you want?" She was confused by the question and tilted her head, looking at him oddly. He thought he detected a bit of impatience on her part.

"Yes," she answered a little coolly. "What else could there be?"

"Frankly, maybe if I were you, I would want to see this guy fired and blackballed from the industry. I would want him to hang publicly. You just described not just a little scam that steals pennies from a bank, but rather a systematic plot to involve you as a sitting duck in a situation that is at least, outrageously improper and at most a felony, a Federal crime. There may even be the possibility of some personal danger. Who knows where these funds go? Maybe just to Atlantic City and the roulette and craps tables, but possibly they go to an offshore account controlled by a criminal enterprise. If this were my situation and it's not, of course, this is you we're talking about, not me, I would want it and this guy put down like a rabid dog."

"That's not really my personality, Michael," she responded. She felt proud to answer this way even though she sensed his disapproval.

"Maybe if I grew up here in New York, I would have beat him with a stick years ago, but I didn't. I was molded to let these sort of things pass as easily as possible, not to be confrontational." She once again watched the minions pass by the window, then continuing, "But sometimes I guess you have no choice but to pull your head out of the sand," she said with some sadness shrouding the finality of the statement.

"Yes you do, Laura, yes you do," Michael said, forcing his opinion on her. He swept his hand toward the window, "This is New York City, I was born and raised here, and if there's one thing I've learned, it's that you can't take shit from anyone. Please understand what I'm trying to say, hear me out." He suspected that his coarse language turned her off. "I don't believe in violence as an answer to anything, nor do I believe in revenge, although I have dreamed about it at times. But with any bully, and that's exactly what this guy is, a bully...whether it's in the schoolyard or in the boardroom, or in a marriage, you must push back to establish your own ground. Otherwise you will surely live with regret eating at you for years while the bully plans another attack on you or moves on to another innocent victim. And here in this situation, you have to do this just to survive because he has sucked you in. It's time to push back, Laura. Don't be scared. Remember that you're in the right and more than likely what this guy is doing is probably some little scam he's trying to enrich himself with. But it is certainly at minimum a fire-able offense and you can't lose your job in this economy. Nor can you risk being investigated by the police. You have no choice but to make copies of all these snapshots, draw up a time line with every detail necessary, including all of the details of how you were treated over the past few years, everything necessary to present your story and bring it immediately to Human Resources on Monday. Tell them you want the police brought in immediately."

She sighed audibly as she knew he was right and she told him so. "Thank you, Michael, for all your help and for listening to me for so long." The light on the street outside was decreasing as the afternoon wore on to the early evening. She leaned forward to look west and could see the spreading magenta over the rooftops of the buildings on the west side, a smattering of wondrous color that always helped her to relax. She leaned back, sighing audibly...

"Where does the time go?" she asked the air. "I'll have to find the courage to do all of this somehow." She started to pack herself up a bit, wiping down the table and throwing her empty cup and the napkins in the garbage. He could see she wanted to leave so he stood up, threw away his own empty cup and moved her chair away so she could move freely. "I have a lot to think about."

"Yes you do, and I'm truly sorry that you are being forced to do this. It really pisses me off. It reminds me of a time many years ago when my mother was similarly tormented by an executive at a big Park Avenue conglomerate." He took her elbow again and guided her to the door. While he was doing so, she turned her body to say thank you and he could feel her well developed bicep. It reminded him of a trip to San Francisco when he was a teenager and a girl he met named Virginia. "Call me Gin, not Ginny, okay?" she used to tell him. He and Gin drove down the coast to Carmel and ran wind sprints on the beach, counted the stars while they rested and then took dinner at an beautiful al fresco place, trying to act like sophisticated players although they were both just nineteen years old. They struck up a conversation with a fiftyish married couple who were friendly, but absolutely boiled on three bottles of locally produced wine. At the conclusion of the evening, the older man kissed Gin on the cheek and Michael noticed him running his hand up her arm. Sneaky bastard, he thought at the time, and he felt guilty now because he realized he just did the same thing. He remembered that at least the man removed his hand before either of them could protest and then vanished out of their lives. The two teenagers returned to the beach to count the remaining stars and to look for Venus and Mars. What a beautiful evening that was. And how strange it was for him to think about that now. They were both at the door of the Starbucks, four hours after they entered. It was breezy now, the May evening retaining a bit of winter strength. A couple of German skinhead tourists barged their way in past them. Michael wanted to smash their faces for their rudeness in his own city. But instead he shrugged his shoulders, held his palm out like a doorman at The Plaza, and she breezed through the door out to the street. He followed her, pulling his jacket around himself to ward off the cold. They turned east heading toward Sixth Avenue, falling perfectly into step like they had on their walk up Broadway the first night they met ten years earlier, when he dropped her off at a dance studio. He wished that evening that he could have joined her. A homeless guy called out to Laura as they passed, "Hey beautiful, please let me take you out. You're so fabulous!" Michael responded for her, but made sure to do so with some humor.

"Hey, be a gentleman, okay?" He turned to her and she looked back at him at the same time. Goodness, she was beautiful. Hai Carumba, he's handsome she thought. They turned left on Sixth Avenue and continued over to Central Park South where they turned right.

"I have held onto many old-fashioned notions of how a man should treat a lady. Sometimes it doesn't go over that well with the average New York woman," he said. It certainly goes over well with me, Laura thought. "It's nice, I like it," was all that she said. They continued east and Michael asked her, "What train do you take?"

"The N train. There's a station over by the park."

"I know it. My mom used to take me to the pond along Central Park South when I was a kid. I would fashion a hook out of aluminum foil and go fishing in the pond with it." She laughed, and then covered her mouth as if she were embarrassed, "I'm sorry, I'm not laughing at you. That's just so funny. Did you ever catch anything?"

"Yes, a cold." They both laughed together. "Where do you live anyway?"

"In Long Island City. I take the N to Queens Plaza and then back-track on the 7 to Vernon-Jackson. I live in a two-family house a few blocks away from the Vernon-Jackson station. It's right down the block from the East River. I think they're building some luxury apartments down there." Yeah, well, maybe not, he thought. That was definitely a subject for another time. One disaster per day.

"Did I ever tell you that I grew up around there?" he asked.

"No, I remember once at one of the parties that you told me that you grew up in Queens, but I didn't ask you where. I originally thought you must have grown up in Manhattan because you seem to have equal amounts street grit and Park Avenue to you." A very interesting combination, she always thought.

"Do you like that combination?" Why not a little flirtation? He may never see her like this again. Might as well have a little fun for the next two minutes before they get to the train station.

"I do," she answered maybe a little too hurriedly. "You have a little James Bond in you, I think." He laughed and explained that James

Bond was much tougher than he could ever be and added that Sean Connery was the best James Bond. They continued down Central Park South past the carriage horses, some of the drivers calling out to them for a ride. Like any New Yorker, Michael would rather be dead than ride in one of the hansom cabs. But maybe with her one day. Yes... maybe he would consider riding in a hansom cab, but only as long as he was with her. They arrived at the entrance to the subway station across the street from the Plaza Hotel and Laura turned to him. Her brow was furrowed and she was undeniably upset. Boy, that happened quickly, Michael observed.

"What's wrong?"

"I just wish I never had to do this," she said. "I just wanted to advance as far as I could in the computer field, make some money, get a little recognition maybe, and accept my fate or fortune knowing I did the best I could." She spit the rest of the words now, reminding Michael that she had some strength and pure Latina heart in her. Better not ever think of her in any other way, he reminded himself. "But these people, these jerks have involved me in something that is possibly, probably illegal and they have ruined my good name. I am pissed off about it!"

She was shaking despite her efforts at self control. He didn't say anything for a minute or so, letting her settle down. Then he decided to get crazy. "Tell you what, I have a silly idea which might balance your head a little bit. It may help you reach the conclusion you can be comfortable with."

"What is it?" she asked. "Whatever it is, I'll take it at this point if it will help me."

"Let's spend the day together tomorrow," he said venturing into dangerous territory. He could practically hear AJ screaming at him all the way from behind her café counter, screaming at him to just peck her on the cheek and let her go home on the subway alone. "We can have a day of culture." She was astonished that he asked her, but intensely curious.

"What's a day of culture?"

"Do you like art?"

"Yes."

"Music?" She shook her head yes once more.

"Baseball?"

"I don't know anything about it. I've never been to a game. The Yankees have a new stadium, don't they?"

"Uh yeah they do...so do the Mets although it's not finished yet either. I'm a Mets fan so maybe we can go see them play. They play the Yankees this weekend so it will be an electric gathering of New Yorkers. Anyway, let me work all this out and we will have a day full of culture, to celebrate all that New York City has to offer and all of this other stuff can be put aside, at least for a day. What do you say? We can meet right here early in the morning."

She was silent in the wake of this offer by Michael. She was having difficulty trying to decide whether to include him among the scores of men who led her on and then bullshitted her in an amazing variety of ways, the art of deception as natural as breathing to most of them. Was Michael showing his true colors now, asking me for this date? Or am I completely overreacting to an offer with no other attachments dangling off the end? She reminded herself that it was she who called him and then got him involved in this situation to a certain degree. He worked for the same company, maybe he could get sucked in somehow because now he also knew about the scam. And if he would have done something like this, if it was so much in the forefront of his mind, certainly she would have heard it from him a long time ago. She was so deep into this wrestling match in her head that she didn't hear him speaking once again and she turned to him in such a way to convey without a trace of doubt that she had not heard a word he just said. She wanted him to know without actually saying it that she well knew he was married and that dating married men was not something she ever wanted to do, regardless of the fact that so many others seemed to be doing it. What did he say?

"This is not for romance, Laura, okay? My family is out of town, they'll be back on Sunday afternoon. I have nothing going on from now until ten-thirty tomorrow night when I will be meeting my friends for a card game." He shrugged his shoulders finishing with, "I probably wouldn't have waited this long to ask you out if I had romance on my mind." He could see her half-smiling, considering his request and he arched his eyebrows in one final plea to her. She was thinking how could it happen that he just articulated what I was thinking?

How unbelievably...natural. Nothing fake about it. Why not spend the day with him? He's proven himself time and time again. And I don't have anything to do tomorrow either. A day of culture...I like it. It's original and interesting, although I would rather see Yankee Stadium than where the Mets play, she thought. Why am I thinking so much? Or maybe I should just sit at home and scroll through endless pages on the internet, looking for advice from people I don't know about... what? My love life? The pain in my knees? Why I did this, didn't do that? Time to answer him.

"Okay, Michael, let's do it. When and where should we meet?"

"How about right here at..." he stroked his chin between index finger and thumb, looking down at the ground, making mental calculations..."Eight-thirty?" he asked snapping his head back up.

"That's good," she answered evenly and they stood there for a moment before she announced that she was going to get going. Michael had his car parked on the east side but there was no way he was going to offer her a ride as much as he desired just that. He truly only wanted to have a perfectly nice day out on the town with Laura so they would always have just that...in case their friendship would remain forever what it had been for the past ten years. Let her take the subway home. At least tomorrow, he would give her a first date that her next ten lovers would never match. For now, he would be perfectly satisfied with that. She smiled and started for the steps, pausing for a moment, moving closer to the wall from which the pond was visible.

"Thanks, Michael, for listening to me today." She continued looking out over the stone wall that separated the street from the very serene setting.

"No problem, Laura. We'll talk more about it tomorrow in between cultural events." He shrugged his shoulders thinking that he would have canceled virtually any other appointment to meet with her and just... talk with her. He knew he was totally interested but he also knew he was a disciplined man, not given to crazy acts. "Tomorrow at eight thirty, okay? I'll dress nice, but casual...you can wear sneakers if you like."

"Okay, Michael, see you here, tomorrow, bye and good night." And she was off down the stairs. Michael stepped into her footprints and looked over the wall to see what she was looking at. The pond was there, where his mother had taken him and his older brother fishing so many Sunday afternoons ago, where he knew she had frolicked on the huge rock at the southern end of the pond, (she had once shown him and her kooky friend a few pictures of herself from years ago) right near where he had fashioned the hooks from the flip tabs on the soda cans. The cherry trees were seconds from full bloom due to the warm weather all of the city was glorifying in the past couple of days. There was a couple on a bench below him holding each other close, not talking but definitely communicating. From his vantage point, he couldn't tell if they were happy or sad. The old-fashioned wrought iron lamps suddenly came to life. He could see a pair of teenagers etching their initials in the bark of an ash that was leaning majestically over the still water and then an older woman, maybe eighty-five or so, straight from central casting as everyone's favorite Jewish bubby, was suddenly at his side from out of nowhere exclaiming privately for him while gesturing over the wall, "Isn't all that beautiful?" But before he acknowledged the old woman, he looked down the subway stairs after Laura, who was now on the bottom step, turning left into the station, now pausing for a moment to look behind and upon seeing him there, waved good-bye before disappearing into the system. He turned back to Sylvia Miles' stand-in, "Yes dear, it most definitely is."

⚓

EVENING

Whathefu, Andre, and Aubrey sat in the Saab in Long Island City, on Vernon Boulevard, which ran parallel, north and south to the island across the East River. Andre had extracted from her Human Resources file that Laura had lived here for several years, in an outwardly shabby but neat three-family house on Forty-Seventh Avenue between Vernon and the river. From their spot, they would be able to see her exit the subway station and she would probably walk right by their car on her way home. She wouldn't ever suspect that she was being watched.

Whathefu liked the neighborhood for its proximity to the city and the development possibilities it obviously held. He had no use for anything that bespoke middle class. He envisioned a grand vision of a vast tourist center complete with golf course and the tallest hotel in

the world. These poor little homes and ugly warehouses would all have
to go. Even just sitting with these two cretins in this shitty car made
his self-appointed lofty sense of self and entitlement turn in on itself.
He closed his eyes, not believing it had been just a couple of days since
he was so close to Kismine's breasts, straining against her silk blouse
in the skidding Ferrari. He would have enjoyed that conquest, maybe.
Then again, maybe he would have enjoyed the young man from a few
nights earlier a little more. He was amazed so many homosexuals were
part of the drifting culture and he saw them not as brothers, but as
a whole new class of human being he could take advantage of. It was
easy to get a blowjob at the drifting scene, unlike with your average
Saudi girl or even many of the American and European women he met
in the fashionable clubs and restaurants and on the beautiful beaches.
And giving the other driver, a nice, very cute guy the same in recipro-
cation wasn't as bad as he thought it would be. He decided he could
and would do it again the first chance he got.

Anyway his father, if he wanted to, if he was a real father, could
fund several such building projects here with just his petty cash and
Whathefu would run it all. Not incidentally, with all the cash flowing
in and out of foreign hands, it would be a perfect money laundering
operation. But even before he killed Kismine, his father never would
have given it a second of thought. It really was tough to be the third
son of a third wife of a Saudi billionaire with far-reaching government
and apparent Wahhabist contacts.

Where was the woman with the great ass? Probably stalking the
hotel bars, looking for a traveling businessman she could claim for
the night. The way these American women give it away disgusted
him although it never stopped him from sleeping with any number of
them. It was so easy to pretend he was a Saudi prince and they would
just faint away. Not all of them, but so many it was becoming hard
to count how many conquests and encounters, difficult to remember
them all. Completely without morals, so many of them were, he con-
curred with the voice in his head, never giving an ounce of thought to
the fact that he was right there physically and somewhat spiritually
with them at the same time.

But he is my father, he always circled back to that...what would
be wrong with his idea? Maybe after we get this job done. He would

have to come forward with his own substantial financial stake. But he had already started thinking of the very thing...why not raise the theft amount to one hundred million? It's not like we have to carry sacks of cash out of the bank. All of it moves in less than a second and then again to a secret account. That was it, he decided. When they find the woman, they will remove one hundred million. The three had circled the block once to get the lay of the land and parked back on the boulevard to stake her place out. The block itself was bleak, but Whathefu did like the little park at the end where you could probably find some solace under a shade tree, looking up occasionally to dream about living and working in the towers of Manhattan, just a half mile away. Maybe he would keep it as some sort of tribute when he built his mini city here. As they turned left past the park, Whathefu could see several large empty lots with construction machinery parked on the side and a trailer that must have served as the project office of a builder. He also thought the large soda sign should be moved over to the other side of the lot in order to accommodate a larger building.

The longer he sat in the Saab station wagon, the disdain he held for the middle classes increased geometrically. Even sitting there was bearable only because he still felt, even though he knew this man was a murderous thug, a strange thrill every time he caught Aubrey's strong jaw in the corner of his eye. He didn't dare try to again engage him in conversation; he could barely look him in the face. This was a real man, thought Whathefu, a soldier who just might be able to carry Islam through the streets of America. He wanted to take in more of him but again didn't dare turn to him or try to catch his eye. Maybe just maybe, at some point in the future, he would be lucky enough to lay down with this man. In the meantime, he could dream, couldn't he? First things first, though...they needed the woman.

Aubrey hated the street and the surroundings mostly because he felt more exposed here than he wanted. There were more and more pedestrians than he thought there would be, although they all seemed to be hurrying to and fro, none of them even glancing in their direc- tion. There were just a few frame multi-families bordered by factories, trucks constantly rumbling by with pickups and deliveries and a lot of traffic on this main street causing more noise. He did like that because he knew noise often was an ally in a stealth approach like this. There were a couple of delicatessens, an old time family-owned hardware store, and a bar on the corner. A Boeing 737 inbound to LaGuardia rumbled overhead. Aubrey hated the overall industrial nature of the neighborhood, wondering who would ever want to live here, not understanding why so many young people in cities seem to prefer neighborhoods like these, the proximity to Manhattan, general goodness of the long-time residents and the cheap rents apparently never occurring to him.

Of course none of these thoughts were shared between the three men in the Saab. All they had in common, beside a shared Muslim faith, was that they were all in on this quest to find Laura and use her to unravel what she did to the computers in order to buy the rest of their lives for them and their dreams and goals. There was just silence between them now, none of the usual banter about ball games, kids, marriage, that any group of men, friends or not, could find some common ground on for a conversation.

Andre was feeling some exhilaration, looking forward to a big payday. What would Fated think of him now? He would be sure to send his friend a snapshot of him and Kismine frolicking on some beach somewhere. He was fancying himself similarly to the guy who married Celine Dion all the while managing her career. Of course there was the evil blue-eyed bastard sitting in the driver's seat he had to deal with. He seemed absolutely soulless, thought Andre. What would a man like that think of his infatuation, no, his perfect love for his Kismine? Would he even be aware of a sliver of beauty in anyone or anything? His strict observance of Islam made Andre nervous. In fact, strict adherence to any religion made Andre nervous. Andre attended services sporadically, stopping by the mosque on Steinway Street because at times he felt a little peace there, which is what he figured one should find in a house of worship. He was shocked at some of the invectives he had witnessed hurled from the pulpits of mosques and churches over the years. That minister there, although he seems to accept the Jews and Christians in the neighborhood, well, he seems to be a fine man and quite devout. Andre's own prayer recitations, his posture while doing so, were just slightly above atrocious.

But this big bastard is like any other convert, on a mission to prove to himself and any others who had been privileged to be born in the faith the total purity of his convictions. He had seen the same type of zealotry in other converts to various religions. They reminded him of farm girls from Kansas and country rubes from Saskatchewan arriving in New York and acting within a week as if they had been here their entire lives. Another brand of pathetic behavior in the American human, he concluded. But Andre certainly wasn't going to talk back to him. He had the physical strength, already demonstrated when he pinned him to the wall in the mosque as if he were a sheet of loose leaf paper and with the violent encounter with the young guy in the leather jacket he and Fated came upon when they arrived on Steinway Street. He also had that cold, hard stare he had seen in the eyes of the martyrs in the Middle East in the videos they produced before blowing themselves into a million bits in some bakery or on a bus.

The thrill of soon-to-be-had easy wealth was exiting his body quickly the more he thought of who he was currently involved in this scam with. He started cursing the day he decided to set up the salami scam to fund his girlfriend's recording career. Why couldn't he be reasonable with her and frankly just look her in the eye and say, Sorry dear, but I can't afford this? Let her go her own way if she freaks out and that would have been it. He wouldn't be here worrying about going to jail—which was going to happen whether he was able to help these clowns steal the money or not. He was going to jail. They had to find her...and silence her as well. He was realizing that now, that if the big bastard didn't finish her off, he would have to. Would he be able to find the will, the strength to do that?

That is, if the big bastard didn't stab him with the vicious-looking knife in his belt, or shoot him with the automatic pistol in his jacket pocket, or just beat him to death with his fists.

He looked out the window and considered Laura's residence. Had he been wrong about her? He had always figured she had some man or men wrapped around her finger, receiving subsidies from all of them here and there for...whatever. Andre heard enough whispered comments about her appearance from others in the office to himself finally acknowledge she was an attractive woman. But he had to target her from the moment she arrived at the bank. How dare she walk in here with her nice smile and think that was going to usurp my experience and college degree? He had came to the conclusion years ago that she must be a kept woman, as any other woman or any employee at all would have quit years ago after all the crap he managed to dump on her. Probably living in some high-rise on the Upper East Side, driving a Mercedes, sunning in the Hamptons. Just keeping the Argent job for the health insurance and to bolster her 401k. Living the life that should be his.

But this was not the city block of a wealthy woman about town, and the small house he had turned his head toward once more was not the sort of place he ever figured she would live. He was realizing slowly how wrong he had indeed been about her. Her elegance, walking through the hallways of the bank with her head always held high, her carriage erect and seemingly pulling her body slightly behind it, was apparently a product of good parenting and good genes along with a desire to carry through on what she learned as an adolescent. Maybe she wasn't a spoiled bitch after all. And she did hang in there all these years. So many of the men he hired and fired over the past ten years didn't match her dedication and toughness in spite of their fancy college degrees.

He slammed his eyes shut to stave off the impending pounding in his temples. In the space of a few minutes he had contemplated killing Laura, then admitted to himself that he had probably been totally wrong about her and, as a manager of a department, probably screwed up when he didn't reward her past diligence, to wondering what it would have been like if he was with her and not Kismine. Dear God, why do I always torture myself this way with all these insane scenarios?

Whathefu had no patience for waiting. All of the velvet ropes of the western world had been open to him since he was a teenager. Even in Saudi Arabia, the third son of a third wife rarely waited or wanted for anything. The exhilaration was leaking out of him as well. The perfect timing of the ugly African's conversation coupled with the luck, as it were, to be partnered/kidnapped with the beautiful soldier next to him sustained him for the first twenty-four hours. At first he couldn't believe how perfectly everything was working. He was tasting his freedom once more. That is until the ugly African blew the whole thing. What horrible luck that the woman discovered his little scam the day before we needed it work. Well, she'll pay once we find her. We have a soldier on the job. With that thought, he turned slightly to surreptitiously admire his controller out of the corner of his eye...he just couldn't help himself.

Aubrey was again surveying the landscape of Vernon Boulevard like it was a Kuwaiti desert, his highly trained eyes sweeping every possible angle. The car was not helping much, as the Saab's windows were large and untinted, affording the passersby on the street too many opportunities to make them. He checked the side view mirror and could see yet another police car leave the 108th precinct which was unfortunately situated a couple of blocks south. Where the hell was this woman? Certainly she had to come home soon. The time for evening prayers was fast approaching and he had no intention of missing them. He needed all of Allah's favor now. For the past few hours he set aside the practicality of finding the woman as it seemed fairly easy to him. Just sit on the house, she had to arrive here at some point. She wouldn't suspect we are here. They couldn't possibly scour the city for one person, especially so in the absence of any decent intelligence on where she might have gone. So it was an easy decision to come down to staking her place out, as sooner or later she would have to show up here, definitely before the weekend was up so she could get ready for work on Monday. In the worst case, he figured, they would have to wait until Sunday afternoon or evening before they had a chance to grab her. So this was all they could do. He allowed his mind to wander with the possibilities this soon-to-be-found wealth would make available to him.

The dictators of the Arab world were as vulnerable as they had ever been. The righteous people who had lived under the heels of these tyrants, Assad, Mubarek, Khadafy, and Ahmadinejad were on the verge of rising up and they would need a new spiritual leader. And it was his convinced opinion that they would want him. Look at how Al-Alwaki was gathering steam in Yemen. He was also an American, but not like Aubrey, who was proud of his soldiering talents and his good looks. Al-Alwaki was a nerdy-looking, skinny little shit who was trying to be the next Khomeini. That wouldn't work with the young people he had seen on the news throwing rocks and challenging the government thugs who were out in force with tear gas and bullets. His vision would be realized through patient discussion with these youngsters who wanted many of the advantages western society offered in the way of education and equality, but also infused with the discipline of being a devout Muslim. He knew in his heart, in his head as well, that he could be a beacon for this population of young people. And the women would like him as well. He could feel the little prince's eyes on him again and he was instantly sickened. He held off on exploding at Whathefu with a great effort, instead growling, "What the hell are you looking at?" The small Saudi man cowered under the verbal lash.

"I was just wondering what you thought our next move would be," Whathefu responded with raised hands. The sudden conversation stirred Andre from his silence in the back seat.

"Are we going to stay here all night?" he asked. As quick as lightning, Aubrey's Glock was in his hand and pointed at Andre's face, barely an inch from his nose.

"Once again for you two, we will do what I say. Period, end of story. And if either of you get out of line, I swear you will pay with your lives. Am I finally being clear enough for you two?"

Andre nodded, his head being the only part of his body that would move as he was consumed with fright. The man's eyes seemed even wilder than yesterday, something he didn't think possible. Slowly Aubrey pulled the gun back over the seat and he rested it in his lap for a second before it came up again, the muzzle sharply smacking into the side of Whathefu's head who threw up his hands, his eyes slamming shut and tearing from the pain. He started his privileged rich man's son whine an instant later, "Why did you...what's the matter with you? We're on the same side, searching for the same woman, we have the same goals." The gun was back in Aubrey's jacket pocket but the knife was out now and again displaying incredible swiftness and control, had the blade right at Whathefu's throat in what seemed like a millisecond. He held it there without a word, the silence from his tormenter causing Whathefu to start to quiver noticeably as if he were seated on a block of ice. Aubrey was struggling to hold his temper as he was ready to wait for this woman and force her to his way of thinking without these two. He spoke calmly and quietly but kept the knife just under Whathefu's chin.

"You," he said, looking the frightened Saudi directly in the eye, "will keep your mouth shut unless you have truly something important and useful to say. I will leave it up to you to determine what I might find useful, but if you're wrong, and you start asking me stupid questions about what happens next or if you make stupid comments about some woman's ass or the viability of a block or neighborhood for development, I will draw this knife right across the middle of your neck and I won't stop until your head lands in your lap. Once again I have to make sure by asking, do you understand?" Whathefu nodded in quick, short bursts so as not to cut his own throat. Aubrey pressed the knife closer to the breaking point of his captive's skin and said, "And stop looking at me like that. I've seen you several times looking at me the way a million queers have looked at me and I can tell you that many of them wound up in the hospital. You will never make it to the hospital." He withdrew the knife and stuck it back in the sheath inside his jacket. Aubrey looked out the windshield continuing to assess their situation.

Right now, he was feeling the need for prayer. The mosque they visited yesterday was only a couple of miles away so it would have to do. He would make sure they stayed in the back as much as possible, away from the other faithful. They could return here and wait until the small hours of the morning and then retire to the safe apartment they stayed in the night before. Then it would all start over again on Saturday until the woman appeared, which she had to do sooner or later. It was likely they would not attend prayers on Sunday so he started to form a proper dua in his mind, a supplication to the will of Allah, a plea for forgiveness.

He looked over to his left at Laura's building, squinting slightly as a light drizzle was falling now, making it more difficult to see anything there. He checked his watch and made calculations for the final prayer of the day, the ishi'a. It's Friday night so it made sense that she was out somewhere, probably partying and whoring herself. That's what they all did. He pinched the bridge of his nose as the memory of his last twenty-four hours started to squeeze his skull. Whathefu and Andre both noticed this but said nothing.

The light was fading now, the last beams from the west now dipping below the towers of Manhattan just across the river. The rain was quickening as well. It was obvious to him now...there was no way they were going to catch her by staking this place out for at least a few hours. Maybe they could check the windows later to see if anyone appeared home.

"Do you know which apartment is hers?" he asked Andre without turning around.

"Her address on her Human Resources card includes 2F which in New York means the second floor in the front," he answered, trying his damnedest to sound confident. Aubrey continued staring at the building, trying to will some life out of it, knowing that was unlikely. It would have to wait until tomorrow probably. We'll do a pass-by after the prayers and something to eat, and if her window is still dark that probably means she has her legs spread somewhere for some man who offered her a cheap dinner. Once again he cursed himself inwardly for worrying about what these non-believers did with their pathetic lives. Time for action. He shifted the car into drive and made a U-turn on Vernon, turning left up by the police precinct and continuing to the corner of Jackson Avenue, which, if he took another left, he remembered, would take him back to the mosque on Steinway Street. He told his passengers, "We go for prayers, then we will get something to eat and check back here one more time for a second stakeout before we go back to the apartment. That's our plan. It would be better to take her tomorrow anyway. The bank will be closed, no one would be around on a weekend, and we wouldn't have to move around with and hold her prisoner tonight."

He wasn't going to wait for a response from either of them and as he figured, he didn't hear a peep other than the blare from a yellow cab's horn washing over them, pushing them through their left turn onto Jackson Avenue, Aubrey staring at the exit of the subway station in the driver's mirror as long as he could, hoping the woman would appear.

—◦◦◦—

It was one of the things she missed most growing up on the farm, the beautiful quiet. City dwellers didn't know what they were missing. No planes flew overhead, no subways rumbled around the town, and there were no yellow cabs with their horns in what seemed like a constant state of honking. She paused for a moment halfway up the stairs of the subway exit, catching a moment of calm before she exited the station on the corner of Jackson Avenue and Vernon Boulevard. She liked the neighborhood mostly for its proximity to the city, but the noise from all the myriad vehicles spilling into the nearby Midtown Tunnel sometimes unnerved her, so she usually waited for a moment before exiting the station to make sure there was no bottleneck of cabs and trucks blaring away. She turned north on Vernon Boulevard, tuning out the hoots from the teenagers spilling out of the deli, and ignoring the highly appreciative stares of the men who passed her on her two-block walk to her street. How is it that not everyone in this city has high blood pressure? she wondered. Not only the noise, but the rudeness of so many, the selfishness of practically everyone, the unwelcome surprises of all shapes and sizes, which she found equally annoying and stressful as the promise of success for everyone the city held.

She crossed Vernon, turning down her block and was about to step onto her stoop when she decided to take a walk to the end of the street. It was only about two hundred yards to the bank of the East River, with not much to admire in terms of beauty on the way so she made a beeline to the edge of the river, to the little park near the soda sign. She listened with closed eyes to the rhythmic slap of the river's tide against the pilings and upon opening them, tried to look deeply into the gray water. It was certainly not the bank of the gentle river that coursed through her family's property, gurgling past hundreds of perfectly placed smooth rocks of varying sizes, the clear water filled with colorful trout that she and her brothers would pluck out of the water with patient hands, cherry and honeysuckle trees along the banks perfuming the air so sweetly in the spring. She recalled sitting there for hours on end, watching and listening to the bubbling water and lifting her nose up in the air to catch every scent, following the polliwogs in the pools and occasionally skipping a stone across to the other side.

She looked out now over the river in her life which wasn't even a river, although you couldn't tell any New Yorker that, scanning from the Queensboro Bridge about a mile north down past the Beekman Hotel and the fancy apartment buildings on Sutton Place, further down to the green windows of the United Nations building. Her eyes settled on a police boat moored in the middle of the river, probably there she surmised to protect the high-minded diplomats from some sort of terrorist attack, most probably an event that had an infinitesimal chance of occurring. She saw it as one more poorly considered allocation of the city's resources.

Laura recalled her years socializing among the U.N. crowd, as smug and elitist a group of people she ever could imagine. She recalled Hans, the handsome and tall charges d' affair for the Luxembourg mission she dated for several years. She enjoyed his company, impressed with his grasp of languages and his ability in a social situation. But she suspected he was somewhat embarrassed by the lack of refined, diplomatic-type social graces in a country girl, although she had enough physical grace and beauty to go around for all of the women she had the misfortune to meet at these events. She started to suspect he drank a little too much when they weren't together, and he was constantly in training for the Olympic flirting team, much of the time in her presence. She could easily recall the last time she saw him. They had been practicing how to say, "How do you do," with the correct amount of...aplomb. It had gone on for two hours that way. "No Darling, try it like this," he repeated over and over again until she wanted to put her hands around his neck the same way she would grab the trout in the river.

She had told him, "I can handle it, you'll see. Have some confidence in me. Don't worry about what these other people think of us. We're supposed to be in love and not interested in what others think of us. If you had wanted to, you could have chosen one of those other women, the same ones I always see hanging around these sorts of things."

"Of course not, Darling, I only want you." He had stood to her side when he said it and his words brushed past her face with a chill, an actual physical sensation like an unwelcome stiff breeze on an otherwise glorious New York autumn afternoon. She never forgot it, the superstitious streak in her left over from the ghost stories her brothers would tell her, that made him seem to her at that moment like some sort of unwelcome visitor from lower earth. Later that night she finally told off one of the 'chosen,' as they frequently saw themselves, another who, with a little liquid courage that was always in abundance at these parties, decided some disparaging remarks about growing up on a farm would spark some laughter. Composed in the face of the obvious insult, and in the wake of hundreds of less obvious affronts, she proceeded to tell the assembled snots the story of Hideyoshi Yoritomo, who in the late 1500's had risen from peasant farmer to be the supreme ruler of Japan until his death, bending even the the emperor's court to his formidable will. She also pointed out that President Bill Clinton and

Abraham Lincoln had risen from less than stellar social backgrounds—in their opinion, not hers—to occupy the White House and the ultimate seat of power in the modern world. Hans was furious with her performance and he told her so later in a verbal whipping that made her feel small, but only for an instant. She looked into his handsome face, topped by his lean body and smooth manner, recalling the trips to Europe and the Caribbean, the lovemaking which was really very nice...and told him to get lost right then and there. These people were self-absorbed asses, she said to him and he countered that they were indeed the beautiful people of this world, and she countered that they were parasites, and apparently you are one of them as well. And he turned on his heel and walked away, never turning back to her for any kind of final look. And she knew that if they turn around to look, they are truly interested in you. That was the last she saw of him.

Almost five years of dating down the drain, an engagement ring in his pocket that she would never wear, ninety-nine percent of the women in New York that would have been aghast that she, a thirty-five-year-old, would turn this guy out the way she did. But she did, and her best friends always told her that they admired her strength in doing so. She wondered what it would have been like with him now, all these years later. He would probably still be handsome and trim, their children would be educated and beautiful, they would probably not have touched each other or exchanged a civil word in years and he would have women installed in cities all over the world for his comfort and amusement, and they would have been posted in some hellholes here and there as part of his foreign service.. She shook her head free of these thoughts. He had a great outer casing with an impeccable resume, but ultimately exposed himself as yet another bland and classless man who didn't have a clue.

She sighed at the memories and they then fast forwarded to the other night with Adam. She could feel her eyes welling, not because she had displaced another potential boyfriend, but the rage she felt along with the astonishment at his cruel brashness. Strange is our life, she thought, as this terrible event also led her to the Long Island office and the discovery of Andre's crimes and her talk with Michael. And now, tomorrow's date with him. She giggled like a little girl, thinking halfway through their meeting that just talking with him was almost as good as most of the sexual foreplay she had experienced in the past ten years. All they did was talk and listen to each other, he provided advice and support and didn't bore her with his own stories. Better than any guy she ever dated.

A rainstorm was starting up and the river turned grayer and angrier astonishingly fast. She turned away to her left to avoid the chilly breeze and looked over a construction site just a short distance away. Wouldn't it be nice to live in one of those high rise apartments they are building around here? Wouldn't it be nice if those people at Argent Bank would recognize my efforts? Wouldn't it be nice if I could open a little café somewhere on Thirtieth Avenue in Astoria, where young people from all over the world could sit in peace and quiet? She was back on her block now and she spent the next thirty steps or so wondering, what would it have been like with Michael in the bed last night, instead of Adam. No, she concluded, I won't get involved in that. But I would like someone to tell me what to wear to a 'day of culture.' And as if on cue, her phone chirped. She could see that it was her somewhat crazy but always amusing, as well as very savvy friend, Angelina. She would have a host of problems to complain about, lists of people she wanted revenge on, setbacks she wanted turned around. For Laura, that's what she needed, to listen to someone else's problems and issues and plans for revenge other than the voice in her head. She flipped open her phone, said hello to her friend, and agreed to meet her shortly at her apartment in Forest Hills.

"Yes, of course. Why not? Sure, I'll stay over. A movie? Sure, sounds fun. Yes, please make your chicken and baked potato dinner; I'm kind of hungry, too. What was the name of the film? *The African Queen*...Humphrey Bogart and Katherine Hepburn? *Charlie and Rosie*? A love story between two people who are completely different? Sounds good. Yes, I can stay over but I have to leave at seven-thirty for an appointment in the morning. Okay, see you in a little while." Laura ran down the block to beat the rain which was threatening to turn into sheets, running upstairs and grabbing some clothes for the next day with Michael and ran out again, making sure not to step on the loose plank at the top of the stairs. Within a minute she was back in the subway, heading out to see her friend.

⸺

J'lome had seen them as soon as they entered his mosque, but he concealed this from the two thugs who seemed to have recruited Andre somehow. Idiots, he thought. Why would they return here after what they did yesterday? And what was Andre doing with them? He was a buffoon, a nowhere man who hadn't a clue about accomplishing anything on his own. He felt he could buy happiness and fulfillment by acquiring...things. Worse, he had the other clown Fated, in his ear much too often. He made a mental note to counsel Andre the next chance he had. He was disturbed that his leading of the prayers was disrupted by these thoughts and he pulled himself back together to finish strongly.

J'lome had been, still is, and would always be, one of the boys although he was a man of the cloth now. He ran with Michael, Vinny, the Burkes, Moose Miller and, God rest their souls, their other friends dead so many years in the towers because of those twisted people and their twisted and broken hearts. J'lome was unrepentant in his public disgust for the attacks of 9/11, earning him the ire of many, most of whom would only put their views forward on anonymous websites and with videos sent to CNN, the BBC, and the *New York Times*, all of which gladly gobbled them up and printed and broadcast their damaging words and thoughts time and time again.

It galled him, the media reports of widespread coordinated attacks on Muslims in the United States, which he refused to believe. Not one of his faithful ever really complained about anything serious, other than what seemed to him to be random acts of drunken racism and stupidity. But he made sure to keep his eyes and ears open for evidence of anything truly over the top in any sense, just to be sure. The neocons and Fox News would have you believe it never happened, and he also knew that to be as false as the head-hunting reports and warning issued by various anti-defamation groups.

It further galled him that the same networks and media outlets were now turning on the government, riding the tide of what they called 'Muslim resentment' against the United States. He remembered driving through Times Square, about a week before George Bush's invasion of Iraq, eyeing some helmet-haired network news teleprompter reader broadcasting on the jumbotron television facing uptown, the exploding graphics and over-the-top enthusiasm for war too much for him. The papers, magazines and the networks wanted it. It wasn't a war for oil as those knuckleheaded anarchists and the super progressives would insist. No, he saw it as a war of ratings, of circulation-busting proportions, of product for the media for years to come. He recalled only Michael out of the whole group not agreeing to invade Iraq, but what did the opinion of some guy in Queens matter? Outside of the city, and in some reluctant-to-admit-it parts of the city, everyone forgot about the big hole in the ground downtown on the West Side. That was only a few miles away from his mosque. From where he decided years ago to make a stand against the nineteen and those who thought like them. No radical ideas were allowed here, just rational discussion. J'lome had picked the name The People's Mosque with ease as well as purpose. He didn't want to convert anyone but instead, he wanted to open Islam to the principles of the other great religions, Judaism, Christianity, Buddhism, as well as the thoughts and concerns of any type of non-believer. "Allah has made all of these people in a certain way, so who are we to judge them to be defective?" was a sermon he delivered countless times during services and in private conversation.

His faith was as strong as it had ever been, he loved all the people who attended his services, who sought his counsel. But he would never allow himself to be played for a fool by any man or woman. So he kept a half an eye on the three in the back and over to the left, the three who were not quite behind the pillar. He easily noticed their attempts to be unobtrusive. Didn't they realize that would make them more obvious instead?

The instincts from the old neighborhood and from inside jail continued to live inside him and they were screaming at him now. He had to remain impassive in the presence of these three, as if maybe he didn't even notice them. Once he was finished and his faithful were standing, talking and milling about, he with the crowd, swallowed by them and therefore unseen by the three, offering a kind word here, a mock admonishment but with an edge to it there, trying to get to his office where he needed to reach out to Vinny immediately about these three. Maybe the kid Charlie Mick was still outside. He hoped so. This situation was wrong and it made him nervous.

⚊

Vinny never left AJ's place for the rest of the afternoon, listening to the Burkes endlessly talking and arguing basketball, Moose Miller chatting with AJ about how to impress his wife more and the importance—in his view—of doing so, young Charlie Mick sitting by until receiving a call from Jackie Stevens about fifteen minutes ago and then leaving the table telling Vinny, "I gotta get back on that thing," listening and hardly ever contributing anything other than jumping in on a communal laugh.

Everyone was pushing the same thesis..."Don't worry Vin, it'll all work out. You and Mikey will find a way through the shit, you'll see. And J'lome, he's praying for everyone as well. I'm tellin' ya, I feel it's all gonna be good." He could feel their fear soaking through their clothing and he appreciated their efforts at putting on a good face and not crumbling to pieces.

He wished Michael was still here, but he knew not to question his friend when he says he has to be somewhere. Anyway, he would be seeing him again tomorrow for the game. He seemed a little jumpy about his appointment. I wonder what it was all about. I'll ask him about it tomorrow.

He hated these diversions from his train of thought. When he was younger, he could concentrate on a problem until he bore a hole through it with the force of his will. Now, in his late forties, not so much anymore. He worried about his friends and the issues in their lives, their finances, wives, girlfriends, other friends, kids. He reluctantly brought them into his deals financially, only after countless discussions about the gamble and the risk did he allow them to invest directly in his various enterprises. The stores, the real estate, the bread routes...everyone had been a fractional owner in all of the partnerships and they all paid off very nicely. Nice, boring businesses that would stand the test of time and would withstand any severe economic downturn. Jobs and prosperity for all of us. And now all of it was on life support.

The River House project...it seemed so perfect at the time. Three buildings, nine hundred or so rental units, a couple of family restaurants, a public park and the offshore beach, a brilliant idea by the Burkes. They had designed a circular beach, about 100 feet from the diameter, that would turn ever so slowly, "so as to ensure a perfect tan and easy access and egress for anyone who is able to just step on an escalator," to sit flush to the bulkhead, on the southern part of the lot. Vinny had argued successfully with the city that this project guaranteed him certain riparian rights to the waterway, and he convinced them to sign off by giving one hundred of the units to low income families, which he had planned to do anyway. How could he have shown his face in the neighborhood if he hadn't?

It took years to put it all together. Sitting on the option for the land, grabbing it immediately as it came up, Vinny already having shaken many hands, endured countless dinners and lunches and banquets with local politicians and city planners years before anyone wanted to fly over Long Island City let alone live there. Carefully refinancing or selling every property, pulling out every dime from refinancing the bread routes, exhausting lines of credit on the electric and plumbing company he shared with the Burkes, everyone's IRA's and 401k's, AJ refinancing her building...what a headache it all had been.

The permits, the legal fees, architects fees, the initial cost for the purchase of the option, it was all from him and his friends. The other capital was put up by some of the money men and women he had met over the years who believed in him. But they were pros. They understood risk and had plenty to back them up in case this went south. Vinny had promised them a certain return for the first three years at which point they would be bought out and the entire project would belong to Vinny, the Burkes, Michael, AJ, Charlie Mick, Moose Miller and J'lome. It was all completely thought out and it was going to work perfectly...until this preservation society stepped in over a fucking sign and that stupid pier. He should have destroyed the pier as a potential health hazard the first day he had the option on the land. But he was involved in the rest of the planning and the building and this was one detail he didn't think he had to deal with. I wanted the project not only for me but for them as well...a permanent place to hang their hat, and a source of income that would always carry them and their families through. He was feeling guilty now...maybe he should have had the real money men pay for the upfront and then bring everyone else in later in the game.

He was thinking back to his dinner with Maxie Carter. Nice lady... smart lady. He liked her even though they came from such different worlds. She seemed to be aware of how lucky she was, to be born into Sutton Place which was a vast improvement over most who grew up in that kind of world. Again, he started to wonder about what she had said at the conclusion of their evening together. Apparently, she believed a solution was at hand for his problem but she couldn't just come out and tell me. I bet that would be a violation of some law or understanding, he figured. She came off to him immediately as a woman with a moral center that couldn't be disturbed by an earthquake. His phone rang just then, and he answered immediately once he saw who was calling.

"You," he said to the caller.

"Are my brother always," J'lome answered.

"What's happening, what's going on"? Vinny asked, not unaware of the slight strain in his friend's voice.

"They're here again, the two guys from yesterday. And they seem to have a member of my flock with them now. I don't think he's a willing participant," he added.

"Are they causing problems again?" Vinny was sitting straight up now, grateful for anything to take his mind away from his troubles with the project and from the Burkes arguing about the NBA. Friday night now, nothing to be accomplished with that anyway until possibly tomorrow. Hopefully the Knicks will win tonight and tomorrow afternoon.

"No, but there's a lot wrong here. I can't be sure, but I think Andre..."

"The fat ugly one?" Vinny interjected.

"Yes, please remember that we are all made in the image of God, my friend."

"Yeah, some more than others, I guess..."

"Actually we can't be sure because no one has seen God, my brother." Vinny grabbed the bridge of his nose to push the headache back. He knew J'lome was right.

"I know that and you know that I know that." There was an

uncharacteristic uncomfortable silence between the two friends. Vinny spoke up, "I'm sorry, bro."

"No, it was me being too judgmental and proud of my beliefs. Forget it and please forgive me." The chill in the air between the two of them thawed quickly, like a glacier at a global warming conference. J'lome continued, "Look, I think something is majorly wrong here, I think these people need to be watched. I am worried about Andre. These guys, especially the big blond one…"

"The good looking one?" Vinny could feel the warmth of his friend's smile over the line.

"Yes," he chuckled, "the movie star. Seriously though, he's bad news. And he's with a rich Arab, a Saudi, I think…these are too incongruous a pair to be just hanging out. And after yesterday, I know 'Brad Clooney' is capable of the rough stuff. Is the kid still with you?"

"No, he split after the meeting. I have him sitting on these guys so he might be outside your place as we speak."

"How did that go?"

"Don't ask."

"Am I going to have to shut the mosque?"

"No, because we might all need a place to stay after the weekend." Vinny shifted forward, his elbows resting on the table, what AJ always called 'his serious pose'. "Listen, if it weren't for you, I would have been in that jail and I know I wouldn't have turned out as well as you have. I owe you for the rest of my life. The mosque stays…forever."

"I'm sorry I doubted you." His tone shifted, "Can you make sure to send the kid over here again, just make sure he did follow them here? Just for another pair of eyeballs."

"Of course, like I said he's not here, but I'll find him. I'm thinking he's probably already there. Keep me informed, okay?"

"I will. Thank you, my friend. I will stop by the game tomorrow to see everyone."

"Really? Are you gonna play?"

J'lome smiled. "You know I can't do that. And lucky for you guys, because with my pipeline to God, I'd wipe all of you out. I'll talk to you later. Thanks, my brother."

"It's nothing…you should know that," Vinny answered. He clicked off and then dialed Charlie Mick. The kid answered on the first ring.

"Where are you"? Vinny fairly barked into the phone.

"I'm outside J'lome's mosque, on Steinway Street," he answered quickly. Vinny smiled and could feel the warmth, the familiar feeling spreading throughout him, when he knew, just knew, that something good was brewing. "I had nothing else going on so this was the last place you asked me to be, so I came back here just in case, you know, you wanted me here for something else." Vinny was immensely pleased but he wasn't about to let him know that, not yet.

"I want you to keep your eyeballs on these three humps..."

"The ones from yesterday?"

"Yeah," he continued, only mildly annoyed by the interruption, "The ones that are hassling J'lome and the rest of his people. They're in the mosque now. I want a call from you every hour for the next forty-eight, even in the dead of night, understand?"

"What do I do with them?" Charlie Mick asked. Vinny barked at him in response.

"Do nothing but watch them. And don't get made, understand? Don't talk to them, don't go near them, don't engage them in any way. Remember to call me and take notes of what you see."

"Okay, got it." Vinny clicked that call off and redialed J'lome.

"You'll be happy to know that the kid showed some initiative and he's actually outside the mosque right now. He's gonna keep an eye on these guys after they leave your place, okay? Forget about them, they are covered."

"Thank you, brother. I will see you tomorrow then?"

"Yes, some time before the game. I'll let you know." He was about to click off the phone when he heard J'lome calling, "No, wait, wait a minute." He stayed on the phone.

"My brother, you know this will work out, it always has before, hasn't it? It was never an easy path for any of us, but look at us now. As we are getting on in age, I think you can see that the grand design of our lives is going to be one of success although probably never overnight for any of us. There are solutions out there, everywhere, to a multitude of problems, ongoing as well as the usual pile of unscripted, unwanted daily crap that lands in your lap." Vinny was stunned by his use of the salty language and told him so.

"I'm not perfect, just forgiven."

"I thought that was for the Christians."

"Whatever...let me look for some inspiration in the Koran for a business project. Should be able to tie it in somehow."

"A little divine intervention would be a nice thing. We'll talk tomorrow, alright? Speak to you then."

"Good night, brother." Vinny clicked off the phone and almost instantly started brooding again. So much shit all happening at once. In his mind, he always spoke like a thug, but never in a business meeting and never in front of a woman. He always wondered if this apparent duality was a sign of some sort of deeper psychological problem.

His rage was starting to smolder again, fighting through his disciplined inner calm. His dream and his friends' all at risk because of this nonsensical preservation society. A group of blue bloods who more than likely were incredibly bored with their lives and got off on screwing around with others. And that wasn't all. He felt his friends were losing their sense of self, the glue that keeps any human being from the edge of the abyss. Home problems, work problems, getting older everyday problems, love and lack of love problems, physical pains popping up all the time now. Boy oh boy, are we all turning into old men before our own eyes?

He forced out the warm feeling from his heart again and it was definitely calming. Maybe it was his dinner with Maxie. It was so unplanned. All of a sudden she was there on the street and a few hours later, they were saying good night as if they both had the best first date of their lives. Strange how it all happened when he was definitely not thinking of love and relationships.

It doesn't happen so quickly, he thought. It's a dance, almost an intellectual exercise figuring out your own feelings beyond the obvious ones in your pants. Vinny was smart enough to realize that no man could ever possibly know the depths of any woman's soul, but somehow she touched his heart...quite effortlessly. He thought again about what she said about the pier. Was she his advocate? He didn't know, but it was apparent to him that a solution was coming around to him, if ever so slowly. He moved to the end of the booth and stood up, a little shaky as he had been sitting and thinking for almost eight hours. He heard one of the few popular songs he was able to sing halfway decently over AJ's sound system.

"But I tell them there's no problems, only solutions," he sang flatly.

"John Lennon you're not," AJ reminded him. He walked over to her, grabbed her by the shoulders and kissed her on the cheek. "Take care sweetness."

"Okay. Hey, are we going to be alright on this thing?" She didn't bother to hide her concern on her face. He turned back to her halfway to the door.

"Yes we are. Somehow it will all work out."

"You want some advice?" she asked. "Something you won't read in a book?"

"Sure, what is it?" She walked right up to him and looked up into his eyes.

"Listen to what a woman you like or admire has to say. There could be some hidden wealth of information in what she says." She smirked a bit, twisting her hips when she said it. He couldn't resist smiling.

"Why do you people keep us guessing all the time? Is this a sport that females love to play against us?" Now she laughed.

"I'll never tell because even though I love all of you guys, you are all still on the other team. I can't divulge industry secrets." He laughed again and turned for the door, waving over his shoulder. He was thinking about what AJ said. Could she have known somehow about his night out with Maxie? Nah, he concluded, still thinking about the tidbit she offered. He disappeared into the increasingly chilly evening, recalling once more what Louis Pasteur once said: "Chance favors the prepared mind." Prepared I will be, he thought, for anything that might come my way. But what could it be?

DAY THREE

MORNING

It was looking like a real winner, thought Michael. It was the weather he was thinking about, because he had not a clue as to how the rest of the day was going to go. He was happy about the card game at least and very much looking forward to it. That part of it would go well. It was always a guaranteed fun time with the boys whether he won or lost.

He had mapped out the day the way an M.I.T. Professor of Physics approaches a lesson plan. He had figured the day had to be equal parts fun, interesting, including hopefully something she had never done before, other than socializing with me, that is, and hopefully it would all hit the mark. And he was going to do it all somehow managing to avoid any romantic overtures. He already had a relationship of sorts with her, strange as its parameters may be to others, and at least if they were never able to consummate anything, be it now or thirty years from now, at least he would put together a date that no other clown would be able to match. If he tried to push anything else on her, their friendship would crumble.

He would give anything to know what her true thoughts were

the first time they met. He often wondered if they were similar at all to his. He had to figure there was some low, low flame living there, staying alive through the years, through other dates for her, both horrible and exciting, through relationships, both horrible and exciting. He was confident that already he had established something with her that none of these other clowns were able to blot out completely.

Then again, it was also entirely possible that he was a total fool, thinking himself a little more important than he really was in this lady's life. Really, what was it? Nothing more than an interesting friendship. He reminded himself once more that he was married, rubbing his left hand which was a little lighter in weight that day, his wedding ring off his hand for the first time. That would remain the only indication of his, what...expectations? If he managed to kiss her good night, then it would be just that. He was looking over the wall into Central Park, where they parted yesterday. He was amazed at all the tourists out on the street at eight o'clock in the morning. The sun was high and climbing higher, everyone was smiling, one of the magical moments when everyone knows spring is finally here. What perfect timing, he thought, as he completed his turn in place and then he saw her.

She was just exiting the subway station at Central Park South and Fifth Avenue, and it hit him immediately how interesting it was that they were able to see each other immediately through the throngs of Europeans and Midwesterners. She was far enough away that he could take her in with just the movement of his eyeballs, not tipping her off that he was actually looking her up and down. He came to the conclusion that she was easily the most beautiful woman in the city. She was wearing a pair of fashionable black jeans that appeared to be cut just for her, tight enough to get attention, but not enough so that all imagination was lost either. Her hair was tied back in a ponytail which further accentuated her sharp features...cheekbones out to here...and she wore a slightly frilly white blouse with a yellow cardigan. She walked toward him on a pair of flats that left her at about five feet nine...what she must look like in a little black dress, heels and a string of pearls, he was thinking...with her smile, she was a perfect complement to the beautiful New York spring day that lay ahead of them. He had to suck in some air so he could speak.

"Good Morning, glad you could make it," he greeted her cheerfully but not overly so. The day just started after all and he didn't want to scare her off.

Her heart was racing from the moment she boarded the subway for the short trip under the East River over to Fifth Avenue. Please just allow me to have a nice, peaceful day, she begged silently. I don't know what is going to happen, or where we're going, or what we're going to do, but I don't want to feel any guilt about it. I'm forty-two years old and I've done everything correct in my life, always played by the rules, and what did it get me? A few nice vacations, some okay relationships, some decent sex...so what? I would like to experience, before I leave this planet, a truly memorable moment with a man. I thought I had one going just a couple of nights ago...well, whatever.

She knew this was a terrible rationalization, but even if she slept with Michael tonight, and then stood at the pearly gates the very next day facing down Jesus and St. Peter, she would know hers had been a proper, not perfect, but very proper life. It was getting a bit lonely, she had to admit to herself. She had very few friends left and the family still after so many years held her in contempt for leaving the old country. She hadn't spoken a word to some of her brothers in over twenty years. None of them had even visited the United States, let alone having tried to settle here, make a go of it in New York or Boston, or L.A, or wherever.

One dream, two dreams, three dreams, dashed. One that never really got started, one that she dabbled with, played with, one that was firmly in her grasp but had to let go as she refused to spend any more time with a man who also loved the bottle. She managed to avoid that kind of prison unlike so many of her old girlfriends and, she suspected, a couple of her sisters-in-law. But she started catching herself wondering if the benefits would have outweighed the burdens and especially the problems looming on the horizon like a thundercloud for a woman like her, for any woman for that matter.

The bucking of the train shook her loose from these poisonous thoughts and she considered herself in the reflection of the rectangular window of the subway door. She liked the colors she picked, the casualness of it, but would he? Well, she considered further, I like it and if he doesn't, well then maybe he isn't what I thought he was. But this isn't romance, she reminded herself for the millionth time in the past twenty-four hours. He even said as such. But would I like it to be? This she asked herself while she held onto the pole, her ankle trying to wrap itself around it, her hands gripping lightly, allowing her body to sway with the rhythm of the train as it hurtled toward the city. She always hated vanity, but she had to admit to herself, I look pretty good, and he will think so as well.

So now she had exited the station, turned to her right to look up Central Park South, where she figured he would be waiting, and was delighted to find him immediately. He was wearing jeans as well, a pair of somewhat ugly brown shoes, and a blue shirt with a polo player logo. His sleeves were turned up slightly to reveal strong wrists and hands. She could see him smile once he saw her and its effect was magnetic, pulling her toward him with the most confident strides she could manage without the slightest hitch of uncertainty. Those eyes of his, a blue that no painter could ever hope to find on his palette, were pulling her in, his voice, the deep resonating sound that spoke words of confidence, humor, and friendship all these years was like a call to her to come home. She answered him a tad too breathlessly, but she was now beyond caring about things like that, "I wouldn't have missed it!"

الله

"I wouldn't miss my morning prayers for anything or anyone," Aubrey told his prisoners/sidekicks/cohorts, whatever. They were heading toward the Saab which was parked further up the street, about one hundred yards away from the door of J'lome's mosque.

He could see the almost indiscernible disdain on each of their faces with the required prayers for members of their shared faith, in spite of dealing with the fear and the enormity of their individual and shared situations. He didn't know what he hated more, the various shades of infidels in this disgusting city or lapsed Muslims like these two. They had the privilege of birth into Islam and they then treat it like an old sweater, only proper to wear when they were comfortable, when it suited them. Ultimately his flashes of anger with them were subsiding quicker now as he was committed to their deaths—along with the woman—as soon as they effected the transfer of the money.

He fully expected within forty-eight hours to be in Europe being introduced to other secret cells his benefactor had told him existed due to his personal sustenance. Aubrey wanted to revive their dormancy and establish their own brand of Islam in Europe, where many of the faithful had settled over the past thirty years under the noses of Europe's racist legions. He was sure he could then supplant Al-Alwaki in Yemen as the most famous American Muslim soldier of The Prophet.

But first he had to get his hands on this woman. He had decided that Whathefu would die in her presence—what purpose did he serve anymore anyway?—this would show her and the fat African—who was whom he really needed for his expertise—how committed he was to this goal and erase any thoughts they might have of trying to escape or defy him.

"When this is over, I could definitely see immersing myself in the faith," said Whathefu. He leaned into Aubrey slightly, "My father is very well-connected in the kingdom, you know..." No shit, you fucking homo, thought Aubrey, he loves and respects me more than you. "And he can open some doors for a man like you," Whathefu continued, sounding like a college recruiter speaking with a high school sports star.

Aubrey told them both, "All of that will be settled later. The only thing we need to concentrate on is to get hold of this woman and to make her do what we want." They approached the car parked about one hundred feet up the block from the mosque, Aubrey indicating to Andre that he should drive. Aubrey rode silently in the passenger seat trying to remember the exact way back to Laura's house. They approached the east end of Queens Plaza, a confusing jumble of intersecting intersections with two branches of the subway roaring over their heads. Andre in a moment of clarity, understood the look on his kidnapper's face and offered, "Don't worry, I know where I'm going." He wanted to know more about what they planned to do so he asked, feeling safer from this man's violence when he was driving the car. "How are we going to do that, you know, get hold of her?" Andre asked him. Aubrey considered a moment before answering. Yes, I do have to engage them to some degree, he admitted to himself. He turned a bit to Andre, who negotiated the twisting lanes smoothly and broke through a crack in the traffic to hurtle along Jackson Avenue.

"Do you know anything about her? Does she date anyone, attend church, jog in the park, anything?" Andre shook his head no and turned left on Twenty-First Street and then a right over to Vernon Boulevard. This way he would avoid driving past the police precinct, he informed Aubrey. He continued west and hung a left on Vernon where they passed several friendly-looking cafés filled with young artist and hipster types eating and drinking. Andre noticed one couple feeding cheesecake to each other and wished he was there feeding his beloved Kismine in the same manner. The evil bastard was continuing to speak and Andre concentrated his listening again, keeping his eyes peeled for a good spot. He pulled in behind a tradesman's van that was just pulling away from the curb. They were near the corner, able to look behind them for the pedestrian traffic exiting the subway. She would have to walk right past them. Andre turned the car off and settled back in the seat.

"You," Aubrey was jabbing his index finger in Andre's upper arm. "You have to talk to her initially. She knows who you are, you're in the same line of work, therefore you speak the same language. You have to make her understand in the first three minutes of when we make contact with her that she has to comply with all our demands. I don't want to hear anything from her except for total obedience. Is she a troublemaker at work, loud or offensive?" he asked.

"No," Andre replied, "When I think of it, she's actually very quiet and studious. It seems sometimes as if she isn't really there in the room with you, she's so quiet." Aubrey liked this and was ready to consider her just another pliable immigrant, no matter how long she had been here.

"If she complains in just the slightest way, that is when I will smash her knee with this," he said, pulling his jacket aside to remind them he had another automatic pistol as if they might have forgotten about the first one or the knife. I'm sure she will be in full compliance after that. All we can do, minus any intelligence on her comings and goings, is sit by her place for the rest of the day. Sooner or later, she has to show up and we will be ready," he told them, twisting toward Whathefu in the back seat, coming down hard on the *will*.

Aubrey told Andre to move a little closer to the intersection to make sure that there be no room for another car to park in front of them. He didn't want anything or anyone blocking their view. He liked the spot, he knew they would find her. She had to come home some-time after all, didn't she?

—⚬—

Michael and Laura entered the park at the southeast corner, dodging multitudes of sketch artists, tourists, and lovers all clamoring for a piece of the great oasis in the center of Manhattan. She wrinkled her nose at the powerful stench of the manure left from the horses pulling the hansom cabs.

"Any real New Yorker would never ride in one of those," Michael told her, pointing at the carriages.

"The horses look sad," Laura replied, clinching her nostrils.

"Better than the glue factory, I suppose." He noticed her holding her nose against the stench and asked, "Didn't you grow up on a farm? I'm surprised that bothers you." She was pleased that he had remem-bered that she had told him a bit about her childhood. He, as a city boy, had listened to her stories of going out into the wild to capture horses and cattle in order to increase the family's herd with amaze-ment. She also told him about how she would be the only one who could break the horses because they didn't trust her brothers. With that he was starting to understand how she got those muscles he could see beneath her sweater and her jeans.

"I think they need more water and better food. It never smelt that bad as I remember, although that was a long time ago."

"Well, if anyone ever asks, you can tell them we talked about shit all day." She blushed at his choice of words. She always hated vul-garity, but had to admit it was a funny line and couldn't help laughing.

"I only rode a horse once. I was sixteen, and I was dating a girl in Connecticut..."he was cut off by her look of pure astonishment. "What's so funny?" He asked her as they continued to stroll past the pond.

"Dating"...she shook her head in a sorrowful way..."That was so impossible for me until I came to America. I was twenty-three years old, could you imagine?" In fact, no, he couldn't believe it. But then again he didn't grow up in rural Argentina with all those brothers. He remembered her rattling off their names one Christmas party, years ago. She was then thinking of Diego...would she have liked him to be here now on this beautiful day? What could he possibly be like now? Did that relationship ever really exist for me at all?

She looked a little lost in thought so he decided to change the subject. They were still walking north, along a path with the pond on their left and he swept his hand out to the water.

"This is where my mother used to take me when I was a kid. I would sit right there," he said, pointing to some rocks that jutted into the water. "There wasn't any fencing here then. The park was a little shabbier than it is now." Laura followed his gesture to see the rocks where he had sat as a boy, taking notice that several turtles were sunning themselves there now.

She said, "Now the turtles would fight you for room."

"Right. Anyway, I would fashion a fishing pole out of a tree branch and use a small piece of tightly wrapped aluminum foil or a soda can flip top in order to fashion a hook. I would sometimes use a shoelace as my fishing line." He looked sideways at her, "I took it out of my sneaker first." She smirked, a cute smirk at that. Make her laugh, his inner voice told him. Every woman you have ever quizzed on the subject told him that a man who made her laugh was a great find.

"Anyway, the little golden perches and larger goldfish they had in here then would come up to the hook I made and basically sit around and laugh at it." Could that be a metaphor for his life? Lots of chances but none of them so far taking the bait? Michael knew he was a successful man by most standards, but he also carried with him the burden of believing that somewhere, somehow, greatness awaited him. And he hungered for it, an escape from the ordinary, from being just another guy from Queens. "Count your blessings," his dear Nana had always told him...so hard it became over time to do that and especially so more recently.

"It's a good thing you didn't become a fisherman," she said, breaking him out of his momentary loss of place. She laughed when she said it and then continued, "Sometimes I laugh when maybe I shouldn't, you know, like when you stub your toe on the corner of your bed and you fall down? I know I shouldn't because someone can be really hurt, but I can't help it. It's gotten me in trouble a few times in the past." They continued past the pond, the Bow Bridge on their left. Not wanting to mingle with the tourists posing for pictures, he guided her slightly east and north again.

"I once saw this guy riding a bicycle down Lexington Avenue, you know, one of these guys with a bicycle designed by NASA, with the yellow jersey, helmet with rear view mirror, and the stupid looking tight shorts? I was stopped at a light and he hit a pothole right next to me and went head over heels over the handlebars and landed in the street flat on his back. I jumped out of the car, and stood over him to see if he was still alive, and as soon as I could see that he was okay, I burst out laughing in his face. I felt bad about it but I couldn't help it."

"So if I laugh at you later if you trip and fall into the horse shit, you won't be angry?" Beaming smile accompanying the question.

"No, I may actually do it on purpose."

"Why?"

"Because I like to hear your laugh and see your smile. A perfect addition to a perfect spring day." He pointed to the roadway as soon as he said it in order to wash the compliment down a bit, "Let's go this way." He did manage to hold her gaze for a moment or two in the wake of his little verbal jewel and then stepped over a low railing into the roadway, she declining his outstretched hand for support.

⚓

Maxie Carter was thinking about how beautiful the breakfast always tasted on a spring day on the balcony, and it depressed her to think it was the only thing she looked forward to anymore. Most married couples look forward to one moment of pleasure per week, that seemed to be the standard of sorts...she did the same thing, but it was with a meal instead of a man.

She was thirty-two, married 'late' as her mother had said more than a few times, but to a good family...her mother also reminded her of that several times per week. She never said anything about what kind of man she was married to.

She had certainly heard that a marriage will usually start to fade within seven years or so. Kids, careers, schedules, added weight, familiarity with each other...all of that combining in quite a simple fashion, unnoticed until the knees and the spirit start to buckle, overtaking any passion that existed at the beginning, when they first saw each other.

"How could I have been so lonely?" she thought, recalling their first date, a blind one although his head and shoulder photo she was provided by her friend looked pleasant enough, even kind of handsome, the first time she looked upon him and gave him the millisecond in length look over that all women seem to be able to do instinctively, she could only come to one unmistakable conclusion: he had a fat ass.

But he was good looking and he was kind of charming and they had a few decent moments. She seriously thought of breaking it off several times before she found herself all of a sudden on an altar nodding yes to an Episcopal priest and then a reception that she did not remember, and a vacation to St. Martin which she remembered for two things. The far end of the beach of the resort being so close to the only airport's runway, would provide comic relief in the way of watching unsuspecting guests being blown off the beach by the thrust of the jets taking off just across the street. The other was that her husband hadn't touched her since the wedding, a behavior to be continued for the duration of the honeymoon.

And so it was for the past four and a half years. They attended smart little parties that were given by smart little people who bored her to tears with the greatest of ease. They did not go to the beach, which she loved to do. They did not go to the movies, which she also loved to do. Their days and evenings were endless. All he had an interest in was trading within his family's massive Merrill Lynch account, which he recently shifted. Her exhortations against lifting the account from the adviser who guided it so well for twenty-five years were ignored. She was horrified at the way he treated him, a decent and honest man who always protected their money while providing pretty decent returns throughout the years. Her husband dumped him as if he were nothing, instead dropping all his money into an account run by someone she had never heard of who had an office in the Lipstick Building on Third Avenue. She was repelled by all his efforts for he created nothing. Flipping papers, making trades, and a recent interest in real estate speculation.

I could be a great law professor or nurse, she mused often, telling herself that it still wasn't too late to start. She still had the bulk of her parent's estate under her control as she would not ever relinquish those precious funds to her husband to be gambled with. The apartment's stock and proprietary lease were in her name only and would remain that way. School would have been simple to accomplish. There was plenty of money and they had no children to look after. And the most boring of school classroom subjects would have been preferable to another dinner party at the newest 'must be seen in' restaurant with her husband's snooty friends. She could find work maybe out at her alma mater St. John's, or she could revive her nurse's license and go back to work at the hospital.

She was enjoying her simple breakfast of Fruit Loops in a bowl with milk, a sliced apple, orange juice and tea on the balcony, overlooking the East River. What a nice day, she thought as she then started to struggle what to make of it. Maybe a walk through the park later. She decided to stop at Shakespeare's statue, at the south end of the mall, to watch the tango dancers. Maybe someone would ask her to dance even. If not, she could walk up to the band shell and take a spin with a young salsa dancer. All of a sudden, her husband banged his way onto the veranda and dropped into the seat opposite her, not even bothering to say hello. He banged his plates on the table but not on purpose. It was just his way of further establishing to anyone who could observe that he really didn't belong in any civilized setting, Maxie thought. He was eating oatmeal and white toast, which she thought described him perfectly. She almost slept out here last night, his snoring was so loud. He snapped his paper open and then folded it into a tiny square so he could read with one hand and eat with the other. Maxie thought this posture aged him about forty years.

Instead of dwelling on the bland uncaring individual in front of her, she allowed her mind to wander, and she didn't have to go far. The impromptu dinner she had with Vinny was at the forefront of her mind. And it was not only the rugged good looks he had, although she could easily see herself on his arm on any street in Manhattan whether they were wearing evening clothes or jeans and tee shirts. She found him fascinating on several other levels as well.

In spite of the obvious tremendous pressures on him, he seemed as cool and collected as an international jewel thief. His intelligence was on display with everything he said and she was quite impressed with the empire he built from scratch, just like her father had. Even when he wasn't speaking about the philosophical works of Hobbes, St. Aquinas and Kant and how he interwove their different views on all aspects of the human existence into his business and social life, he seemed completely at ease with himself. No self or even unconscious touching and retouching of his body or his arguments. He said what he wanted to say and he believed in it totally. He was fairly well dressed last night, but not in anything that was meant to impress because of the label. She was astonished to learn he usually purchased all his business clothes at the thrift store on Seventeenth Street in Chelsea, which contributed all of its profits to AIDS-related causes. None of her friends would ever think of looking in the window of a thrift shop, let alone buying something there. They wouldn't even buy something wholesale...'too Jewish' they would say.

His friends and his relationship with them also fascinated her. Not only for their longevity, but also for their apparent cement-like foundation, unshakeable and permanent. He depended upon them as much as they depended upon him. They were almost symbiotic in their appearance to an outsider. She frowned thinking of her own 'friends' who laughed at the 'dese, dem, and dose' people who mostly lived in the outer boroughs of New York City. The firemen, cops, sanitation workers and yes, the teachers and maybe even the nurses as well. Maxie had a St. John's law degree, but wanted to be a professor of law, rather than a partner in a big firm. Maxie recalled how so many of the firemen and police officers rushed into the towers, and she recalled her tears at their fates and her disgust at her husband's attitude of indifference toward these brave men and women. To him and his collection of people he called friends, the neighborhoods of Long Island City, Sunnyside, Astoria and Jackson Heights just across the river were nothing more than places to be driven through on the way to the Hamptons. They were all so wrong because she knew it was in these small two-family homes, apartments and tenements that the best and brightest minds of America's future were being nurtured. Her grandparents started their sweater business in a factory on Colden Street in Flushing and it was filled with immigrants of every stripe and shade, and she clearly recalled her grandfather describing each and every one of them as his family, the reason for his success. When the factory burned down in 1973, he paid all the wages of each employee for one year until he reopened. In her eyes her grandfather was a true American hero. She smiled at the thought of the dinner once again and found herself looking forward to seeing his ruggedly handsome face once more, eating number fifteen and number twenty nine at the nice restaurant downtown, and talking about anything other than interior design, the newest place to be seen, the latest...whatever.

"Maxie," her husband addressed her from across the table, as if he were about to give an order to a secretary, "I got a call from Calvin Waples this morning about the Pepsi sign project. Is it dead?" He never looked up from his commodity and stock tables as he asked the question. She refused to answer until he looked at her. It took about ten seconds, but he finally put his paper down and looked over the table at his wife for his answer.

There was something she didn't like in the way he asked the question, as if the answer to some riddle were riding on the answer. What the hell did Calvin Waples and his ultra snotty wife have to do with her role on the Preservation Commission and the building project?

"What do you mean by that?" she answered intentionally rudely with a question of her own, eating the slices of apple with her fingers, wiping the juice away on her faded old jeans. He looked at her with obvious distaste which is exactly why she continued to do it. Next time I'm going to suck the fruit's residue noisily off my fingers.

"Is it dead and finished, that's what I meant by it, it's a simple question." He turned back to his paper halfway through the question. Her fury was rising like steam in an overheated nuclear reactor.

"I am not in any position to kill a project, as you so put it. I'm not interested in killing anything but rather preserving what is good and irreplaceable in the city. The name of the board I sit on is called the Sutton Place River and Environmental Preservation Society, in case you've forgotten. I need to remind you we have no official powers, especially in a case like this whereby everyone in government in the city has put a stamp of approval on it." He laughed at her response into his newspaper which he began to raise in the middle of her answer and took another spoonful of oatmeal into his mouth. Maxie wondered if she hit him hard enough would the spoon penetrate the back of his throat and sever his spine.

"No one wants this deal to go through for this River House project, don't you understand that?" he asked her as if she were a simpleton. His face was buried in his paper when he asked but he then dropped it on the table with a slight flourish once the last syllable of the statement passed his teeth. She had always thought her colleagues' fierce opposition to the placement of the sign was entirely unwarranted and frankly, a bit silly if not outright stupid. There were more important environmental issues affecting the waterways of the city and more significant buildings to be considered for landmark status instead of a stupid sign. The steam was working its way up through the valve of her patience.

"What on earth are you talking about?" she asked, with the right touch of annoyance in her voice. She wanted his attention now and the framing of her query was supposed to guarantee just that. He turned in his chair and faced her now. What a dog he is, she was thinking, so easy to push and pull according to her whim.

"Calvin Waples and his investors, including your colleagues on the Preservation Commission, thought they had the option on the land sewed up some time ago and were furious to learn that Mr. Malloy had acquired it. Now, with the outer boroughs looking more and more attractive for development, they want it back." He settled back in his chair and swiveled one quarter-turn like a turn-of-the-century robber baron, picking up his paper again and his spoon, clinking it around the ceramic bowl to scoop up the last remnants of the oatmeal. The steam was at the top of the pipe and the whistle was about to blow. It was speaking again...

"In addition, his wife Tiff-Whitney always wanted the red glow of the sign to play into her windows just right. Something about capturing the natural sheen of the silk paneling she had picked out." He was smiling when he said it, as if he were sure his wife would fall right in line with the joke. "The angle gets ruined if the sign is moved further north on the lot, as the project design calls for."

"Also as the construction permit issued by the city has allowed it to be," she retorted. Maxie was sitting straight up now, barely able to control herself. Her husband casually waved the comment away.

"Ultimately that won't mean anything if the two male members of your august body have anything to do with it." She thought of the other two members of the board. Were they in on some back room deal? She asked him so. He opened his paper again, ready to fold it once more into perfect little rectangles like some half-assed origami practitioner. Was he convinced this made him look more...urbane? The way a smoker thinks he looks tougher with a Marlboro dangling from his mouth? "Of course they get a piece, they get their tribute. They're the ones who reached out to the bank holding Mr. Malone's mortgage commitment."

"Do you think you're in some kind of mafia?" she shouted at him. "Are you aware you sound like Tony Soprano and Hyman Roth?" She leaned back in her chair, the disgust dripping from every pore, looking out over the river at the stalled, almost dead project...five hundred jobs. Apartments for hundreds of families and others who can't afford to live over here in the city. And she was apparently a patsy in it, set up by this spineless bastard. She turned back to the building just south of theirs where Calvin Waples and his horribly entitled little wifey lived with their perfect terrace, perfect children, and their slightly less than perfect silk paneling. The steam control was now nonexistent and Maxie leaped from her seat and brought both palms crashing flat on the table, overturning the glasses of orange juice and water she set out. Her husband jumped in fright in his seat, disrupting his rectangles.

"Who the hell do you think you are, screwing around with people's lives and their livelihoods?!" she yelled at the top of her lungs, the question one long angry inflection Her husband tried to be defiant and dropped the paper on the table, causing it to fan out to its original shape.

"Maxie!" he quietly but angrily exclaimed, swiveling his puny head here and there as if someone else were within earshot on the twenty-fifth floor, "Your language, please," admonishing her as if she were a child which had the effect of enraging her further. She grabbed his newspaper and flung it into the wind, the pages separating and falling like drunken seagulls all over the East River Drive.

"My language? That's what you're concerned with, my language? Who in God's name is going to hear us up here anyway?" she retorted. He was starting to stand but she commanded him to sit with an extended index finger, "Stay in that fucking chair!" She came around to his side of the table, put her right hand on the back of his chair, her left flat on the table and bore into him with her eyes.

"Are you telling me that I am now involved in a plot to steal this land out from underneath this entrepreneur, a man who fought and sweated his way through life, someone who created something from nothing, just so this little witch wife of your mealy-mouthed Ivy League friend can have her paneling glow properly? And also enrich yourselves with development of the land after you've stolen it? Do you people even have a plan for the property? Who the hell do all of you think you are?!"

"We happen to be..."

"Shut the fuck up!" She backed away from the table, throwing her hands up in the air and leaned up against the wall. She was so enraged, she didn't know what to do. She didn't know if she wanted to jump off the porch or throw him off. More than four years of listening to this scheming, squirreling little Napoleon, screwing with people's lives and dreams, and all because he wanted to play the role of determinator. Who should fail, who should succeed, what type of career she should pursue, how often, and where. What was wrong with her? She could practically hear her father screaming the question at her from the heavens. She noticed a flock of Canada Geese flying in a V formation coming in from across the river. It startled her, the perfection of their movements, the large number of birds—there were almost thirty, she figured—the configuration appearing very unusual to her. One of the geese suddenly broke away, and headed north, up the river and over the Fifty-Ninth Street Bridge. She regained her composure and looked down at him, still sitting in his chair, still shocked into submission by her outburst.

Tiredly she spoke again, "This is a beautiful project, a perfect project for the waterfront of Queens, one that will enhance the view of everyone who has an apartment in this building, did you ever think of that?" She angrily stared at the man who seemed to be shrinking before her eyes. He was mute under her lash. "I thought so, pompous dummies, all of you. How about the jobs this project would produce, hmmm? Did that ever cross your minds? How about just making one more stretch of waterfront in this city a little more beautiful and pro-ductive? New York City makes less use of its waterfront than any other city in the country. Taxes would be collected, other jobs would be available in small businesses that would open up around the project, I could go on for an hour about the virtues of this development."

"But Calvin wanted to get hold of the land again. It's better for us if he does it. He's our friend so we would get a piece and he would build something probably nicer than this other person has in mind." She stared at him uncomprehendingly, overwhelmed by his failure to grasp this situation for what it truly was, his lack of knowledge of the site's plans, what she possibly wanted to do for a living and how this sort of subterfuge would tarnish her career permanently before it started, his appalling selfishness and apparent ease of acceptance of the sort of dishonest and slimy backroom maneuvers her father always cautioned her against. "It's never worth it, Maxie, I don't care how much money you can make," he would tell her over and over.

"You know what? Fuck Calvin and his neurotic little shrew of a wife. If he were on the ball, the option would have been his." Her husband had opened his mouth to protest but she silenced him again with her index finger, which she pointed at him like a samurai's blade. She continued, "Had he envisioned the future like this man has, if he sweated to get his financing together in time as this man did, and if he assembled a build-and-design team that got all the permits together as once again, this man did...if he even tried to do any of that, then maybe he would have the option. But he didn't do shit and that's exactly what he got, shit on his pointy little face." She allowed him ten seconds to respond, which was just a breather for her, as she had no interest in what he had to say.

"I don't think I care for your language, Maxie, first of all. And second of all, I care even less for your approach to this problem." She stared in amazement at the boldness of this person, her husband...how did that happen, really? Obviously she was never within his narrow field of vision.

"What you're doing is illegal. I am a licensed attorney, and you have me mixed up in the sort of shenanigans that could land someone in jail. Calvin is screwing with a process that possibly involves public funds, definitely public agencies, did you ever even think of that one?" Her hands were on her hips and she was towering over him, mocking him with the question. She continued, "Well I am not going to jail for anybody, especially you." She turned and stormed through the door, the wake caused by her abrupt departure creating a breeze on his face. He could see her grab her coat off the rack, the one she bought at the Barney's off-price sale years before, that was the dominating thought in his mind while his eyes were following her, wanting to stop her from heading out the door. He jumped out of his seat and followed her.

"Maxie. Maxie!" He was trotting a bit across the wide room. Finally he caught her elbow and spun her around. She looked at him as if she was going to kill him right there and then, but he had to make his final stand.

"You have to realize that you're in it as well now whether you like it or not. In addition, you can not divulge anything about what I've told you this morning. You are my attorney as well as my wife." He crossed his arms after he said it and Maxie was wondering if she was going to hear him pronounce, harumph! She leaned into him almost seductively, and took his tie loosely in her hands...who wears a tie to breakfast anyway?...she did like the feel of the silk as she kneaded the fabric between index finger and thumb. She gripped it, but did not pull his head down as she really wanted to do.

"I just want you to know two things. First, I am removing myself from all aspects of your personal life and all present, past, and future business interests. Secondly, I am filing for divorce tomorrow. I don't know what ever came over me, that I would allow someone like you to touch me. But I now know exactly what you are and it sure doesn't feel or sound like a man, at least not the kind of man I want in my life." She released his tie, turned the knob and pulled the door open but stopped halfway and faced him once more.

"Remember this is my apartment, I am on the stock and lease alone. I want you out of here tomorrow. Stay at the club...or Calvin's. Or go see that other oily bastard out in Montauk you gave all your money to, Bernie what's-his-name. But don't be here when I return."

"I suppose you will spend the night with your developer friend, hmmm?" Instantly, almost as if she had never left, she was back in the room, facing him down.

"Excuse me?"

"I know where you went Thursday night. I have some connections in this town, you know."

"You had me followed?" Her eyes were narrow slits.

"I got a call," the smugness returning.

"So you know that I went to dinner with Mr. Malloy last night? Well I'll tell you something. All your little snitch would have been able to tell you was that we only spoke with each other...never kissed or touched. You know what we spoke about? Anything and everything. Except for his project. Never once did he mention it. And that right there tells me that he has more integrity in his little finger than you have in your whole body." She was holding her pinky in the air and let it drop into a fist for a second before she brought her hands by her side again.

"Frankly I found him fascinating, not because of his good looks of which he has plenty, but because he engaged me in an entertaining conversation about his upbringing, his friends and his devotion to them, his different philosophies of life and circumstances. He was a brilliant conversationalist and I enjoyed his company completely. All of the slimy U.N. diplomats and their hookers and your suckass friends with their shitty little parties you dragged me to all these years...a bunch of hypocritical, elitist, racist, anti-Semitic bastards, not one of whom could find their own ass with both hands unless their daddy helps them out." She had raised her speech in volume with each passing syllable. But she once again had her composure in hand and started for the door.

"He never made a pass at me and I never felt that he was all of a sudden going to lean in for a kiss. He impressed me with his broad knowledge in a wide variety of subjects and his ability to convey interesting points of view in a concise manner. I can't even remember the last time you and I had such a conversation, or if we ever had one at all."

"His project is dead, Maxie. You have to accept it."

"Unless there is evidence that fraud is involved or if the pier comes down by itself," she answered. She quickly added, "I told him that, by the way, but he already knew it. We're finished, you and I, the marriage is over. I would rather spend the next twenty years looking for a man who can stimulate me intellectually, screw me creatively and vigorously, and who would never ask me to invest all of my trust money with some guy named Bernie which sounds like a name for a fucking teenager, not a businessman, who doesn't even send you a fucking monthly statement when you ask for it." She was exiting once again now, but not before reminding him to pack and leave before she returned. She didn't slam the door behind her and he was he was glad she hadn't. The neighbors might complain.

⚊⚊

Twenty minutes of slow walking brought Michael and Laura up to Shakespeare's statue, at the south end of the mall that led to the band shell and Bethesda Fountain. It was among his favorite places in the park. The early spring shoots were just starting to add a tincture of green to the scenery. There were hundreds of people out now, just walking or sitting, watching the show walk by.

"I sometimes dance tango here on Saturday nights during the summer," Laura said. "It's free, it's nice."

"It was always a major drawback with me when it came to dating because I didn't dance," he confessed. No problem with it now because he wasn't ever going to really date this lady. He shuddered at the memory of having to go to a disco once in a while in the late 1970s with his friends, standing there like a statue, hating the music, the culture. "Tango looks like fun, though. I actually took a few turns at a milonga held in an open square in Amsterdam many years ago. I think I still remember the basic Argentine step." She often wondered why he had never asked her to dance at any of the office Christmas parties and now she had at least half the answer and it made her feel good for some reason.

"I am so surprised that you even know what a milonga is. Most New Yorkers wouldn't know what that word means." Laughing a bit now, she followed up with, "Were you any good?"

"No, it was just an event I ran into by accident when I was on vacation there. I remember it was called, 'La Noche de Elegance'. A lady from Peru taught me the basic steps...she wore a green blouse and jeans and I thought she was beautiful, and the uhh friend I was with said that for me, it was more like 'La Noche de Blusa Verde' instead of the night of elegance." He turned to face her. "I was blessed and cursed with a great memory. La Noche de Blusa Verde and other moments like it, I will remember forever. I even remember her socks as well... they had embroidered bicycles on them. Amsterdam is full of bicycles and those people take their bike riding seriously."

"Did you ever see her again?"

"No, I went to the casino after the milonga and won a few thousand Euros at roulette. Number nine was the winner." The next thought was shared equally by them although of course, they couldn't know it: I will not dance tango with him/her...probably.

"Let's make it around the statue just once, let's see what you remembered from your Peruvian lady from long ago," she suggested without thinking, he then taking her elbow gently and moving her to an area where they could start even before she finished her suggestion. "We won't be late for...wherever we're going?"

Who gives a shit?

"Yeah probably, but it's okay. We can be a little late to our second stop as well." The Yankees will probably win anyway. He was moderately terrified now as his dancing skills were never, well...existent. What the hell.

"Let me apologize in advance for stepping on your toes." He took her into a semi-embrace and rocked back and forth a bit to get their timing together. This was the closest they ever stood next to each other, the first time they ever touched. The Peruvian lady came back to him with her lessons. He could see in his mind's eye her beautiful hair piled on top of her head, her magnificent hips, alluring eyes, and enduring patience with a young student with two left feet. "Don't push heavily with your left hand, keep it away from your body, don't look to your right, lean in a little bit, bend your knees." He counted out a tango beat and stepped back, to the left, then stepping outside and turning his torso slightly to the right leading with his right foot, he continued with his left bringing them together, forward with the left again while she stepped smartly into a cross and he ended the step by stepping right and bringing his ankles together, leading her gently but firmly throughout the step. He started to step away, but she squeezed his hand, beckoning him to stay.

"No, no...let's do this some more, one complete turn around the fountain. I'd like to try a few things," she said. She couldn't believe she had established such a nice dancing connection with him so quickly. Laura had talent on the dance floor, but always felt stiff and unable to relax, causing more than a few partners to grow frustrated with her and tell her to loosen up before they dance again. But she could feel

Michael's gentle but firm grip on her hand, the roll of his chest, and when she gracefully lifted and placed her left arm around his shoulders, she was greatly pleased with the shape of his body. He had compelled her movements very well, never pushing too hard or stepping outside their circle.

"How can I refuse?" he replied.

So around the fountain they went in that fashion, ignoring the stares of the tourists, several of whom were snapping photos of them, she helping him to turn her into a series of ochos at the end of which she stepped into an embellishment that resulted in her leg wrapping itself around his momentarily before she snapped it off in a powerful and elegant fashion. It took almost ten full sets of the basic step before they finished their revolution around the statue. They had started in a casual semi-embrace but had finished much closer, his hand slipping toward the middle of her back, just under her shoulder blade. She felt her left breast pressing against his chest. Time to release, she thought and backed away from him, holding his forearms as she stepped backward.

"That was lovely, thank you. You're actually pretty good for a beginner. I'd bet you would be great after a few more milongas," she told him quite honestly.

"Thanks," he replied, getting a little red in the face. He looked down at the ground like a kid in the schoolyard. A young tourist approached, took their picture and told them they looked soooo cute together.

"It's a lot like drumming, what with the improvisational possibilities and of course you have to keep good time. That I can do, but the actual dancing, well, I'm a little stiff." He turned toward her. "My friend's wife once said to me I had a little Patrick Swayze in me." He smiled to set up the very necessary self deprecating remark. "I told her that I guess maybe I did if she believed so, but he was definitely better looking, richer, had a better body, he was a famous celebrity, aaannnd...a much better dancer. "Shall we?" he inquired with a raise of his eyebrow, gesturing toward the path that led through the mall. She was thinking then that as nice looking as Patrick Swayze was in that movie in which he played a dance instructor, she preferred Michael's company.

There were hundreds of people on the mall on this fantastic spring day, its wide expanse and rows of benches on both sides providing ample opportunity for bucket drummers, jugglers and some pretty decent street magicians to showcase their talents. Tourists from the four corners of the world were milling about, soaking in the atmosphere. They covered about one hundred yards also soaking it in.

"Where are we going? Do you have a destination or are we making this up as we go?" she asked. He answered with a question of his own.

"Do you like art?"

"Sure, are we going to the museum?" She hoped not as she wanted to stay out in the sun on this glorious day. And she wanted him all to herself.

"No, not the museum, too many people and the Metropolitan is too big. It's such a nice day I don't want to spend all day inside, right?" He looked at her askance and she thankfully agreed, shaking her head no.

"I'm not some big art student, but I've always liked Monet's work and I saw that a gallery up on Seventy-Seventh Street is having an exhibition. We should be able to see everything in about an hour at the most, and then we'll be on our way to our next stop."

"Great. I like the outdoors, I grew up in the outdoors and I love all types of athletics and games that you can play outside."

"Well, the next place we are going is an athletic event, but we will be sitting and watching." An inspirational thought hit his mind then. "Actually, maybe we can do something athletic, I'll work on it while we're being cultural at the gallery. I hope you like it." I will, she thought, as long as you continue to be so charming, funny, and... simply irresistible. She sniffed at the air, much in the way a comical resident of some European palace might do so.

"We'll see," she said, looking sideways at him with an impish smile, her cheeks starting to hurt from the workout his humor had been giving them since the morning. He caught her comment with perfect timing, coughing some imaginary phlegm into his hand like an English banker with a severe head cold.

"Onward, your Majesty. Mr. Monet is waiting for your perusal of his works." They continued up the mall, laughing together as if they were the only people in the park, looking very much like teenagers in love. All the tourists loved them as much as the flowering trees and a quite a few more snapped their picture.

—ﷲ—

Tony Craig, Federal Agent, twenty-seven years on the job with some of the worst postings an FBI Agent could ever have, was boiling mad at the moment. He stepped out of his boss' office in downtown Manhattan wondering what it would be like to just go back in and shoot the man he just met with, the head of the New York office of the FBI, Biff Chetlington. Tony had entered the academy with Chetlington and they quickly became enemies, a doing that was strictly of the latter's choosing. He had entertained many theories over the years as to why the man had targeted him virtually from the day they met. Maybe it was Tony's good looks, combined with a calmness that made women quietly swoon whenever they met him. Maybe it was that he was six feet two and one hundred ninety-five pounds of muscle and sinew and that he could take a punch as well as give one. Another theory was the innate ability Tony brought to the job, an ability to read a situation quickly and accurately, especially in the area of human nature, this he had learned in the streets of Woodside, Queens, just a couple of subway stops away from Sunnyside on the 7 train. His father's side of the family had a great number of men—and later women—who had chosen to join the ranks of the NYPD. Most had made Detective or better. Tony had the first one's Patrolman certificate hanging on his wall. It was signed by Theodore Roosevelt, then the Police Commissioner, dated at the turn of the century. He loved to listen to these men and women talk about their cases, never letting on that he was listening probably more intently then some of them were. He loved hearing about the people involved in criminal matters...why did they do it? Most of the crimes his Uncles would talk about came down to appallingly bad decisions and/or timing. In one example, a woman is shot, hit by an apparent stray bullet. Apparently she was the pillar of her society, doing God's work her entire life, not abandoning the mean streets and housing projects and their citizens although her family had begged her to countless times. Something like this, he recalled them agreeing, it goes nowhere, maybe a few days' investigation until the brick wall hits you full in the face and the case goes cold because something else even worse happens so quickly as to put an amazing tragedy similar to this one on the back burner.

Another story...a young mother and her teenage daughter gunned down in broad daylight. No one on a busy street sees a thing, of course, because to talk to the cops about anything is considered sacrilege in many of these neighborhoods, but this isn't a case of a lonely church lady with no friends or social life. These victims had family, friends, co-workers...all of whom immediately pointed to the ex-boyfriend, who had been jealous of anything and everything he could think of throughout the short, tumultuous relationship he shared with the single parent: her own daughter, a boyfriend from umpteen years ago, the woman's own ex-husband whom she hadn't seen or heard from in over ten years. It took them fifteen minutes to get an address, another hour before he showed up, and the confession was heard in the station house in time for lunch.

He remembered how riled they still were about the church lady, though. They wouldn't let go of it, they were like snarling dogs each with a grip on the last bone. He listened to how they 'scoured' the neighborhood, which he took to believe was that they beat the shit out of every mutt they could find until something, anything useful came out of them. After a few weeks of this, something did fall out of the broken mouth of a local loser. The nice church lady apparently liked to take in an occasional movie at the Center Theater on Queens Boulevard and this person swore she had a date with her. A man...hmmm, all her family said she led a sheltered life. Maybe not so sheltered. Can we examine her personal effects a little more closely please? they asked of her family.

A card was found hidden in the binding of a personal diary, a boring Hallmark type of greeting, the extra prose it contained..."You are the colour in an otherwise drab and gray world"...was all. No signature, no envelope, maybe some fingerprints later, but this was 1967. The forensics then were not as sophisticated as they are now. Tony had to meet Uncle Pete that afternoon for an afternoon Met game. The new rookie pitcher Seaver was starting. He found them all around Uncle Pete's desk poring over this card as if it were the Dead Sea scrolls, concentration screwing their faces and deepening the lines on their foreheads. Several of them had hands as greasy as a mechanic's from running their fingers through their brylcreemed hair in some attempt to massage more blood into their brains to help find something about this one tiny possible clue. When Tony looked at the card, he had only one thing on his mind. That it was twelve-thirty and the game started at one o'clock. "C'mon, Uncle Petey, let's get out of here. Can't these other guys pick up the Brit you're looking for?

Eight large Irish heads swiveled toward him at that moment. He was instantly frightened by their scowls. These men had been the fathers he never had and were always patient and loving. Now they looked as if they wanted to strangle him for interrupting them.

"What did you just say?" This from his Uncle Pete, a decent man married to his mother's cousin, a serene ex-seminarian whose voice never rose above a whisper but was so tough and strong he once opened a coconut on a vacation in Jamaica with his bare hands, karate chopping a slice out of it in front of an astonished Jamaican gardener, then ripping the husk apart, spilling the water inside on the sandy soil. The gardener had flung his machete in the air and skillfully brought the coconut down and Uncle Pete, in an apparent effort to show how tough a New York cop was, did him one better. Tony was looking at those hands now resting on his uncle's desk, the fingers clasped in a show of control, but his knuckles were white. He asked the question again and Tony stepped forward and stabbed his index finger at the card, which his Aunt Marie, 1st Grade NYPD Detective, grabbed out of mid-air, before he could touch it.

"Because we don't spell color that way. With a 'U,'" said Tony. He punched his mitt to indicate to Uncle Pete they should be going. The adults all looked down at the card...and smiled. After a few quick orders from Uncle Pete, they all dispersed and Seaver that day mowed down twelve Houston Astros and the Mets won seven to two. Baseball games in those days only took a little more than a couple of hours and by the time Uncle Pete got back to the station house, the others had brought in one Paul Madison, a British national who quickly admitted that he was upset that the church lady rejected his suggestions for romance and he felt his only chance at redemption was to shoot her down. They all thanked Tony for his help but swore him to silence that it was he who figured it out. No sense confusing the chief of Detectives, right?

Two years and two days later, the same crowd was sitting in Uncle Pete's den on Long Island late at night, glued to the television in anticipation of the first human stepping onto the surface of the moon. A little before eleven o'clock, as Armstrong came down the ladder, Tony's ditzy Aunt Riki continued her daylong speculation on the fate of the astronauts once they opened the hatch to descend to the surface. Earlier, the guests had been treated to such gems as 'Would they be hit by some fast-acting disease?' "Maybe there was a predatory moon animal lying in wait for them...maybe another civilization living on the dark side of the moon would invade the side that faces earth to rid itself of the interlopers."

"You never know," she offered as Armstrong stood above the lunar surface, "maybe they will sink into the surface of the moon when they step off the ladder." This was actually picked up by the rest of the group and given tacit legitimacy as the astronaut stepped cautiously down the ladder. Tony swiveled his head around at the adults, who were all sitting on sofas and chairs maneuvered from around the house for the best angle.

"Hey Aunt Riki, dontcha think the spaceship woulda sunk into the ground? It's heavier than a guy, right?" He held their collective gaze for a moment, the men started to laugh uproariously, Uncle Pete pointing out to Aunt Riki..."Gotta admit the kids got you there, Rik," which earned him a playful sock on the shoulder. Tony was glad he was able to make them laugh, what a great feeling. But when he turned back to the television, Armstrong was already on the moon and Cronkite was asking about the quote he just heard from the astronaut. Tony was pissed off he missed the moment of the century just so he could be the wise guy in the room. He thought of that moment often in the many years that have passed since, and he was recalling it right now.

He had done okay he thought for a poor Italian/Irish kid, raised by a single mother as so many had been in the old neighborhood—everyone's place where they grew up was the 'old neighborhood' whether it was Astoria, Woodside, Sunnyside, Rego Park, or Elmhurst—altar boy at St. Sebastian's, baseball and basketball for the CYO teams, sometimes latching onto a PAL team which he loved because he was able to meet other kids from neighborhoods close by who didn't share his heritage, skin color, religion, or observations on life. He knew what a great education it was along with learning how to play the game he loved even better.

His mother decided early on that he would not fall prey to the drinking marathons in the bars along Roosevelt Avenue, filled with Ralph Kramden-type dreamers, outright losers, and not a few IRA gun runners and boosters. Too much heroin was filling up the streets as well, making these respectable-looking, working class neighborhoods as junkie-filled as any of the wastelands of Bedford-Stuyvesant and the South Bronx. She had grasped the depth of his intellect early on and was determined not to let him be educated at Long Island City, or Bryant High School, where shootings and stabbings were more common than college-ready young men and women.

He and his mother had driven around New England every weekend for several months, interviewing at Exeter in New Hampshire, Choate in Connecticut, Berkshire in Massachusetts, finally settling at a school that had prep status, but was fading from its past glory in the carefree early 1970s, Trinity-Pawling. The main reason was that a scholarship was available for a young man like Tony, who possessed not only excellent grades but supreme athletic skills as well. He was a great pitcher, basketball player and soccer star, never seeming to run out of breath as he traversed the field or court as if it were his own private domain. His leadership skills were apparent from his first day on the campus, the seniors drawn to him even though he was two years younger. The handful of female day students all longed for his company.

The friends he made there were different from his friends in Woodside, kids who had fathers who taught ambition and confidence and molded their sons in their own images, not anyone else's. No rock star, no teacher nor social philosopher reached the ears and brains of these kids as deeply as the messages they received from their older siblings and parents. They were taught to think they were special, royal even, a concept that was so simple to Tony he decided if he ever had a son, he would raise him the same way. Sure many of these kids were held up by trust funds, but he also watched most of them push ahead with their dreams and ambitions with total abandon, as if they didn't have a pot to piss in or a window to throw it out of...nothing at all to lose.

These were friendships he wanted to nurture so that they turned into lifetime relationships and frankly, with all the connections that grew out of such a society. He had no interest in mining his friends' social networks for strictly personal gain, he wanted to belong, to transform himself from just another guy from the old neighborhood into a man who was a part of the fabric of the upper reaches of society, a respectable man about town, someone his uncles on the force would be proud of.

He brought this philosophy of living his life to Boston College, where he got good grades, had many fun times and even fell in love with a girl he met at a party who didn't speak much English but just enough that they both knew something was there. He could still see her sitting in the room, strangely ignored by most of the others in the room because of her less than perfect language skills, or was it because she was so beautiful? Is that why she wasn't being approached? She had a purplishly-patterned dress and a string of pearls and when she crossed her legs and rested her head on her hand, she looked like Sophia Loren in her early twenties. They became friends quickly and he learned to love her quickly, but she had other plans for her life that couldn't include him, namely, moving back to South America. He tried to spend as much time as he could with her, but one day his knock on her door brought only the gnarled face of the landlord, the scratchy voice that went with it informing him that she had left permanently for her hometown. She left him a letter that was so full of love he accepted her reasons and apology for leaving in the middle of the night through real tears...but she had to return to care for her parents. She also left him a picture from the night they had first met...it was exactly how he remembered her and he carried it with him to this day. He never had a serious relationship after that. Plenty of women...but none that stayed around longer than six or seven months, frustrated by his unwillingness to commit.

He would walk by her house from time to time and look up to her window on the third floor, hoping against hope that she would appear and flash him that warm smile and wave to him, indicating that she would be down in a moment, knowing all the time that she was eight thousand miles away and thinking of other things, other situations, other men. It never failed to profoundly depress him but he couldn't stop himself.

He was accepted right away into the FBI Academy upon graduation from law school, always earning good grades once again as well as the respect of his peers. He attended law school at night, graduating in two years, never bothering to take the bar exam because it was an FBI agent he wanted to be, not someone doubled over in a cubicle in some white shoe law factory in Manhattan or Chicago or Boston, checking comma placement and poring over endless reams of dry testimony searching for that one kernel of truth that would lead to more billable hours and the opportunity to destroy someone's life or business.

But maybe he should have done just that. Maybe, probably, he should have insisted to the girl in the purple dress that they get together in spite of the distance. He could travel to South America once a month, maybe even move there. Maybe it would have been more difficult for her to leave knowing that he had some sort of plan for life that included love and peace and happiness. She seemed a little put off by the idea of being with a cop...what was an FBI agent but a cop with a fancier badge?...she told him stories about the police corruption she had seen in her home country and others throughout Central and South America. He had hoped that his desire to uphold the law for everyone equally, the way it always should be, would shine through and become obvious to her, but apparently it wasn't going to happen and he knew once again that his reticence in sharing his true feelings with virtually anyone would continue to hurt him personally and ultimately professionally.

More than twenty years now wearing the Federal badge, he was thinking at that moment. Twenty- seven years of bad postings, crap assignments, promotions that went to others less deserving than he and overall plain old shit duty. The political game just wasn't his strong suit and it never would be. He knew just enough, learned from his days at Trinity-Pawling, to be consistently on the periphery of a situation, but never at the center. Or even tied to or close with anyone at the center. He had no rabbi, foolishly believing that his own dogged self-determination would shine through and it would be obvious to anyone who even looked a little bit at his record.

Chetlington was always hanging around his career like a freaking spider, Tony feeling his privileged, manicured hand in most of the postings and transfers and less-than-wonderful assignments that didn't take into account in the slightest his natural investigative skills. He didn't consider himself a paranoid individual. He was standing by when Chetlington received the heavily desired postings in New York or

Los Angeles or foreign assignments in Paris or Rome. All of the shitty counterfeiting jobs he ran down in Anchorage or the bank robbery in Helena that he was assigned to always seemed to have Chetlington's stamp. This order or that recommendation coming from an associate or friend or college buddy of...Chetlington's. There was a pattern there, he felt, but Tony was always busy working these small cases, shuttling here and there, and never bothered to really look into it or even speak to Chetlington about it. All of a sudden, it was 2007 and he had so many years in, and the great break was not going to come in his career, he was finally accepting that now, and he seriously started to contemplate his retirement. Maybe go to her home city and sit in sidewalk cafés for the rest of his life hoping the girl in the purple dress would happen by one day. He would be like that dog that faithfully sat outside Shinjuku Station in Tokyo for years waiting for his master to return, unaware that the man whom he followed to the train every day had died earlier that afternoon.

Finally the posting he had wanted his entire career materialized as part of an expansion in the New York office in a department dedicated to sniffing out homegrown terrorist suspects and sleeper cells. He had spent the past several years there working with good, dedicated, smart people who figured, quite simply, that with our porous borders and open society, that there must be underground activity worth checking beyond the clowns in white sheets and hoods and the occasional madman like Timothy McVeigh. Tony had developed and maintained strong contacts within the NYPD and they seemed to trust him instinctively, something that was a bit lacking among his Federal colleagues.

Maybe he should have just stayed home and been a cop for the city, was a standard torture routine he ran through his brain several times a week. By now he would have had made First Grade Detective, had a house in Putnam or Suffolk County with some kids and a nice wife for whom he would buy a purple dress. He would have built up a huge pension, probably a hundred grand a year for the rest of his life. But the eventual conclusion to that never-ending conversation with himself was always the same, You didn't choose that path; you chose this one. And now, it was truly blowing up in his face as he walked back to his desk in the wake of one of the most infuriating conversations of his life.

"Biff," he started once he realized he was losing his boss' interest, "I'm telling you, this guy is up to no good. And I'm not only talking about what he did to his wife." Chetlington was now leaning back in his chair, staring at the ceiling, thoroughly uninterested in what Tony was saying.

"Honestly how do you know?" he asked, holding his hands out palms up which he then slapped down on his thighs in a peevish, frustrated manner. The door to his office was open and everyone else could hear what was going on.

"I received a call from an old friend, from the old neighborhood we both grew up in."

"Oh, that's great, another of your buddies from the local force, another flunky cop brought in to screw things up for us." His hands were now straightening his lapels and he then threw them up in the air, coming to rest behind his head. His pomposity surprised even Tony, who thought by this time in his life he had seen it all in terms of people who thought who they were.

He really started bristling a half second later at the haughtiness of the comment, the putdown of the NYPD from a fellow law enforcement officer. He continued, in spite of the chilly atmosphere Chetlington was creating. He would not allow himself to be swayed by this man, not now, never again. And especially not with this situation because he set himself going forward with the belief once it landed in his lap that something big was going on. He hoped he was right about that. Because his career would either finally take off, or go down in flames with this one.

He replayed the call he received four days ago. It was not unexpected on any day that Dom Antonio would call, and call often. Tony was his one remaining lifeline from a close circle of friends who finally grew tired of his constant stories about Donna, his wife of ten years. How the last conversation the two of them had was as she hid from the choking, billowing smoke that was filling the Windows on The World restaurant, a few minutes after Flight 11 out of Boston slammed into the north face of World Trade Center tower number one. How he kept reassuring her that the firemen would get her out, knowing in his heart that she probably wouldn't make it as he stared up at the enormous hole and flames from the relative safety of Vesey Street. How they talked about their trip to the Caribbean just the year before, their plans for children, how she really wasn't feeling well that morning and was going to cancel her meeting, only to be overruled by Dom, telling her she absolutely should go to meet with the bankers who wanted to hear about her new restaurant plans, "Don't worry honey, they'll love you the way I do."

And those were his last words to her, as the line suddenly only started to transmit the cries and screams of other men and women in the room with her. The last human voice he heard was that of a nameless young man assuring her, "Donna, it'll be okay." And then World Trade Center tower two fell and the line went dead. Shortly thereafter, after running a mile or so uptown, he stood on the roof deck of their condo on Union Square and watched the second building drop from his view, to be replaced by an upside down mushroom cloud. He always wanted to know the identity of that young man, who was attempting to reassure his wife that she would not die a horrible death that day. He wanted to tell his family how appreciative he was of their son's bravery, but he was never able to ascertain who he was.

He never recovered Donna's body, still to this day thousands of victim's remains are still unidentified. One day he knew he would get a call as the dedicated people of the Medical Examiner's office were certain to work until all of the bits and pieces of bodies were identified positively. Of course that couldn't happen if she were completely atomized, as he had overheard many tourists by where they now called Ground Zero describe the pulverizing force of the collapsing buildings as they stood on Church and Vesey Streets and posed for pictures in front of the devastation.

He spent the next two years living inside a bottle of Jack in an abandoned cabana in Atlantic Beach, occasionally venturing out to watch the piping plovers race back and forth, chased up the beach by the fading energy of the waves.

In that same time, many of his friends had more mundane tragedies to wrestle with, such as divorce, bankruptcy, sick parents. And therefore, it was so easy for everyone to forget about Dom...poor Dom, who would become nothing more than a topic of discussion at an occasional gathering..."Anyone seen Dom lately?"...or an example of human spirit thoroughly broken, indisputable proof that you could actually die of a broken heart.

Tony, who had no wife, no siblings, found out about Dom at his own mother's funeral where after the graveyard service, he stood around by the limousines on the same block through Calvary Cemetery that Vito Corleone's funeral was staged, and the question came up..."Has anyone seen Dom?"

Tony had been chasing a counterfeiting ring operating in, of all places, Pierre, South Dakota, for the past nine months, somehow settling in there enough to manage to bust the perpetrators. The locals there, a strong, hardy people for sure, were more amazed in the wake of the busts that he was from Queens than that he was an FBI agent. At the cemetery, he was stunned to hear about the quick slide into lifelessness that his friend had taken. He ordered the funeral parlor's limousine to take him out to Atlantic Beach where he found Dom, half-crazy with his first bottle of Jack Daniels behind him, ranting like a madman at Bush, Islam, theocrats...anyone he could blame for Donna's murder.

"Dom, what are you doing? What's happening to you?" He chose his words very carefully as he knew this man had been a great street cop with the NYPD, tough on the local shitheads, loving and respectful to the citizens of his patrol sector. Now on extended indefinite leave, Tony hoped he was still one who regarded words and their nuances more telling than a perp running away from a scene. Not what have you done to yourself, but what are you doing going forward was what Tony wanted to know. Big difference. But not now, as Dom's first reaction to the question was to take a swing at Tony, bottle in hand, that missed his head by an inch or two and thank goodness for it because he would have killed him had he connected.

Dom's momentum carried him forward and Tony caught him in the gut with his knee, expelling all the air in his lungs and the entire contents of his stomach. Enraged, Dom stood somehow, but Tony cracked him with an perfect uppercut, his fist nestling perfectly in the space between Dom's lower mandibles, knocking him backward, stumbling like the great Bavaro with three defenders hanging on his back for twenty feet, refusing to go down, but ultimately giving way to the slope of the beach as well as the force of Tony's blow, aided further by the liquor he had consumed daily for the past seven hundred or so days. He fell into the sand with such force that the Piping Plovers ran *into* the water—possibly for the first time in the history of their species. Tony begged any deity he could think of at that moment to keep Dom from coming after him again.

But instead he stayed in a supine position in the sand, the cool incoming tides running around his upper body, soaking everything from his head to his waist. The Piping Plovers took flight to Rockaway and Tony sat down on the ridge of the beach, with his head between his knees. He started to cry softly for the dear sweet lady he just buried, the angel who put her life aside for him and by doing so punched his ticket for a decent life. It was when his shoulders started shaking from the sobbing that Dom finally sat up out of the water, his hands behind him, supporting him. He started at Tony as if he had awoken from a dream.

"What's your fucking problem, eh?" he asked. What do you have to cry about?" Tony lifted his head from between his knees, realizing just then that Dom didn't know.

"I buried my mom today." Dom leaned back on one elbow, the tide continuing to roll in around him but still looking as comfortable as if he were luxuriating on an expensive leather couch.

"I'm sorry, Tony, she was a great lady. She always made those cinnamon rolls we all loved, always made me feel welcome in your house." The two friends looked at each other, and Dom answered his question.

"I'm disappointing Donna, that's what I'm doing. She always hated drinking and now look at me. I haven't eaten a decent meal in two years but I've gained twenty pounds from the whiskey. She wouldn't have anything to do with me if she could see me now."

"You're probably right. But she would have kicked your ass, gotten it in gear, gotten you straightened out before you fell too far."

"Yeah, she would have." Tony could see that he was far away once again...he was on the phone with her again, he could hear the others in the room with her, alternating between hysterical and soothing.

"But she can't because she's dead. She's dead, Dom, she was never found and she's dead. So now, it's up to me to fix you up and get you back on your feet because she can't. And if I meet her in purgatory one day I know she'll get on my case big time if I don't do this for you and her." He stood and walked down to his friend and kneeling in front of him, spoke directly into his face.

"You're so fucked up that even a skinny Fed like me was able to kick your ass. But that's okay, I always liked a challenge." He grabbed his old friend's shoulders and shook him slightly.

"I will not watch you kill yourself any longer. I'm sorry I was away for a while but I'm here now. And if Donna could be here she'd agree with me. You know that." Dom shook his head in agreement, the movement causing waves of pain behind his eyeballs.

"She'd want you to stop drinking, start exercising again, retire if you want to...how many years do you have on the job, twenty? Twenty-three?"

"Twenty-four. Holy shit, how did that happen?" They both laughed at one of the most common exchanges between men of a certain age.

"Twenty-four years. That's a lot of pension. You could get out of New York, head on down south maybe. Donna would insist that you find another girl and make her happy, right? You know that's exactly what she would tell you to do."

"I know, I know." Tony stood up and offered Dom his hand to help him stand.

"So then get started. Be a Nike commercial. Just do it. I will help you as much as possible. Let's go make a fucking plan right now to pull you out of the abyss."

Six months later, six months free of any type of alcohol, five months free of cigarettes, running four miles every day on the beach instead of laying on it like a drunken manatee. Reading, writing, recording his thoughts. Reaching out to friends, apologizing for his invisibility. "Don't be ridiculous, Dom, we all know why..." that was the standard, honest answer he got from all of them. Older, busier, but all the bonds intact. Amazing how that happens. He was now thirty pounds lighter, in the best shape he had been in for years, he was retired with a pension that paid all his bills quite easily. He was loving life again...never forgetting, but living in the present.

He decided to move to South Carolina where he accepted a post of a civilian investigator for the Parris Island Military Police. Tony had made a few calls to clear him through...you'll love it, I'm tellin' you...

the weather is nice and you can beat up some Marines occasionally." Dom was an Army man. "The salary with your pension will make you live like a robber baron down there."

Six months later, he was beating up one drunken Marine per month, dating a bevy of Southern belles whose husbands had moved on to younger models, and hitting the golf courses with regularity. He finally picked up his settlement for Donna's death and he spent it lavishly on his friends, paying for a college education here, paying down a mortgage there, helping to seed a dream or business all over the place. Sometimes he and his favorite lady of the moment would skip over to Bermuda and swim in the most beautiful water either of them had ever seen.

Tony was glad he had made sure to stop in a few times when he was shuttling between crap assignments, wondering if he should have set himself up with this gig Dom now had. It was a beautiful feeling, saving a human being. And therefore it was no surprise that he would hear from him a couple of days ago, but the urgency in his voice, well that was a surprise.

"Tony, this guy here, something suspicious is up with him, something is majorly wrong."

"It just sounds like a bad marriage, Dom. What was his assignment?" Tony asked.

"He was an Army guy, can you believe that shit? He was involved in deadly training, hand-to-hand combat, knife fighting, pistols, that sort of shit. Real close order stuff, kind of like a Jason Bourne type, like when you can't beat your enemy by dropping a laser guided bomb down his chimney, when you're in his face, mano to mano. He could probably kill you with a band-aid, this fucking guy. Anyway he was the best at it, career guy, all-American type, beautiful wife who is now in the hospital and near death by his hand."

"So bust his ass, reduce his rank and get the wife a good divorce lawyer, Dom. I mean, it all sounds so routine to me. Sad, but routine."

"You don't get it my friend. This guy was the face of the Army. Movie star looks, big tall bastard...he and this lady, some recent Miss Cotton Bowl or something like that, they were the future Mr. and Mrs. Republican governor for the state of South Carolina on their way to the White House. A few years ago, while serving overseas in some sand land, he has some sort of awakening."

"Of a religious kind?"

"Exactly. Apparently he was involved in all kinds of nasty wet work over there, rough interrogations, targeted assassinations, a whole bunch of shit that makes the Geneva Convention authors retch their guts out. It obviously affected him because upon his return, he resigned from his local church and started preaching about U.S. world imperialism and the injustice of the Crusades and world domination by the Jews through the stock market and the media, really caustic shit. Anyway, the other day he punched out a chaplain, a Colonel no less, and although the good father wouldn't press charges, the MP's showed up and he beat the shit out of both of them, apparently with the greatest of ease."

"Dom, I'm still waiting to hear about why this guy interests me so much. I mean, I'm not blowing you off, but this is barely above garden variety asshole husband type of stuff."

"Listen, it gets better. He then goes home just in time to see his cutey-pie Miss Southern belle wifey tipping a grocery delivery boy."

"Jesus, just when she thought he was at church? This sounds like a bad romance novel."

"No, no...it's not like that. He's an eighteen-year-old kid whose old man is a civilian employee at the base. He set up a side job for himself doing all of these deliveries for all the wives, picking up dry cleaning, the kids, the car from the mechanic, they all love him. So this guy sees his wife giving the kid a tip for the deliveries and apparently she smiled at him and maybe Mr. Army Ranger thought something more was just transacted. He goes nuts, accusing the wife of teasing the young man into a state of *pre-fornication*."

"Did he actually say that?"

"Just that way, *pre-fornication*. The kid then thinks out loud a little too much for this guy, maybe he just uttered...Huh? And he wallops the kid, sends him off the stoop and lucky for the kid, he lands kind of on all fours and is in a position to take off. He was the one who called it in."

"I'm afraid to ask what happened to this woman."

"Bad scene. She's unconscious, probably gonna survive, but he beat her to a pulp. Fractured skull, four missing teeth, two broken arms from trying to fend off his attacks. She recalled him yelling all sorts of crazy shit during the beating."

"Like what?"

"Koran stuff, quoting verses about a woman's loyalty and responsibility for the happiness of her husband, how we need Sharia law in America, infidels, final judgment, and all this other crap. On the one hand, this poor lady had a front row seat to some of the most vicious spousal abuse I've ever seen, but she had the presence of mind to also register what he was saying and how unusual it was. She described it as a leopard shaking off its spots. She was so confused by what he was saying that it almost numbed her from the pain of the blows. Like I told you, we're talking about real church going Southern folks, and now he's going off about Allah and Muhammad."

"Dom, I gotta tell you I'm totally distressed hearing this terrible story, but I still don't see what I'm supposed to do with this."

"Here it is for ya. In the middle of the beating, he gets a phone call. The wife says he disappeared into the bedroom to answer a phone that's ringing in there."

"A phone she doesn't know about?"

"Exactly. She can hear him grunting in Arabic."

"He speaks Arabic?"

"Apparently he learned it over there. It all sounded like gibberish to her, but she understood the last two words clearly."

"Let me guess...Allah Akbar?"

"Right. And just like that, as if he were in a trance of some kind, out the door he goes into the car and heads off. We got a hit a couple of hours later on the car's EZ-Pass that he was headed north on I-95. By now the MP's are at her door and she's being taken to the hospital and when the MP's search the bedroom, they find a secret drawer with a Koran, a list of phone numbers, and several pre-paid phones, all for use in calling the Middle East. They also found an Arabic dictionary and unfortunately, what they didn't find, were his two Glocks. So apparently he's armed and on his way to either meet someone or take care of something in your town."

Tony was back in the office armed with this tip in front of his asshole boss, who was now setting an appointment for dinner at Jean

Georges, possibly the most celebrity-laden and most expensive restaurant in the city. Good to remain anonymous, you jerk, he was thinking, as he started in once again on his sale of this string of unusual behavior by a decorated soldier. Chet started waving him off immediately.

"So correct me if I'm wrong, but this just sounds like another hick who found a life in the Army and went off a little bit on the missus when she didn't bring him his beef jerky in time. Why are we dealing with this?" he asked Tony impatiently.

"A further search of the premises also turned up maps of many major American cities, and many videos of Awlaki, the American who is now in Yemen making all sorts of YouTube rants, and becoming a bit of a star in the Jihadist community," answered Tony. How could this guy be so blind? What is his problem? Tony came around his desk abruptly to check on what Chet was concentrating on so intently on his computer screen. He was hoping it would be something related to this case. But instead it was the menu at the restaurant. Tony figured he just wanted to act cool in front his friends by ordering in French and here he was practicing while one of his agents was trying to sell him on the idea of a home grown jihadist in their midst, definitely armed, quite possibly dangerous as hell, apparently on his way to New York and absolutely capable and motivated to do some pretty harmful shit. Finally Tony exploded...

"Listen to me dammit!" That kind of got Chet's attention. The man Tony Craig wanted to beat the hell out of at that moment peered slowly over his reading glasses and with barely-concealed dislike looked away from the screen at Tony like a DMV worker at 4:45 on a Friday afternoon answering to a desperate motorist who needed his license renewed at that moment. Tony continued again...

"I had the one cop you allowed me to use for this..."

"Another loser," Chet responded automatically, starting to turn his attention back to the screen with the French menu. Chet regarded local cops the way anarchists regard anyone with a full time job...with thinly veiled contempt. "His own Lieutenant wants to dump him." The struggle to maintain what was left of his composure took all of Tony's strength.

"...tail this prick and he wound up out at Kennedy Airport where he picked up this guy," he said, shoving the photo of Whathefu in front of the menu. "Do you know this person?"

"No, but I bet you're going to tell me."

"He is the son of one of Saudi Arabia's wealthiest businessmen. And he is meeting an American soldier, one who just fled his post after nearly killing his wife, quoting the Koran to anyone who will listen after receiving an inbound call from Saudi Arabia on a secret cell phone, screaming about Sharia law and Allah Akbar and all other kinds of shit." Tony cocked his head to one side. "Aren't you the least bit interested in this? Obviously the soldier was contacted by someone in the kingdom who then sent some kind of envoy, a family member no less, to meet with him." He leaned in closer to Chet, "Isn't he, the father, a subject of one of our investigations?" he asked.

"Need to know, Tony, need to know," Chet answered dismissively.

"Chet," Tony began somewhat wearily, "I have given twenty plus years to this agency, to this badge. And from day one I just went with the flow, helping out, doing whatever I could to be a team player. I was everyone's utility man...writing their reports, cleaning up their sloppiness, taking inventories of evidence, spending too much time in the worst postings an agent could have, doing all the menial tasks, always being the good soldier. Well, I also picked up a lot along the way. And I'm telling you that this guy is here for a very bad reason and we have to concentrate on him. There are too many unusual pieces all seeming to come together." Tony sat down on the edge of his desk which he knew Chet hated but he had to tower over him some way at that moment, he had to be the bigger dog in the fight.

"I grew up on these streets in Queens where a lot of these guys seem to be hanging around. I have a pretty decent inner sense of some things and right now it is clanging like a church bell. You have to let me see this thing through. Let me have more manpower, at least for a couple of days, let's see where this pair goes and whom they speak to."

"Have to?" Chet stood up quickly, "Have to?" he asked again, almost laughing the question out of his mouth. "I don't have to do anything for or to you if I choose not to."

And there it was Tony thought. A slight stumble on the part of Mr. Perfect. Do anything...to me? Why would he say that?

"What is it, Chet?" he asked quietly, like a gulag investigator questioning a spy he was on the verge of breaking. "Help me understand here and now what exactly it is that you have held against me all these years? And don't insult my intelligence by denying it, you just dropped your drawers. I can understand why you wouldn't want to do anything for me, as I'm not one of your ass-kissing, suck-up Ivy League buds. But *to* me? What did you mean by that?" Silence for a full minute followed. Tony knew, as any good salesperson knew, there was a time to just shut the hell up and wait for an answer. Chet looked over at him again and leaned forward, his elbows on the desk. Tony wouldn't move from where he was perched for the last two minutes.

"I loved her, you know."

"Who?" Tony never saw this coming. He suspected, expected a multitude of other reasons for his banishment from any of the exciting work his agency did every day. But what was this?

"Carly Lisa." From the Taft School...don't you even remember?" he practically shouted after seeing the bewilderment on Tony's face.

"Yes, I remember her, barely. She was a cheerleader. We were sixteen. We met at a dance sponsored by the Miss Porter's School, so what about her?" All Tony could really truly remember about her was that she was a typically snotty Upper West Side girl with great tits. It hit him then like a jolt of electricity.

"Are you telling me that I have endured a flood of career insults and political marginalization orchestrated by you and your buddies including crap postings, total absence of any appreciation for all the grunt work I took care of while you and your political allies were standing up in front of television cameras—blowing your covers as Federal agents by the way—all because some little girl blew you off for me at some suckass dance for teenagers some thirty-five years ago?!" Tony was astounded at the revelation. The release of this information by Chet seemed to propel him off the chair as if he were a balloon that just lost its tie.

"Yes, dammit, that's why!" he shouted. His nostrils were flaring like Secretariat's in the stretch run at Belmont. Tony was stunned that he could be so angry still, about a teenage fling gone wrong. "You made me look like a fool that night and I vowed never to forget it. And I didn't. I was thrilled when I found out you were at the academy. I knew that was a gift from heaven and I have played you like a puppet ever since. You're right...all of the postings, all of the short shrift you received...that was my work, my fingerprints all over everything and I enjoyed every minute of it." Tony seriously didn't know what to feel hearing all of this. Should it be pity, anger, or full blown rage?

Should he tell this pitiful fool how life really works, that things happen for a reason? Should he inform him that he found out years later at a reunion at Trinity-Pawling that Carly Lisa, the selfish spoiled little girl Chet loved, was actually a witch in training? That she discarded Tony about one minute after she visited his modest, two-family in Woodside, having mistakenly concluding his confidence and manners were the product of some upper crust background, not a nice little Irish lady who was a secretary in Manhattan?

Should I tell him that she did indeed grew into a real beauty, and snagged herself some Harvard MBA type, moving or maneuvering him into a classic six on Park Avenue that he could only afford if the bonuses kept on coming, a vacation home in the Hamptons that he never got to visit because he was always working to keep up with her demands, that she pushed out a couple of kids that she promptly pushed into the hands of two different nannies, that she started screwing the doorman in full view of everyone in the building and when confronted by this and evidence of her other illicit affairs, blew him out of the water with her dad buying her the best divorce money could buy, as well as getting her now ex-husband fired from Wall Street and turning his kids against him to boot? Should I tell him how much of a favor I actually did for him? The weariness was spreading over Tony like oil over a cormorant swimming through an environmental disaster. But it didn't suffocate him like some poor bird. He discarded the pity, the anger...and went with the rage. I mean fuck it, he concluded...I'm fifty-two years old, I can do other things in the investigative field, and this clown can't touch my pension. I hate that my only true love, this agency and the thousands of dedicated professionals who were a part of it, was leaving him. And all because of this smug little fuck. He pushed aside the flap of his jacket and placed his palm on the butt of the Glock pistol and stared at Chet with as much hate and indifference as he could muster.

"I should shoot you right fucking now," he said, the flat monotone of his voice and the frankness of his delivery startling Chet, who really thought he might do it.

"But not for the reason you think," Tony continued, still speaking flatly. "I never hated you, Chet, but I do now. Because people have probably been injured, possibly killed because of your impossibly narrow-minded and selfish view of every situation that has passed under your nose in the years since you've been a Special Agent in Charge. Let me ask you a question that I long suspected. Were you part of the thinking that blew off that agent in Phoenix who wanted to warn the public about Arabs training to fly airplanes prior to 9/11? He always complained that the higher-ups wouldn't listen to him. Today I see so much effort still devoted to chasing down the remnants of the mob here in New York. Why? So you can get a production deal for some Hollywood film on all of this shit? All the time you spent the last two summers chasing down a couple of art fraudsters? You liked that crowd out there in the Hamptons, didn't you? In the meantime, really important information and the educated hunches of your agents are being ignored so you can go to dinner at expensive restaurants and meet with film producers and literary agents." Chet held his hands up to stop Tony from continuing and Tony obliged him. He wanted to see how much further this clown could bury himself.

"Alright, Tony, fine...now you know. But did you ever think that maybe your tour was good for you? You were mostly out of harm's way." He leaned forward on his elbows, rubbing his hands together mischievously, sensing a point of rationality that would play well with Tony. A small point that he would try to build into a well-researched, acceptable reason like a slick small-town politician would utilize in order to improve his position. But Tony also leaned forward in response and placed his hands flat on Chet's desk.

"I didn't join the bureau to become a clerk, a gopher for you types," Tony said, still with the dead voice.

"What types are you talking about?" Tony was astonished yet again at the ineptitude of this man to read a situation. How did he ever rise so far in this organization?

"Mush-mouthed, spineless egoists, a politician who would put his own agenda first no matter if it was correct or not, no matter who gets hurt or compromised. A selfish little shit in other words." Tony jumped up again and headed around Chet's desk once more. This time Chet didn't follow him with his gaze but instead trained it out the window of his office in search of a nod from a friendly face, a potential ally. To his horror, there was none.

"Where are you going?" Chet's voice was cracking slightly with fear and concern, the pitch rising like a Koufax fastball.

"Right here once again," replied Tony full of confidence in what he was doing and saying, perching himself once more on the edge of the desk, leaning into his opponent once more. "Here is my view, simply stated...homegrown terrorism is a growing threat. They are real and they are here, in New York and Detroit, and Chicago and a thousand little towns just sitting and waiting for a signal from overseas while they insert themselves into the fabric of American society. They will not fly stolen airplanes next time. Instead they will walk through Central Park with a Kalashnikov they will just pull out of the trunk of their car. Or maybe some guy will stuff his underwear with a load of Semtex when he boards a subway train. Or maybe someone, a man or a woman will wear a burqua into a shopping mall or a supermarket with a couple of pistols and a few grenades. The new politically correct bureau and unfortunately a lot of the local police precincts won't stop these people until it's too late for fear of being branded a profiling racist. The guy who arrived in the city on Thursday is here for a reason, he met the Saudi's son for a reason, and I am going to find out why." He was leaning closer and closer to Chet, his voice lowering a bit with each passing word.

"I don't give a damn what you think of me or my theory or what your friends in Human Resources think of the report you're going to put together regarding this meeting. Fire me if you like. I have my pension which you can't touch and very little worldly needs." He was almost nose to nose with Chet now and his voice was barely above a whisper.

"But I am going to follow this through to the end of this weekend with or without your sanction or assistance. This guy told his wife he would be back early next week to finish her off, so that tells me he has some sort of assignment he needs to complete quickly. I am going to find out what that assignment is and, at the conclusion of this weekend, I will either nail him to the wall or I will drop my badge and gun on your desk and walk out of here. But if I feel in any way shape or form that you are hindering my investigation, if you try to thwart these efforts of mine, I will come back here and fucking bury you."

Tony lingered for a moment, hoping that Chet would try something physical, but that was too much to hope for. So he quickly hopped off the desk and started for the door. Pausing there, he said loud enough for everyone within earshot to hear.

"All you really needed to do, Chet, old boy, was make Carly laugh. That's all most women want from a man." Chet jumped from behind the desk and rushed toward his office door, which Tony had just turned from.

"I don't need women advice from the likes of you," he yelled at Tony's back as it continued on its way away from him, somehow managing to sound completely feeble even though his voice was raised. What a pathetic counter, thought Tony. He turned to speak over his shoulder without breaking stride.

"You're right, the only advice you should take from me is to not forget what I just told you. See you Monday." He then turned right through the heart of the cubicle farm, and then he heard Chet once more, this time with vigor.

"You're finished, Agent Craig, done, finito. No matter what happens this weekend with your stupid, bullshit hunch. You could bring me Bin Laden's head on a platter and I would still make sure you get buried in this agency, buried!"

You've already done that you little shit, Tony thought as he pushed through the glass doors to the vestibule where he caught the elevator to the street. I allowed it to happen for years, but not anymore. I will bring these guys' heads to you on a platter but the reception I get for it will not be like what you have planned, my friend. He arrived in the lobby and strode purposefully through the double doors to the street. He stood there for a few seconds drinking everything about the city into every sensory input in his body. I love this place, he thought. It's my hometown and I'll be damned if these guys plan anything here that could hurt it. I have to get back to the old neighborhood, he concluded quickly. These guys were last seen hanging around in Astoria near the mosque on Steinway Street. Wasn't the Imam there one of the gang of younger kids from years ago? He figured he should be able to run something down if he reached out for some old friendships. Hopefully, they would remember him because if he did return to the office on Monday empty-handed, it would be to visit the Human Resources office, as his career at the FBI would be over. He walked briskly up the block to hop the subway back to Queens.

—⊶—

LATE AFTERNOON

"I grew up down that block, on the corner," Michael said to Laura as they rode the number 7 train between the Lowery and Bliss Street stations in Sunnyside, Queens out to Shea Stadium.

"This neighborhood is always mentioned in the real estate sections of the papers and magazines," she replied. "Nice restaurants, cultural diversity, decent schools, you know, the typical points a broker would point out to a prospect." For him it was a million places he already visited or walked past a million times about a million years ago. There were also old lessons on the streets out the window of the train that he learned as well and he was struggling to remember all of them now.

He was daydreaming again, looking out at the White Castle where he bought donuts for eight cents apiece and those disgusting but delicious burgers for twelve cents when he was a kid, playing back in his mind their stroll down the mall and dance at the statue.

They had left the gallery, sat for a couple of hours in the park slowly eating ice cream cones while watching the tourists, strolled through Tiffany's and Bergdorf's, and then headed back to the subway out to Queens. It was a perfect spring day for a leisurely stroll with no particular destination. It was just warm enough the past couple of days to nudge several of the cherry trees to life, their full pink and white petals providing a delicious alternative to the brown splotches of the grass and the gray apartment buildings that towered over Fifth Ave. He was starting to remember that he actually did have the evening laid out time-wise so he gently prodded the day along to keep everything moving. After all, a bored girl is a dangerous girl.

He loved it when she commented that they were walking almost in sync, their strides matching each other perfectly, like a Marine marching band. I'd bet if I had my arm around her waist, with my pinkie and ring finger just barely slipped inside the waist of her jeans, the way he always wanted to walk with a girl, and held her so close that our hips were touching, we still wouldn't break stride. Have to remember to do that some day.

"I remember the first night we met, we took the walk up Broadway after the holiday party."

"Yes," she replied as evenly as possible, actually recalling every step, every moment, especially the way the tourists parted for them as if they were on the red carpet. Much as if they were a royal couple out on the town among the commoners.

"It's nice that we are matched well that way, it's actually uncomfortable to walk with someone who is either too short or tall or just a plodder. As a native New Yorker, I'm used to moving along at a pretty good clip, I hope you don't mind."

"I don't mind," she answered, deciding to play with him a bit. "I'll bet I can outrun you in a race." His mouth twisted in mock speculation.

"Are you sure? I was always pretty quick."

"We'll see later. Maybe we'll have a race somewhere."

They continued back along the path they took earlier, the sun higher now, bathing them in a warm glare that bounced off the pond. More than a few young women were now sunbathing on the lawn on their left, their bodies glistening and tight and he didn't give a shit. She turned to him and asked about their next destination with the enthusiasm of a teenager.

"Do you like baseball?" he asked in response to her question.

"I've never been to a game, actually. I watched a little bit on television once, but honestly it seemed a little boring," she said, playfully wincing. He answered quickly and confidently.

"You weren't watching with the right person. Baseball can move slowly between pitches, of course, especially with the egoistic, preening players we have now, but there is so much happening on every little play that if you understand the nuances of the game, you can see a lot. I'll try to teach you some of it, okay?"

"So I guess we are going to a baseball game?"

"It is a day of culture, so we should include some baseball in the day. Plus, I seem to remember you telling me once that you like sports, didn't you?"

"I did...and I do, but I like to play, not sit and watch." Oops, she thought, act a little appreciative, maybe you'll like it this time. She recalled the only time she went to a baseball game at Yankee Stadium, taken there by some lout whose name escaped her, who screamed at every player's every move, complained about their salaries and lack of hustle, and spilled beer on her. Well, at least Michael wasn't a classless lout, but baseball...ugh. Oh well.

"Well...let's give it a shot. We'll be going to Shea Stadium, that's where the Mets play."

"Oh, you're not a Yankees fan? I thought everyone in New York is a Yankees fan."

"It only seems that way. My dad took me to my first game at Yankee Stadium in 1967. I wanted to see my favorite player as a kid, Mickey Mantle. At that point his career was almost over, he was a shell of his former self, but to me he was, well...Mickey Mantle. Even his name was pure baseball magic. He had the most magnificent combination of power and speed and he also had to deal with many difficulties with the press and the fans when he took over center field from Joe DiMaggio, who was a legend in Yankee-land and The Mick, in spite of taking over for a legendary player who frankly never made it easy for him, established himself as a star in New York in spite of growing up in a small town in Oklahoma. And you know what happened when I finally got to see him in person? He was booed every time he came to bat. I was seven years old and I wanted to beat the crap out of all those so-called Yankee fans, and I cried all the way home. My dad, who was a Brooklyn Dodgers fan, then took me to see the Mets play the next day, and all the fans were happy and their new pitcher, a future hall of famer named Tom Seaver, pitched a shutout and two years later, the Miracle Mets of 1969 won the World Series and the Yankees were ensconced in last place. I cut out of school to see the fifth and last game of the World Series, snuck into the stadium with some friends, and then ran out onto the field when they won. I remember it like it was yesterday." He turned toward her, trying to measure the skepticism in her face, and was relieved to see that she actually seemed interested in what he was saying. Or at least she was a great actress.

"Look, if it totally bores us, we can always leave early," he continued. "It could be interesting because the Mets are playing the Yankees tonight, so the crowd will be lively."

Now rumbling along the metal elevated portion, past where the train tracks take a left to head up Roosevelt Avenue, she was aware that he continued to stare blankly out the window at the passing neighborhood, where all she could see were apartment buildings, some restaurants and bars, a White Castle and a huge cemetery when the train tracks started to bend away from Queens Boulevard. But he seemed to be reliving something, he seemed so lost in it all. Did she know him well enough to ask what he was thinking?

"So what are you thinking?"

Of course he would answer her truthfully. At some point in the future when maybe they were dating, but certainly not now. He was thinking of the wholly natural way they slipped through the gallery halls, appreciating the paintings without trying to sound like an art student. Just commenting on colors and shapes, drawing disdain from other patrons because to them, Michael & Laura were almost Philistine-like in their basic proletarian appreciation of Monet's work. Assholes.

And then the dance. He hadn't danced in untold years, and hadn't danced tango save for that one night in Amsterdam with A.J. so long ago. But the pieces of the step came back to him so quickly and their ability to walk down the street in perfect stride was even more evident when they moved around in a circle in their imaginary milonga. He wanted to tell her that this was the most fantastic moment he had spent in years, primarily because of the uniqueness of its spontaneity and the seamless participation in the moment by them, two people who never had stood closer than three feet from each other for the past ten years. I loved it, Laura, and I hope you did, too.

He turned from the window and looked around the subway car. It had started to fill rapidly as they continued past Woodside into Jackson Heights. He could hear good natured arguments and a few mild taunts from jersey-clad twenty-somethings...some of whom Michael figured would be punching each other out later...about Jeter versus Reyes, Clemens versus Piazza, the kid in the Mets' system, former Yankee Ron Davis' kid as a matter of fact, who would one day remind them of Mattingly. Fifty years earlier, it was all the same conversation, except no one wore jerseys and the arguments were about Mickey, Willie, and the Duke and the subway cost a dime. Everything worth anything to a kid cost about a dime in those days. Were decisions easier then? Or were they just made because doing the right thing meant just that, nothing else but that, and said decisions were not run through a mill of psychiatrists, lawyers, and committees?

"I was just trying to think of a way to put the game of baseball into perspective for you, as someone who didn't grow up in the states," he answered. "Do you hear these people?" he asked her, his eyes sweeping the car to indicate everyone else but them.

"Yes, are they really angry with each other or is it just for show?" Maybe there was a little concern in her voice. She could recall the *futbol* matches in her hometown and how those games very often brought out the worst in people.

"No," he replied quickly as he sensed some trepidation, some nervousness with some reason as two knuckleheads decked out in team colors, complete with hats, wristbands, and two hundred dollar jersey replicas, were vehemently arguing over whether Guidry's magnificent 25-3 season in 1977 was greater than Seaver's dominating 25-7 in the magical summer of 1969.

"Although I'll bet a few of them will get a little wild before long. I promise we'll avoid them as much as possible and remember there will be cops all over the stadium." He looked directly into her face when he said, "You have nothing to worry about here."

The train carrying Michael and Laura and countless childish arguments lumbered the rest of the way through Elmhurst, Corona, and they now pulled into the Willets Point station. He held her elbow, pausing her momentarily, so they wouldn't get caught up in the throngs exiting for the game, the car emptying quickly save for a few elderly Asians, presumably heading home to their enclave in Flushing which was the next and last stop.

They finally exited and followed behind the crowds, which quickly swallowed them up once they crossed the traverse from the subway across Roosevelt Avenue and down the spiral staircase which deposited them near the home team's parking lot, beyond the right field stands. When he was a kid and begged the likes of Cleon Jones, Ron Swoboda, Bud Harrelson and even the great Yogi Berra for an autograph, they mostly obliged through the rolled-down windows of their Chevy station wagons. Nowadays, the players drive Lexuses and Corvettes with the occasional Lamborghini thrown in and your chance of an autograph in this same spot was the same as catching a foul ball that night, about a million to one.

"One thing, Michael," as she interrupted his thought.

"What's that?" He started walking west, toward the gate that would lead them to their seats along the third base side.

"Please make sure to teach me about this, so I understand, okay? I don't want to just sit here without any idea of what I'm looking at."

"Of course I will," his voice assuring and true. "Baseball is a great game for many reasons, but for one most of all," he continued.

"What's that?" The enthusiasm was back in her voice, good...let's keep it that way he thought.

"Baseball is a great game because you don't have to be tall like in basketball, full of brute strength as in football or hockey or boxing, fast as in soccer or most track and field events, you don't even have to be in very good shape with a perfectly sculpted body. Some of the greatest players looked like me, not too tall, no big muscles, not very fast, but they had the unique ability to throw and hit a baseball. Tony Gwynn, for example, was the best hitter I ever saw, but he was kind of fat. So was Babe Ruth. David Wells and Mickey Lolich were also very big guys, but they had golden left arms and they could throw the ball wherever they wanted it to go. Mel Ott was only about five feet three, but he hit 511 home runs. And those were in bigger ballparks against arguably better pitchers." He could see that he had her attention.

"Sometimes even a mistake is a good thing. If a pitcher throws a ball that fools the batter and he manages to only tap the ball a little bit, that can sometimes create havoc with the infielders which can lead to a mistake by the defense, and all of a sudden, a game that seemed well in hand was now turning to the other team's favor. I'll give you a little play-by-play and point things out to you before and while they happen. Here we are," he announced, guiding her to the turnstiles where they handed over their tickets and entered the stadium.

—◆—

The trio waiting on Laura at that moment were once again sitting in the Saab on the corner of Vernon Boulevard and Forty-Seventh Avenue. They had just returned from a local pizza place with some sandwiches and slices. Anyone passing them on the street wouldn't think anything of them other than a few guys waiting on a friend to get on the way somewhere to watch the big game.

Across the street and a few blocks down was the bulky presence of the 108th New York police precinct. Aubrey made extra sure his subjects behaved normally and didn't signal anyone on the street or in the store. The police presence didn't concern him as much. The precinct was in the middle of its four o'clock to midnight shift and he didn't think many patrol cars would be cruising a block away from home base. Plus he was not a wanted man here in New York.

The Military Police in South Carolina, they'd want to talk to him, that was sure. But for what? A simple wife beating would be hushed over. A mandatory period of estrangement from his wife and some other out-of-town duties for a short time and it would blow over. Amazing, though, that his controller called him right at that hour. The cheating bitch has no idea how she was saved because he felt confident at the time that he had the right to kill her.

He was silently chastising himself for his lack of better judgment. He just should have walked out the door, never to return, uncomplaining and seemingly oblivious to his wife's casual screwing around. What did it matter anymore? he asked himself so often, although he had no proof of her infidelity. There actually was none, but the silent scenarios he created in his mind at the slightest suggestion of impropriety were driving him crazy as he saw her screwing strange men, old boyfriends, and maybe even a woman or two at every opportunity.

Ever since he embraced the word of Allah, and then decided to become a devoted follower of Wahhabism, he felt a purpose in his life that he could truly latch onto. His controller, Whathefu's father, quickly became the father he never had. He saw in Aubrey perhaps what his own third son of a third wife would never become, tall, strong, and brave.

The girls in Aubrey's teens, already drawn to him for his excessively good looks, the nights at the beach with his long-forgotten friends in high school drinking the hours away and smoking joints were so far behind him now the recollections of them, if they ever could be lifted out of the dusty reaches of his memory, would be a blur. Any bit of it that he did recall with any clarity did not stir any fondness in his heart for a particular moment, no matter how pleasant at the time.

The Army had been his home since his enlistment right out of high school, fourteen years earlier. It was the natural path for an unconnected kid out of West Virginia. He dove into the training, each bead of sweat, every challenge thrown at him further proving to him that he was further and further away from his despicable alcoholic parents. Those memories he could recall and often did.

How did those two stubby, shabby people produce a six foot four inch modern David, complete with movie star looks? everyone always whispered. Was he adopted? He was a star football and basketball player, the only memories he looked back upon with some happiness. The camaraderie he felt with his teammates was genuine and the games provided the basis of the physical work he would excel at later from basic through Ranger training.

There was also a practical side to his successful high school sports career.

His old man enjoyed the beatings he administered to his son, probably liked it better than sex, Aubrey concluded many years ago. His father delivered all sorts of blows to every area of his body and head with various instruments all the while insulting the perfection of his son's visage and body. Aubrey realized finally that some sort of twisted jealousy was at work here when his father cracked him in his face with a wrench. Not only was Aubrey born with magnificent facial structure and muscles that were smooth and hyper-twitchy, he was also given unusually hard bones. They were like New Hampshire granite. That particular blow would have lifted any other man's cheekbone under his scalp, but Aubrey somehow managed to recover, much to his father's astonishment.

Many a linebacker found out the hard way that the skinny-looking tight end not only had good hands, but hit them like a freight train on his way up the field. He never broke a bone, stretched a ligament, or sprained a joint. Resiliency was his middle name. But the bruises from his father's beatings remained, which he was lucky enough to attribute to the violence of the football and impromptu rugby games in which he regularly engaged.

"So you're a little less good looking today, Mr. Movie Star," his father told him once he got over his initial disappointment and shock that his son was still standing. "You'll be pretty again soon, looking like a butt fucking, cocksucking faggot."

"You and Mom brought me into this world, Dad," Aubrey calmly explained. "The two of you made me look this way, I didn't ask for it," he continued as his mother entered the room, a tumbler of Wild Turkey in her hand, a Kool cigarette wobbling between her lips. She spun her son around, took him by the lower jaw, burning him slightly with a stray live ash from the Kool in the process, and swiveled his head back and forth sending new spasms of pain into Aubrey's nervous system, surveying the damage inflicted by her husband on her son's face. She released him, drew on the Kool, and took a long swallow of the whiskey.

Her open palm smacked into the side of his face where the wrench had been just a minute before, her bulldog-like features showing no empathy for her only child's pain as she spit out her opinion, "Don't talk back to your father!"

And so it went on and on until he left for the Army and so it is now that he was sitting in this car on this disgusting street in yet another morally bankrupt city with these two assholes, neither of whom apparently had any idea how close they were to the end of their days on this planet. Their chittering filled the car like a swarm of trapped mosquitoes, the buzzing of their voices around his head annoying him to no end. But he decided long ago that he would endure it until he had the woman. That's all he needed, he concluded quickly. The woman can put this together for him. All he had to do to motivate her was to shoot Whathefu in front of her.

This woman, she could be the key to his dream of becoming a rock star in the Islamic world. He envisioned a general Arab uprising, starting in one of the North African states, such as Tunisia or Egypt, that would then spread to the rest of the disaffected youngsters of these despot-led countries. It was bound to happen according to his way of thought...he knew from his time abroad that these people lived under the heels of hereditary kings and sons of fathers who held onto power through threats of and implementation of real violence. It was strictly a matter of time. And he would then be in a position to step right in to lead them. He further envisioned the re-drawing of the borders of the Middle Eastern Arab states, maybe Iran as well, into one

Pan-Arab superpower that the rest of the world would never ignore again. And he would sit on top of it in this dream of his, as soon as he could drain this bank of enough money to finance his plan. Maybe a string of madrassas across the United States? He wanted to slam his fist into the wheel of the car suddenly recalling his situation in South Carolina. Was anyone able to trace him up here? He had to move quickly to get his escape and plan for domination of the *umma* going, and it frustrated him to have to sit here like a cop on a stakeout. Why couldn't at least all of this have happened on a weekday when he could be sure she would be home soon? But that would also mean that the bank would be open tomorrow and they wouldn't be able to do whatever work needed to be done to sabotage the computer system. The mosquitoes started buzzing again, sounding to him like a vuvuzela band at an African soccer match.

"I am going to move back home and ask my lady to marry me," Andre was saying. "And then I will make her a star," he added effusively. "She will be adored by every man in the Muslim world. She has the voice of a bird, the face of an angel, and she is as virtuous as she is beautiful."

"Maybe if she is as beautiful as you say, she can cross over into Europe and maybe South America," offered Whathefu. "I have many business and social contacts in the entertainment industry, just the right people to help your lady friend." They sounded like two posers at a C-list party in West Hollywood.

"Maybe we can have the honor of opening your new cabaret. She can do a few sets, I'm telling you, people will love her!" he exclaimed. Whathefu had told him of a restaurant idea that had come to him in a dream the previous night. Middle Eastern cuisine with an Asian flair, a full bar of course, as he would cater mostly to infidels. Dancing girls, belly dancers, beauties all of them of course, along with an all male wait staff that he would pick personally, hmmm. He kept that part of the dream to himself of course. "They would love it in London and Paris. It would easily be the new place to be. And as soon as things cooled down here, maybe we could open something in New York through intermediaries. We could keep our names out of it."

Whathefu winked at Andre as if their deal was already signed, sealed, and delivered and only the two of them knew it.

Aubrey was feeling the pangs of hunger stabbing him repeatedly and even though the turkey and Swiss cheese sandwich he bought at the deli was sitting in his lap, he couldn't begin eating. His frustration was boiling over again, his collective rage at the two mosquitoes in his midst, the anger at his wife's disgusting behavior with the young man, the tips of his fingers so close to his dreams that he could practically scratch the new paint off them and still...he had to sit here and bide his time. A patient warrior is the most dangerous kind, his Army instructors had told him and he always found it interesting that his Arab father told him the very same thing. "Always be patient," both camps continuously cautioned, "otherwise you will expose yourself and your men to unnecessary harm."

His window of opportunity opened just twenty-four hours ago with this assignment to watch this ungrateful little shit. And then, what a gem that fell into his lap! The opportunity to instantly be able to finance so much, including a new life beyond the borders of this wretched country and their laws. With the money, he could secretly fund so many operations.

How hard could it be to send a group of young athletic jihadists loaded with automatic weapons and grenades, rushing south through Central park from 110th Street, mowing down anyone they could find? Just over two miles of mostly flat ground, with it all being over before the police ever got there, ending at the south end of the park with a mass martyring. So easy to plan and start. Or maybe the subways... how hard would it be to blow up a few trains? Or buses? Just pay off the families of the bombers for their sons' contribution to the destruction of Western culture, no problem.

Maybe something at the baseball stadiums? How hard would it be for a few strapping young men to get into the stadiums through the outfield stands, again with automatic weapons and grenades? The difference with this plan would be that he would have many more waiting outside for the terrified baseball fans running out into apparent safety, only to meet their makers in the same spot where they scalped their tickets just an hour before. And it would all be caught on television. Yes, the stadiums would be better...but why not both on the same day?

And he wouldn't be quick to take credit for it either, unlike those Palestinian fools or bin Laden. Only later, once he had established himself as a true beacon of wisdom for the *umma,* would he let it be known that they were his operations. So easy...no security here...why hasn't anyone even tried to park a car full of explosives on any random street in Manhattan? They don't check any vehicles going over the toll-free bridges into Manhattan. Why not drive five of them into the city one day and set the timers for one hour? One on Forty-Seventh Street, where all the Jew diamond merchants worked, one near Wall Street, one on Fifth Avenue, and maybe another in the East or West Village, where all the liberal anarchists lived. So many of those types tried to sympathize with the cause, but they were not welcome. They were just another brand of infidel, never to be trusted, always to be considered expendable for the slightest reason.

Where was this woman? he asked himself for the hundredth time in the past hour. Certainly she should have come home at least once, to change for an evening out. Maybe she was on a date, he thought, and therefore the possibility was high she wouldn't even come home tonight if she met someone who could talk her out of her clothes.

So many of the women he met before his marriage were so quick to settle for just any man. So many settled for a no-strings-attached relationship with traveling businessmen who visited their city every few weeks. A phone call, some small talk, a cheap dinner, and then she pulls her dress over her head and fucks him in return. Just like that. Pigs, he concluded...sluts to be giving themselves up so easily. Dammit, where was this bitch. He checked his watch again and saw that it was approaching eight o'clock. He dropped his wrist back into his lap impatiently, and stared out his passenger window down Laura's block for possibly the hundredth time. Maybe she was sleeping, a little nap before going out. Did these two idiots ever consider that? The buzzing again, it was starting once more and he feared for these two as they still had no idea how tantalizingly close they were to their ends.

"I'm telling you, Whathefu, you would love her. She sings like a bird and she is sooo beautiful," Andre cooed in the manner of the besotted man, practically wrapping his arms around himself in admiration of... himself, tearing off a hunk of his chicken sandwich, the top slice of bread slipping away because of the lime and mustard sauce the counterman suggested he try, and he laughed so very hard when it dropped into his lap and on the passenger seat of Aubrey's car. Whathefu started to laugh with him, but he was really laughing at Andre, already tuning the African bastard out, his plans having nothing to do with him or his girl-friend. But he didn't laugh for long as Aubrey exploded at the jocularity between these two while they were in the middle of an operation he was putting together in a catch as catch can fashion.

"Shut up, SHUT UP, the both of you!" he exploded, wiping the errant piece of sandwich off Andre's seat. He started into Andre's eyes with pure hatred, "You eat like a pig, you know that? Why didn't you just order yourself a big greasy pork sandwich, you fat fuck?" He spun around to face Whathefu, who was already cowering, thanking his lucky stars that he was in the back seat, although he was daydreaming at that moment of being in the front seat where he could blow the handsome soldier while they drove around the city. Aubrey turned his body to face front again and took the first bite of his food, realizing that he needed energy for later. This outburst at the two idiots drained him so quickly he felt his blood sugar dive like a rock. He spoke to the windshield silently, with no urgency in the movement of his lips. His disdain for these two was at an all time high, but he was feeling some comfort in the fact that he would kill them both within the next twenty-four hours.

"We have nothing, unless we find this women. No plans, no singing careers, no beaches in Rio, no cabarets or development plans. And once we find her, we need to kidnap her, force her to do what we want, and then kill her. Do the both of you understand this completely? That there is no other way to pull this off?" He wasn't about to wait for an answer so he continued.

"I also have my dreams that could easily be financed by the riches this scheme has to offer. I will kill anyone who gets in the way or screws this up." He turned to Andre, who sat transfixed with his sand-wich still in his raised hand, still in mid-chew, and then to the back at Whathefu, who was still trying to make himself as small as possible in the corner of the seat. "So eat your food, keep your mouths shut and your eyes and ears open. Be alert and try to fucking concentrate on the task at hand!" He kept his gaze a little longer on the two of them to further his points, and then turned to this window where he could see Laura's two-family home about fifty meters away. Where the hell is this bitch? he asked himself as he continued to methodically chew on his turkey and Swiss.

The game was moving quickly and Michael was certainly glad for that. Today's modern baseball game typically stretched longer than three hours, with myriad pitching changes, sloppy play, mandatory television commercials, combined with music pumped over the stadium's public address that was positively deafening, even to a heavy metal fan. But after the first hour, the Yankees and the Mets were locked in a classic pitcher's duel, accentuated by flawless defense on both sides. Matsui hit one out for the Yankees and their fans went crazy. A group of young twenty-somethings a few rows away with differing uniform replicas, started in with each other.

"See those guys," Michael said to Laura, pointing toward the groups of opposing New York baseball fans. "I'll bet you a dollar they start to fight soon." She looked a little worried at that.

"Will it get bad? How can you tell?"

"Don't worry," he countered, "There are cops everywhere. And ninety-nine percent of the people in this stadium, even though they may be passionate fans, also know that at the end of the day, it's unimportant, just a silly game. But you know how some people can get." He looked past her slightly, just to keep an eye on the youngsters, one of whom was now standing, looking away from the game, goading a fat guy in a Keith Hernandez jersey into a brawl. Michael had to fight the urge to turn the other way to check if one of the yellow jacketed security guys was around or maybe a cop.

Endy Chavez belted one out in the fifth off Andy Pettitte to give the Mets the lead and the stadium erupted with cheers. Michael could see Laura was jazzed by the excitement pulsating through the large crowd and he didn't dare interrupt it with an inane comment like "Waddya think?" Her smile, as she stood cheering and clapping for something that she probably didn't understand completely, was as wide as her face would allow, her cheekbones straining against her skin with the effort, her teeth probably bright enough to light the entire stadium. Finally the applause died down and she sat back down, almost out of breath from cheering and clapping and the general excitement.

"That was great!" she exclaimed, followed by a humorously perplexing look, "But what happened?"

He went on to explain the home run, how the score changed, the significance of a lefty batter not known for power hitting a 400-foot fly ball against a crafty lefty pitcher who was approaching legendary status in the eyes of Yankee fans, Willie Randolph's brilliant decision to let Chavez swing away where others expected he wanted the next pitch taken.

"That's what I meant earlier by that baseball can seem boring at times, but every pitch, every play, has so much behind it. The guy who just hit the home run has forever achieved legendary status with Mets fans for probably the best catch in baseball's history, ever. And that was in the playoffs just last year. Maybe they'll show it." He pointed to the large TV screen in center field. And as if he had a magic wand, in tribute to Endy Chavez taking Andy Pettitte over the wall, the screen replayed...The Catch against the Cardinals in the playoffs. Laura was very impressed with the athleticism of the play as well as the clutchness of it, coming in the playoffs, taking a sure home run away.

"I always appreciate people who can perform well under that kind of pressure," she said. She looked away at the youngsters again, Michael following her gaze and noticing that several more were standing now, their caps turned around backward in the fashion that Michael openly hated. I need to perform under pressure over the next few days, she was thinking, and I hate it. Why should I have to be in this position? I didn't ask for it. Why do so many of these people seem to be delighted in the suffering of others? She turned to look at Michael again, who looked a little concerned. Why am I here with this married man? was her final thought. He raised his eyebrows and cocked his head to the side, beckoning a comment on her status from her. She had to admit, she enjoyed his economy of words. So many of the men she had dated in the past never shut up.

"I'm okay," she said, beaming again. "I was just thinking too much." She leaned in to say quietly, "Those young guys seem to be about ready to fight. What's wrong with them? I hate that kind of behavior." Michael shrugged his shoulders in response.

"Idiots," was all he could offer.

"I meant to ask you earlier," she started, wanting to change the subject, "what happens to the balls that get hit into the seats?"

"Whoever catches it, keeps it. People fight for the ball sometimes; it's considered a great souvenir."

"Did you ever catch one?"

"Actually I did, but I was helped by the third base coach who saw it drop from my grasp back onto the field and he picked it up and gave it to me. So I don't know if that counts or not."

"How do you know when it's coming?

"You don't. But if a lefty batter is up at the plate, there is a better chance of him hitting a ball over to this side of the stadium. A right-handed batter would more likely hit it over there," he informed her like a physics professor, gesturing to the seats over by and above the Mets dugout.

"Look, that's Hideki Matsui, a left-handed batter up at the plate. If he is late swinging on a pitch, the ball will head over this way, either a line drive, or a pop-up, or it may land lower in the box seats or if he really hits it hard, it could go all the way to the top of the stands. But it will come over here, to this side of the stadium." They were sitting in the Loge section, jutting over the box seats, between third base and home plate in what Michael always considered the best seats in the house. "I wanted you to see the whole field and all the players and I personally think it's better up here," he had told her.

New pitcher Joe Smith was working Matsui away with his slider which had finally made its appearance in the game, Matsui letting the first two go by and gaining a 2-0 count with his excellent batting eye. Smith then tried a fastball, ninety-three miles per hour and out over the plate, but Matsui was expecting another hard slider so his swing was a millionth of a second too late and he lofted a foul ball toward the stands on the third base side, right in their direction.

"Oh my," Michael said to no one in particular, then he grabbed Laura's elbow to make sure she was seeing the flight of the ball, telling her, "this belongs to us." The youngsters to their right were too busy still jawing with each other and the couple in the box in front of

Michael and Laura had just departed for beers and hot dogs. This one belonged to him Michael knew, it was his.

He cupped his hands close to his chest, recalling a lesson from his father years before. He could see the old man, many years before, could see him clearly in his mind as he held his hands under his heart and told his son, "The answers to most problems, to your most pressing questions about life, can usually be found right here." But maybe that approach wouldn't work for this situation, he started to think. He then raised his hands over his head, forming a cup that he hoped the ball, which had already reached its apex and was now on its way down to him, would settle into nicely. All of a sudden however, he was back in right field in second grade Little League, stuck out there because he couldn't catch a cold, let alone a fly ball.

Laura was cowering slightly beside him as she realized he was focused on the ball coming down and not on anything else including falling over on her. Most of the rest of the stadium was following its flight, wishing they had a chance at a foul pop-up, hoping that they would see a good play in the stands. Matsui was knocking the dirt from his spikes.

I have to catch this, was the last thought Michael had before the ball bounced off the heel of his hands and into the lap of a ten-year-old off to his left to the absolute delight of the kid as the stadium swelled with groans and catcalls. Michael sat down, turned to Laura and holding his palms up muttered, "manos de piedras," hands of stone...better known as the nickname for Roberto Duran, the great Panamian boxing champion. He was smiling as he said it and she loved his humility and it was indeed a fairly humiliating moment for him. Just then his phone chirped, and he answered, "Hello," without also dropping it.

"Nice fucking hands, Mikey, you still can't catch shit." Michael laughed as he recognized the voice of his old friend Josh Evans, who continued, "Who is the pretty girl with you?" Michael stood up quickly and looked around the stadium. "Where are you? How did you see me?"

"Look up here, to your left, in the red hat," and Michael was able to catch his friend's broad smile under the brim of a red baseball cap even from this distance as long as he kept waving and he could also see that he was holding a pair of binoculars. Of all the luck, Michael thought as he continued, "Josh, gotta go now, enjoy the rest of the game and let's talk during the week." He clicked off the phone without awaiting a response. Jesus, how could I be so unlucky to be seen here with Laura, in the midst of all these people? How does anyone ever conduct an affair without getting caught? he was in the middle of thinking when the young fans off to their right started duking it out. The cops on duty at the stadium were all over them in an instant and as they were being escorted out to the cheers of the patrons seated around them, Laura commented that she was impressed with the way Michael had predicted the outcome. He in turn smiled in a 'what me' kind of way, but he was thinking that he would love to be able to predict the outcome to this evening. As well as a million other things.

EARLY EVENING

Moose Miller had just completed one circumlocution of Manhattan in the boat and although this was one of the more pleasurable aspects of being a member of the harbor patrol of the New York City Police Department, it did not bring any joy into his heart the way it usually did. As he headed north in the East River out of his headquarters in Brooklyn at Harbor Charlie, he passed by the construction site and the Pepsi sign. He could see the construction trailer sitting on the huge site almost forlornly, like the kid who didn't get chosen in for the game.

He had one hundred fifty thousand dollars invested in the project with Vinny and the others, all of his life's savings. If this didn't work itself out somehow, he would be broke at forty-five years of age. He already had twenty years in on the job, could retire with a great pension, but it wouldn't be enough to keep his wife and three kids going. They lived in a three-family rental in Astoria just off Thirty-First Avenue that was surrounded by boisterous cafés filled with young eastern-European wannabe tough guys, along with younger girls from Estonia, Lithuania, and Ukraine with skirts so tight and short, they shouldn't have bothered. His wife was furious with him for the recent problems with the site although she thought it was a great idea at the start. Never being one to keep secrets from his spouse, he told her at once of the difficulties causing the investment to teeter on the edge of the abyss and she let him have it with both barrels.

He hated those confrontations with her...how could anyone be so adept at being right all of the time? He loved his wife, cherished his kids, but there were times he just wanted to ask her point blank what she wanted from him, what did she expect from him, what did she think she was getting into, marrying a cop fifteen years her senior, someone who loved the job and who frankly had no other prospects, no sideline business like so many other cops and firemen with their bars, on the quiet plumbing and contracting gigs, nothing but his dreams?

He was on the thirty-six footer for this shift, a sixteen-hour affair that was filled mostly with boredom punctuated by occasional moments of excitement and too often, a decade's worth of despair for the average man. In about a month the floaters would appear, the unfortunates who drowned in the waterways ringing Manhattan, kept on the bottom for months by the cold water and strong currents or just by being snagged on something on the riverbed, the gases in their corpses inflating them and forcing them to the surface. Some days throughout May while the rest of the city was enjoying the new spring's warm weather, the flowers in the park, pickup ball games, or dusting off the golf clubs, he was pulling as many as three bodies from the water per day. Suicides, accidents, crime victims, each with a different story as to their demise but all with the same ending. He was lucky, he knew, never to have had to recover a child. Others in the unit were not so lucky in that respect.

It was a beautiful night, the stars crisply bright and the usually ferocious current and unpredictable movement of the river seemingly placated by the full moon. The current was outbound, heading south past The Battery into the harbor and out past the Verrazano Bridge.

He wasn't expecting any of bin Laden's buddies to fire a missile into the green building housing the world's diplomats but an assignment was an assignment, and he had to stay alert. What was it Vinny had said earlier? A quote from Pasteur—boy did he love his quotes— "Chance favors the prepared mind." His pilot this night was a new kid with connections out the wazoo, Laurence Martin the Third or Fourth or something like that. In uniform for only one year, and now he was piloting the boat that Moose had to wait eleven years for. He probably had his eye on driving the commissioner within two years and maybe he was even going to law school at night so that he could parlay his N.Y.P.D. experience into a political career.

Moose Miller loved the water, and boats, and felt especially privileged to be part of the Harbor Unit. He couldn't understand some of the complaining he heard from his fellow officers, especially when it came to giving VIP's tours around the harbor. "What the fuck, you wanna walk a beat in Bedford-Stuyvesant instead?" he would counter. He had met many heads of state, movie and television stars on these tours and he thought he had the best job in the department, especially the day when he was ferrying Nicole Kidman around one morning and then Julia Roberts later in the same day. He remembered what the wife had to say about that. "Does that get you a medal or a promotion or something? If not, I'm not interested." He was lost in thought recalling this moment when he realized the rich kid was speaking to him.

"Moose, I need a favor."

"What is it?" he answered without looking at the former, and possibly still, young yachting enthusiast. Moose Miller on the other hand learned the waterways around the city working on the tugboats for eight years before he got his chance to join the department. The young cop stepped out from behind the wheel and approached Moose in the stern of the boat to apparently speak in private although they were alone on the craft. What does this kid want from me? he was thinking.

"My current love interest is on the water tonight and she'll be stopping by in about fifteen minutes. I think you know her, the Victoria's Secret model, Gail Nelson? You know her, right?"

"Sorry, I don't," Moose responded with as little enthusiasm as he could, "I have my own three aspiring models and ballplayers at home and they help to keep me out of the more fashionable places around town." Ignoring the not-so-subtle jab at his jet set lifestyle, the young cop droned on.

"She'll be dining tonight at her parents' in Westchester and the old man will be taking his sloop down the river and out east to the Hamptons. She would like to be dropped off here." Moose stopped what he was doing and stared at the kid.

"Waddya mean, here?"

"Well, that's the favor I need from you. After the shift, I'm supposed to meet her at her penthouse on Union Square and stay for the weekend. But I can tell she needs a little, uh, something from me because she's going to be hitting the clubs in Chelsea and if I take care of her, it will help her keep her pants on until I see her later." There was only one question Moose could have asked at that moment.

"Are you telling me you want to abandon the post, leave me alone on this boat while you bang your fucking model girlfriend? Just so she is satisfied enough to wait for you later? Are you out of your fucking mind?" Laurence Martin the third or fourth...definitely the last if Moose Miller had his way, put up his hands in a pleading kind of way.

"Come on, no one will ever know. And it's not like anyone is going to come by to check on us either." He leaned over the starboard gunwale and looked upriver. "Look, I can see the outline of the sloop's mast now. They'll be here in a few minutes." He ducked back into the wheelhouse and retrieved a bag which apparently contained some personal items. He returned to the starboard side of the boat and started waving at the approaching sloop which Moose guessed was about a fifty-five footer, a beautiful and graceful vessel that he could tell was being piloted well. It had to be to make it down the Hudson, through the Harlem River, through Hell Gate and to here. After a few more minutes the sloop changed course slightly to come alongside. The kid turned back to him.

"I'll be back in a couple of hours," he said, stepping from the patrol boat onto the beautiful yacht, tossing his bag to a crew member. He turned to Moose and infuriated him to no end when he said, "Just cover for me, it'll be good for your career some day." With that the sloop moved off down river, leaving Moose Miller alone on the boat praying that he wouldn't be receiving another visit from Internal Affairs about this new situation. Moose then made sure to cover his ass by calling after the young cop as he started to embrace the beautiful young woman who just appeared on deck who was apparently this Gail Nelson, "Don't for a fucking second expect me to cover if the Lieutenant or Sergeant calls in looking for you," which was answered by a casual kind of go fuck yourself sort of brusheroo wave behind Ms. Nelson's back. The sloop continued to move off to the kind of evening Officer Miller would never know...and that didn't bother him at all. What did bother him was how it seemed as if everyone in his circle, save for the boys, personally, professionally, were targeting him as someone you could manipulate. And he didn't like that one bit.

─·ıl·ı·─

Vinny was sitting in his office in the trailer on the construction site just a couple of hundred yards away from where Moose Miller was contemplating the possible end of his career. Interestingly enough, Vinny was doing the same thing. He was reading for the tenth time the stack of warning letters from creditors he was holding in his hands, all of whom expected to get paid with the initial release of funds from the construction loan for the work they had done so far...once the funding from the construction loan had come in, *sigh*. All of his remaining properties were now mortgaged to the nines, loans he also expected to start to pay off with the initial release and totally later on once the complex was finished and the rents started to come in. All in all a very well-ordered and thought-out plan brought to its knees by a trio of blue blooded assholes.

He thought yet again about Maxie. What a wonderful woman she seemed to be, too bad she was married. Strange that she would accompany him to dinner that way. What was really on her mind? he wondered. She didn't seem the type for a one-nighter. Not that Vinny believed she would be sent to hell without an electric fan if she just wanted to get laid...maybe her husband was a jerk who hadn't touched her in years...but she didn't strike him that way.

What did she mean about the pier? It seemed to him that she suspected something was amiss with her counterparts on the Preservation Board, but she also didn't seem ready to depart from their condemnation of the project. He bunched up the warning letters and hurled them against the wall in a rare fit of frustration and fury. He then had a strange recollection of his last girlfriend years before, a passionate woman who liked to throw her clothing against the wall of his bedroom when they disrobed for sex. They both delighted in this mindless exercise...he was convinced he was the only man who got the signal from his girlfriend that she was ready for loving by throwing her blouse at him.

He decided he needed some air and stepped into the doorway of the trailer which was facing northwest over the East River, the twinkling lace of lights somehow making the somewhat unattractive-by-day Queensboro Bridge look as beautiful as any structure in the city. He leaned out further to train his gaze toward the United Nations building, holding onto the inside of the door to keep from spilling down the stairs. He could see the Harbor Unit launch holding steady in the outbound current and although he couldn't make out anybody on the vessel, he knew Moose Miller was on the craft. It comforted him to know he was so close by, even though Vinny was on land and Moose wasn't. He certainly wasn't going to go run out on the pier to call to him either. It pissed Vinny off to no end that Moose was being hung out the way he described yesterday, all because of some drunken fool of a lieutenant he was forced to cover for who didn't have the good sense to say no thanks to the bartender and then smashes up his patrol car. He needed to have a long talk with his friend once he got a handle on his problems with the bank and his creditors. Because frankly if he didn't, his resulting problems would dwarf Moose's. Vinny's gaze backtracked north, stopping and lingering for a longish moment on the ritzy high rises on Sutton Place. He didn't know which one Maxie lived in, but he was pretty sure it was one of the few right on the river between Fifty-Second and the base of the bridge.

Vinny called the Burkes to check on their schedule and they assured him that they would be arriving on time much in the way Willis Reed walked out on the Madison Square Garden floor a long, long time ago in one of the most iconic of New York sports memories, "We'll be there just before tip-off but we promise to make a dramatic entrance." He smiled, but couldn't laugh or make a sarcastic remark. He wondered if they realized that when he clicked off the phone. He then dialed Charlie Mick for an update.

"Hello, Vinny."

"Where are you right now?"

"Strange, but I'm only a couple of blocks away from you, on Vernon and Forty-Seventh Avenue. The monkeys are staking out someone or something about a quarter of the way down the block."

"How do you know that?"

"Well," the young man started as he felt the first beads of sweat form on his brow. Talking with Vinny was like talking with his father, God rest his soul. He continued, "They are parked on the southwest corner, as far away as they can get without losing sight of the row of two-families on the block. They don't seem to ever look this way. The big one is at the wheel and I can see him staring intently down the block most of the time. A few minutes ago he seemed to give his other clowns a dressing down of sorts, but then he returned to looking out the driver's window, nowhere else. All of his concentration seemed to be down the block. I wondered if he were looking for you because of the confrontation at J'lome's, but he can't see you down there, they're too far away. That's uhh, why I believe that."

"Okay kid, you're doing good. Stay there until midnight and then come down to the game. But make sure you get the plate number first." He clicked off the phone once again. He knew he didn't have to call Michael because he said he would be out somewhere and would most definitely show up on time at ten-thirty or a little earlier. Mikey...Vinny shook his head thinking about his friend...he also wanted him to start thinking about himself for once in his life. He loved him regardless of his flaws, but would like him to just once do just that. Something for him, and only him. He dialed J'lome quickly as he hadn't spoken to his lifelong brother-friend all day and as long as he could remember, not a day went by when they didn't speak, not even when J'lome was in the clink for four years. Strangely, it went straight to voice mail. J'lome was always available for his flock or for anyone else in any kind of trouble. He'll try him again later...probably with one of the visitors to the mosque...at least the cell call would be registered and he would know Vinny called.

He wondered again about her but just for a brief second. Where was she tonight, who is she with and what is she doing? And knowing that finding any answers to those questions outside the door, on this almost dead construction site were about as likely as the male members of the preservation society, apology and retractions in hand, walking through the door. He turned back into the trailer to set up the space for the game with the chips, the beer, the table and chairs the boys would be using soon in their card game.

Maxie Carter was dead tired from walking the streets of Manhattan for most of the day. When she stormed out of the apartment earlier in the wake of her argument with her husband, she just turned south and walked zombie-like down Second Avenue all the way to the East Village, where she window- shopped in the vintage stores, loving the strange patterns, textiles, and accessories. She stood in front of one store and the shopkeeper, a twenty-one-year-old with as many piercings as someone attacked by a crazed porcupine invited her inside, gave her a cup of delicious Japanese green tea, and proceeded to dote on her as if she were a billionairess let loose in a Madison Avenue boutique with her soon-to-be ex-husband's American Express card.

She was impressed with the young woman's knowledge and salesmanship and she promised to come back again while she was paying for the multi-colored stones strung on a gold chain she fell in love with. It only cost one hundred dollars but it was more beautiful than any of the overpriced gold and diamond encrusted stuff that her husband bought for her.

She continued downtown, cross town on Canal Street, and then down Broadway all the way to Battery Park, where she was startled by the relocated statue of the orb that had once stood in the plaza between the towers of the World Trade Center. She hadn't known it was moved there. She hated the sculpture when it was in the middle of the fountain in the plaza. Just another suitcase full of wasted taxpayer money on a piece of shit of so-called art. But here, set among the beautiful trees and tranquility of the park, with its scars and dents from the falling debris of the planes and the buildings plainly visible, it radiated a certain kind of noble strength.

She lingered in the park for an hour or so, taking delight in the tourists from Nepal, New Mexico, and Nigeria lining up for the trip to Ellis Island and the Statue of Liberty. She briefly considered joining them as she had never visited either place in all her years in New York City but she realized that she would be trapped over there, a slave to a timetable when all she wanted to do was walk and think. So she headed up the west side instead, first stopping at The Wintergarden where she bought a Mr. Softee vanilla cone with chocolate sprinkles and sat on the back steps overlooking the lower Hudson and a small marina. She watched families pile into their yachts for a trip, where?

Out to the Hamptons? Or maybe down the Intracoastal to Miami? Lots of roller skaters here along with many strong-looking young men in shorts and big sneakers as well. Probably headed over to the basketball courts near Stuyvesant High School.

She lingered a bit longer watching a couple in their early fifties, the both of them good looking and refined. She loved how they walked together, like a pair of high school students in love. And she was amazed when they sat on the grass next to one another, not even with a blanket! The man was wearing a well tailored suit and tie and the woman was in a beautiful black dress with pearls and very nice high heels. And there they were, in about five thousand dollars of clothing and jewelry, just sitting together her head on his shoulder, he whispering something to her, she administering a playful slap on his shoulder in response. The scene made Maxie smile and then start to weep almost immediately after as this was the sort of moment she craved in her own life and she had to fight back any realization with all her strength that maybe it would never happen.

Maxie bit the last part of her cone, wiped her mouth free of the sticky residue and tossed the napkin in a receptacle. She started navigating northward up the newly developed path, the Hudson to her left and the new condos of Battery Park City to her right. She had never been through here, but she remembered when this part of the city was nothing more than landfill created from the rubble displaced by the building of the World Trade Center. The buildings, almost all new condominium units for sale, were sleek and seemed well built. It's a whole new neighborhood, she thought to herself, with supermarkets and cafés, close to Wall Street and other financial business locations, most with a hell of a view. It made her think again of the project in Queens she had helped vote down.

She came by a basketball court that was filled with games of all levels of play, old guys against old guys, Latinos against each other, Chinese players also keeping mostly to themselves, the faster, heavy-duty games filled with sleek young men of all ages and races sweating and straining. Maxie had to admit most of them looked pretty good...and they seemed to be good players as well. At the far end of the courts, were another couple who seemed to be dating and they were playing basketball together, some sort of foul shooting contest, the man running after all of the woman's wayward shots, never complaining about it once.

She knew what she had to do. There was no way she was going to allow this fraud to go through. The consequences didn't matter to her as long as she was able to look herself in the mirror and be happy that she did the right thing. This project was necessary for the economy and for the housing it provided, period. To prevent it at this point for the reasons her husband laid out to her, made her think of Czars, Kings, Shahs, and various Presidents for life. The exact kind of people she loathed the most. And this harassment directed at Vinny's project was emblematic of the behavior of public officials in those types of republics. She felt like a member of the Duvalier or Hussein family being part of the cover-up and she hated that fact almost as she hated her husband for so casually getting her involved in it. She would have to go to the police, CNN, the *Times*...no, not the *Times*...the *Post*. The *Post* would love this.

She continued north along the river, the on-shore breeze blowing her hair back and lifting the corners of her mouth into a smile upon her features. A young man smiled at her as she passed Thirty-Eighth Street and she demurely lowered her eyes and continued on. She stopped by the Circle Line dock, where hordes of tourists from Littleton, Colorado, South Egremont, Massachusetts, and Boynton Beach, Florida queued up for the several hour boat ride around Manhattan, easily the best tourist boat ride available in the United States. Moms and dads with their kids living in other cities, the kind of people and cities her husband and his friends would often deride as culturally bankrupt backwaters full of big hair, bible thumping, and fat butts. But it was apparent to Maxie, a Sutton Place resident for most of her life, that these were her fellow Americans and most of them if not all, looked a hell of a lot more happy than any of her neighbors in the building.

She continued to Fifty-Seventh Street and decided to turn east back toward the apartment. She would make her announcement to her husband of her intentions and then pack a few things to hold her over for a week or so at a girlfriend's house. A shiver went through her at that moment as she was crossing the wide expanse of the West Side Highway, the drivers heading north itching to get through the last traffic light before the highway opened up. Who would she call?

Maybe she wouldn't bother calling anyone. She wasn't interested in any opinions except her own, she soon realized as she reached Tenth Avenue. She could stay at her grandparents' house out in Sagaponack. It would still be closed this early in the season, the furniture covered by white sheets, the fridge empty. No problem, she concluded in an instant, they have take-out there. I'll just walk the beaches for days and speak to no one but the seagulls. She resolved to clean out her life of anyone or anything that did not contribute positively to it as her journey was wrapping up...she was now at Fifth Avenue where, if her former girlfriends were with her, would have forced her to detour into Tiffany's or Bergdorf Goodman. She shook her head at the silliness of it. How many miles have I covered? she started to wonder. It must be close to ten or so. The fatigue was really starting to set in as she crossed Madison and approached Park Avenue. The fatigue wasn't the only sensation settling in. It was also the apprehension of what she was about to do. She felt right about it in her heart, her brain, and in the pit of her stomach, but the effort of it all would drain her—the arguments over the splitting of assets. He would make an effort to get the apartment which she would never allow to happen. Her grandparents' house out east had her name alone on the deed as well but she could see him making a play for it. She knew this to be true as well as she knew her own name. She took a deep breath to steel herself for the challenge but still found it difficult. The light changed and she started across the street just as a pedicab driver, the new scourges of New York City streets, brushed past her almost running her down.

"Open your fucking eyes, you dumb bitch!" he yelled at Maxie over his shoulder continuing down Park Avenue at half speed practically daring her to say or do something. As scared as she was a moment ago, her fear turned in on itself and what came out was pure rage. She took off after the pedicab driver and grabbed the handbrake as soon as she drew up to him, effectively grinding his ride to a halt and immobilizing him.

"Hey, bitch, you're assaulting me!"

"No asshole, this is assault," she answered, adding a slap with the back of her hand that cracked across his face like a bullwhip. "Try stopping for the red light next time and if you can't do that, try stopping for a pedestrian as we always have the right of way, and if you can't even do that, then do all of us a favor and move back to whatever part of the world you fucking came from!"

"Uhh, I'm from Boston."

She released the brake and walked across the downtown lanes of Park Avenue and when she reached the median she turned back to the stunned pedicabber, "Then fucking get going back there. And don't come back to my city until you know how to behave. Fucking moron." She checked the uptown lanes before crossing against the light—which she always believed is a New Yorker's birthright—and continued east toward her apartment and the showdown with her husband which she was now relishing. All she had to do in order to retain her strength and conviction was imagine him as a pedicab driver.

⁂

Tony Craig had also spent the greater part of his day just wandering the streets of Western Queens, not blankly as Maxie had but with a certain sense of purpose that brought him to many places from his past. He had an appointment later that couldn't be moved up so he needed to kill some time. Any old girlfriends to look up, or old acquaintances he could call? No, not around here and not any that he would want to speak to who were from the dreary places he had been for the past twenty-plus years.

"Don't ever make a habit of visiting the past," his mother always said. "By visiting the past, you color what is happening in the present with the negative paint the past usually provides you with, and as a result you can screw up what is possible for the future. You can't change any of it, so why bother? The world is full of men who wonder how many blow jobs their wives gave to other men before they met, who watch a Yankee game actually thinking if they just gripped the baseball slightly different twenty-five years earlier, then maybe they would have been on the field in the Bronx. Why didn't I make that call, shake that hand, think of that...thing? The unidentifiable 'thing' that all losers refer to. Let me tell you what that 'thing' is, my son... simple confidence." He could recall the conversation word for word which occurred the night before he left for his first posting...in Fargo,

North Dakota. He still couldn't believe so many years later, that his mother had used the phrase 'blow job'.

"With confidence in yourself and in your convictions and yourself, you can get past anything. The girl who breaks your heart, the job that doesn't work out, the dream that fades long before it can become realized. Because you will know without any doubt that whatever happened previously, whatever someone said to or about you, wherever your life diverged from its chosen path, all of that is a mystery and as a result totally unimportant to whatever, wherever, or whomever you are dealing with in the present time. Please, my son, don't ever forget that. If there is one lesson I can give you for the rest of your life, it is that."

What his mother didn't know was that revisiting his past on his stroll through Woodside, Jackson Heights, and Sunnyside was just like studying for the big test the night before. All around him on what would have appeared to anyone observing as nothing but a seemingly aimless walk, were the kind of people and places that would have told him straight to his face if anything about him was bullshit. Not that he was out to seek advice from anyone. He could just listen to it on the street like some kind of radio advice show with the volume on low. Except that the audience was just him and there were several thousand advisors all talking to him at once.

At the Remax Real Estate on Northern Boulevard he stopped at in the hour or so since he left his office. There he listened to stories of great sales and profits in the previous two years, but the listings were starting to hang around a little longer and the banks were acting a little strangely.

At Murray's Auto Parts on Corona Avenue, where Tony had worked a couple of summers for the old man who owned the joint then, what was his name...Mackineer or something like that. The nephews that took it over were happy with their little operation, speaking Spanish well enough to do business with all the local Dominican, Puerto Rican, and Mexican mechanics, adapting well...but they were very aware of the big box threat looming over small businesses just like theirs. "The landlord is talking about offers for the building to same developer who's gonna triple the rents, I hear. That's for the stores and the apartments as well. Lotsa freakin' greed out there. Gonna ruin everything."

And so it went at the Columbian Restaurant in Astoria on Broadway a couple of blocks away from the subway. He ordered a Pollo Fajita for dinner and added a fig in sweet sauce with cheese kind of thing that had a name that was unpronounceable, but it was delicious. The cute waitress told him she was glad most of the place was full, but it was Saturday night. And the tips were a little smaller here and there, she added, and she could also see a little tightness on some of the faces of her favorite customers, save for a few lucky ones.

And that was really all there was in your life. An opportunity that comes along that you feel you must stake yourself on and go with it no matter what the consequences. Otherwise, all you'll have to look forward to will be days and nights torturing yourself about what you should have done, comparing yourself to others who took a different path, made different decisions that seemed to always work out for them.

For Tony Craig, he was sure that there was plenty of money coming into America from various Middle East interests and governments. He was convinced that these transfers of sums were sometimes massive in nature and done right under everyone's noses. The 9/11 hijackers accomplished their heinous deeds for less than a half million dollars. He long suspected wealthy business interests across the Middle East and in Saudi Arabia, particularly, he knew that they were behind the building and funding of hundreds of madrassas, the same places that fueled the hatred of the nineteen young men who boarded the planes that terrible Tuesday morning and the thousands of others who danced in the streets of Gaza, Aden and, unbelievably, on the Brooklyn Heights Promenade across the river from the towers proclaiming their glee that afternoon. He firmly believed this was the first stop in preventing another attack as well as the funding of what he referred to as 'homegrown terrorists,' which included in his mind many emotionally disturbed, easily manipulated ne'er-do-wells, ex-cons as well as soldiers on active duty.

It took him months to convince anyone of his beliefs, something he initially figured would take a few days given the evidence he presented along with his theory. As Bernstein and Woodward said in the hallways of *The Washington Post* during the early days of the Watergate investigation, "Follow the money."

He threw off the disdain of his bosses and plunged ahead, even using some off-duty N.Y.P.D. Officers for surveillance at his own expense. Trying to convince Chetlington to help arrange for occasional joint task force work with the police in New York had been more of a chore than he could have imagined. All he was able to arrange after an endless harangue was a harbor cop with no stake out experience, available only on his off time and again, Tony had to pick up most of the expense of this very minor operation. He didn't even know who this harbor cop was as he was only able to wrangle him at the last minute, giving him instructions over the phone.

His annoyance with his superiors was beyond measure. Could Chet have him blanketed so effectively that no one else in the office knew he existed? It all seemed so obvious to him. This Special Forces soldier he was tracking exhibited truly suspicious behavior immediately after beating his wife to within an inch of her life. It came out that he had changed upon his return from duty overseas, adopting a position sympathetic to the Islamist cause. There was the call right in the middle of the brawl that was traced from Saudi Arabia. And immediately following all of that was his way-over-the-speed-limit trip up the New Jersey Turnpike and over to Kennedy Airport, where he just happened to meet with one of the sons of the one of the wealthiest businessmen in the Saudi Kingdom. It was all too much to be a coincidence of any kind. Something was going on, Tony was convinced of it, and he was ready to throw his career down the tubes in case he was wrong.

He decided, after finishing his fajita and tipping the impossibly cute waitress thirty percent, to visit J'lome, whom he had not seen in enough years to be confident he would be remembered. But he knew he could drop a few names to gain entry into the man's confidence. J'lome, although he never contacted the FBI to his knowledge, was one of the few Imams in the city that had taken a public position in support of being a contact for information to prevent further terrorist strikes in the city, which did not endear him to many in the New York *umma*. He said publicly that he had been extremely dismayed that not as many of his fellow Muslims would not publicly condemn the nineteen from 9/11 and others like them. He differed with many of his colleagues in that he found the Muslim community in New York ready and willing to help the law enforcement community rid the country of radicals. He would always bring up Chapter 4, Verse 60 in the Koran:

*O ye who believe! Obey Allah, and obey his messenger and those
who are in authority from among you.*

The vast majority of these people just want to live their lives, root
for their teams, raise their sons and daughters and be left alone, he
told Imams from all over the Unites States and Europe. Strange, he
would point out, was that the safest countries on the planet for any
Muslim man or woman to raise a family and live a decent life complete
with the nourishment of his or her faith were the United States and
Israel. Not exactly who you expect to hear from on CNN or read about
in the *New York Times*, but that's another story, Tony always reminded
himself. He headed east on Broadway, flipping open his phone, dialing
information and hating the robotic information service—'Is this a
business or residential listing?'—that finally gave him the number he
was looking for, the call going through and a mercifully quick arrange-
ment made, tremendous luck that the man remembered him, and he
flipped the phone closed, turned up his collar and continued to make
his way past innumerable restaurants and bars and small businesses of
all types all the way up to Steinway Street where he turned left and
headed toward The People's Mosque.

J'lome was usually home at this time of day, after a long day tending
to the many problems of his congregants as well as leading all the
prayer sessions for the day. But he was expecting Tony Craig shortly,
who he did in fact remember from the Police Athletic League basketball games. A tough player a few years older than J'lome and the rest
of the guys, tough but never dirty, he remembered Tony as one who
was able to hit from eighteen feet in his sleep as well as box out the
toughest man on the court and rip any rebound out of the air within
his reach with one hand. They lost touch when Tony went away to
some boarding school and J'lome went to jail, but J'lome was glad to
see how well Tony had done for himself and was totally pleased that
he was taking an interest in keeping an eye on the radical elements of
his beloved Islam. J'lome knew that it was these misinformed, brain-
washed, pathetic losers who had been indoctrinated from birth in
the madrassas of Pakistan, Yemen, and Saudi Arabia who posed the

greatest threat to the members of his mosque and their families and all other Muslims, not rising interest rates, a bad economy, or media-fueled phantom and sometimes not-so-phantom hatred of all things and persons Muslim. He rose to answer the knock at the door, feeling his knees wobble a bit and what was that, a creaky sound coming in the old joints? Even for a man of God, it was tough to get old. He pulled the door open to see Tony Craig waiting, looking up and down the block for any prying eyes.

"Salaam Aleikum."

"Aleikum Salaam, my old friend," answered Tony. They half embraced warmly and J'lome pointed him into his office. "Can I get you anything?"

"No, I'm good. I ate dinner before coming over."

"Astoria has a lot of really great ethnic restaurants around now. The neighborhood is really thriving."

"I can see that. I walked up Broadway and it was filled with young people going this way and that, nice cafés and some vintage clothing stores. It's nice to see. Remember what it was like around here in the mid-seventies?"

"I'd prefer to forget it. A lot of what was going on here then sucked me into a bad life, bad habits. You were lucky to escape it, Tony. I remember when you went away to that school, all of us thought it was a bad idea, but in retrospect it was a brilliant move by your mom." Tony was genuinely moved by J'lome's words and recollections and he had to steel himself to keep the tears in their ducts. J'lome being a well-practiced man of the cloth recognized this and helped Tony stem any embarrassment by asking a question to get him talking and thinking again. He lifted his open palm to the chair Vinny had sat in just a short time ago and beckoned Tony to take a seat.

"So what did you want to see me about? What's going on?" he asked.

"I just wanted to alert you to a couple of people we are keeping an eye on. I know they were hanging around the neighborhood for a couple of days and I thought they might have stopped in here." He started looking through his pockets for the photographs of Whathefu and Aubrey and struggled for a few seconds as they were stuck on a loose loop of thread in the breast pocket of his jacket. He continued as he pulled the photos out with some annoyance, creasing them in the process, thankful they were still recognizable, "I had a harbor patrol cop watching these guys for me but I had to pull him off early because of budget constraints." J'lome leaned forward at that.

"Budget constraints? Don't you work for the Federal government? Or was it the Farmingdale Bureau of Investigation you work for?"

"Yeah, can you believe that? I found out earlier that there were personal and political forces at work here, people plotting against me, but I'm hoping this situation will resolve itself in such a way to ameliorate my office problems." He handed the photos over. "These are the guys we're looking at. One is a Special Forces man who is A.W.O.L. from his unit and the other is the son of one of the wealthiest men in Saudi Arabia. They hooked up at Kennedy Airport yesterday and the last time I spoke to the harbor cop, he saw them near here."

J'lome studied the photos for less than a second, the astonishment spreading over his face like an oil slick in choppy waters. He looked over the top of them at Tony Craig, who easily detected the change in his contact's demeanor.

"What? What is it? Do you recognize them? Have you seen them?"

"Yes, they were here...twice in fact, for prayers. The first time they were here, the blond guy started a ruckus outside the mosque and I had to give him and his friend here," J'lome was tapping the photo of Whathefu, "the word." Tony was bursting out of his skin at this information.

"Do you know where they went? Who they're with?" he blurted out the question like a high school girl looking for a wayward boyfriend.

"Like I said, they came here alone but they left with one of the guys who is a casual attending member of the mosque, a banker named Andre, a bit of a lost angry soul. He works in the computer department of Argent Bank. Do you know it?" he asked and Tony nodding with what he thought was not too obvious of a yes, who hasn't heard of Argent Bank? J'lome continued, "They came back once the next day all together, but there was something strange about the whole thing. The big guy, he wasn't your typical-looking Muslim; he was a blond, all-American type. His posture during prayers was perfect and he seemed too devout, fanatical almost. He looked like he was trying a little too hard, you know what I mean? Andre was with them again and it seemed to me that he was with them against his will."

"And this guy Andre, he works for a bank, in the IT department?" Please confirm for me the answer I heard just a moment ago, thought Tony.

"Yes," J'lome answered, adding, "although even if he tried to explain it to me, I wouldn't get it. I'm still very much a pencil and paper guy," he added with a smile.

The whole thing was taking shape in Tony's mind slowly but surely. He kept trying to knock his suspicions down, but he just couldn't do it. Special Forces soldier takes a call from the Middle East, he had been exhibiting an interest in Islam in the months prior to that, he meets the son of a wealthy Saudi businessman, who had been suspected of funding madrassa and preaching anti-Americanism quietly, while meeting with Western bankers and hedge fund managers and enjoying the pleasures of Western society denied to so many in his own country the rest of the time. And these two hook up with a classic ne'er do well, a loser, someone who has a perpetual black cloud over his life, who just happens to be some sort of technology professional for one of the largest banks in the country. How long would it take this guy to steal millions of dollars from the bank, maybe during off hours, and then disappear? Probably about five seconds was Tony's concluding thought. He was embarrassed to realize that J'lome had continued and he missed the first few sentences as the crystals began to form in his mind.

"What? I'm sorry, my friend, I was lost in thought. What did you say?"

"After the confrontation yesterday outside, I noticed Charlie Mick watching the whole thing like he was filming a movie. I don't know if you remember his father, the other Moose, Mikey Busy, not Moose Miller the harbor cop..." They both stopped in mid thought, realizing the irony of it, their jaws almost hanging down in unison .

"The kid from the old neighborhood who was part of your gang way back when, he's a harbor cop?" Tony asked. "I wonder if it could be the same guy who was sitting on these two."

"Right, small world...but anyway, after the confrontation, I noticed Charlie Mick a short distance from the door. I remember thinking it strange that he would be standing there. Vinny told me later that Charlie Mick would be his eyes on these guys for the next few days, not to worry about them. So I suspect that the kid is sitting on them as we speak." J'lome reached for his phone which he had silenced for this meeting with Tony. He showed the flashing red light to Tony that indicated a message was recently left and once he checked the history, he saw it was Vinny who tried to call a short while ago and he told this to Tony Craig while hitting redial. J'lome angled the phone away from his mouth in order to ask Tony a question.

"Do you remember Vinny Malloy? That's who I've been referring to."

"I do remember him somewhat. Tough guy, smart...made something of himself in real estate, right?" J'lome shook his head in the affirmative. Tony could hear the voice on the other end of the line answer the call and J'lome greeting him in return.

J'lome continued, "You know I'm here with a blast from the past, Tony Craig, do you remember him? He remembers you a bit as well. Yeah, the years, where did they go? Anyway, look...it turns out that Tony is interested professionally in the guys from yesterday. Yeah, we talked about that as well, him and Moose Miller, although we don't know if it's true or not, small world, right. Anyway, is Charlie Mick still on these guys?" Tony sat there transfixed, feeling the edges of the crystals coming together even more precisely in his brain.

"Okay, thanks. I'll send him over there. Be well and play with skill tonight and give my blessings to everyone." J'lome clicked off the phone and set it upon his desk.

"Vinny says that the kid is still shadowing your guys and that they seem to be staking out a two-family house in Long Island City, down the block from Vinny's construction site" J'lome told Tony. "Why don't you head over there? The construction site is where the Pepsi sign is."

"What's he building there?" J'lome twisted his face in apparent dismay at the question.

"Nothing right now, but you never know what God has in store." He stood and Tony did as well. "I'm sorry, but I have to get somewhere. Dispute resolution. Please stop by here any time, you are always welcome," he continued, holding his hand out to Tony, who took it warmly although he was already halfway out the door trying to catch up with his brain which was somewhere on the East River shore right about now. "Hey, hold on a minute, Tony." The FBI man turned, a little nervous out here on the street in full view of...anyone. He waited for J'lome's question.

"How could you not know the name of the cop handling your surveillance?" Tony looked up and down the block again before answering.

"I ordered up the surveillance myself. My office wouldn't buy my theory so I went in my pocket and paid the cop's overtime, I thought it was that important. He took the assignment without telling me his name so he wouldn't have to pay taxes on the money." J'lome stared at him uncomprehendingly.

"Law enforcement in this country has to keep their eyes open for elements. Anyone who doesn't think so doesn't understand anything," J'lome said, Tony not missing the resignation in his voice as he finished. But he had no time for a philosophical discussion at the moment. "I'll be back, J'lome, thanks for your time," and he walked down Steinway Street, turning at the corner to head toward the East River.

—⊪—

The number 7 train was filled with jubilant Mets fans and glum but still supremely confident Yankee fans on the way back to Brooklyn, the Bronx and the city after the Mets' win. Laura and Michael huddled near the front of the first car, both holding the ceiling to floor pole, both taking care to not allow their hands to touch. The game reminded Michael of baseball in the 1960s, when a typical low-scoring game was over in two hours. No endless pitching changes, no player daring step out of the box as much as these guys do today. But this game was a throwback in that it was over quickly and they were on the train headed back toward Manhattan. It was ten minutes to eight and Michael considered them lucky to have caught the express which was hurtling along the el above Roosevelt Avenue like the Cyclone roller coaster.

"Hey," he said to her as they rocked back and forth, "it's still a little early. Do you want to go listen to some music? I'll have you back at your place by ten-thirty, I promise. That's when my card game starts anyway." Had to make it sound very, very casual, he figured. Don't show too much interest, don't frighten her or ruin this magical day and night.

It was a Saturday night and I ain't got nobody...Laura remembered the lyrics to the song. She was somewhat but not overly so, surprised by the swiftness of her decision in her mind. Yes, of course, the pleasure center of her brain screamed at her, doing ferocious battle with her moral center which told her to politely decline, that she had an appointment early in the morning. For lack of a better idea, she decided to play it coy.

"I don't know, let's see," she replied, turning to face the front of the subway car and getting a view out the windshield of the train's path. They were at Woodside now, a busy station that sat above the Long Island Railroad tracks that even the express stopped at. Her own stop, Vernon-Jackson, was about ten minutes away. The cacophony of the Yankees versus Mets arguments washed over the whole car and for her it was welcome only for the fact that she wanted to think about all this some more. The day has been wonderful so far, one of the best dates she had ever been on.

But that nagging question was still hanging in the air: What the hell am I doing here? And she came up with the same simple answer every time, I'm going out for a casual evening with a co-worker I have known for many years without a single trace of inappropriate contact. Olympic champion-type discipline at work here. So what was wrong, really? It was the follow-up that counted in a situation like this one. And after tonight, she would not ever again have any contact with Michael Pierce under any circumstances outside of the bank. And it would be easy to do. She would just act the same as she always had when they saw each other. Always out in the open, friendly conversation with him in the office hall or at the Christmas party, no e-mails, phone calls—everything no matter how trivial or circumstantially happenstance to be just coincidence and limited to two minutes of exchange. In ten years Michael had never done any of those things, but if all of a sudden he decided to after this day, she would have to cut him off at the knees, a skill most intelligent and enlightened men realize all women possess, some more than others with various differences in methodology, but all considered equally deadly and final. What a bitch I am, she concluded as the train pulled into Hunter's Point Avenue. What happened? Vernon-Jackson was the next stop. She looked away and there was Michael, who had apparently quietly edged up near her at the front window and she quickly deduced that he was not there intruding on her thoughts or space but was kind of watching out for her. The exchanges between the fans were getting a little louder, more guttural...something about Cone and Doc had to come to the Yankees for their no-hitters...what was wrong with these guys? Do they really consider these arguments to be important? If she had been alone she undoubtedly would have been concerned. But she felt none of that with this very unselfish man standing beside her. The doors opened at Hunters Point and several of the baseball fans left, bathing the car in a moment of quiet and civility. The doors closed, the brakes released their grip with a whoosh of air and the train lurched forward. She didn't even have the luxury of a long ride between stations to think a little more.

"So what do you think, do you have a little more time?" Michael asked. He added quickly, "I really do have to be here in this neighborhood at about ten-thirty for a card game with my friends, so I can ride back here with you and walk you to your door. It's directly on the way."

She looked straight into his blue irises as if she was trying to read something on the cortex of his brain, searching for the slightest evidence that he was another Adam. The train entered the station, the conductor announcing the stop and letting everyone know the next stop is in Manhattan. She looked out the door at the platform she waited on every day and truly for the first time in her life she had a 'what the hell' moment and decided to fly with the situation. No way was she going to sit in her apartment tonight waiting for...anything. For the next ninety minutes, she was going to live. She said nothing as the doors closed and she remained where she stood and then slowly turning back to the windshield, the train entering the long tunnel under the street which held the Saab containing Aubrey, Whathefu and Andre, the street she lived on, Vinny's construction project site, then under Moose Miller's boat, on its way to the city. Michael joined Laura at the window, remarking as he leaned up against the glass that he always loved looking out the first car's window, even when they were traveling through the tunnel. He didn't check her reaction, but he might have seen a flash of mild astonishment on her face and it took all her control not to blurt out that she was about to say the same thing.

—·—

Fred and Ryan Burke were finishing up some work on one of Vinny's buildings in Astoria. They had spent most of the day lying on their backs, cutting pipe, rerouting wires, unclogging drains, and installing security cameras and buzzer systems. Vinny always believed in taking care of his tenants and that meant never in his career having to attend landlord/tenant court to answer for violations or allowing unsafe conditions to stagnate and therefore multiply. The city had hundreds of landlords who blamed the tenants for everything, and probably many of them were correct in their assertions from time to time, but Vinny Malloy without being asked patched holes in walls, fixed broken windows and doors as soon as it happened and his tenants loved him for it. As a result, the rents were always there on time and the complaint box was usually empty.

The Burkes were tired and irritable and the only things they could agree on were that they loved their new girlfriends, Lisa and Ellen, and that the Knicks were going to suck for years to come but not as bad as the once-storied St. John's basketball program. They also agreed that the card game later tonight was a welcome relief from, well...the world and they would even allow Mikey to go on and on about his and J'lome's victory in the NCAA pool, despite the fact that they didn't know shit about the players and teams, without jumping him and beating him to a pulp. It was a night to look forward to of laughs, beers, fart jokes and winning hands. Fred's phone went off while he was under a bathroom sink while fitting a reluctant elbow joint and he bumped his head on the pipe in reaction to the unexpected noise. He could see in the screen the call was from Vinny and he had a sinking feeling that maybe the card game was off. He answered the call with a question.

"The game's not canceled is it?"

"No, why do you ask? Are you paranoid?"

"We're just looking forward to the game, that's all. Everyone going to be there?"

"Everyone except for J'lome. Mikey will be here a little before eleven, maybe earlier, I guess you guys will be done about the same time, and Charlie Mick will be here as well. Moose Miller is on duty and he may stop over later unless we're all dead to the world by then."

"Let's play until the sun comes up," Ryan Burke interjected. Vinny laughed as Ryan never missed the opportunity to play a game, to entice one more hand out of everyone.

"Just make sure to get here on time but take care of everything first, okay? Do you guys have the truck with you?" He was referring to the old Pepperidge Farm bread truck they used for their electrician and plumbing work.

"Yeah, we were going to leave it at the garage in the building and take the car down there, why?"

"Do me a favor and bring the truck around here. I need some things moved and I could load them in the truck, so bring it, alright?"

"Done. See you at ten-thirty or so." Both parties clicked off their phones. Vinny went back to his serious contemplation of his construction loan problem—and everyone else's as well, which was the real problem for him, and the Burkes went back to finishing up the work they started earlier. They were nothing if not fastidious about their trade as well as their schedules and were proud of being just about the only contractors in New York City who knew how to manage their time effectively. They figured they would be able to turn down Vinny's block at about twenty-five minutes after ten and walk in the door of the construction shack exactly on time.

⚬

Michael and Laura ascended the stairs of the Christopher Street station in the West Village, dodging the tourists, gay couples and screeching teenagers from the outer boroughs and suburbs. Laura felt a little nervous on the busy, crowded, loud avenue at first and almost took Michael's arm instinctively but thankfully her brain kicked in and instead she drew a deep breath to calm herself.

"I used to know a small place over there," Michael said to her, pointing past the triangular park separating them from The Stonewall Inn and several sets of men making out as passionately as two people possibly could. She felt slightly ashamed and immature at her private negative reaction to them and their public displays. "But the NYU kids discovered it recently and it's now a bit crowded. I'll feel like a babysitter in there. Let's go over here. I think you'll like it," he continued, pointing south down Seventh Avenue, guiding her to a jazz club/restaurant called Garage. Inside they went, passing the doorman who bobbed his head slightly as they passed, glad to have a classy looking couple entering the club instead of the usual snotty jazz aficionados, drunken suburbanites and college kids who couldn't get into the little place over on Christopher Street. Michael was hoping that she hadn't been here some other time with some other clown.

Inside there was a trapezoidal shaped bar that ran along the windows looking out on Seventh Avenue; the other side of the bar was close to a small stage where the four-piece band was skimming along in 7/8 time. Laura looked around and could see the space was kind of elegant and the proprietors managed to accomplish this without the place looking like an obvious tourist magnet. Although it was a large room, there was a local tavern feel to it. Michael guided them to the middle of the bar with the windows behind them and faced the band, their backs to the traffic on the avenue.

"Would you like something?" he asked, raising his hand in the direction of the bartender.

"I'll have what you're having," she replied, hoping that he wasn't going to order a martini or something like that, a hard drink.

"I'm going to get a beer, okay with you?" He started to turn fully to the bartender, his eyes still on Laura, awaiting a response. She nodded her approval and he ordered two Guinness. "Have you ever had one of these?" he asked her as he handed over a glass stein full of what looked like thick muddy water.

"Uhh, no...is this beer?"

"It's Guinness. Made in Ireland. It's a different taste, you can tell that just from the look of it. Kind of smoky. Kind of strong, frankly, but we're only going to have one and then we'll head back, right? Try it...if you hate it we'll just get something else. Wait until the foam rises completely and then taste it."

"How long do the bubbles take?" To her it looked like a silt storm in a glass.

"A few minutes. Here," he continued moving over and indicating a spot on the bar. "Put it down here and let's watch the band. These are pretty good players." She moved up to the bar and set her glass down on a coaster the barmaid placed down just in time. The silt storm raged, the band was quietly burning along, and they each were sharing the same thought at that moment: How would it be if we leaned up against each other a little bit here at the bar? Just kind of settle in under his shoulder/under my shoulder...but they instead concentrated on the guitarist for a minute who was now up from his stool, wailing away on a hollow-bodied Gibson.

The bartender, a tough-looking woman named May brought their change back to them. Michael pocketed some of the bills, leaving a couple on the bar ensuring a bit of decent service from her in the immediate future. The bubbles were now almost gone, the Guinness looking as black as a night in the woods or ten miles off the coast on a late night fishing trip. Michael reached for his and he nodded at Laura, indicating it was time. She took her glass and they turned to each other as the band finished with a flourish.

"Here's to a day of culture," he announced, and raised his glass for a taste. When he brought the glass back, it left a tan mustache on his upper lip which he licked away like a child would at the end of a glass of breakfast milk. He smiled and bade her to try it. She lifted the glass to her mouth hesitantly and sipped, tasted, tilted her head in surprise, and drank more. "It's not bad; I like it," she said. "But it definitely seems strong."

"It is. But we're only going to have one. Are you hungry?"

"Actually, yes. The hotdogs didn't fill me up and I'd like to have something healthy."

"You didn't like them?"

"Oh no," she answered in almost mock alarm, "they were delicious. But I think I may not want to ever read the ingredients."

"You got that right. They have a coconut shrimp thing here that's delicious. It has a dipping sauce that's kind of sweet. Do you want to try it? We can eat it here instead of getting a table." As if by magic two stools opened up, one behind Michael that he just leaned back onto. The other was behind Laura and she turned away to pull it closer to him. The barmaid came by again and they ordered the coconut shrimp. He checked the clock on the far wall and saw that it was twenty to ten. The next band was on in ten minutes. The shrimp would arrive in a few minutes and it seemed as if he would indeed get her home by ten-thirty and he would then continue down the block to the card game. Perfect, he thought. Michael loved these little games with times and routine. He hated to be late and he equally hated rude surprises.

A trio of men in their mid-thirties entered the club and headed down their way and settled at the bar behind Michael's back. They were all dressed well and spoke in respectful tones. One of them, a black guy who looked more regal than any three kings you could name let his eyes linger on Laura for a split second longer than Michael would have liked. He found himself wondering if he had any right to say anything if she decided to engage these attractive men in a conversation. Of course he knew he didn't and this annoyed him. They each took new swigs of their respective Guinness and as soon as they put them down, the shrimp arrived. She licked the foam from her upper lip and Michael almost had a heart attack in response.

She took the first piece of shrimp in her fingers and passed it through the sauce before biting it in half. Her eyes closed as she savored the perfect coconut batter. "This is delicious, I love it," she told him.

"How about the Guinness? Is it growing on you?" he asked in response, picking up a piece of the shrimp and biting off the meat all the way to the tail. So nice for a man to act like a man, Laura thought. Too many prissy males in this city who would never have eaten with their fingers in front of me. She raised her glass and took another swallow, shaking her head yes and she set it back down.

"I think it is, it's definitely an acquired taste, but I believe I like it."

The next band's members were milling about the small stage setting up their instruments for the next set. Michael and Laura could see them across the room if they looked forward across the bar area and past the patrons sitting on the other side of the trapezoid. The guitarist was tuning, the sax player was searching in his case for a new reed for his horn, the drummer was raising and tilting the cymbal stands and the snare drum in what seemed an endless combination of possibilities, trying to find the right placement and angles on a house drum set. The bass player stood by as if he were able to begin playing perfect notes any time of day or night. After a few minutes of tuning and manipulating their instruments, they launched into a flurry of notes and rhythms that blended as well as musicians could hope for, creating a groove even the most inept person could easily dance to.

"They're good, don't you think?" Michael asked Laura as the band was a few minutes into their first number. She turned to him with another piece of shrimp in her mouth, biting down on it before she answered.

"Delicious, and I love the dipping sauce. The beer goes well with it, too." Michael hesitated for a perfect moment before going on.

"I was asking about the band," he deadpanned.

"Oh, I'm sorry" she stammered, quickly chewing and swallowing the shrimp then seeing him start to smile slowly, widening as the seconds passed, they both started to laugh together, like lovers who are so comfortable with each other they can do anything together no matter who's watching and judging, having given up any sense of shame or embarrassment or self-consciousness when they were together.

She took the last shrimp and leaned forward, stepping up on her toes and stuffed it in his mouth, a comical angry expression on her face. "You trapped me," she said in mock accusatory form. He threw his hands up in the air as he answered.

"I did nothing," he said, sounding like every guilty-as-sin guy who appeared at an arraignment, "except make you laugh."

Yes, Michael, you did, she thought...thank you for such a selfless natural gift to this woman, so much better than any trip to Europe or a diamond necklace. She tried to remember the last time a man was able to make her laugh so easily, and she couldn't remember even one except for Diego, who so many years ago who was able to coax a belly laugh out of her at any moment.

Am I pathetic or what? she asked herself. Quickly she had her answer and it was no, instead I am more aware at this point of my life of what is truly important and what is truly valuable. Screw the fancy parties, the ski trips to Aspen, all of it. Thank you, Michael Pierce, who I hardly know but whom I have been waiting for my entire life. Thank you for restoring a semblance of joy in my heart. If you are ever not married, I will slay any woman who gets in my way on my ride into your heart.

"Yes you did," she replied to him and added, "thanks." At that, Michael's heart was bursting with desire. "It doesn't seem too difficult for me to coax that smile out of you. The next time I need a little extra light, I'll think of the brightness of the smile you just treated me to."

Cheesiness heaped upon lameness, but who cares? I am not concerned that I am married. I'm having the date of a lifetime and its reassuring in the least to know that I have something still going on as far as the opposite sex is concerned. He drained his Guinness, wiped the last of the dipping sauce from around his mouth and signaled the barmaid for the bill. "I'll be right back," he said, rising from his stool, "the bathroom is in the back of the club if you need it. Do not think about paying the bill, it belongs to me."

He walked to the end of the bar, turned right past the hostess stand, left again in front of the stage where he gave a discreet thumbs-up to the drummer and continued to the back of the room where he disappeared behind the beaded drapes that separated the bathrooms from the main room.

⚬

Maxie Carter was dead tired not just from walking around Manhattan all day, but the kind of disheartening feeling that comes from being mentally exhausted. This, of course, was the result she expected from her fight with her husband and the never-ending contemplation of divorce from that moment on. She was back on Sutton Place but had no desire to return to her apartment. Instead she strolled past the building toward the same small sitting where she encountered Vinny the night before and plopped down on the same bench and stuck her legs out straight, looking like a marathon runner who just crossed the finish line. She stared across the East River at Vinny's construction site. She could see the Pepsi sign sitting right in the middle of it with about two hundred yards of room northward for it to be moved to without anyone ever noticing. All of a sudden she heard footsteps and then someone calling her name.

"Miss Carter? Is that you?" She turned slowly, too tired to show any alarm, and she could see two people approaching, a man and a woman. Their steps were tentative, almost as if they were stalking her but not causing her to feel threatened. She recognized them as soon as they stepped into the light from the street lamp. It was Samuel and Nellie Iberico, the husband and wife team of superintendents for the building.

"Yes, Samuel, how are you? Hello, Nellie."

"Good evening, Miss Carter." Maxie genuinely liked these people. Hard-working immigrants from a farm town somewhere in Peru, they had worked in the building for as many years as Maxie could remember. Ridiculously polite, dedicated to working hard for all the residents of her building. Never saw them with anger tightening their faces, never heard a harsh word between them. She firmly believed she was the only one in the building who ever said hello to them, the rest of the residents believing themselves way above people like the Ibericos. Maxie, more than a few times, had to inform some of the more indiscreet ones that these people raised two sons on their meager salaries, both of whom were stellar students at St. John's University. In her eyes they were more substantial human beings than virtually any resident of Sutton Place.

"Why are you sitting out here all by yourself? It's getting chilly," Samuel said, a hint of genuine concern in his voice. Maxie smiled sadly, turned back to looking out over the river and then answered, not wanting to look these fine people in the eye.

"No reason really, just relaxing, looking at the stars." Samuel and Nellie exchanged quick glances at each other, wondering if the only person they liked in the building where they had worked for the past twenty years was going a little loco...like the rest of the people in the building.

"Well uhh," Samuel started, "we just wanted to say thank you for the extra work Mr. Carter arranged for us." Maxie turned back to them at this revelation with a perplexed look. She had never known her husband to even acknowledge the Ibericos in person, let alone offer them work.

"What are you talking about, what work?"

"On the sign, over there," he said pointing across the river to the Pepsi sign. "Mr. Carter asked us to paint the sign structure and the railings of the little pier the same color with the same paint. At first we thought we'd need a large crew and we would have to split the five thousand dollars with many others, but we worked through the night and got it done, just by ourselves. He told us it didn't have to be very neat, just fast. We have family down in Los Sauces, which is a small farming town in Amazonas state in Peru, and we sent them part of the earnings. It really helped them out a lot, so please tell Mr. Carter we said thank you." They smiled and said good night, turned to leave, but then Samuel stopped and commented further.

"I was surprised he would want the pier painted. It really should be torn down. It's very, how you say...rickety? Muy peligrosa." He turned and left, his wife taking his arm, the two of them walking in perfect tandem.

Maxie stared after them, not wanting to move lest she shake the thought that was building in her mind, crystallizing and taking shape into a theory. What was it that she remembered years ago...it happened with the Landmarks Committee...something about paint and a development downtown in SoHo. And then she had it. It was about another builder who bought a run-down factory and planned on turning it into condos. Many residents of the block objected to the project and advocates for the Landmarks Preservation Committee stepped in and scraped away the paint on the window casings, the railings, and other parts of the structure and determined through spectrographic analysis that the paints matched and, as a result, not only could the developer not paint the building the way they wanted—a nice off-white, as Maxie recalled—but also, since the developer's building was attached to the buildings on either side, they further determined that no part of the building's facade could be changed. All because the earliest layers of paint matched each other from over one hundred years ago. Everyone connected with the project thought it was absurd at the time, garnering some media support in the *Post* mostly, but then it was quickly forgotten as the collective attention of the city moved on to other matters. But the developer's plans for the building ultimately fell apart and the building remained as it had for years, a nasty, rotting, non-tax-producing hulk.

And then Maxie made one more connection. That building was snatched up later that year in the wake of the developer's default on the construction loan by one of her husband's friends in what was now apparent to her a scam using the power of the Landmark Committee. She wondered how much money flowed to her husband for his influence and how many times it had happened before. She looked across the river again at the construction site of Vinny Malloy. She recalled his impassioned pleas to the committee to approve his project...for the desperately needed market rent units, the development of the long-neglected waterfront in Long Island City, the increase to the tax base of the city, etc.

And she was a part of the conspiracy now. Couldn't testify against her husband. Might now be subject to all sorts of investigations including the IRS, the possibility of criminal charges, at the very least she would be paraded on the front pages of the tabloids and the local news, publicly humiliated. The thought of it all made her shiver with fear and dread.

She stood abruptly and quickly and headed west toward Grand Central Station. She didn't know which subway would take her to Long Island City but she figured it couldn't be that hard to figure out. It must be the first stop after emerging from under the river. After that she would just make her way to the river and look for the red glow of the Pepsi sign and then the door to Vinny's construction trailer, where she would tell him everything she knew about the paint, everything she believed about the conspiracy to steal his project, and everything else she wanted to say to a man who had thoroughly captured her imagination. She was walking swiftly now and when she was halfway down the block, she broke into a trot and then into a full run, hoping with each step she was closer to her own redemption and salvation from the steel wool coat her husband placed squarely on her shoulders so many years ago.

Vinny was sitting in the shack watching the clock, patiently waiting on the arrival of the Burkes, Charlie Mick and Michael for the start of the card game. He found himself desperately needing this break from his real life which had taken a major turn for the worst the past few days. Other than meeting the woman Maxie, with whom he seemed to share some sort of semi-spiritual connection, nothing had gone right. He slapped his hands on his knees, his patience worn out all of a sudden, the frustration and anger threatening to spill out of his body like a geyser. There was not a chance he could allow any of the boys to see that happen so he stood and went to the door of the shack and looked to his left, out over the river, past the spindly pier out to the harbor patrol boat that he knew Moose Miller was commanding tonight. His eyes swept back to the Pepsi sign and he was compelled all of a sudden to walk right up to it and give it a look, as if it were an enemy giving him the evil eye.

He sniffed the air as he walked the several hundred yards toward the sign, the tar smeared years ago on the ancient pilings still throwing off a scent that he found unusually pleasant. He knew that the olfactory was probably the most powerful of the human senses when it came to bringing one back to a long lost memory and the air right now brought him back to 1973 or so, swimming in the foul water of the East River, the environmentalists not having garnered enough political strength yet to do anything about it. Mikey, the Burkes, Ping the Router, Charlie Mick's dad, J'lome, Moose and some other loose kids from the neighborhood didn't care about the garbage floating by. All they knew was the water was cool and it was free and it was the greatest of adventures, all of them cheating death each and every time they dove in.

He was able to recall those days quite easily and they never failed to warm his heart, no matter what the demand on his intellect or his soul at the moment he dialed them up. They were like a favorite movie in the DVD player of his mind. As he drew up to the base of the sign however, the images faded away replaced by the hum of the massive neon tubes.

He was surprised when he realized his teeth were grinding and his hands were balled into fists. He took a deep breath and stepped away from the sign, looking up at it as he stepped backward. He couldn't help it and he decided to let it out in a primal scream of rage that even the fish in the river were probably able to hear. "Why, you stupid, short-sighted, blood sucking assholes...why are you doing this?!" he raged over and over at the moon, the span of the Queensboro Bridge, the Pepsi sign itself and the surrounding factories. He spun around as if he were in a drunken stupor and somehow righted himself like a dancer finding his feet again after a mistake by an inexperienced partner. He exhorted his blistering rhetorical questions at the four corners of the globe, as if he were desperately looking anywhere for an answer, a solution, at the very least some kind of plausible explanation. The thrust of his movements carried him away from the sign over to the pier. The sign was not speaking to him at this moment but maybe the pier would. He was standing on the bulkhead in less than a minute staring at the jerry rigged structure. No way would he step out on it like he did when he was a kid, he didn't want to go swimming here anymore. After a few minutes of silent contemplation, he found himself not able to shake off the nagging man in his brain who maybe had picked up on the primal screaming. There was something unusual about the structure...his sixth sense was now whispering it to him but he needed it to yell at full volume because he just wasn't seeing it. The lights of the bridge were twinkling on the uneven surface of the swift waters of the East River and the moon was full, casting its reflected light on this cloudless evening like a halogen lamp. Something was pulling at him, he could feel it, but he still couldn't wrap his head around it.

His thoughts were interrupted by the chirp of his cell phone which he pulled from his pocket with a touch of annoyance. Why are the guys calling me now? They should all be here soon, he thought to himself as he checked the number. It was coming up private, which made him frown. Probably a wrong number, but then again you never know. Maybe it was the president of the bank telling him it was all a joke and that the loan would close tomorrow. He punched the talk button and barked a hello into the ear of the caller.

"Hello, Vinny, this is Tony Craig. Do you remember me? I'm sorry to be calling you out of the blue like this at such an unusual hour." Vinny with his unparalleled prowess for recall did in fact remember Tony as one of the slightly older kids from the neighborhood, a bit of a loner due to the fact there were plenty of fourteen-year-old kids and an equal number of twenty-year-olds, but strangely very few seventeen-year-olds so he was always a little left out of things. Vinny remembered him as a good guy, pretty decent athlete, with a strong-willed mother who packed him off to some fancy boarding school which was about the last time anyone from the neighborhood saw or heard from him.

"Yeah sure, Tony, I remember. How are you doing? Been a long time." Part of the question actually came out as one word, howyudune. The ladies in California he encountered during a vacation there loved it when he said hello to them that way. It made them feel like a gangster was in their midst. He and Mikey visited San Francisco a few times in their early twenties once they found the local girls to be mostly tired of the local males—if you could call them that—with their severely shaved and toned bodies, perfectly coiffed hair, and ridiculously fashionable clothes. Many of the California boys went to the beach wearing gold chains, bracelets and rings, drenching themselves in Aramis cologne. Their cars were highly polished, their fingernails were polished and their speech was also polished so much that one could see straight through to their essence, which was in most cases, not made of anything substantial. He and Michael had a field day with the local talent, just by speaking to them in the patois of Sunnyside and Long Island City.

"Fine, how are you? Long time, I know. Lots of changes for all of us."

"That we all have in abundance, a never-ending series of ups and downs but we're doing okay mostly. What's up? Not that I mind hearing from an old acquaintance, but I heard somewhere years ago you were a Federal Agent and I can't help but wonder what this is all about." He was always the smartest one, Tony thought, best to come at him straight on.

"Can I come by your construction site in a little bit? I just left your friend J'lome...I know he told you I was coming over, but I thought I should call, all the same."

"He's closer to a brother than a friend with me," said Vinny.

"I know that. It's been years since I saw him last and I reached out to him earlier tonight. He's a good man. He told me how to get hold of you." Vinny pondered the situation for a second or two and then invited Tony over. "You know how to get here?"

"Of course...I grew up here, remember? See you in about a half hour. I'm walking, I need the exercise." Vinny clicked off the phone and looked back at the pier wondering what it was trying to tell him. He regarded this phone call from a person buried deep in his past, another guy who got out of the old neighborhood, as a positive development, one that he somehow believed would offer up a solution out of the blue. That was always the best way, when the solutions just came at you when you least expect them.

"Howyudune?" The man speaking with Laura turned at the comment/ question to face his questioner. Michael had him profiled in about a millisecond. Tall, athletically built black man, with shoulders out to... here, as Tom Wolfe used to describe women's fashions of the eighties, ridiculously handsome with the natural bearing of a king. His clothing was impeccable, a beautiful tan checked jacket with leather elbows that must have set him back a thousand bucks and a black low necked sweater. He was about six foot three...a little taller than Michael, but built like an Olympic sprinter or maybe a small forward. His teeth were like perfect white Chiclets and his accent was New England prep school all the way. He could either beat the shit out of Michael within two minutes or debate him under the table regarding the current state of affairs of each and every country or republic on each and every continent on the planet.

"Fine, thank you. How are you tonight?" The question was slightly taunting which rankled Michael Pierce's Irish a little bit. Well, he had to remind himself, he was also tall and kind of handsome and he would give any man a good fight, although he would lose his share. He would definitely lose one with this guy. He was surprised at how jealous he was that this man was speaking with Laura. Did he even have a right to be jealous? Isn't it at all possible that Laura was beguiled by this handsome man and hoped that Michael—the married guy—would just disappear? Whatever. There was only one thing for him to do.

"Great, we're doin' great." A little of the street might work here so Michael decided to lose the 'g' in doing. He moved with absolute confidence in order to offset his crude speech and settled in next to Laura and without taking his eyes off her asked if she wanted another drink. He struggled to maintain the level pitch of his voice. He could see she had drained the last of her Guinness.

"No," she replied, pushing away from the bar. "We should be going soon. I'll be right back." She looked back at the king in the checked jacket and demurely excused herself. She glided away toward the other side of the club, both men keeping their eyes on her as she moved through the tables, dodging the waiters with the grace of a figure skater. The king was addressing him now and Michael heard not Yale, not Choate, but Brooklyn.

"She your lady?" Michael did not immediately turn to face him as he followed Laura all the way with his gaze until she parted the drapes and disappeared. He loved to watch her walk. How should he answer? With some truth? Something like, Well, I'm married but my wife is away and I'm with her for the weekend because we have basically lusted after each other for ten years now without even a phone call between us until two days ago and this is really our first date but again, because I'm married, it will never go any further; therefore, if you want to ask her for her phone number it's okay.'

Or should he play the part of her man? After all, for at least today, he was her man in the sense that they would begin the day together and end it together. So he was responsible for her in a certain way. And frankly, he was finding it difficult to imagine her out on a date with someone else at this point. They were getting physically closer as the night went on, more comfortable with each other, their friendship growing in intensity with each passing minute. He noticed a few times during the day that Laura was watching him with what seemed to be more than a passing interest. Michael knew he was acting ridiculous, and quite selfish, but he didn't care.

"Yeah, she is."

"You're a lucky guy. She's fantastic."

"You're right, she is. We're both lucky," he added quickly and self-assuredly. He further added, "She's a great lady. I'm sorry I came on a little strong earlier. I wouldn't have if you weren't so goddamn handsome." Michael smiled at the comment and the king slapped him playfully on the shoulder, almost dislocating it.

"I gotta tell you, I'm very disappointed that you two are together. I was about to get down on my knees and beg her for a date. Even Stevie Wonder could see she's a cut above the average New York woman." Slick mother this guy is, Michael thought. Smooth, suave and he has the bone structure of one of Michelangelo's models. Time to blow him off despite the fact that he had more of a right to speak with Laura about what she was doing next Thursday night than Michael did. Well, screw this guy and his superlative presentation.

"She is, believe me. That's why I grabbed her a long time ago and that's why I intend on keeping her around." He looked past the king, past the bar and the band, across the club toward the drapes that led to the bathrooms. "What the hell do women do in there?" he asked no one in particular as the king retreated momentarily to the comfort of his court.

The cool water Laura was splashing on her face at that moment was one of the most delicious feelings, one of the great physical sensations, and it was helping her to shake her head clear of so many confusing thoughts. Chief among them, really the only one that counted for her at that moment was how she would feel about herself if she wound up spending the entire evening with Michael. Her checklist was complete as far as Michael was concerned in terms of him as a potential lover. He passed the looks test about one-third of a second after they first met more than ten years before. She would never admit it to him directly, in spite of her long ago spontaneous blurt regarding her surprise that such a handsome man worked for Argent Bank. She still couldn't believe she said it.

Maybe one day she would let him know how he took her breath away that first time he looked straight through her with those beautiful blue eyes. Maybe she would never tell him, even if somehow they did manage to get together at some point in the future. After all, every woman has to keep some secrets from her man, even if they were happily married for fifty years.

Her mind was like a gyroscope on roller blades in her skull, spinning swiftly and leaning to and fro. Part of her just wanted to jump into the pool of those blue eyes, the color of which reminded her of the waters surrounding the most beautiful Caribbean beaches. She wanted to lean into his body, his strength supporting her weight, her ear close enough to hear his heart skip a beat when she did so. Her fingers would be like the free-ranging roots of a bamboo tree, not craving a drop of water, but rather the sensation of running them through his hair while he was in the middle of doing...whatever he wanted to.

She found herself delving once more into the fantasy she played in her mind many times in the past ten years, more so in the past few years, and at least several times since they sat down together in the Starbucks on Fifty-Seventh Street. She wanted to grab that thick mane of sandy hair and pull him away from between her legs where he had just spent the last twenty minutes or so and slide him up her body as if she were pulling a wool blanket over herself to ward off an early morning winter chill and not stop until she pulled him even with her and he would just enter her with the greatest of ease, no problem with lubrication, not too small, not too large, no need to reach down and give him direction, just to be filled completely and there he would stay, nibbling gently on her lower lip, one strong hand cupping her butt cheek, lifting her lower spine into a more comfortable position, he able to perfectly balance his body on his remaining limbs to spare her the weight of his two hundred pounds, staying there, deeply imbedded, not even having to move back and forth, just the pulse of his penis touching her enough to nudge her to the brink of orgasm, like an adult hawk nudging each of her brood to the edge of the nest for their first attempt at flight. In her mind and view, a perfect blend of patience as well as caveman-like urgency, an innate understanding of what a woman wants and needs from her lover, but not pushing aside what he also wanted, the drive to make his woman feel loved, beautiful, and desired after each and every lovemaking session.

"You finished honey?" The question was delivered by a scratchy voice somewhere behind Laura in the tiny bathroom. Her head was still in her hands, the rivulets of water she splashed onto her face not yet falling past her sharp features back into the basin. Her face became almost red hot with embarrassment, convinced the intruder behind her could read her thoughts.

"Yes, sorry," she answered, shaking the water from her hands and reaching for a paper towel. "I was lost in thought."

"It must have been a great one." Laura turned slowly toward this woman whom she had never seen before. She was annoyed with her. Does she think she knows anything about me, that she can read my thoughts? "What are you talking about?" she asked, a sharpness in her voice.

"Oh," she smiled knowingly at Laura, not at all unsure of herself or frightened in any way, "I just figured the brain cloud you were just experiencing had to do with some man. For me, it's always about this one wild adventure I had with this guy many years ago. He was wonderful in every way." Laura continued drying her hands, not giving a damn about this intruder and her past, but somewhat fascinated to peer into her brain a bit. She continued, "He knew how to reach me, read me, and touch me in every single way, physically and spiritually."

"Where is he now?" Laura asked her, her tone friendlier. She tossed the crumpled paper towel in the waste, smoothed her hair. She was answered with an audible sigh, a universal signal to the beginning of a story laden with lament, similar to thousands of stories being told by women across the country every day, about the one guy they never should have let get away. Laura was replaced at the basin by the woman who had introduced herself as Roz Schwartz, born and raised in the Village.

"Don't know," Roz answered as she, too, splashed some water in her face. She looked at Laura in the reflection in the mirror, she also allowing the water to just drip off her face. "But I wish I did. I let some bullshit problems with work, bad horoscopes, some aches and pains, whatever I could find for an excuse to drive him away. I don't blame him. You know, I used to look pretty good then, but you know what men say? Show me a good looking woman and I'll show you a man who's tired of sleeping with her. For all of our bitching about the male of the species, we never look at ourselves and our own peccadilloes and idiosyncrasies. Don't look at me like that, I'm pretty smart. I have a good vocabulary. I'm a doctor of medicine actually." Laura smiled. She was beginning to like this woman. Roz stood and turned from the sink and ripped a couple of paper towels out of the dispenser.

"Is that your guy out there?" she asked Laura.

"Yes," she blurted out, surprised at the quickness and decisiveness of her answer. Was she defending her turf? Was Michael her turf? Well tonight he was. He's a dreamboat answered Roz. "He have good manners? Goodness, that turns me on. I once slept with a young man at medical school just because he held the door open for me." Laura blushed at Roz' comment before answering.

"He does in fact. And I like good manners as well. It's a lost form of behavior in today's modern, feminist world." Roz leaned in conspiratorially, "Is he a good lay as well?" The question insulted Laura immediately and she didn't care if she would be thought of as a prig. She started for the door without answering and then parted the drapes, stepping into the room once more. Her eyes lasered past the band, the waiters, the bickering and bantering couples, and found Michael where she left him but she could see him speaking with the handsome black man who introduced himself to her when Michael was away.

Goodness, was he arguing with him? She recalled that so many of the men she dated in the past thought they were being sexy and alluring to her when they acted confrontational in public. She hated it, absolutely hated that kind of attitude. She was praying Michael was not that type of man as she swept past the stage, the drummer losing one of his sticks as he noticed her gliding along. She passed the underscore of the bar and drew up to Michael, now close enough to hear the conversation.

"The Knicks will never win anything as long as the Dolans own the team."

"It's a shame you can't fire the owners." The king looked past

Michael and nodded slightly, who then turned to see Laura drawing up to him. She was beaming, but about what? He didn't care, because her smile was absolutely perfect, and it was for him only. He smiled back and her heart skipped a beat as it became apparent he was able to make some sort of friendly conversation with a man he didn't know, someone half the men she had known in her life would have challenged in one way or another, the other half quietly dismissing him as just another nigger.

"Missed you...are you ready to go?" She looked up to him with her eyes only, hoping to send an obvious signal to anyone and everyone who might be watching that this was her man, if only for about another forty-five minutes. She nodded and he started to turn to the door after saying good-night to the king.

"The bill's paid, so shall we?" Unconsciously he offered his arm and she took it, making it easier for him to angle her to the door. They were out on Seventh Avenue now, dodging throngs of tourists, NYU students, gay men, and street hustlers of all types. Laura kept her hand on his arm as they made their way to the Christopher Street subway station for the train back to Queens, all the while not noticing the appreciative stares of the diverse crowds on the street they left in their wake.

⸺

It was one of those perfect evenings in New York City, Vinny was thinking, at least weather-wise. It would be a couple of months before the humidity settled in like an unwelcome neighbor. The air was pleasantly cool, the last bit of winter struggling to stave off the onset of blooming flowers, smiling upturned faces and the meat of the baseball season. There were some stiff breezes to be sure, especially at the edge of the river where Vinny still stood looking out at the opposite shore.

That was where the real cold still was, in the hearts of the blue bloods on that facacta Landmark Committee and in the swirling water just a few feet away. The river never really warmed up ever, because of its swift currents. Vinny figured the temperature on this May evening to be less than fifty degrees. Not bad for an air temperature after a brutal winter, but capable of chilling a swimmer to the bone within a few minutes.

Vinny was himself getting chilled now in the increasingly breezy evening and he considered going back to the shack to warm up a bit. Tony Craig would find him there, he'd leave the door open and he would be drawn to the light from inside. It would draw him in...the light. The light from the office lamps would find their way outside and illuminate the steps into the shack. If they were stronger or in closer proximity...to something metallic...or something with a reflective quality to it...he stared into the water again and could see the reflection of the lights from the bridge, little white dots playing over the small swells the maddening current changes coaxed from the river. The stars to a lesser extent, but definitely the full moon was there and off to the right, he could pick out a rosier glow from the red Pepsi sign on the water. What was wrong with this picture? His rage, which had been effectively bottled up for the past two days except for his short outburst earlier, was still at a boiling point. Time was running out and he was losing his grip on the situation with every passing minute. There was something there, however. He knew it, sitting out there in the blackness of the water, mocking him, taunting his intellect, trying to will the answer out of him.

Millions of dollars, close to five hundred jobs, and the personal savings of all his close friends was at stake. He looked across the river to where he and Maxie met the night before last and then to the right at the beautiful coops of Sutton Place. Why don't you want these buildings and the park here? he wanted to scream. So he did, Why?!" His voice boomed out over the waters and he wondered if Moose Miller could hear him. He only yelled the question once, any more would have qualified as whining.

"Why, what?" came a voice from behind him, one that startled Vinny and angered him all at once. How did he allow someone to sneak up on him like this? He knew the answer. Because he was losing himself in his problem. He squinted at the man approaching him who was about twenty feet away but couldn't make out who it was. Vinny answered the question with one of his own.

"Who are you?" Can I help you?" It was not a friendly request. Vinny started moving his feet forward and to the side a bit, the way a great outfielder will when the pitcher is in his windup, so he could make a move quickly, without hesitation once the ball is struck. The man thankfully slowed and spread his hands in the universal New York City gesture that said, What, you don't understand? Tony Craig then added, "Wasn't that you I spoke to earlier? Or did J'lome give me the wrong number? It's Tony, Tony Craig. I don't know if you remember but I actually went swimming here with you once about a hundred years ago." Vinny eased considerably, like a balloon that suddenly was untied, the air whistling out sounding like a little girl that just discovered a caterpillar in her hair.

"Holy crap, Tony, you scared the shit out of me." Vinny and Tony advanced until they were a couple of feet apart and the look on both men's faces showed that bit of recognition that could never be erased completely even after so many years. The two men shook hands warmly but did not embrace and then stepped back for an appraisal of each other.

"You look good, Vin. And from what I hear you're doing well, too."

"I heard you were a Fed. We lost track of you when your mom sent you to that fancy high school upstate. I remember your mom, how is she?" Vinny realized his mistake quickly as Tony looked at the ground, kicked at a stray pebble and told him of his loss in a supremely sad voice.

"I'm sorry Tony. I kind of remember her, it was so long ago. She obviously was a great lady because she took care of you unlike so many other mutts in this neighborhood." He smiled, not being able to resist his next comment. "I remember she used to make cinnamon rolls late in the summer and hand them out to everyone. They were impossibly delicious." Vinny could still remember the aroma of Mrs. Craig's cinnamon rolls wiping out the not-so-pleasant smells of the average Queens street in late August. Tony smiled in return, genuinely touched that Vinny had remembered. "Anyway," Vinny continued, "what brings you here? What's going on? Tell me about being a Fed, what's it like for you?"

"Too many Ivy Leaguers, you know the type, I'm sure. Too many of them running the bureau. A total lack of people who really know the streets. I originally thought I'd be able to bring the smarts I learned on the streets around here into the bureau and make them work well in conjunction with the Fed apparatus. Instead I have spent the last twenty-five years answering to people who are more interested in their summer homes, getting manicures and appearing on television. But that's another story for another time. I can't relate to them, but I can't do without them."

"Sounds like you're talking about women." Both men chuckled at the oldest, shared between all men, inside joke there was.

Tony then went on for another ten minutes, telling Vinny about the original tip on Aubrey possibly coming north after the near-fatal beating of his wife, his concerns about domestic terrorism particularly in the military, Aubrey's call to the middle east, the tailing of him to the airport, and the necessity of pulling the tail off the three.

"How could you lose him there? How could a fucking budget shortage influence something like this when it seems so close to the tip of a possible iceberg?"

Tony continued, ignoring the question, his comments punctuated by shakes of the head and sighs of frustration. He gave Vinny a brief history of his career in the bureau and reluctantly, his outburst in his office a few hours earlier. He hated admitting to a loss of face more so than the actual event. "I think it's an important issue regarding the security of this country and that's why I got the NYPD to give up a harbor cop to tail these guys for me and I was lucky that they stopped in at J'lome's mosque after the cop had to leave and go on duty. Otherwise I might have lost them permanently." He fished a cigarette out of his pocket, cupped his hand to get the match lit on the first try and shook the flame out, flipping it into the water. He inhaled and blew the smoke out quickly and turned back to Vinny, who was slapping the side of his head.

"Shit, Tony, I ran into those guys at the mosque. J'lome called me, said he was having some trouble and frankly, I was in the mood for a fight at the time." He laughed quickly and then continued, "Do you see that boat out there?" he asked, pointing out toward the United Nations building? That's your harbor cop, Moose Miller. He's coming by here later tonight for a game of cards if he can still keep his eyes open once his shift ends." Tony was staring out at the river, still unable to believe how all of this was falling together. This is why the bureau had to start trusting people on the street. He switched gears then, remembering to stay on track in the middle of this blast from the past with an old acquaintance.

"J'lome told me that you had someone still following these guys?" Please let it be true he didn't say.

"Yeah. I put the kid Charlie Mick on them. Partly because I needed him to learn some things, partly because I was also a bit concerned about these guys. Especially the big guy."

"That's the special forces guy we're looking at. Do you know where they are right now?"

"Uhh..how about right up the block? You might have actually passed them on your way here."

"You mean, they're right around here still? All three of them?" Tony couldn't believe what he was hearing. Vinny nodded.

"I just heard from Charlie Mick a few minutes ago. These three guys have been sitting on a house just off Vernon Boulevard for twenty-four hours. And no, we don't know who lives there," he said anticipating the obvious question. Tony looked out at the water again, took a long pull on his cigarette, and flicked it into the dark water.

"I have to go check this out, see it for myself. Exactly where is the kid right now?" Vinny pulled his phone out, called Charlie Mick and got his exact location which he then gave to Tony. "What's the best way to get there? I want to approach them from the rear. Is it this block I go up or this one?" he asked, pointing toward the streets that ran at ninety degree angles to Vinny's construction site. Before he left he added, "I'd like you to show me around the site, see your plans for this when I wrap this thing up. I can see already that it'll be a great place. This thing here with these three guys could maybe be just a piece of shit, I don't know."

"Maybe this Saudi kid has some money laying around. Tell him I'll let him in for a piece if he comes up with some funds. By the way Tony," he asked, putting his arm around his old acquaintance's shoulder and leading him back to the entrance to the site, "Do the Feds ever get involved with a possibly corrupt city agency filled with snotty bluebloods?"

NIGHT

The tension in the Saab was mounting with every passing moment. Aubrey mostly brooded silently, disgusted by the two with him, hating every fiber of their existence. The only way he was able to keep himself calm was to remind himself that he was going to personally put the lights out on each of them within the next twenty-four hours, or even sooner depending upon when this woman shows up.

"I'm getting bored just sitting here doing nothing," Whathefu offered, apparently not learning anything about Aubrey in the past day and a half, who just finally made his decision how he was going to snuff this Saudi snot-nose. It would be fists and feet only, he decided— no gun, no knife, no club to aid in his beating the life out of this twerp. He would drag it out as well, much in the way some feudal lords in Japan would boil their enemies in a large pot a little at a time, stretching out the torture and the agony sometimes for hours on end.

Still the snot-nose had a point. It was just after ten o'clock now on a Saturday night and if she was the whore he was convinced she was, then she would not be coming home at all this night, instead setting herself up with whomever bought her a dinner and a few cheap drinks. They were all the same, these women, he believed firmly. He was also getting antsy just sitting here, his discipline being tested every moment that passed without Laura in their line of vision. Sooner or later they would have to be more proactive in their search for her, but how in such a vast metropolis? Where could they possibly start?

Maybe she was indeed a moderately modest woman as the African described her, out for a movie by herself with maybe a little window shopping on the side. But she could be just like his wife, screwing delivery boys and whoever else on the base or in the town who gave her a wink and a nod. Once again he cursed himself for the beating he administered to her, more so for his lack of control rather than the shame he should have felt for beating a woman. He really just should have given her a hard slap across her face and left without a word was what he was thinking, as if he were rehashing a failed sales presentation. Give her a nice crack, let her fucking think about it, what he was going to do when he returned, goddammit to hell! He raged at himself, his stupidity, his lack of focus in his mind...fuck her and every woman like her. Why couldn't his benefactor have called just five minutes earlier? Most probably he would not have even had the time to deliver so many blows to her ribs and legs if the call came earlier. He sighed and slumped in his seat a little, as he always wanted to since he was a kid and was feeling overwhelmed but hardly ever did for fear of his old man screaming that he would tie a broomstick to his ass to straighten him up. What does any of that matter anymore, he began in his cortex again as he pulled himself out of the abyss of doubt. What does it care? Because he was now on this mission which unexpectedly brought him this tremendous possibility, an opportunity to realize his dreams of spreading the word of The Prophet around the world. Strange how that happens in life, that something can grow out of nothing so effortlessly. He turned to Whathefu with his decision already made. It was really all they could do.

"We're staying here until I say so," he growled at Whathefu who cowered once again under the weight of Aubrey's anger, but much in the way of a faithful dog that just won't leave, no matter how much the master beats him. Aubrey picked up on it somehow and muttered under his breath, "Little fucking queer, a disgrace to your entire family." His eyes locked on Andre in the back seat as he checked the mirror for the thousandth time in the last half hour and he, too, shrunk under his gaze, turning away to watch a group of smiling young people, two men and their girlfriends on the sidewalk who just turned the corner, probably headed to Manhattan, he figured. Aubrey's last thought before his eyes left Andre's was that he hoped this fat African would be provided a better brain by Allah in the next life. Pathetic, overweight loser, another dog to some woman. Stealing all that money from his employer and for what? To finance an operation overseas? To start his own mosque, one with real Islamic values, not like that pathetic place they visited and prayed in the past two days? No, nothing virtuous at all. Just so he could impress some woman. He looked past Andre out the large back window and started.

"Hey," he said to Andre, "Check that one out, is it her?" Andre turned around to see a woman, but he could tell even from here this one was shorter, not as athletically built as Laura. It was definitely not her. The hair was shorter as well, he could see that now. The woman disappeared down the next block, heading toward the river. "That wasn't her." She always came to work on time, thought Andre. Her excellent attendance record at Argent Bank didn't matter so much now on a Saturday night, but in retrospect, he had to admit again that she never seemed like a big party girl. Therefore she should come home soon, at least he hoped so. He gazed at the latest passersby on the sidewalk and thought of Kismine, who he would have firmly in his life once the riches were in his grasp. Where are you now, my kitten? He was annoyed now but didn't show it as the pig American was speaking again.

"Are you sure? Should I circle the block?" Andre nodded, "The hair and height were wrong. It wasn't her," he stated with utter conviction. He wanted to get back to his dream about Kismine right away. Well, Aubrey figured, if it was her, then she would come back up the block from the river. In either case, they could clearly see when anyone approached the house from either direction.

—⊷—

"Otra vez," Kismine whispered into the young man's ear as she accepted another powerful thrust that drove her kneecaps closer to her ears. It was the only Spanish she knew, and it was all she needed to know at the moment. "It means, once again, or do it again," he explained to her so gently, so lovingly. She had been aware of his eyes on her ever since the first recording sessions, not letting anyone else know but her, not coming near her or speaking to her, but allowing his eyes to linger on hers for what seemed an eternity, punctuated by a boyish smile and a look away. His guitar playing was so incredibly fluid and pure sounding, pushing out simple but perfect layovers during the chorus that she never would have thought of. She felt a certain indescribable sync with him for all the songs they recorded after that, and especially the piece they wrote together the other day, when Andre had to run out to his job. His little freakin' computer job, she thought at the time. They were listening to the radio when Carlos Santana's classic, "Oye Como Va" came over the air. She had never heard the song before and was floored by the rhythm section, the vocals, and especially Carlos' guitar playing. "How about the organ solo?" he asked and they both laughed...she got his silly sense of humor instantly and it was at that moment she knew she would never speak with Andre again.

And now here she was in his apartment, doing exactly what she wanted. Making love with this beautiful man in such a way that Andre could never imagine. "I'm only in my early twenties," she said aloud accidentally, breaking her lover's perfect rhythm for a moment. "What did you say?" he asked, he positioned perfectly for another thrust, but resting just outside. She smacked his ass and said what she wanted to say, "Your cock is so hard in my pussy, Otra Vez!" The resulting shock wave of pleasure made her almost black out, her orgasm so intense that she almost hit his nose with her forehead as her body bucked like a wild mustang, she starting to almost laugh out loud thinking she could do this all day long.

———

Maxie Carter was walking down a deserted street flanked by low-level factories, one that she might have normally felt a little nervous about but at the moment she was full of purpose and didn't allow any fear to seep in. She knew she was going in the right direction because she could see across the river to the United Nations building and the other luxury high-rises in the city. Up ahead she noticed a man exit from behind a cyclone fence. The man was pulling his trench coat tightly around him as he started up the block toward her and for a moment she was uneasy. But he passed by her quickly, his head down as if he were trying to conceal himself, never looking in her direction, as if he were only a block from home on a frigid winter evening, complete with an arctic wind force-fed into the canyons made by all the tall buildings in the city. She could have been naked and he wouldn't have noticed. Good, keep on going, mister. She turned around when she reached the corner and could see the man was still heading in the opposite direction with clear determination in his step.

She pulled her own determination together and headed toward the open fence she saw the man exit from. She peered in hesitantly, the poorly illuminated site throwing her off stride for a moment and then she quickly recognized the trailer she saw from the bench on the other side of the river. Off to the right was the Pepsi sign, mostly invisible to her from here except for the faint reddish glow in front of it and there, about the length of a football field away, she could see the outline of a man she knew from here was Vinny Malloy. She could see he was near the edge of the property, on the bulkhead...was he working on the problem? Was he figuring it out? she wondered as her legs carried her forward with more energy than she knew she had. She closed to within about fifty yards and then called out, "Mr. Malloy!" Vinny turned immediately thinking, Jesus, this is the second time someone snuck up on me tonight. Got to get a dog. He was glad it was a woman as he never felt threatened by a woman—at least not physically—and he was amazed when he realized it was Maxie, and he walked out to greet her, smiling broadly. He liked her simple ensemble of jeans and a jacket, her slightly bobbed hair framing her face perfectly...perfectly at least for his eyes.

"What are you doing here?" he asked as she drew right up to him.

"I'm here to set things right, Mr. Malloy."

"Vinny."

"Right, I'm sorry...Vinny." He turned back to the water and beckoned her to follow. She did and in a minute they were at the water's edge, looking at the pier. "I think I figured something out here," he said to her, not averting his gaze from the unsteady-in-the-least-looking, wood and metal pier. She said nothing, fascinated by his concentration.

"Somehow, something is different here, I know it is. I just can't nail it down."

"No reflection," she said. Vinny turned back to her with a perplexed look on his face and then swiveled his head back to the pier. He smiled as it came to him in a rush. "No reflection. Exactly." He ran off to the sign leaving her in his wake, inspected it closely and she could see him shaking his head and clapping his hands as he ran back to her. "Flat paint. It doesn't reflect the lights off the bridge and the moon," he said. He leaned out over the first few planks of the pier, but did not step out on it, examining the railings. He was grateful for the full moon tonight and said a silent thank you to whomever controlled such things. "This thing was recently painted as well as the sign. Flat paint on top of the glossy paint that was always there that used to reflect the lights of the sign and the bridge."

"Yes," she answered. "It was painted with the same paint as the sign, at the same time. Both times it was some shade of black, certainly different in texture and darkness and unfortunately for whoever

did this, flat paint. I doubt that even you would ever have noticed."
He shook his head slowly. "I wouldn't have ever bothered looking at
something like that. And I love details," he added, turning back to
face her. "But I am still kind of surprised to see you here. Pleased, but
still surprised." She drew her jacket a little closer in response to a bit
of a breeze off the water and nodded at the shack, "Do you have some
heat, maybe a little coffee in there? I'm kind of cold and if you can
fix me a cup of black coffee with two sugars, I'll tell you all about it."
Vinny pursed his lips, cocked his head jauntily, raised his hand in the
direction of the shack and beckoned her in its direction. He believed,
when they arrived at the stairs, that for the first time since he could
remember, that he was falling in love.

———

The number 7 train lurched out of the Grand Central stop, several
levels below the famous ceiling under which thousands of suburban
commuters every day crisscrossed the big room in search of their train
back to four bedrooms and full finished basements full of...not much.
Within seconds the train was hurtling under the East River to Queens.
The sudden pick-up of speed threw Laura off balance and she practically fell into Michael's arms and instinctively placed her hands flat on
his pectorals to slow her movement forward. Her face burned crimson
red and she pulled away quickly.

"Sorry. Sometimes I can lose my balance, even after so many years
of riding the trains."

"No, don't worry about," Michael responded. "It's okay. It's good
to have Irish toes when riding the subway." She looked up at him,
thoroughly confused."

"Irish toes. That's when the second toe is a little longer than usual.
It keeps the average Irishman from teetering forward after a few too
many Guinness'. That longer toe kicks in unconsciously and pushes
the body back to an upright position before it loses its center completely and hits the ground." She smiled and lightly punched his arm.

"That's silly."

"Well I guess so...but it's still okay that you bumped into me. Don't
worry about it."

No, it's not okay, she wanted to scream. It's not okay that I am out on this perfect date with this fantastic man who I want in my bed within the next five minutes. For the first time in her life, she was feeling a warmth in her loins without someone or herself actually touching her body. It was merely the thought of this man in her arms, of her in his, that was turning her on, more so than any man she had known previously, all of whom had to work fairly hard at getting her turned on. All Michael had to do was just stand next to her.

Yes, Michael, she wanted to scream, it is true that the first moment I laid eyes on you ten years ago, my brain turned to jelly and my heart exploded and I blurted out things to you that I never told any man even after dating some of them for more than a year.

Yes, I so appreciated your honesty with me all these years unlike that pig Adam and I also could so easily determine that you have a good moral compass along with those lovely blue eyes and full head of sandy hair. But I also like to think I have a good moral compass as well and I am fighting a battle within myself right now I never thought I'd have to fight. So many men, committed to other women, lying to me and to so many other women over the years. How could they live with themselves? Laura often wondered. She would have more appreciated it if they announced that all they wanted was someone they could have a quick bang with every couple of weeks or so. At least there was some speck of honesty in that although the lack of morality would have always bothered her and it didn't mater anyway because that was not who she was or wanted to be. She never could have truly enjoyed herself lying underneath another woman's man, no matter his level of bedroom talent.

I don't want any part of another woman's man, the sneaking around, the quick shower afterward, the lonely holidays and birthdays, the feeling of being used, like an old dish rag, when being dropped off at my door only to see him leave to go have dinner with his family. I want what I want. I want, no, I crave love and silliness, I want a man with sexy good looks that he can achieve in less than five minutes in the bathroom. I want a man who knows what he is doing when the mood is in the air between us...before, during, and after lovemaking. I want him to make me feel like the only woman in the world each and every time he holds me close. I want an athletic man who can run as fast as me, an elegant man who can hold his own socially and intellectually at the fanciest dinner party in town. I want this man to be able to speak with a head of state as easily as he speaks to a deli clerk and I want him to appreciate how hard the deli clerk works to make a living. I want him to be able to swing me across a dance floor as if he were Gene Kelly and then engage me in a farting contest later on in the evening. She could feel the train start its incline and she knew they were past the halfway point in the tunnel under the river. She looked up at Michael and silently marveled at his eyes which seemed to shift from green to blue every few seconds. She wondered what made them do that. She held his gaze for a few seconds and it was during this short period that Michael wondered if he had ever looked into a face as lovely as hers.

Not the slightest diminishing of electric attraction had occurred in the ten years since they met. Each and every time he had seen her in the hallway of the bank or at the Christmas party...no matter what she was wearing or what mood she was in, she was easily the most beautiful woman he had ever seen. His guilt was profound, mulling over these types of thoughts. Not about the beauty thing...after all beauty was truly only skin deep, but he wasn't ever out on the prowl trolling for women in the bars or online. He reminded himself once again the whole thing these past ten years with Laura was all accidental.

Except for this day and evening of course.

He figured he had about ten minutes left with her and that saddened and delighted him at the same time. You never know about the twists and turns an individual life can make...maybe one day he would see her socially again. He knew absolutely that he wouldn't think of calling anyone else for a date if he were ever single again. After all these years, with the way she was holding his gaze just a little too long right now...wow, look at the way her hair falls around her shoulders...it was still simple for him to admit that she was quite simply the most beautiful woman he had ever seen. Not just met in person, but seen anywhere. The straight line of her jaw, the figure, the slightly sleepy brown eyes that reminded him of a delightful afternoon nap, one that you don't wake from with a headache, the tiniest wisp of makeup that he could detect, the nice personality...he thought about it often enough over the years to now know without any doubt that if he could build a woman, this is what he would build. All the tourists in the Village thought so. Even the gay guys were checking her out, their eyes taking all of her in as if she were Tom Brady or something. I can't imagine not ever being turned on by her, even if we made love fourteen times in the next four days.

The last time he made love to Georgia she actually yawned in the middle, which wouldn't be so bad maybe if at that precise moment he thought he was really reaching her, turning her on, touching her perfectly.

But there was no way he could pursue anything with Laura beyond this one time date. The only accomplishment to spring out of that would be the destruction of their relationship. If it is to be, it will come about naturally, or not at all. He stretched up to his full height to relieve some pressure in his lumbar spine, the result of walking around with her all day.

"Everything alright?" The words floated out of her mouth like tiny butterflies that once lighted on his eardrums made it seem as if they were made strictly to hear her voice. He smiled down at her, desperately wanting at that moment to lift her chin just so and kiss her like she's never been kissed before. The train then filled with light as it burst out of the dark tunnel into the Vernon-Jackson station, the lurching action now separating them a bit more, momentarily dulling the growing heat between them.

"Yes, it's all good," he answered as the train screeched to a stop. He lightly touched her elbow and guided her to the door, a group of young Eastern-European tough guys headed probably to the cafés in Astoria to ogle the largest collection of too-tight skirts in the metropolitan area stepping aside for them. What a gentleman, she thought once again, almost sighing audibly, but catching herself just in time. They stepped clear of the closing doors, and walked straight into the old style, floor-to-ceiling turnstile, passing through it one at a time. Michael heard the conductor call out to watch for the closing doors as they headed up the stairs to Vernon Boulevard.

⚮

Vinny and Maxie were talking about the project over coffee and cheesecake in the construction shack. She was pleased to see how neat and ordered it was. Her father had a desk like that. He had shown her the blueprints and mockups of the buildings, the park, and the floating beach and was not only amazed at the attention to detail but also how everything seemed to rise off the table into a three dimensional picture of the finished project as a result of the completeness of the presentation. She would much rather look out across the river on her terrace at a place like this rather than emptiness, which is what was always there, except of course, for the Pepsi sign.

She had only needed a few minutes to rehash the scene with her husband from earlier in the day. Vinny had listened with rapt attention, interrupting only to question her about the other participants in the scheme to take the property out from underneath him. Somewhere, he figured, there's a banker or a lawyer or real estate broker or someone like that behind these people and he was going to figure out who it is. He suddenly had a warm feeling spread throughout his bones thinking about how delicious it would be to find out who was screwing with him behind his back so he could blow them out of the water.

"What are you smiling about?" she asked. "I think it's something else beside figuring out the problem with the pier. You have a very contented look on your face." Vinny was mildly startled that Maxie Carter, a society woman whom he barely knew, from the other side of the river, was able to read him so accurately. He was similarly startled with himself when he realized with astonishing speed and clarity what he wanted to say to her. With the confidence of ten men, he leaned forward to be able to look directly into her face. At that moment, his cell phone rang. "Just a moment," he said as he flipped it open with his thumb, barking into the speaker, but not angrily, "What?!"

"It's us," replied Fred Burke, who was at the wheel of the converted Pepperidge Farm bread route truck, his brother Ryan in the passenger seat, baseball cap on backwards, peeling a banana. "It's game six versus Houston and Starks is currently two for twelve or something like that from the floor and he's not slowing down so we know nothing is going to get better." Maxie could hear the conversation as Vinny set the phone to speaker causing a bemused expression to cross her face.

"What are you talking about? English please." He could hear the other Burke brother answer.

"The brakes and suspension in this piece of shit are completely shot. We're going to have to retire her, I think. Once we pull up to your place, it's parked forever. Do we have enough money to get something new? Otherwise we're gonna have to start taking the bus to our appointments." Fred continued, "This truck is definitely Scott Layden with problems, Vin. We have to retire her, set her up as a permanent museum piece somewhere. Otherwise we're going to tip over like Eddie Curry on roller skates after an all you can eat brunch. Seriously bro', we gotta do something. Are we gonna be able to?"

"That truck is going nowhere. Just get it here without killing yourselves. Everything is working out, I have it all covered," he said, smiling at Maxie. "Hey, maybe we can set it up at the edge of the complex, by the floating beach as a permanent Mr. Softee truck."

"I like that," both Burkes replied in unison. Fred took over the conversation again, "Kind of like Ewing going from a defensive paint presence to a shooting center. I like it. Look, we'll be over in fifteen minutes, we're just finishing up here at El Paso Gardens, the building by the park."

"Okay, just take it easy on the truck, I really like this idea about the Mr. Softee thing. I want that truck back here in one piece. You guys, too."

"Do you love us that much?"Ryan asked.

"No, just your money, which I'm going to take from you at will. See you later." Vinny clicked off the phone and closed it, seamlessly turning his attention to the lady he had only met a couple of days earlier, a lady from another world, with whom he was rapidly falling in love.

"What do you want to do with the rest of your life Maxie?" he asked her. She could easily see his genuine interest in her.

"I never told you this, my soon-to-be-ex-husband was ashamed of it amazingly, but I want to go back to nursing. I graduated with honors from nursing school but when I got married..." She paused for a moment, thinking about it and all of a sudden she snapped her head up, her eyebrows arched.

"I mean what kind of man wouldn't want a nurse as a wife, right?" In any event, I married a guy who was nice at first, he was...appropriate, I guess. Anyway, he wanted me to go to law school. He did pay for it, by the way; I'll give him that. In his crowd, that's what everyone seemed to aspire to. What a dead career that is, unless you're a D.A. having a good time putting felons away, which I actually wanted to do, but even that wasn't good enough for him. He wanted me to do real estate or securities law. I realize now all he wanted was to use me instead of paying for his own representation. What a jerk." She looked away, sniffling a bit.

"I did all of these things for all the wrong reasons," she added sadly. Vinny extended his hand so that his fingertips were under her chin. He lifted her head ever so gently and looked right at her. "Don't feel so bad about that. Most people do. And very few of them ever escape. You're about to."

"I'm scared. But I'm confident also." Vinny leaned back at this comment and smiled. "Now I know you're smart," he said to her as he poured her another cup of coffee.

⸺

Tony Craig was walking north on Vernon Boulevard on the west side of the street, his mind racing ahead of him toward two possible con- clusions. One not-so-far-off-the-chart conclusion being the end of his career with the FBI, a career marked by countless hours of inane drudgery and lack of the kind of success he always envisioned, the other a possible 180 degree turnaround in said career if something comes out of this little surveillance he put together which was based upon a hunch, started by a...sadly, in these times...run of the mill domestic crime four hundred miles down the interstate from where he now stood. He started calculating his pension as he passed by hard- ware stores, delicatessens and a church. He then switched over to his acceptance speech to head the New York office. The first thing he would do is send Chetlington to...where? Maybe Fargo. Let him freeze his ass off for a few years. See if Jean-Georges delivers up there.

Up ahead and across the street he noticed a hulking figure leaning out of a doorway briefly. Even from a half block away he knew who it was. The kid looks like his father, he thought, at least from the neck down. He started across the boulevard at a sharp angle and then noticed the Saab on the opposite corner from the kid facing toward him. He kept his eyes lowered, but not overly so...even the slightest attempt to be unobtrusive would alert someone with good instincts. He was thankful he was wearing dark jeans and a black coat. He could easily blend into the neighborhood. He used to live here. This was his place, not theirs. He was only thirty feet from the Saab and he dared not look their way lest that was the singular moment that Aubrey might refocus his attention his way and catch the resulting almost imperceptible hitch in his step, the look of interest that would then remove his composure, possibly resulting in a deadly response. He hoped the kid had some brains about him. He was crossing the double yellow line in the middle of Vernon Boulevard, eyes on a spot ten feet in front of him as he progressed, careful not to raise his eyes to the kid. He would have to give him some kind of verbal pass as he walked by, something to entice the kid into following him to a safe place where they could speak. He decided it had to be up the block, away from the boulevard where the lighting was brighter. He felt the presence of people off to his right and he could see in his peripheral vision a woman and a man walking together, but not as lovers. He paid them no mind and continued to Charlie Mick's post.

"There she is!" blurted Andre, pointing through the large rear windshield of the station wagon as he spoke. Aubrey reached between the bucket seats and grabbed his outstretched arm, pulling it down. He hissed at the man in the back seat. "Get down on the seat, hide your face, now!" he whispered but with the venom of a cobra in every word. He averted his eyes, staring down at the gearshift and the ignition in the center console and spoke in an equally quiet but venomous tone to Whathefu who seemed to be in a state of delayed elation at the sudden turn of events. "Look down here where I'm looking, turn your face away from the window." Aubrey raised his eyes enough to appraise the two people walking by. The man was tall, older than him, but looked somewhat fit. His hands were in his pockets and he was smiling as he talked with the woman.

He took the woman in as best he could as they passed the car. She passed by between the man and the car, and he could see that she was indeed athletically built and moved well. She seemed in his quick once-over to be modestly dressed for a woman who lived in a city full of sin and debauchery. She had her head turned toward the man, obviously enjoying and paying attention to what he was saying. He lifted his head to see a bit more with each additional step past the car they took. The two of them had passed by without seeming to notice their car or its occupants, which pleased Aubrey greatly. The last thing he wanted was a confrontation in public. They had to get in the apartment and do it there.

Michael and Laura started to angle their steps toward the building on the corner, Aubrey checking to make absolutely sure they were headed to her place and not a corner bar or the deli. Andre lifted his head then and following his captor's gaze, turned to see Laura turn the corner with some man who looked vaguely familiar to him. Then he had it. He worked for the bank, but Andre didn't know what department. He didn't give a damn about any other part of the company but his own and never bothered to speak with anyone else that he didn't absolutely have to. He indubitably knew he never spoke to the man, but he figured at least that he was married as Andre had noticed his wedding band on the infrequent occasions that they were in the kitchen together.

"Fucking whore," he spat. "She's been out on one date with this guy and she's taking him into her home." He turned to his two other cohorts both of whom were now looking into the backseat at him, "He's married, too. What the hell is he doing out with her on a Saturday night?" he asked them. He turned to watch them again, following them with his unblinking stare making their way down the block, now crossing over to her side of the street.

Although Aubrey detested the woman's apparent looseness with her morals, he had no interest in the opinions of others on the subject right now, especially the African's. He spoke to them both in a calmer tone now, drawing them in conspiratorially, hoping to displace any fear they might have at their now very much in reach moment of glory and redemption. If only they knew, he thought, how close to death they are. So easy to manipulate, these two!

"You have to be quiet from here on in. Any extra sounds or voices could alert them to our presence," he half-whispered to them both, seeing that he had their rapt attention. "What you say about her may be true, and probably is true," directing his gaze to Andre, "but that is not central to our mission. All we need from her are the passwords to restart the computer. The man, whoever he is and whatever he's doing with her, means nothing to us or our mission and is therefore expendable. She is not. Do you understand?" Whathefu and Andre both nodded yes, not questioning anything, to Aubrey's relief. He hoped that just maybe these two would ultimately prove useful in grabbing the woman.

"We let them get comfortable for a couple of minutes. Maybe the man is going to leave her at the doorstep and go on his way. Maybe he will enter her apartment, only to leave a few minutes after he uses the bathroom. The point is, we have to make this simple and quiet. We will give them ten minutes before we move in."

"But she's a fucking whore!" Andre half roared. "She's probably in bed with him already!"

"I said quiet!...you fucking idiot. Just listen to me and keep your mouth shut." He was gritting his teeth as he said it, his stomach was churning and his brain was racing. He was trying to whisper his comments as a Doberman might if it could talk. Could he afford the ten minutes? he was wondering. Maybe not. He knew the police precinct was a few blocks away, but would they have been alerted to his presence in New York by now? No, not yet...definitely not yet. Maybe in a few days, but definitely not by now. But he also couldn't tip his hand too quickly. He didn't want the man there although he was sure he would kill the woman's lover in less than a minute. But that would be noisy. And messy. Let the situation play out. He was conducting this operation on a catch-as-catch-can basis with a couple of pinheads as his partners. He had to see what happened with the man.

Maybe she was a whore, but that wouldn't be a problem. Catching them unawares, naked in bed, completely vulnerable just might work in their favor. But they were going to wait for ten minutes and he told his cohorts so. He knew he needed the time as well. The tension of the wait in the car was wearing him down like a desert sun. Better to try and get as fresh as possible before moving in. But no longer than ten minutes. He knew time was not his friend. But he was listening to his gut, moving the fear and concern about imminent capture for the beating of his wife aside for his greater goal, the capture of the woman, the forcing of the passwords from her, and the deaths of these two in the car with him. And maybe the man and the woman as well. In twenty-four hours or less, I want to be on a plane to Saudi Arabia and my new life with my money. His decision was made. He knew how he would lay it out. He drew the two passengers in the car into his confidence again as he leaned into them as if they were lifelong friends. He had two Glock pistols in his jacket. He took one out of his side pocket. He removed the clip and cleared the chamber, and after emptying the clip save for a single round, handed it to Andre and whispered, "Here's what you are going to do."

Charlie Mick was tired from standing in one spot for hours. He would have been more physically comfortable if he were running back and forth in a basketball game at the courts in Astoria Park. This standing around like a tree was for the birds. These guys aren't going anywhere or doing anything. He considered going back to Vinny's car to sit there, but it was parked up the block and he didn't want these guys to disappear in the minute or two it would take him to walk back to where he was parked.

He was antsy waiting for the call from Vinny to drop this surveillance and get to the card game. He loved taking his father's place with his friends, loved the jokes and the camaraderie. He knew he had to learn to control his primal emotions with these guys if he were to get anywhere with them, Vinny was adamant about that. But he desperately wanted to hate someone for what happened to his dad and his dad's friends on 9/11.

One of his dad's best friends was a Muslim and Charlie Mick often wondered what he was thinking when the floor fell out from beneath him and he started hurtling toward the street, being ground up...atomized was how the mayor so tactfully put it. Did he hate his fellow Muslims for ending his life so early and violently? His head hurt as he thought of every debate he listened to on the street and in the media, politicians decrying the Islamization of Europe and America, war hawks like Rumsfeld foolishly shaking both fingers in the air at a White House press conference insisting that America could fight a two front war in the Middle East and North Korea if necessary.

The conspiracy idiots and the apologists, the families of the victims with their protracted calls for a memorial and payouts, to so much of the international community and their visceral hatred of anything American, and even to much of America. It seemed to him that so many people outside of New York have completely forgotten what happened here.

His dad always told him that Vinny was the smartest and toughest man he had ever known and he advised his son to seek his counsel if anything ever happened to him. That was a decision he didn't even have to make as Vinny came to the house late in that fateful day to check on his friend, and finding Charlie Mick alone, crying, watching the TV, a cell phone in his hand with the redial button jammed sideways by repeated pressing, a little boy who was now an orphan, having lost his mother to her ruthless selfishness and laundry list of addictions while still in his infancy. His father didn't even keep a picture of her anywhere in the house. "Do you know where my dad is?" he had asked Vinny with all the hopefulness and trust a little boy could muster. Vinny didn't lie to him, "I'm sorry kid, we think he was caught in the building with Khan and Ping the Router. But we really don't know where he is. Until your dad shows up, I'll be your dad along with everyone else. Come to my place here, let's write and leave a note for your dad so he doesn't worry about you when he gets home."

And he went to Vinny's apartment and never left, being raised through the years by a collection of his dad's friends, his mother never bothering to show up again even after he was paid a million dollars by the government as a result of his father's death. Vinny forced him to put it into the bond account with their friend Tommy who worked on Wall Street and the interest paid him nicely but his frustration and anger at the loss of his dad grew like the interest on the account. He missed his dad still to this day. He was the one who stayed with him after his mother walked out. His loyalty to the man was as fierce as that of any lioness defending her cubs. And now it was to Vinny and the others.

He felt like an idiot, a failure all day and yesterday because of what he had said outside of J'lome's mosque. J'lome was the man who visited him most often in the wake of his dad's murder, teaching him everything from how to construct a good sentence to the Pythagorean Theorem to how to fake right and go left into the paint. And he insulted the man and his faith today, worse yet, in front of Vinny, his best friend and Charlie Mick's de facto father. Not too smart. Well he would show them he could handle anything, that he could change the course of his anger. And he would do so by staying right here until Vinny said different.

It was then that he noticed some movement off to the left, a man walking diagonally across the street somewhat toward him and a couple crossing over the opposite way. The man with the woman looked familiar, and he was startled when he realized it was Michael Pierce. Who was the woman with him? Charlie Mick could see that she was tall and that her hair moved nicely around her shoulders, and also that it wasn't his wife Georgia. Probably headed to the card game and maybe he just started talking to the woman while they walked along the street. Michael was like that...friendly, could talk to anyone about anything. He kept his eye on them as they turned the corner and he thought he detected some movement in the car. And then he was startled again as the man drew near quickly and started talking to him without breaking stride.

"Charlie Mick, I'm an old friend of your father's, Vinny told me you were here, follow me up the block in one minute," the man aid to him in a muted tone. Who the hell was this guy? Charlie thought, as Tony continued past him. He ached to turn to follow after him but he refused to take his eyes off the car. Tony Craig ducked behind a large maple tree that was uprooting the sidewalk and the curb and whistled softly by cupping his hands tightly together and blowing through the first knuckle of his thumbs which emitted a low pitch whistle that would catch Charlie's attention but not be loud and shrill enough to carry any further. After about ten seconds, Charlie Mick started up the block, keeping close to the buildings, taking refuge in their shadows until he reached the tree. He looked down the block and seeing no one there, crossed the sidewalk quickly on a line and stepped behind the tree with the older man. He regarded Tony Craig whom he didn't recognize at all. The kid concluded quickly that this man had a presence about him that proclaimed him as a no-nonsense kind of guy, as well as realizing that he had some kind of insane intensity going on about something and it was Vinny's voice in his head then reminding him that listening is twice as important as talking. He leaned into the man so that their voices could be kept low and listened to him start talking without any further introduction.

***

"It must be nice living near the river, you probably get a nice breeze in the summer," Michael told Laura as they ambled along the sidewalk. He couldn't recall which place was hers among the row of two-family homes that lined the block. This is perfect. He would drop her here and then continue down the block to the game.

"Yes, but in the winter the wind coming up this block can be terribly cold. Sometimes it can drive you backward and it makes my eyes water by the time I get to the door."

"That just makes it feel better when you finally get inside." He could see her widening the distance between them slightly as they progressed down the block. He started to shuffle his feet a bit to slow their progress, to extend their time together in any way he could.

"You don't have to walk me all the way home, Michael," she said.

"Well I'm going this way anyway. My friend is developing the lot at the end of the block so I'm going to continue past your place down there for our card game. Some of the others might be there by now."

"Oh."...a little disappointed that he had, in fact, already had another appointment later, an assurance that he never had any intention of going any further on this date with her. She had apparently forgotten that he had told her about the game earlier, or maybe she wasn't listening to him then, letting the less-than-positive wave of information pass over her like an unwanted breeze. She realized that she never should have expected anything different from him. Ten years had passed since they first met, ten years of staring at each other across a room or speaking together only in a hallway filled with people. Many nice conversations filled with information, insight, good opinions that she agreed with mostly, and humor. But never a phone call, never a dance together at the holiday party, never even an e-mail. Well there were a few about him playing music somewhere, but he always started so late. She probably should have gone at least once she was realizing now. She looked away slightly, not sure if she was more filled with respect for him than desire. What the hell, she figured, you may as well as admit it to yourself finally. That was, admit that although she had never been in his arms, she wanted to be not only for his obvious physical attractiveness, but also for the reason that he was a decent, tender man, a true gentleman.

She wanted to melt into his arms right then, and it was not the first time she felt this way tonight. Somehow she knew that his kisses would be soft on her lips, never pressing against her teeth, never sticking his tongue down her throat like this one and that one from her past. She knew that he would know to lightly suck on her lower lip and grab her darting tongue lightly between his front teeth, always holding her closely but not overly firmly, playing with but never pulling her hair, slurping her skin or grinding himself into her. She knew instinctively that his lovemaking would be the perfect combination of passion and patience, of talent and joyful discovery. She was sure he would be full of all sorts of interesting maneuvers as well, some of which she already knew, some of which she wouldn't, but the ones she was acquainted with would be enhanced by her admiration for this man. He was talking to her again and she was becoming annoyed with herself at the constant daydreaming she was falling into, lessening her attention on him. She turned back to him and kept walking, but a little slower this time.

"Besides, what kind of gentleman would drop you off anywhere but your front door?" He flashed her a perfect smile accompanied by a raising of his eyebrows. "Hmmm?" She was daydreaming again, trying to decide what to do. Her stoop was just steps away. The vapor lamps on the street seemed to play with the color of his irises, shifting them from blue to green and then back. It was as if she were in a black and white world with his eyes providing the only color. It was at that exact moment that she decided to ask him in for a few minutes. There was no way this date was going to end at the stoop. She was not walking up those steps alone. She would make him some homemade juice or a nice shake with real fruit, slice up an apple or two and add some dates and figs she found at the fruit stand in Union Square for them to share, they would sit down with at least three feet of space between them at all times, maybe listen to some music, and then he would leave for his card game with his buddies. That was it, that's the plan, period, the end.

"You have a bit of old-fashioned manners, Michael," she said evenly.

"A lot of women don't like that anymore," he responded.

"Sorry, but I disagree. I have known some tough women in North and South America, and I know they would always appreciate a man who treats them like a lady. As long as it is not a put-on, or done in a showy manner. Naturally is the best, when something is done or a feeling is felt without any influence other than that it is the right thing to do."

"Well for me, being a gentleman was how I was able to get girls in college. I didn't have much money or a car. I once had a date with the most beautiful girl in the school, Anna Maria Rivera." He swooned comically for her and continued, "I held the door for her once while a bunch of my friends walked past me, not allowing her to pass first, thinking I was holding it for them. I loved all those guys, Stevie, JP, Lou, Oggie, and Dave, but they blew it that day."

"How did the date go?"

"Terrible. Only because she was much more mature than I was, I had a bit of an edge to me then and quite frankly, I think she was scared of me. I also think her family would have disapproved of me. But if you asked her today, that is, if she even remembers who I am, at least she would have told you that I was the perfect gentleman that evening if not anything else."

The smile again. The warmth was undulating throughout her body now and in no way was she trying to control it. It would have been impossible anyway, so she decided to allow these feelings to wash over her, if only to use them as a measuring stick for any man she might date in the future. What was he thinking at this moment? She would kill to know.

Michael was at that moment thinking of all the liaisons with various women he had experienced through the years, business and social. Really none of them were like this, not even with Georgia, he was sad to admit to himself; through all the years of no social contact with Laura, he had developed an undeniable bond with her which grew steadily somehow, nurtured only by itself...like it had its own life. It was an understanding between them, held together at first and then strengthened by trust, honesty, and loyalty. He never once even thought of making a pass at her, not even jokingly. If he had, he knew the trust would have been irretrievably broken.

He felt like a king walking with her through the streets of the

Village earlier, in the ballpark and in Central Park. Every time she walked, sat, or turned to him, her allure struck him like it was the first time he laid eyes on her. There was no bad angle to her. And she was nice as well, with an apparent strong moral center topped off by a bit of an adventurous streak...I think. She angled a bit more away from him and he was momentarily convinced that she could read his thoughts and was turned off by what he was thinking but instead she drew up to a stoop that led to a small platform with a red door, apparently her place. Now was the time, might as well go for broke. He checked his watch quickly, it was ten-fifteen. He figured he could stay for a few minutes and be at the game on time. There was no way he was going to leave her here on the street, with a handshake, at least he hoped it would happen that way. He certainly couldn't force himself into her place. So he said the first thing that came into his mind, cursing himself for sounding so incredibly lame.

"It's never polite to refuse a lady's invitation to sit for a few minutes at the end of an evening. As long as you don't overstay your welcome." He stared right at her, hoping that he didn't ruin the entire evening, their friendship, and any future friendship or whatever was in their future by his inept line. He hoped that she could see that he just didn't want to end this amazing evening, not just yet, and that by sitting for a few minutes with her in her place would further cement their already unique relationship. He was amazed at what she said next.

"Why don't you come up for a cup of coffee? It will keep you awake for your card game and you'll win more money that way."

"You got it," he said as they both stepped onto the platform. He waited slightly behind her as she fumbled for her keys. He was surprised when the door opened outward, its arc to open nearly covering the small area where they were standing, commenting to her that she should have her landlord fix the door. Make it open inward. "Hah," she replied over shoulder as she stepped inside a tiny vestibule and opened a heavier door that did swing inward. "I've been after him to fix a loose plank at the top of the stairs. Every day I have to remind myself not to step on it. One day I'm going to go right down to the bottom. Be careful of it when you get to the top of the stairs," she said as the front door closed behind them.

The two men behind the tree fifty yards up the block from where

Michael and Laura just entered the small building had their heads together speaking quietly. Charlie Mick, now satisfied that Tony was indeed from the old neighborhood and that Vinny did in fact send him here, told him everything about the past two days, from the initial fight outside J'lome's mosque—leaving out the racial slur that he uttered that got Vinny so upset—right up to the point where the two of them converged a few minutes ago.

Tony asked him, "And they're just sitting there all this time? No movement around the car, they didn't get out and go anywhere?"

"No, just a couple of times to go to the deli on the corner for something to eat which they brought right back to the car."

"Where else did they go? They had to move around a bit, didn't they?"

"They went out to Long Island and spent some time in an office building."

"How long were they there?"

"Not long. They came running out though, as if they had just missed someone. I followed them to the train station and they ran up onto the platform, but they didn't get on the train, they missed it. They came back to J'lome's mosque to pray I guess a couple of times. Oh right, I forgot...they went to another office building in the city before they went to Long Island. Other than all that, they have just been sitting here, watching the street." Tony Craig rubbed his chin, thinking furiously. What was the common connection between all of this? What are they waiting here for? Charlie Mick sensed his consternation and added what he saw just before Tony happened upon him.

"I don't know if this is important or not, but I just saw Mikey Pierce and some woman enter the building down the block. You almost bumped into them when you were crossing over to see me."

"Did you recognize the woman? And is that Michael Pierce from Sunnyside you're talking about?"

"Yeah, we're all from there. I didn't know the woman, though. It wasn't his wife. I wonder what they're doing there." Tony regarded the young man closely.

"Get your head out of Page Six. It's entirely possible they are just friends," Tony informed him.

"Most people believe that's impossible, you know. For a man and a woman to be just friends," Charlie Mick countered.

"Yeah, well, kid, you know most people have as much brains as God gives a goose, don't forget that. And don't believe everything you hear, no matter who says it. Men and women can be friends. It's rare, but it can happen." Tony looked out from behind the tree to see if anything was happening with the car and its occupants and saw nothing out of place. Maybe the woman and Mikey Pierce were just walking by and maybe they are screwing each other. All he knew for sure was that this situation had better jell soon otherwise his next act with the bureau was saying goodbye to the receptionist. He peered around the tree again and then back at Charlie Mick. "Let's stay here and keep an eye on this together. Let's see what happens. If it's nothing but a waste of time, I'll join you at the card game."

—※—

Michael and Laura made their way to the second floor in the two-family house, turning left at the top of the stairs, stopping in front of her door where she once again fumbled for her keys. Michael stayed a step or two behind her, looking back at the loose plank she had pointed out. She finally found the key and pushed it into the lock and, looking over her shoulder, invited Michael in. Before entering he pointed back at the floor.

"You know, it's easy to fix that. All you need is a couple of nails on the far end and it will stay." He followed her into the apartment. "Do you have a hammer?"

She closed the door, shaking her head, "No...just coffee."

"Coffee won't help your floor."

"I know, that's why I have some dates and apple slices as well."

"Oh, well, that'll do it. Maybe I could use the date pit as a hammer."

Michael stayed at the door and watched Laura step into the small apartment, which appeared to be a one bedroom, about seven hundred square feet.

"I have some old cake in the fridge, maybe by now we can use it as glue." She smiled at her own joke and bid Michael into the flat. Her heart was beating so strongly it felt as if she were living inside a taiko drum. This was the first man she had ever allowed inside this apartment. She stepped into the kitchen, a sideways affair about three feet wide and looked through the cupboard for cups and the coffee, momentarily nervous that maybe she didn't have any that were clean enough. She stuck her head back out and saw Michael still lingering by the door.

"Michael, please sit down. How do you like your coffee?" He looked up quickly and jerkily made his way into the apartment.

"I don't drink coffee often, but when I do, I take it black, please, with two sugars." He sat at one end of the couch that was in the middle of the room and crossed his legs. He leaned forward and flipped through a few magazines that were on the table in front of him.

What the hell am I doing here? he asked himself as he listened to Laura rummaging in the kitchen. A moment later, he heard the sound of water running into a pot, followed by the ignition of the gas stove, and the clink of cups against their saucers. He looked around the small apartment and liked what he saw. On one wall were several photographs of the Andes Mountain range, waterfalls and various flowers, many of which he did not recognize but looked to be orchids. There was a bookcase filled with textbooks, some classic English novels, and others in Spanish. He smiled when he noticed the two little stuffed penguins on the top shelf. In the window to the left of the bookshelf, he could see that she had planted some tomatoes in a plastic box that hung outside. A single white orchid stood on the sill on the inside. On another other wall there hung a classical guitar, adorned with dried rosebuds. He didn't even want to look toward her bedroom.

He heard her stepping out of the kitchen and he turned to see her with a tray in her hands that held two cups of steaming coffee and a small dish for each of them with two dates and half an apple, nicely peeled and sliced. Good...he was getting a little soft around the middle. A large cheesecake slice would just sit in his body like nuclear waste. He could see she was concentrating hard on not spilling anything, tiptoeing into the room, looking down at him and smiling-laughing, staring at the tray with her mouth open now, her lips forming a perfect O, and then looking up at him with a big smile as she continued into the room more confidently and set the tray on the low table, removing the cups and saucers.

"I put the sugar in already, two right?" She sat on the opposite end of the three-pillow sofa and angled her body toward him, her knees pressed together.

"Yeah, thanks," Michael answered, stirring the hot drink in such a way as to not clink the inside of the cup. Somehow, he knew he didn't want any extraneous sensory input now, no unexpected sounds or tastes, or anything else to see. He couldn't believe he was here with her, he was thinking, as he finished his silent stirring and placed the spoon back in the saucer. He quickly raised the cup to his lips mostly because he couldn't think of anything to say at that moment. He nodded toward the somewhat old-fashioned Pioneer stereo sitting on a makeshift wall unit made up of cinderblocks and square pieces of polished wood, its multi-components and separate KLH speakers reminding him of college dorm life.

"I bet you get a nice warm sound out of that system. What kind of music do you listen to?" he inquired. She gestured to the bookcase, "You can take a look there and see if there's anything you like." He took another sip and set the cup down and picked himself up off the couch to choose something to listen to but not before selecting a date to chew while he considered which music to pick.

If Adam were here, he would have made fun of my stereo, Laura thought. All of his bright shiny toys, the latest technology, all substance and style with absolutely no depth at all. She watched Michael from behind as he ran through her meager collection of music. He seemed to like the dates as she noticed that he swallowed the meat in about two seconds, expertly nibbling it around the pit.

"I thought you were going to chew the apple and date a little bit more." He turned toward her, a look of confusion on his face.

"It's so delicious it doesn't take much chewing. I just kind of squeeze it between my tongue and the roof of my mouth and squeeze it down my throat."

"How can you enjoy it that way?" she asked. He picked out a CD and was reading the back of the jewel box as he answered.

"I don't know, that's just how I eat it. They're delicious, where did you find them?" She nodded out the window, "In the farmer's market in Union Square, I love the stuff from there." She added, "I have to let food sit on my tongue for a while. Kind of savor it, you know?" He looked up from the CD and could see that she was sipping her coffee now, with an odd look on her face. He held the CD out for her to inspect it. "How about this one? I don't know who this is but I see he plays a classical guitar and I always loved the sound as I may have told you some other time. Let's play this."

Laura put her cup down and came around the table to take the CD from Michael. She checked the list of songs until she found the one he wanted. Her hand was shaking a little as she pushed the on button for the receiver, the equalizer, and the disc player. As the song started, she found herself back home, about twenty-five years before. She was a teenager in love then, her family already stating the obvious, that they were thoroughly displeased with Diego. The night before the bus ride to the seminary and her new life, they had made an arrangement to see each other after everyone in the town was asleep.

They sat in the moonlight, contemplating...impossibilities. Such as running away together, making a life together in America. Getting married, children, chasing dreams. And he had brought his guitar to sing for her that night, and the song he played over and over for her was this one here, the one Michael picked out on the Camilo Sesto CD. Laura refused to ignore the symbolism of this act. Although her experiences over the past twenty-five years had done nothing if not set her feet firmly on the ground, she still retained a deep spirituality about life. She still somewhat believed in the alignment of the stars and planets, bio rhythms, and signs and signals of all types. And as she put the CD in the player and the warm sounds of the guitar floated out of the speakers and filled the small apartment, she was back on the bank of the river, the moon was above and the night was most magical. But it wasn't Diego here now, and they weren't children anymore. This is my apartment and it was Michael Pierce, a man she has known and admired for ten years here, not anyone else. And he had to leave in ten minutes...must absolutely leave, she reminded herself, so she slowly hurried back to her end of the couch and picked up her coffee because she had no idea of what to say to him at that moment. He turned to her and offered a date. He leaned back easily on the sofa and listened to the music for a moment before he turned back to her.

"This is really nice," he said. "It reminds me of, well, I don't know but...I know this is crazy, but it reminds me of when I was seventeen. And there was this girl I liked. And we sat on the beach one night and listened to music and the waves breaking on the shore and it was beautiful, and that was the last night I ever saw her. She moved with her family somewhere the next day and I never got a forwarding address. I always wondered what happened to her." Laura took the date and swallowed it almost in one gulp as he told the story, at least being careful not to choke to death on the pit.

—⁂—

Andre hesitantly stepped away from the car and made his way toward the corner. He turned back once and could see Aubrey waving him on, much in the same way a frustrated pet owner would wave a family dog away from the dinner table. He turned back without a return gesture and continued on the journey out of his body and his life as he knew it. He turned the corner and was now out of sight of the car with Aubrey and the Arab kid. For a moment he considered fleeing, but he then heard the car start up and he could hear them behind him turning into Laura's street. They pulled ahead of him slowly and parked on her side of the street but not quite in front of her house. As he drew near the car, the driver's window came down a few inches. He stopped there to listen to Aubrey once again.

"You know what you have to do?"

"Yes," Andre nodded in acknowledgment.

"You know how you're going to get them out of there?" Another nod from Andre.

"Then get it done. Remember, quiet and quick. We'll be down here. If you're not back in three minutes, we're coming in." Andre nodded again like a bobble-head statue in the hands of a three-year-old. He stepped away from the car and walked up to the small porch, climbing the three steps as tiredly as if he were running an uphill marathon. He was holding a thin but stiff sheet of plastic in his right hand and he slipped this in between the door and the jam, the way Aubrey showed him, the lock opening much easier than he thought. He didn't look back at his compatriots as he noiselessly stepped into the vestibule.

The stairs were right in front of him, just three feet inside the front door and past a second door which he opened once again with the plastic sheet, leaving it ajar. He looked up and to the left and he could see the door to her flat there. He drew a deep breath and started up the stairs, leaning up against the wall as he advanced upward on the outside of each step to minimize the chance of any of them creaking. His pace was painfully slow as he was terrified of either Laura or her boyfriend opening the door before he reached the top.

He was surprised that he wasn't as terrified about what he was going to do. Up until now, it had been nothing more than just talk. But in a few moments, he was going to get inside her apartment and kidnap her and her date. Just that could land him in prison for the next who knows how many years. But the crazy bastard in the car downstairs just might decide to kill her and the guy with her to get what he wants. And then he would be an accessory to murder, even if he didn't pull a trigger. Life in prison, no chance for parole, a Federal prison as well because of the kidnapping charge.

He was one third of the way up the flight of stairs and as he turned his head to the left, he could now see her door. What was going on behind it? he wondered as he took a couple more steps. He was grateful that the building was apparently well maintained and it helped his whirling psyche that his progress was turning out to be as silent as a cat moving through an alley. He stopped two-thirds of the way and stared at the door, wishing that he could see through it and catch a glimpse of Laura's life. What was she really like? He had worked alongside her for more than ten years but he had to admit now that he knew nothing about her life, her dreams, her fears. She always seemed so quiet and demure, but he had seen it with his own eyes that she was fornicating with a married man. He detected soft music. That's good, it would make it easier for him to approach the door. He took two more steps, almost to the top now, he put his hand inside his jacket pocket and gripped the Glock pistol that Aubrey had given him, recalling the instructions the brute had given him.

"There is only one bullet in this magazine my friend. That's so you don't get any ideas other than getting that woman out of the apartment. If you have to, put a round into the leg of her lover. Make sure you don't hit her. But don't be stupid with this. Just show them the gun and more than likely they're going to follow your instructions. Remember that you have to make it to her door on the second floor without alerting anyone to your presence."

Andre was fingering the weapon in his pocket, surprised that it was not bulkier. He looked up at the door again and frowned. He began to hate her. How dare she have a man in her apartment who was not her family member or her husband? He started to grit his teeth involuntarily, as his rage was beginning to boil up toward his brain. How dare she act like a whore in front of the whole city, walking around with this man, wherever they were, whatever they were doing, like some sort of animal without any concern for the sensibilities of other, more righteous individuals like himself and his darling Kismine? Even after one year, he still had not held his beloved in his arms and Andre knew it was because her virtue was more important to her than any riches or fame. This Laura, she was just another American whore, one the city would not miss. He set his jaw, steeled his intestines, gripped the pistol, keeping it in his pocket, and continued climbing silently to the top of the flight of stairs, stepping to the left at the top to shorten the distance, if but for a couple of feet only, to her front door. Behind that door held the answer to the life he always dreamed of and he wanted it to start as soon as possible. And if he needed to shoot someone in order to get it started, so be it.

He recalled again Aubrey's instructions, "Announce yourself as the police if she doesn't have a peephole in the door. This way she can't ask to see your badge before she opens the door. Try to camouflage your voice. If she does have a peephole, announce yourself as the next door neighbor and tell her there may be a problem with a fire or a leak that has to be addressed immediately. Set your ear to the door when you speak so she will only be able to see the side of your head. If you don't get an answer within ten seconds of your second set of raps on the door, kick it down and get in there. More than likely they'll be in the sack with each other if she doesn't answer quickly. Remember, I am giving you exactly three minutes once you enter the building before I move in, so don't dawdle or suddenly decide that you're not going along with this anymore. If I detect that to be the case, I'll kill you and believe me, I'll get this woman to do what I need her to." With that thought, Andre made his way to Laura's door.

"Whoa, what the fuck is this?" Charlie Mick announced as he looked over Tony's shoulder down the block and past the boulevard to where Laura's house was. Tony whirled around and stepped quickly behind the tree, pulling the kid behind as well. They both watched around the tree trunk as Andre made his way to the two-family house, stopping to apparently fumble with the door lock, and then disappear inside. Tony felt the sweat starting at his hairline as he struggled with his next decision.

"What should we do?" That was a question Tony was not immediately prepared to answer. A thousand possibilities ran through his mind in a millisecond like a thousand little tornadoes racing across a cornfield. But sometimes, the answer was obvious and easy.

"We do nothing. Let's see how this plays out."

"I'm thinking that something just started and it could get ugly quickly." Tony checked his watch.

"We give it five minutes. Then I'm going to go in for a closer look."

"What do you want me to do?"

"I want you to go to the card game. I don't know what I have here, but I do know it could get hairy and I can't have anything happen to you. This is my play and mine alone." Tony put up his hand to stop Charlie Mick from commenting further. "Listen, go to the game, tell Vinny that I dismissed you. I'm telling you, it will be okay with him." Charlie Mick looked Tony hard in the eye and then agreed to leave but not before reminding him to tell Vinny that he ordered him away from this scene. Tony nodded agreement and with that, Charlie Mick turned up the block, away from Vernon Boulevard at the older man's suggestion so that the occupants of the Saab on the corner wouldn't see him. Tony wanted as little movement on the street as possible. He couldn't control the pedestrians or any other cars up and down the boulevard, but here was one person he could direct, one tiny little thing he could control and what man would ever not jump on that?

They sat closer to each other now, listening to the music float out of the speakers and around the room. The room seemed so much smaller, much in the same way places and things one experienced in youth are smaller when viewed with the eyes of an adult. A visit to an old classroom, favorite park or the tree you once carved your initials in with your favorite girl. They are all so much smaller and manageable once viewed through more experienced eyes, as well as usually more boring and not nearly as much fun or intimidating as they once were.

Laura and Michael were like moths drawn to a common flame in the sitting room of her shrinking apartment. The coffee and food was delicious and were in fact just what they needed as they were in a moment that Laura heard the girls in South America usually describe as 'el puente para amor'...the bridge to love. They were now sharing the middle cushion of the three-cushion sofa with their inside legs leaning toward each other ever so imperceptibly, like two leaning towers of Pisa.

That common flame was lit not this night, but ten years earlier in the first ten seconds of their friendship. If they had both been single that night, there would be no doubt that a first date would have been planned before the end of the evening, a 'momentito privado'—another favorite expression of the girls in Laura's hometown—would have been experienced by the end of the month, cohabitation after a year and marriage a year after that. There could be no other possibility for these two. That is, if they were available for that kind of shared existence. The night they met, they had a common thought hours later, when Laura was in the apartment she then shared with her boyfriend at the time, a former Olympic skier who was starting a Formula One racing career and Michael was with Georgia at some trendy rooftop bar surrounded by pompous suits. Neither of them knew it, but they both wondered at about the same time if they had missed their chance for something special. Michael came to the conclusion easier than Laura did. Quite simply, he deduced that if he were not married that night he met Laura, he would have broken off any relationship he had at that time to date her. Even if it were with Georgia.

The years passed and the frustrations and shortcomings of relationships filled both of their lives, Laura passing through a series of encounters shared with some nice guys, filled with an occasional vacation, some fun times, some decent sex, a few marriage proposals, but nothing that touched off an inner flame that she always thought should be present in a love relationship between a man and a woman. For Michael, it was the same but for the fact that there was only one woman through the same span of time...he worked on the advancement of his career, the stepping up in society, the birth of his only child, and he tortured himself virtually every day with the horrible 'what if' question, which always sent him into spasms of guilt whenever he looked into the eyes of his little girl.

Michael started slightly at the conclusion of the song. He could have fallen asleep then, he was so comfortable on Laura's couch, in these simple surroundings with no central vacuum or air conditioning, no dishwasher and no 24-hour security guard at the front gate of the development. The music had settled him into a world class kind of peace and tranquility. He then looked over at Laura who seemed similarly lost in some sort of dream. He wondered where she was in her mind at that moment. He knew where he was. He was sitting next to the most beautiful woman in New York City, sitting on her couch in her place. He reached for his cup of coffee, drained the final bit left in the cup, and set it back down gently. He could feel her watching every move he made, which made him reluctant to look up from the coffee table. The CD player skipped to the next song, an up-tempo number that snapped them both out of their dreamy lassitude.

"I had a great time today with you, Laura," he told her. How did she get so close to me on the couch? he wondered. I can smell her perfume and I can now see the pulpy parts of her lips that I never noticed before because I was never this close to her. He continued, struggling to retain some semblance of composure, "I hope you did as well. I never had a day of culture before." She leaned forward slightly, raising her chin which elongated her neck, her lovely neck which seemed as if it was necessary to deliver the answer to his question. Why lie? she asked herself.

"Michael, it was the best date, most perfectly planned and executed date I have ever had. Frankly," she continued, but now looking away slightly for a moment, bringing those lovely soft brown eyes back to look directly into his, "I always knew it would be this way if we ever went out socially. We spent so much time together for the past ten years without anything tangible passing between us, that when it finally happened it was as beautiful and natural as any other stretch of time I have ever experienced." She shifted her weight on the couch, the movement bringing her closer to him, her chin not quite as high as it was a moment ago, her eyes raised to meet his in that way that only women can do. He had to say it, say it now, throw it in her face like a cold shower, do it now, his brain shrieked. He shifted on the couch slightly, turning his body more toward hers, she not moving an inch, watching him closely, scrutinizing his movements.

"Ummm, it would be natural for me to say at this point, uhh, that maybe we should do this again. Really soon as a matter of fact. But"...his voice trailed off at that point and his eyes drifted to the plate with the date pits and the empty cups. And there it was for her, just like that, she thought, the bittersweetness of this beautiful day, of every time he charmed and warmed her heart with a simple hello or expression of good cheer on a day of darkness at that damn bank. His wit and intelligence always out front of his perfect height and good looks, looking so, mmmm, in his well-tailored suits, compelling her to tell him exactly how she felt, that she wanted him all to herself, no other women allowed but here he was doing the right thing, the proper thing, the only thing just as he had for the past ten years. She reached out and touched his forearm with her right hand, a gesture any woman knows is one of tremendous intimacy although it might not appear so to the more Cro-Magnon type of men found in such large numbers well...everywhere.

"I know, Michael." She let her fingers curl around his arm, and she was pleased to feel sinewy strength there. She now shifted her body forward without abandon. They were in each other's personal zones now, she still holding onto him, pressing slightly with her fingertips. Would he see this as an invitation to her bed or a good-bye squeeze? She didn't know herself what she was trying to convey. She was operating on autopilot.

"I'm so glad we had this day, Michael. I'll never forget how you set aside your personal time to help me through my problem at the office. I just couldn't think of anyone to trust, anyone else I figured would have the insight and opinions I could accept without question. You built that up over the years with me and it is as strong a foundation as I have ever had with anyone else. Maybe...sometime in the future... there will be more moments for us. Moments that we can enjoy, uninterrupted by anyone or anything." She was actively leaning forward now, her eyes taking on a dreamy quality.

"It truly was my pleasure," he answered, also leaning forward a little more, making sure not to move so much that she would be compelled to remove her hand. His decision was made then, and it was final. I will not let this moment pass without kissing her just once, I refuse to allow one more "What if" to infiltrate my thoughts. I have to kiss this woman, taste her, smell her, and finally run my fingers through her hair. And then, it would be off to the card game at Vinny's construction trailer for a few beers, a few winning hands, a bunch of fart jokes and other sophomoric behavior and the never-ending camaraderie between he and his friends from the old neighborhood.

He leaned in now without hesitation, her eyes widening in anticipation for an instant, then softening and closing a bit, her grip loosening on his forearm, the fingers instead of leaving starting to move up past his elbow to his bicep. "I know I won't either forget or regret this moment," he whispered. He had to make sure that she was the one to lead him at this point. No way would he force himself into a soul kiss with her. The static electricity charges on their bodies were ready to leap from one to another as their lips drew closer and their heads tilted to receive each other. Michael and Laura both again shared a common thought, that they were glad they both tilted the same way. Laura usually titled her head to the left to kiss a man. Most men wanted it the other way, to the right. But not Michael...in spite of the obvious guilty verdict they would both receive in moral court, she realized she was going to enjoy this kiss immensely. Another common thought passed unknowingly between them as their lips were almost brushing each other...'I wanted to kiss these lips from the first time I saw them.' But then the magic spell was broken by three sharp raps on the door followed by a booming voice announcing the police needed to speak with whoever was in the apartment.

—◦—

Vinny was caught looking over Maxie's shoulder, caught dead to rights by her checking the clock, but she didn't feel insulted. She laughed at him and swatted his shoulder playfully. "I know you're expecting your friends shortly. I don't want to overstay," she said, twisting in her seat to look for her purse. Vinny leaned forward quickly and grabbed her elbow, beckoning her to stay. She dropped the purse on the floor.

"You can stay a little while longer. Here, have another cup of coffee. You can meet some of my friends maybe. They'll like you. I don't know how you'll feel about them, but I know they'll like you." She settled back in the seat and he released her elbow, which he hadn't grabbed with much vigor, just a light touch on the underside. "Are you going home tonight?" he asked her. She felt some of the strain start to enter her body again in spite of the firmness of her decision, the overall rightness of her position.

"I don't know, probably not. I have a girlfriend or two that may still remember me from the old days. I haven't spoken to them in years. I hope they take my call. If not, I'll just find a hotel and stay there."

Vinny smiled warmly at her as he said, "There's always a construction shack in Queens available in case the Waldorf or the Plaza don't work out." He poured her what he considered to be a final cup of coffee. She wrapped her fingers around the porcelain cup, which warmed them nicely while she lightly blew on the steaming liquid. She looked up at Vinny as she did so, who seemed the picture of contentment at that moment. She laughed as she asked, "What? What is it? You look like a contented pussycat."

"I always believed that there are only solutions in life. There aren't any problems worth worrying about. If it's cancer, then you have to worry. But not all the rest of the shit that clogs our minds every day, thwarting our progress, our pursuit of happiness. Things you did in the past, things you didn't do. Decisions you wish you could have another chance to make differently, what a waste of time. You didn't take that job because you didn't have the nerve to try. You didn't marry that young man or young lady because you didn't love him or her enough. You didn't leave them sooner than you should have because you didn't want to take charge of your own life. I have spent most of my life looking for solutions to my problems as well as my friends' problems. But tonight, Maxie, tonight, you brought me a solution to the major problem in my life that helps not only me but all my friends as well. And I will never forget it, ever." He suddenly leaned forward and took her by the shoulders and kissed her hard on the lips, releasing her after a few seconds. But she wouldn't have any of that. She flung herself at him, and lost herself in the greatest kiss she ever had, wrapping her arms around Vinny so tightly he couldn't breathe. Several minutes passed before they came up for air. There was only one thing left for them to do, and that was to show each other that they wanted this to continue. It was Vinny's suggestion that sealed it.

"Let's go back to that restaurant for number fifteen and number twenty-nine tomorrow, what do you say?"

"I say, absolutely!" And with their plans for the beginning of the last relationship of their lives settled, they embraced once again, this time taking their sweet time about it.

—⊷—

The Burke brothers were arguing about next year's NBA draft as they turned the Pepperidge Farm delivery truck left on Vernon Boulevard from Ditmars, a few miles north of Laura's house. The frame of the ancient vehicle squealed as its springs struggled to hold the vehicle straight through yet another turn taken a bit too quickly. Ryan Burke chided his younger brother as he braced himself, easily detecting that the vehicle was starting to lose its center of gravity.

"I told you to take it easy, Fred, what's your problem? You take advice like Stephon Marbury." The groaning of the chassis and the older brother stopped as they straightened out and continued south toward the massive span of the Queensboro Bridge, the lights lining its span twinkling through a rapidly developing fog. "So what were you saying?" he asked his brother.

"I was saying that this card game is perfect timing for all of us. It's good for everyone to get together."

"Better than getting together to lick our financial wounds. There won't be too many laughs at a get-together like that." The brothers lapsed into silence, both thinking about their futures in case the project falls apart. They would have to re-adjust their careers, join the unions, and take plumbing and electrical work assignment handouts from assholes who could give a shit how well you worked. The brothers Burke loved working together and being together unlike so many siblings who could barely stand to open a Christmas card from their brother or sister, let alone have them over for dinner.

"We're pretty lucky guys, Freddy, you know that?" He looked over at his brother.

"Well, we are on the right side of the dirt. That's a good start. There are so many of us that are no longer here. I often wonder about Ping and the others. Where they are? What they're doing?" Ryan Burke wasn't used to philosophical tidbits from his brother. Thinking too deeply made him nervous, causing him to spew cosmically challenging questions like a fiery Baptist preacher toward a wayward congregation. Fred drove the old truck like an old man with a hat and Florida plates down the boulevard, not looking over at his brother. He instead looked in his oversize driver's side mirror as a taxi's horn blared behind them. He stuck his arm out and waved the impatient driver on, refusing to holler a single invective at the jerk.

"I wonder what they would do in this situation if they were still here. I sometimes feel, with their deaths, we are a depleted team, even though I have faith in Mikey and Vinny."

"You mean like when Bernard King went down with that knee injury? Should I get out of the truck and start punching the asphalt?" Ryan was referring to the heartbreaking scene of the Knick star slapping the Madison Square Garden floor, the severity of his injury immediately apparent to everyone in the Garden. "We did get Ewing in the draft lottery the next year because of the bad finish that followed. You never know."

"Right, but Patrick missed what, thirty games the next year?"

"Thirty-two to be precise. We did get Pitino to coach the team the next year, and we did get Mark Jackson to run the offense."

"So what are you telling me?" Fred asked as yet another cab driver hurtling down the boulevard leaned on his horn. He wanted to yell at the driver as he passed, but he quickly swallowed the epithets, the curses, the hatred and the annoyance that was sitting on the tip of his tongue. He too, had learned so much from Vinny. Keep things cool, never yell because that's when you not only lose any argument, but you also sound like an idiot. Once again, but more casually, more in control this time, he waved the cabbie onward.

"I'm telling you that positive thinking is necessary in a spot like this. Vinny has brought us all so far, it's a great thing we hitched ourselves to him. We've all been friends now since we're like ten years old, so now is not the time to get full of negative waves." Fred regarded his older brother with as much skepticism as he could show in his tired features, and it pained him to do so.

"You sound like Phil Jackson with all that zen shit." Ryan figured he had his brother turning the corner of gloom now and he smiled at him, loving him more than anyone else in the world.

"You mean Phil Jackson who won about eighty championships with the Bulls, the Lakers, and the Knicks? Maybe we should listen to someone like that, with that track record." Ryan screeched to a halt for a red light, causing some of the equipment that lined the inside walls and floor to rush forward.

"What the fuck is the matter with you?" Fred yelled at his brother, who turned to face Ryan, his visage contorted with slightly less than mock anger. The light turned green and the vehicle behind him inched forward. Ryan looked through the rear windows and could see the distinctive blue license plates of an ambassador's vehicle. Don't you dare fucking honk at me, he thought to himself. He turned to his brother again.

"I *am* trying to think positively bro', because that's all I can do. We have all our dough in this project and Vinny is great, I know that and he loves us and we can trust him one hundred percent, I know all of that. I also know that we were smart to work with him all these years. The distributions from our little pieces of the real estate and the money we would always earn working on the buildings would always keep us in good green. But we are in big fucking trouble here and if you don't fucking mind, I'm going to worry about it as much as I like. Don't worry, by the time we get to the game, I'll be a new person, full of smiles and fart jokes, but right fucking now, I feel like when Michael Ray Richardson said..." his brother repeated the famous quote for his brother, "The ship be sinking."

The light turned yellow and then quickly red, and the ambassador's driver tapped his horn a few times, very much in a courteous way, not in a blaring, annoyed, move-the-hell-out-of-the-way common to drivers with Jersey plates and yellow cabbies. But Fred jumped out of the truck, walked up to the limousine carrying the ambassador to wherever the little shit was going, and informed the good man and his driver that due to their diplomatic status, the police would not be able to arrest him for beating the shit out of him. Ryan jumped out as well to support his brother who, upon seeing a look of real concern on his older brother's face, jumped back in the Pepperidge Farm truck without another word, waving the ambassador on once the light turned green again. "That was stupid bro'...really stupid," Ryan calmly told his brother. Fred waited a moment while he pushed his fists into his eyeballs in an attempt to rid himself of his shame before continuing along Vernon Boulevard in silence, now only about a mile away from Michael and Laura, Tony Craig, two desperate men in a Saab, and another with a gun in his hand for the first time in his life about to commit his first kidnapping.

—∎—

Tony Craig was furiously playing the scene in his mind as it was unfolding in front of him, trying to check every angle, consider any possibility as to why the black guy, Andre was his name, he reminded himself, who works at the same bank with Michael Pierce in the computer department, entered the building. Maybe the woman who lives in the apartment knows him professionally, maybe she works for the bank. Then again, maybe she's a hooker and she's entertaining Michael before he goes to his card game and maybe this black guy is her next client. He damned himself for such crazy thoughts. The woman and Michael had been laughing and talking together strolling along Vernon this time looking like soon to be lovers, obviously comfortable in each other's company, the kid had told him. It seemed apparent to Charlie Mick even from a distance that they enjoyed being with each other.

Maybe she was a toy for Michael. A little biscuit he kept on the side. He'd been married a long time. How long could he hold out if a nice looking woman like this one gave him the green light? They were halfway down the block from where Tony hid behind the tree and the kid even mentioned she was attractive looking, with great lower body movement and obvious physical strength. But somehow, Tony wasn't buying an affair between them. They acted close, but the way friends acted...the kid didn't see anything that suggested intimacy. But they were close to it, he was pretty sure of that.

And now the black guy going up to her apartment apparently. What the hell was this about, a love triangle? No, it couldn't be because any man attending a surreptitious meeting between his girlfriend or wife and another man would go by himself. No man would expose himself as a cuckold in that fashion to another man. Even if he had bad intentions in mind, he would do it himself. The two guys he was in the Saab with eliminate that possibility, so what was it? It could only be that the woman was wanted by these three, but for what? Did she work at the bank with the black guy? Couldn't be that she was up to no good with these guys. Even though there were more and more women becoming radicalized Islamists, they were found mostly in the Arab states in the Middle East. There was no jihadist woman as far as he knew who was a threat here on American soil. Or so he hoped. He didn't trust anyone anymore, though he was feeling better about being near people he grew up with, on streets he knew. But still, what the hell was this all about?

It had to be, it was really the first thought he had but his bureau training taught him to consider anything over and over, to move as far away from the obvious as you could and see how many times it dragged you back. Michael was out with this woman, apparently all day, and although Tony didn't know why they were together, it seemed on the surface to be social in nature. Vinny told me just a few minutes ago that he expected Michael at the construction site for a card game so he doesn't have enough time to even have a quickie.

With Andre however...his approach to the building was not direct, his steps were those of a homeless man, bent against the onrushing next few minutes of his wretched existence. Tony recalled now noticing that Andre looked back toward the Saab once or twice as he advanced on the small building. He was receiving instruction from there, had to be. The Army guy...he would be the one who would presumably instruct this bank executive in doing something very illegal, possibly violent...the car is moving now to the opposite corner. Are they keeping an eye on the black guy, making sure he doesn't try to escape? Who the hell really knows? Tony looked at his watch, hacking it to count off exactly three hundred seconds...five minutes, at which time he was going to advance on the building somehow, get inside, and find out what the hell was going on. He figured it was either five minutes to the end of his career in the bureau, or five minutes away from saving his career in the bureau.

⚜

Laura and Michael retreated back to the left and right cushions of the couch as if the magnetic pull that was so irresistible just a second earlier completely reversed its field. Michael looked at the door, ran his fingers through his hair, feeling not a little relieved, and then at Laura, who shrugged her shoulders and got up from the couch to answer.

"Sorry, I can't imagine what this is all about," she said as her face turned as red as a tomato. Michael shook his head with a half-smile to show her it was nothing to be concerned about. He was surprised to see her blush so obviously. She was embarrassed to be interrupted like this, like we were in a college dorm room instead of two adults in their own home, he figured, which frankly, he found a little endearing. He watched how she moved around the table with the empty cups and plate and toward the door. He started to pull himself together for his exit, checking pockets for keys, wallet, phone...sitting forward on the couch so he could then stand without ripping a meniscus.

I wonder if there is a woman in the world at this very moment experiencing a worse case of bad timing such as mine right now, Laura was pondering, as she moved to the door, a perplexed look and mild confusion clouding her features. What the hell could this be? she wondered. Michael noticed the door had no peephole and was about to remind her to ask for another confirmation of who was there before she opened the door. She couldn't be that naive, that trusting, could she? He stood, deciding not to say anything as this was her place and he wouldn't think any further about making any kind of decision for her, lest he be insulting, treating her like a country rube. He decided also to stand because someone seeing him lounging on the couch might suspect something had passed between them, something a little more tangible than what really transpired between them to an unknowing eye. But at some point in the future, he would definitely tell her about the neighborhood not being so safe despite what New York magazine says, and to please be careful. Maybe this is a good thing, this interruption, he started to think. They never touched lips although he was certain she wanted to kiss as much as he did. Oh well, at least he knew she wanted to and that would have to do. In a few minutes he would leave—maybe a kiss on the cheek at the door—and he would be at the game with the boys and tomorrow he would go to the airport to pick up Georgia and Sally with a clear conscience.

⁓

Andre could hear her steps approaching the door from outside in the hall and he pulled the gun out of his pocket and gripped it tightly it in his right hand, his index finger outside the trigger guard, as Aubrey instructed him. He was surprised at himself realizing how comfortable he was. Did he really have this ruthlessness in him his whole life, to be awakened now in this way, by a stranger who never saw him until a couple of days ago? He lowered his left shoulder as Aubrey also instructed him to do, ready to drive it into the door as soon as it cracked open. He figured that maybe she had one of those security chains on her door and to be absolutely sure he could gain entry quickly, he would have to blow through the door. Maybe knock her down. Take the man by surprise, show them the gun immediately. Use as little words as possible. He had only about one and a half minutes left before the goon squad in the car entered the building. He had only ninety seconds left in his life as he once knew it.

⁓

Laura turned to Michael again as she reached for the doorknob, leaning forward a bit, not standing directly in front of the door. She shrugged her shoulders once more. "I'm sure this will just take a moment." Michael nodded, smiling back at her warmly, not allowing her to see his own annoyance at being interrupted. He was about to remind her to ask again who it was when she turned the handle and at once, the room exploded. The door slammed open before she even had a chance to let go of the knob, nearly taking her hand off at the wrist. Michael was knocked back on the couch by the sudden burst of violence, the door splintering at the hinges, hanging now at a wild angle, the security chain that offered no resistance to Andre's two hundred and twenty pounds ripped from the wall coming to rest at Michael's feet, and then finally by the husky black man who burst into the room, touching the ground to slow his forward progress. The man, Michael thought, didn't look athletic at all, pudgy and soft, but he managed to land slightly forward, supported by his left hand...the one without the gun, Michael now saw. Who was this guy? He looked strangely familiar.

Laura had screamed for a second, an inward cry from being startled mostly, not by fright. But she was frightened with what she saw in front of her now. Andre stood up to his full height and pointed the gun in her face from two feet away.

"Whoa, just a minute, just relax," Michael said, holding his palms out in front of him. He lifted himself off the couch as slowly as a rose unfolding on a warm day so as not to startle the intruder. He now started to recognize Andre as someone he had seen walking the halls in Laura's office, not knowing his name or his function at the bank. He kept this realization to himself as somehow maybe it could be used to his advantage. His mind was racing ahead to the next thing he had to do whatever it was. He wished he could take a moment to watch a few clips from the latest Jason Bourne movie and copy some moves from the fight scenes. The problem was the guy with the gun controlled the situation so he had to let it play, look for a way out. He knew that the 108th Police precinct was just a few blocks away from where they were now and that comforted him to a degree. Better than being somewhere in the middle of some fucking suburb, where the police station could be miles away and the patrol cars mostly stayed on the main roads writing tickets for speeders and others who flick a cigarette out the window. If they managed to break free from this clown, that's where they had to run to. He hoped Laura knew where the precinct was as well. She must...she walks past it every day on the way home.

"Shut up you," Andre retorted angrily and clumsily to Michael's plea and then turned his attention back to Laura, the gun still pointing at her face. Michael saw a look of defiance somewhere in her eyes, beyond the fear and incomprehension. "Sit down, both of you, now!" Andre barked, the both of them listening and obeying silently and slowly returning to the couch this time both choosing the middle as if to huddle for protection. The guy checked his watch and looked out her window and then turned his attention back to Laura.

―――

"Guys, where are you?" Vinny growled into his phone. Maxie Carter had stepped into the shack's bathroom a moment earlier to freshen up before her trip back to the city. She decided she didn't want to be in the way of his meeting with his friends, She was a little nervous about their reaction to her, being part of the Landmark Committee and all.

Vinny's annoyance was evident as all he wanted at this moment was to start the game. The stress of the past couple of days was dripping off him like a wax candle left at a crazy angle and he wanted to exit from that situation into a totally opposite scene of beer, cards, and fun. Of course he would tell everyone about Maxie's story and their discovery of the paint job designed to connect the two structures. He needed to talk to Mikey most of all. Even though tomorrow was Sunday, they would need to find the owners of the bank and let them know the landmarking problem was history. But that would be later... after he cleaned every one of them out. Maybe he would ask Tony Craig to come back, it was certainly good to see him, Vinny always enjoyed running into an old face. Maybe he could sic him on the assholes who tried to derail his project. How great would that be? His phone came to life as the Burkes answered in unison.

"We're on Vernon Boulevard, by the Board of Education book building. We'll see you in five minutes."

"Okay, see you then. How's the truck holding up?"

"The truck is great as long as you don't have to steer it, or use the brakes, or make a turn at even a moderate speed," answered Fred. Ryan added, "It's in as good shape as Rudy T's cheekbone after it said hello to Kermit Washington's fist.

"Guys, do me a favor and lay off the basketball metaphors, just for one evening, alright? I've got a million things going on in my head and I can't allow any additional clutter. Waddya say?"

"Right, will do. See you shortly. And Vin?"

"Yeah?"

"Who wore number fifty-two for the Lakers in 1971?"

"*Happy* Hairston," Ryan said, coming down hard on the 'Happy.' Vinny couldn't help but smile as he heard the Burke brothers laughing in unison over the wire.

"Just get the fuck over here and bring all your money." He ended the transmission before they could answer. It was going to be a great night. He went to the door again and looked out over the river. He saw

Moose Miller's boat there again. Maxie then came out of the bathroom and after he gave her a quick once over he found it easy to conclude that it was going to be a great life going forward as well.

—ılı—

"Andre, what the hell are you doing? Have you lost your mind?" Laura demanded of the pudgy guy with the gun. Michael winced at her words, desperately wanting her to watch how she dealt with this guy, but he just sat there silently waiting and watching for any opportunity to do...anything. He slowly started to stand again ready to implore this guy to relax but was met only with Andre growling at him again to sit down, this time leveling the automatic at Michael's torso. He couldn't miss me from there, Michael supposed as he sat back down, this time a little closer to the edge of the seat. Andre turned his attention back to Laura, who now was also seated on the edge of the furniture.

"You bitch, you goddamn bitch, you couldn't leave things well enough alone, things that were none of your business. You had to poke around and screw around with other people's lives. Always asking questions, always getting in the way!" The man, Michael noticed, was punctuating his comments with the gun as if it were one of the iron rulers the nuns used to beat him with in Catholic school. He prayed that the trigger wasn't set to some hyper-sensitive position.

It was then Michael realized who this guy really was. He was the one Laura had called him about, the one who was running the scam she discovered. Holy crap, he thought, how desperate could this idiot be? He probably didn't have a violent bone in his body before this night, but he was out of his head now, coming here with a gun, surmising quite properly that he was facing arrest and prosecution for what he had done. Michael also realized that her apartment must have been watched for some time. It wasn't by accident that he appeared at her door just after we arrived. Michael wondered if he had a posse of friends with him outside as backup. Just then Laura started shouting back at Andre and Michael's blood pressure began to rise as her defiance burst forth and her voice now was as big and strong as a mountain.

"You pathetic loser, stupid bastard, Andre, I didn't set out to spy on you. All I wanted to do was to clear my name. It was obvious someone was using my passwords and in order to save my job, my reputation, I was forced to look into the situation out at the Long Island office. I had no idea of what I would find once I got there." She was spitting the words at this guy, Michael noticed, real hatred oozing out of her. He didn't know whether to feel proud of her for her show of defiance, of putting her fear aside—which he always advised anyone to do in a tough situation—or to tell her to shut the hell up before this clown got so angry he would lose the last bit of control he had and start blasting away.

Her eyes, so lovely and soft just a few moments ago, were now blazing with molten fire. There was no stopping her, all of the frustrations pouring out of her and not even Joan of Arc was going to stop it. Even the clown was stunned by her outburst, the gun no longer pointed directly at her, his arm lowering inch by inch, Michael keeping his eyes glued to Andre, drinking in all his movements, searching for any possible weakness or hesitation to be exploited at the right time whenever that could be.

"You fucking assholes, all of you in the department trying to screw around with my career, with my life as if it were a fucking game! As if I traveled five thousand miles to a new country and culture, learning a new language, leaving my family and friends behind just so that a group of half-assed, talentless toads led by the likes of you could take advantage of me. You have no idea what I've been through so far in my life mostly because you never bothered to ask, never bothered to try to get to know me even just a little bit. All you fucking men, all of you all of my life treating me like an accessory, never as an equal, just a pretty face and a firm body just to show off to friends. Meanwhile not one of you, except for this man here"—she jerked her thumb at Michael—"knew how to hold me, how to make love to me...just a bunch of losers who wouldn't know what to do with a real woman if you ever had the chance." Michael was stunned at her language, he never heard her utter even the gentlest criticism, as well as humbled that she included him as the one man in her life that apparently knew what to do with her even though he had never even kissed her. She must have great fantasies about me, he concluded. He would have to ask her about that when and if he got the chance. He was broken out of this reverie by Andre lunging at her, the gun now pressed against her temple, Laura finally quieting down, bending under the weight of the fat bastard with the gun.

"Shut up, you bitch whore!" he yelled at the top of his lungs. Good, Michael thought, I like that. Make a lot of noise. Let someone hear and call the cops. Just four blocks away from the precinct house. Fucking dummy. I'll beat the shit out of you later when I get the chance for yelling at her this way and threatening us. Michael stood, not too quickly to alarm the intruder, his hands once again palms up, in a pleading fashion.

"Hey, hey, just relax. If you're here for a robbery just take what you want and leave," Michael said to Andre, who straightened up and once again trained the gun on Michael. Andre stared Michael back into his seat on the edge of the couch, something that would have never worked if he didn't have the gun.

"You I don't need; however, she's coming with me. I have work for her to do."

"What work?" asked Laura, quieter now.

"You are going to accompany me and my associates back out to the Long Island office and you are going to undo all of the damage to the computers you did. We are then going to reset the passwords you changed..."

"I'm not going anywhere with you, *maricon*." Michael was strangely turned on by her cursing but he hoped at the same time that this guy didn't speak Spanish. Andre brought the gun back to her head with a jerking motion that indicated to Michael this guy was getting increasingly nervous. He was therefore increasingly prone to a mistake, and Michael reminded himself again that he had to keep his wits about him and keep an eye open for an opportunity. He noticed now the gun didn't appear to be cocked, but Michael had never fired a pistol in his life save for a weekend at Greenwood Lake with his father so many years ago.

"Who are your associates?" Michael queried Andre. Had to divert his attention somehow get him talking, maybe create an opportunity. But Andre didn't even look at him when he answered. Was he regaining his boldness or was he just set on a path that he now realizes is incredibly wrong but he can't reverse himself from?

"That's none of your business, no one you need to know about. Like I said before, I don't need you. I need her and she's coming with me." With that final word, Andre leaned forward and grabbed Laura by the arm and jerked her violently to her feet, then started pulling her toward the door. Michael stood up again, quickly this time, ignoring the reality of the gun.

"I'm not letting you just walk out of here with her. That's not going to happen." he said, trying to summon up his best Irish menace. Andre looked into his cold blue eyes and somehow was able to detect the steel slowly filling the spine of Laura's...whatever. Fine, he thought, let this bastard try this defiant Sir Lancelot crap with the American beast downstairs. He held Laura at arm's length and waved the gun at Michael.

"Very well then, you can come along with her." Andre then guided Laura through the door, walking backwards, his right hand tightly gripping her left elbow, the Glock now in his left, pointed at Michael's torso. Andre beckoned Michael through the door as he backed through it, looking over his left shoulder and quickly turning back. Laura looked back at Michael as she stepped through the door and he hoped the look he gave her was somewhat reassuring. The fact of the matter was that he was terrified. At the least, he was looking at some sort of physical altercation outside the house. Who the hell were these associates the guy spoke of? And what were they made of? Michael couldn't help trying to visualize them as the three edged toward the staircase.

———

"What do you want me to do?" Whathefu asked Aubrey as they approached the stoop to Laura's house. They had left the protection of the car a half a minute ago, Aubrey thinking that the African was more than likely going to screw this up somehow and that meant he had to be in some sort of position to take over. He cursed himself for not just busting the door down, putting a round between the eyes of the man and pistol whipping the woman into unconsciousness. He could have then carried her out of the house and by now, they would have been on the Long Island Expressway, on their way back to the office where the African said he could implement his scam again.

"Step inside quietly, don't slam the door, and see if you can hear anything. Do not go upstairs. If you don't hear anything, hold your hand up like this." Aubrey held up his hand as if he were waving good-bye. "If you do hear something, then step back outside and nod to me. Remember, don't let the door slam." Aubrey hated giving instructions to these two idiots. Even though they were godless and therefore condemned for all eternity, the soldiers in his squad wouldn't have to be told what to do. This operation would have been over in thirty seconds without a shot or a scream from the woman. Not a single neighbor would have heard a thing. He parked himself at the bottom of the stoop looking up and down the street, his eyes coming back to Whathefu, who tentatively started up the three steps to the front door.

—※—

Michael knew several things about the situation as Andre continued backing up toward the stairs. The guy was an amateur, unsure of himself; the 108th precinct was just a few blocks away, a building bursting with real professionals who would relish taking this guy in; this was his neighborhood and he knew every nook and cranny of it; and also that his own friends were very, very near. In spite of it all, he felt very strong and capable. It had been a while since he was in a real brawl, but he had plenty of street fights in his early years and he was still fairly fit and at just under two hundred pounds, a fairly formidable human being. Laura looked back at him again, and he nodded at her and he believed she felt his strength with this quick glance but he couldn't be sure. Maybe he looked scared shitless to her and as a result she would lose all hope in him at that moment. Who knows with women, right?

Michael thought this guy was looking a little more confident once they were out of Laura's apartment. Michael looked back over his left shoulder, realizing that he didn't close the door. Ignoring his natural inclination to step back and pull the door closed, he glanced down over the railing toward the front of the building. He thought for an instant about leaping over the railing and down to the first floor, but dismissed the thought just as quickly. Either his knee or his ankle would collapse and render him lame in more than one way. The guy with the gun would have a clear shot at him from up on high and frankly, what kind of man would Michael Pierce be, abandoning Laura that way? His thoughts were interrupted by Andre grunting an order to the both of them.

"Just move it along, slowly and quietly, the both of you." He backed against the wall to apparently let Laura descend the stairs first. He still had the gun in his left hand, almost flush against the wall. Now he turned his body slightly toward Michael to gauge his progress behind Laura's. Michael started to think that maybe it was best for them to get out of the building and somehow make a break for the 108th precinct. He struggled to keep his wits about him when all of a sudden, the wooden floor creaked, the board Laura warned Michael about earlier not able to support all of Andre's weight. Andre was momentarily thrown by the slight loss of balance, but looked as if he would be able to recover in just a second.

That is if Laura hadn't also been keeping a close eye on the man before her who invaded her home and privacy and ruined what was otherwise one of the best days of her life. Her hatred of Andre at that moment was total. She may have looked like a terrified woman to anyone who was observing the unfolding situation, but her brain was working just like Michael's, though hers was country and his was city born and bred. Whereas he was hopefully using his New York street smarts to unlock a potential solution to their current problem, she was in her mind back at the farm, waiting for an opportunity to use the skills she learned from her older brothers. She remembered how they would bunch their fists and throw their bodies behind a two-handed punch to the rumps of thousand pound steers and horses to guide them into a stable or to the water trough when they were acting ornery. She as always amazed that these powerful animals would respond immediately to these blows and her brothers would tell her to always make sure to concentrate a punch where the balance of the person absorbing the blow would be affected most.

When she realized that Andre stepped on the loose plank and lost his balance, she knew her opportunity was at hand. Please, please Michael, follow up my next actions well. I'm sorry that I can't convey my thoughts to you...which may not be the best of ideas as some of my thoughts about you will remain secret even if we wind up married for twenty-five years...but please be alert and resourceful. You've never failed me in our strange but fulfilling friendship, please don't fail me now.

And that was the last thought through her head before she launched a powerful two-handed blow that caught Andre in the chest, on the border of his pectoral and rib cage, knocking him back into the wall and giving her the opportunity to break free. She ran past him and started to take the stairs two at a time. Andre recovered quickly from the two fisted punch and, fully enraged now, veins popping on his forehead, his aorta struggling with the sudden surge of blood pressure, lifted the Glock in his left hand to sight the weapon down the stairs at Laura's back. It would be an easy shot, he realized with satisfaction, one that anyone would be able to make, even someone like himself who had never held a gun in his life. His anger at that moment was at an all-time high, the bile rising in his throat not at his captivity for the past forty-eight hours, not at his inability to finance his girlfriend's dream with his measly salary supplemented by his meager scam, but at the outrage he felt at the physical effrontery just visited upon him by Laura. That was going to get him past the fact that he had never even been in a street brawl, let alone shoot someone in the back. He started to sight along the barrel of the gun, thinking it would be easy just to put one in her shoulder, just to wound her.

Just then, Michael was revisiting an old memory just as Laura had done a moment earlier. He was completely jazzed by Laura's physical rebuke of Andre—What a girl!—and for a moment he had completely forgotten about the gun. Michael was only a few feet away from him when Andre recovered from the blow that momentarily sent him teetering and now he was gripped by the horror that Andre was no longer an inexperienced buffoon but instead a motivated killer.

It was Vinny that suggested it to him, that was, to sneak into Madison Square Garden on the night of March 8th, 1971. The other guys in the neighborhood tried to steal, buy, gamble, even work for tickets to any one of the closed circuit venues that were showing the fight. But not Vinny. He wasn't sitting next to anyone he didn't want to for the fight. And he wasn't going to watch it on some movie screen.

"What are we gonna sit next to some clown who just had a garlic and pickle sandwich who farts so much he could play a clarinet with his ass? I got a way to get into the Garden. Do you remember that old guy from the other side of the boulevard, Ricky Pergolis?"

"The Greek guy? The one who had the pizza place on Astoria Boulevard ?"

"Right. Remember when I kicked the shit out of that jerk from the Bronx who was busting up his beloved Wurlitzer?"

"And then later on in the same day, you managed to help his favorite sister carry her groceries into her new house on Fifty-Second Street. Yeah, I remember him. So what?" Vinny looked at Michael at that moment as if he were an idiot.

"Mikey you have to learn the value of favors, my friend. I helped the Greek out twice that day, and he never forgot. I mean I'm just a kid but he knew that I knew he had to take care of me, had to do the right thing."

"I still don't get it," Michael replied. "How does this help get us into the Garden for the fight?"

"Remember his daughter? The one that married that cop from Maspeth?"

"Yeah? So?" Vinny's disapproval at Michael's reply was total.

"Are you stupid? Or are you just not thinking? He's a cop, Mikey. He's working the Garden tonight for the fight. And he's gonna sneak us in."

And so that was how it happened that Vinny and Michael sat ringside with the likes of Frank Sinatra, Woody Allen, and Norman Mailer. They watched Burt Lancaster doing the color commentary and thousands of others, tough guys, connected types, pimps with their fur coats and hats, the women with them bursting out of their outfits, Michael and Vinny just a couple of kids who had seen plenty by that tender age agog at the innumerable sights and sounds.

It was a fantastic fight, truly the fight of the century. Ali was jabbing Frazier relentlessly through the first five rounds, Smokin' Joe unable to catch up to the faster, more fleet Ali and unleash his superior punching power. But Ali started to slow in the sixth round, Frazier started finding his jaw and his ribs and in the early moments of the fifteenth round launched what many have called the most perfect punch in the history of the ring, a left hook that started way down here...and just exploded into Ali's jaw, sending him to the canvas. Michael and Vinny had snuck down from the cheap seats and were then at a perfect vantage point behind Frazier and they each saw him start to leap with the punch and they each close enough to feel the concussive power of that left hook as surely as all the others in the Garden that night heard the impact of glove on jaw. It was the greatest moment at a live sporting event for each of them and they never forgot it, never tiring of telling the story to whomever would listen of the night they snuck into the Garden and watched Joe Frazier retain not only the heavyweight title, but his dignity as well.

So it was thirty six years later that Michael found himself on a balcony in a two-family house, with a woman—not his wife—and a maniac pointing a gun at her in the wake of her desperate escape attempt, and he knew what he had to do. He felt his right foot brushing up against the bottom rail of the balcony and he brought his left fist up from way down here, closing the fingers individually starting with the pinky, turning his hand into a block of hardness, making sure not to tuck the thumb inside and together with the torque provided by pushing off the railing's base launched himself at Andre much in the same way Frazier did that same night so many years ago.

Andre never saw it coming, at least not soon enough to do some-thing about it. Michael's fist landed on the right side of Andre's face, his middle knuckle landing just below Andre's cheekbone, his tightly bunched fist cracking the bone, spraying the wall with a mixture of saliva, blood, and a bicuspid. Andre's head spun to the left rendering him senseless, but incredibly not unconscious. If someone had been observing, it would have looked like that famous photograph of Rocky Marciano landing a right cross on the face of Ezzard Charles, twisting it into a monstrous looking visage that only a mother could love.

Andre's body followed the path of his face which was to say that he twisted like a sapling past its breaking point in a hurricane and landed on his back at the top of the landing. Michael raced past him, but Andre grabbed Michael's thigh as he was trying to get past, which only had the effect of propelling Andre down the stairs on his back like a body surfer riding a wave in reverse posture, fighting the small chop, desperately trying to get something out of a typically weak east coast swell, the gun now out of his hand, clattering end over end down the stairs ahead of them both. Michael had a horrible vision of the gun going off accidentally as it spun down the stairs and he checked Laura's progress and saw that she was almost to the door. She didn't seem to be interested in stopping anytime soon and Michael thought she would be able to run through a brick wall at that speed.

Laura burst through the door, treating it like one of the beasts on the farm. All she knew was that freedom beckoned to her on the other side and nothing was going to stop her. She felt a strange heaviness on the front door as she exited the building but she paid it no mind as she gulped the cool night air, which energized her instantly and she took off as if she were pursued by a hungry tiger toward the river...away from the 108th Precinct.

—◦—

Tony Craig was startled out of his dizzying stroll through all the questions and possibilities that were dangling in front of him like an infant's mobile by the figure bursting through the door, knocking the skinny Saudi kid to the sidewalk from the impact. Now has to be the time, he realized and he started to quickly walk, almost trotting toward Vernon Boulevard, his eyes fixed on the door, the figure lying prone on the sidewalk, the big guy now moving briskly toward the door all the while ignoring his partner, and on the woman running like Flo Jo down the block toward the river. Whatever these guys had in mind was going awry in the least. His weapon, a 44 Magnum, was out of his shoulder holster, pointed downward and held against his leg in an almost futile effort to be unobtrusive with it.

—◦—

Whathefu was knocked straight back off the three step stoop to the sidewalk by the sudden impact from Laura's hasty exit. For an instant he glimpsed the woman as she continued past him, not pausing for an instant to check on him. What a bitch, he was somehow able to surmise as he flew through the air, his brief flight ending by landing hard on his head and shoulders on the sidewalk. He crumpled instantly on impact, stunned mostly by the amazingly quick turn of events. Where there was nothing happening, all of a sudden the situation was exploding all around him. He hoped Aubrey would come to his aid and he did see the beautiful soldier approach him with, what is that? A quizzical look? Not one of concern? He noticed Aubrey had his gun out and was now watching the woman race away from them, noting immediately her amazing speed. He was surprised at how fast she was, deciding it was fear that was propelling her mostly, not any type of athleticism. Most American women were sloths, he was convinced of that, tough on the outside but ready to fall apart at a moment's notice. That adrenaline rush would run out quickly and his soldier would be able to run her down in about ten seconds even if she were one hundred yards ahead. But where was the African he was thinking in the next moment that Michael followed Laura through the door, putting his shoulder into it, blowing it open once again, and leaping off the stoop like Beamon, landing squarely on Aubrey's upper torso like a sack of flour, knocking him to the ground as easily as Lawrence Taylor tossed a lead-footed offensive linemen out of his way.

Amazingly, Michael found himself on all fours with his wits in control. He didn't have time to brace himself for the impact as he was loose with his limbs when he passed through the door and didn't sustain any injury when he knocked the bigger Aubrey to the floor. Becoming aware then of the sprawled body of Whathefu on the sidewalk as well, Michael immediately deduced these guys were the partners of the kidnapper. And as soon as he saw another gun in the hand of the big guy, he knew it was time to get out of there. It felt as if he ran into a brick wall when he landed on Aubrey...if the guy was waiting for him he would have been able to absorb the contact. Michael heard fading footsteps to his right and to his horror saw that it was Laura running toward the river. She'll be trapped there. Doesn't she know the cops are just a few blocks away? Where the hell is she going? He pushed himself off of Aubrey's body and took off after her, calling her name at the top of his lungs.

—⚜—

Tony Craig was now half walking, half running toward the corner, still keeping his weapon at his side, hoping against everything that he wouldn't be seen by the two men who were now slowly raising themselves from the sidewalk. Was that Michael Pierce who just ran out after the woman? Had to be. Where was the first man, the Black man who entered the building? He turned his head to the right once he arrived at the corner to check for oncoming traffic and had to slow himself for an old working man's truck that was lumbering slowly and cautiously toward him.

Andre turned his head to the right and was noticing that the molding at the base of the wall at the bottom of the staircase he just slid down needed a paint job. He then noticed the gun Aubrey had given him not ten minutes earlier lying on the ground just past his head. He quickly rolled over, pushed himself off the floor, picking up the gun in one sweeping motion and headed for the door, all the time struggling to get his feet under him as he was still feeling the effects of Michael's left hook and the pounding his head took sliding down the stairs. He was hoping that his new friends had stopped Laura and the other guy from getting away. Friends, he thought...how strange I should think of them as my friends or allies, he pondered to himself as he made his way to the stoop just in time to see Aubrey on one knee, pointing his own gun at Andre's torso.

The Burke brothers turned the corner onto Forty-Seventh Avenue with as much care as Fred could muster. The truck was now barely able to make the turn without flipping over, its suspension system was so bad.

"The truck turns like a fifty-year-old white guy plays defense," Ryan observed. His brother smiled at the clear path back to peace between them. Ryan continued, "Slow and no ability to play angles, to cut corners."

"Aren't you describing slow twice there? Don't carry on too much with your metaphors, who are you, Clyde Frazier? Leave the fifty-year-olds alone, we'll be there soon." Just then Fred leaned forward to get a better view of what was happening down the street. Ryan had turned to remind his brother that they had been speaking in metaphors since they could talk at all. One brother was confused by what he saw, the other horrified. It caused them both to say the exact same thing at the same time, "What the hell is that?"

Aubrey could see the woman and the man she was in the apartment with sprinting down the street. Although he was surprised at the woman's speed, he knew he would be able to run them both down rather easily, he was by far the greater physical specimen. But first, he had to do away with this African who failed so miserably. With the computer knowledge the little prince had, he would be able to extract what he needed from the woman. He was on his knee now, the gun in his right hand, his left gripping his right wrist to steady his aim, his powerful wrist fighting back against the recoil as he fired two rounds into Andre's abdomen, doubling him over, the only sound escaping his mouth being the whoosh of air knocked out of his lungs by the bullet's impact. The round ripped through Andre's stomach and liver, spilling digestive juices, blood and bile throughout his abdominal cavity. Unfortunately for Andre, the bullet didn't as much nick his spine, the severing of which would have at least saved him from the searing pain that would start in about five seconds and that would stay with him until he died, which would be in about ten agonizingly slow minutes. Andre continued to slump to the ground, winding up in a sitting position against the house, his left hand clamped over the wound, feebly trying to staunch the flow of fluids that were starting to gush out of him at a rate he was astounded by. The tangibility of the pain filling his gut was like the mother of all gas pains, as if it were fueled by salmonella laced tacos, empanadas, and the hottest of red peppers, topped off by a gastrointestinal tract blockage that refused to let him even fart away some of the discomfort. His eyes went wide as the pain peaked a second after he hit the ground, even wincing in response was painful. It was so bad he couldn't even conjure up a new level of hatred for his kidnapper, who was standing now, looking down the block at Laura and the other guy, looking back to the Arab and saying, "Just leave him here, you come with me to get those two. And like an apparition he was gone. Whathefu lingered at the stoop for a moment, only able to turn his palms up in apparent commiseration, and he then took off down the block calling after Aubrey, neither of them uttering a word of comfort to the dying man.

—⚹—

"That guy...he just shot the other guy on the stoop!" Fred cried. But

Ryan didn't see what transpired in the previous few seconds and although he could hear his brother, he wasn't listening to him. He was concentrating on the huffing and puffing vehicle which seemed to be on its absolute last legs and on what appeared to be a couple of people fleeing the scene.

"Hey is that Mikey running up the street? Looks exactly like him," he answered his brother's exclamatory statement.

"It is him, catch up quickly, like Ty Edney going coast to coast." Ryan slammed the gas pedal to the floor and the engine roared to life with probably the last push of torque the old truck will ever have. The engine on this piece of shit was still halfway decent, Ryan said to himself. Thank goodness I'm not turning until the end of the block. Within a few seconds they were almost abreast of Michael, who was flagging a bit as he pursued Laura.

"Hey man, what's going on?" Fred Burke beseeched Michael from his perch in the passenger seat. Michael hadn't even turned toward the vehicle when it drew up to him, his concentration fixed totally on gulping oxygen into his lungs and catching Laura before she made a wrong turn away from the police precinct.

"Catch up to her!" Michael yelled, pointing up the block to the figure running in the distance as the truck slowed slightly, maneuvering himself alongside to be able to jump onto the back. Ryan knew immediately that Michael wanted a ride on the bumper the way they used to years ago when they went skitching through the streets of the city after a snowstorm. A quick look in the rear view mirror told him why. The big bastard who just shot the fat bastard was now running after them, and fast. Wait a minute, what was he doing? Getting down to one knee. Aiming...at us! He could feel Michael's weight on the back bumper, the springs groaning a bit even with just a couple hundred pounds of extra weight. There were cars parked on either side of him, no way to swerve to avoid the shot that was coming his way. Besides, that would throw Mikey off the back and he would possibly hit this woman they were about to catch up to. Hopefully this guy whoever he is, was as good a shot as Chris Dudley was from the free throw line.

Laura was sprinting as she had from her days on the farm, trying to race one of the new foals, or get away from one of her older brothers or one of the numerous lecherous men from the surrounding towns who had stalked her relentlessly through her mid teens. Thank goodness she wore the flats today, although she once beat one of her old boyfriends in a footrace through Central Park while wearing high heels. It was the last date for them as the man...what was his name? can't remember...couldn't bear to be beaten by a woman. She could hear Michael desperately calling her, but she allowed her fear to consume her, knowing it would enable her to drive her legs like the pistons of a Maserati, to rely only on herself to get away from Andre and his thug friends. For a few seconds she didn't hear Michael calling her name and momentarily thought that maybe she had been abandoned by him. Thank goodness for this truck coming up behind me. Maybe it will block Andre's friends from seeing me. Laura kept her legs pumping as she moved to the side of the street, allowing the truck to pass and was completely startled to hear Michael again calling her name, the strong voice much closer now, and now he was suddenly beside her, riding the back of the truck like it was a snowmobile.

"Get on!" he yelled to her and she obeyed immediately, grasping his extended arm. She jumped on the back bumper and knelt as low as she could for balance as Michael banged the roll up door of the truck with his open palm, bellowing to the driver to move it, Move It Now!

—※—

Tony Craig himself started to move more quickly now. He didn't see what just transpired because his line of vision was momentarily blocked by the Pepperidge Farm truck, but he heard the two shots. All law enforcement men and women recognize that sound for what it is immediately while the average citizen expects a more Hollywood-like explosion when a gun is fired. He pulled up to the stoop a few seconds later and came upon Andre clutching his abdomen, the red stain spreading further and beginning to pool beneath him. Tony knew the man was gone, a horribly painful way to go as well. He had seen others with the same type of wound and he knew this man, whoever he was, didn't have much time left. He bent down close to Andre who barely had the strength to look up, and spoke softly to him.

"Where did they go? Your two friends. Tell me now." Andre slowly turned his head and looked down the street and Tony then saw the truck picking up speed...was that someone on the bumper...and as he stood up from the stoop, he could see the big bastard in the middle of the street in a combat position, taking aim at the truck. He quickly dialed J'lome, thankful that he was the kind of man who picked up on the first ring. He was talking and leaning down the block at the same time, the third person about to abandon Andre in his final minutes.

"J'lome, Tony here, just listen. Your friend is here, he's hurt bad. Get over to Forty-Seventh Avenue, just west of Vernon Boulevard. Call an ambulance immediately and the local precinct. I have to get going, my suspect is getting away." Tony clicked the phone off and then bent back toward Andre. "You made some bad choices for friends, pal. In your next life, you'd be smart to try to do better." And with that he took off down the block in pursuit of Aubrey, without even a glance over his shoulder. Just then Andre's phone beeped, announcing the arrival of a text message. From Kismine! My love, he thought, she will give me the strength I need to live again. He opened the message and read...

> 'Andre. I am leaving New York tomorrow for Los Angeles with my new boyfriend Carlos. Thanks for everything and nothing as well. I can't waste time anymore. Bye, and I hope we can still be friends.'

With his last second of strength, he pressed the delete button on her message, lest anyone find out he was dumped in such a way, his pride, his sorely misplaced pride, leading him by the hand even now, toward an endless sleep.

—⁌⁍—

Aubrey was more enraged than he had ever been. More so than on the battlefield, even more so than when he was convinced his wife had betrayed him. The truck was pulling away from him as he knelt in the middle of the street, his gun arm extended toward the back of the truck, struggling to center his aim with the notoriously inaccurate weapon from more than fifteen feet, on Michael. It's the woman I need, not him, he understood as he fired off a burst of five quick rounds, the bullets stitching a concave pattern of holes in the rollup door above Michael's head, the cop killer rounds easily passing through the thin metal door directly into the truck's compartment. Michael banged on the door three more times, yelling at the top of his lungs, "Go, GO, GOOO!"

"Step on it, this fucking guy is crazy. He's shooting at us!" Fred yelled to his brother.

"We'll be alright, we're far away and this guy shoots like John Starks in a game seven." For the first time he could remember, Fred was not interested in basketball, his entire focus was now staying on the correct side of the cemetery dirt.

"If I remember correctly, Starks did make three out of nineteen that night and since there's only two of us in the truck, those be odds I don't like. Move this pig now! Get the fuck away from this guy," Fred barked once again at his brother, twisting left in the seat to get a view of the guy with the gun through the small windows fitted into the roll-up door. The truck picked up speed quickly as the engine and transmission seemed to find a second wind and Fred could now see them putting some distance between them and Aubrey. All they had to do was make a left and it was a few blocks to the 108th where there were a ton of cops.

Aubrey steadied himself once more, all his training, all his love, all his hate, all his desire and frustration wrapped up into a ball of determination as he fired once more, this time three shots passing between the foot of space between Michael and Laura's heads, all the rounds blasting through the door once again as the truck approached the end of the block. Aubrey leaped to his feet as soon as the last bullet left the chamber and he started his sprint again after his prey.

"Goddammit!" Ryan clamored as one of Aubrey's bullets found his left elbow, smashing into the joint, splintering it. He couldn't help his reflexive action of drawing his wounded arm downward, his thumb catching one of the spokes of the steering wheel, throwing the old truck into a sharp left turn it was never designed to negotiate a day out of the factory. The suspension wasn't holding, the brakes were failing, and the truck leaned sickeningly to the right, nothing to stop it, finally tipping over on its side like an overweight brontosaurus, depositing Ryan into Fred's seat, his head hitting his brother's hip point and opening a bloody gash on his temple.

Laura was propelled through the air by the bumper going far more than horizontal and somehow flew over Michael's body without touching a hair on his head as if they were professional contortionists, making the landing stick like a gymnast, thanking all the horses that threw her off their backs in her early teen years when she was trying to break them. It was important then to land on your feet and get moving quickly in case the horse decided to step on your head. Michael managed to slide backwards down the bumper aided by his grip on the door handle and the sickeningly slow rate of descent of the truck, and was able to kick himself free of the vehicle once it plopped on the asphalt, but he came up with a nasty case of road burn on his butt and upper back. Stay awake, don't black out, he told himself as he watched the truck land on its side and slide along about ten more feet before stopping. He could hear the Burkes screaming inside and his brain hungered for an answer. He looked back down the block and could see the big bastard was now up and running and bearing down on them quickly. Where was Laura? He frantically twisted and turned to see her running not down the block to the left, toward the police precinct and safety, but instead she went the other way toward the entrance of Vinny's construction project. He got to his feet, not wanting to leave his friends, but he then noticed Aubrey change his direction slightly to pursue Laura. Aubrey didn't care about the Burkes, he reasoned, so Michael chose to leave his friends and go after Laura, suddenly desperate to keep her from entering the construction site, leaving herself with no retreat. To his horror, she then not only entered the poorly lit area, it seemed as if she made a beeline for it, speeding through the fence. Was she trying to shake the guy with the gun? Stupid! He'll know you're in there, he's right behind us, he can see where we're going! Have to go after her, she doesn't know her way around the site. In the middle of a sunny day not being pursued by a murderous maniac, it's a very dangerous place to be running around. Once again he yelled to her as he brought himself to his feet, "Laura! Stop! Don't go in there!" as she disappeared into the dark beyond the entrance.

Tony Craig inwardly cursed his less than average ability with a firearm, otherwise he could have taken out these two from behind. He had the drop on them, at least he was ninety-nine percent sure he was still unknown to the two other men who were in the car with the dead guy. At least he wasn't wearing the fancy wingtips so many of the others in the office favored. Bunch of posers, they just want to look good to bust some goddamn stockbrokers. His gum and rubber soled shoes may have looked clunky and cheap alongside a nice pair of brogues, but they allowed him to be fast and quiet.

He bent his knees more and leaned into the breeze coming off the river to aid in his forward movement because he figured the skinny one of these two would go to finish off the truck drivers, who were now crawling out of the back door of the truck which had popped open when it rolled on its side. Just seconds before, he watched Michael and Laura somehow drop and roll to safety, a miraculous effort by the both of them. The woman was some athlete and he was glad that Michael kept himself in shape as well, dumb luck not playing an insignificant part in it. They better have some more luck in them before this is over. Any number of balding, twenty pound overweight desk-flyers would have still been on the ground, broken and bleeding. He saw the two of them take off, into the site where he had met Vinny just a short time ago. That he didn't like. The big bastard was gaining on them with each step and it was not conceivable they would be able to pull off a U-turn and get out of there. It was their roach motel. He could see that the truck drivers were now both out of the back door of the truck which had rolled up with the impact of the accident, one of them appearing to be seriously hurt, but they were on their feet at least and they were being ignored by the skinny one, who followed his partner into the construction site without as much as a glance at the truck's occupants. Tony continued after them as quickly and silently as he could, struggling to recall the layout of the place he had visited just ten minutes or so earlier.

<hr />

"I have always thought that kissing and lightly sucking on the lower lip of a woman was much better then mouth mashing, what do you think?" Vinny asked Maxie who was sitting with him on the same side of the card table, her legs folded over his under the table. Her arms were around his neck and all of her senses were alive with the moment.

"Mmmm," was her reply, continuing to enjoy herself for the first time in years. He was holding her perfectly, tightly enough to confirm his real interest and make her feel so comfortable and protected, but loosely enough to let her maneuver and not feel restricted. She was about to tell him with real words this time exactly how wonderful she felt when he suddenly jerked his head away, his eyes suddenly ablaze, senses tuned like those of a lioness hearing a metallic click while nursing her cubs.

"What is it?" she was asking as Vinny gently moved her legs away without answering her question, slipping out from behind the table. He stepped over to the door of the trailer, Maxie brushing her hair out of her eyes, settling herself, waiting for his answer, wondering what was happening. Her own senses had been so tuned into his kiss and being in his arms that she would not have noticed if a grenade went off by her ear. He stopped short of the door, passing it by to instead look out the louvered window at the far end of the trailer.

"Didn't you hear that? It sounded like a car crash." He turned back to her, "You really didn't hear anything?" She smiled adorably at him, shaking her head no and he melted in spite of his sixth sense currently yelling into his brain. She then raised herself up in the chair, cocking her ear toward the sudden sound of feet crunching on the uneven ground somewhere outside. "That I heard. It sounds like someone running."

Michael was one hundred feet inside the site by now, still screaming to Laura. He knew of a hole in the fence surrounding the site to the north. He had seen some kids sneaking in a couple of days earlier and had meant to mention it to Vinny but it had wandered away from his brain what with everything else of the past couple of days. But how do I direct her that way? Jesus, she was a fast runner. He was surprised at his own stamina, grateful that he stopped smoking a couple of years earlier, but convinced that he, too, was working on a rush of adrenaline, which frightened him, increasing the chemicals in his body that overrode the pain in his bad right knee, the ankle he broke playing basketball when he was thirty and the pulmonary something that was sure to pop like Vesuvius any moment now.

Michael knew the trailer was off to the left, at the south end of the site. He could see the lights on in the window, Vinny waiting there for the game to start. Didn't he hear the crash? Hopefully he did and called the cops. But wouldn't he have come out of the trailer to investigate? What's he doing in there, setting out the chips and whatnot? The door was closed and he couldn't see anyone outside. Just then he made out the sound of another shot from his pursuer, a wild one at that, but he still was able to hear the bullet sizzle through the air over his head. Laura was about fifty feet ahead of him and she seemed to be heading toward the trailer, but he couldn't be sure. At this rate it would only be a few seconds before she hit the bulkhead and would have to go either left or right or into the water. He would have to catch her soon and then lead her northward along the river's edge to the hole in the fence.

They both heard the shot and both recognized it for what it was although Maxie had only heard a gunshot in the movies. Vinny went for the door immediately, instructing Maxie to get on the floor and stay out of sight. He ripped the door open, realizing what a mistake that was as the light from inside the trailer was as bright as Sirius and not only made his silhouetted frame in the door a perfect target, it also blinded him from seeing anything that was more than ten feet away. Aubrey, who was fifty feet behind Michael, wheeled as the first beam of light hit his retina and he squeezed off one round on the run like a Kamakura archer on horseback. He was royally pissed off that he couldn't pick off the woman and the man on the back of the truck. If he was only twenty feet or so closer to them during the dash down the street, he could have calmly put a round in the man's thigh and a couple more in the truck's tires. But he knew he had this guy in the door dead to rights.

The bullet slammed into Vinny's shoulder like a meteorite, spinning him around and sending him to the floor, the fire in his shoulder starting even before he landed. Maxie was speechless, and Vinny turned his gaze to her, wincing through the horrible pain, hoping against hope that she could keep herself together. To his relief, she didn't scream in terror, instead ripping the tablecloth off the card table—which was the only card table that always used a tablecloth due to too many cards being casually flipped from dealer to player, a card sliding off the edge of the table, ruining many of Vinny's great hands because a flipped card didn't land as it should have, revealing itself to the rest of the players—and immediately bunching it into a compress that she pressed against Vinny's shoulder. She could see the bullet did tremendous damage and was impressed that he was still coherent and able to pull himself to a semi-sitting position. She pressed the tablecloth with all her strength, trying to staunch the flow of blood. Vinny nodded to her, directing her attention across the trailer. "Get me my phone, please." Maxie jumped to her feet and brought back the two-way and gave it to him, watching him closely as he speed dialed, not a little astounded at his control as he punched the send button and lifted the phone to his ear with his good arm.

Moose Miller morosely watched the scene on the northbound East River Drive coupled with a cool detachment to the carnage just a hundred feet away. He had looked up from his book instantly when he heard the squeal of tires followed by the sickening crunch of metal as a couple of idiots who were racing up the drive on their rice rocket motorcycles collided with each other and then into the back of a yellow taxi that was traveling only about twenty miles per hour because the Egyptian cabbie was arguing with his passenger, turning all the way backwards in the bench-type front seat to get in the face of the New Yorker in the back seat about the Israelis and the Palestinians.

Moose called in the accident but kept his position in the river in front of the United Nations building. There was nothing for him to do at the accident scene as he was unable to tie up to the bulkhead on the Manhattan side of the river. Besides, he couldn't leave the boat because he was still alone, his partner not as yet returned from his fling with the model on the sailboat. He was unsure if he would be written up for not reporting his young partner's absence. The easy thing to do was to call the accident in, let the guys in the radio cars have the call, let them work it out.

It reminded him of the time a hugely fat, amazingly drunk guy jumped into the river about one hundred feet north of his present position. The man went under like a stone and Moose knew there was no chance to pull him out so all he could do was put out the buoy over where the man went down and wait for a dive team. He was roundly cursed by a group of bystanders, vilified for being a coward, for not diving in after the victim. Don't they know that it is December and that the water is freezing and that I could never get that man off the bottom? We'll find him sometime in the spring, he thought as he pondered yet again why anyone would take their own life. He felt naked and alone and thoroughly useless as he watched the radio cars and the ambulances come upon the scene, the traffic slowing to less than a crawl, the cars filled with gawkers who couldn't resist viewing the wreckage.

It became unusually quiet with the absence of the drone of the uptown traffic speeding by. Moose was able to hear the water lap against the hull of the boat and the cries of a few gulls heading upriver. It was just after the last of the gulls honked its presence that his sense was jarred by a sharp report. Was that a shot? He looked back at the cops tending to the injured on the Drive, trying to determine by a raised head, any sign of diverted attention, if they also heard anything. He was on the river and they were not, the open water amplifying sounds that seemed to skip over its surface like a flat stone. He was sure he heard something and he turned around to the Queens side of the river and he immediately noticed the light pouring from the open door of the construction shack. That was unusual, he thought. It's a little breezy out here, the difference between daytime and nighttime temperatures about twenty degrees. Vinny always liked it warm and therefore never left a door or window open unless it was eighty degrees.

He reached for a pair of binoculars and trained them on the bulkhead, starting his sweep from the northern end of the site as he wanted to make sure to catch someone before they disappeared into the darkness, away from Vinny's open door. And then he could indeed see someone, a woman it looked like, seemingly running straight for the bulkhead. Who the hell was that and what was she doing? Was she going to jump in? He quickly dropped the binoculars and stepped into the pilot house to bring the boat around, his instinct telling him that something was going on over there and that it probably wasn't right. His phone rang at that moment and he flipped it open but didn't acknowledge the caller immediately as he simultaneously started to wrestle with the wheel, but he could clearly hear someone yelling through the tiny earpiece, Archie, get over here now, now NOW!"

Laura turned on a dime to the right once she heard the shot and now she picked up on Michael's shouted instructions to follow the bulkhead north, toward the bridge, away from the trailer. She was close to the water now and she tried to carefully pick her way along its length, but it was becoming more difficult as she had less and less light to guide her. Another round slammed into the ground just a few feet in front of her and it stopped her in her tracks. Now the fear gripped her like a vise and she desperately searched for any exit. Michael was coming up fast behind her now and could see the indecision in her movements and as he was about to call out again for her to continue in the same direction she was originally headed, where it was darker and this bastard behind us would have a more difficult time hitting anything, he realized with horror that she was going to run out on the pier. Oh sweet Jesus, no, don't do that, he wanted to scream but his voice wouldn't work. What else could he do but follow her there? She pulled up at the last ancient plank, about fifteen feet out into the East River, and Michael caught up with her a second or two later.

"It's not good here," he said as he drew even to her and he hated himself as he always did whenever he blurted out something obvious. But he saw no derision in her face as she turned back to him, just her eyes widening with fear as Aubrey suddenly appeared on the horizon, no longer running but walking confidently toward them. Michael stood between Laura and their approaching killer, putting his hand around her waist, holding her sideways to give him less of a target, unsure of what, if anything there was to do.

Aubrey slowed considerably, sauntering up to the bulkhead, realizing that he had his prey cornered, the gun now loosely at his side. But that didn't abate his anger at the sudden turn of events of the last few minutes, his plans for the stolen money that was not yet stolen slipping away. The man was holding the woman closely so his aim would have to be perfect. One round right into his forehead would drop him like a stone and then he would dash in to keep the woman from going into the water with her date. With a bit of luck he could have her in the car inside of five minutes, on their way back to Long Island to put the fat African's computer back together.

"Hey, be careful. This dock can't support all of our weight," Michael called out to the tall powerful man as he stepped onto the structure. His warning went unheeded as Aubrey continued onto the dock. There was only ten feet between them now, and Michael could see him smirking which pissed him off.

"Who the hell are you? What do you want with us?" Michael buzzed Aubrey with the query, struggling to keep the quaver from his voice. He could feel Laura's grip tighten on his arm as he spoke. He was wondering about the dock and its staying power as Aubrey advanced a couple of steps more before stopping again. Michael thought he could hear an engine rumble to life somewhere out on the water, but he fought the urge to turn around. His brain told him that Moose Miller was on duty just a few hundred yards away...did he hear the shots? Did anyone think to call him? Was that his boat?

"I only want her," the giant calmly answered. Aubrey extended the hand without the gun and beckoned Laura to follow him back up to the bulkhead. But she didn't budge.

"What do you want with me? What happened to Andre?" she stammered, not moving an inch from the end of the pier.

"I need your computer expertise. I want you to put his computer back together so we can steal some money. I have big plans for that money and I'm not going to let you screw it up."

"Why not just use Andre and his damn expertise?" Oh, the insanity of it, all she considered in the middle of this impossible situation. Here was this guy telling me he wanted my expertise when I have spent most of the last year arguing with Andre about how much expertise I really had. Fucking men, I hate them all.

"You mean the fat African?" Aubrey realized just then that he never knew Andre's name. He chuckled venomously. "He's no use to anyone anymore. He's dead by now on your front doorstep. If you want to join him, well that will be your decision entirely." Laura's hand went to her mouth in horror. Don't be frightened, she screamed at herself. He just admitted that he needs you, he's not going to kill you. He knows that only you know the passwords.

"I only want you, honey. Your boyfriend is not necessary," Aubrey continued matter of factly as he raised the gun again and Michael could see that the next bullet to leave that barrel was going to land somewhere behind him in the East River shortly after it traveled through his brain out the back of his skull.

Michael didn't think as the ancient muscle memory that propelled him off this very pier thirty-five years before kicked in. He grabbed Laura around the waist, his left hand mid-torso, just under her lowest rib, and dove into the water taking her with him. He screamed at her in the middle of their plunge toward the icy water to take a deep breath, his last syllable leaving his mouth just before they hit the water. The East River water temperature was in the low fifties. Not bad for a stroll through Central Park, but positively frigid for the average adult human. It felt as if he were being scratched with needles of dry ice all over his body. Michael kicked furiously as soon as he was under water to keep from surfacing too soon, holding his depth as soon as his ears started to hurt so he could be as undetectable from the surface as possible. The only problem was holding his breath long enough before he surfaced. The problem of whether or not Laura was able to hold her breath wasn't entering his mind. She wasn't struggling against his grip and he thought he could feel her legs furiously kicking as well. The cold water was wrapping itself around him like a boa constrictor made of hot needles, sapping his strength, constricting his chest, the burning sensation from oxygen depletion moving up his throat in concert with the biting cold of the river seeping into his marrow.

Aubrey was stunned at Michael's sudden athletic movement, furious with himself for not anticipating anything like it. Diving into that freezing, swirling water dressed like he is would be a forbidding task for the toughest Navy SEAL, he was easily concluding as his mind was racing ahead to his next move. Their escape wouldn't work out for them, he knew. The man's desperate move would ultimately turn out to be nothing more than a mere delay. The river water was swirling, the currents powerful and unpredictable. Even if this guy is a champion swimmer, he wouldn't be able to stay down more than twenty seconds, less because he's fully dressed, even less because he's pulling a body along with him. Five more seconds, that was all he had left, Aubrey calculated, and as soon as I see his head rise out of the water, I'm going to put a hole in it. His would be the first to rise for air, his effort at pulling her along keeping her a millisecond behind him. But where, where will he appear? Aubrey's concentration was totally fixated on the surface of the black water, waiting for any change any indication of where they might surface. The tide was moving at crazy angles, five feet of water going north, a little whirlpool over there, the next twenty feet out, the water flowed south...but much slower or so it seemed. Aubrey was used to the currents of the smaller rivers he remembered fishing and skipping stones in when he was a boy. The river back then ran one way, its descent shaped and maneuvered by a landscape you got to know because it was always the same. This river here was so very different, so much larger, and it was taking all of his concentration to expand his vision to include the widest angles, his hearing aided by the cupping of his left ear, the Glock held straight out over the end of the pier waiting for a target, his mouth slightly open. His knees remained slightly bent, ready to pivot with precision and balance here or there. His concentration wouldn't be shattered by anything, unless it was the heavy footsteps of Whathefu pulling up behind him, having just run out onto the pier, not for a second thinking the spindly structure was anything unlike the same piers at marinas and private homes around the Mediterranean that he hopped and skipped onto throughout his life. He slowed his pace quickly and clumsily, as if he were a fighter plane being grabbed by a cable a second after its wheels touched down on the flight deck.

—illi—

She was thinking about the many times she visited San Carlos as a child, running through the cold mountain stream that ran out of the foot hills of the Andes. She always felt energized after she returned to the farm after a week or so there, visiting relatives who were living in Chile, not realizing until many years later that those experiences helped her develop a great wind. That was certainly helpful in this present situation, Laura managed to think to herself through the pain of the cold water. It felt like a bath given by your most hated aunt who used a Brillo pad on your bare skin. Luckily she heard and under-stood Michael's bellow, her surprise reaction at being pulled off the pier helping her to draw as full a lungful of air as was possible. She knew she could hold her breath for over a minute, but that was in a contest with her brothers at the bottom of a pool filled with much warmer water. When she knew that all she had to do to escape was to push off the bottom of the pool and break the surface of the water with a wide grin.

Of course swimming in all her clothing was another matter entirely. Especially when she was gripped around the waist by a man, who at the end of the day she hardly knew, being pursued by a killer she didn't know at all. What the hell was going on? Andre would have been fired for just stealing the money, she was sure of that. But what more had he gotten himself into, and me as well? Her life was out of her control now and it was that simple fact that started her shivering even before she hit the water. The fear that a bunch of men were again currently in control of her life hit her hard and she allowed her fury to take over her thoughts instead. All thoughts other than surviving this night were eliminated. But at least Michael was different than all the others, she allowed. I knew he wouldn't abandon me, I knew in my heart always that he wouldn't disappoint me.

She was kicking furiously in a bid to help Michael and she lost her shoes at some point during the effort. Several times their ankle bones clicked together and the cold water did little to dampen the jarring pain. His arm around her waist gave her an unusual feeling of calm. It was almost sexual the way he held her so tightly against his body, his forearm flat against her stomach, just a few inches above her pubic bone. She could detect the power in the sweeping probes of his right arm, the downward thrust unrelenting in its search for forward progress. But how long could he continue? And how can he know how long I can hold my breath? With these thoughts starting to cloud her brain, she tried to match his strokes to maximize the effort.

That effort was starting to take its toll on Michael after about ten seconds. He unfortunately did not grow up high in the Andes Mountains, but at sea level in Queens. Countless hours of laps in the pools of the beach clubs he and his friends would sneak into in Atlantic Beach, thousands of waves waited on by treading water past the last barrel, caught, and body-surfed into shore, as well as all the summer afternoons he entered these very waters gave him a hard, lean body that he carried well into his mid thirties; a problem that he was now in his mid forties. That he was doing all of this under duress with a body under his arm, in his clothing, no less, was a little more than he expected at this point in the evening. It should have been about now that Fred Burke would be trying to bluff with nothing in his hand, Michael then sweeping the table clean of all the chips. He suddenly remembered his hatred of swimming in cold water.

He knew he dove deep enough to remain undetected from the surface. This was not the Caribbean with its crystal clear waters guaranteeing fifty foot visibility with gentle tides. But it was impossible for him to tell how much progress he had made since entering the water. He figured he had been under for about ten seconds and would have to surface within the next ten. The current could have kept him perfectly in place, rising for his last gulp of air just a few feet away from where he jumped in. And he would never know until he came up. He was grateful for Laura's help. He could feel her kicking powerfully as well as pulling at the currents with her other arm. He was glad to see that she was a woman who wouldn't take any shit, who somehow would grasp a situation by its throat, and manage to do so with not a little bit of grace and style included somewhere. At least this time.

The basketball games with the Burkes on the concrete playground on Forty-third Street that started the creaking in his knees and lower back when he passed forty were now overwhelming him more than the need for oxygen. But he was not yet convinced he was far enough away. That big bastard had shot with that pistol pretty well, just missing us on the back of the truck. I have to breathe shortly and so does she. Maybe a few more seconds, a few more kicks and strokes, maybe, just maybe, he would remind himself that as an Irish Capricorn he was most probably at least genetically and in the opinion of the Zodiac, the most stubborn and determined strain of human being on the planet. Three more strokes, that was all he determined they would have energy for before they surfaced and with an effort to point their progress south to further throw the bastard with the gun off, surface quickly, gulp another lungful and down again. The second set of underwater kicking and stroking would take them away from the range of the Glock and they could then float as far as they could, mirthfully to be spotted before the swirls of the river dragged them down.

—◦—

Whathefu's arrival on the pier infuriated Aubrey who was fixated on where Michael and Laura should surface. Maintaining his concentration on the roiling black waters was requiring an inhuman effort. One shot, that's all I need, he kept telling himself. But I need to see them first, the doubts would answer just as quickly. He could hear Whathefu behind him breathing heavily as he dropped to his knees in exhaustion from the run down the block. Aubrey detected a tiny shift in the structure but ignored it. He didn't ignore what the little Arab boy yelled next however, he just filed it for future reference, to be reviewed in about two seconds.

"There's someone behind us, and he's got a gun!"

I have to breathe now was Michael's decision. His lungs and joints were on fire and he could feel Laura's kicks slowing. Please Laura, he screamed in his mind's voice, make sure you gulp air and not water when we surface, please make sure your timing is perfect, because I probably have to take you under again.

⸻

Aubrey heard them breaking the surface and the desperate inhaling of oxygen from two pairs of straining lungs and his body sprang into action. He dropped a few inches further into a combat stance, his already extended arm having to move only about ten degrees from his guesstimate of where he would see them next, his trigger finger now inside the guard. They were only thirty feet away, the currents, the cold water, and the clothing having impeded any more progress. Good for me, bad for them, he thought as he squeezed off a shot and saw then both heads quickly disappear below the surface. He was sure he hit the man and expected them to surface again in a second or two. Whathefu was yelling behind him now like a cheerleader, jumping up and down, "You hit him, I heard it, yeah!!" Aubrey's concentration on the water's surface was now broken. Not by Whathefu's intrusions, but by the slow, almost imperceptible but clearly unstoppable lean of the dock and what he heard next which sent a greater chill through him than the water in this river ever could.

⸻

"F.B.I.! Drop the gun! Get the fuck off the dock! The both of you walk back this way, hands in the air, now!" Tony Craig held his position on the bulkhead not only because he had lateral movement up here, but he remembered what Vinny had told him earlier about how weak the structure was. Aubrey stood quickly to shore up his balance, too quickly for Tony's comfort level, and he quickly stepped to his left, unleashing a shot that struck Aubrey in the right shoulder blade right on its edge splitting it in two, the pain causing him to double up with a guttural roar, rendering the arm almost useless, the big man dropping to his knees.

There is usually very little or no warning with structural failure. Frequent inspections keep most bridges from toppling into the ravine or river they traverse...as long as the local government takes care of business, of course, but if you have a spindly structure anchored poorly, built haphazardly probably one hundred years before for some local to get a better angle on the stripers running up to the Sound, exposed to brutal weather patterns and a steady patter of feet over the years, sooner or later it's going to go if one isn't careful.

Sometimes there is a moan, seemingly giving the twisting and failing metal a soul, an ungodly sound that small and large structures suffering a catastrophic failure produce. Other times, depending on the type of structure, vibrations or even extreme undulations offer a taste of what will soon follow. But not in the case of the little dock on the East River in the shadow of the bridge and the Pepsi sign in Long Island City. It instead just dropped into the water with nary a squeak or a ripple, mere milliseconds after Aubrey's shoulder exploded and his body weight then dropping so perfectly suddenly, at the most perfect spot on the already weakened structure.

Aubrey pitched forward, hitting the water like a kid doing a cannonball off a diving board, the awful cold helping him to clear his head and taking away much of the pain from the bullet. Fucking F.B.I! He must have had some connection to his wife and the Military Police in South Carolina, an event he had almost forgotten about as his plan to dominate the Muslim media world unfolded since the moment Andre stepped from the bathroom in J'lome's mosque and the plot to steal the money commenced. His mind was so beyond twisted that he still believed there was a chance he could pull it off. He had swum mile after mile during his constant physical training and conditioning. He knew where the man and the women were and he could catch them and still get the woman back to land in one piece to do what he wanted her to. The fate of his 'partner' never entered his mind as he began his first stroke.

Whathefu fell onto his butt and then pitched forward entering the water head first like a four-year-old learning to dive for the first time. The cold river felt like a thousand scorpions stinging him over and over again. Unfortunately for the young Saudi, an insignificant third son of a third wife, he had never swum in water other then the heated pools in his father's mansions or in the warmest coastal waters of the Caribbean, Hawaii and the Mediterranean. The shock of hitting the frigid East River was so that it suddenly caused his mouth to fly wide open and as soon as he righted himself underwater, the effect was the same as the old science experiment from second grade where the teacher pushes a cup down into a basin filled with liquid and the air keeps the liquid out...until you turn it over. The experiment works with any container you turn over in a liquid environment and as a result of this scientific certainty, Whathefu's lungs filled with the cold vile water in seconds as he righted himself, paralyzing him instantly and leaving him standing on the riverbed weighted down perfectly by the water balloons in his chest that used to breathe oxygen, the last vision to caress his retinas being the pearls of lights on the bridge that usually led him to the parts of the beautiful skyline of the city he so desperately wanted to be a part of and would never see again.

Moose Miller swung the boat around hard to starboard. He wanted plenty of room to maneuver past the southern tip of Roosevelt Island and U Thant Island, named in honor of the former Secretary General of the United Nations. The island is small, barely one hundred by two hundred feet, made up of refuse and landfill deposited there by William Steinway of piano making fame, and is used exclusively by an endangered species of cormorant. Moose was always amazed that no weekend boater ever ran up on the island with their Chris Craft or Cigarette racing boat as there was only a tiny, barely discernible light on the top of a spindly tower signaling the island's presence in the channel. Now was not the time to make haste and run aground. He also could not push the throttles to full power if he wanted to be able to hear any cries of warning or shouts for help as well as avoid running anyone over. His river pilot's mind instantly calculated the very short course and limited speed he was going to use. He figured he needed about twenty seconds to arrive near Vinny's site. What the hell was going on there?

Tony Craig had watched the pier collapse, not believing his good and bad luck. The turn of events was so sudden and startling, he was left speechless except for a soft cry of surprise that he could not suppress. The last time he was so paralyzed by an event was when a woman he had been dating, in an attempt to bend a fairway drive around a century-old oak blocking a straight shot to the green, instead hit the oak and somehow the ball ricocheted around the lower branches of the tree and landed back in the golf cart like a grenade. He and the woman had laughed for days later and they were convinced that if they videotaped the event, it would have had a million hits on YouTube.

There was no way he was going in the water. He knew he wouldn't last more than a minute. He remembered how treacherous these currents were from the one or two times he joined Vinny and his younger friends here for a swim. They had playfully taunted him after his final refusals to dive in the water, but he was a man who had always known his limitations. His decision was made in an instant. He raised his gun, steadied his stance, and fired five shots at Aubrey, emptying the huge revolver, the impacts on the water from the quickly spent rounds like the concentric circles left by a stone skipping over the surface of a still lake. Tony realized he had almost zero chance of hitting anything from this range; he was astonished by the soldier's physical strength and speed in the water in spite of his wounded shoulder. His target was already about thirty feet away and Tony knew all he could do was use the gun as a noisemaker and maybe, just maybe, he could put another round in this bastard.

Moose Miller was no longer a casual weekend-type of boater. When he wasn't on the job, he now stayed on land with his kids, preferring parks and softball games to the water skiing and fishing of his youth. When he was the pilot, as he was now, forced into it because of the sudden departure of his partner to go get laid, he was as alert as a chimpanzee that smelled a panther nearby. The gunshots unleashed by Tony Craig had their desired effect, although he would have preferred to blow his target's head off. The flash of the gun, the sharp crack of the contained explosions grabbed Moose Miller's attention instantly and his senses were drawn to some sounds of thrashing in the water. He passed U Thant Island safely and pushed the throttles forward, urging the boat ahead, quickly guiding it toward the construction site's bulkhead. He could see as he got closer that there were actually several people in the water, the two in front apparently attempting to escape from the third.

Aubrey knew his strength of body and mind. His confidence that he could catch these two, dispatch the man here in the water, and get the woman back to land was without question. But his anger overwhelmed him and he foolishly stopped his progress to raise himself up in the water to attempt another shot. The bullet whizzed harmlessly over the heads of Michael and Laura, but it also caught the attention of Moose Miller who had just raised the glasses once more to his eyes hoping to get a clear idea of what the hell was going on before he got to the scene.

Michael had heard the shot and felt death coming to him like the morning sun, eventual and unstoppable. But the bullet didn't reach its mark, missing as the first one shot from the pier and he continued his torturous swim toward, whatever, wherever. The water was unbelievably cold, but thank goodness the current was at its weakest, apparently changing from inbound to outbound. But his limbs were not just freezing. He was greatly fatigued by too little exercise, too many past cigarettes not yet completely cleaned out of his lungs and the fact that he was weighted down by his clothing. He was working on auto pilot now, his right arm pulling him forward, his legs kicking with all he had. His left arm was still securely around Laura's waist and thankfully he could feel her legs moving. He had a sudden terrible thought that maybe she was dead but he then felt her grip tighten on his forearm as if she were massaging it. She has to breathe, and so do I and I don't want to surface yet, but I have to. Their heads broke the water and Michael whipped his around quickly to get his bearings. They were more than fifty feet away from the pier now and the current had taken them another fifty feet south. This was the furthest out Michael had ever been in the river. Years earlier, he and his friends hadn't dared to jump in off the dock without holding a safety line that was tied to the bulkhead. He and Laura were treading water now, floating along with the tide, breathing only a touch easier now, working their legs the best they could, the cold water sapping their strength with each passing second. Michael turned his attention to Laura, looking straight into her eyes.

"Just keep kicking, alright?" he said between shivers. "The current will take us to safety." He knew there was no real place either north or south where they could climb out of the water, but she probably didn't know that.

Laura fed off Michael's calm and powerful self-control. The man is a management genius, she thought, amazed that he was holding it together in the middle of all this craziness. Ten minutes ago she was sitting on her couch with him just a millisecond away from a kiss she had craved for ten years. Now she was in the freezing water of the East River without a life preserver or a paddle. Never in her life had she ever felt so cold. She swiveled her head, starting to look around as the current suddenly pulled them south even faster, as if they just stepped on an airport pedestrian walkway. The irresistible power of the water didn't scare her, however; it was what she saw when she looked back at the dock. Michael noticed her eyes widen at something in the distance and he knew what it was before she screamed.

"Michael! Michael! He's coming!" she screamed, oblivious of anything other than her own fear. Michael turned and now he could see the big bastard coming their way, swimming awkwardly on his side for some reason, but still making ground. There was pure evil in his eyes, sprinkled with a vast amount of determination, his lips stretched across his face. Animalistic grunts accompanied each of Aubrey's strokes, making him sound like a female tennis player rocketing a backhand down the line. Maybe he's injured, Michael thought, but still, there was no way he wanted to fight this guy in the water. Or on land for that matter. Hitting Andre in the face was one thing, but grappling with this guy was another, especially in the water. In the very, very cold water whose currents were starting to become a bit violent in their shifting of direction. Tiny little white caps were appearing and now Michael was becoming exponentially fearful of drowning.

Aubrey's shoulder was blinding him with pain from the moment he entered the water. But his physical prowess and the unmatchable self-determination that made him the formidable soldier he was allowed him to push ahead toward his targets. When he was twenty feet away from Laura and Michael he stopped and also began to tread water. He hung in the roiling waters like an orca stalking a seal trapped on an ice floe, staring at the man and the woman with ill-concealed malevolence. Michael wondered momentarily if the gun would work in the water.

Aubrey laughed maniacally, his head thrown back, the powerful sternocleidomastoid muscles of his neck standing out like bridge support cables. He pointed the gun at them, treading water effortlessly.

"You're both fucking dead," he screamed in a voice that probably could be heard over an elevated subway as it barreled along above the streets. "Everything is gone now and nothing matters to me anymore except your deaths. But first I want you, you fucking bitch. You are coming with me to do my bidding and then I'll decide how you'll die." He punctuated his last comment with the gun and Michael was sure at that moment he was going to pull the trigger so he dove under the water again pulling Laura along with him for one last desperate lunge for their lives. Just before his head disappeared under the water, he heard another shot from Aubrey's gun and then a rumbling, a throaty growl he wouldn't have expected at that moment, accompanied by a blinding light which reminded him of all the stories he had heard of near-death experiences, the victims all consistent in their description of a light pulling them to their final destination.. He was convinced for a moment that he was hit by the last shot and that he was on his way to see Jesus and he thought, Please...please save this lady and please, please, someone help me remember the words to the Act of Contrition prayer.

⁂

The spotlight on Moose Miller's boat swept east from the two people in the water toward the sound of yet another shot and it then rested upon a third person, who was apparently pursuing the other two. What the hell is this all about? he asked himself. He pushed the throttles forward to intercept the shooter, the boat's prow lifting from the sudden surge of power. He was there in a few seconds, cutting off Aubrey's line of sight. Moose pulled back on the throttles then into reverse to hold his position, the boat's transmission screaming with the effort, as soon as he reached a point where he could stop the pursuit of the shooter, soon enough so as not over run him. The wake shot out from the boat and reached Aubrey quickly, knocking him off balance in the water. Moose jumped out of the pilot's house, grabbing a life ring as he went to the other side of the boat to check on the two people in the water. Leaning over the gunwale, he could now see to his horror that it was Michael and some woman, the cold starting to take them, the color drained from their faces, Michael's hand now reaching to Moose from about fifteen feet away. He tossed the ring to them, making sure they grabbed hold, yelling to them to hold on, that he'd be right there for them.

Moose heard and felt the next shot from Aubrey. It creased his right temple, stunning him, but not even coming close to knocking him down or scaring him away. Instead it had the opposite effect. He turned to the other side of the boat where he could now see the shooter raising his gun and aiming for a truer second chance and it seized him then, all of the rage that had been bottled up by the gentle giant for years—the bypassing at promotion time for guys with a 'rabbi' in the department, the friends and colleagues lost on 9/11, bin Laden still not caught, his shitty apartment and the constant complaining about it from his wife, she never making an effort to go to work and make a few bucks to help out, the public never appreciating what a cop has to go through every day on this job, instead choosing to jeer the badge at every opportunity. The bosses at One Police Plaza, married to their computer stats, all of them little politicians, their street smarts and policing talents wasted away from years behind a desk but still controlling every man and woman who pulls on a uniform every day and walks a beat like it was a board game.

The money always short at the end of the month, his joints always hurting from the frequent jumps in the water during the winter, the depression that grasped at him whenever he had to bring a young person out of the gloomy depth of the waterways that surrounded the city. His one final stab at financial freedom with his investment of his entire life's savings and his pension in Vinny's project almost dead, his wife certain to make good on the promise to leave him if the whole thing fell apart. The snotty looks from others at the temple, knowing he didn't wear a jacket and tie to work and that he didn't have an advanced degree of some sort. The dreams, the desires, the hopes, all seemingly flattened at age forty-seven, and now this moment. Now this motherfucker shooting at him. He yelled at Aubrey, who swam a few feet closer to him, Moose thanking him for his stupidity as he felt under the gunwale for the gaff, an eight-foot staff made of hard ash that was topped by a metal point with a large hook turning back on the shaft.

"Police, put the gun down now!" Aubrey's response was to raise the weapon and Moose could see he was directly in his sights. He stepped nimbly to the side to ruin his aim and then stabbed at Aubrey's head with the gaff straight on. In spite of his own wound and the chill of the water sapping his strength and swimming ability, Aubrey managed to duck just in time, the gaff passing over his head, only grazing him. However Moose connected when he pulled the gaff back for another try at Aubrey's head, driving the hook under Aubrey's chin. Like an angler who just landed a marlin, he jerked the gaff with all of his strength, propelled by his personal pissed-offness as well, so many things and people and situations that lay, he believed, beyond his control...the effect being that now he had Aubrey impaled, the hook traveling through his lower jaw, severing his tongue, and burying itself two inches deep into his palate. Moose was instantly reminded of that matador on the front page of the *Post* who was impaled by the bull much in the same way. But he wasn't finished with this bastard. He roughly pulled Aubrey, who was now paralyzed with shock by the horrible injury, closer to the boat like a tuna brought up out of the canyons and now with good leverage established and maintained so that the gaff would not snap, lifted him halfway out of the water and kept him there by jamming the end of the gaff under the right angle created by the starboard gunwale and the transom.

"That'll quiet you down now, won't it, you fucking cocksucking asshole?!" He hurried to the other side of the boat, knowing that Michael and the woman had already been in the water much too long. It was a fair chance that they would be lost already in the last few seconds, the currents taking them south past the bridges, the Statue and the Narrows out to the deep. Two people on the ring was one too much. Please, Jesus Lord, let them be there.

***

Tony Craig was watching everything play out from the bulkhead. He could see that Moose Miller—boy was he glad that this one particular officer was available when he needed a pair of eyes at the airport—had caught Aubrey. He could see the soldier hanging off the side of the boat like a tuna, a sight that thrilled and chilled him at the same time. The boat blocked his view of the other two, the woman from the bank and Michael Pierce. He hoped that they were still alive. He could see Moose Miller leaning over the opposite gunwale but couldn't tell if he was able to help them or if he was scanning the surface of the water for any further trace of them. He had to get there, had to take control of the soldier and the situation. He also needed the woman if she was still alive. But how could he get on the boat with the dock gone and the police boat too big to pull right up to the bulkhead? All of a sudden he had an idea and reached for his phone.

***

Steve North was piloting his Coast Guard Zodiac craft through Hell Gate, the shallow draft of the boat and its powerful twin outboard engines moving him through the treacherous waters fairly easily. One more pass down the east side of Manhattan and he would be at the Coast Guard station in Staten Island. He was tired, the work sometimes inclined toward monotony as he checked every inch along Manhattan's east and west side, guiding the highly maneuverable craft into the spaces between the piers, moving slowly along the bulkheads, making sure there were no packages left behind by some visiting Islamist, but it was important.

The Zodiac was a small warship, designed for the fast attack in case mischief on the waterways of New York was the next way Al Qaeda decided to go. But the years since 9/11 have passed without another terrorist incident, and there were some in government, local and Federal, that were now calling for austerity, so that monies set aside for security in New York could be used for protecting a bridge or little-used Federal building in Bumfuck, USA. He was thinking about making a high-speed run down the East River, bursting out into the harbor once he passed the Battery and then home to Staten Island – while he still could – when his phone rang. He could see who it was on the screen. He was always glad to hear from Tony Craig, his old college friend from Boston, although the calls between them were more and more infrequent.

"Tony, what's cookin' eh? he asked, hoping that he was in the city. Maybe a beer later so they could play catch up.

"Steve, please tell me you're on duty tonight."

"I am, why? What's up?"

"Please also tell me you're in the Zodiac."

"I am. Now you tell me what's happening before you ask me another question."

"Listen, I'll tell you when you get here. I am at the bulkhead by the Pepsi sign in Long Island City. There is a bad guy being held on the NYPD harbor patrol boat in the river. I need to get to that boat and I need a fast and secret ride downtown with a couple of passengers. When can you be here?" He heard an engine roar to life over the phone before he heard the answer to his question.

"Three minutes."

Michael figured he had about two minutes left in his life. The appearance on the scene by Moose Miller certainly gave him a lift, another reserve of strength, but now he was fading fast. Even if he were swimming in the beautiful aqua of the Caribbean Sea, he would be dog tired and in need of a break. This was nothing like that. Every way it could be different was so, and in the most negative fashion. He started dreaming of a lazy swim off the shore of some deserted island with just a few palm trees and parrots for company. And Laura, of course. What would she look like in a nice white bikini, her skin magnificently bronzed by the sun, her hair perfectly messy from the sea breezes and ocean salt. He snapped himself out of it quickly, thinking that dreaminess at a moment like this could only lead to death. And it wasn't his time.

He wanted to see Sally again, console her when her heart was broken, guide her thoughts properly through all the problems life was going to throw at her in spite of his efforts to shield her from them, and to walk her down the aisle with a nice young man who loves and respects her. He wanted to play cards with his friends and laugh at Charlie Mick's ridiculous jokes, to have farting contests with the Burkes and J'lome, to enjoy the kind of laughing that produces no guffaw, no sound, just a bunch of guys straining to keep their ribs from breaking.

I want to see the hard winters of New York City die time and time again, to see the Cherry Blossoms at the Botanical Garden in Brooklyn bring us all back to life. I want to hear the crack of a wood bat out at Shea Stadium, the giggle of a young girl, the pounding of the surf at the beach. I want to eat pizza and hot dogs with brown, not yellow mustard, and sliced steak with plum sauce like my old friend Johnny Winter used to make in the parking lot in The Meadowlands before a Giant game. I want to reach out to other friends I haven't been able to see as much as I wanted.

I want to hear that bin Laden is captured, tried, and executed and that somehow, world peace has been accomplished. I want to come up with some kind of idea that may give eyesight to the blind, a house to a homeless mother, or just I little bit of hope to a disillusioned man.

I want to see if I can find the love that I once had for Georgia, although I don't know if that's possible. If not, I will respect and protect her with all my strength for all my remaining days and I will go live alone somewhere in some shitty apartment and find comfort and peace somehow. I want to lie in a hammock under an awning on a summer afternoon while a thunderstorm hammers away at the heat and humidity, the drumbeat of the raindrops lulling me into a perfect sleep. I want to hit a two hundred fifty yard drive that unzips the fairway of the third hole at Split Rock Golf course, followed by a fairway drive to within thirty yards of the green, followed by a perfect pitch that lifts the ball to the heavens and drops it within two feet of the hole, topped off by a putt that drops my Calloway into the hole from the backside. All I want is a par...it doesn't have to be a birdie. I want to take the baseline with my left hand, breaking the ankles of some young kid in a pair of two hundred dollar Nike sneakers who had been sneering at the old white guy a few seconds before, going up and under the basket laying it in over my shoulder perfectly like the original Pearl, Mr. Monroe.

I want to hold Laura in my arms and make love to her three times a day for five days in a row.

I don't want to die here in this filthy cold waterway. There is so much to do.

"Mikey, MIKEY!" The growl of Moose Miller's voice brought him back to the present. He could feel Laura shaking him and starting to kick her legs again, a bit feebly but she was doing it. What a girl! Moose was now only about five feet away, leaning over the gunwale, trying to stretch his arm as much as possible. Where was the gaff? Michael wondered. Why doesn't he reach for us with the gaff? he wanted to shout, as he also started to move his legs, however feebly. It was then he was frightened for the first time. I want to get back home. I want to see Georgia and hold her and tell her I love her. Sometime after this crazy evening ends I will tell Laura how much I love her as well and I will promise her I will look for her sometime in the future if that's what my karma brings. I don't care if you're in love with someone else then, I will wait as long as I have to. If it can't be you, then I will remain alone for the rest of my life for to even try to look into another woman's eyes would be as fruitless an exercise as beating the surf back with a broom.

He looked at the beautiful woman struggling against her own flagging strength and her fear of imminent death, and he smiled at her in spite of everything. He had to offer her something now, something she would always remember. What else but humor? Moose Miller grabbed his outstretched hand and pulled him to the side of the boat where he managed to grab and hang onto one of the rubber bumpers that was hanging off the side.

"Hang on there, Mikey. You, too, honey. I have to secure this other bastard first." There was no way Moose was going to bring this lady on the boat with Charlie the Tuna hanging there. Michael gripped the bumper with renewed strength and wrapped his arm around Laura's waist, his palm flat against her stomach, not caring that he was touching her bare skin uninvited.

"See," he started, looking into her eyes as deeply as he possibly could, "I told you I had good friends, right?" She stared back at him and he couldn't tell what she was thinking. She had that peculiar-to-women, uncomprehending kind of look that indicates either lifetime unconditional love or pure as driven snow hatred and disgust. Moose pulled Aubrey into the boat, dropping him on the deck and finished securing his prisoner with handcuffs on his ankles and wrists, keeping the gaff in place in case he tried to do anything that resembled an escape. A little twist of that thing would dissuade him quickly.

Michael considered telling Laura the joke about the cheeseburger that walked into a bar, but still that uncomprehending stare was there. He chose silence and a tighter grip on her waist. Was it hatred, disgust, or something else? She reached up with her arms, releasing her grip on the bumper and threw her arms around his neck, burying her face in his neck. "Hold me, Michael. I need you, I want you to hold me." How could he resist such a command?

Just then Moose Miller placed his beefy hands on the gunwale and spoke to Laura while reaching for her under her armpits.

"He has a terrible sense of timing, lady, but don't hold it against him. Come on, dear, let me help you." He was struggling to separate the two people in the water, the woman's hold on Michael's neck vise-like, Moose's lower back starting to ache and his prisoner was sprawled out on the deck behind him and his eyes were off him for longer than he would like.

"Come on, honey, let me help you." Finally she released her grip on Michael's neck and allowed Moose to pull her into the boat and immediately upon finding herself on firm footing she jumped up from the floor and helped Michael into the boat. They both collapsed on the deck, Laura resuming her hold on Michael as if he were a favorite toy that had just been found after an hour-long search at the park. Michael looked past her head at the quizzical face of his friend and waved his hand as if to say, Don't ask, I'll tell you all about it later. All of a sudden, Laura released her hold again and sat up. Looking around the boat she quickly saw the body of Aubrey sprawled on the other side of the boat handcuffed, horribly wounded, but for the first time in her life, she had no compassion for a human being as she got to her feet and kicked Aubrey in the side of his head.

"Fucking men! I hope you die, you piece of shit!" And with that she collapsed back onto the deck and started sobbing, Michael was off the floor now, he as well wanting to deliver a Tom Dempsey drop kick to Aubrey's head but instead noticing a blanket rolled up in a space under the gunwale and unfurling it, sitting next to Laura, she folding her legs over his, he wrapped the blanket tightly around them, the warmth slow in coming but there somewhere in the immediate future. He looked at Moose, who was staring off into the distance. What is he looking at?

"Moose, please take us somewhere warm, where we can get out of these wet things and away from this jerk-off," Michael requested, his teeth chattering and Laura shaking under the blanket.

"Yeah I will, but we got company. Let me check this out and don't worry about this guy, he's not going anywhere."

—◦—

Steve North eased the Coast Guard Zodiac boat up against Moose's boat silently and expertly and someone the harbor cop vaguely recognized stepped up to greet him. He had the impression something was going on that was above his pay grade not only because of the presence of the Zodiac but also because it happened so fast and there were no lights spinning on the Coast Guard boat. Someone wanted this to be quiet. The older guy in the suit started speaking and he recognized the voice as his Fed controller.

"Hello, Officer Miller," the man started, "I'm Tony Craig." He flipped open his credentials which Moose scrutinized over the gunwale. "I'm glad to meet you finally. You did good work on the surveillance and with this guy here," he said looking down at the still unmoving body of Aubrey. "He secure?"

"He ain't goin' nowhere." He looked down at the still prone body and then back at Tony. "I guess you had the right premonition about this guy."

"Just a lucky guess. It wouldn't have worked out if I didn't keep up some old contacts. Strange that it all came back to the people I knew growing up in this neighborhood."

"Are you from here? You know, I'm sure this is the first time we've met but I think I recognize you."

"Maybe you do. But that was a long time ago and we have to complete this operation here and now. We have plenty of time later for reminiscing. I need for you to help me with these two people. We will secure and take care of them. Wait here for me; I'll be back in about a half hour. Think you'll be alright here, uh...why are you alone? Where's your partner?"

"Long story. I'll deal with that later in my own way. Do what you gotta do, and get back here safe. This guy here isn't going anywhere. I'm calling it in now so you don't have long to do what you have to do."

"Tony." It was Steve in the Zodiac. "I have to get this rig back to Staten Island soonest, we have to roll now. Get your passengers together and let's go." Tony and Moose helped Michael and Laura up off the deck and, without letting go of each other, they stepped into the Zodiac in perfect unison, the blanket still tightly wrapped around them. Tony Craig jumped back aboard the Zodiac and told, no asked, Steve North to get them down to Battery Park in a hurry. He flipped open his phone to call yet another old friend he hadn't spoken to in a long time.

Larry Lazar was a lucky man. Having given up a lucrative yet boring legal career years before, he was now able to look out at his little empire from his balcony. Actually he needed to be on the street to do that, as his empire consisted of owning thirty-five mostly two-bed-room apartments in a recently constructed building in Battery Park City, the neighborhood near the World Trade Center site which was where Maxie walked through earlier. Larry quite correctly figured that many financial district professionals would want to live down here and therefore sold everything he had and mortgaged the apartments to the hilt some ten years earlier and paid them all off just last year. The average rent in one of his two bedrooms was thirty-five-hundred per month. Multiply that by thirty-five apartments and it is easy to see why Larry was a happy man. Not even a call late at night from a number he didn't recognize could faze him. He flipped open the phone and said hello, a rare person in New York City who was able to perform this simple function without a trace of anxiety about who might be calling.

"Larry, this is Tony Craig."

"Holy shit, bro, what a great surprise. How have you been, where have you been? What are you, water skiing?" The high-pitched whine of the Zodiac's twin outboard Evinrudes made it difficult to hear anything. Tony bent over facing away from the engines, jamming the phone into his ear as much as he could to hear Larry's voice. He had to hold onto the gunwale and bend his knees to keep his balance as the boat raced down the East River to the southern tip of Manhattan.

"Larry, listen to me, I have a major problem and you're the only one who can help me. I'm sorry to call you out of the blue like this..."

"Don't be ridiculous, man. I always told you that I would take your call anytime, anyplace. What's happening and where are you? I can hardly hear you." The Zodiac continued down the east side of Manhattan, passing under the Williamsburg, Manhattan, and soon the Brooklyn Bridge, the overhead pounding of the traffic on the bridges adding to the cacophony of noise.

"Larry, please tell me that you have a free apartment. Is it possible that one of your places is not rented right now? Empty and hopefully furnished? I desperately need a secure place to hide a couple of people for just one night. You can bill it to the Federal government." There was a moment of silence on the line and Tony was bracing himself for a negative answer.

"Tony, do you remember the night we went upstate when we were eighteen? When we drove five hours to Utica for some stupid frat parties? We were supposed to meet about a hundred girls and drink gallons of beer and laugh our asses off. But all those WASPy kids were in our faces all night and then I had to belt that one asshole and his friends jumped me and who was the only one who dove in to help me? I remember it was you, my friend. You and I beat the crap out of those guys and when we got on the Thruway for the ride home, I never felt better in spite of the pain. You know why?" He continued talking without waiting for an answer.

"Because you were there for me that night, a half-Italian, half-Irish Catholic like yourself, jumping into a fight to help a Jew. And I know you took a few kicks to the gut and a few shots to the face, but you didn't back down and we got out of there with our dignity and our faces intact. I don't know about Catholics, but a Jew will never forget that, do you understand? So stop worrying about that. We haven't spoken in a few years, so what? We'll get around to that later."

"Do you have a place for me, Larry? Please tell me yes." The Zodiac was passing the southern tip of Manhattan now, Steve North slowing the craft down, waiting for Tony to give him instructions.

"I do, but it's only a one bedroom, is that okay? Its empty but furnished, I kicked out the renters I had in there and changed the locks. I still have their furniture, towels, and some clothing even, which they will never see again unless they pay me my rent. Do you know where..."

"I do. Meet me in the lobby in fifteen minutes, okay? Thanks." He clicked off the phone and asked Steve to drop them off at the marina by the Wintergarden, the glass structure across the street from Ground Zero. "Bring us in silently, Steve, okay?" As if the request referred to all types of sounds, Steve just nodded his agreement.

Eight minutes later Tony was helping Laura and Michael out of the boat, asking Steve to wait outside the marina for five minutes and then to come back in to pick him up. There was no way he wanted to draw any attention to where he was depositing these two. He had to have them safe and secure until the morning. That meant no hotels, nothing with an electronic trail, no busy streets. For this purpose, Larry's building was perfect. The doormen were all refugees from the former Yugoslavia, funny genial types who would turn into ferocious Grizzly bears if someone tried to get into *their* building. Tony was sure that Larry gave these guys about a thousand bucks each at Christmas in tribute for their dedication to the building and for handling any repairs, leaks, or painting in each of his apartments throughout the year. Their loyalty would be unquestioned and Tony made sure to ask Larry that there was a crew of them available.

Right on time Larry was in the lobby and he was able to see this was a real situation as soon as the three of them entered the lobby. He took notice of the two people who were walking together like Siamese twins, wrapped and hidden under a blanket like an Afghan woman living in a Taliban-controlled area of that wretched country. And there was Tony, whom he hadn't seen in a few years with one arm wrapped around the people in the blanket, the other waving Larry over, who just pointed at the elevator bank, indicating the destination. He pressed the button and addressed Tony, keeping it all business for the moment.

"What do you need from me, bro?" Larry asked as the elevator arrived and they stepped inside, Tony facing Laura and Michael toward the wall, away from the elevator camera. Tony waited to answer until the doors were closed and the cab started its ascent.

"I need these people to be perfectly comfortable until noon tomorrow. I assume the utilities are on and there are some supplies for them?" Larry was getting mildly upset at the obvious gravity of this thing, the secrecy of this thing whatever it is and the oily stink seeping out from underneath the blanket was only making him more nervous. But he was always a lot tougher than he appeared to others in the courtroom, the basketball court, or anywhere else.

"It's all good, like I told you."

"Can I have a couple of your Yugoslavians for the door? I can't have anyone, and I mean anyone, I don't care what kind of badge they show, coming to this door." Larry clearly could hear the urgency in his friend's voice. He could catch up on the years with him later or tomorrow. First he had to assure him all would be well here.

"Yes, Tony," he answered, putting a hand on his friend's shoulder. I'll have someone in the stairwell and someone on the floor all night. Plus, I can lock off this floor from the elevator. Only a resident giving notice to the lobby doorman will be able to get up here. How's that?" The cab started to slow as they reached the top floor. Good location, Tony reasoned, looking up and down the hall before exiting the cab. Larry turned to the right and headed to the end of the hall which had no other doors. He explained as he fumbled for some keys.

"The former owner of this unit combined the five original apartments and promptly fell behind on his maintenance and mortgage payments. I bought the note and gave him six months to get himself right, but he didn't, so it's all mine now. I split this one unit off from the rest. I had it rented to some jerk-off equities trader, but he didn't know what on-time payments meant, so he's gone as well." He looked over his shoulder at Tony and the blanket twins as he inserted the key and turned the lock. "You're lucky, my friend," he said as he pushed open the door. Two weeks ago I had everything all rented out. Good timing for you." Tony ushered the two inside, asking Larry to wait for him, hoping that he wouldn't be insulted if he kept him in the hallway for a moment. Laura and Michael peeled the blanket off their heads and let it drop to the floor. Tony could see they were exhausted and he knew he had to make this quick. He put his hands on their shoulders and spoke directly to them.

"This has been a terrible night for you both, I know that. But you made it out and you're both going to be okay. No one will come near this apartment; you're all alone up here. I will be back at about eleven-thirty tomorrow morning with some food. Do not open the door for anyone except me. Do not leave, do not make a phone call. I'm going back to Long Island City to clean up the rest of all of this, whatever it is. But you two are safe. Clean up and go to sleep. I'll see you in the morning and will debrief you then."

"Hold it," Michael croaked. "How are Vinny and the Burkes?" Tony didn't know, but he told them as he was half in and half out the door that they were fine, hurt but not permanently. "Don't worry about anything other than yourselves for the rest of the night," and he closed the door quietly.

They never had trouble speaking with each other at all of the Argent Bank Christmas parties for the past ten years. The few random times they saw each other in the hallways of the bank were always pleasant, the both of them never at a loss for genuine conversation. They never spoke about the weather, she never asked him where interest rates were going, he never asked about the computer department. That was something Michael always liked about Laura and she about him. And it continued throughout the day of culture, which was not marred even once by an uncomfortable silence or a discussion about their jobs.

But in this beautiful apartment, spacious but somehow managing to be cozy as well, with huge windows looking west and south, so high up that you could imagine being able to see the Golden Gate on a clear day, they stood apart, silently contemplating the last half hour or so. Neither looked at each other and no words were spoken until Michael sat on the edge of the couch and pointed weakly toward the bathroom.

"Why don't you use the shower first?" Her response was a barely perceptible nod in agreement, and she wordlessly headed for the bathroom. If they had been dating for several years, he would have naturally figured that she was angry at him.

She disappeared through the door and he heard the water of the shower start a few minutes later. He was surprised she didn't lock the door, at least he didn't hear the bolt click into place. He wondered if that meant she trusted him more now, after this terrible experience of the last hour. He felt like laughing as he thought that if he and Laura were having an affair, all he would have to do is take a shower and dry off, change into some spare duds he would have kept in the trunk of the car, and drove home to Georgia and Sally with a perfectly manufactured lie.

He certainly wouldn't have told anything about their affair, had they been conducting themselves that way. He could never understand the need for unloading oneself to a spouse in such a manner, bringing the hurt out into the open. How utterly selfish that seemed to Michael. Just do your thing if you have to and get it over with without embarrassing your other half. Don't shit where you eat was the stock New York City phrase for anyone contemplating boinking the cute secretary down the hall or your friend's girlfriend or a woman who needed a release from her bland life. There are many bridges and tunnels connecting the boroughs of New York and it was wise to use them if you needed a release from the sameness, the uselessness of what you considered your life to be.

There would be nothing told about how smart they looked together, the way they were able to walk together perfectly in sync, like ballet dancers sans choreography laid out for them but rather the bumps and grinds of the city providing a source of inspiration for every half-step and pivot. He would keep forever secret how the multitudes in the Village stepped aside as they walked on the sidewalk, how the tough guy with the tattoos and the bulging muscles just had to comment on how good they both looked together. He never would relate how obvious it seemed that other couples were comparing their own relationships with them. And they weren't even having a relationship, just a day of culture whatever the hell that was. How could he ever explain this day to anyone else?

Right now, however, they were no longer that beautiful couple taking over the city just by being there. Instead they were exhausted, scared, angry, scared, wet and cold and scared and lucky to even be alive. It was hard to believe that they were on the verge of a kiss a little over an hour ago. Living in their own little world, lost in what they could only describe as a completely natural and honest state of being between them.

Michael stood up quickly as if one of the springs in the couch just blew through the fabric and goosed him and walked into the bedroom toward the sound of the shower. He pressed his nose up against the floor to ceiling window and looked west over the Hudson River. His temples were throbbing not only with the aches of the exertion in the river coming to roost in the absence of any further adrenaline but also with his perception of the naked woman showering just beyond the door to his right.

Screw all this, he thought to himself. I almost died tonight and I don't know why. If I didn't get involved with her life and her problems, I would be at the card game right now. Instead I have an ache in my forehead, back spasms that won't quit, and a line of questioning tomorrow from a bunch of Feds that has to begin and end before I leave for the airport to pick up Georgia and Sally.

Of course it won't end in time and I'll be late to La Guardia to pick them up and the whole thing will unravel before I'm even out of the goddamn airport. And I'm going to tell her that nothing happened and that nothing will happen tomorrow, and that nothing ever happened in the many years of marriage and dating we have had but it will go nowhere. I might as well make love to Laura tonight because if I'm going to be guilty in everyone's minds I might as well have enjoyed the experience.

The shower turned off just then and Michael felt suddenly guilty as if he were spying on her although she couldn't have known he was just outside the bathroom door. But he made no effort to leave. He quickly came to the conclusion that she wouldn't mind that he was standing there waiting his turn. And if she did, well...he was beyond caring what anyone else thought.

The shower was very hot and Laura welcomed it as it was the only way she would be able to dispel the chill that infiltrated her marrow. Usually she preferred a colder shower as she believed it would keep one's skin tighter.

She savored the pulsating jets of water shooting through the shower's double headed system, thinking about what a great idea it was to have the two shower heads at once, having never seen it before. One shower head was angled to come straight down on the crown of her head and the other on the back of her neck and shoulders, which were just starting to return to their normal position. The steaming cascade of water was amazingly effective in clearing her head of all the crap that had occurred in the past hour. She knew Andre was dead and that the guy who chased her down the street with the gun had been subdued and arrested by Michael's friend. She had briefly glimpsed the horrid sight of the gaff protruding from Aubrey's mouth when she first rolled onto the deck of the boat but for the first time she could remember, she didn't give a damn for someone in such obvious pain.

Now her mind was like a blank chalkboard. There was no more Andre and his schemes and games. No more issues with work as all of her fears of retribution were now erased. There was no more thinking about the awful night with Adam just a couple of days ago, a situation that now seemed positively comical in comparison to the events of this day. She knew she had to deal with that situation emotionally at some point, but not now.

She felt so strong and full of life in the shower, as if she could handle anything. I mean in the past twelve hours, she resisted sleeping with one of the most irresistible men in the city...certainly the best man she had ever met. And then she thwarted her own kidnapping and possible murder, with his help. All he wanted to do was have a nice night and then go see his friends. Boy, did he get a lot more than he bargained for on this date.

Not in any other decent person's eyes could she have been judged a weakling before now, but the events of the day of culture with Michael crystallized for her what she truly wanted in her life in terms of personal achievement as well as what she wanted from a man. She wanted this particular brave, handsome, strong man...how unfair it would be to judge any other man she might meet in the future to Michael now, after all they'd been through.

But I won't have him until he is available, truly available in his heart and mind as well as legally. And if he never is available, then any other man who crosses her path would have to measure up to this one and if they came up short, they were gone. Cut off at the knees with a detached savagery, a skill that every woman had at her fingertips whether she was from Chile, France, Indonesia, or the East Village, regardless of race, economic status or religious persuasion. She decided right there and then that she would never take any shit from anyone ever again.

She squeezed a dollop of liquid soap into the coarse washcloth and started to scour every inch of her body. She then squeezed an extra helping of shampoo into her scalp and rubbed the East River out of her hair. She wondered if this apartment was a two bedroom, but even if it was she had no intention of sleeping alone here tonight. At least she wanted to make sure she was clean when she got into the bed. She squeezed the last of the shampoo from her hair and turned off the shower and toweled herself off. The white bathrobe she found hanging on the door was warm and comfortable and she stepped through the door without hesitation, hoping that he hadn't fallen asleep in his wet clothes.

Michael heard the door opening but he didn't turn from the window. He could see her reflection in the glass and he realized this was one of the only times he had seen her bare legs. They looked great, her calf muscles contracting beautifully with each step. Her hair hung over her face like backward dreadlocks. There was a glow to her that he could see even in the window's reflection. She probably scrubbed the hell out of her body...maybe she was glowing with anticipation as well?

"The shower is really nice," he heard her say. "Keep it hot and use a lot of soap and shampoo so you get all the filth from the river off your body. Let the water flow over your forehead so your eyes get really clean." He nodded wearily and trudged toward the bathroom without looking at her, and she couldn't help but feel a bit disappointed that he didn't acknowledge her as she strangely felt kind of sexy in the bathrobe. He must be feeling the same exact release of stress I was feeling before I jumped in the shower, she figured. Maybe he will be uplifted by the cleansing as I've been, she figured as she lifted back the blanket and slipped into the bed, instantly luxuriating in the cool crisp sheets, the warmth of the blanket providing a delicious contrast.

Laura lay there for a minute listening to the shower, trying her damnedest to imagine it was instead a tropical cloudburst outside the window of her hotel in Bali. Tomorrow...tomorrow, she promised herself, she would stop these little fantasies because they were nothing more than a waste of her time. She rolled on her left side and then her right, and then back again, punching and folding the pillow just right so she could achieve maximum comfort, much in the same way a flounder settles itself in the seabed to hide from predators. Virtually every man she shared a bed with either chided, laughed at, or acted highly annoyed at this routine at the start of their relationship, always casting an instant pall over events that were either about to happen or had just happened.

"I'm just trying to get comfortable," she would tell them, "Why should such an insignificant peccadillo trouble you so? I always thought those are the types of things that bind a couple that is truly in love closer together." The last comment was usually delivered with the sort of iciness that guaranteed a quick exit in the morning with the possibility of a follow-up date virtually unfathomable. Laura had no patience for that sort of behavior. Say it once like that and you reveal the next twenty years to me. And I'll be damned if I spend one additional minute with anyone who treats me like this. Her friends told her she was the pickiest woman in New York and Laura didn't mind the moniker one bit. She was going to be even pickier from this day forward.

The water for the shower was clearly audible through the door and it made her think of a recurring daydream she enjoyed since some of her earliest days at the seminary. A thunderstorm would be rolling over some tropical island and she would be relaxing in a hammock on a porch of a simple but comfortable house and the winds would start to blow in before the raindrops reached her position, chilling her, and at that moment a beautiful man would appear with the perfect blanket, no scratchy wool, not too heavy, just enough to keep the goosebumps at bay, wrapping it around her as if he read her mind, tucking her feet under the folds and then gently slipping in beside her, the hammock not reacting to the extra bulk at all, the both of them instinctively understanding that no words were necessary, simultaneously awed by and protected from the power of the raging storm. She sighed audibly at the same time she finished her nightly flopping exercise, finding just the right spot on the bed and the pillow to ensure a dreamless sleep.

The water stopped and she could hear him pushing the shower curtain aside and stepping out, then pulling the curtain closed. One point in his favor, she always hated the wet curtain remaining folded against the wall, a veritable petri dish for mold. He was toweling off vigorously or so she imagined from the quick short rubbing sounds and the quick short breaths that bled through the door. She turned off the lamp on the night table as she heard Michael snap the water off the towel, hang it up and pull on the other bathrobe she remembered hanging there with the one she was now wearing. The room was not quite dark thanks to a beautiful full moon that cast a comfortable glow through the large windows. It felt like a scene in a Hitchcock movie or a silver-based photograph from the last century, the images clear but only distinguishable by differing shades of gray. She noticed with a jump in her heartbeat the light under the bathroom door go out and Michael then stepped through, finger combing his hair. All in all, he spent about one-twentieth of the time Adam spent in the bathroom prior to their disastrous night together. Clearly Michael was the sexier man as well as the better man.

She watched him with her eyes only as he walked to the other side of the king sized bed and to her relief he slipped under the covers without a word or a moment's hesitation. She allowed a few seconds of silence to pass before speaking.

"It's comfortable here isn't it?" She couldn't think of anything else to say and hoped that she didn't sound ridiculous. She turned on her side and faced him. He was laying on his back breathing easily and rhythmically as if he were doing breathing exercises. She liked the way his chest rose when he drew a breath. He kept his eyes closed as he answered, the rhythm of his chest never stopping.

"Yes, yes it is." He then took a very deep breath which she took as a sign that nothing further was going to be said or shared between them that evening. Just as well. The shower only did so much to wash away the night's terrible turn of events. She launched again into her pillow punching, flopping fish routine to get comfortable, apologizing to Michael while she was doing so.

"Why are you apologizing for something like that? You're just trying to get comfortable in a strange bed. Don't worry about it." She finished quickly and turned her head toward him, slightly startled to see he was now on his side looking at her. They had about three feet of space between them on the bed and without another word, she left the comfortable nest she made for herself and he simultaneously made his way across to her to like a sidewinder. He slipped his left arm under her neck and his right went over her hips, his hand flat on the small of her back. He pulled her gently toward his body, her right arm also slipping underneath his neck, her fingers entangling themselves in his hair, her left under his right arm, ending up over his shoulder, her fingers locking in on his hair and the muscles descending from his neck to his shoulder. She straightened out her body and the soles of her feet found the tops of his and she stayed there as if she were a little girl having her first slow dance with an older uncle who was teaching her to move correctly by allowing her to stand on his shoes. She felt his hands tighten their hold on her around her scapulas and in the small of her back and at that moment, there were no two human beings holding each other so tightly anywhere to be found in the city.

He angled his face perfectly toward hers and completed the kiss that was started earlier in the evening. It was sweet and gentle, tender and delicious, passionate and patient all at the same time. It was the best kiss either had ever had.

"Pleasant dreams, Laura," he whispered.

"Dulce suenos, Michael," she answered back, the blackness of the night and their fatigue finding them simultaneously, the both of them tumbling into the abyss of deep REM sleep together.

⚊ ▎ ⚊

The early morning sun acted as the perfect alarm clock, gradually warming the room and bathing it in natural light which awakened Laura slowly and gently with its caress. She turned her face toward the warm beams, allowing them to bathe her face as if they were liquid instead of light. She never woke from a night's sleep so easily. Even on the farm, she was the last to crawl out of bed to milk the cows and feed the chickens.

She slipped out from underneath the covers and stood up to her full height, raising her arms to the ceiling, stretching her body to its maximum point, realizing then that her normal aches and pains in her lower back, her shoulder, her feet were curiously vanished giving her the strange idea that somehow she lost some long time acquaintances, they'd been with her so long. There was a full-length mirror on the wall opposite the bed and she took a look at herself. The fact that she was naked didn't startle her as much as her total comfort with it.

There were a number of times in the past when she slept naked at home or on the farm or with a lover, but never had she felt the confidence boost she reveled in now, loving the freedom of it. She slowly ran her fingernails along her flanks, her taut stomach, letting her fingertips linger for an extra second on her nipples, which stood immediately at her touch.

On a cedar chest at the foot of the bed she found a yellow silky dress. She picked it up and dropped it over her head, the fabric shimmering like a gentle snowfall of diamond dust flakes as it dropped over her shoulders, back, and rump with some minimal assistance from a shake of her hips, ending its journey a few inches below her knee. The dress perfectly hugged her butt and breasts, a couple of spaghetti straps holding it in place. She pirouetted in front of the mirror, loving the manner in which the dress flared at the bottom when she moved even slightly, the supple material allowing its wearer to show off the muscular curve of her thighs. She loved how the yellow contrasted with her tanned skin and jet black hair. She thought it strange at how she was able to just slip it on without worrying about having to smooth any wrinkles. She didn't pause for a moment to consider her tan and when she got it.

She stepped forward into a breakfast nook of some sort, liking the openness of this space. There seemed to be no walls separating the rooms, just half-columns set into the outside walls which changed color as one progressed from sleeping space to eating space to sitting and relaxing space. Nothing there to impede one's progress.

On a glass table she took in a tray of delicious-looking pastries and slices of mango. There was also a dish of vanilla ice cream, the real kind with dark spots of vanilla speckling the white surface here and there. There was also an open carafe of Orangina, the ice cubes floating on top not having lost their sharp edges though they had been in the liquid for...how long? she wondered. She plucked a slice of mango from the bowl, drawing it along the curve of the top of the ice cream scoop and placed it on her tongue, savoring the delicious fruit for a few moments before finally almost reluctantly biting into the fleshy treat.

Laura picked up the bowl of ice cream and mango slices and stepped forward out to a deck of polished wood. There was a wicker table that seemed to grow out of the deck that held a single service and she picked up a spoon that she used to scoop a large chunk of the ice cream and a couple of pieces of mango, this time gulping them down quickly, the cold ice cream tingling against her teeth. Still holding the bowl, she moved toward the edge of the deck and lightly leaned against the railing, mesmerized by the amazing blue color and clearness of the water. It was only then that she realized the house was built on stilts about one hundred feet off the beach and the water here was quite deep. What an amazingly peaceful place, she thought, as she surveyed her surroundings, taking in the lushness of the mountains behind the beach, itself a perfectly-shaped crescent lagoon without a single footprint thus guaranteeing her some privacy, and the most tranquil waters she ever imagined.

She closed her eyes and concentrated. She could hear nothing except for the rustling of the fronds of the palm trees and the gentle lapping of the water against the pilings holding the structure above it all. There were some birds singing, but she didn't know what kind they were. It didn't matter because their voices were lovely, the perfect complement to the silence that otherwise enveloped this place. No subways, no sirens, no angry people arguing.

She opened her eyes again and looked down the perfectly white ribbon of sand and she was able to see Michael now as he was stepping from the water, shaking the excess from his hair then brushing it back from his face. She just watched him, not surprised to see him here, just glad that he was. She was glad that she could watch him from afar, admiring his movements as he arched his back with his hands behind his legs, the power in his shoulders and torso evident even from this distance. The best I will ever have had, she decided as she picked up the bowl with the mango and ice cream and the single spoon and started back through the hut, finding the exit as if she had been here a thousand times before, making her way along the raised wooden footpath to the crushed coral sand.

Michael laid down on his back on the black blanket, the warmth it absorbed from the early morning sun a welcome change from the usual chill he felt upon exiting the water on Long Island. He propped himself on his elbow and stared out at the lagoon, convinced that it was the cleanest water he had ever swum through. The water was so warm he couldn't even feel it on his skin. About thirty feet offshore there was a coral formation with a shape that reminded him of the Rose Bowl. The upper lip of the natural obelisk was only a foot or so below the surface of the water, but it quickly dropped away to a flatter surface with pockets of small coral and brain-shaped formations here and there. The colors of the multitudes of fish were dazzling, reminding him of the kaleidoscopes he played with as a kid. The reds, greens, yellows and blues could never be reproduced by any colorist or artist, no matter how hard they tried or for how long. Michael spent what seemed like hours in the bowl, trying to get the trust of each angel and clown fish...they always approaching but never allowing his touch. He figured it was a game they were playing with him. The bowl was big enough for him to swim counter clockwise faster and faster with ease, most of the time just lumbering along like a whale shark in an aquarium. After a few minutes, all the fish which had deftly eluded his touch now tailed him like a multicolored comet's tail. He couldn't even remember coming up for a breath. He rose to the surface slowly, and went over the lip of the coral Rose Bowl, barely kicking his feet so as not to disturb the fishes' tranquility, not feeling a bit of burning in his lungs as he did so.

His face broke the surface with hardly a ripple. It was as if the water here was denser than most, velvety in texture, no doubt full of minerals. He twirled around like a top surveying his surroundings, orienting himself. The majestic cone-shaped rock formations that formed offshore thousands of years ago were scattered around the outer edge of the lagoon perfectly. They were like sentries, keeping the hordes of pasty, loud European tourists from the cruise ships at bay. Behind him was the most perfect ribbon of sand, a fantastic arc of white that seemed to grudgingly allow the water to lap at its edge, the ripples from the wide lagoon touching it ever so gently. A city boy, he was compelled to gaze at the mountains in the background in awe, then focusing closer on the palm trees that ringed the back of the beach, the birds sitting in them as multi-colored as the fish he just visited, their songs sweet and pleasant to his ears.

He turned over and backstroked lazily to the shore, his powerful legs straight out from his body, not bent at the knee but kicking with controlled strength and purpose. There was no thrashing around in the water allowed here. It wasn't a posted rule, just one that was understood by him instinctively. His fingertips scraped the bottom and he turned his body over, bringing his knees to his chest and as soon as he gained a firm foothold he stood and strode toward the blanket.

The air was absent of any humidity at all which had the effect of drying his body and hair almost before he got to the blanket. Just a couple of shakes of his head whipped his hair dry, not making him dizzy as it sometimes did. He wasn't tired, but he laid down anyway and looked past his body back at the water. He felt strangely...taller and a bit leaner but couldn't explain why and decided not to worry about it as he always wanted to be a little taller and leaner anyway. He always asked his girlfriends to picture him that way if he ever made an appearance in any of their dreams.

He was thankful for the solitude. Not that he didn't mind a little socializing, but here there were none of the discussions and arguments that never failed to ultimately squeeze his temples together...global warming, socialism versus capitalism, Mets versus Yankees, Democrats versus Republicans, men versus women, us versus them. The most elusive quality and quantity of peace and quiet he ever could hope to experience was here, right now. He was thinking that he could lay here for hours as he slowly turned on his other side and it was then that he noticed Laura stepping off a footpath that led from a thatched-roof hut constructed on piles over the lagoon.

Maybe the clean air here helped his eyesight because he could see her clearly. Even from this distance he could discern all he had always appreciated about her in a physical sense at least. The wavy black hair, the well-toned arms, the curve of her thigh pushing against the dress, the very yellow dress that he had always imagined her in. Daydreamed of her in. He loved her posture, always a straight back, head held high with powerful, confident strides pulling her forward, her carriage about a millionth of a second ahead of her well-defined jawline and sculpted cheekbones. He pulled his legs closer and rested his body on his straightened arm, his hand flat on the blanket. It was like watching his favorite scene in his favorite movie, he realized, taking in all the movements of her body, enjoying them individually, a concert of female beauty, each step bringing her closer and each luscious characteristic into greater clarity. But this wasn't a movie he could rewind, this was happening and ending at the same moment, a truly unique experience that he reminded himself not to waste in any way. By this time in his life, he had watched, noticed, semi-leered, and occasionally privately drooled over thousands of beautiful women on the streets and beaches of New York, in the subways, and on the Great Lawn in Central Park. But this woman was walking out of his dreams into his life and he sure wasn't going to stop her.

The sand felt so good on her feet, the relentless pounding and washing of the coral fragments and seashells for countless centuries leaving a wonderful consistency. The years of working in the fields, dancing, and trudging along in high heels from office to office, up the subway steps, down the staircase in her home had left her feet in a permanent state of tiredness. But here, on this morning, they felt lighter and more alive than they had felt in years. She shifted over to where the water met the sand and she skirted the edge of it, letting the water gently run through her toes. The sensation was delicious and she moved back up on the beach, the water so warm and inviting she was almost tempted to lift the dress over her head and dive in. Couldn't do that now she knew... there were other things first. Strange how the sand didn't stick to her feet even though they were wet.

Not a speck of litter was in sight. The only evidence of non plant or animal life was the bowl she carried, the black blanket, his bathing suit and her dress. Otherwise it was if humans had never touched this small part of the world, until now. It was all theirs, only theirs, and Laura knew they would enjoy it uniquely as only they could. The quiet was intoxicating; it reminded her of the beautiful cloudless nights of her youth far away from the city when she would lay in the grass and dream of the boldest things to do, places to go, things to work on once she arrived, somewhere. Thoughts that would shock any member of her family. Forget the people at the seminary. She reveled in the privacy of those thoughts, that secret world that she—and every other woman in the world—had in her heart. Today was the day she was going to let all of that go, if but for only a few minutes.

She looked out over the lagoon and then back to the mountains as she continued toward Michael, whom she could tell had noticed her by now. Look at him waiting there, a real friend, someone who supported me in my darkest hour of need, who made me laugh through the years when we never even stood closer than three feet from each other. We held our ground, knowing that ours, if it did happen, would be the most special of relationships between any man and woman. And yes, Michael, I'll never verbalize it to you, but I wanted you from the moment I saw you and through all the bad dates, boring relationships, and average lovemaking I have endured in the last ten years, I did wish it was you all those times and not those...clowns I was with. Thank you, my dear, for being honest with me...such a rare trait these days in a man.

So many of them had charm and talent and some had looks in abundance, a few were pretty decent kissers, but none had a clue how to truly reach me, to caress my heart. You did it effortlessly, naturally. And you have never even held my hand.

She continued in a straight line toward him and as she drew closer, could clearly see his smile. He looks good in that black bathing suit, she was thinking. She allowed her eyes to roam along his body, appreciating the long, strong legs, taut but not overly cut abdomen, and the ease with which he moved, no wasted motion, like a star athlete. He was sexy in her eyes by what he didn't do as much as what he did and said. He never put off any negative waves in all the time she had known him. Certainly he had his share of ups and downs in the past ten years like anyone else, but she never detected anything but pure joy when they saw each other. Was it her? Did she interest him that much? Or was he just able to handle his problems on a daily basis and maintain some sort of equilibrium through the daily madness of life in New York? Now that was sexy. Too many wimps in the city. Where was a Marc Antony in modern-day New York? A man who waited for his Cleopatra through any storm, unashamed to be open with his woman about his desires and emotions because he was bleeding confidence in his love for me and mine for him? He knows I am coming for him, but does he stare at me like those leeches on the subway? No, not at all, nothing like that.

We know each other now, we built our friendship over time much in the same way carbon becomes a diamond. But with no pressure...this man never even outright flirted with me—although I could see it in his eyes—not like the drunken spring breakers she encountered in Florida on that vacation a few years ago or the traveling businessmen who seemed to think that somehow they were entitled to lay down with me after a first date or a drink bought at some bar. She found it unbelievable that there was a single woman alive that would respond favorably to those types. And there were even a few, if they had worked just a little harder, been a little more patient, asked me a little nicer, I would have opened up to them. And maybe then, I never would have told Michael within seconds at our first meeting—Jesus, was that embarrassing, I never said anything like that ever—how handsome he looked in his suit and tie.

She wanted to know the nature of his touch, was it soft or strong? Loving and passionate, or a perfect combination of both? Maybe he was a secret cave man, fumbling his way along? No, not this man. He was like a cuddly tiger, she just knew it. It was then she realized that he had never touched her before. She giggled with anticipation like a schoolgirl, quickly regaining her composure, bringing her head erect once more, brushing away a stray lock of hair, her lips pursed and ready for anything. She did feel like Cleopatra—"I want that one there, deliver him to me at once"—welcoming Marc Antony back from a long and arduous campaign somewhere in North Africa or ancient Persia. She wanted to know everything about him...and she couldn't even bother to think of a reason why she shouldn't.

I love that girlish smile, Michael was thinking as Laura approached, I'd give a million of anything to know what she was thinking about right now. And what's with the bowl? Michael didn't interrupt this meeting with unnecessary bullshit small talk or questions. Instead he drank in her every movement as she sat comfortably on her haunches on the blanket beside him. The curve of her thigh was advertising itself through the fabric of the dress. Boy, did she look good in yellow.

She sat there in that manner for a few moments looking down at him and then leaned sideways, her upper body supported by her elbow while the bowl remained perched perfectly in her hand. Michael didn't even bother hiding his appreciation of her as his eyes strayed to her legs—the dress was hiking up them a little bit now—which were stretching out to way out there, somewhere near the horizon. As he brought his eyes back to hers they made stops at her calves, her knees and thighs. Her hips were an insane brand of curvy, dipping away to a trim waist and he couldn't stand it anymore so he jumped over the rest of her straight to her eyes...those eyes and those lips, and the mane of black hair that framed it all so wonderfully...the most alluring woman he had ever seen.

I need to kiss her now, he decided, and so he leaned forward and up, a hint of a smile appearing and then a dash of seriousness as he approached her.

I have waited for this kiss for more than ten years, she was thinking. But I am Cleopatra, as every woman really is, and I want him to mostly come to me. Then of course, at that moment, I am all his. He was approaching her now, no hesitation on his part, no fear on hers, and he put his hand on her cheek and she knew at that instant that this man's touch, so warm and loving, was the one she craved since she was a teenager. The touch she knew in her heart only he possessed. And there it was as he kissed her gently, remaining there for a few seconds, not pushing her lips against her teeth or mashing his tongue inside her mouth.

He allowed a few moments to pass before he tentatively flicked the tip of his tongue against the inside of her upper lip, which caused her open her mouth more and she allowed a soft moan to escape which he took as a cue to run the back of his hand up past her ear, catching her head in the bend of his elbow— gee, it's nice that she bends her head to the left to kiss, not many others do that—and positioned like this they simply devoured each other with the kind of passion that had been building for so long.

"I'm a little hungry," she said as they pulled away from each other, their lips expressing their reluctance to part with an intimate, smacking sound that would not be noticed by anyone else even if they were in a crowded room. Somehow I know he'll like the mango, and she relaxed back on her haunches and deftly fed him one of the pieces of fruit and followed by scooping some of the ice cream with her fingertips and placed it on his tongue. Who needs utensils?

Michael then took the plate and offered her the fruit in the same way, Laura licking the slightly melted ice cream from his fingertips which he found amazingly erotic and stimulating. How did it stay so cold for so long? he wondered as she, in turn, took the bowl and fed him once more, this time her fingertips licked clean by him. That's a first, he realized suddenly, and he wondered why that was so important. The manner in which they were sharing the mango and *ice cream was more erotic and more of a turn-on than any other conventional sexual stimuli, from alcohol to a thong, could ever hope to be.*

The mango and ice cream was now finished and neither could really remember what happened to the bowl, it just vanished somehow to somewhere. She sat up on her haunches again and Michael immediately took to stroking her thigh, marveling at its strength and symmetry. The curve of her quadricep was blowing his mind. He enjoyed how his fingers glided over the silky material of the yellow dress but he longed to touch her skin. It has to be like velvet, he thought, as one of his strokes caught the hem of her dress and he pulled it up to her hip. He could see in her eyes and hear the short intake of breath that this simple gesture made her heartbeat race and he was pleased.

This is a throwback woman, he conjectured, one that believed that a string of pearls with a simple black dress was infinitely sexier than anything found in a Victoria's Secret catalog, that the most simple of gestures could either begin or end an evening, and that the pulling up of the dress was definitely one of them. For the first time in his life he had no doubt which way a woman was going to react.

I wish I could feel his hand on my skin, she was thinking.

I would love to touch her and explore every inch of this leg was what he was thinking.

Apparently she decided to show him the way as she then stood, bracing herself automatically for the jolt of sciatica pain she has experienced for the past year or so but thankfully it never materialized. Was it the rush of adrenaline coursing through her veins that blanketed the discomfort she got used to feeling in her hip? she was wondering. Whatever, it's nice to be able to stand like a young woman again, without having to think about planting your feet correctly beforehand.

He remained in his supine position, gazing up at her in awe. Her toes were fidgeting a bit and their tips brushed against his ribs. He thought she had nice feet. I always hated my feet, but they look nice today, she was thinking, as he gently squeezed each toe in sequence. His eyes started their journey upward again and now he raised himself into the same position she was in just before, back on his haunches. He didn't think about the pounding his knees had taken on the asphalt courts in Sunnyside that left them with about ten percent of the cartilage left. He found himself sitting back rather comfortably, his face now at a level with her hips...those magnificent hips he had first seen from behind more than ten years before.

A gentle zephyr whispered its way across the water and it caught the hem of her dress and flapped it noiselessly against her upper calves. She turned her upper body toward the ocean to catch it as if she were a parachute. The sun was a little warmer now and the unexpected breeze was delicious, hardening her nipples and blowing her hair once again into her eyes which she brushed away so gracefully. She looked back down at him in a way which had the effect of a starter's pistol.

Michael ran his hands north on the outside of her body starting from her ankles up the outside of her thighs, the tips of each finger discovering every contour of her legs, the tight calves, the multi-aforementioned quadriceps, even a pair of dimples just above her knees. His touch was semi forceful to try to show both sides of his sexuality, the patient and passionate...the cuddly tiger. She's bursting with passion, this woman is...he knew it now, which he anyway had always figured somehow. I wonder if anyone ever stirred her like this before. He hoped so for her sake, then dismissed the unnecessary misplaced thought; unintentional as it was it had no place here and now and probably never. His hands were gripping her hips now, his fingers gently kneading her butt, the palms attached like suction cups to the skin just below where her pelvis sharply jutted. She could see he was maybe just a little too fascinated with her legs and frankly she wanted him to move this along a little bit before her head exploded. She was asking him something and he could hear her voice now, as sweet as it was the first time she ever spoke to him.

"How is the water?" Her fingers were now playing with his hair, twirling the locks playfully, her lips slightly parted.

"Quite simply the most beautiful water I have ever swam in," he answered, still not looking up at her. Now she pulled gently at his hair, beckoning him upward. I want him to stand right next to me, I want his body to slide right up against mine, she tried to order telepathically.

He stood slowly, rolling the dress up as he ascended up her body, stopping for a moment to marvel at her muscular yet very feminine abdomen. Michael kissed her lightly between her navel and her trimmed black pubic hair, allowing his tongue to linger in her belly button for a few moments. Once again there was the soft moan. Thank you, dear, for letting me know...he disliked it when a woman just laid there and didn't express herself. He felt another gentle tug on his hair and he rose slowly as if he were on a leash. As he did so, he pulled his bathing suit from his waist and it fell perfectly to his ankles as he rose to his full height. He could feel her foot reach between his legs to hold them secure, allowing him to step out of the way of the trunks like a dancer.

His penis was stiffening rapidly and was now standing almost straight up. She reached for him and her hand wrapped around it and she softly stroked him, no friction amazingly, her grip not causing any kind of discomfort. He was now as hard as blue steel, the tip of his penis cutting a path through her bush, she was raising her arms now and he pulled the dress over her head and casually tossed it aside. I like the way he did that, she thought...the way he just flung the garment out of the way.

I need both hands for this woman, he thought as he cupped her face gently but kissed her hard, their tongues probing relentlessly. Michael sucked a bit noisily on her lower lip and she responded by doing the same with his upper lip, their tongues resorting to a wrestling match, their mouths almost wide open at this point. An idea came to him and he stepped back a bit, knelt down again, and scooped up a bit of the still very cold ice cream—so that's where it disappeared to—and let it lay on his tongue. As if this whole experience was choreographed by Balanchine, she parted her legs slightly and he reached behind her and cupped her ass in both hands, pulling her toward him and upward, burying his chilled mouth and tongue in her pussy.

Her grip on his hair tightened but the pain was quite bearable to Michael as he found her clit, his cold tongue sending shock waves of pleasure through her body, the heat and the cold fighting each other for her attention. His hands held her in place and she was glad that they weren't sticky or grimy...how did that happen? she wondered for a millionth of a second because really...what does that matter? This was unlike anything she had ever felt before, not just the alternating sensory storm on her clitoris, but the fact that she was standing here like an Egyptian queen being serviced this way was intensely erotic. She never lost her balance even when she leaned her head back, opening her mouth and closing her eyes. "Me gusta," she purred as her left hand released its grip on Michael's hair and went to her erect nipple, kneading it gently. Laura was loving his strong hands on her butt and thighs, not only providing her balance, but also letting her know in no uncertain terms that he loved her body.

He moved his hands upward again and he was cupping her cheeks once more, giving them a little love tap in between the flicks of his tongue on her labia, a gentle pull on her clit with his lips, all of it a wonderful dance that she found more satisfying at this point than any other she had ever had. And there was a lot more to come, literally and figuratively.

I always knew there would be no awkwardness between us, Michael thought, as she parted her legs just a little more, followed by another gentle tug on his hair beckoning him upward once again. What exquisite timing, I was just thinking of something I always wanted to do. I want to share this new experience with her.

Michael stood slowly, his tongue cleaning itself of vaginal juices on her skin as it moved past Laura's abdomen, pausing for a moment at her right nipple—which somehow he knew was more sensitive than her left—and now at almost his full height his almost painfully erect penis entering her with no resistance. The moan this act elicited from both Laura and Michael would have been audible to anyone within a half mile of them.

She closed her legs slightly, locking him inside her, his cock the perfect length and girth, the warmth and strength of his penis touching every part of her vaginal wall. In her earlier life there had been bigger, longer, fatter ones, but none of them had compelled her to even think that this penis was the perfect one for her. "Your cock is so hard in my pussy," she whispered into Michael's ear. "I've wanted you from the very first moment I saw you," was all that he could muster in response. Why bother coloring it like a Shakespearean sonnet? What he told her was the unbridled truth, unable to be interpreted in any other way. He felt at that moment, whether it be true or not, that he was maybe the only man who had coaxed such a comment out of her. And why should that matter? Why did he give a shit about such nonsense? He was angry at himself for allowing his thoughts to wander in such a way, what was the point if nothing—other than to ruin the most perfect moment he had ever had, the privilege of holding this woman in his arms.

"Hold my neck tightly," Michael was saying to Laura as he tapped her right thigh. He could feel the sinewy strength in her lean forearms and biceps squeeze so hard his neck muscles had to fight back lest he pass out from lack of oxygen. She lifted her leg and it slipped into the bend of his left elbow. A second later, aided by a slight hop she settled her left leg in the bend of his right elbow and he stood straighter that he had in years, never quite able to listen to his old man who chided him relentlessly for his bad posture. He felt physically stronger than he had in years. He bent his spine backward as far as he could, still able to keep his balance, the action serving to bury his penis deep inside her. Her eyes rolled up as far as they could in response, her eyelids fluttering, the pleasure overtaking her, the connection with Michael total and complete. He was thrilled *that the bad discs in his back that sometimes made it so hard to even sleep comfortably did not hamper him now.*

"Walk with me, Michael, carry me to the water now." *She could barely get the words out, she knew somehow the natural buoyancy would help Michael with her weight and she wanted to do anything to keep this wonderful connection together. He started ambling toward the water, taking care with his steps...can't make a misstep now. The action of his stride and the resulting movement of his hips created a rhythm inside her that Laura had never felt during lovemaking before, even with those men who weren't inept clowns in bed. The movements of his shaft were infinitesimal if measured by standard measure, but the effect for her was not unlike a largely unnoticeable tremor in the earth's crust which could only be measured using the most sensitive seismograph. She was sure she couldn't come this way, but it was certainly quite the experience and she tried to clear her mind completely so she could concentrate.*

"Me gusta mucho, mi tigre mas fuerte." *He was thankful of his ability to pick up languages, which was a great skill to have growing up in Queens. Yes, my dear, today I am definitely your very strong tiger.*

"Si, yo tambien me gusta querida." *There were no broken shells at the water's edge, no holes to trip in, only the deliciously warm water washing over his feet, the mud seeming to provide him with a little more traction. The sea bottom sloped gently downward, the water quickly reaching the soles of her feet, her concentration not wavering from Michael's connection with her. The water reached her butt and she now felt more and more weightless. She was glad Michael could take a bit of a break, she knew she wasn't one of those emaciated women she saw all around New York, eating a few leaves during the day and then running themselves into the ground later in overpriced gyms. Now the water covered their hips and was approaching their midsections, the ocean enveloping them like a magic blanket.*

"The water is great," *she told him,* "like liquid velvet." *She had never made love in the water before...the thought to do so never really occurred to her...and why was that? A lack of imagination on her part or her lover's parts? Oh what the hell, why am I thinking about that now?* "Oh, what are you doing?" *she whispered into Michael's ear as he positioned himself over a dark shape just to his right...where did that come from?*

"I want to sit down." *How fortunate that he was able to find the only piece of coral that seemed to be the correct shape, height, and wasn't made of some material that would rip the skin from the back of his legs. He settled onto his new found chair and the action filled her vagina again with his penis...the water providing a wonderful weightlessness that allowed them both to be very content with the rhythmic movement of their bodies helped along by the gentle waves and tides in the lagoon. They remained this way for a few minutes until Michael discarded his cuddly persona and became the tiger again, grabbing her ass and pulling her forward and backward that had the most amazing effect on her most sensitive spot, just inside her vagina and below her clitoris, the back and forth which would have been tiring and uncomfortable in a bed or on a kitchen chair but here in this water was producing these tiny little orgasmic bursts in her that were increasing with intensity slowly but evenly. Oh si... thank you for sitting down, she was thinking.*

His actions were becoming more primal, his pulling and pushing more furious, and he was turned on more so when he watched her with her eyes half closed, her lips parted her arms no longer around his neck, just her hands clasped behind his head. After a few minutes, even with the adrenaline coursing through his body and the weightless effect the water was affording them, fatigue was beginning to set in and he slowed his pulling and pushing. She was also panting from the effort and she leaned into him again as he stopped, now wrapping her legs around his waist and he also held her as close as he could, his face buried in her neck, all the time their connection never faltering.

"Michael, make love to me now," she commanded. In the bend of his elbows went her legs again, a small wave appearing out of nowhere to aid in his motion of standing up. Back to the blanket he headed, her arms tight around his neck once more. Once he was there, he was able to drop slowly to his knees without his meniscus and cartilage screaming with pain and, as if he were able to adjust the pull of gravity along the strip of beach, continued slowly downward until she lay on her back. She kept her knees up alongside him and he remained on his elbows and knees as much as possible so as to give her some room to breathe. "I can't believe my sciatica isn't acting up again, it always hurt in this position."

Michael steadied himself on the points of his body, a reminder of when none of his joints used to hurt even after hours on the basketball courts, running circles around suburban players and taking on young men from the city ten years his junior. Laura reached behind her and pulled her hair out from underneath her back and settled her head back down, staring up at him. So lovely she is, he thought as he began a slow steady rhythm, allowing only half of his penis to enter her vagina before withdrawing. Every eight or nine slow thrusts would then be followed by one deeper, more powerful, Michael slipping his right hand under her butt...the most perfect ass he had ever seen...lifting her slightly so his thrust would reach as deep as he could. Each plunge into her elicited another soft moan from Laura, nothing like those ridiculous women in a porn film, but the sort of sound that let a man know that he is making love correctly, bringing his partner to newer and better heights of pleasure.

Now is the time for me, Laura thought to herself. She was basking in a glow she hadn't felt in years, and precious few times in the past due mostly to her own insecurities and her lover of the moment's ineptness. But this man here, he has strength and vitality and the stamina of a triathlete. She lowered her legs to her side, Michael somehow understanding completely what she wanted to do. He moved his knees on the outside of her legs and moved them closer together with light pressure. They locked their gaze on each other, Michael waiting for something to interpret, some sort of sign of what she needed. She was the leader now. Laura lifted her fingers to his mouth and he sucked and slurped on them... without losing a drop...and she placed her left hand at the base of his skull... her hand was so warm...he could feel each individual fingertip gently kneading the muscles there, which had given him so much trouble over the years but not now...and she moved her right hand to her clit and started manipulating and stroking in the same way she discovered one amazing revelatory night when she was twelve years old.

Michael stayed just inside her vagina, increasing the size and shape of his penis by contracting his buttocks, which was just enough for Laura to feel and appreciate. What beautiful timing and rhythm he has, she thought. She took her hand from behind his neck and held it under her right breast...her more sensitive one...commanding him again, "Kiss my tit"...and his body dropped enough and his neck stretched to the perfect length where he was able to wrap his lips around her nipple, which sent a miniature explosion through her chest.

"Otra vez, Michael,"...and at her command he plunged deeply into her, but not so hard as to bruise her cervix and he was able to do this plunging somehow without sliding up her body at the same time, pulling her skin against the grain, hurting her, and as with one of her former lovers, banging the crown of his head into her jaw. When he withdrew back into his slow, pulsing rhythm, she felt as if all of her insides were being turned inside out, including her brain which was tuned into just a few random thoughts about the conversations she had with her girlfriends in the past about their boyfriends and their exploits. She was working her fingers furiously now, and she started to laugh quietly remembering the stories of colored lights and shaking legs and slapping bodies, none of which

especially excited her...it all seemed so comical to her at the time, and painful as well. She tried to discern then if they were lying to her about all that...her own experiences seemed so limited in the face of their bragging and although she certainly had many pleasant moments with her old boyfriends and lovers, not one of them ever once gave her an orgasm with their penis. Her friends made it seem that their men's penises were some kind of magic wand, that worked by the simplest of touch, like the orgasmatron in the movie Sleeper.

"Otra vez," she cried softly again and once more Michael lifted his lips from her nipple which he had been sucking on in such a way that was noisy, but produced a high intensity vibration that was better than anything made by Hitachi...his plunge this time was deeper, longer than before somehow and her hips were now starting to burn as if she were on a bed of hot coals. The girl- friends left her consciousness along with everything else outside of this moment and as he began his withdrawal, she grabbed his butt, whispering..."Stay." It would be...just another moment...her manipulations were furious now... can I hurt myself this way...what is he thinking right now...such strength and stamina...how can he maintain this posture, but oh, please continue..to..do...so.

And now in the future she would be able to wade into a conversation about orgasms and sex and a true connection with someone as the rush started to overtake her senses, the fire in her hips moving like a stain throughout her body, shimmering along the surface of her muscles, expanding every artery, vein, and capillary in her body to the breaking point, her vaginal walls starting to contract, wrapping itself around Michael's hard, muscular penis and then all of the fire, all of the liquid fire that had surged throughout her bloodstream made a mad rush back to her vagina which exploded in waves of pleasure... masturbation times ten...tricks with her eyes as colors burst all around her... liquid pouring out of her along with the last bit of oxygen in her lungs...her head jumping off the blanket almost hitting Michael squarely in the nose but somehow he anticipated her reaction...how did he do that, how did he know... she started laughing again because here she was in her early forties, ten lovers behind her, and she had never known the limits of her own passion, of her body...until now...with this man. She removed her hand from her groin and settled back with both her hands on his neck, pulling him down for the best kiss he's ever had. At least she had hoped it was. Then she grabbed his butt with her right hand and gave him a tap to let him know how wonderful, how beautiful, desired, and loved she felt at that moment and also to snap him into action for the sake of his own pleasure.

What a woman, Michael thought to himself for perhaps the thousandth time in the last five minutes. All of their lovemaking had been as natural as if they had practiced for this moment in front of a mirror for the past year. But it instead was entirely uncontrived and richly exquisite in not only the spontaneity of the moment, but the naturalness of it all. No hesitation, no embarrassment, no wondering if this position was right or wrong, no thoughts about past lovers and those experiences, nothing but pure unadulterated joy and love, yes...love because anyone with half a brain knows lovemaking is so much better when you are in love.

He finished off the kiss she just laid on him and his inner tiger felt unleashed with her slap on his butt, like a jockey's whip on the haunch of a thoroughbred rounding the turn at Belmont. His thrusting became a study in controlled fury as Laura urged him on, slapping his butt and whispering "Me Gusta" in his ear...her other hand running through his hair again mussing, grabbing and pulling...glad I'm not bald...thinking about nothing other than what a turn-on it was to make love to a woman like this, who completely handed herself over to him at this moment...not as a subservient, not as some bored suburban—or urban for that matter—housewife who was practically running through her day book in her mind for tomorrow's appointment while her boyfriend, husband or lover was hoping, praying that he was somehow connecting with her, all the while ignoring the arms at her side, the legs flat against the bed, the head turned toward the window, or even the occasional but still very audible and obvious yawns. I had my orgasm, I feel wonderful...now it's your turn. A model of simplicity.

The trigger, the fuse, was now lit deep in his groin and he had no intention of slowing its progress. No change of rhythm now to last a little longer, no thinking of baseball players, as Woody Allen once so hilariously suggested, to prolong the moment of passion. No, none of that was going to take place now. The flames and the lava inside his body were boiling now, the liquid fire moving its way up his shaft shooting into Laura, the globules of warm come spraying her vaginal walls and cervix like champagne against the MVP's head in the winning locker room, the connection between Laura and Michael now complete and nothing at all would ever be able to change it. They laid together when he was fully emptied, their breathing long and hard, both participants completely spent. Michael's penis was still hard as blue steel, still buried in the folds of Laura's vagina, still pulsing with strength as if it had a mind of its own, Michael knowing he could keep on going but no, this was not some kind of athletic event. He wasn't going for some kind of record here. He already knew without asking that he had shared the ultimate lovemaking experience with Laura...it was the same result and feeling for both of them.

He lifted himself off of her, her eyes following his as he laid beside her, his breathing still slightly labored, his body sliding down her luscious, sweaty body until he was able to lay his forehead on her stomach. He could hear the beat of her heart, and actually see a tiny pulsating ripple travel to her abdomen. Both of her hands now were gently kneading his scalp, a wonderful sensation that conveyed her love for him without a single word. After a few minutes he lifted himself off her completely and laid at her side, giving her a break from his weight but pulling her closely for a final message. I can feel him still...I can't believe his cock is still hard, how does he do that?'

"Laura," he whispered near her ear as he kissed her cheek with more affection than she had ever known, "Te Amo."

"Michael, mi amor, mi tigre," she murmured, the both of them then falling into an abyss of darkness that was measureless in its vastness, quiet, peace, warmth, and comfort.

EPILOGUE

MORNING

The morning sun entered the room through the tall windows like a hammer, causing Michael Pierce to awaken suddenly and start to sit straight up in the unfamiliar bed as if the pillow were loaded with a spring. Laura's arms were still around his neck impeding his progress... how did that happen?...and his sudden movement didn't immediately awaken her or release her grip. Michael fell back onto the pillow with a flourish, unable to come to grips with where he was as the dream was that real, so real he could recall all of it. He looked over at Laura, who was now snuggling against him and smiling in her sleep. A series of soft taps on the door jarred them both completely out of their sleepiness.

"You okay in there?" came the voice of Tony Craig, not instantly recognizable to Michael. Neither answered, both wanting to fall back into the abyss of their amazing shared experience which neither realized the other knew about. They were both lying on their sides again, still clad in their borrowed bathrobes as they were when they succumbed to sleep some ten hours earlier and it was becoming apparent to both of them how unique the previous evening was although it was still somewhat unclear to them, probably because maybe only a few couples on the planet shared what they shared the night before.

Laura acknowledged their connection fearlessly by speaking first, "I had a tremendous dream, a most realistic experience, I felt like I was swimming in the most beautiful blue water." Michael, still on his side and staring out the window, could feel her eyes on him, searching for a signal that she wasn't going crazy. "I was with you on the same beautiful beach," he answered, joining her in the acknowledgment but not wanting to mention the sexual experience in the dream at this time. He looked back to her and somehow they both knew what went on in their minds without actually mentioning it. Tony Craig knocked on the door a bit more strongly this time and Michael responded without removing his eyes from Laura's, "Yes, we're okay." The knocking stopped and Michael heard a muffled voice on the other side of the door giving some kind of instructions to the guards. He started to sit up, suddenly glad he was still wearing the bathrobe.

"Laura, why don't you use the other room to get dressed unless you want to use the shower again."

"No," she answered while pushing the bed covers off, allowing Michael a flash of a deliciously muscled leg, "I don't need a shower. Just give me a minute to get my act together." And she slipped into the bathroom, lightly closing the door behind her. Michael took this opportunity to slide out from under the heavy blankets and plant his feet on the floor. His body was aching now, the exertion of the previous night revisiting him in the form of pulled muscles and aching joints. He allowed his head to sag between his legs as if he were trying to stave off faint.

The dream with Laura...it was so...unbelievably real, he thought, so real he expected to wake up on the beach to a good morning kiss from her and possibly another go around. He swiped at an itch on the tip of his nose, sniffing his fingertip expecting to find her scent on him but there was nothing there. He stood and opened his robe, disappointed not to see any trace of sand, sweat, or dried bodily fluids that one would expect after a steamy sex session. What he also noticed was that this was the first morning in memory that he didn't wake with a raging erection.

Michael threw off the robe and pulled on a pair of sweats and a tee-shirt that was several sizes too large, but at least was comfortable and dry. He moved toward the window and looked down at Battery Park and then further out past the Statue of Liberty out to the Narrows and the majestic span of the Verrazano Bridge. From this height he could just about see all the way out to Ambrose Light. When he was a kid, he recalled sitting on the back of a chair in the living room of the apartment on Forty-Seventh Avenue in Sunnyside staring for hours at the kids in the park across the street, the people on the sidewalk and the cars rolling by. He laughed to himself as he regarded the potential change in quality and quantity of his dreaming when he was a kid if he had this view. He heard the door opening and turned away from the window.

Laura came out of the bathroom running her fingers through her hair, which was falling forward over her face. She was walking like a hunchback while she did this and then after a few steps, threw her head back settling her locks into place perfectly, better than any salon stylist could have done. Michael thought she looked as beautiful as she did in the silky yellow dress of their dream. Their dream? He still wasn't absolutely sure they shared the same dream, but he suspected it was so. Still he wasn't going to mention it...until much later. He pointed with a nod of his head in her direction, indicating her own set of oversized, shapeless sweatpants.

"Are those comfortable? They look great on you." She smiled and turned a little red at his compliment.

"You mean my fuzzy pants and socks? My only girl cousin and I had thick warm stuff like this and that's what we used to call them." She was hugging herself and smiling while she was telling him this little story, a nugget from her life that maybe never would have come up at any other time with anyone else but now it seemed so natural to share it with him. The tears then started to come as they stared intensely at each other from across the room and what else was there for them to do except to complete what had started the night before. They crossed the room wordlessly toward each other and embraced tightly, Michael's face buried in her hair, Laura's arms wrapped tightly around his neck as if they were diving back into the East River. Her sobs were soft in his ears and he started to stroke her head as if she were his steady lover, the one woman in the world he wanted and had in his life and as if it was his only responsibility at the moment. He tried to hold her in such a way without needing any words or further explanation and convey to her that somehow...all was going to be well going forward. The knocking started at the door again, this time a little more insistent. Michael whispered into Laura's ear, still stroking her head gently, "Let's let the world back in." Her reaction was to hug him tighter and then step back a moment later, her hands on his shoulders now and she sniffed and wiped her nose with her sleeve and shook her head yes, forcing out a smile at the end of her acknowledgment. Michael released her and crossed the room answering the second series of knocks with typical early morning annoyance, "Yeah, yeah.. be right there." He made sure to look through the peephole and once seeing Tony Craig on the other side, unlocked and opened the door. Tony let himself in, quickly surveying the space, apparently, Michael thought, in an effort to clear the room. Laura had somehow disappeared into the bathroom when he was letting him in and she reappeared a moment later, this time with a non-committal, very serious businesslike look on her face. Her hair was pulled back in a tight pony tail and the room got a little chillier. The reality was back. They were the victims of a crime, and her posture and mannerisms in front of the FBI agent said it was time to do the woman thing and be unreachable and unreadable. Did we really share that dream? Michael figured she was just being coy with the situation with Tony Craig in the room. Tony spoke to her, "I'd like to take you to my office. We need to get a statement from you about everything that happened over the last few days. The implications of this reach further than you might think." She turned to him with a hard look on her face, one that Michael had never seen before...at least not on her.

"I'm not a simpleton, Mr. Craig. I know all about the ugliness in the world and that it has now infected my life. I managed to avoid most of it in my lifetime but I have seen much more than I'll ever care to admit and I understand evil very well," she answered sharply, then adding, "I want Michael to be there." The vote of confidence thrilled him for just a moment as Tony Craig slowly shook his head no. "It's really necessary to do this separately. We'll compare your stories afterward. This will help us to truly clarify what you have seen, heard, and done over the past few days. It's really the best way. I can give you a ride home later and have someone outside your place so you feel safe."

"Which I never will again, but I know that's not your fault." Boy can she get chilly quickly, Michael was thinking. "Do we need to do this now? At this moment?" she asked, the pent-up stress dialing up her annoyance quotient. Tony stepped up to her and held her hands as he answered.

"I know you and Michael here have been through hell and back. One moment you're out on an evening together and the next you're close to drowning in the river while someone is trying to shoot you. I can't believe you look so together after such a harrowing event. To be truthful, I decided last night to break protocol, which usually is to interview a witnesses immediately in order to take advantage of a clear mind and the lack of opportunity to think too much about what occurred. That way you can avoid having events being colored, time lines becoming hazy or forgotten entirely. But I figured after seeing you in the boat, you would have never survived that process, the both of you had to come down from the trauma of the evening and find some comfort, a feeling of safe harbor." There was an endless silence that followed which Tony answered to very smoothly, "And I gather that happened here last night. That's good, I'm glad." He held her hands tighter and shook them a little bit for emphasis. "It's important that you come now, please...you can trust me," he said, looking to Michael for help, who then stepped up to her and took her by the elbow, turning her to face him. They looked right into each other's eyes, the chill gone, Tony no longer in the room, they were in the dream again as she felt his concern for her, his total being at that moment centered on gaining her trust on this before he even said the words.

"Laura, this guy is okay. Some of my friends know him from the old neighborhood and that's enough for me. He did jump into the situation last night without a care for his own life, with his chief concern being our safety and brought us here. I'm telling you I also think you should go with him now. It is better that we tell our stories separately." He turned to Tony asking, "Do I have your word that she gets treated like a queen and that you or some of your men will look after her?"

"Absolutely."

"When do you want to see me?"

"As soon as possible."

"I have to go to the airport now," Michael told them, re-entering his life as he knew it just a couple of days ago, "but I can see you maybe later this afternoon if that will be all right." Tony nodded and added, "I'll be outside, see you in a minute." They stood silently waiting for the door to close. When the metallic snap of the bolt was heard, they again turned to each other, not on the precipice of a shared dream, but here on Sunday morning in this room, not having made love but keenly aware of something that passed over, under, and through them, leaving a permanent impression of...what? Something certainly. Michael wondered if he would ever know or if they would ever articulate it to each other. For all he knew, he might never see her again after this one moment. The both of them were drinking each other in again without any words at all and it seemed decided by both of them that too many words now would be like too much sugar in your coffee.

"Michael," her hands on his chest now, standing so very close, ridiculously close, closer than last night when they were still dry, "Michael, you are the greatest man I have ever met in my life. I look forward to seeing you again. Somehow I know we'll see each other again."

"At least at the Christmas party later this year, right?" Her eyes dropped a little at the comment, and he felt awkward. Did he misspeak somehow? He tried to speak directly into her brain through some kind of telekinesis. But she looked up and smiled sadly a moment later.

"Thank you for saving me last night, Michael. I know somehow I'll see you again. I think maybe we owe the world that. I think we could really show all of them what love and respect between a man and a woman is really all about if given the chance. Her eyes went wide and she buried her head on his chest laughing, and exclaiming, "Wow... how philosophical!" She was right up on him now, his arms around her, fitting so perfectly around her ribcage, holding her body against his own. She stood on her toes and kissed him for a few seconds, ending it with a drawn-out smack that was as delicious as Michael always thought it would be. They locked eyes halfway through the smack portion of the kiss and it was glorious, the connection between them absolute, inviolable, unforgettable, unbreakable, unmatchable. At least we have that, Michael thought, as he stepped away from her, starting for the door. He stopped there, his hand on the knob. "Yes, Laura, I believe we will see each other again as well. Please always be well and please call me any time, even at 2:00 in the morning if you need to, or want to." She nodded, her lips drawn tight now, Michael knowing it was time. He opened the door and Tony was there with a few burly friends. Laura stepped up to Tony with as much confidence as any other woman in New York and announced she was ready to leave. Michael stayed in the door, Tony reminding him to call as soon as he is back from the airport, then barking an order to one of the bull-necks to stay with him until he was clear of the building. The elevator took an interminably long time and when it arrived they all started to enter but, as Michael had hoped, the perfect cherry to this experience had also arrived when she turned to take one last look at him, to speak with her eyes only to him, the others oblivious, that dazzling smile now on her face directed only to him...for him alone, and he figured it could sustain him through anything he had to face for a long time.

—ılıı—

The ride to Kennedy Airport felt longer than usual, the streets of western Queens yelling out to him, calling to him with memories, many so wonderful and good, so many bad, so many dripping with despair. He wasn't all that interested in getting to Kennedy in a hurry. He fought the voice in his head that told him nothing was there for him. But he told his wife that he would pick her and their child up at the airport on Sunday so that's what he was doing. No friends to see today anyway, no baseball to watch until later, no beach to walk on, nothing interesting to read.

Thirty-Ninth Place and Queens Boulevard...it was noisy here, hey! Remember when you dropped Wally with one punch because he called your new girlfriend a nigger? There was where the old Orbit restaurant was, a diner with sad-looking paintings of the solar system all over the walls but also with a decent motorized mobile of the planets that he found fascinating when he was a kid. He used to drive his old man nuts in those days sitting in the booth by the street by insisting on trimming off the edges of his grilled cheese before eating it. Why...why would such an insignificant thing infuriate him so?

Cherry Valley Dairy on the corner of Forty-Second Street, where his friend's troubled older brother borrowed his hairbrush one day and proceeded to hold up the store with it. Across the street at the gas station the air hose was still there, where he sat for two hours on a cold winter day long, long ago stitching together a blowout in the inner tube of his bicycle's front tire because he had no money to buy a new one. Today if he wanted, he could just go out and buy a new bicycle instead of fixing the tire.

Here was the old Sunnyside Gardens where he watched the roller derby, maniacs on skates, pound for pound tougher than any modern NFL player. Wrestling was big here, the marquee lit up with names like Gorilla Monsoon, Ivan Putski, and Chief Jay Strongbow. Further up the boulevard closer to Bliss Street, the shopping hub of Sunnyside, where he bought brand new Converse sneakers—'Cons' as they were known to everyone—for ten bucks, the only sneaker anyone would be caught dead wearing, although Pro Keds opened the market up a bit later on. The old Abraham & Strauss, where he eyed the red Stingray bicycle for weeks, showing it to his mother, trying to gauge her reaction to the twelve dollar price tag and he didn't try to stop the tears from welling up as he recalled the Christmas morning when he turned the corner in the apartment and saw it there waiting for him.

The boulevard was opening up now, the number Seven train screeching around the bend that would carry it up Roosevelt Avenue, past Irish bars that were involved with most of the gun running to the IRA in the 1970s, Latino restaurants and Pakistani and Indian and Bengali shops filled with colorful clothing and the smell of spices that were so wonderful they could lift you out of your shoes.

There was the site of the old Lucky Lounge, once a topless joint, now some sort of community outreach center where he saw his first naked *woman's* breast. The first time was that horrible day at the local junior high school when that tough chick from Brooklyn pulled off the sweater of the gentle Persian girl sitting next to him. He couldn't recall her name, but he was still able to mentally dial up the horror on her face as her nakedness and shame was revealed to the waiting eyes of all the kids in Mrs. Grandes' Spanish class. He often wondered if she ever got over that horrible experience and if she also balled her fists at the first sign of any type of or hint of reproach...as he had started to do so much more in the past few years.

He was running a little early so he decided at the last minute to take the Brooklyn-Queens Expressway, inducing the ire of several cabbies as he cut across three lanes to head back down Maurice Avenue, which would lead him back west for a mile or so before spilling onto the BQE. He stopped at the light and surveyed Maurice Field where he played endless amounts of baseball and softball about a million years ago.

He turned right when he had the green, pausing to let the drivers and truckers who thought the first few seconds of a red light were really yellow make their way through the intersection. He continued west along the service road and entered the BQE from Forty-Third Street. In seconds he was speeding along the rise over the Kosciuszko Bridge, the city on his right, a spectacle he was never able to drive by without looking out at the fractured, but still beautiful skyline.

The Williamsburg Bridge ramp was on his left, so he maneuvered into the middle lane early in order to avoid the usual rush of New York traffic that decides at the last minute to swing over for an exit. The expressway traffic was thankfully light as it was Sunday and he was able to keep the car going at a good clip, a little more than fifty miles per hour. Quickly he came upon the exits for the Manhattan Bridge and the Brooklyn Bridge. He could see tourists by the hundreds walking along the paths on the older span, holding hands, in love with the city and all it had to offer to them. In the area of the road that ran underneath the promenade in Brooklyn Heights, he could see intrepid souls in kayaks pushing off the piers for a jaunt around the mouth of the East River. He shuddered thinking about what it would be like to get caught out in those waters without a life vest. The current would whisk you right past your friends before you could get a word out of your mouth.

He continued along the highway heading for the side of the split in the road that would take him to the Shore Parkway. There across the Narrows was Staten Island where he had taken a bunch of loans in a new building project many years ago. The developer had his hand out the entire time and his profit on those deals was scant, but it got him going in the business, more deals came out of it, more contacts that he didn't have to pay for, people who just wanted a job done well. The way it should be...always enough money to go around, why bother with sucking everyone dry for their nickels and dimes, was there any dignity in that at all? He didn't think so. The kite fliers were out early in the field just past the span of the huge bridge, their homemade creations diving and rising, the tails multi-colored and beautifully whooshing through the currents of air, little sweet candy pieces thrown randomly against the blue morning sky.

As the Belt Parkway continued east toward the airport he realized why he jumped off Queens Boulevard so abruptly. The streets all the way out to the Grand Central Parkway would have called out to him incessantly, the memories of fights, and girls, and tears, and victories here and there too much for him to think about now right now. He felt equally blessed and cursed to have been given such a strong memory. He could recall so much in vivid detail and colors even, he could hear the voices and remember the looks on the faces of those who were around him at those moments, but he didn't want to so much of the time. Too much despair and pain on those streets, within those memories. The highway would allow him to breeze along, the hum of the radial tires and the accompanying rhythm of the myriad cracks in the road keeping the voices at bay, the taunting at a minimum.

The parachute jump of Coney Island was off to his right and he was brought back to the trips to the arcades and Nathan's about a million years ago. The animal farm's indoor zoo, the scooter cars they would ride all day. All for the price a subway token. The girls on the beach and the tough guys up around Surf Avenue all fascinated him then and he knew they would now as well. Do you ever really change? Is he the same man, same person today that he was yesterday, last year...or thirty-five years ago?

The traffic was really moving now and the ghosts and taunting went away completely. He was feeling drowsy so he turned on the radio and opened his window, the blast of air rushing in serving to bring him back to life, this life with all its contemplations and decisions, all of them coming at him and everyone else, for that matter, as if they were being fired from a hidden machine gun nest. What would be waiting for him at the airport? Maybe a new beginning or the beginning of the end. He gripped the steering wheel as he headed south on 678, determined to be prepared for anything like those old National Rifle Association bumper stickers, 'Make love not war, but be prepared for both.'

He pulled into the correct parking lot and amazingly found a spot somewhat near the terminal's entrance. He pulled in, turned off the ignition and placed the ticket he just received from the automated attendant into the slot of the car's CD player so that half of it still stuck out. Couldn't lose it there, he reasoned, as he started to gather up the piles of paper on the driver's seat, then decided to leave them there, thinking the inch or two of single-spaced prose would make him look to the arrivals like a mad professor with a hundred English 101 compositions to grade. He trudged out of the parking garage, the sharp glare of the sun causing his eyes to squint which made him feel drowsy again, angling toward the exact same spot where he had always picked up his wife and child.

He had always run his plan for the rest of his life through his mind every day from his teen years right up until now. He believed John Lennon was absolutely correct when he sang to his own little boy that 'Life is what happens while you're busy making other plans.' What a wonderfully profound lyric. Today he was wondering about separation and divorce and bankruptcy. Certainly hadn't figured those events into his plan for life, but then again who would?

How would he handle it? The pain of it all, the tears not only from his wife but from his kid as well. His kind of memory...boy oh boy, those scenes would live there until his last days. How would it affect his kid? Cutting, drinking, tattoos? Would that be the path the kid would take? It would be all his fault. The money? Who gives a shit... that was truly how he felt. He would downsize in a minute if he could and feel great about it. Too many people buying up property they had no business buying anyway, probable equity shortages and higher property taxes in their futures along with asshole neighbors and burst pipes.

The kid and me, he thought, that's all that matters right now. He had reached the point of no return regarding the whole business. He recalled the only decent advice his father had ever given him: 'Do what's right for yourself and you will invariably do what is right for everyone else as well.' It always sounded so selfish but it was ringing true for him now. In any event the moment of truth was walking through the revolving doors of the terminal in the form of his wife and child and a few pieces of luggage. He lurched forward upon seeing them, reaching for the heaviest of the bags. There were no open arms for him, as he expected, but at least he got a sunny greeting from the kid.

"Hi, Dad." A hug and kiss followed and immediately following, the placing of the ear buds for the newest Ipod in the outer ear, inserted as deeply as possible, the deafening thump of the modern music clearly audible to him a few feet away. His wife already had her phone at her own ear, lighting a cigarette and starting across the street. She pointed in the general direction of where she believed the car to be and he nodded yes, and they all headed that way, the handing-off of responsibility to him now complete. If he had another arm, she would have just hung the remaining two small bags on him as if he were a coat rack. The early returns were not looking promising. Once again, he felt like a glorified butler.

"How was the trip?" Only the child answered but how his words were heard over the pulsating music was incomprehensible to him.

"It was okay." He could see the small hand manipulating the volume control, probably turning it up to full blast. That would be it, he figured. How he hoped that he could be a source of information for his kid later in life, during the teen years, early career and marriage days and so on. Maybe a conversation of more than three sentences, that would be very nice. Right now he was merely a chauffeur. I guess that wasn't all that bad. At least the kid said hello. They arrived at the car and he popped the trunk and carefully placed the bags there. His wife waited by the passenger door, phone still at her ear. "Okay", she was saying to...someone, anyone, "We're getting in the car, I'll talk to you later." He opened the door for her and his wife plopped into the seat and started to text someone. The kid jumped in the back, pulling the door shut and he then walked around the back of the car to the other side, carefully opening and shutting the door, not wanting to show how royally pissed off he was at this chilly reception after three days. He paid the four dollars for barely fifteen minutes of parking... how could New York state not have any money with all these fees?— and eased the car out of the lot toward the airport exit. His wife finished her text and then picked up the papers he had left on the floor.

"What's this, you write a freakin' novel while I was gone?" She started to thumb through the pages, reading here and there, trying to comprehend all the words and thoughts while browsing quickly. A look of annoyance was spreading on her face, the lines on her forehead deepening, her concentration becoming more pronounced. Hank Fredericks had known this woman for close to twenty years and her heart may have been a deep ocean of secrets like any other woman's, but her face was as easy to read as a comic book.

"Just something I put together over the last few days. Maybe you'll find it interesting," he told her. She continued to read here and there, asking "What's with these fucking dreams and who the hell are Michael and Laura?" She looked up at him and studied his face for an answer as she fished another smoke out of her pocket, lighting it and rolling down the window. He hated the smoke and she knew it, especially with their child in the car. He remained silent, not wanting to answer as all the questions he had were in those pages and she would have to figure it out for herself. Fair? Probably not. But who said life was fair?

He hit the Belt Parkway again and continued east to his suburban town and his suburban street and his overtaxed house. The music thumped in the ears of his child in the backseat and the typed pages in the hands of his wife flew by before her eyes, the sucking of the cigarette becoming more furious, her concentration on the words and ideas his mind spit out lingering here and there.

The rest of his life was ahead of him now and he wanted to get on with it immediately, no matter how, why, or when, because of or with whom. But to get on with it, oh yeah...that was going to happen no matter what. Starting right now.